The Tower of London

A Historical Romance, Illustrated

CW01082869

William Harrison Ainsworth

Alpha Editions

This edition published in 2024

ISBN : 9789357966351

Design and Setting By
Alpha Editions
www.alphaedis.com
Email - info@alphaedis.com

PREFACE.

It has been, for years, the cherished wish of the writer of the following pages, to make the Tower of London—the proudest monument of antiquity, considered with reference to its historical associations, which this country or any other possesses,—the groundwork of a Romance; and it was no slight satisfaction to him, that circumstances, at length, enabled him to carry into effect his favourite project, in conjunction with the inimitable Artist, whose designs accompany the work.

Desirous of exhibiting the Tower in its triple light of a palace, a prison, and a fortress, the Author has shaped his story with reference to that end; and he has also endeavoured to contrive such a series of incidents as should naturally introduce every relic of the old pile,—its towers, chapels, halls, chambers, gateways, arches, and drawbridges—so that no part of it should remain un-illustrated.

How far this design has been accomplished—what interest has been given to particular buildings—and what mouldering walls have been informed with life—is now to be determined:—unless, indeed, it may be considered determined by the numbers who have visited the different buildings, as they have been successively depicted by pen and pencil, during the periodical appearance of the work.

One important object the Author would fain hope his labours may achieve. This is the introduction of the public to some parts of the fortress at present closed to them. There seems no reason why admission should not be given, under certain restrictions, to that unequalled specimen of Norman architecture, Saint John's Chapel in the White Tower,—to the arched galleries above it,—to the noble council-chamber, teeming with historical recollections,—to the vaulted passages—and to the winding staircases within the turrets—so perfect, and so interesting to the antiquary. Nor is there stronger reason why the prison-chamber in the Beauchamp Tower, now used as a mess-room, the walls of which, like a mystic scroll, are covered with inscriptions—each a tragic story in itself, and furnishing matter for abundant reflection—should not likewise be thrown open. Most of the old fortifications upon the inner ballium-wall being converted into private dwellings,—though in many cases the chambers are extremely curious, and rich in inscriptions,—are, of course, inaccessible. But this does not apply to the first-mentioned places. They are the property of the nation, and should be open to national inspection.

It is piteous to see what havoc has already been made by alterations and repairs. The palace is gone—so are many of the towers—and unless the progress of destruction is arrested, the demolition of others will follow. Let us attempt to preserve what remains.

Opposite the matchless White Tower—William of Orange by the side of William the Conqueror,—is that frightful architectural abomination, the Grand Store-House.

It may not be possible to remove this ugly and incongruous structure. It is not possible to take away others that offend the eye at every turn. It is not possible to restore the Tower to its pristine grandeur. But it *is* possible to prevent further mutilation and desecration. It *is* possible to clear the reverend and massive columns of Saint John's Chapel, which look like giants of departed days, from the thick coat of white-wash in which they are crusted,— to sweep away the presses with which its floors are cumbered, and to find some other equally secure, but less interesting—less sacred, in every sense, depository for the Chancery rolls. It *is* possible to render the same service to the magnificent council-chamber, and the passages leading to it,—it *is* possible to clear the walls of the Beauchamp Tower,—and it *is*, also, possible and desirable, that the public should be admitted to these places, in which they have so strong an interest. The visiter to the Tower sees little—and *can* see little of its most curious features. But it is the hope of the writer, that the day is not far off, when all that is really worth seeing will be accessible. In this view, the present publication may not be without use.

To those, who conceive that the Author has treated the character of Queen Mary with too great leniency, he can only affirm that he has written according to his conviction of the truth. Mary's worst fault as a woman—her sole fault as a sovereign—was her bigotry: and it is time that the cloud, which prejudice has cast over her, should be dispersed. "Let us judge of her dispassionately and disinterestedly," says Griffet *; "let us listen to the testimony of those who have known her, and have had the best means of examining her actions and her discourse. Let us do this, and we may perhaps discover that the reproaches which Protestant writers have heaped upon her have been excessive; and after a strict and impartial examination of her character, we may recognise in her qualities worthy of praise." To this authority may be added that of Mr. Patrick Fraser Tytler, and Sir Frederick Madden, the latter of whom, in his able introduction to the *"Privy Purse Expenses of the Princess Mary,"* has most eloquently vindicated her.

* *Nouveaux Eclaircissements sur l'Histoire de Marie, Reine*

d'Angleterre. Adressés à M. David Hume. 1760.

Presuming upon the favour which the present work has experienced, the Author begs to intimate that he has other chronicles of the old fortress in contemplation, which he hopes to find leisure to produce. Those who desire further insight into its history and antiquities, are referred to Mr. Bayley's excellent and comprehensive work on the subject,—a publication not so much known as it deserves to be, and from which much important information contained in the present volume has been derived.

It would be unpardonable in both Author and Illustrator, were they to omit to allude to the courtesy and attention they have experienced from the gentlemen connected with the different departments of the Tower, as well as from the occupants of the various fortifications. They beg, therefore, to offer their cordial acknowledgments to Major Elrington, fort-major and acting governor; to Edmund L. Swift, Esq., keeper of the regalia; to Robert Porrett, Esq., F. S. A., of the Principal Store-keeper's Office; and George Stacey, Esq., of the same; to Thomas Hardy, Esq., F. S. A., keeper of the records in the Tower; to Lieutenant Hall, barrack-master; and to many others.

The Author's best thanks are, also, due to Sir Henry Bedingfeld, Bart., of Oxburgh Hall, Norfolk, (the lineal descendant of the Lieutenant of the Tower introduced in the following pages,) for his obliging communications respecting his ancestor.

"And so," to adopt the words of old Stow, in his continuation of Holinshed's Chronicle, "craving a favourable acceptation of this tedious travail, with a toleration of all such faults, as haply therein lie hidden, and by diligent reading may soon be spied (especially by the critics), we wish that they which best may, would once in their life grow resolute and at a point in this laudable kind of study, most necessary for common knowledge, little or much to exercise their head and hand. Finally, beseeching God to bless these realms, and its ever precious jewel, our gracious Queen Victoria, and the infant princess newly given to us; to save them as the apple of his eye; and to protect them with the target of his power against all ill,—the Chronicler, in all humility, takes his leave."

Kensal Lodge, Harrow Road, November 28, 1840.

BOOK ONE

I.—OF THE MANNER IN WHICH QUEEN JANE ENTERED THE TOWER OF LONDON.

ON the 10th of July, 1553, about two hours after noon, a loud discharge of ordnance burst from the turrets of Durham House, then the residence of the Duke of Northumberland, grand-master of the realm, and occupying the site of the modern range of buildings, known as the Adelphi; and, at the signal, which was immediately answered from every point along the river where a bombard or culverin could be planted,—from the adjoining hospital of the Savoy,—the old palace of Bridewell, recently converted by Edward VI., at the instance of Ridley, bishop of London, into a house of correction,— Baynard's Castle, the habitation of the Earl of Pembroke,—the gates of London-bridge,—and, lastly, from the batteries of the Tower,—a gallant train issued from the southern gateway of the stately mansion abovenamed, and descended the stairs leading to the water's edge, where, appointed for their reception, was drawn up a squadron of fifty superbly-gilt barges,—some decorated with banners and streamers,—some with cloth-of-gold and arras, embroidered with the devices of the civic companies,—others with innumerable silken pennons to which were attached small silver bells, "making a goodly noise and a goodly sight as they waved in the wind,"— while others, reserved for the more important personages of the ceremony, were covered at the sides with shields gorgeously emblazoned with the armorial bearings of the different noblemen and honourable persons composing the privy council, amid which the cognizance of the Duke of Northumberland,—a lion rampant, or, double quevée, *vert*,—appeared proudly conspicuous. Each barge was escorted by a light galley, termed a foist or wafter, manageable either by oar or sail as occasion demanded, and attached to its companion by a stout silken tow-line. In these galleys, besides the rowers, whose oars were shipped, and in readiness to be dropped, at an instant's notice, into the tide, and the men-at-arms, whose tall pikes, steel caps, and polished corslets flashed in the sun-beams, sat bands of minstrels provided with sackbuts, shalms, cornets, rebecs, and other forgotten musical instruments. The conduct of the whole squadron was entrusted to six officers, whose business it was to prevent confusion, and who, in the small swift wherries appointed to their use, rowed rapidly from place to place, endeavouring by threats and commands to maintain order, and keep off the crowd of boats and craft of all sorts hurrying towards them from every quarter of the river. It was a brilliant and busy scene, and might be supposed a joyous and inspiriting one—more especially, as the object which had called together this assemblage was the conveyance of a young and lovely sovereign to her throne within the Tower. But it was not so. Young and lovely as was that sovereign,—rich,—richer, perhaps, than any of her sex,—in endowments of mind and person,—illustrious and royal in birth,—professing and supporting a faith, then newly established throughout the country, and which it was feared, and with reason, might be greatly endangered, if not wholly subverted, if another and nearer claimant of the crown, the Princess Mary, had succeeded to the inheritance; still, with all these high recommendations,—though her rights were insisted upon by the ablest and most eloquent divines from the pulpit, though her virtues, her acquirements, and her beauty were the theme of every tongue;—as she was not first in the succession, and, above all, as she had been invested with regal authority by one who, from his pride, was obnoxious to all men,—her father-in-law, the Duke of Northumberland,—the Lady Jane Dudley's accession was viewed by all ranks and all parties with mistrust and apprehension. In vain had the haughty duke brought her with a splendid cavalcade from Sion House to his own palace. No cheers greeted her arrival—no rejoicings were made by the populace, but a sullen and ominous silence prevailed amongst those who witnessed her entrance into the capital. It is true that her youth and surpassing beauty excited the greatest interest. Murmurs of irrepressible admiration arose at her appearance; but these were immediately checked on the approach of Northumberland, who, following closely behind her, eyed the concourse as if he would enforce their applauses; and it was emphatically said, that in pity of the victim of his soaring ambition, more tears were shed on that occasion, than shouts were uttered. On the 9th of July, Lady Jane Dudley—better known by her maiden title of Lady Jane Grey—had been made acquainted with her exalted, but, as she herself (with a sad presentiment of calamity) pronounced it, her fatal destiny. Edward the Sixth had breathed his last, three days previously. His death had been kept carefully concealed by Northumberland, who hoped, by despatching false messages, to have secured the persons of the princesses Mary and Elizabeth. But intelligence of her brother's death having been communicated to the latter, she avoided the snare; and the duke, finding further dissimulation useless, resolved at once to carry his plan into execution, and proclaim his daughter-in-law queen. With this view, and accompanied by several members of the privy-council, he proceeded to Sion House, where she was then living in retirement, and announced to her that the late monarch had declared her by his letters-patent (an instrument which he had artfully obtained) his successor. Jane refused the proffered dignity, urging the prior claims of Edward's sisters; and adding, "I am not so young, nor so little read in the guiles of fortune, to suffer myself to be taken by them. If she enrich any, it is but to make them the subject of her spoil. If she raise others, it is but to pleasure herself with their ruins. What she adorned but yesterday, is to-day her pastime: and if I now permit her to adorn and crown me, I must to-morrow suffer her to crush and tear me to pieces. Nay, with what crown does she present me? A crown which has been violently and shamefully wrested from Catherine of Arragon, made more unfortunate by the punishment of Anne Boleyn, and others who wore it after her; and why then would you have me add my blood to theirs, and be the third victim from whom this fatal crown may be ravished, with the head that wears it?" In this forcible and feeling language she couched her refusal; and for some time she adhered to her resolution, until at length, her constancy being shaken by the solicitations of her relatives, and above all by the entreaties of her husband Lord Guilford Dudley, to whom she was passionately attached, she yielded a reluctant assent. On the following morning, she was conveyed, as has been just stated, with great pomp to Durham House, in the Strand, where she received the homage of her subjects, partook of a magnificent banquet, and tarried sufficiently long to enable the duke to collect his retinue to conduct her in state to the Tower: it being then the custom for the monarchs of England to spend the first few days of their reign within this ancient fortress. It is with the moment of her departure for this palace and prison of crowned heads, that this chronicle commences.

The advanced guard of the procession was formed by a troop of halberdiers dressed in striped hose of black and tawny, velvet caps decked at the side with silver roses, and doublets of murrey and blue cloth, embroidered on the front and at the back with the royal blazon, woven in gold. Their halbert staves were covered with crimson velvet, fastened with gilt nails, and ornamented with golden tassels. Filing oft on the right and left, they formed two long lines, extending from the gateway of the palace to the foot of the plank communicating with the barge nearest the shore. A thick rayed cloth was then unfolded, and laid down between them by several attendants in the sumptuous liveries of the Duke of Northumberland. This done, a flourish of trumpets resounded from within; a lively prelude arose from the musicians on the water; and two ushers with white wands marched at a slow and stately pace from the portal. They were followed by an officer bearing the mace; after whom came another carrying the sword of state; then several serjeants of the city guard, in their full accoutrements, and with badges on their sleeves; then the garter king-at-arms in his tabard; then several knights of the Bath, each having a white laco on his sleeve; then their esquires; then the judges, in their robes of scarlet and coifs; then the bishop of Ely, who, in his character of lord high chancellor, wore a robe of scarlet, open before, and purfled with minever; then the aldermen, likewise in cloaks of scarlet; the sheriffs; and, finally, the lord mayor, Sir George Beame, in a gown of crimson velvet, and wearing the collar of SS.

Sufficient time having been allowed for the embarkation of these important personages, who, with their attendants, filled several barges, another flourish of trumpets was heard, fresh symphonies resounded from the river, and the heads of the different civic companies, in their robes of state, descended and departed. Many an eye tracked their course along the river, which flamed like a sheet of molten gold beneath its glittering burthens. Many an ear listened to the measured sweep of their oars, and the softening cadences of their minstrelsy; lingering, enchanted, on the sight and sound till both faded away in the distance. Still, though a thousand pulses beat high, and a thousand hearts throbbed, not an acclamation was raised, not a. cap thrown in the air, not a scarf waved. The same silence, that had prevailed during the morning, prevailed now. Queen Jane, it was evident, was not the choice of her people.

Meanwhile, two venerable persons had presented themselves on the stair-head. These were Cranmer, archbishop of Canterbury, and Ridley, bishop of London. They were attired in the scarlet simar, and surplice with its snowy lawn sleeves, proper to their order, and were engaged in deep converse together. The austere course of life prescribed to, and pursued by, the fathers of the Reformed Church, had stamped itself in lines of unusual severity on their countenances. Their demeanour was grave and singularly dignified, and such as well beseemed their high ecclesiastical rank. Arrived at the last step, Cranmer raised his eyes, and, after glancing around as if in expectation of some greeting from the multitude, observed to his companion, "This silence of the people likes me not, my lord: disaffection, I fear, is abroad. This is not the way in which our good citizens are wont to receive a triumph such as his Grace of Northumberland has prepared."

"Your Grace is in the right," replied Ridley. "The assemblage before whom I pronounced a solemn exhortation this morning at St. Paul's Cross,—when I proved, as I trust, satisfactorily, that Mary and Elizabeth are excluded from the succession on the score of illegitimacy,—received my discourse with murmurs of disapprobation. Vainly did I tell them if they accepted Mary they would relapse into darkness and idolatry: vainly did I enlarge on our young queen's virtues, and show them that she was prepared to carry into effect the wise ordinations of her pious predecessor. They made no answer,—but departed, as men resolved not to be convinced of their error."

"These are signs indeed of troublous times," sighed Cranmer; "and, though it is not given to us to foresee the future, I cannot but fear that a season of bitter persecution of our church is at hand. Heaven avert the day! Heaven preserve queen Jane, who will prove our surest safeguard! Had Mary ruled———"

"Had that false bigot ruled," interrupted Ridley, frowning at the idea, "your grace and I should, ere this, have changed places in the Tower with Gardiner and Bonner. But should what you fear come to pass; should evil times arise, and Rome and her abominations again prevail; should our church need a martyr, she shall find one in me."

"And in me," rejoined Cranmer, fervently.

While this was passing, twelve French gentlemen in splendid habiliments, consisting of pourpoints of white damask, barred with gold, short mantles of crimson velvet, lined with violet taffeta, and carnation-coloured hauts-de-chausses, took their way down the steps. These galliards, who formed the suite of M. Antoine de Noailles, ambassador from Henry the Second of France, were succeeded by a like number of Spanish cavaliers, the attendants of M. Simon Renard, who fulfilled the like high office for the emperor Charles the Fifth. Dressed in suits of black velvet, entirely without ornament, the Spaniards differed as much from the airy and elegant Frenchmen in gravity and reserve of manner, as in simplicity of apparel. Their leader, Simon Renard, was as plainly attired as his followers, his sole decoration being the Toison d'Or: but of all that brilliant assemblage, perhaps there was none so likely to arrest and rivet attention as this remarkable man; and as he is destined to play no inconsiderable part in this history, it may be worth while to take a narrower survey of his personal appearance. Somewhat above the middle height, and of a spare but muscular frame, he had a dark complexion, rendered yet more sombre in its colour from the contrast it presented to his grizzled board and moustaches. His eye was black and flaming, his nose long and hooked, and he had astern searching glance, which few could withstand. There was something mysterious both in his manner and character which made him universally dreaded; and as he never forgave an offence, nor scrupled at any means of gratifying his vengeance, it was not without reason that he was feared. A subtle politician and skilful diplomatist, high in the favour of the most powerful sovereign in Europe, with apparently inexhaustible funds at his command; inexorable in hatred, fickle in friendship, inconstant in affairs of gallantry, suspected of being mixed up in every political intrigue or conspiracy, Simon Renard had been for some time the terror and wonder of Edward's court, and had been regarded with suspicion and jealousy by Northumberland, who looked upon him as a dangerous opponent. During Edward's lifetime frequent quarrels had occurred between these two crafty statesmen; but now, at this desperate conjuncture, the duke deemed it prudent to forget his animosity, and to conciliate his antagonist. More of a courtier, and not less of a diplomatist, but without the skill, the resolution, or the cunning of his brother ambassador, De Noailles would have been no match for Renard had they been opposed: and, indeed, his inferiority was afterwards signally manifested. But they were now united by common bonds of animosity: both were determined enemies of Northumberland—both resolved upon his overthrow, and that of the queen he had placed upon the throne.

No sooner had the ambassadors entered their barge, than withdrawing out of earshot of their attendants, they commenced a conversation in a low tone.

"How long will this farce last, think you?" inquired De Noailles, with a laugh.

"Not a day—not an hour," rejoined Simon Renard, "if these suspicious and timorous English nobles will but act in concert, and confide in me."

"Confide in *you?*" said De Noailles, smiling. "They fear you more than Northumberland."

"They will not succeed without me," returned Renard, coldly. "Mark me, De Noailles, I, Simon Renard, simple bailli of Amont in the Franche-Comté, and an unworthy representative of his Majesty Charles the Fifth, hold in my right hand the destiny of this fair land of England."

"Ha! ha! ha!" laughed De Noailles. "You have learnt to rhodomontade at the court of Madrid, I perceive, Monsieur le Bailli."

"This is no rhodomontade, messire," rejoined the other, sternly; "were I to join with Northumberland and Suffolk, I could establish Jane upon the throne. Acting with the privy council, who, as you well know, are, like ourselves, the duke's secret enemies, I shall strike the sceptre from her grasp, and place it in the hand of Mary. Nay more, I will tell you that if I had not wished to ensure Northumberland's destruction, I would not have suffered him to proceed thus far. But he has now taken a step which nothing can retrieve."

"My hatred of him is as great as your own, M. Renard," observed De Noailles, gravely; "and I shall rejoice as heartily as yourself, or any of his enemies, in his downfall. But I cannot blind myself to his power. Clinton, the Lord High Admiral, his fast friend, is in possession of the Tower, which is full of armed men and ammunition. The royal treasures are in his hands; the troops, the navy, are his—and, as yet, the privy council have sanctioned all his decrees—have sworn obedience to Jane—have proclaimed Mary illegitimate, and deprived her of her inheritance."

"They shall eat their own words," replied Renard, in a sarcastic tone. "But it is time, De Noailles, to admit you to my full confidence. First, swear to me, by the holy Evangelists, that I may trust you."

"I swear it," replied De Noailles, "provided," he added, smiling, "your scheme has nothing treasonable against my liege lord, Henry the Second."

"Judge for yourself," answered Renard. "There is a plot hatching against the life of Northumberland."

"Mortdieu!" exclaimed the French ambassador; "by whom?"

"To-night you shall meet the conspirators," replied Renard.

"Their names?" demanded De Noailles.

"It matters not," answered the other; "I am their leader. Will you make one of us?"

"Willingly," rejoined the Frenchman. "But how is the duke to be put to death?"

"By the headsman," replied Simon Renard. "He shall die the death of a traitor."

"You were ever mysterious, messire," observed De Noailles, drily; "and you are now more mysterious than ever. But I will join your plot with all my heart. Pardieu! I should like to offer Northumberland's head to Queen Mary. It would be as acceptable as that of Cicero to Fulvia."

"My gift shall be yet more acceptable," rejoined Simon Renard, sternly. "I will offer her the fairest and the wisest head in England—that of Queen Jane."

During this conference, the procession had been increased by several members of the privy-council, consisting of the Earls of Arundel, Shrewsbury, Huntingdon, and Pembroke, the Lords Cobham and Rich, with divers other noble and honourable persons, among whom Sir William Cecil, principal secretary of state, (afterwards, the great Lord Burghley.) must not pass unnoticed. Pembroke and Cecil walked together; and, in spite of their forced composure, it was evident that both were ill at case. As a brief halt took place amongst the foremost party, Cecil seized the arm of his companion, and whispered hurriedly in his ear, "We are lost, my lord. Your messengers to the queen have been arrested; so have my trusty servants, Alford and Cayewood. Luckily, their despatches are in cipher. But Northumberland's suspicions once aroused, his vengeance will not be slow to follow. There is yet time for escape. Can we not frame some excuse for landing at your lordship's residence, Baynard's Castle? Once within the Tower, I tremble for our heads."

"My case is not so desperate as yours," returned the earl, firmly; "but were it so, I would never fly while others are left to pay the penalty of my cowardice. We have advanced too far to retreat—and, be the issue of this project what it may, I will not shrink from it. Simon Renard is leagued with us, and he alone is a match for Northumberland, or for the fiend himself, if opposed to him. Be of good cheer. The day will yet be ours."

"Were I assured of Renard's sincerity," replied Cecil, "I might, indeed, feel more confidence. But I have detected too many of his secret practices—have had too much experience of his perfidy and double-dealing, to place any faith in him."

"You wrong him," rejoined Pembroke; "by my soul you do! As we proceed, I will give you proofs that will remove all apprehensions of treachery on his part from your mind. He has proposed a plan.—But of this anon—for, see!—all, save ourselves, have entered the barge. Do you mark how suddenly the weather has changed? A thunder-storm is gathering over the Tower. 'Tis a bad omen for Northumberland."

"Or for us," rejoined Cecil, gloomily.

The sudden change in the weather, here alluded to, was remarked and commented upon by many others besides the Earl of Pembroke; and by most it was regarded as an evil augury against the young queen. The sky had become overcast; the river, lately so smiling, now reflected only the sombre clouds that overshadowed it; while heavy, leaden-coloured masses, arising in the north-east, behind the Tower, seemed to threaten a speedy and severe storm in that quarter. Alarmed by these signs, several of the more prudent spectators, who preferred a dry skin to the further indulgence of their curiosity, began to urge their barks homewards. The majority of the assemblage, however, lingered: a glimpse of a queen so beautiful as Jane was reputed, appeared to them well worth a little personal inconvenience.

Meanwhile, a loud and prolonged trumpet-blast proclaimed the approach of the Duke of Northumberland. He was accompanied by the Duke of Suffolk, the father of the queen. Nothing more majestic can be conceived than the deportment of the former—nothing more magnificent than his attire. His features, though haughty and disdainful, with a fierce expression about the mouth and eyes, were remarkably handsome and well-formed. His figure was tall and commanding, and there was something which is generally associated with the epithets chivalrous and picturesque in his appearance. John Dudley, Duke of Northumberland, who by his genius and rare abilities as a statesman had elevated himself to the lofty position which he now held, could not be less in age than fifty. But he had none of the infirmity of years about him. His forehead was bald, but that only gave expanse to his noble countenance; his step was as firm as a young man's; his eye as keen and bright as that of an eagle. He was habited in a doublet of white satin, with a placard or front-piece of purple cloth of tissue, powdered with diamonds and edged with ermine. Over this he wore a mantle of cloth of silver, pounced with his cipher, lined with blue velvet, set with pearls and precious stones, and fastened with a jewelled clasp. From his neck was suspended the order of the Garter, while in his hand he carried the silver verder belonging to his office as grand-master of the realm. The Duke of Suffolk was scarcely less magnificently arrayed, in a doublet of black cloth of gold, and a cloak of crimson satin flowered with gold, and ribanded with nets of silver. He also wore the order of the Garter. Suffolk was somewhat younger than his companion, of whom he stood, as indeed did all the other nobles, greatly in awe. He had well-formed features, a fine figure, a courtly air, and affable and conciliating manners; but though a man of unquestionable ability and courage, he wanted that discernment and active resolution which alone could have preserved him from the dangers and difficulties in which he was afterwards involved. His qualities have been admirably summed up by Holinshed, who describes him as "a man of high nobility by birth, and of nature to his friend gentle and courteous; more easy indeed to be led than was thought expedient, nevertheless stout and hardy; hasty and soon kindled, but pacified straight again, and sorry if in his heat aught had passed him otherwise than reason might seem to bear; upright and plain in his private dealings; no dissembler, nor well able to bear injuries; but yet forgiving and forgetting the same, if the party would but seem to acknowledge his fault and seek reconcilement; bountiful he was, and very liberal; somewhat learned himself, and a great favourer of those that were learned, so that to many he showed himself a very Maecenas; as free from covetousness, as devoid of pride and disdainful haughtiness of mind, more regarding plain-meaning men than clawback flatterers." Such, as depicted by the honest old chronicler above-named, was Henry Grey, Duke of Suffolk, father of Queen Jane.

Just as the two dukes emerged from the portal, a slight commotion was heard in the outer court, and a valet, stepping forward, made a profound reverence to Northumberland, and presented him with a paper. The duke broke the silken thread and seal with which it was fastened, and ran his eye rapidly over its contents. His brow darkened for an instant, but as speedily cleared, and a smile of fierce satisfaction played upon his lips. "Traitors!" he ejaculated in an under tone, turning to Suffolk; "but I have them now; and, by God's precious soul! they shall not escape me."

"What new treason has come to light, brother!" demanded the Duke of Suffolk, uneasily.

"Nothing new,—nothing but what I suspected. But their plots have taken a more dangerous and decided form," replied Northumberland, sternly.

"You do not name the traitors,—but you speak of the privy-council, I conclude?" observed Suffolk.

"Ay, brother, of the privy-council. They are all *my* enemies,—*your* enemies,— the *queen's* enemies. This scroll warns me that a conspiracy is forming against my life."

"Heaven forbid!" ejaculated Suffolk. "Surely, our English nobles are not turned assassins."

"The chief mover in the dark scheme is not an Englishman," returned Northumberland.

"It cannot be the light-hearted De Noailles. Ha! I have it: it is the plotting and perfidious Simon Renard."

"Your Grace is in the right," replied Northumberland; "it *is* Simon Renard."

"Who are his associates?" inquired Suffolk.

"As yet I know not," answered the other; "but I have netted them all, and, like the fowler, will spare neither bird of prey nor harmless songster. I have a trick shall test the true metal from the false. What think you, brother?—a letter has arrived from Mary to this false council, claiming the crown.".

"Ha!" exclaimed Suffolk.

"It is here," continued Northumberland, pointing to a paper folded round his silver staff. "I shall lay it before them anon. Before I depart, I must give orders for the proclamation. Bid the heralds come hither," he added to the attendant; who instantly departed, and returned a moment afterwards, followed by two heralds in their coats of arms. "Take this scroll," continued the duke, "and let the Queens Highness be proclaimed by sound of trumpet at the cross at Charing, in Cheapside, and in Fleet-street. Take with you a sufficient guard, and if any murmuring ensue let the offenders be punished. Do you mark me?"

"We do, your Grace," replied the heralds, bowing. And, taking the proclamation, they departed on their behest,—while the duke, accompanied by Suffolk, entered his barge.

Preceded by two trumpeters, having their clarions richly dressed with fringed silk bandrols, displaying the royal arms; a captain of the guard, in a suit of scarlet bound with black velvet, and with a silver rose in his bonnet, next descended the stairs, and announced, in a loud and authoritative voice, that her Highness the Queen was about to embark: an intimation, which, though received with no particular demonstration of enthusiasm or delight by the spectators, was, nevertheless, productive of considerable confusion among them. The more distant wherrymen, who had been hitherto resting tranquilly on their oars, in their anxiety to secure a better position for their fares, now pressed eagerly forward; in consequence of which many violent collisions took place; great damage was sustained by the foremost boats, some being swamped and their owners plunged in the tide; while others, bereft of their oars, were swept away by the rapid current. Amid this tumult, much struggling and scuffling occurred; shrieks and oaths were uttered; and many blows from sword, dagger, and club were dealt, and requited with the heartiest good-will. Owing, however, to the exertions of the officers, no lives were lost. The drowning persons were picked up and carried ashore; and the disputants compelled to hold their peace, and reserve the adjustment of their differences to another, and more favourable opportunity. By the time Jane appeared, all was comparatively quiet. But the incident had not tended to improve the temper of the crowd, or create a stronger feeling in her favour. Added to this, the storm seemed fast advancing and ready to burst over their heads; the sky grew darker each moment; and when a second discharge of ordnance was bred from the palace walls, and rolled sullenly along the river, it was answered by a distant peal of thunder. In spite of all these adverse circumstances, no delay occurred in the procession. A magnificent barge, with two large banners, beaten with the royal arms, planted on the foreship, approached the strand. Its sides were hung with metal scutcheons, alternately emblazoned with the cognizances of the queen and her consort; and its decks covered with the richest silks and tissues. It was attended by two smaller galleys—one of which, designated the Bachelors' barge, was appropriated to the younger sons of the nobility: the other was devoted to the maids of honour. In the latter was placed a quaint device, intended to represent a mount with a silver tree springing from it, on which was perched a dove with a circlet of diamonds around its neck, bearing an inscription in honour of the queen, and a crown upon its head. No sooner had the royal barge taken up its position, than a train of twenty gentlemen, in doublets of black velvet and with chains of gold, stepped towards it. They were followed by six pages in vests of cloth of gold; after whom came the Earl of Northampton, lord high chamberlain, bareheaded, and carrying a white wand; and after the chamberlain, appeared the Lady Herbert, younger sister of the queen, a beautiful blonde, with soft blue eyes and silken tresses, accompanied by the Lady Hastings, younger sister of Lord Guilford Dudley, a sprightly brunette, with large orient orbs, black as midnight, and a step proud as that of a Juno. Both these lovely creatures—neither of whom had attained her fifteenth year—had been married at the end of May—then, as now, esteemed an unlucky month,—on the sumo day that the nuptials of the Lady Jane Grey took place. Of these three marriages there was not one but was attended with fatal consequences.

Immediately behind her sisters, with the laps of her dress supported by the bishops of Rochester and Winchester, and her train, which was of great length and corresponding magnificence, borne by her mother, the duchess of Suffolk, walked queen Jane. Whatever disinclination she might have previously shown to undertake the dangerous and difficult part she had assumed; however reluctantly she had accepted the sovereignty; nothing of misgiving or irresolution was now to be discerned. Her carriage was majestic; her look lofty, yet tempered with such sweetness, that while it commanded respect, it ensured attachment. Her attire—for the only point upon which Jane did not conform to the rigid notions of the early religious reformers was in regard to dress—was gorgeous in the extreme; and never, assuredly, was rich costume bestowed upon a more faultlessly beautiful person. Her figure was tall and slight, but exquisitely formed, and gave promise, that when she attained the full maturity of womanhood—she had only just completed her sixteenth year, and (alas!) never *did* attain maturity—her charms would be without a rival. In mental qualifications Jane was equally gifted. And, if it is to be lamented that her beauty, like an opening flower, was rudely plucked and scattered to the breezes, how much more must it be regretted, that such faculties as she possessed should have been destroyed before they were fully developed, and the fruit they might have produced lost for ever! Reared in the seclusion of Bradgate, in Leicestershire, Jane Grey passed hours which other maidens of her tender age are accustomed to devote to amusement or rest, in the severest study; and, long before she was called upon to perform the arduous duties of her brief life, she had acquired a fund of knowledge such as the profoundest scholars seldom obtain. If this store of learning did little for the world, it did much for herself:—it taught her a philosophy, that enabled her to support, with the constancy of a martyr, her after trials. At the moment of her presentation to the reader, Jane was in all the flush and excitement of her new dignity. Everything around her was dazzling and delusive; but she was neither dazzled nor deluded. She estimated her position at its true value; saw through its hollowness and unsubstantiality; and, aware that she only grasped the shadow of a sceptre, and bore the semblance of a crown, suffered neither look nor gesture to betray her emotions. Her dress consisted of a gown of cloth of gold raised with pearls, a stomacher blazing with diamonds and other precious stones, and a surcoat of purple velvet bordered with ermine. Her train was of purple velvet upon velvet, likewise furred with ermine, and embroidered with various devices in gold. Her slender and swan-like throat was encircled with a carcanet of gold set with rubies and pearls, from which a single and almost priceless pearl depended. Her head-dress consisted of a coif of velvet of the peculiar form then in vogue, adorned with rows of pearls, and confined by a circlet of gold. At her right walked Lord Guilford Dudley—a youthful nobleman, who inherited his father's manly beauty and chivalrous look, with much of his ambition and haughtiness, but without any of his cunning and duplicity, or of his genius. He was superbly attired in white cloth of gold, and wore a collar of diamonds. Behind the queen marched a long train of high-born dames, damsels, youthful nobles, pages, knights, esquires, and ushers, until the rear-guard was brought up by a second detachment of halberdiers. Prepared as the mass of the assemblage were to evidence their dissatisfaction by silence, an involuntary burst of applause hailed her approach, and many, who thought it a sort of disloyalty to Mary to welcome a usurper, could not refuse to join in the cheers.

At the moment Jane was crossing the railed plank leading to her galley, a small wherry, rowed by a young man of slight sinewy frame, clad in a doublet of coarse brown serge, and wearing a flat felt cap, on which a white cross was stitched, shot with marvellous rapidity from out the foremost line of boats, and, in spite of all opposition, passed between the state barges, and drew up at her feet. Before the daring intruder could be removed, an old woman, seated in the stern of the boat, arose and extended her arms towards Jane. She was dressed in mean attire, with her grey locks gathered beneath an ancient three-cornered coif; but her physiognomy was striking, and her manner seemed far above her lowly condition. Fixing an imploring glance on the queen, she cried—"A boon! a boon!"

"It is granted," replied Jane, in a kind tone, and pausing. "What would you?"

"Preserve you," rejoined the old woman. "Go not to the Tower."

"And wherefore not, good dame?" inquired the queen.

"Ask me not," returned the old woman,—her figure dilating, her eye kindling, and her gesture becoming almost that of command, as she spoke,— "Ask me not; but take my warning. Again, I say—Go not to the Tower. Danger lurks therein,—danger to you—your husband—and to all you hold dear. Return, while it is yet time; return to the retirement of Sion House—to the solitudes of Bradgate.—Put off those royal robes—restore the crown to her from whom you wrested it, and a long and happy life shall be yours. But set foot within that galley—enter the gates of the Tower—and another year shall not pass over your head."

"Guards!" cried Lord Guilford Dudley, advancing and motioning to his attendants—"remove this beldame and her companion, and place them in arrest."

"Have patience, my dear lord," said Jane, in a voice so sweet, that it was impossible to resist it—"the poor woman is distraught."

"No, lady, I am not distraught," rejoined the old woman, "though I have suffered enough to make me so."

"Can I relieve your distresses?" inquired Jane, kindly.

"In no other way than by following my caution," answered the old woman. "I want nothing but a grave."

"Who are you that dare to hold such language as this to your queen?" demanded Lord Guilford Dudley, angrily.

"I am Gunnora Braose," replied the old woman, fixing a withering glance upon him, "nurse and foster-mother to Henry Seymour, Duke of Somerset, lord protector of England, who perished on the scaffold by the foul practices of your father."

"Woman," rejoined Lord Guilford, in a menacing tone, "be warned by me. You speak at the peril of your life."

"I know it," replied Gunnora; "but that shall not hinder me. If I succeed in saving that fair young creature, whom your father's arts have placed in such fearful jeopardy, from certain destruction, I care not what becomes of me. My boldness, I am well assured, will be fearfully visited upon me, and upon my grandson at my side. But were it the last word I had to utter,—were this boy's life," she added, laying her hand on the youth's shoulder, who arose at the touch, "set against hers, I would repeat my warning."

"Remove your cap in presence of the queen, knave," cried one of the halberdiers, striking off the young man's cap with his staff.

"She is not my queen," rejoined the youth, boldly; "I am for Queen Mary, whom Heaven and Our Lady preserve!"

"Peace, Gilbert!" cried Gunnora, authoritatively.

"Treason! treason!" exclaimed several voices—"down with them!"

"Do them no injury," interposed Jane, waving her hand; "let them depart freely. Set forward, my lords."

"Hear me, sovereign lady, before I am driven from you," cried the old woman, in accents of passionate supplication—"hear me, I implore you. You are going to a prison, not a palace.—Look at yon angry sky from which the red lightning is flashing. A moment since it was bright and smiling; at your approach it has become black and overcast. It is an omen not to be despised."

"Hence!" cried Lord Guilford.

"And you, Lord Guilford Dudley," continued Gunnora, in a stern tone,—"you, who have added your voice to that of your false father, to induce your bride to accept the crown,—think not you will ever rule this kingdom,—think not the supreme authority will be yours. You are a puppet in your father's hands; and when you have served his turn, he will cast you aside—or deal with you as he dealt with Lord Seymour of Dudley,—with the lord protector, *by the axe*,—or, as he dealt with his sovereign, Edward the Sixth, *by poison*."

"This passeth all endurance," exclaimed Lord Guilford;—"away with her to prison."

"Not so, my dear lord," said Queen Jane. "See you not that her supposed wrongs have turned her brain? She is faithful to the memory of the lord protector. If my reign prove as brief as she would have me believe it will be, it shall never be marked by severity. My first act shall be one of clemency. Take this ring, my poor woman," she added, detaching a brilliant from her taper finger, "and when you need a friend, apply to Queen Jane."

Gunnora received the costly gift with a look of speechless gratitude; the tears started to her eyes, and she sank upon her knees in the boat, burying her face in her hands. In this state, she was rowed swiftly away by her grandson, while the loudest shouts were raised for the munificence and mercy of Jane, who was not sorry to hide herself behind the silken curtains of her barge.

At this moment, a loud and rattling peal of thunder burst overhead.

Seated beneath a canopy of state, supported by the richest silken cushions, and with her tiny feet resting upon a velvet footstool, adorned with her cipher and that of her husband interwoven with love-knots, Jane proceeded along the river; her heart oppressed with fears and forebodings, to which she gave no utterance, but which the storm now raging around with frightful violence was not calculated to allay. The thunder was awfully loud; the lightning almost insupportably vivid; but fortunately for those exposed to the tempest, it was unattended with rain. Lord Guilford Dudley was unremitting in his assiduity to his lovely consort, and bitterly reproached himself for allowing her to set forth at such a season. As they approached that part of the river from which the noble old gothic cathedral of St. Paul's—one of the finest structures in the world, and destroyed, it is almost needless to say, by the Fire of London, when it was succeeded by the present pile—was best seen, Jane drew aside the curtains of her barge, and gazed with the utmost admiration upon the magnificent fane. The storm seemed to hang over its square and massive tower, and flashes of forked lightning of dazzling brightness appeared to shoot down each instant upon the body of the edifice.

"Like me, it is threatened," Jane mentally ejaculated; "and perhaps the blow that strikes me may strike also the religion of my country. Whatever betide me, Heaven grant that that noble pile may never again be polluted by the superstitious ceremonies and idolatries of Rome!"

Viewed from the Thames, London, even in our own time, presents many picturesque and beautiful points; but at the period to which this chronicle refers, it must have presented a thousand more. Then, gardens and stately palaces adorned its banks; then, the spires and towers of the churches shot into an atmosphere unpolluted by smoke; then, the houses, with their fanciful gables, and vanes, and tall twisted chimneys, invited and enchained the eye; then, the streets, of which a passing glimpse could be caught, were narrow and intricate: then, there was the sombre, dungeon-like strong-hold already alluded to, called Baynard's Castle; the ancient tavern of the Three Cranes; the Still-yard; and above all, the Bridge, even then old, with its gateways, towers, drawbridges, houses, mills, and chapel,-enshrined like a hidden and cherished faith within its inmost heart. All this has passed away. But if we have no old St. Paul's, no old London Bridge, no quaint and picturesque old fabrics, no old and frowning castles, no old taverns, no old wharfs—if we have none of these, we have still *the Tower;* and to that grand relic of antiquity, well worth all the rest, we shall, without further delay, proceed.

Having passed beneath the narrow arches of London Bridge, the houses on which were crowded with spectators, and the windows hung with arras and rich carpets, the royal barge drew up at the distance of a bow-shot from the Tower. Jane again drew aside the curtain, and when she beheld the sullen ramparts of the fortress over which arose its lofty citadel (the White Tower), with its weather-whitened walls relieved against the dusky sky, and looking like the spectre of departed greatness,—her firmness for an instant forsook her, and the tears involuntarily started to her eyes. But the feeling was transient; and more stirring emotions were quickly aroused by the deafening roar of ordnance which broke from the batteries, and which was instantly answered from the guns of several ships lying at anchor near them. By this time, the storm had in a great measure subsided; the thunder had become more distant, and the lightning only flashed at long intervals. Still, the sky had an ominous appearance, and the blue electric atmosphere in which the pageant was enveloped gave it a ghostly and unsubstantial look. Meanwhile, the lord mayor and his suite, the bishops, the privy council, the ambassadors, and the Dukes of Northumberland and Suffolk, having disembarked, the wafter having the charge of the royal galley drew it towards the land. Another "marvellous great shot," as it is described, was then fired, and amid flourishes of trumpets, peals of ordnance, and ringing of bells, Jane landed. Here, however, as heretofore, she was coldly received by the citizens, who hovered around in boats,—and here, as if she was destined to receive her final warning, the last sullen peal of thunder marked the moment when she set her foot on the ground. The same preparations had been made for her landing as for her embarkation. Two lines of halberdiers were drawn up alongside the platform, and between them was laid a carpet similar to that previously used. Jane walked in the same state as before,—her train supported by her mother,—and attended on her right hand by her husband, behind whom came his esquire, the young and blooming Cuthbert Cholmondeley.

Where there are so many claimants for attention, it is impossible to particularize all; and we must plead this as an apology for not introducing this gallant at an earlier period. To repair the omission, it may now be stated that Cuthbert Cholmondeley was a younger branch of an old Cheshire family; that he was accounted a perfect model of manly beauty; and that he was attired upon the present occasion in a doublet of white satin slashed with blue, which displayed his slight but symmetrical figure to the greatest advantage.

Proceeding along the platform by the side of a low wall which guarded the southern moat, Jane passed under a narrow archway formed by a small embattled tower connected with an external range of walls facing Petty

Wales. She next traversed part of the space between what was then called the Bulwark Gate and the Lion's Gate, and which was filled with armed men, and passing through the postern, crossed a narrow stone bridge. This brought her to a strong portal, flanked with bastions and defended by a double portcullis, at that time designated the Middle Tower. Here Lord Clinton, Constable of the Tower, with the lieutenant, the gentleman porter, and a company of warders, advanced to meet her. By them she was conducted with much ceremony over another stone bridge, with a drawbridge in the centre, crossing the larger moat, to a second strong barbican, similarly defended and in all other respects resembling the first, denominated the Gate Tower. As she approached this portal, she beheld through its gothic arch a large assemblage, consisting of all the principal persons who had assisted at the previous ceremonial, drawn up to receive her. As soon as she emerged from the gateway with her retinue, the members of the council bent the knee before her. The Duke of Northumberland offered her the keys of the Tower, while the Marquess of Winchester, lord treasurer, tendered her the crown.

Queen Jane's entrance into the Tower.

At this proud moment, all Jane's fears were forgotten, and she felt herself in reality a queen. At this moment, also, her enemies, Simon Renard and De Noailles, resolved upon her destruction. At this moment, Cuthbert Cholmondeley, who was placed a little to the left of the queen, discovered amid the by-standers behind one of the warders a face so exquisitely beautiful, and a pair of eyes of such witchery, that his heart was instantly captivated; and at this moment, also, another pair of very jealous-looking eyes, peering out of a window in the tower adjoining the gateway, detected what was passing between the youthful couple below, and inflamed their owner with a fierce and burning desire of revenge.

II.-OF THE INDIGNITY SHOWN TO THE PRIVY COUNCIL BY THE DUKE OF NORTHUMBERLAND; AND OF THE RESOLUTION TAKEN BY SIMON RENARD TO AVENGE THEM.

When the ceremonial at the Tower gate was ended, Queen Jane was conducted by the Duke of Northumberland to an ancient range of buildings, standing at the south-east of the fortress, between the Lanthorn Tower, now swept away, and the Salt Tower. This structure, which has long since disappeared, formed the palace of the old monarchs of England, and contained the royal apartments. Towards it Jane proceeded between closely-serried ranks of archers and arquebusiers, armed with long-bows and calivers. The whole line of fortifications, as she passed along, bristled with partizans and pikes. The battlements and turrets of St. Thomas's Tower, beneath which yawned the broad black arch spanning the Traitor's Gate, was planted with culverins and sakers; while a glimpse through the grim portal of the Bloody Tower,—which, with its iron teeth, seemed ever ready to swallow up the victims brought through the fatal gate opposite it,—showed that the vast area and green in front of the White Tower was filled with troops. All these defensive preparations, ostentatiously displayed by Northumberland, produced much of the effect he desired upon the more timorous of his adversaries. There were others, however, who regarded the exhibition as an evidence of weakness, rather than power; and amongst these was Simon Renard. "Our duke, I see," he remarked to his companion, De Noailles, "fears Mary more than he would have us believe. The crown that requires so much guarding cannot be very secure. Ah! well, he has entered the Tower by the great gate to-day; but if he ever quits it," he added, glancing significantly at the dark opening of Traitors Gate, which they wero then passing, "his next entrance shall be by yonder steps." Jane, meanwhile, had approached the ancient palace with her train. Its arched gothic doorway was guarded by three gigantic warders, brothers, who, claiming direct descent from the late monarch, Harry the Eighth, were nicknamed by their companions, from their extraordinary stature, Og, Gog, and Magog. Og, the eldest of the three, was the exact image, on a large scale, of his royal sire. By their side, as if for the sake of contrast, with an immense halbert in his hand, and a look of swelling importance, rivalling that of the frog in the fable, stood a diminutive but full-grown being, not two feet high, dressed in the garb of a page. This mannikin, who, besides his dressed figure, had a malicious and ill-favoured countenance, with a shock head of yellow hair, was a constant attendant upon the giants, and an endless source of diversion to them. Xit—for so was the dwarf named—had been found, when an infant, and scarcely bigger than a thumb, one morning at Og's door, where he was placed in the fragment of a blanket, probably out of ridicule. Thrown thus upon his compassion, the good-humoured giant adopted the tiny foundling, and he became, as has been stated, a constant attendant and playmate—or, more properly, plaything—of himself and his brethren. Unable to repress a smile at the ludicrous dignity of the dwarf, who, advancing a few steps towards her, made her a profound salutation as she passed, and bade her welcome in a voice as shrill as a child's treble; nor less struck with the herculean frames and huge stature of his companions,—they were all nearly eight feet high, though Magog exceeded his brethren by an inch;—Jane ascended a magnificent oaken staircase, traversed a long gallery, and entered a spacious but gloomy-looking hall, lighted by narrow gothic windows filled with stained glass, and hung with tarnished cloth of gold curtains and faded arras. The furniture was cumbrous, though splendid,—much of it belonging to the period of Henry the Seventh, though some of it dated as far back as the reign of Edward the Third, when John of France was detained a prisoner within the Tower, and feasted by his royal captor within this very chamber. The walls being of great thickness, the windows had deep embrasures, and around the upper part of the room ran a gallery. It was in precisely the same state as when occupied by Henry the Eighth, whose portrait, painted by Holbein, was placed over the immense chimney-piece; and as Jane gazed around, and thought how many monarchs had entered this room before her full of hope and confidence,—how with all their greatness they had passed away,—she became so powerfully affected, that she trembled, and could with difficulty support herself. Remarking her change of colour, and conjecturing the cause, Northumberland begged her to retire for a short time to repose herself before she proceeded to the council-chamber within the White Tower, where her presence was required on business of the utmost moment. Gladly availing herself of the suggestion, Jane, attended by her mother and her dames of honour, withdrew into an inner chamber. On her departure, several of the privy-councillors advanced towards the duke, but, after returning brief answers to their questions, in a tone calculated to cut short any attempt at conversation, he motioned towards him two ushers, and despatched them on different errands. He then turned to the Duke of Suffolk, who was standing by his side, and was soon engaged in deep and earnest discourse with him. Aware that they were suspected, and alarmed for their safety, the conspiring nobles took counsel together as to the course they should pursue. Some were for openly defying Northumberland,—some for a speedy retreat,—some for the abandonment of their project,—while others, more confident, affirmed that the Duke would not dare to take any severe measures, and, therefore, there was no ground for apprehension. Amid these conflicting opinions, Simon Renard maintained his accustomed composure. "It is plain," he said to the group around him, "that the Duke's suspicions are awakened, and that he meditates some reprisal. What it is will presently be seen. But trust in me, and you shall yet wear your heads upon your shoulders."

At the expiration of a quarter of an hour, the Queen, who had been summoned by Lord Guilford Dudley, reappeared. The great door was then instantly thrown open by two officials with white wands, and, attended by Northumberland, to whom she gave her hand, traversing a second long gallery, she descended a broad flight of steps, and entered upon another range of buildings, which has since shared the fate of the old palace, but which then, extending in a northerly direction, and flanked on the right by a fortification denominated the Wardrobe Tower, connected the royal apartments with the White Tower. Taking her way through various halls, chambers, and passages in this pile, Jane, at length, arrived at the foot of a wide stone staircase, on mounting which she found herself in a large and lofty chamber, with a massive roof crossed and supported by ponderous beams of timber. This room, which was situated within the White Tower, and which Jane was apprised adjoined the council-chamber, was filled with armed men. Smiling at this formidable assemblage, Northumberland directed the Queen towards a circular-arched opening in the wall on the right, and led her into a narrow vaulted gallery formed in the thickness of the wall. A few steps brought them to another narrow gallery, branching off on the left, along which they proceeded. Arrived at a wide opening in the wall, a thick curtain was then drawn aside by two attendants, and Jane was ushered into the council-chamber. The sight which met her gaze was magnificent beyond description. The vast hall, resembling in all respects the antechamber she had just quitted, except that it was infinitely more spacious, with its massive roof hung with banners and its wooden pillars decorated with velvet and tapestry, was crowded to excess with all the principal persons and their attendants who had formed her retinue in her passage along the river, grouped according to their respective ranks. At the upper end of the chamber, beneath a golden canopy, was placed the throne; on the right of which stood the members of the privy-council, and on the left the bishops. Opposite to the throne, at the lower extremity of the room, the walls were hung with a thick curtain of black velvet, on which was displayed a large silver scutcheon charged with the royal blasen. Before this curtain was drawn up a line of arquebusiers, each with a caliver upon his shoulder.

No sooner was the Queen seated, than Northumberland, who had placed himself at the foot of the throne, prostrated himself, and besought her permission to lay before the lords of the council a despatch, just received from the Lady Mary; which being accorded, he arose, and, turning towards them, unfolded a paper, and addressed them in a stern tone as follows:— "My lords," he began, "it will scarcely surprise you to be informed that the Lady Mary, in the letter I here hold, given under her signet, and dated from

Kenninghall in Norfolk, lays claim to the imperial crown of this realm, and requires and charges you, of your allegiance, which you owe to her, and to none other,—it is so written, my lords,—to employ yourselves for the honour and surety of her person only; and furthermore, to cause her right and title to the crown and government of the realm to be proclaimed within the city of London and other places, as to your wisdoms shall seem good. Now, my lords, what say you? What answer will you make to these insolent demands—to these idle and imaginary claims?"

"None whatever," replied the Earl of Pembroke; "we will treat them with the scorn they merit."

"That may not be, my lord," observed Queen Jane; "your silence will be misconstrued."

"Ay, marry will it," rejoined Northumberland, glancing fiercely at the Earl; "and your advice, my lord of Pembroke, savours strongly of disloyalty. I will tell you how you shall answer this misguided lady. You shall advertise her, firstly, that on the death of our sovereign lord, Edward the Sixth, Queen Jane became invested and possessed with the just and right title in the imperial crown of this realm, not only by good order of ancient laws, but also by our late sovereign lord's letters patent, signed with his own hand, and sealed with the great seal of England, in presence of the most part of the nobles, councillors, judges, and divers other grave and sage personages, assenting to and subscribing the same. You shall next tell her, that having sworn allegiance to Queen Jane, you can offer it to no other, except you would fall into grievous and unspeakable enormities. You shall also remind her, that by the divorce made between the king of famous memory, King Henry the Eighth, and the lady Catherine her mother, confirmed by sundry acts of parliament yet in force, she was justly made illegitimate and unheritable to the crown of this realm. And lastly, you shall require her to surcease, by any pretence, to vex and molest our sovereign lady Queen Jane, or her subjects from their true faith and allegiance unto her grace. This, my lords, is the answer you shall return."

"We will consider of it," cried several voices.

"Your decision must be speedy," returned the Duke, scornfully; "a messenger waits without, to convey your reply to the Lady Mary. And to spare your lordships any trouble in penning the despatch, I have already prepared it."

"Prepared it!" ejaculated Cecil.

"Ay, prepared it," repeated the Duke. "It is here," he added, producing a parchment, "fairly enough written, and only lacking your lordships' signatures. Will it please you, Sir William Cecil, or you, my lord of Pembroke, or you, Shrewsbury, to cast an eye over it, to see whether it differs in aught from what I have counselled as a fitting answer to Mary's insolent message? You are silent: then, I may conclude you are satisfied."

"Your grace concludes more than you have warrant for," rejoined the Earl of Pembroke; "I am *not* satisfied, nor will I subscribe that letter."

"Nor I," added Cecil.

"Nor I," repeated several others.

"We shall see," returned Northumberland: "bring pen and ink," he added, motioning to an attendant, by whom his commands were instantly obeyed. "Your grace of Canterbury," he continued, addressing Cranmer, "will sign it first. 'Tis well. And now, my lord Marquess of Winchester, your signature; my lord Bedford, yours; now yours, Northampton; yours, my lord chancellor; next, I shall attach my own; and now yours, brother of Suffolk. You see, my lords," he said, with a bitter smile, "you will be well kept in countenance."

While this was passing, Simon Renard, who stood among the throng of privy-councillors, observed in a whisper to those nearest him,—"If this despatch is signed and sent forth, Mary's hopes are ruined. She will suspect some treachery on the part of her friends, and immediately embark for France, which is what Northumberland desires to accomplish."

"His scheme shall be defeated, then," replied Pembroke; "it never shall be signed."

"Be not too sure of that," rejoined Renard, with a scarcely-repressed sneer.

"And now, my lord of Arundel," said the Duke, taking the document from Suffolk, "we tarry for your signature."

"Then your grace must tarry still longer," replied Arundel, sullenly, "for I am in no mood to furnish it."

"Ha!" exclaimed Northumberland, fiercely,—but, instantly checking himself, he turned to the next peer, and continued: "I will pass on, then, to you, Lord Shrewsbury. I am assured of *your* loyalty. What! do you, too, desert your queen? God's mercy! my lord, I have been strangely mistaken in you. Pembroke, you can now prove I was in error. You fold your arms—'tis well! I understand you. Rich, Huntingdon, Darcy, I appeal to you. My lords! my lords! you forget to whom you owe allegiance. Sir Thomas Cheney,—do you not hear me speak to you, Sir Thomas? Cecil, my politic, crafty Cecil,—a few strokes of your pen is all I ask, and those you refuse me. Gates, Petre, Cheke,—will none of you move? will none sign?"

"None," answered Pembroke.

"It is false," cried Northumberland, imperiously; "you shall *all* sign,—*all!* vile, perjured traitors that you are! I will have your hands to this paper, or, by God's precious soul! I will seal it with your blood. Now, will you obey me?"

There was a stern, deep silence.

"Will you obey him?" demanded Renard, in a mocking whisper. "No!" answered Pembroke, fiercely.

"Guards!" cried Northumberland, "advance, and attach their persons."

The command was instantly obeyed by the arquebusiers, who marched forward and surrounded them.

Jane fixed an inquiring look upon Northumberland, but she spoke not.

"What next?" demanded Pembroke, in a loud voice.

"The block," replied Northumberland.

"The block!" exclaimed Jane, rising, while the colour forsook her cheek. "Oh! no, my lord,—no."

"But I say yea," returned the Duke, peremptorily. "'Fore Heaven! these rebellious lords think I am as fearful of shedding blood as they are of shedding ink. But they shall find they are mistaken. Away with them to instant execution."

"Your grace cannot mean this!" cried Jane, horror-stricken.

"They shall have five minutes for reflection," returned the Duke, sternly. "After that time, nothing shall save them.'"

An earnest consultation was held among the council. Three minutes had expired. The Duke beckoned a sergeant of the guard towards him.

"You had better sign," whispered Simon Renard; "I will find some means of communicating with her highness."

"We have reflected," cried the Earl of Pembroke, "and will do your grace's behests."

"It is well," answered Northumberland. "Set them free." As soon as the guard had withdrawn, the council advanced, and each, in turn, according to his degree, subscribed the despatch. This done, Northumberland delivered it to an officer, enjoining him to give it instantly to the messenger, with orders to the latter to ride for his life, and not to draw bridle till he reached Kenninghall.

"And now," continued the Duke, addressing another officer, "let the gates of the Tower be closed, the drawbridges raised, and suffer none to go forth, on pain of death, without my written order."

"Diable!" exclaimed De Noailles, shrugging his shoulders.

"Prisoners!" cried several of the privy-councillors.

"You are the queen's guests, my lords," observed the Duke, drily.

"Do you agree to my scheme now?" asked Renard, in a deep whisper. "Do you consent to Northumberland's assassination?"

"I do," replied Pembroke. "But who will strike the blow?"

"I will find the man," answered Renard.

These words, though uttered under the breath of the speakers, reached the ears of Cuthbert Cholmondeley.

Shortly afterwards, the council broke up; and Jane was conducted with much state to the royal apartments.

III.-OF THE THREE GIANTS OF THE TOWER, OG, GOG, AND MAGOG; OF XIT, THE DWARF; OF THE FAIR CICELY; OF PETER TRUSBUT, THE PANTLER, AND POTENTIA HIS WIFE; OF HAIRUN THE REARWARD, RIBALD THE WARDER, MAUGER THE HEADSMAN, AND

NIGHTGALL THE JAILOR: AND OF THE PLEASANT PASTIME HELD IN THE STONE KITCHEN.

Cuthbert Cholmondeley, it may be remembered, was greatly struck by a beautiful damsel whom he discovered among the crowd during the ceremonial at the Gate Tower; and, as faithful chroniclers, we are bound to state that the impression was mutual, and that if he was charmed with the lady, she was not less pleased with him. Notwithstanding her downcast looks, the young esquire was not so inexperienced in feminine arts as to be unconscious of the conquest he had made. During the halt at the gate, he never withdrew his eyes from her for a single moment, and when he was reluctantly compelled to move forward with the procession, he cast many a lingering look behind. As the distance lengthened between them, the courage of the damsel seemed to revive; she raised her head, and before her admirer had reached the extremity of the lofty wall masking the lieutenant's lodgings, he perceived her gazing fixedly after him. She held by the hand a little curly-haired boy, whom Cholmondeley concluded must be her brother,—and he was perplexing himself as to her rank,—for though her beauty was of the highest order, and her lineaments such as might well belong to one of high birth, her attire seemed to bespeak her of no exalted condition,—when an incident occurred, which changed the tenor of his thoughts, and occasioned him not a little uneasiness. While she remained with her eyes fixed upon him, a tall man in a dark dress rushed, with furious gestures and an inflamed countenance, out of the gateway leading to the inner line of fortifications on the left, and shaking his hand menacingly at the esquire, forced her away. Cholmondeley saw her no more; but the imploring look which she threw at him as she disappeared, produced so powerful an effect upon his feelings that it was with difficulty he could prevent himself from flying to her assistance. So absorbed was he by this idea, that he could think of nothing else;—the pageant, at which he was assisting, lost all interest for him, and amid the throng of court beauties who surrounded him, he beheld only the tender blue eyes, the light satin tresses, the ravishing countenance, and sylph-like person of the unknown maiden. Nor could he exclude from his recollection the figure of the tall dark man; and he vainly questioned himself as to the tie subsisting between him and the damsel. Could he be her father?—Though his age might well allow of such a supposition, there was no family resemblance to warrant it. Her husband?—that he was scarcely disposed to admit. Her lover?—he trembled with jealous rage at the idea. In this perplexity, he bethought himself of applying for information to one of the warders; and, accordingly, he addressed himself to Magog, who, with Xit, happened to be standing near him. Describing the damsel, he inquired of the giant whether he knew anything of her.

"Know her!" rejoined Magog, "ay, marry, do I. Who that dwells within this fortress knows not fair Mistress Cicely, the Rose of the Tower, as she is called? She is daughter to Dame Prudentia Trusbut, wife of Peter the pantler—"

"A cook's daughter!" exclaimed Cholmondeley, all his dreams of high-born beauty vanishing at once.

"Nay, I ought rather to say," returned the giant, noticing the young mans look of blank disappointment, and guessing the cause, "that she *passes* for his daughter."

"I breathe again," murmured Cholmondeley.

"Her real birth is a mystery," continued Magog; "or, if the secret is known at all, it is only to the worthy pair who have adopted her. She is said to be the offspring of some illustrious and ill-fated lady, who was imprisoned within the Tower, and died in one of its dungeons, after giving birth to a female child, during the reign of our famous king, Harry the Eighth," and he reverently doffed his bonnet as he pronounced his sire's name; "but I know nothing of the truth or falsity of the story, and merely repeat it because you seem curious about her."

"Your intelligence delights me," replied Cholmondeley, placing a noble in his hand. "Can you bring me where I can obtain further sight of her?"

"Ay, and speech too, worshipful sir, if you desire it," replied the giant, a smile illuminating his ample features. "When the evening banquet is over, and my attendance at the palace is no longer required, I shall repair to the Stone Kitchen at Master Trusbut's dwelling, where a supper is provided for certain of the warders and other officers of the Tower, to which I and my brethren are invited, and if it please you to accompany us, you are almost certain to behold her."

Cholmondeley eagerly embraced the offer, and it was next arranged that the dwarf should summon him at the proper time.

"If your worship requires a faithful emissary to convey a letter or token to the fair damsel," interposed Xit, "I will undertake the office."

"Fail not to acquaint me when your master is ready," replied Cholmondeley, "and I will reward you. There is one question," he continued, addressing Magog, "which I have omitted to ask.—Who is the tall dark man who seems to exercise such strange control over her? Can it be her adoptive father, the pantier?"

"Of a surety no," replied the giant, grinning, "Peter Trusbut is neither a tall man nor a dark; but is short, plump, and rosy, as beseems his office. The person to whom your worship alludes must be Master Lawrence Nightgall, the chief jailor, who lately paid his suit to her. He is of a jealous and revengeful temper, and is not unlikely to take it in dudgeon that a handsome gallant should set eyes upon the object of his affections."

"Your description answers exactly to the man I mean," returned Cholmondeley, gravely.

"Shall I bear a cartel to him from your worship?" said Xit. "Or, if you require a guard, I will attend upon your person," he added, tapping the pummel of his sword.

"I do not require your services in either capacity, as yet, valiant sir," replied the esquire, smiling. "After the banquet I shall expect you."

Resuming his place near Lord Guilford Dudley, Cholmondeley shortly afterwards proceeded with the royal cortege to the council-chamber, where, being deeply interested by Northumberland's address to the conspiring lords, he for an instant forgot the object nearest his heart. But the next, it returned with greater force than ever; and he was picturing to himself the surprise, and, as he fondly hoped, the delight, he should occasion her by presenting himself at her dwelling, when Simon Renard's dark proposal to the Earl of Pembroke reached his ear. Anxious to convey the important information he had thus obtained to his master, as soon as possible, he endeavoured to approach him, but at this moment the council broke up, and the whole train returned to the palace. During the banquet that followed, no opportunity for an instant's private conference occurred—the signal for the separation of the guests being the departure of the Queen and her consort. While he was considering within himself what course he had best pursue, he felt his mantle slightly plucked behind, and, turning at the touch, beheld the dwarf.

"My master, the giant Magog, awaits you without, worshipful sir," said Xit, with a profound reverence.

Weighing his sense of duty against his love, he found the latter feeling too strong to be resisted. Contenting himself, therefore, with tracing a hasty line of caution upon a leaf torn from his tablets, he secured it with a silken thread, and delivering it to an attendant, commanded him instantly to take it to the Lord Guilford Dudley. The man departed, and Cholmondelcy, putting himself under the guidance of the dwarf, followed him to the great stairs, down which he strutted with a most consequential air, his long rapier clanking at each step he took. Arrived at the portal, the young esquire found the three giants, who had just been relieved from further attendance by another detachment of warders, and, accompanied by them, proceeded along the ward in the direction of the Gate-Tower. Sentinels, he perceived, were placed at ten paces' distance from each other along the ramparts; and the guards on the turrets, he understood from his companions, were doubled. On reaching the Gate-Tower, they found a crowd of persons, some of whom, on presenting passes from the Duke of Northumberland, were allowed to go forth; while others, not thus provided, were peremptorily refused. While the giants paused for a moment to contemplate this novel scene, an officer advanced from the barbican and acquainted the keepers of the inner portal that a prisoner was about to be brought in. At this intelligence, a wicket was opened, and two heralds, followed by a band of halberdiers, amidst whom walked the prisoner, stepped through it. Torches were then lighted by some of the warders, to enable them to discern the features of the latter, when it appeared, from his ghastly looks, his blood-stained apparel, and his hair, which was closely matted to his head by the ruddy stream that flowed from it, that some severe punishment had been recently inflicted upon him. He was a young man of nineteen or twenty, habited in a coarse dress of brown serge, of a slight but well-proportioned figure, and handsome features, though now distorted with pain and sullied with blood, and was instantly recognised by Cholmondelcy as the individual who had rowed Gunnora Braose towards the Queen. On making the discovery, Cholmondeley instantly demanded, in a stern tone, of the heralds, how they had dared, in direct opposition to their sovereign's injunctions, to punish an offender whom she had pardoned.

"We have the Duke of Northumberland's authority for what we have done," replied the foremost herald, sullenly; "that is sufficient for us."

"The punishment we have inflicted is wholly disproportioned to the villain's offence, which is little short of high treason," observed the other. "When we proclaimed the Queen's Highness at Cheapside, the audacious knave mounted a wall, flung his cap into the air, and shouted for Queen Mary. For this we set him in the pillory, and nailed his head to the wood; and he may think himself fortunate if he loseth it not as well as his ears, which have been cut off by the hangman."

"Ungrateful wretch!" cried Cholmondeley, addressing the prisoner, his former commiseration being now changed to anger; "is it thus you requite the bounty of your Queen?"

"I will never acknowledge a usurper," returned Gilbert, firmly.

"Peace!" cried the esquire; "your rashness will destroy you."

"It may so," retorted Gilbert, boldly; "but while I have a tongue to wag, it shall clamour for Queen Mary."

"Where are you going to bestow the prisoner?" inquired Gog from the foremost herald.

"In the guard-room," replied the man, "or some other place of security, till we learn his grace's pleasure."

"Bring him to the Stone Kitchen, then," returned Gog. "He will be as safe there as anywhere else, and you will be none the worse for a can of good liquor, and a slice of one of Dame Trusbut's notable pasties.'"

THE STONE KITCHEN.

"Agreed;" rejoined the heralds, smiling; "bring him along." While this was passing, Cholmondeley, whose impatience could brook no further delay, entreated Magog to conduct him at once to the habitation of the fair Cicely. Informing him that it was close at hand, the giant opened a small postern on the left of the gateway leading to the western line of fortifications, and ascending a short spiral staircase, ushered his companion into a chamber, which, to this day, retains its name of the Stone Kitchen. It was a low, large room, with the ceiling supported by heavy rafters, and the floor paved with stone. The walls were covered with shelves, displaying a goodly assortment of pewter and wooden platters, dishes and drinking-vessels; the fire-place was wide enough to admit of a whole ox being roasted within its limits; the chimney-piece advanced several yards into the room, while beneath its comfortable shelter were placed a couple of benches on either side of the hearth, on which a heap of logs was now crackling. Amid the pungent smoko arising from the wood could be discerned, through the vast aperture of the chimney, sundry hams, gammons, dried tongues, and other savoury meats, holding forth a prospect of future good cheer. At a table running across the room, and furnished with flagons and pots of wine, several boon companions were seated. The chief of these was a jovial-looking warder who appeared to be the life and soul of the party, and who had a laugh, a joke, or the snatch of a song, for every occasion. Opposite to him sat Peter Trusbut, the pantler, who roared at every fresh witticism uttered by his guest till the tears ran down his cheeks. Nor did the warder appear to be less of a favourite with Dame Potentia, a stout buxom personage, a little on the wrong side of fifty, but not without some remains of comeliness. She kept his glass constantly filled with the best wine, and his plate as constantly supplied with the choicest viands, so that, what with eating, drinking, singing, and a little sly love-making to Dame Trusbut, Pibald, for so was the warder named, was pretty well employed. At the lower end of the table was placed a savage-looking person, with red bloodshot eyes and a cadaverous countenance. This was Mauger, the headsman. He was engaged in earnest conversation with Master Hairun, the bearward, assistant-keeper of the lions,—an office, at that time, of some consequence and emolument. In the ingle nook was ensconced a venerable old man with a snowy beard descending to his knees, who remained with his eyes fixed vacantly upon the blazing embers. Seated on a stool near the hearth, was a little boy playing with a dog, whom Cholmondeley perceived at once was Cicely's companion; while the adjoining chair was occupied by the fair creature of whom the enamoured esquire was in search. Pausing at the doorway, he lingered for a moment to contemplate her charms. A slight shade of sadness clouded her brow—her eyes were fixed upon the ground, and she now and then uttered a half-repressed sigh. At this juncture, the jolly-looking warder struck up a Bacchanalian stave, the words of which ran as follows:—

With my back to the fire and my paunch to the table,

Let me eat,—let me drink as long as I am able:

Let me eat,—let me drink whate'er I set my whims on,

Until my nose is blue, and my jolly visage crimson.

The doctor preaches abstinence, and threatens me with dropsy,

But such advice, I needn't say, from drinking never stops ye:—

The man who likes good liquor is of nature brisk and brave, boys,

So drink away!—drink while you may!—

There's no drinking in the grave, boys!

"Well sung, my roystering Pibald," cried Magog, striding up to him, and delivering him a sounding blow on the back—"thou art ever merry, and hast the most melodious voice and the lustiest lungs of any man within the Tower."

"And thou hast the heaviest hand I ever felt on my shoulder, gigantic Magog," replied Ribald; "so we are even. But come, pledge me in a brimmer, and we will toss off a lusty measure to the health of our sovereign lady, Queen Jane. What say you, Master Trusbut?—and you, good Hairun—and you, most melancholic Mauger, a cup of claret will bring the colour to your cheeks. A pot of wine, good dame, to drink the Queen's health in. But whom have we yonder? Is that gallant thy companion, redoubted Magog?"

The giant nodded an affirmative.

"By my faith he is a well-looking youth," said Ribald—"but he seems to have eyes for no one excepting fair Mistress Cicely."

The Stone Kitchen.

Aroused by this remark, the young damsel looked up and beheld the passionate gaze of Cholmondeley fixed upon her. She started, trembled, and endeavoured to hide her confusion by industriously pursuing her occupation of netting. But in spite of her efforts to restrain herself, she could not help stealing a sidelong glance at him; and emboldened by this slight encouragement, Cholmondeley ventured to advance towards her. It is scarcely necessary to detail the common-place gallantries which the youth addressed to her, or the monosyllabic answers which she returned to them. The language of love is best expressed by the look which accompanies the word, and the tone in which that word is uttered; and this language, though as yet neither party was much skilled in it, appeared perfectly intelligible to both of them. Satisfied, at length, that she was not insensible to his suit, Cholmondeley drew nearer, and bending his head towards her, poured the most passionate protestations in her ear. What answer she made, if she made answer at all to these ardent addresses, we know not, but her heightened complexion and heaving bosom told that she was by no means insensible to them. Meanwhile, Og and Gog, together with the heralds and one or two men-at-arms, had entered the chamber with the prisoner. Much bustle ensued, and Dame Potentia was so much occupied with the new-comers and their wants, that she had little time to bestow upon her adoptive daughter. It is true that she thought the handsome stranger more attentive than was needful, or than she judged discreet; and she determined to take the earliest opportunity of putting a stop to the flirtation—but, just then, it happened that her hands were too full to allow her to attend to minor matters. As to Peter Trusbut, he was so much entertained with the pleasantries of his friend Ribald—and so full of the banquet he had provided for the Queen, the principal dishes of which he recapitulated for the benefit of his guests, that he saw nothing whatever that was passing between the young couple. Not so a gloomy-looking personage shrouded behind the angle of the chimney, who, with his hand upon his dagger, bent eagerly forward to catch their lightest whisper. Two other mysterious individuals had also entered the room, and stationed themselves near the doorway. As soon as Dame Trusbut had provided for the wants of her numerous guests, she turned her attention to the prisoner, who had excited her compassion, and who sat with his arms folded upon his breast, preserving the same resolute demeanour he had maintained throughout. Proffering her services to the sufferer, she bade her attendant, Agatha, bring a bowl of water to bathe his wounds, and a fold of linen to bind round his head. At this moment, Xit, the dwarf, who was by no means pleased with the unimportant part he was compelled to play, bethought him of an expedient to attract attention. Borrowing from the herald the scroll of the proclamation, he mounted upon Og's shoulders, and begged him to convey him to the centre of the room, that he might read it aloud to the assemblage, and approve their loyalty. The good-humoured giant complied. Supporting the mannikin with his left hand, and placing his large two-handed sword over his right shoulder, he walked forward, while the dwarf screamed forth the following preamble to the proclamation:—"*Jane, by the grace of God Queen of England, France, and Ireland, Defender of the Faith, and of the Church of England, and also of Ireland, under Christ on earth the supreme head. To all our loving, faithful, and obedients, and to every of them, greeting.*" Here he paused to shout and wave his cap, while the herald, who had followed them, to humour the joke raised his embroidered trumpet to his lips, and blew a blast so loud and shrill, that the very rafters shook with it. To this clamour Og added his stunning laughter, while his brethren, who were leaning over a screen behind, and highly diverted with the incident, joined in lusty chorus. Almost deafened by the noise, Dame Trusbut, by way of putting an end to it, raised her own voice to its utmost pitch, and threatened to turn Xit, whom she looked upon as the principal cause of the disturbance, out of the house. Unfortunately, in her anger, she forgot that she was engaged in dressing the prisoner's wounds, and while her left hand was shaken menacingly at the dwarf, her right convulsively grasped the poor fellow's head, occasioning him such exquisite pain, that he added his outcries to the general uproar. The more Dame Trusbut scolded, the more Og and his brethren laughed, and the louder the herald blew his trumpet—so that it seemed as if there was no likelihood of tranquillity being speedily restored—nor, in all probability would it have been so without the ejectment of the dwarf, had it not been for the interference of Ribald, who at length, partly by cajolery, and partly by coercion, succeeded in pacifying the angry dame. During this tumult, the two mysterious personages, who, it has been stated, had planted themselves at the doorway, approached the young couple unobserved, and one of them, after narrowly observing the features of the young man, observed in an under-tone to his companion, "It *is* Cuthbert Cholmondeley—You doubted me, my lord Pembroke, but I was assured it was Lord Guilford's favourite esquire, who had conveyed the note to his master, warning him of our scheme."

"You are right, M. Simon Renard," replied the earl. "I bow to your superior discernment."

"The young man is in possession of our secret," rejoined Renard, "and though we have intercepted the missive, he may yet betray us. He must not return to the palace."

"He never *shall* return, my lords," said a tall dark man, advancing towards them, "if you will entrust his detention to me."

"Who are you?" demanded Renard, eyeing him suspiciously. "Lawrence Nightgall, the chief jailor of the Tower."

"What is your motive for this offer?" pursued Renard.

"Look there!" returned Nightgall. "I love that damsel."

"I see;" replied Renard, smiling bitterly. "He has supplanted you."

"He has," rejoined Nightgall; "but he shall not live to profit by his good fortune."

"Hum!" said Renard, glancing at Cicely, "the damsel is lovely enough to ruin a man's soul. We will trust you."

"Follow me, then, without, my lords," replied Nightgall, "and I will convey him where he shall not cause further uneasiness to any of us. We have dungeons within the Tower, from which those who enter them seldom return."

"You are acquainted, no doubt, with the secret passages of the White Tower, friend?" asked Renard.

"With all of them," rejoined Nightgall. "I know every subterranean communication—every labyrinth—every hidden recess within the walls of the fortress, and there are many such—and can conduct you wherever you desire."

"You are the very man I want," cried Renard, rubbing his hands, gleefully. "Lead on."

And the trio quitted the chamber, without their departure being noticed.

Half an hour afterwards, as Cuthbert Cholmondeley issued from the postern with a heart elate with rapture at having elicited from the fair Cicely a confession that she loved him, he received a severe blow on the head from behind, and before he could utter a single outcry, he was gagged, and forced away by his assailants.

IV.—OF THE MYSTERIOUS OCCURRENCE THAT HAPPENED TO QUEEN JANE IN SAINT JOHN'S CHAPEL IN THE WHITE TOWER.

On that night Lord Guilford Dudley was summoned to a secret council by his father, the Duke of Northumberland, and as he had not returned at midnight, the Lady Hastings, who was in attendance upon the Queen, proposed that, to while away the time, they should pay a visit to St. John's Chapel in the White Tower, of the extreme beauty of which they had all heard, though none of them had seen it. Jane assented to the proposal, and accompanied by her sister, the Lady Herbert, and the planner of the expedition, Lady Hastings, she set forth. Two ushers led the way through the long galleries and passages which had to be traversed before they reached the White Tower; but on arriving at the room adjoining the council-chamber which had so lately been thronged with armed men, but which was now utterly deserted, Jane inquired from her attendants the way to the chapel, and on ascertaining it, commanded her little train to await her return there, as she had determined on entering the sacred structure alone. In vain her sisters remonstrated with her—in vain the ushers suggested that there might be danger in trusting herself in such a place at such an hour without protection—she remained firm—but promised to return in a few minutes, after which they could explore the chapel together.

Taking a lamp from one of the attendants, and pursuing the course pointed out to her, she threaded a narrow passage, similar to that she had traversed with the Duke in the morning, and speedily entered upon the gallery above the chapel. As she passed through the opening in the wall leading to this gallery, she fancied she beheld the retreating figure of a man, muffled in a cloak, and she paused for a moment, half-inclined to turn back. Ashamed, however, of her irresolution, and satisfied that it was a mere trick of the imagination, she walked on. Descending a short spiral wooden staircase, she found herself within one of the aisles of the chapel, and passing between its columns, entered the body of the fane. For some time, she was lost in admiration of this beautiful structure, which, in its style of architecture—the purest Norman—is without an equal. She counted its twelve massive and circular stone pillars, noted their various ornaments and mouldings, and admired their grandeur and simplicity. Returning to the northern aisle, she glanced at its vaulted roof, and was enraptured at the beautiful effect produced by the interweaving arches.

While she was thus occupied, she again fancied she beheld the same muffled figure she had before seen, glide behind one of the pillars. Seriously alarmed, she was now about to retrace her steps, when her eye rested upon an object lying at a little distance from her, on the ground. Prompted by an undefinable feeling of curiosity, she hastened towards it, and holding forward the light, a shudder ran through her frame, as she perceived at her feet, *an axe!* It was the peculiarly-formed implement used by the headsman, and the edge was turned towards her.

At this moment, her lamp was extinguished.

Queen Jane's first night in the Tower.

THE BY-WARD TOWER.

V.—OF THE MISUNDERSTANDING THAT AROSE BETWEEN QUEEN JANE AND HER HUSBAND, LORD GUILFORD DUDLEY.

JANE NOT appearing, and some time having elapsed since her departure, her sisters, who were anxiously awaiting her return in the room adjoining the council-chamber, became so uneasy, that, notwithstanding her injunctions to the contrary, they resolved to go in search of her. Accordingly, bidding the ushers precede them, they descended to the chapel; and their uneasiness was by no means decreased on finding it buried in darkness, and apparently empty. As they gazed around in perplexity and astonishment, a deep-drawn sigh broke from the northern aisle; and, hurrying in that direction, they discovered the object of their search, who had been hidden from view by the massive intervening pillars, extended upon a seat, and just recovering from a swoon into which she had fallen. Revived by their assiduities, Jane was soon able to speak, and the first thing she uttered was a peremptory order that no alarm should be given, or assistance sent for.

"I am now well—quite well," she said, with a look and in a tone that belied her words, "and require no further aid. Do not question me as to what has happened. My brain is too confused to think of it; and I would fain banish it altogether from my memory. Moreover, I charge you by your love and allegiance, that you mention to no one—not even to my dear lord and husband, should he interrogate you on the subject,—how you have just found me. And if my visit here be not remarked by him—as is not unlikely, if he should remain closeted with the Duke of Northumberland,—it is my will and pleasure that no allusion be made to the circumstance. You will not need to be told, dear sisters, that I have good reasons for thus imposing silence upon you. To you, sirs," she continued, addressing the ushers, who listened to her with the greatest surprise, "I also enjoin the strictest secrecy;— and look well you observe it."

The solemn and mysterious manner in which the Queen delivered her commands quite confounded her sisters, who glanced at each other as if they knew not what to think;—but they readily promised compliance, as did the ushers. Supporting herself on the arm of Lady Herbert, Jane then arose, and proceeded at a slow pace towards the eastern stair-case. As she was about to turn the corner of the aisle, she whispered to Lady Hastings, who walked on her left—"Look behind you, Catherine. Do you see nothing on the ground?"

"Nothing whatever, your highness," replied the other, glancing fearfully over her shoulder. "Nothing whatever, except the black and fantastic shadows of our attendants."

"Thank Heaven! it is gone," ejaculated Jane, as if relieved from a weight of anxiety.

"What is gone, dear sister?" inquired Lady Herbert, affectionately.

"Do not ask me," replied Jane, in a tone calculated to put an end to further conversation on the subject. "What I have seen and heard must for ever remain locked in my own bosom."

"I begin to think a spirit must have appeared to your majesty," observed Lady Herbert, whose curiosity was violently excited, and who, in common with most persons of the period, entertained a firm belief in supernatural appearances. "Every chamber in the Tower is said to be haunted,—and why not this ghostly chapel, which looks as if it were peopled with phantoms? I am quite sorry I proposed to visit it. But if I am ever caught in it again, except in broad daylight, and then only with sufficient attendance, your majesty shall have free leave to send me to keep company with the invisible world for the future. I would give something to know what you have seen. Perhaps it was the ghost of Anne Boleyn, who is known to walk;—or the guilty Catherine Howard,—or the old Countess of Salisbury. Do tell me which it was—and whether the spectre carried its head under its arm?"

"No more of this," said Jane, authoritatively. "Come with me to the altar."

"Your majesty is not going to remain here?" cried Lady Hastings. "I declare positively *I* dare not stop."

"I will not detain you longer than will suffice to offer a single prayer to Heaven," rejoined the Queen. "Be not afraid. Nothing will injure, or affright you."

"I am by no means sure of that," replied Lady Hastings. "And now I really *do* think I see something."

"Indeed!" exclaimed Jane, starting. "Where?"

"Behind the farthest pillar on the right," replied Lady Hastings, pointing towards it. "It looks like a man muffled in a cloak. There!—it moves."

"Go and see whether any one be lurking in the chapel," said Jane to the nearest usher, and speaking in a voice so loud, that it almost seemed as if she desired to be overheard.

The attendant obeyed; and immediately returned with the intelligence that he could find no one.

"Your fears, you perceive, are groundless, Catherine," observed Jane, forcing a smile.

"Not altogether, I am persuaded, from your manner, my dear sister, and gracious mistress," rejoined Lady Hastings. "Oh! how I wish I was safe back again in the palace."

"So do I," added Lady Herbert.

"A moment's patience and I am ready," rejoined Jane.

With this, she approached the altar, and prostrated herself on the velvet cushion before it.

"Almighty Providence!" she murmured in a tone so low as to be inaudible to the others, "I humbly petition thee and supplicate thee, that if the kingdom that has been given me be rightly and lawfully mine, thou wilt grant me so much grace and spirit, that I may govern it to thy glory, service, and advantage. But if it be otherwise—if I am unlawfully possessed of it, and am an hindrance to one who might serve thee more effectually, remove, O Lord, the crown from my head, and set it on that of thy chosen servant! And if what I have this night beheld be a fore-shadowing and a warning of the dreadful doom that awaits me, grant me, I beseech thee, strength to meet it with fortitude and resignation; so that my ending, like my life, may redound to thy honour, and the welfare of thy holy church." While Jane was thus devoutly occupied, her sisters, who stood behind her, could scarcely control their uneasiness, but glanced ever and anon timorously round, as if in expectation of some fearful interruption. Their fears were speedily communicated to the ushers; and though nothing occurred to occasion fresh alarm, the few minutes spent by the Queen in prayer appeared an age to her companions. There was something in the hour—it was past midnight,—and the place, calculated to awaken superstitious terrors. The lights borne by the attendants only illumined a portion of the chapel; rendering that which was left in shadow yet more sombre; while the columned aisles on either side, and the deeply-recessed arches of the gallery above, were shrouded in gloom. Even in broad day, St. John's Chapel is a solemn and a striking spot; but at midnight, with its heavy, hoary pillars, reared around like phantoms, its effect upon the imagination will be readily conceived to be far greater.

Already described as one of the most perfect specimens of Norman ecclesiastical architecture, this venerable structure, once used as a place of private worship by the old monarchs of England, and now as a receptacle for Chancery proceedings, has, from its situation in the heart of the White Tower, preserved, in an almost unequalled state, its original freshness and beauty; and, except that its floors are encumbered with cases, and its walls of Caen stone disfigured by a thick coat of white plaster, it is now much in the same state that it was at the period under consideration. It consists of a nave with broad aisles, flanked (as has been mentioned) by twelve circular pillars, of the simplest and most solid construction, which support a stone gallery of equal width with the aisles, and having an arcade corresponding with that beneath the floor is now boarded, but was formerly covered with a hard polished cement, resembling red granite. The roof is coved, and beautifully proportioned; and the fane is completed by a semicircular termination towards the east.

Old Stowe records the following order, given in the reign of Henry the Third, for its decoration:—"And that ye cause the whole chapel of St. John the Evangelist to be whited. And that ye cause three glass windows in the same chapel to be made; to wit, one on the north side, with a certain little Mary holding her child; the other on the south part, with the image of the Trinity; and the third, of St. John the Apostle and Evangelist, in the south part. And that ye cause the cross and the beam beyond the altar of the same chapel to be painted well and with good colours. And that ye cause to be made and painted two fair images where more conveniently and decently they may be done in the same chapel; one of St. Edward, holding a ring, and reaching it out to St. John the Evangelist." These fair images—the cross—the rood,—and the splendid illuminated window, are gone—most of them, indeed, were gone in Queen Jane's time—the royal worshippers are gone with them; but enough remains in its noble arcades, its vaulted aisles, and matchless columns, to place St. John's Chapel foremost in beauty of its class of architecture.

Her devotions over, Jane arose with a lighter heart, and, accompanied by her little train, quitted the chapel. On reaching her own apartments, she dismissed her attendants, with renewed injunctions of secrecy; and as Lord Guilford Dudley had not returned from the council, and she felt too much disturbed in mind to think of repose, she took from among the books on her table, a volume of the divine Plato, whose Phædo, in the original tongue, she was wont, in the words of her famous instructor, Roger Ascham, "to read with as much delight as some gentlemen would take in a merry tale of Boccace," and was speedily lost in his profound and philosophic speculations.

In this way the greater part of the night was consumed; nor was it till near day-break that she was aroused from her studies by the entrance of her husband.

"Jane, my beloved queen!" he exclaimed, hastening towards her with a countenance beaming with delight. "I have intelligence for you which will enchant you."

"Indeed! my dear lord,'" she replied, laying down her book, and rising to meet him. "What is it?"

"Guess," he answered, smiling.

"Nay, dear Dudley," she rejoined, "put me not to this trouble. Tell me at once your news, that I may participate in your satisfaction."

"In a word, then, my queen," replied Lord Guilford,—"My father and the nobles propose to elevate me to the same dignity as yourself."

Jane's countenance fell.

"They have not the power to do so, my lord," she rejoined gravely; "I, alone, can thus elevate you."

"Then I am king," cried Dudley, triumphantly.

"My lord," observed Jane, with increased gravity, "you will pardon me if I say I must consider of this matter."

"Consider of it!" echoed her husband, frowning; "I must have your decision at once. You can have no hesitation, since my father desires it. I am your husband, and claim your obedience."

"And I, my lord," rejoined Jane, with dignity, "am your queen; and, as such, it is for me, not you, to exact obedience. We will talk no further on the subject."

"As you please, madam," replied Lord Guilford, coldly. "To-morrow you will learn the Duke's pleasure."

"When I do so, he shall know mine," rejoined Jane.

"How is this?" exclaimed Dudley, gazing at her in astonishment. "Can it be possible you are the same Jane whom I left—all love—all meekness—all compliance?—or have a few hours of rule so changed your nature, that you no longer love me as heretofore?"

"Dudley," returned Jane, tenderly, "you are dear to me as ever; and if I accede not to your wishes, do not impute it to other than the right motive. As a queen, I have duties paramount to all other considerations,—duties which, so long as I *am* queen, I will fulfil to the best of my ability, and at every personal sacrifice. Be not wholly guided by the counsels of your father,—be not dazzled by ambition. The step you propose is fraught with danger. It may cost me my crown, and cannot ensure one to you."

"Enough," replied her husband, apparently convinced by her arguments. "We will postpone its further consideration till to-morrow."

When that morrow came, Dudley's first business was to seek his father, and acquaint him with the manner in which his communication to the Queen had been received. The haughty Duke appeared surprised, but imputed the failure to his son's mismanagement, and undertook to set it right. With this view, he repaired to the Queen's apartments, and on obtaining an audience, informed her that he and the lords of the council had resolved to place her husband on the throne beside her. Her answer differed in nothing from that which she had returned to Lord Guilford, except that it was couched in a firmer tone; but it had this addition, that she was well aware of his Grace's object in the proposal, which was, in effect, to obtain possession of the supreme power. In vain arguments, entreaties, and even threats, were used by the Duke: Jane continued inflexible. Northumberland was succeeded by his no less imperious spouse, who, with all the insolence of her arrogant nature, rated her daughter-in-law soundly, and strove to terrify her into compliance. But she, too, failed; and Lord Guilford was so enraged at his consort's obstinacy, that he quitted the Tower, and departed for Sion House, without even taking leave of her.

Perplexed as he felt by Jane's conduct, Northumberland was too well versed in human nature not to be aware that a character however soft and pliant may, by the sudden alteration of circumstances, be totally changed,—but he was by no means prepared for such a remarkable display of firmness as Jane had exhibited. The more he considered the matter, the more satisfied he became that she had some secret counsellor, under whose guidance she acted, and with the view of finding out who it was, he resolved to have all her motions watched. No one appeared so well fitted to this office as his daughter, the Lady Hastings; and sending for her, he extracted from her, in the course of conversation, all particulars with which she was acquainted of the mysterious occurrence in St. John's Chapel. This information filled Northumberland with new surprise, and convinced him that he had more to dread than he at first imagined, and that the schemes of his enemies must be in full operation. His suspicions fell upon Simon Renard, though he scarcely knew how to connect him with this particular occurrence. Dismissing his daughter with full instructions for the part he desired her to play, he continued for some time brooding over the mystery, and vainly trying to unravel it. At one time, he resolved to interrogate Jane; but the reception he had recently experienced, induced him to adopt a different and more cautious course. His thoughts, however, were soon diverted from the subject, by the onerous duties that pressed upon him. Amongst other distractions, not the least was the arrival of a messenger with the intelligence that Mary had retired from Kenninghall in Norfolk, whither he had despatched a body of men to surprise her, and retreated to a more secure post, Framlingham Castle—that she had been proclaimed in Norwich—and that her party was hourly gaining strength in all quarters. Ill news seldom comes alone, and the proud Duke experienced the truth of the adage. Other messengers brought word that the Earls of Bath, Sussex, and Oxford, Lord Wentworth, Sir Thomas Cornwallis, Sir Henry Jerningham, and other important personages, had declared themselves in her favour.

While he was debating upon the best means of crushing this danger in the bud, a page from Lady Hastings suddenly presented himself, and informed him that the Queen was at that moment engaged in deep conference with M. Simon Renard, in St. Peter's Chapel. On inquiry, the Duke learned that Jane, who had been greatly disturbed in mind since her husband's departure, had proceeded to St. Peter's Chapel—(a place of worship situated at the north end of the Tower Green, and appropriated to the public devotions of the court and household,)—accompanied by her mother, the Duchess of Suffolk, and her sisters, the Ladies Herbert and Hastings; and that the train had been joined by the Earls of Pembroke and Arundel, De Noailles, and Simon Renard—the latter of whom, when the Queen's devotions were ended, had joined her. Tarrying for no further information, the Duke summoned his attendants, and hastened to the Tower Green. Entering the chapel, he found the information he had received was correct. The wily ambassador was standing with the Queen before the altar.

INTERIOR OF ST. PETER'S CHAPEL.

VI.—OF THE SOLEMN EXHORTATION PRONOUNCED TO THE GIANTS BY MASTER EDWARD UNDERHILL, THE "HOT-GOSPELLER," AT THEIR LODGING IN THE BY-WARD TOWER; AND OF THE EFFECT PRODUCED THEREBY.

In spite of the interruption occasioned by the dwarf, the evening at the Stone Kitchen passed off pleasantly enough. Dame Potentia was restored to good humour by the attentions of the jovial warder, and the giants in consequence were regaled with an excellent and plentiful supper, of which Xit was permitted to partake. Whether it was that their long fasting, or their attendance at the state-banquet, had sharpened the appetites of the three gigantic brethren, or that the viands set before them were of a more tempting nature than ordinary, we pretend not to say, but certain it is that their prodigious performances at the table excited astonishment from all who witnessed them, and elicited the particular approbation of Ribald, who, being curious to ascertain how much they *could* eat, insisted on helping them to everything on the board, and, strange to say, met with no refusal.

With the profuse hospitality of the period, all the superfluities of the royal feast were placed at the disposal of the household; and it may therefore be conceived that Peter Trusbut's table was by no means scantily furnished. Nor was he disposed to stint his guests. Several small dishes which had been set before them having disappeared with marvellous celerity, he called for the remains of a lordly baron of beef, which had recently graced the royal sideboard. At the sight of this noble joint, Og, who had just appropriated a dish of roast quails, two of which he despatched at a mouthful, uttered a grunt of intense satisfaction, and abandoning the trifling dainties to Xit, prepared for the more substantial fare.

Assuming the part of carver, Peter Trusbut sliced off huge wedges of the meat, and heaped the platters of the giants with more than would have satisfied men of ordinary appetites. But this did not satisfy them. They came again and again. The meat was of such admirable quality—so well roasted—so full of gravy, and the fat was so exquisite, that they could not sufficiently praise it, nor do it sufficient justice. The knife was never out of Peter Trusbut's hands; nor was he allowed to remain idle a moment. Scarcely had he helped Og, when Gog's plate was empty; and before Gog had got his allowance, Magog was bellowing for more. And so it continued as long as a fragment remained upon the bones.

Puffing with the exertion he had undergone, the pantler then sat down, while Ribald, resolved not to be balked of his pastime, entreated Dame Potentia to let her guests wash down their food with a measure of metheglin. After some little solicitation, she complied, and returned with a capacious jug containing about three gallons of the balmy drink. The jug was first presented to Magog. Raising it to his lips, he took a long and stout pull, and then passed it to Gog, who detained it some seconds, drew a long breath, and returned it to Dame Trusbut, perfectly empty. By dint of fresh entreaties from the warder, Dame Potentia was once more induced to seek the cellar; and, on receiving the jug, Og took care to leave little in it for his brethren, but poured out what was left into a beaker for Xit.

They were now literally "giants refreshed;" and Peter Trusbut, perceiving that they still cast wistful glances towards the larder, complied with a significant wink from Ribald, and went in search of further provisions. This time he brought the better half of a calvered salmon, a knuckle of Westphalia ham, a venison pasty with a castellated crust of goodly dimensions, a larded capon, and the legs and carcass of a peacock, decorated with a few feathers from the tail of that gorgeous bird. Magog, before whom the latter dainty was placed, turned up his nose at it, and giving it to Xit, vigorously assaulted the venison pasty. It soon became evident that the board would again be speedily cleared; and though he had no intention of playing the niggardly host on the present occasion, Peter Trusbut declared that this was the last time such valiant trenchermen should ever feed at his cost. But his displeasure was quickly dispelled by the mirth of the warder, who laughed him out of his resolution, and encouraged the giants to proceed by every means in his power. Og was the first to give in. Throwing back his huge frame on the bench, he seized a flask of wine that stood near him, emptied it into a flagon, tossed it off at a draught, and declared he had had enough. Gog soon followed his example. But Magog seemed insatiable, and continued actively engaged, to the infinite diversion of Ribald, and the rest of the guests.

There was one person to whom this festive scene afforded no amusement. This was the fair Cicely. After Cholmondeley's departure—though wholly unacquainted with what had befallen him—she lost all her sprightliness, and could not summon up a smile, though she blushed deeply when rallied by the warder. In surrendering her heart at the first summons of the enamoured esquire, Cicely had obeyed an uncontrollable impulse; but she was by no means satisfied with herself for her precipitancy. She felt that she ought to have resisted rather than have yielded to a passion which, she feared, could have no happy result; and though her admirer had vowed eternal constancy, and pleaded his cause with all the eloquence and fervour of deep and sincere devotion—an eloquence which seldom falls ineffectually on female ears— she was not so unacquainted with the ways of the world as to place entire faith in his professions. But it was now too late to recede. Her heart was no longer her own; and if her lover had deceived her, and feigned a passion which he did not feel, she had no help for it, but to love on unrequited.

While her bosom alternately fluttered with hope, or palpitated with fear, and her hands mechanically pursued their employment, she chanced to raise her eyes, and beheld the sinister gaze of Lawrence Nightgall fixed upon her. There was something in his malignant look that convinced her he read what was passing in her breast—and there was a bitter and exulting smile on his lip which, while it alarmed her on her account, terrified her (she knew not why) for her lover.

"You are thinking of the young esquire who left you an hour ago," he observed sarcastically.

"I will not attempt to deny it," replied Cicely, colouring; "I am."

"I know it," rejoined the jailer; "and he dared to tell you he loved you?"

Cicely made no reply.

"And you?—what answer did you give him, mistress?" continued Nightgall, furiously grasping her arm. "What answer did you give him, I say?"

"Let me go," cried Cicely. "You hurt me dreadfully. I will not be questioned thus."

"I overheard what you said to him," rejoined the jailer. "You told him that you loved him—that you had loved no other—and would wed no other."

"I told him the truth," exclaimed Cicely. "I do love him, and will wed him."

"It is false," cried Nightgall, laughing maliciously. "You will never see him again."

"How know you that?" she cried, in alarm.

"He has left the Tower—for ever," returned the jailer, moodily.

"Impossible!" cried Cicely. "The Duke of Northumberland has given orders that no one shall go forth without a pass. Besides, he told me he was returning to the palace."

"I tell you he is gone," thundered Nightgall. "Hear me, Cicely," he continued, passionately. "I have loved you long—desperately. I would give my life—my soul for you. Do not cast me aside for this vain court-gallant, who pursues you only to undo you. He would never wed you."

"He has sworn to do so," replied Cicely.

"Indeed!" cried Nightgall, grinding his teeth, "The oath will never be kept. Cicely, you must—you *shall* be mine."

"Never!" replied the maiden. "Do you suppose I would unite myself to one whom I hate, as I do you?"

"Hate me!" cried the jailer, grasping her arm with such force that she screamed with pain. "Do you dare to tell me so to my face?"

"I do," she rejoined. "Release me, monster!"

"Body of my father! what's the matter?" roared Magog, who was sitting near them. "Leave go your hold of the damsel, Master Nightgall," he added, laying down his knife and fork.

"Not at your bidding, you overgrown ox!" replied the jailer. "We'll see that," replied the giant. And stretching out his hand, he seized him by the nape of the neck, and drew him forcibly backwards.

"You shall bleed for this, caitiff!" exclaimed Nightgall, disengaging himself, and menacing him with his poniard.

"Tush!" rejoined Magog, contemptuously, and instantly disarming him. "Your puny weapon will serve me for a toothpick," he added, suiting the action to the word. And, amid the loud laughter of the assemblage, the jailer slunk away, muttering interjections of rage and vengeance.

Nightgall's dark hints respecting Cholmondeley were not without effect upon Cicely, who, well aware of his fierce and revengeful character, could not help fearing some evil; and when he quitted the Stone Kitchen, an undefinable impulse prompted her to follow him. Hastily descending the stairs, on gaining the postern she descried him hurrying along the road between the ballium wall and the external line of fortifications, and instantly decided on following him.

On reaching the projecting walls of the Beauchamp Tower, behind which she sheltered herself, she saw that he stopped midway between that fortification and the next turret, then known as the Devilin, or Robin the Devil's Tower, but more recently, from having been the prison of the unfortunate Earl of Essex, as the Devereux Tower. Here he disappeared. Hastening to the spot, Cicely looked for the door, through which he must have passed; and after some little search, discovered it. Pushing against it, it yielded to the pressure, and admitted her to a low passage, evidently communicating with some of the subterranean dungeons which she knew existed under this part of the fortress.

She had scarcely set foot within this passage, when she perceived the jailor returning; and had barely time to conceal herself behind an angle of the wall, when he approached the spot where she stood. In his haste he had forgotten to lock the door, and he now, with muttered execrations, hastened to repair his error; cutting off by this means the possibility of Cicely's retreat. And here, for the present, it will be necessary to leave her, and return to the Stone Kitchen.

The attention which must otherwise have been infallibly called to Cicely's disappearance was diverted by the sudden entrance of a very singular personage, whose presence served somewhat to damp the hilarity of the party. This was Master Edward Underhill—a man of some ability, but of violent religious opinions, who, having recently been converted to the new doctrines, became so zealous in their support and propagation, that he obtained among his companions the nick-name of the "Hot-gospeller." He was a tall thin man, with sandy hair, and a scanty beard of the same colour. His eyes were blear and glassy, with pink lids utterly devoid of lashes, and he had a long lantern-shaped visage. His attire was that of a gentleman-pensioner.

Rebuking the assemblage for their unseemly mirth, and mounting upon a stool, Master Underhill would fain have compelled them to listen to a discourse on the necessity of extirpating papacy and idolatry from the land—but he was compelled, by the clamour which his exordium occasioned, to desist. He was, moreover, brought down, with undue precipitation, from his exalted position by Xit, who creeping under the stool, contrived to overset it, and prostrated the Gospeller on the floor, to the infinite entertainment of the guests, and the no small damage of his nose.

This incident, though received in good part even by the principal sufferer, served to break up the party. Apprehensive of some further disturbance, and not without fears that the giants might indulge as freely with the fluids as they had done with the solids, Dame Trusbut took advantage of the occurrence to dismiss her guests, which she did without much ceremony.

It was then for the first time that she noticed the absence of Cicely. Not being able to find her, the recollection of the handsome esquire, and of the attention he had paid her, rushed to her mind; and with a dreadful foreboding of impending misery, she despatched her husband to the palace to make inquiries after him; while she herself went to the gate—to the ramparts—everywhere, in short, that she thought it likely she could gain any information,—but everywhere without success.

The giants, meanwhile, with Xit, betook themselves to their lodgings in the By-ward Tower. The herald and the men-at-anns, who, it may be remembered, had charge of the prisoner Gilbert, not having received any further instructions respecting him, accompanied them thither. They were also attended by Master Edward Underhill, who was bent upon admonishing them, having been given to understand they were relapsing into papacy.

INTERIOR OF THE BY-WARD TOWER.

Arrived at the entrance of the By-ward Tower, the giants volunteered to take charge of the prisoner till the morning—an offer which was gladly accepted by the herald, who, intrusting him to their care, departed. But the Gospeller was not to be got rid of so easily. He begged to be admitted, and, partly by entreaties, partly by a bribe to the dwarf, succeeded in his object. The first care of the giants, on entering their abode—an octagonal chamber of stone, about sixteen feet wide, and twenty high, with a vaulted coiling, supported by sharp groined arches of great beauty, springing from small slender columns,—was to light a candle placed in front of an ancient projecting stone fireplace. Their next was to thrust the prisoner into the arched embrasure of a loop-hole at one side of it.

The walls of the chamber were decorated with the arms and accoutrements of the gigantic brethren,—the size of which would have been sufficient to strike any chance-beholder with wonder. Over the embrasure in which they had placed the prisoner, hung an enormous pair of gauntlets, and a morion of equal size. Here was a quiver full of arrows, each shaft far exceeding a cloth-yard in length—there a formidable club, armed with sharp steel spikes; while the fire-place was garnished with a couple of immense halberts. Having drawn a large pot of wine, which they first offered to their guest, who refused it, they each took a deep draught; and informing Underhill, if he was still resolved to hold forth, he had better commence without further delay, they disposed themselves to listen to him.

Placing a small table in the centre of the chamber, Og seated himself opposite it, and took Xit upon his knee; while Gog sat down beside him, and Magog supported his huge bulk against the wall. Divesting himself of his cap and sword, and placing an hour-glass on the table, the Hot-gospeller then opened a small volume, which he took from beneath his cloak; from which he began to read certain passages and to comment upon them in a vehement tone.

Edward Underhill the "Hot Gospeller" preaching to the Giants in the On-ward or Gate Tower.

His exhortation opened with a burst of rejoicing on the accession of Queen Jane—in which he pronounced terrible anathemas against all those who sought to restore the fallen religion. Perceiving the fierce gaze of the prisoner fixed upon him, he directed his chief thunders against him, and, excited by his subject, soon worked himself into a state approaching to frenzy.

In this strain he continued for some time, when a sound arose which drowned even his vehemence. Overcome with drowsiness, the three giants, who for a short time vainly endeavoured to attend to the discourse of the Gospeller, had now sunk into a comfortable slumber—and the noise which they made was tremendous. In vain Underhill endeavoured to rouse them by thumping the table. Gog gazed at him for an instant with half-shut eyes, and then leaning on Og's shoulder, who, with head dropped back and mouth wide open, was giving audible proof of his insensible condition, he speedily dropped asleep again. Such was the astounding din, that the Gospeller could not even make himself heard by the dwarf, who, perched on Og's knee at a few paces' distance, stared in amazement at his gesticulations.

More than an hour having passed in this manner, the Hot-gospeller, whose energies were wholly exhausted, came to a pause; and after menacing his insensible audience with proportionate punishment in the next world—especially the idolatrous prisoner, whom he threatened with gesture as well as with word—he closed his volume, and prepared to depart. With some difficulty the three giants were awakened; and it was only by the assistance of Xit, who tweaked their noses and plucked their beards, that this could be accomplished.

Just as Master Underhill was taking his leave, Dame Trusbut arrived in the greatest tribulation. The fair Cicely was nowhere to be found. Her husband had been to the palace. Nothing could be heard of the young esquire; nor could Lawrence Nightgall be met with. In this emergency, she had come to entreat the giants to aid her in her search. They agreed to go at once—and Xit was delighted with the prospect of such employment. Accordingly, the door was locked upon the prisoner, and they set forth with the distracted dame.

As soon as he was left alone, Gilbert surveyed the chamber to sec if there was any means by which he might effect his escape. An idea speedily occurred to him: by the help of one of the halberts he contrived to free himself from his bonds, and then clambered up the chimney.

VII.—HOW CUTHBERT CHOLMONDELEY WAS THROWN INTO A DUNGEON NEAR THE DEVILIN TOWER; AND HOW A MYSTERIOUS FEMALE FIGURE APPEARED TO HIM THERE.

On recovering from the stunning effects of the blow he had received, Cuthbert Cholmondeley found himself stretched on the floor of a gloomy vault, or dungeon, for such he judged it. At first, he thought he must be dreaming, and tried to shake off the horrible nightmare by which he supposed himself oppressed. But a moment's reflection undeceived him; and starting to his feet, he endeavoured to explore the cell in which he was confined. A heavy chain, which bound his leg to the floor, prevented him from moving more than a few paces; and, convinced that escape was impossible, he sank upon the ground in despair.

Unable to assign any cause for his imprisonment, and wholly at a loss to imagine what offence he had committed, he taxed his brain as to everything that had recently happened to him. This naturally directed his thoughts to the fair Cicely—and with her gentle image came the recollection of the malicious countenance and threatening gestures of Lawrence Nightgall. Remembering what Magog had told him of the jealousy and vindictive nature of this person, and remembering also that he had heard him described as the chief jailer, he felt that he need seek no further for the motive and the author of his imprisonment.

The assurance, however, which he had thus gained, afforded him no consolation, but rather tended to increase his disquietude. If he had been a prisoner of state, he might have hoped for eventual release; but placed in the hands of so remorseless and unscrupulous an enemy as Nightgall had shown himself, he felt he had little to hope. This consideration filled him with anguish, which was heightened as he thought of the triumph of his savage rival, who by some means—for he seemed desperate enough to have recourse to any expedient—might possess himself of the object of his passion. Fired by this thought, Cholmondeley again sprang to his feet, and strove with all his force to burst his bondage. But the effort was fruitless; and by lacerating his hands, and straining his limbs, he only added bodily torture to his mental suffering. Exhausted at length, he sank once more upon the floor.

By this time, having become habituated to the gloom of the place, he fancied he could make out that it was an arched cell of a few feet in width, and corresponding height. The only light admitted was from the entrance, which appeared to open upon a passage branching off on the left, and upon a further range of dungeons extending in the same direction.

Not altogether unacquainted with the prisons of the Tower, Cholmondeley felt against the walls to try whether he could find any of those melancholy memorials which their unfortunate inmates delighted to bequeath to their successors, and which might serve as a clue to the particular place of his confinement. But nothing but the smooth surface of the stone met his touch. This circumstance, however, and the peculiar form of the cell, induced him to think that it must be situated beneath, or at no great distance from the Devilin Tower, as he had heard of a range of subterranean dungeons in that quarter: and, it may be added, he was right in his conjecture.

The cell in which he was thrown was part of a series of such dreadful receptacles, contrived in the thickness of the ballium wall, and extending from the Beauchamp Tower to the Devilin Tower. They were appropriated to those prisoners who were doomed to confinement for life.

Horrible recollections then flashed upon his mind of the dreadful sufferings he had heard that the miserable wretches immured in these dungeons underwent—how some were tortured—some destroyed by secret and expeditious means—others by the more lingering process of starvation. As the latter idea crossed him, he involuntarily stretched out his hand to ascertain whether any provisions had been left him; but he could find none.

The blood froze in his veins as he thought of dying thus; his hair stiffened upon his head; and he was only prevented from crying out to make his lamentable case known to the occupants of any of the adjoining cells, by the conviction of its utter futility. But this feeling passed away, and was succeeded by calmer and more consolatory reflections. While in this frame of mind, Nature asserted her sway, and he dropped asleep.

How long he remained thus, he knew not; but he was awakened by a loud and piercing scream. Raising himself, he listened intently. The scream was presently repeated in a tone so shrill and unearthly, that it filled him with apprehensions of a new kind. The outcry having been a third time raised, he was debating within himself whether he should in any way reply to it, when he thought he beheld a shadowy figure glide along the passage. It paused at a short distance from him. A glimmer of light fell upon the arch on the left, but the place where the figure stood was buried in darkness. After gazing for some time at the mysterious visitant, and passing his hand across his brow to assure himself that his eyesight did not deceive him, Cholmondeley summoned courage enough to address it. No answer was returned; but the figure, which had the semblance of a female, with the hands raised and clasped together as if in supplication or prayer, and with a hood drawn over the face, remained perfectly motionless. Suddenly, it glided forward, but with a step so noiseless and swift, that almost before the esquire was aware of the movement, it was at his side. He then felt a hand cold as marble placed upon his own, and upon grasping the fingers they appeared so thin and bony, that he thought he must have encountered a skeleton. Paralysed with fright, Cholmondeley shrunk back as far as he was able; but the figure pursued him, and shrieked in his ear—"My child, my child!—you have taken my child!"

Convinced from the voice that he had a being of this world to deal with, the esquire seized her vestment, and resolved to detain her till he had ascertained who she was and what was the cause of her cries; but just as he had begun to question her, a distant footstep was heard, ands uttering a loud shriek, and crying—"He comes!—he comes!"—the female broke from him and disappeared.

Fresh shrieks were presently heard in a more piteous tone than before, mixed with angry exclamations in a man's voice, which Cholmondeley fancied sounded like that of Nightgall. A door was next shut with great violence; and all became silent.

While he was musing on this strange occurrence, Cholmondeley heard footsteps advancing along the passage on the left, and in another moment Lawrence Nightgall stood before him.

The jailer, who carried a lamp, eyed the captive for a few moments in silence, and with savage satisfaction.

"It is to you, then, I owe my imprisonment, villain," said Cholmondeley, regarding him sternly.

"It is," replied the jailer; "and you can readily conjecture, I doubt not, why I have thus dealt with you."

"I can," resumed the esquire; "your jealousy prompted you to the deed. But you shall bitterly rue it."

"Bah!" exclaimed Nightgall. "You are wholly in my power. I am not, however, come to threaten, but to offer you freedom."

"On what terms?" demanded Cholmondeley.

"On these," replied the jailer, scowling—"that you swear to abandon Cicely."

"Never!" replied the esquire.

THE TRAITOR'S GATE.

"Then your fate is sealed," rejoined Nightgall. "You shall never quit this spot."

"Think not to move me by any such idle threat," returned Cholmondeley. "You dare not detain me."

"Who shall prevent me?" laughed the jailor, scornfully. "I, alone, possess the key of these dungeons. You are their sole occupant."

"That is false," retorted the esquire. "There is another captive,—a miserable female,—whom I, myself, have seen."

"Has she been here?" cried Nightgall, with a look of disquietude.

"Not many minutes since," replied the other, fixing a scrutinizing glance upon him. "She came in search of her child. What have you done with it, villain?"

Cholmondeley had no particular object in making the inquiry. But he was astonished at the effect produced by it on the jailer, who started and endeavoured to hide his confusion by pulling his cap over his brows.

"She is a maniac," he said, at length, in a hoarse voice.

"If it be so," rejoined the esquire, severely; "she has been driven out of her senses by your barbarous usage. I more than suspect you have murdered her child."

"Entertain what suspicions you please," replied Nightgall, evidently relieved by the surmise. "I am not accountable for the ravings of a distracted woman."

"Who is she?" demanded the esquire.

"The names of those confined within these cells are never divulged,'" returned the jailer. "She has been a prisoner of state for nineteen years."

"And during that term her child was born—ha?" pursued Cholmondeley.

"I will answer no further questions," replied Nightgall, doggedly. "One word before I depart. I am not your only enemy. You have others more powerful, and equally implacable. You have incurred the displeasure of the Privy Council, and I have a warrant, under the hands of its chief members, for your execution. I am now about to summon the headsman for the task."

"Then your offer to liberate me was mere mockery," observed the esquire.

"Not so," replied the other; "and I again repeat it. Swear to abandon Cicely, and to maintain profound silence as to what you have just seen, and I will convey you by a secret passage underneath the Tower moat to a place of security, where you will be beyond the reach of your enemies, and will take the risk of your escape upon myself. Do you agree to this?"

"No," replied Cholmondeley, firmly. "I distrust your statement, and defy your malice."

"Obstinate fool!" growled the jailer. "Prepare to meet your fate in an hour."

"Whenever it comes it will find me prepared," rejoined the esquire.

Nightgall glared at him fiercely for a moment from beneath his shaggy brows. He then strode sullenly away. But his departure was prevented by Cicely, who suddenly appeared at the mouth of the dungeon.

"You here!" he exclaimed recoiling, and trembling as if an apparition had crossed his path. "How have you obtained admittance?",

"It matters not," she answered. "I am come to purchase your prisoner's freedom."

"You know the terms?" rejoined the jailer, eagerly.

"I do," she replied; "and will comply with them when you have fulfilled your share of the compact."

"Cicely!" cried Cholmondeley, who had been to the full as much astonished at her unexpected appearance as the jailer. "Cicely!" he cried, starting to his feet, and extending his hands towards her. "Do not consent to his proposal. Do not sacrifice yourself for me. I would die a thousand deaths rather than you should be his."

"Heed him not," interposed Nightgall, grasping her arm, and preventing her from approaching her lover; "but attend to me. You see this warrant," he added, producing a parchment. "It is from the Council, and directs that the prisoner's execution shall take place in such manner as may best consist with despatch and secrecy. If I deliver it to Manger, the headsman, it will be promptly obeyed. And I *shall* deliver it, unless you promise compliance."

"The villain deceives you, dear Cicely," cried Cholmondeley, in a voice of anguish. "The Council have not the power of life and death. They cannot— dare not order my execution without form or trial."

"The Council will answer for their actions themselves," rejoined Nightgall, carelessly. "Their warrant will bear me and my comrades harmless. Mauger will not hesitate to act upon it. What is your determination, Cicely?"

"Free him," she replied.

"Recal your words, sweet Cicely," cried Cholmondeley, throwing himself at her feet, "if you have any love for me. You doom me to worse than death by this submission."

"Cholmondeley," she replied in a mournful voice, "my resolution is taken, and even you cannot induce me to change it. The opening of our love has been blighted. My heart has been crushed, almost before it knew for whom it beat. It matters not now what becomes of me. If my life could preserve yours, or restore you to freedom, I would freely yield it. But as nothing will suffice except my hand, I give that. Think of me no more,—or think of me only as another's.'"

"That thought were madness!" groaned Cholmondeley.

"Master Lawrence Nightgall," continued Cicely, "you say you can conduct the prisoner beyond the walls of the Tower, Bring me back some token that you have done so, and I am yours."

"Willingly," replied the jailer.

"Retire then for a moment, while I arrange with him what the token shall be."

Nightgall hesitated.

"Refuse, and I retract my promise," she added.

And the jailer, with a suspicious look, reluctantly left the cell.

"Cicely, my beloved," cried Cholmondeley, clasping her in his arms, "why— why have you done this?"

"To preserve you," she replied, hurriedly. "Once out of this dungeon, I can bring assistance to liberate you."

"Indeed!" ejaculated Nightgall, who, having placed his ear to the wall, lost not a syllable of their discourse.

"It will be unavailing," replied Cholmondeley. "No one will venture to oppose an order of the Council. You must make known my case to Lord Guilford Dudley. Take this ring. Explain all to him, and I may yet be saved. Do you hear me, Cicely?"

"I do," she replied "And I," added Nightgall.

"In case you fail," continued the esquire, "the token of my escape shall be"— And placing his lips close to her ear, he spoke a few words in so low a tone, that they escaped the jailer. "Till you receive that token treat Nightgall as before."

"Doubt it not," she answered.

"I am content," said the esquire.

"I see through the design," muttered the jailer, "and will defeat it. Have you done?" he added, aloud.

"A moment," replied Cholmondeloy, again pressing the damsel to his bosom, "I would sooner part with my life's-blood than resign you."

"I must go," she cried, disengaging herself from his embrace. "Now, Master Nightgall, I am ready to attend you."

"In an hour I shall return and release you," said the jailer, addressing the prisoner. "Your hand, Cicely."

"I will go alone," she replied, shrinking from him with a look of abhorrence.

"As you please," he rejoined, with affected carelessness. "You are mine."

"Not till I have received the token. Farewell!" she murmured, turning her tearful gaze upon Cholmondeley.

"For ever!" exclaimed the youth.

And as they quitted the cell, he threw himself despairingly on the ground.

Issuing from the outer door of the dungeon, Cicely and her companion took their way towards the Stone Kitchen. They had not proceeded far, when they perceived several persons approaching them, who, as they drew nearer, proved to be Dame Potentia, Xit, and the giants.

"What have you been doing, Cicely?" inquired her adoptive mother, angrily. "I have been searching for you everywhere!"

"You shall know anon," replied the maiden. "But come with me to the palace. I must see Lord Guilford Dudley, or the Duke of Northumberland, without a moment's delay."

"Warders," interposed Nightgall, authoritatively: "go to Master Manger's lodging in the Bloody Tower. Bid him hasten with two assistants, and the sworn tormentor, to the dungeon beneath the Devilin Tower. He will know which I mean. Justice is about to be done upon a prisoner."

"Oh no—no—do not go," cried Cicely, arresting the giants. "He does not mean it. He is jesting."

"Go home, then, and do not stir forth till I bring you the token," rejoined Nightgall, in a deep whisper.

"In Heaven's name, what is the meaning of all this?" cried Dame Potentia, in amazement.

"I will inform you," replied the jailer, drawing her aside. "Your daughter was about to elope with the young esquire. I detected them trying to escape by the secret passage beneath the moat, of which you know I have the key. Lock her within her chamber. Pay no attention to her tears, entreaties, or assertions. And, above all, take care no one has any communication with her."

"Trust me to guard her," rejoined Dame Potentia. "I know what these court-gallants are. They will venture anything, and contrive anything, when a pretty girl is concerned. But what has happened to the esquire?"

"He is safe for the present," answered Nightgall, significantly.

Cicely, meantime, had availed herself of their conversation, to whisper a few words to Xit.

"Take this ring," she said, placing the ornament given her by her lover, in the hands of the dwarf, "and fly to the palace. Show it to Lord Guilford Dudley, and say that the wearer is imprisoned in the dungeons beneath the Devilin

Tower. Assistance must be speedily rendered, as he is ordered for immediate and secret execution. Do you understand?"

"Most precisely, lovely damsel," replied Xit, kissing her hand, as he took the ring; "and I guess the name and condition of the prisoner, as well as the nature of the interest you take in him."

"Fly!" interrupted Cicely. "Not a moment is to be lost. You shall be well rewarded for your trouble."

"I desire no higher reward than your thanks, adorable maiden," replied Xit. "Your behests shall be punctually obeyed." So saying, he disappeared.

"Come, young mistress," cried Dame Potentia, seizing her adoptive daughter's arm, "you must to your chamber. You have led me and your father, and these worthy warders, a pretty dance. But you shall lead us all where you list, if I let you out of my sight in future."

And thanking the giants, who had looked on in speechless astonishment, she dragged Cicely along with her.

"Remember!" whispered Nightgall, as he walked a few paces by the side of the latter.

"I shall expect the token in an hour," she answered in the same tone.

"You shall have it," he rejoined.

With this, he halted, and retraced his steps. The others then separated. Cicely was conveyed to the Stone Kitchen; and the giants, after looking in vain for Xit, and calling to him repeatedly but without effect, returned to the By-ward Tower. Just as they reached it, a shot was fired from the battlements, and was immediately answered from those of the Middle Tower. Other reports followed. And, alarmed by the sounds, the huge brethren hastily unlocked the door of their lodging, and entering it, to their infinite dismay, found the prisoner gone.

VIII.—HOW GILBERT ESCAPED FROM THE BY-WARD TOWER, AND SWAM ACROSS THE MOAT; HOW OG HUNG XIT UPON A HOOK; AND HOW LAWRENCE NIGHTGALL BROUGHT THE TOKEN TO CICELY.

Gilbert having freed himself from his bonds, and clambered into the chimney in the By-ward Tower in the manner previously related, ascended without any inconvenience, except what was occasioned by the pungent smoke arising from the blazing fagots beneath, until he reached the level of the upper story, where another fire-place, connected with the passage up which he was mounting, so narrowed its limits, that it seemed scarcely possible to proceed further. The sound of voices in the chamber on this floor also alarmed him, and for some minutes he suspended his labour to listen. But as nothing occurred to disturb him, and it was evident, from the conversation of the speakers, that he had not been noticed, he presently resumed his task, and redoubling his efforts, soon vanquished all obstacles, and gained the opening of the chimney.

Here a fresh difficulty awaited him; and one for which he was wholly unprepared. The smoke found a vent through a small circular opening or louver, as it was termed,—for there was no chimney-top to disperse it to the air,—in the battlements. Through this opening he must necessarily creep; and, provided he could accomplish the feat, he had to elude the vigilance of the sentinels stationed on the roof of the turret. Luckily, the night was profoundly dark; and the gloom, increased by a thick mist from the river, was so intense, that an object could scarcely be discerned at a foot's distance. Thus favoured, Gilbert resolved to hazard the attempt.

Watching his opportunity, he drew himself cautiously through the louver, and without being noticed by the sentinel, who was standing beside it, crouched beneath the carriage of a culverin. In this state, he remained for a short time, meditating what course he should next pursue, and nerving himself for some desperate attempt, when a door at the side of the southern turret suddenly opened, and three men-at-arms, the foremost of whom carried a torch, came to relieve guard.

Aware that he should now infallibly be discovered, Gilbert started to his feet, and drawing a dagger which he had picked up in the giants' chamber, stood upon his defence. The movement betrayed him. Though confounded by his appearance, the sentinel nearest him presented his partizan at his breast and commanded him to surrender. Gilbert answered by striking up the man's arm, and instantly sprang over the battlements.

A loud splash told that he had fallen into the moat. The men held the torch over the side of the turret. But it was too dark to distinguish any object below. Presently, however, a noise was heard in the water that convinced them the fugitive was swimming for the opposite bank. One of the soldiers instantly discharged his caliver in the direction of the sound,—but without effect.

This served as an alarm to the guards posted on the western ramparts, as well as to those on the Middle Tower, both of which commanded this part of the moat, and other shots were immediately fired. A signal was then rapidly passed from tower to tower, and from portal to portal, until it reached the Bulwark-gate, which formed the only entrance to the fortress on the west, and a body of armed men carrying lights instantly sallied forth and hurried towards the side of the moat.

Gilbert, meanwhile, swam for his life. Guided by the torches, which served to discover his enemies rather than to betray him, he effected a secure landing, But before he had climbed the steep bank, he was observed by a soldier, who, making towards him, shouted to his comrades for assistance. In the struggle that ensued, the torch borne by the soldier was extinguished, and bursting from him, Gilbert darted at a swift pace up Tower-hill. His pursuers were close upon him. But, well acquainted with the spot, he contrived to baffle them, by flinging himself beneath the permanent scaffold, then standing upon the brow of the eminence, and thus eluded observation. As soon as his foes had passed, he struck off swiftly to the left, and leaping a low wall, skirted All-hallows Church, and speedily gained Tower-street.

While Gilbert was flying in this direction, his pursuers finding themselves at fault, hastened back, and endeavoured to discover some trace of him. Some mounted the steps of the scaffold to see whether he had taken refuge on its blood-stained planks,—some crept under it,—others examined the posts of the neighbouring gallows,—while a fourth party flew to the postern gate, which defended the southern extremity of the city wall, in the hope that he might have been stopped by the watch. All, however, it is needless to say, were disappointed. And after some time had been fruitlessly expended, the whole party returned to the Tower to report the unsuccessful issue of their expedition.

Meanwhile, the report of the musquetry had reached the ears of Lord Clinton, the constable, who, attended by the lieutenant, the gentleman-porter, and a numerous patrol, chanced to be making the round of the fortifications at the time, and he descended to the gates to ascertain the cause of the alarm. On learning it, he immediately summoned the herald and the gigantic warders to his presence, and after sharply rebuking the former for neglect, ordered him into custody till the morning, when he proposed to take the duke's pleasure as to his punishment. He then turned to the giants, who tried to soften his displeasure by taking the blame upon themselves, and telling them he would listen to their statement when the herald was examined, and, in the interim, they would be answerable with their lives for any further dereliction of duty, he dismissed the assemblage, and returned with his train to the ramparts.

Among those who had been gathered together in the guardroom near the By-ward Tower,—where the foregoing examination took place,—were Nightgall and Xit,—the latter having just returned from the palace, after a vain attempt to deliver his message to Lord Guilford Dudley, who, it has been already stated, was engaged at the time in secret conference with the Duke of Northumberland, and could not therefore be spoken with.

Ever on the alert, and suspicious of those around him, Night-gall overheard Og question the dwarf as to the cause of his absence; and perceiving, from Xit's manner, that he had some secret to communicate, he contrived to approach them unobserved. He then learnt the message with which the dwarf had been entrusted by Cicely, and enraged at her endeavour to overreach him, snatched the ring from him as he was displaying it to the giant, and threatened him with severe punishment, if he dared to meddle further in the matter.

As soon as he had recovered from his surprise, the affronted mannikin drew his rapier, and making several passes at Nightgall, would have certainly wounded him, if he had not dextrously avoided the blows by interposing the huge bulk of the giant between him and his assailant. The fury of the dwarf was so excessive, and the contortions into which he threw himself so inconceivably diverting, that Og could render him no assistance for laughing. Thrusting his sword between the giant's legs,—now cutting on the right, now on the left,—Xit tried in every way to hit the jailer, and must have succeeded, if Og, who was by no means desirous to have blood shed in so ridiculous a fray, and who enjoyed the pastime too much to speedily terminate it, had not prevented him.

Gog, moreover, having on the onset disarmed Nightgall, he could not protect himself except by keeping under the shelter of the giant. Foiled in his attempts, Xit's indignation knew no bounds, and exasperated by the derisive shouts and laughter of the spectators, he threatened to turn his sword against Og if he did not deliver up the jailer to his vengeance. This only produced louder roars of merriment from the by-standers; and the dwarf, whose passion had almost deprived him of reason, uttering a shrill scream like a child robbed of its plaything, threw himself on Og's leg, and scrambled up his body, with the intention of descending on the other side, and exterminating his foe.

This feat raised the merriment of the spectators to the utmost. Og suffered the imp to ascend without opposition, and clinging to the points of the giant's slashed red hose, Xit drew himself up to his broad girdle, and then setting one foot on the circlet of raised gold thread which surrounded the badge on his breast, soon gained his shoulder, and would have leapt from thence upon his foe, if Og, who began to think it time to put an end to the sport, had not seized him by the leg as he was in the act of springing off, and held him at arm's-length, with his heels upwards.

After many useless struggles to liberate himself, and menaces of what he would do when he got free, which, as may be supposed, only provoked still further the laughter of the by-standers, Xit became so unmanageable, that Og fastened him by his nether garments to a hook in the wall, about fourteen feet from the ground, and left him to recover himself.

Thus perched, the dwarf hurled his rapier at Nightgall's head, and replied to the jeers of the assemblage by such mops and mows as an enraged ape is wont to make at its persecutors. After the lapse of a few minutes, however, he began to find his position so uncomfortable, that he was fain to supplicate for release, to which, on receiving his assurance of quieter conduct for the future, Og consented, and accordingly unhooked him, and set him on the ground.

Nightgall, meanwhile, had taken advantage of this diversion, to leave the Guard-room, and hasten to the Stone Kitchen.

Dame Potentia was just retiring to rest as the jailer reached her dwelling, and it was only by the most urgent importunity that he succeeded in obtaining admission.

"Your pardon, good dame," he said, as the door was opened. "I have that to tell Cicely, which will effectually cure her love for the young esquire."

"In that case, you are right welcome, Master Nightgall," she replied; "for the poor child has almost cried her pretty eyes out since I brought her home. And I have been so moved by her tears, that I greatly misdoubt, if her lover had presented himself instead of you, whether I should have had the heart to refuse to let him see her."

"Fool!" muttered Nightgall, half aside. "Where is she?" he added, aloud. "I have no time to lose. I have a secret execution to attend before day-break."

"Yours is a butcherly office, Master Nightgall," observed Peter Trusbut, who was dozing in an arm-chair by the fire. "Those secret executions, to my mind, are little better than state murders. I would not, for all the power of the Duke of Northumberland, hold your office, or that of Gilliam Mauger, the headsman."

"Nor I yours, on the same fee, Master Pantler," rejoined Nightgall. "Tastes differ. Where is your daughter, good dame?"

"In her chamber," replied Potentia. "Ho! Cicely, sweetheart!" she added, knocking at a door at the end of a short passage leading out of the kitchen on the right. "Here is Master Nightgall desires to speak with you."

"Does he bring me the token?" demanded the maiden, from within.

"Ay marry, does he, child," replied the dame, winking at the jailer. "Heaven forgive me the falsehood," she added,—"for I know not what she means."

"Leave us a moment, dear mother," said Cicely, hastily unfastening the door. "Now, Master Nightgall," she continued, as Dame Potentia retired, and the jailer entered the room, "have you fulfilled your compact?"

"Cicely," rejoined the jailer, regarding her sternly, "you have not kept faith with me. You have despatched a messenger to the palace."

"Oh! he is free," exclaimed the maiden, joyfully,—"your plans have been defeated?"

Nightgall smiled bitterly.

"My messenger cannot have failed," she continued, with a sudden change of countenance. "I am sure Lord Guilford would not abandon his favourite esquire. Tell me, what has happened?"

"I am come to claim fulfilment of your pledge," rejoined the jailer.

"Then you have set him free," cried Cicely. "Where is the token?"

"Behold it," replied Nightgall, raising his hand, on which her lover's ring sparkled.

"Lost!—lost!" shrieked Cicely, falling senseless upon the floor.

The jailer gazed at her a moment in silence, but did not attempt to offer any assistance. He then turned upon his heel, and strode out of the room.

"Look to your daughter, dame," he observed, as he passed through the Stone-kitchen.

IX.—OF THE MYSTERIOUS MANNER IN WHICH GUNNORA BRAOSE WAS BROUGHT TO THE TOWER.

Hurrying along Tower Street, and traversing Eastcheap and Watling Street—then narrow but picturesque thoroughfares—Gilbert,—to whom it is now necessary to return,—did not draw breath till he reached the eastern extremity of St. Paul's. As he passed this reverend and matchless structure—the destruction of which, was the heaviest loss sustained by the metropolis in the Great Fire—he strained his eyes towards its lofty tower, but the gloom was too profound to enable him to discern anything of it beyond a dark and heavy mass.

"Thou art at present benighted, glorious fane!" he cried aloud. "But a bright dawn shall arise for thee, and all thy ancient splendour, with thy ancient faith, be restored. If I could see Mary queen, and hear mass solemnized within thy walls, I could die content."

"And you shall hear it," said a voice in his ear.

"Who speaks?" asked Gilbert, trembling.

"Be at St. Paul's Cross to-morrow at midnight, and you shall know," replied the voice. "You are a loyal subject of Queen Mary., and a true Catholic, or your words belie you?"

"I am both," answered Gilbert.

"Fail not to meet me then," rejoined the other, "and you shall receive assurance that your wishes shall be fulfilled. There are those at work who will speedily accomplish the object you desire."

"I will aid them heart and hand," cried Gilbert.

"Your name?" demanded the other.

"I am called Gilbert Pot," answered the youth, "and am drawer to Ninion Saunders, at the Baptist's Head, in Ludgate."

"A vintner's boy!" exclaimed the other, disdainfully.

"Ay, a vintner's boy," returned Gilbert. "But, when the usurper, Jane Dudley, was proclaimed at Cheapside this morning, mine was the only voice raised for Queen Mary."

"For which bold deed you were nailed to the pillory," rejoined the other.

"I was," replied Gilbert; "and was, moreover, carried to the Tower, whence I have just escaped."

"Your courage shall not pass unrequited," replied the speaker. "Where are you going?"

"To my master's, at the Baptist's Head, at the corner of Creed Lane—not a bow-shot hence."

"It will not be safe to go thither," observed the other. "Your master will deliver you to the watch."

"I will risk it, nevertheless," answered Gilbert. "I have an old grandame whom I desire to see."

"Something strikes me!" exclaimed the other. "Is your grandame the old woman who warned the usurper Jane not to proceed to the Tower?"

"She is," returned Gilbert.

"This is a strange encounter, in good sooth," cried the other. "She is the person I am in search of. You must procure me instant speech with her."

"I will conduct you to her, right willingly, sir," replied Gilbert. "But she says little to any one, and may refuse to answer your questions."

"We shall see," rejoined the other. "Lead on, good Gilbert."

Followed by his unknown companion, about whom he felt a strange curiosity, not unalloyed with fear, Gilbert proceeded at a rapid pace towards his destination. The whole of the buildings then surrounding Saint Paul's, it is almost unnecessary to say, were destroyed by the same fire that consumed the Cathedral; and, though the streets still retain their original names, their situation is in some respects changed.

Passing beneath the shade of a large tree, which then grew at the western boundary of the majestic edifice, Gilbert darted through a narrow entry into Ave Maria Lane, and turning to the left, speedily reached Ludgate, which he crossed at some fifty paces from the Gate—then used, like several of the other city portals, as a prison—and, entering Creed Lane, halted before a low-built house on the right. The shutters were closed, but it was evident, from the uproarious sounds issuing from the dwelling, that revelry was going on within. Gilbert did not deem it prudent to open the street door, but calling to his companion, he went to the back of the tavern, and gained admittance through a window on the ground floor.

"They are having a merry rouse," he observed to the other, "in honour of the usurper; and my master, Ninion, will be too far gone to notice aught except his guests and his sack brewage, so that I may safely conduct your worship to my grandame. But first let me strike a light."

With this, he searched about for flint and steel, and having found them, presently set fire to a small lamp hanging against the wall, which he removed and turned, not without some apprehension, towards the stranger.

His glance fell upon a tall man, with an ample feuille-morte coloured cloak thrown over his left shoulder, so as completely to muffle the lower part of his features. Gilbert could see nothing of the stranger's face, except an aquiline nose, and a pair of piercing black eyes; but the expression of the latter was so stern and searching, that his own regards involuntarily sank before them. A bonnet of black velvet, decorated with a single drooping feather, drawn over the brow, added to the stranger's disguise. But what was revealed of the physiognomy was so striking, that Gilbert was satisfied he should never forget it.

Something, indeed, there was of majesty in the stranger's demeanour, that, coupled with his sinister looks and the extraordinary brilliancy of his eyes, impressed the superstitious youth with the notion that he was in the presence of an unearthly being. Struck by this idea, he glanced at the stranger's feet, in expectation of finding one of the distinctive marks of the Prince of Darkness. But he beheld nothing except a finely-formed limb, clothed in black silk hose and a velvet shoe, above which hung the point of a lengthy rapier.

"I am neither the enemy of mankind nor your enemy, good youth," observed the stranger, who guessed the cause of Gilbert's apprehensions. "Bring your grandame hither, and take heed how you approach her, or your looks will alarm her more than mine do you."

It was not without reason that this caution was given. Gilbert's appearance was ghastly in the extreme. His countenance was haggard with the loss of blood; his garments torn and saturated with moisture; and his black dripping locks, escaping from the blood-stained bandage around his head, contrasted fearfully with the deathly paleness of his visage. Acknowledging the justice of the suggestion, Gilbert decided upon proceeding in the dark, that his appearance might not be observed.

Accordingly, he crept cautiously up stairs, and returned in a few minutes with his aged relative. Gilbert found the stranger in the same attitude he had left him, and his appearance startled Gunnora, as much as it had done him.

Crossing herself, she glanced uneasily at the mysterious stranger. From him her eye wandered to Gilbert; and terrified by his haggard looks, she cried in a tone of anxiety, "You have suffered much, my child. The ill news reached me of the shameful punishment with which you have been visited for your loyalty to your true Queen. I heard also that you had been conveyed a prisoner to the Tower; and was about to make suit to the gracious lady, Jane Dudley, in your behalf. Was I wrongfully informed?"

"No, mother, you were not," replied Gilbert. "But heed me not. There stands the worshipful gentleman who desires to speak with you."

"I am ready to answer his questions," said Gunnora. "Let him propose them."

"First, let me tell you, dame," said the stranger, "that your grandsons devotion to Queen Mary shall not pass unrequited. Ere many days— perchance many hours—shall have passed, he shall exchange his serge doublet for a suit of velvet."

"You hear that, mother," exclaimed Gilbert, joyfully.

"Who are you that make him the offer?" asked Gunnora, stedfastly regarding the stranger.

"You shall know, anon," he replied. "Suffice it, I can make good my words. Your presence is required in the Tower."

"By the Lady Jane,—I should say by the queen?" rejoined Gunnora.

"By the Privy Council," returned the stranger.

"What do they seek from me?" demanded the old woman.

"To testify to the death of his late Majesty, King Edward the Sixth," replied the other.

"Ha!" exclaimed Gunnora.

"Fear nothing," rejoined the stranger. "The council will befriend you. Their object is to prove that Edward was poisoned by Northumberland's order. Can you do this?"

"I can," replied Gunnora. "My hand administered the fatal draught."

"Yours, mother!" ejaculated Gilbert, horror-stricken.

"Prove this, and Northumberland will lose his head," said the stranger.

"Were my own to fall with it, I would do so," replied Gunnora. "My sole wish is to avenge my foster-son, the great Duke of Somerset, who fell by Northumberland's foul practices. It was therefore when all the physicians of the royal household were dismissed, and the duke sent messengers for empirical aid, that I presented myself, and offered my services. When I beheld the royal sufferer, I saw he had but short space to live. But short as it was, it was too long for the duke. A potion was prepared by Northumberland, which I administered. From that moment his highness grew worse, and in six hours he was a corpse."

"It was a cursed deed," cried Gilbert.

"True," replied Gunnora, "it was so, and Heaven will surely avenge it. But I did it to get Northumberland into my power. The king's case was past all remedy. But he might have lingered for days and weeks, and the duke was impatient for the crown. I was impatient too—but it was for his head. And therefore I did his bidding."

"Your vengeance shall be fully gratified," replied the stranger. "Come with me."

"Hold!" exclaimed Gunnora. "How will his testimony affect the Lady Jane?"

"It will deprive her of her crown—perchance her head," rejoined the stranger.

"Then it shall never be uttered," replied Gunnora, firmly.

"Torture shall wring it from you," cried the stranger, furiously.

The old woman drew herself up to her full height, and, regarding the stranger fixedly, answered in a stern tone—"Let it be tried upon me."

"Mother," said Gilbert, striding between them, and drawing his dagger, "go back to your own room. You shall not peril your safety thus."

"Tush!" exclaimed the stranger, impatiently. "No harm shall befal her. I thought you were both loyal subjects of Queen Mary. How can she assume the sovereign power while Jane grasps the sceptre?"

"But you aim at her life?" said Gunnora.

"No," replied the stranger, "I would preserve her. My object is to destroy Northumberland, and restore the crown to her to whom it rightfully belongs."

"In that case I will go with you," returned the old woman.

"You will fall into a snare," interposed her grandson. "Let him declare who he is."

"I will reveal my name to your grandame, boy," replied the stranger. And advancing towards Gunnora, he whispered in her ear. *

The old woman started and trembled.

"Hinder me not, Gilbert," she said. "I must go with him."

"Shall I accompany you?" asked her grandson.

"On no account," replied the stranger, "unless you desire to be lodged in the deepest dungeon in the Tower. Be at the place of rendezvous to-morrow night, and you shall know more. Are you ready, good dame?"

Gunnora signified her assent; and, after a few parting words with her grandson, the latter unfastened a small door, opening upon the yard, and let them out.

They were scarcely clear of the house, when the stranger placing a silver whistle to his lips, blew a call upon it, which was instantly answered by a couple of attendants. At a signal from their leader they placed themselves on either side of Gunnora, and in spite of her resistance and remonstrances, dragged her forcibly along. The stranger, who marched a few yards in advance, proceeded at so rapid a pace, that the old woman found it utterly impossible to keep up with him. She therefore stood still, and refused to take another step. But this did not avail her, for the two attendants seized her in their arms, and hurried forward as swiftly as before.

Though bewildered and alarmed, Gunnora did not dare to cry out for assistance. Indeed, they did not encounter a single passenger in the streets, until, as they were descending Budge-row, they heard the clank of arms, and beheld the gleam of torches borne by a party of the watch who were approaching from Can-wick-street, or as it is now called, Cannon-street.

Turning off on the right, the stranger descended Dowgate-hill, and gained Thames-street before he had been remarked. A short time sufficed to bring him to St. Mary-hill, up which he mounted, and entering Thames-street, and passing St. Dunstan's in the East on the right, and the ancient church of All Hallows Barking on the left, he reached Great Tower-hill.

By this time, the vapours from the river had cleared off. The stars had begun to peep forth, and the first glimpse of day to peer in the east. By this light, and from this spot, the stern and sombre outline of the Tower, with its ramparts—its citadel, and its numerous lesser turrets, was seen to great advantage. On the summit of the Hill appeared the scaffold and the gallows already noticed.

Pausing for a moment, and pointing to a range of buildings, the summits of which could just be distinguished, to the south of the White Tower, the stranger said—"Within that palace Northumberland now reposes, surrounded by a triple line of fortifications, and defended by a thousand armed men. But if you will only reveal all you know, ere another week has passed his head shall be laid on that scaffold."

"The last time I beheld that fatal spot," returned Gunnora, "my foster-son, the Duke of Somerset, was decapitated there. If I can avenge him upon his foe, I shall die content."

"Obey my directions implicitly, and you *shall* do so," rejoined the other.

"How are we to enter the Tower?" asked Gunnora.

"Not by the ordinary road," replied the other, significantly. "But we shall be observed if we linger here. Forward!"

Crossing the Hill in the direction of the City Postern, the stranger suddenly wheeled round, and, under cover of a low wall, approached the moat. Exactly opposite the Devilin Tower, and the bastion occupying the north-western anglo of the exterior line of fortifications, stood at this time, at a little distance from the moat, a small low building. Towards this structure the stranger hastened. As he drew near it, he glanced uneasily at the ramparts, to ascertain whether he was observed. But though the measured tread of the sentinels and the clank of arms were distinctly audible, he remained unperceived.

Unlocking the door, the whole party entered the building, which was apparently deserted. After a moment's search, the stranger discovered a spring in the floor, which he pulled, and a trap-door opened, disclosing a long and steep flight of steps, at the foot of which sat a man with a mask, bearing a torch.

No sooner did this person hear the noise occasioned by the opening of the trap-door, than he hastily ascended, and placed himself in readiness to guide the party. On gaining the level ground, it was evident, from the dampness of the arched roof of the passage, and the slippery surface of the floor along which they trod, that they were far below the bottom of the moat. Traversing this damp dark passage for more than a hundred yards, the humid atmosphere gave place to a more wholesome air, and the ground became drier.

Hitherto, the passage had been about three feet wide and seven high, and was arched and flagged with stone. But they had now arrived at a point where it became more lofty, and their further progress was checked by a strong door plated with iron, and studded with nails. Taking a huge key from his girdle, the man in the mask unlocked this ponderous door, and, admitting the party, fastened it behind him. He then led them up another stone stair-case, similar in all respects to the first, except that it did not ascend to more than half the height. This brought them to a vaulted gallery, from which three passages branched.

Pursuing that on the right, and preceded by his masked attendant, the stranger strode silently along. As she followed him, Gunnora noticed several strong doors in the wall, which she took to be entrances to dungeons. After threading this passage, the party ascended a third short flight of steps, at the top of which was a trap-door. It was opened by the guide, and admitted them into a small stone chamber, the walls of which appeared, from the embrazures of the windows, to be of immense thickness. The roof was groined and arched. In the centre of the room stood a small table, on which some provisions were placed. A small copper lamp, suspended from the roof, threw a sickly light around, and discovered a little pallet stretched in a recess on the right.

"You are now in the Bowyer's Tower, in the chamber where it is said the Duke of Clarence was drowned in the butt of malmsey," observed the stranger. "Here you will remain till your presence is required by the Council."

Gunnora would have remonstrated, but the stranger waved his hand to her to keep silence, and, followed by his attendants, descended through the trap-door, which was closed and bolted beneath.

INTERIOR OF THE BOWYER TOWER.

X.—HOW THE DUKE OF NORTHUMBERLAND MENACED SIMON RENARD IN SAINT PETER'S CHAPEL ON THE TOWER-GREEN; AND HOW QUEEN JANE INTERPOSED BETWEEN THEM.

It will now be proper to ascertain how far the Duke of Northumberland was justified in his suspicion of Queen Jane's conduct being influenced by some secret and adverse counsel. After the abrupt departure of Lord Guilford Dudley for Sion House, as before related, she was greatly distressed, and refused at first to credit the intelligence. But when it was confirmed beyond all doubt by a message from her husband himself, declaring that he would not return till she had acceded to his request, she burst into tears, and withdrew to her own chamber, where she remained for some time alone.

When she re-appeared, it was evident from her altered looks that she had suffered deeply. But it was evident also, from her composure of countenance and firmness of manner, that whatever resolution she had formed she would adhere to it.

Summoning the Earls of Arundel and Pembroke to her presence, she briefly explained to them that she had heard, with infinite concern and uneasiness, that the council had proposed to raise her husband to the throne, because she foresaw that it would breed trouble and dissatisfaction, and greatly endanger her own government.

"Your highness judges rightly," replied the Earl of Pembroke. "It will be said that in thus elevating his son, Northumberland seeks only his own aggrandisement."

"And it will be truly said, my lord," rejoined Jane. "But if this is your opinion, why was your voice given in favour of the measure?"

"No man is bound to accuse himself," replied Pembroke.

"But every man is bound to speak truth, my lord," rejoined Jane. "Again I ask you, why your assent was given to this measure, which, by your own admission, is fraught with danger?"

"The Duke of Northumberland is my enemy," replied the Earl, sternly. "Had this step been taken it would have ensured his destruction."

"You speak frankly, my lord," rejoined the Queen. "But you forget that it must have ensured my destruction also."

"I am a loyal subject of your majesty," replied the Earl of Pembroke, "and will shed my last drop of blood in the defence of your crown. But I will not submit to the Duke's imperious conduct."

"And yet, my lord, you owe your own dignity to him," rejoined Jane, sarcastically. "Sir William Herbert would not have been Earl of Pembroke but for the Duke's intercession with our cousin Edward. For shame, my lord! you owe him too much to act against him."

"*I* owe him nothing," interposed the Earl of Arundel, "and may therefore speak without risk of any such imputation as your majesty has thrown out against Lord Pembroke. If the overweening power of the Duke of Northumberland be not checked, it will end in his downfal, and the downfal of all those with whom he is connected."

"I thank you for your counsel, my lord," replied the Queen; "and, setting down much to your private animosity, will place the rest to loyalty to myself."

"Your highness will be speedily satisfied of the truth of my assertion, if you refuse compliance with Northumberland's demands," replied Pembroke. "But you will find it, unless you have recourse to strong measures, a difficult and a dangerous game to play."

"To one who, though so young in years, is yet so old in wisdom as your majesty," added the Earl of Arundel, "it will be needless to say, that on the first decisive movement of your reign—as on that of a battle—depends the victory. If you yield, all is lost. From this one step the Duke will estimate your character, and become either your servant or your master. From his conduct, also, you will know what to expect from him hereafter."

"My resolution is taken, my lords," returned the Queen.

"The course I have resolved upon in reference to the duke, you will learn when I meet you in the council-chamber, where he will be present to speak for himself—and, if need be, defend himself. My desire is that my reign should begin and proceed in peace. And, if you hope for my favour, you will forget your differences with his grace, and act in concert with me. In asserting my own power, I trust I shall convince him of the futility of any further struggle with me, and so bring him to a sense of duty."

"Your majesty may depend upon the full support of your council," rejoined Arundel.

"I doubt it not, my lord," replied Jane. "And now to the business on which I summoned you. It may have reached you that my dear lord has departed this morning for Sion House, in great displeasure that I have refused to comply with his wishes."

"We have heard as much," replied both noblemen.

"My desire is that you hasten after him and entreat him to return with all speed," pursued Jane.

"Your majesty then consents!" exclaimed Pembroke, hastily.

"Not so, my lord," replied the Queen. "I will raise him to his father's rank. He shall have a dukedom, but not a kingdom."

"I would counsel your majesty to reflect ere you concede thus much," observed Arundel.

"I have already said that my resolution is taken," replied the Queen. "Repeat what I have told you to him, and entreat him to return."

"*Entreat* him!" echoed Pembroke scornfully. "It is not for your highness to entreat, but to command. Obedience sworn at the altar by the lips of the Queen of England, is cancelled as soon as uttered. Your husband is your subject. Empower us to bring him to you, and he shall be at your feet within an hour."

"My pleasure is that you literally fulfil my injunctions, my lords," replied the Queen. "Lord Guilford Dudley was the husband of my choice. When I gave my hand to him at the altar, I had no thought that it would ever grasp a sceptre, Nor, till I obtained this unlooked-for—and, believe me, most unwished-for dignity,—did the slightest misunderstanding ever arise between us. But now that I am compelled to sacrifice my affections at the shrine of duty,—now that I am Queen as well as consort—and he is subject as well as husband—this disagreement has occurred, which a little calm reflection will put to rights."

"What if his lordship should refuse to return with us?" asked Pembroke.

"You will use your best endeavours to induce him to do so," replied Jane, a tear starting to her eye, and her voice faltering in spite of her efforts to maintain her composure. "But if you fail, I shall at least be satisfied that I have done my duty."

"Your majesty's commands shall be obeyed," replied Pembroke. "But we must have your licence to go forth—for we are detained as prisoners within the Tower."

"You shall have it," replied Jane. And she immediately wrote out the order.

"The passport must be countersigned by the duke," said Pembroke. "The gate-keepers will not hold this sufficient authority."

"How!" exclaimed Jane, reddening, "Am I not Queen? Is not my authority absolute here?"

"Not while the duke holds his high office, gracious madam," returned Pembroke. "His followers give you the *name* of Queen. But they look up to him as sovereign."

"My lord, I need no assurance that you are Northumberland's mortal enemy," replied Jane.

"I am your majesty's loyal subject," replied the earl. "And if your passport be respected, I will confess that I have wronged him."

"And if it be not, I will confess I have wronged *you*, my lord," rejoined Jane. "The royal barge is at your service.—An usher shall conduct you to it."

So saying, she motioned one of her train, to attend them, and the two nobles bowed and departed.

As soon as they had quitted the royal presence, Pembroke observed to his companion:—

"We have now effected a quarrel, which will end in Northumberland's destruction and Jane's dethronement. Simon Renard will so fan the flame, that it shall never be extinguished."

As the Earl anticipated, the Queen's pass was refused—the warders declaring that their instructions were to suffer no one to go forth without the Duke's written order. They then returned to the palace. It was some time before they were admitted to the Queen, as she was engaged in the angry conference previously-related with her mother-in-law. When the Duchess had departed, they sought an audience.

"How, my lords," cried Jane, turning very pale; "do I see you again so soon?"

"It is as I informed your highness," replied the Earl of Pembroke, laying the order on the table. "The Duke is master here."

"Ha!" exclaimed the Queen, starting to her feet, "am I deserted by my husband—braved by the Duke—and treated like an infant by his imperious dame? I cry you pardon, my lords, you have *not* deceived me. You are my loyal subjects. Oh! I could weep to think how I have been deluded. But they shall find they have not made me queen for nothing. While I *have* power I will use it. My lords, I bid you to the council at noon tomorrow. I shall summon Lord Guilford Dudley to attend it, and he will refuse at his peril."

"Have a care, gracious madam, how you proceed with the Duke," replied Pembroke. "Your royal predecessor, Edward, it is said, came not fairly by his end. If Northumberland finds you an obstacle to his designs, instead of a means of forwarding them, he will have little scruple in removing you."

"I shall be wary, doubt it not, my lord," rejoined Jane. "To-morrow you shall learn my pleasure. I count on your fidelity."

"Your majesty may safely do so," they replied. And with renewed assurances of zeal, they departed.

"Her spirit is now fairly roused," observed Pembroke, as they quitted the palace. "If she hold in the same mind till to-morrow, it is all over with Northumberland."

"*Souvent femme varie, bien fol est qui s'y fie,*" observed Simon Renard, advancing to meet them. "Let me know how you have sped."

The Earl of Pembroke then related the particulars of their interview with the Queen.

"All goes on as well as I could desire," observed Renard. "But she must come to an open rupture with him, else the crafty Duke will find some means of soothing her wounded pride. Be that my task."

Taking their way slowly along the outer ward, the trio passed under the gloomy gateway of the Bloody Tower, and ascended a flight of steps on the left leading to the Tower Green. Here (as now,) grew an avenue of trees, and beneath their shade they found De Noailles, who instantly joined them. Renard then entered into a full detail of his schemes, and acquainted them with the information he had received through his messengers, in spite of all the Duke's precautions, of the accession in strength which Mary's party had received, and of the numbers who had declared themselves in her favour. He further intimated that his agents were at work among the people to produce a revolt in the metropolis.

As they proceeded across the Tower-green, the Earl of Pembroke paused at a little distance from the chapel, and pointing to a square patch of ground, edged by a border of white stones, and completely destitute of herbage, said—

"Two Queens have perished here. On this spot stood the scaffolds of Anne Boleyn and Catherine Howard."

"And ere long a third shall be added to their number," observed Renard, gloomily.

Shaping their course towards the north-east angle of the fortress, they stopped before a small turret, at that time called the Martin Tower, and used as a place of confinement for state offenders, but now denominated the Jewel Tower, from the circumstance of its being the depository of the regalia.

"Within that tower are imprisoned the Catholic Bishops Gardiner and Bonner,'" remarked Arundel..

"Let Mary win the crown, and it shall be tenanted by the protestants, Cranmer and Ridley," muttered Renard.

While the others returned to the Green, Renard lingered for an instant to contemplate the White Tower, which is seen perhaps to greater advantage from this point of view than from any other in the fortress. And as it is in most respects unchanged,—excepting such repairs as time has rendered necessary, and some alterations in the doorways and windows, to be noted hereafter,—the modern visitor to this spot may, if he pleases, behold it in much the same state that it appeared to the plotting Spanish ambassador.

THE WHITE TOWER.

Rising to a height of nearly a hundred feet; built in a quadrangular form; terminated at each angle by a lofty turret, three of which are square, while the fourth, situated at the northeast, is circular, and of larger dimensions than the others; embattled; having walls of immense thickness, exceeding fourteen feet, and further strengthened by broad flat buttresses, dividing the face of the building into compartments; lighted by deep semi-circular-arched windows;—this massive stronghold, constructed entirely of stone,—and now in some parts defaced by a coating of mortar and flints,—occupies an area of an hundred and sixteen feet on the north and south, and ninety-six on the east and west. At the south-east corner is a broad semi-circular projection, marking the situation of St. John's Chapel, already described. The round turret, at the north-east angle, was used as an observatory by the celebrated astronomer, Flamstead, in the reign of Charles the Second. The principal entrance was on the north, and was much more spacious than the modern doorway, which occupies its site.

At the period of this chronicle the White Tower was connected, as has already been mentioned, on the south-east with the ancient palace. On the south stood a fabric called the Jewel-house; while at the south-western angle was another embattled structure of equal elevation and dimensions with the By-ward Tower and the other gates, denominated the Coal-harbour Tower. These, with the Lanthorn Tower and the line of buildings extending in an easterly direction towards the Broad Arrow Tower, have totally disappeared, and the White Tower is now disconnected with every other edifice. For centuries it has stood, and for centuries may it continue to stand! Within its walls the old monarchs of England have held their councils,—within its vaults prisoners have sighed,—from its gates queens have come forth to execution!—Long may it flourish as a fearful memento of the past!

On the present occasion, it presented a stirring picture. From a tall staff, planted on the roof, floated the royal standard. Cannon bristled from its battlements, and armed men were seen marching from post to post on its platforms. Before the principal entrance four warders were stationed; and in front troops of arquebusiers and archers were passing under the review of their leaders. The sound of martial music filled the air; pennons and banners fluttered in the breeze; and pikes, steel caps, and corslets glittered in the sunbeams. Amid these warlike groups, the figures of the gigantic warders and their diminutive attendant, Xit, caught the eye of Renard, and filled him with astonishment:—the former being taller by the head and shoulders than the mass of their companions, besides far exceeding them in bulk and size of limb; while the latter, with more than ordinary pretensions to the dignity of manhood, had scarcely the stature of a child. It must not be omitted in the description of the White Tower that the summits of its four turrets were surmounted by large vanes, each decorated with a crown, in the hollows of which, as in our own time, the jackdaws were accustomed to build.

After gazing at this magnificent structure for a few minutes, and indulging in the emotions which its contemplation inspired, Simon Renard followed his companions, and resumed his discourse. They had again adverted to Jane, when the door of the principal entrance of the White Tower was thrown open, and, attended by the Duchess of Suffolk and the Ladies Hastings and Herbert, the subject of their conference issued from it and proceeded on foot towards St. Peter's Chapel. The road was immediately cleared by her attendants, and the three gigantic warders and their tiny companion marched before her, and planted themselves on either side of the chapel door. Glancing significantly at his companions, Renard motioned them to follow him, and hurried towards the sacred pile.

"What! you a rigid Catholic, M. Renard." observed Pembroke, "about to attend Protestant worship? Hopes may be entertained of your conversion."

"Stronger hopes may be entertained that I shall restore the ancient worship," muttered Renard, as he entered the chapel, and took his place unobserved by the Queen behind one of the columns of the aisle, while she advanced to the altar.

Erected in the reign of Edward the First, the little chapel of St. Peter ad Vincula (the parochial church—for the Tower, it is almost needless to say, is a parish in itself), is the second structure occupying the same site and dedicated to the same saint. The earlier fabric was much more spacious, and contained two chancels, with stalls for the king and queen, as appears from the following order for its repair issued in the reign of Henry the Third, and recorded by Stow:—"The king to the keepers of the Tower work, sendeth greeting: We command you to brush or plaster with lime well and decently the chancel of St. Mary in the church of St. Peter within the bailiwick of our Tower of London, and the chancel of St. Peter in the same church; and from the entrance of the chancel of St. Peter to the space of four feet beyond the stalls made for our own and our queen's use in the same church; and the same stalls to be painted. And the little Mary with her shrine and the images of St. Peter, St. Nicholas, and Katherine, and the beam beyond the altar of St. Peter, and the little cross with its images to be coloured anew, and to be refreshed with good colours. And that ye cause to be made a certain image of St. Christopher holding and carrying Jesus where it may best and most conveniently be done, and painted in the foresaid church. And that ye cause two fair tables to be made and painted of the best colours concerning the stories of the blessed Nicholas and Katherine, before the altars of the said saints in the same church. And that ye cause to be made two fair cherubims with a cheerful and joyful countenance standing on the right and left of the great cross in the said church. And moreover, one marble font with marble pillars well and handsomely wrought."

Thus much respecting the ancient edifice. The more recent chapel is a small, unpretending stone structure, and consists of a nave and an aisle at the north, separated by pointed arches, supported by clustered stone pillars of great beauty. Its chief interest is derived from the many illustrious and ill-fated dead crowded within its narrow walls.

Here rested, for a brief season, the body of John Fisher, Bishop of Rochester, beheaded in 1535, for denying the king's supremacy—"a prelate," says Holinshed, "of great learning and of very good life. The Pope had elected him a cardinal and sent his hat as far as Calais. But his head was off before his hat was on, so that they met not." Next to Fisher was interred his friend, the wise, the witty, the eloquent Sir Thomas More, whom Hall, the chronicler, hesitates whether he shall describe as "a foolish wise man, or a wise foolish man,"—and who jested even on the scaffold. His body was afterwards removed, at the intercession of his daughter, Margaret Roper, to

Chelsea. Here also was interred the last of the right line of the Plantagenets, Margaret, Countess of Salisbury, the mother of Cardinal Pole. The venerable countess refused to lay her head upon the block, saying (as Lord Herbert of Cherbury reports),—"'So should traitors do, and I am none.' Neither did it serve that the executioner told her it was the fashion:—so turning her grey head every way, she bid him, if he would have it, to get it as he could: *so he was constrained to fetch it off slovenly.*"

Here also was deposited the headless trunk of another of Henry the Eighth's victims, Thomas Lord Cromwell, the son of a blacksmith, who, having served as a common soldier under Bourbon, at the sack of Rome, entered Wolsey's service, and rose to be Grand Chamberlain of the realm. Here, in Elizabeth's reign, were brought the remains of Thomas Howard, Duke of Norfolk, who aspired to the hand of the Queen of Scots. And here also were laid those of Robert Devereux, the rash and ill-fated Earl of Essex. Under the communion-table was interred, at a later date, the daring and unfortunate Duke of Monmouth, who fell a sacrifice to his ambition. And to come down to yet more recent times, beneath the little gallery at the west of the chapel, were buried the three leaders of the rebellion of 1745—Lords Kilmarnock, Balmerino, and Lovat.

There were four other graves, which, as being more nearly connected with the personages introduced in this chronicle, it will be proper to notice separately. Before the altar, on the west, a plain flag bore the inscription "*Edward Seymour, Duke of Somerset, 1552.*" On the next grave to that of the great Lord Protector was written "*Katherine Howard,*" and on the adjoining stone, "*Anne Boleyn*" These two queens,—equally unfortunate, but not, perhaps, equally culpable,—perished within five years of each other—the latter suffering in 1536, the former in 1541. Close to the wall on the right, a fourth grave bore the name of "*Thomas Seymour, Baron Sudley.*" Seymour was brother to the Duke of Somerset, and Lord High Admiral of England; and the only stain on the Protector's otherwise reproachless character is, that he signed his death-warrant, and declined to use the power he undoubtedly possessed, of procuring his pardon. The fiery and ambitious Admiral was beheaded in 1549.

Between this grave and that of Anne Boleyn intervened a plain stone, unmarked by any inscription, and indicating a vacant tomb. Beneath this flag, eighteen months after the execution of his victim, the Duke of Somerset— and barely six weeks from the day on which this chronicle opens—was deposited the headless trunk of the once all-powerful and arrogant Northumberland.

The service over, as the Queen was about to depart, Simon Renard advanced to meet her. Returning his ceremonious salutation by a dignified greeting, Jane, with a look of some surprise, inquired the cause of his presence..

"I might have chosen a more fitting season and place for an audience with your majesty," replied Renard, in the low and silvery tone which he could adopt at pleasure. "But I have that to communicate which emboldens me to break through all forms."

"Declare it then, sir," replied the Queen.

Renard glanced significantly at her. She understood him, and motioning her attendants to withdraw to a little distance, they obeyed; and Lady Hastings seized the opportunity of despatching a messenger to her father to acquaint him with the circumstance, as already related.

What was the nature of the disclosure made by the wily ambassador to the Queen, it is not our present purpose to reveal. That it was important was evident from the deep attention she paid to it; and it was apparent, also, from her changing looks and agitated demeanour, that her fears were greatly aroused.

As Renard proceeded, her uneasiness increased so much that she could scarcely support herself, and her attendants were about to hasten to her assistance, when a gesture from the ambassador checked them.

Different inferences were drawn by the various witnesses of this singular interview. But all were satisfied of the ascendancy which Renard had, in some manner, acquired over the youthful sovereign. While glances of triumph were exchanged between the conspiring lords, who watched them from their station in the aisle, the greatest misgivings were experienced by the Ladies Hastings and Herbert. Unable to comprehend the mystery, they were so much struck with the peculiar expression of Jane's countenance, which precisely resembled the look she wore after the mysterious occurrence in St. John's Chapel, that they could not help thinking the present conference had some relation to that event.

Renard's manner, indeed, was so extraordinary that it furnished some clue to the nature of his discourse. Casting off the insinuating tone and deferential deportment with which he had commenced, he gradually assumed a look and accent of command, and almost of menace. His figure dilated, and fixing his black flaming eye upon the trembling Queen, he stamped his foot upon the vacant grave on which he was standing, and said, in a voice so loud that it reached the ears of the listeners, "Your Majesty will never wear your crown in safety till Northumberland lies here."

Before any answer could be returned, the door of the chapel was suddenly thrown open, and the Duke presented himself. A momentary change passed over Renard's countenance at this interruption. But he instantly recovered his composure, and folding his arms upon his breast, awaited the result.

Unable to control his indignation, the Duke strode towards them, and flinging his jewelled cap on the ground, drew his sword.

"M. Renard," he exclaimed, "you are a traitor!"

"To whom, my lord?" replied Renard, calmly.

"To me—to the Queen," rejoined the Duke.

"If to be your grace's enemy is to be a traitor, I confess I am one," retorted Renard sternly. "But I am no traitor to her majesty."

"It is false!" exclaimed the Duke, furiously. "You are her worst and most dangerous enemy. And nothing but the sacred spot in which you have sought shelter, prevents me from taking instant vengeance upon you."

Renard smiled disdainfully.

"Your grace threatens safely," he said, in a taunting tone.

"Insolent!" exclaimed the Duke, roused to a pitch of ungovernable fury. "Draw and defend yourself, or I will strike you dead at my feet."

Queen Mary interposing between Northumberland & Simon Renard

"Put up your sword, my lord," cried Jane, throwing herself between them. "You forget in whose presence you stand."

"No!" exclaimed Northumberland, "I do not forget. I am in the presence of one who owes her authority to me—and who holds it through me. The same power which made you queen, can as readily unmake you."

"Your majesty will now judge who is the traitor," observed Renard, sarcastically.

"I do," she replied. "I command your grace," she continued, authoritatively addressing Northumberland, "to quit the chapel instantly."

"What if I refuse to obey?" rejoined the Duke.

"Your grace will do well not to urge me too far," replied Jane. "Obey me, or take the consequences."

"What are they?" cried the Duke contemptuously.

"Your arrest," said the Earl of Pembroke, laying his hand upon his sword, and advancing. "If his grace will not submit himself to your highness's authority, we will compel him to do so."

"Jane!" said the Duke, suddenly controlling himself—"be warned before it is too late. You are in the hands of those who will destroy you."

"On the contrary," rejoined Renard, "her majesty is in the hands of those who will uphold her, and destroy *you?*

"No more of this," interposed the Queen. "If you are, what you profess yourselves, my faithful subjects, you will reconcile your differences."

"Never!" exclaimed the Duke. "Let M. Renard look to himself."

"Another such menace, my lord," said Jane, "and I place you in arrest."

"Threatened men live long," observed Renard. "I beseech your majesty not to place any restraint upon his grace."

"Will your highness grant me a moment's speech with you!" said Northumberland, sheathing his sword.

"Not now, my lord," replied Jane. "To-morrow, at the council, you shall be fully heard. And I charge you, by your allegiance, to cease all hostilities till then. Have I your knightly word for this?"

"You have," replied the Duke, after a moment's reflection.

"And yours, M. Renard?" continued the Queen, turning to him.

"Since his grace has passed his word I cannot withhold mine," replied the ambassador. "But I give it with reluctance."

"Your grace will not fail to attend the council to-morrow," said Jane.

"If your highness desires it I will not, undoubtedly," replied the Duke. "But since you decline to act upon my advice, there can be little need for my presence."

"My wishes—my commands are, that you attend," rejoined the Queen.

"Your wishes *are* commands," rejoined the Duke. "I will be there."

"Enough," replied Jane. "M. Renard, you will accompany me to the palace."

As the ambassador was preparing to depart, he perceived Northumberland's cap lying at his feet.

"Your grace's hat," he observed, pointing to it. And glancing significantly at Jane, he added, in an audible whisper, "Would the head were in it!"

"Ha!" exclaimed the Duke, laying his hand upon his sword. "But you are safe till to-morrow."

Renard made no reply, but with a smile of exultation followed the Queen out of the chapel.

XI.—HOW THE DUKE OF NORTHUMBERLAND WAS PREVAILED UPON TO UNDERTAKE THE ENTERPRISE AGAINST THE LADY MARY.

At noon on the following day, the Council was held as appointed by the Queen. In the meantime, alarming intelligence having been received of the accession which Mary's party had obtained, it became absolutely necessary that immediate and decisive measures should be taken against her.

As soon as the Lords of the Council, including the two ambassadors, Renard and Noailles, were assembled, and the Queen had taken her seat upon the throne, the Earl of Pembroke stepped forward, and thus addressed her:—

"It is with infinite concern that I have to apprise your majesty that news has just been brought that Sir Edward Hastings, with an army of four thousand men, has gone over to the Lady Mary. Five counties also have revolted. Your highness is already aware that the Earls of Sussex, Bath and Oxford, Lord Wentworth, Sir Thomas Cornwallis and Sir Henry Jerningham, have raised the commoners of Suffolk and Norfolk. Lord Windsor, Sir Edmund Peckham, Sir Robert Drury, and Sir Edward Hastings, have now raised those of Buckinghamshire. Sir John Williams and Sir Leonard Chamberlain have stirred up a party in Oxfordshire, and Sir Thomas Tresham another in Northamptonshire. These rebels with their companies are now marching towards Framlingham Castle."

"The revolt must be instantly checked," rejoined Jane. "An army must be sent against her."

"To whom will your majesty entrust its command?" inquired the Earl of Pembroke.

"To one well fitted for the office,—my father, the Duke of Suffolk," answered the Queen.

"My advice is, that it be given to the Duke of Northumberland," said the Earl of Arundel. "Wherever he has carried his arms—in Scotland and in France— he has been victorious. The recollection of the defeat sustained by the rebels at Dussindale will operate in his favour. His grace has every recommendation for the office. Having achieved the victory of Norfolk once already, he will be so feared that none will dare to lift up a weapon against him. Besides which, I need scarcely remind your highness, who must be familiar with his high reputation, that he is the best man of war in the realm, as well for the ordering of his camps and soldiers, both in battle and in the tent, as for his experience and wisdom, with which he can both animate his army and either vanquish his enemies by his courage and skill, or else dissuade them (if need be,) from their enterprise."

"My voice is for Northumberland," cried Cecil.

"And mine," added Huntingdon.

"We are all unanimous," cried the rest of the Council.

"Your grace hears the opinion just given," said Jane. "Will you undertake the command?".

"No," answered the Duke, bluntly. "I will shed my blood in your majesty's defence. But I see through the designs, of your artful council, and will not be made their dupe. Their object is to withdraw me from you. Let the Duke of Suffolk take the command. I will maintain the custody of the Tower."

"Do not suffer him to decline it," whispered Simon Renard to the Queen. "By this means you will accomplish a double purpose—insure a victory over Mary, and free yourself from the yoke he will otherwise impose upon you. If the Duke of Suffolk departs, and he is left absolute master of the Tower, you will never attain your rightful position."

"You are right," replied Jane. "My lord," she continued, addressing the Duke, "I am satisfied that the Council mean you well. And I pray you, therefore, to acquiesce in their wishes and my own.".

"Why will not your highness send the Duke of Suffolk, as you have this moment proposed?" rejoined Northumberland.

"I have bethought me," replied the Queen. "And as my husband has thought fit to absent himself from me at this perilous juncture, I am resolved not to be left without a protector. Your grace will, therefore, deliver up the keys of the Tower to the Duke of Suffolk."

"Nay, your majesty,"—cried Northumberland.

"I will have no nay, my lord," interrupted the Queen peremptorily. "I will in nowise consent that my father shall leave me. To whom else would your grace entrust the command?"

The Duke appeared to reflect for a moment.

"I know no one," he answered.

"Then your grace must perforce consent," said the Queen.

"If your majesty commands it, I must. But I feel it is a desperate hazard," replied Northumberland.

"It is so desperate," whispered Pembroke to Renard,—"that he has not one chance in his favour."

"The Council desire to know your grace's determination?" said Arundel.

"My determination is this," rejoined the Duke. "Since you think it good, I will go,—not doubting your fidelity to the Queen's majesty, whom I shall leave in your custody."

"He is lost!" whispered Renard.

"Your grace's commission for the lieutenantship of the army shall be signed at once," said Jane; "and I beseech you to use all diligence."

"I will do what in me lies," replied the Duke. "My retinue shall meet me at Durham House to-night. And I will see the munition and artillery set forward before daybreak."

A pause now ensued, during which the Duke's commission was signed by the whole Council.

"It is his death-warrant," observed Renard to the Earl of Arundel.

"Here is your warrant, under the broad seal of England," said the Earl of Pembroke, delivering it to him.

"I must have my marches prescribed," replied the Duke. "I will do nothing without authority."

"What say you, my lords?" said Pembroke, turning to them.

"Agree at once," whispered Renard—"he is planning his own ruin."

"Your grace shall have full powers and directions," rejoined Pembroke.

"It is well," replied Northumberland. "My lords," he continued with great dignity, addressing the Council, "I and the other noble personages, with the whole army that are now about to go forth, as well for the behalf of you and yours, as for the establishing of the Queen's highness, shall not only adventure our bodies and lives amongst the bloody strokes and cruel assaults of our adversaries in the open fields; but also we leave the conservation of ourselves, children and families, at home here with you, as altogether committed to your truth and fidelity. If," he proceeded sternly, "we thought you would through malice, conspiracy, or dissension, leave us, your friends, in the briars and betray us, we could as well, in sundry ways, foresee and provide for our own safety, as any of you, by betraying us, can do for yours. But now, upon the only trust and faithfulness of your honours, whereof we think ourselves most assured, we do hazard our lives. And if ye shall violate your trust and promise, hoping thereby of life and promotion, yet shall not God account you innocent of our bloods, neither acquit you of the sacred and holy oath of allegiance, made freely by you to the Queen's highness, who, by your own and our enticement, is rather of force placed therein, than by her own seeking and request. Consider, also, that God's cause, which is the preferment of his word, and fear of Papists' entrance, hath been (as you have heretofore always declared,) the original ground whereupon you even at the first motion granted your good wills and consents thereunto, as by your handwritings appeareth. And think not the contrary. But if ye mean deceit, though not forthwith, yet hereafter, Heaven will revenge the same."

"Your grace wrongs us by these suspicions," observed the Earl of Arundel.

"I will say no more," rejoined the Duke, "but in this perilous time wish you to use constant hearts, abandoning all malice, envy, and private affections."

"Doubt it not," said Cecil.

"I have not spoken to you in this sort upon any mistrust I have of your truths," pursued the Duke, "of which I have always hitherto conceived a trusty confidence. But I have put you in remembrance thereof, in case any variance should arise amongst you in my absence. And this I pray you, wish me not worse good-speed in this matter than you wish yourselves."

"We shall all agree on one point," observed Pembroke aside to Renard— "and that is a hope that he may never return."

"If your grace mistrusts any of us in this matter, you are deceived," rejoined Arundel, "for which of us can wash his hands of it. And if we should shrink from you as treasonable, which of us can excuse himself as guiltless. Therefore, your doubt is too far cast."

"I pray Heaven it be so," replied the Duke, gravely. "Brother of Suffolk, I resign the custody of the Tower to you, entreating you, if you would uphold your daughter's crown, to look well to your charge. I now take my leave of your highness."

"Heaven speed your grace," replied Jane, returning his haughty salutation.

"Farewell, my lord," said the Earl of Arundel, "I am right sorry it is not my chance to bear you company, as I would cheerfully spend my heart's blood in your defence."

"Judas!" muttered the Duke.

Upon this, the Council broke up, and Jane returned to the palace, accompanied by the Duke of Suffolk, the two ambassadors, and others of the conspiring nobles.

"We may give each other joy," said Pembroke to Renard, as they walked along—"we are at last rid of Northumberland. Suffolk will be easily disposed of."

"Queen Mary shall be proclaimed in London, before tomorrow night," rejoined Renard.

Meanwhile, the Duke, attended by the Marquis of Northampton, the Lord Grey, and divers other noblemen, entered his barge, and proceeded to Durham House. On the same night, he mustered his troops, and made every preparation for his departure, As he rode forth on the following morning through Shoreditch, great crowds collected to see him pass. But they maintained a sullen and ominous silence.

"The people press to see us," observed the Duke, in a melancholy tone, to Lord Grey, who rode by his side; "but not one saith God speed us!"

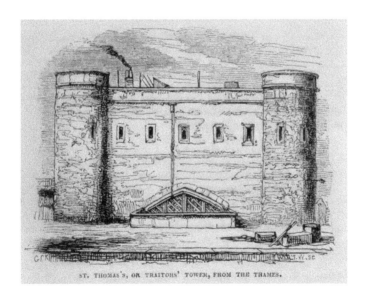

ST. THOMAS'S, OR TRAITORS' TOWER, FROM THE THAMES.

XII.—HOW MAGOG BECAME ENAMOURED OF A BUXOM WIDOW, YCLEPED DAME PLACIDA PASTON; HOW HE WENT A WOOING; AND HOW HE PROSPERED IN HIS SUIT.

ON the night of the Duke of Northumberland's departure, as the three gigantic warders and their dwarfish attendant were assembled in their lodging in the By-ward Tower, preparatory to their evening meal, the conduct of Magog, which had been strange enough throughout the day, became so very extraordinary and unaccountable, that his brethren began to think he must have taken leave of his senses. Flinging his huge frame on a bench, he sighed and groaned, or rather bellowed, like an over-driven ox, and rolling his great saucer eyes upwards, till the whites only were visible, thumped his chest with a rapid succession of blows, that sounded like the strokes of a sledgehammer. But the worst symptom, in the opinion of the others, was his inability to eat. Magog's case must, indeed, be desperate, if he had no appetite for supper— and such a supper! Seldom had their board been so abundantly and invitingly spread as on the present occasion—and Magog refused to partake of it. He must either be bewitched, or alarmingly ill.

Supplied by the provident attention of the pantler and his spouse, the repast consisted of a cold chine of beef, little the worse for its previous appearance at the royal board; a mighty lumber pie, with a wall of pastry several inches thick, moulded to resemble the White Tower, and filled with a savoury mess of ham and veal, enriched by a goodly provision of forcemeat balls, each as large as a cannon-shot; a soused gurnet floating in claret; a couple of pullets stuffed with oysters, and served with a piquant sauce of oiled butter and barberries; a skirret pasty; an apple tansy; and a prodigious marrow pudding. Nor, in this bill of fare, must be omitted an enormous loaf, baked expressly for the giants, and compounded of nearly a bushel of mingled wheaten flour and barley, which stood at one end of the table, while at the opposite extremity was placed a nine-hooped pot of mead—the distance between each hoop denoting a quart of the humming fluid.

But all these good things were thrown away upon Magog. With some persuasion he was induced to take his seat at the table, but after swallowing a single mouthful of the beef, he laid down his knife and fork, and left the rest untasted. In vain Og urged him to try the pullets, assuring him he would find them delicious, as they were cooked by Dame Potentia herself:—in vain Gog scooped out the most succulent morsels from the depths of the lumber pie, loading his plate with gobbets of fat and forcemeat balls. He declined both offers with a melancholy shake of the head, and began to sigh and groan more dismally than ever.

Exchanging significant looks with each other, the two giants thought it best to leave him to himself, and assiduously addressed themselves to their own meal. By way of setting him a good example, they speedily cleared the chine to the bone. The gurnet was next despatched; and a considerable inroad made into the lumber pie,—three of its turrets having already disappeared,—when, as if roused from a trance, Magog suddenly seized the marrow pudding, and devoured it in a trice. He then applied himself to the nine-hooped pot, and taking a long deep draught, appeared exceedingly relieved.

But his calmness was of short duration. The fit almost instantly returned with fresh violence. Without giving the slightest intimation of his intention, he plucked his cap from his brow, and flung it at Xit, who chanced at the moment to be perched upon a stool stirring a great pan of sack posset, set upon a chafing-dish to warm, with such force as to precipitate him over head and ears into the liquid, which, fortunately, was neither hot enough to scald him, nor deep enough to drown him. When he reappeared, the mannikin uttered a shrill scream of rage and terror; and Og, who could not help laughing at his comical appearance, hastened to his assistance, and extricated him from his unpleasant situation.

By the aid of a napkin, Xit was speedily restored to a state of tolerable cleanliness, and though his habiliments were not a little damaged by the viscous fluid in which they had been immersed, he appeared to have suffered more in temper than in any other way from the accident. While Og was rubbing him dry,—perhaps with no very gentle hand,—he screamed and cried like a peevish infant undergoing the process of ablution; and he was no sooner set free, than darting to the spot where Magog's cap had fallen, he picked it up, and dipping it in the sack-posset, hurled it in its owners face. Delighted with this retaliation, he crowed and swaggered about the room, and stamping fiercely upon the ground, tried to draw his sword; but this he found impossible, it being fast glued to the scabbard. Magog, however, paid no sort of attention to his antics, but having wiped his face with the end of the table-cloth, and wrung his bonnet, marched deliberately out of the room. His brothers glanced at each other in surprise, and were hesitating whether to follow, when they were relieved from further anxiety on this score by Xit, who hurried after him. They then very quietly returned to the repast, and trusting all would come right, contented themselves with such interjectional remarks as did not interfere with the process of mastication. In this way they continued, until the return of Xit, who, as he entered the room, exclaimed, with a half-merry, half-mischievous expression of countenance, "I have found it out—I have found it out."

"Found out what?" cried out both giants.

"He is in love," replied the dwarf.

"Magog in love!" ejaculated Og, starting. "Impossible!"

"You shall be convinced to the contrary if you will come with me," rejoined Xit. "I have seen him enter the house. And, what is more, I have seen the lady."

"Who is she?" demanded Gog.

"Can you not guess," rejoined Xit.

"The fair Cicely," returned the giant.

"You are wide of the mark," replied the dwarf—"though, I confess, she is lovely enough to turn his head outright. But he is not so moonstruck as to aspire to *her*. Had I sought her hand, there might have been some chance of success. But Magog—pshaw!"

"Tush!" cried Og, "I will be sworn it is Mistress Bridget Crumbewell, the Bowyer's daughter, who hath bewitched him. I have noted that she hath cast many an amorous glance at him of late. It is she, I'll be sworn."

"Then you are forsworn, for it is *not* Bridget Crumbewell," rejoined Xit— "the object of his affections is a widow."

"A widow!" exclaimed both giants—"then he is lost."

"I see not that," replied the dwarf. "Magog might do worse than espouse Dame Placida Paston. Her husband, old Miles Paston, left a good round sum behind him, and a good round widow too. She has a bright black eye, a tolerable waist for so plump a person, and as neat an ancle as can be found within the Tower, search where you will. I am half disposed to enter the lists with him."

"Say you so," replied Og, laughing at the dwarf's presumption, "then e'en make the attempt. And such assistance as we can render, shall not be wanting; for neither Gog nor I—if I do not misapprehend his sentiments—have any desire that our brother should enter into the holy state of matrimony."

"Right, brother," rejoined Gog; "we must prevent it if possible, and I see not a better way than that you propose. If it does nothing else, it will afford us excellent pastime."

"Excuse me a moment," observed Xit. "If I am to play the suitor to advantage, I must change my dress. I will return on the instant, and conduct you to Dame Placida's dwelling."

So saying, he withdrew for a short space, during which he arrayed himself in his holiday garments. "Magog will have no chance," he observed, as he strutted into the room, and glanced at his pigmy limbs with an air of intense self-satisfaction; "the widow is already won."

"If she be as fond of apes as some of her sex, she is so," replied Og; "but widows are not so easily imposed upon."

The two giants, who, during Xit's absence had entirely cleared the board, and wound up the repast by emptying the nine-hooped pot, now expressed themselves ready to start. Accordingly, they set out, and, preceded by Xit, shaped their course along the southern ward, and passing beneath the gateway of the Bloody Tower, ascended the hill leading to the Green, on the right of which, as at the present time, stood a range of buildings inhabited by the warders and other retainers of the royal household.

Before one of these Xit stopped, and pointing to an open window about six feet from the ground, desired Gog to raise him up to it, The giant complied, when they beheld a sight that filled them with merriment. Upon a stout oak table—for there was no chair in the domicile sufficiently large to sustain him—sat Magog, his hand upon his breast, and his eyes tenderly fixed upon a comely dame, who was presenting him with a large foaming pot of ale. The languishing expression of the giant's large lumpish features was so irresistibly diverting, that it was impossible to help laughing; and the lookers-on only restrained themselves, in the hope of witnessing something still more diverting.

Magog's Courtship

Dame Placida Paston had a short plump (perhaps a little too plump, and yet it is difficult to conceive how that can well be,) figure; a round rosy face, the very picture of amiability and good humour; a smooth chin, dimpling cheeks, and the brightest and merriest black eyes imaginable. Her dress was neatness itself, and her dwelling as neat as her dress. With attractions like these, no wonder she captivated many a heart, and among others that of Magog, who had long nourished a secret passion for her, but could not muster courage to declare it—for, with a bluff and burly demeanour towards his own sex, the giant was as bashful as a shamefaced stripling in the presence of any of womankind.

With the tact peculiarly belonging to widows, Dame Placida had discovered the state of affairs, and perhaps being not altogether unwilling to discourage him, having accidentally met him on the Tower Green on the day in question, had invited him to visit her in the evening. It was this invitation which had so completely upset the love-sick giant. The same bashfulness that prevented him from making known his attachment to the object of it, kept him silent towards his brethren, as he feared to excite their ridicule.

On his arrival at her abode, Dame Placida received him with the utmost cordiality, and tried to engage him in conversation. But all without effect.

"I see how it is," she thought; "there is nothing like a little strong liquor to unloose a man's tongue." And she forthwith proceeded to a cupboard to draw a pot of ale. It was at this juncture that she was discovered by the observers outside.

Magog received the proffered jug, and fixing a tender look on the fair donor, pressed his huge hand to his heart, and drained it to the last drop. The widow took back the empty vessel, and smilingly inquired if he would have it replenished. The giant replied faintly in the negative,—so faintly, that she was about to return to the cupboard for a fresh supply, when Magog caught her hand, and flung himself on his knees before her. In this posture he was still considerably the taller of the two; but bending himself as near to the ground as possible, he was about to make his proposal in due form, when he was arrested by a tremendous peal of laughter from without, and, looking up, beheld Xit seated on the window-sill, while behind him appeared the grinning countenances of his brethren.

Ashamed and enraged at being thus detected, Magog sprang to his feet, and seizing Xit by the nape of the neck, would have inflicted some severe chastisement upon him, if Dame Placida had not interfered to prevent it. At her solicitation, the mannikin was released; and he no sooner found himself at liberty, than, throwing himself at her feet, he protested he was dying for her. Perhaps it might be from a certain love of teazing, inherent even in the best-tempered of her sex, or, perhaps, she thought such a course might induce Magog more fully to declare himself; but whatever motive influenced her, certain it is that Dame Placida appeared by no means displeased with her diminutive suitor, but suffered him, after a decent show of reluctance, to take her hand.

Thus encouraged, the dwarf was so elated, that springing upon a chair, he endeavoured to snatch a kiss. But the widow, having no idea of allowing such a liberty, gave him a smart box on the ear, which immediately brought him to the ground.

Notwithstanding this rebuff, Xit would have persevered, had not Magog, whose feelings were really interested, begun to appear seriously angry. Seeing this, he judged it prudent to desist, and contented himself with entreating the widow to declare which of the two she preferred. Dame Placida replied, that she must take a few hours to consider upon it, but invited them both to supper on the following evening, when she would deliver her answer. Having given a similar invitation to the two giants outside, she dismissed the whole party.

XIII.—OF THE STRATAGEM PRACTISED BY CUTHBERT CHOLMONDELEY ON THE JAILOR.

Several days had now elapsed since Cholmondeley was thrown into the dungeon, and during that time he had been visited only at long intervals by Nightgall. To all his menaces, reproaches, and entreaties, the jailor turned a deaf ear. He smiled grimly as he set down the scanty provisions—a loaf and a pitcher of water—with which he supplied his captive; but he could not be induced to speak. When questioned about Cicely and upbraided with his perfidy, his countenance assumed an exulting expression which Cholmondeley found so intolerable that he never again repeated his inquiries. Left to himself, his whole time was passed in devising some means of escape. He tried, but ineffectually, to break his bonds, and at last, satisfied of its futility, gave up the attempt.

One night, he was disturbed by the horrible and heartrending shrieks of the female prisoner, who had contrived to gain access to his cell. There was something about this mysterious person that inspired him with unaccountable dread; and though he was satisfied she was a being of this world, the conviction did not serve to lessen his fears. After making the dungeon ring with her cries for some time, she became silent, and as he heard no sound and could distinguish nothing, he concluded she must have departed. Just then the unlocking of a distant door and a gleam of sickly light on the walls of the stone passage announced the approach of Nightgall, and the next moment he entered the cell. The light fell upon a crouching female figure in one corner. The jailor started; and his angry ejaculations caused the poor creature to raise her head.

Cholmondeley had never beheld anything so ghastly as her countenance, and he half doubted whether he did not look upon a tenant of the grave. Her eyes were sunken and lustreless; her cheeks thin and rigid, and covered with skin of that deadly paleness which is seen in plants deprived of light; her flesh shrunken to the bone, and her hands like those of a skeleton. But in spite of all this emaciation, there was something in her features that seemed to denote that she had once been beautiful, and her condition in life exalted. The terror she exhibited at the approach of the jailor proved the dreadful usage she had experienced. In answer to his savage ejaculations to her to follow him, she flung herself on her knees, and raised her hands in the most piteous supplication. Nothing moved by this, Nightgall was about to seize her and drag her away, when with a piercing scream she darted from him, and took refuge behind Cholmondeley.

"Save me!—save me from him!" she shrieked; "he will kill me."

"Pshaw!" cried the jailor. "Come with me quietly, Alexia, and you shall have a warmer cell, and better food."

"I will not go," she replied. "I will not answer to that name. Give me my rightful title and I will follow you."

"What is your title?" asked Cholmondeley, eagerly.

"Beware!" interposed Nightgall, raising his hand menacingly. "Beware!"

"Heed him not!" cried Cholmondeley; "he shall not harm you. Tell me how you are called?"

"I have forgotten," replied the terrified woman, evasively. "I had another name once. But I am called Alexia now."

"What has become of your child?" asked Cholmondeley.

"My child!" she echoed, with a frightful scream. "I have lost her in these dungeons. I sometimes see her before me running and clapping her little hands. Ah! there she is—coming towards us. She has long fair hair—light blue eyes—blue as the skies I shall never behold again. Do you not see her?"

"No," replied Cholmondeley, trembling. "How is she named?"

"She died unbaptised," replied the female. "But I meant to call her Angela. Ah! see! she answers to the name—she approaches. Angela! my child!—my child!" And the miserable creature extended her arms, and seemed to clasp a phantom to her bosom.

"Alexia!" roared the jailor, fiercely, "follow me, or I will have you scourged by the tormentor."

"He dare not—he will not,"—cried Cholmondeley, to whom the wretched woman clung convulsively. "Do not go with him."

"Alexia," reiterated the jailor, in a tone of increased fury.

"I *must* go," she cried, breaking from the esquire, "or he will kill me." And with a noiseless step she glided after Nightgall.

Cholmondeley listened intently, and as upon a former occasion, heard stifled groans succeeded by the clangour of a closing door, and then all was hushed. The jailor returned no more that night. When he appeared again, it was with a moodier aspect than ever. He set down the provisions, and instantly departed.

While meditating upon various means of escape, an idea at length occurred to the young esquire upon which he resolved to act. He determined to feign death. Accordingly, though half famished, he left his provisions untouched; and when Nightgall next visited the cell, he found him stretched on the ground, apparently lifeless. Uttering a savage laugh, the jailor held the light over the supposed corpse, and exclaimed, "At last I am fairly rid of him. Cicely will now be mine. I will fling him into the burial-vault near the moat. But first to unfasten this chain."

So saying, he took a small key from the bunch at his girdle and unlocked the massive fetters that bound Cholmondeley to the wall. During this operation the esquire held his breath, and endeavoured to give his limbs the semblance of death. But the jailor's suspicions were aroused.

"He cannot have been long dead," he muttered, "perhaps he is only in a trance. This shall make all secure." And drawing his dagger, he was about to plunge it in the bosom of the esquire, when the latter being now freed from his bondage, suddenly started to his feet, and flung himself upon him.

The suddenness of the action favoured its success. Before Nightgall recovered from his surprise, the poniard was wrested from his grasp and held at his throat. In the struggle that ensued, he received a wound which brought him senseless to the ground; and Cholmondeley, thinking it needless to despatch him, contented himself with chaining him to the wall.

Possessing himself of the jailor's keys, he was about to depart, when Nightgall, who at that moment regained his consciousness, and with it all his ferocity, strove to intercept him. On discovering his situation, he uttered a torrent of impotent threats and execrations. The only reply deigned by the esquire to his menaces, was an assurance that he was about to set free the miserable Alexia.

Quitting the cell, Cholmondeley turned off on the left, in the direction whence he imagined the shrieks had proceeded. Here he beheld a range of low strong doors, the first of which he unlocked with one of the jailor's keys. The prison was unoccupied. He opened the next, but with no better success. It contained nothing except a few rusty links of chain attached to an iron staple driven into the floor. In the third he found a few mouldering bones; and the fourth was totally empty. He then knocked at the doors of others, and called the miserable captive by her name in a loud voice. But no answer was returned.

At the extremity of the passage he found an open door, leading to a small circular chamber, in the centre of which stood a heavy stone pillar. From this pillar projected a long iron bar, sustaining a coil of rope, terminated by a hook. On the ground lay an immense pair of pincers, a curiously-shaped saw, and a brasier. In one corner stood a large oaken frame, about three feet high, moved by rollers. At the other was a ponderous wooden machine, like a pair of stocks. Against the wall hung a broad hoop of iron, opening in the middle with a hinge—a horrible instrument of torture, termed "The Scavenger's

Daughter." Near it were a pair of iron gauntlets, which could be contracted by screws till they crushed the fingers of the wearer. On the wall also hung a small brush to sprinkle the wretched victims who fainted from excess of agony, with vinegar; while on a table beneath it were placed writing materials and an open volume, in which were taken down the confessions of the sufferers.

Cholmondeley saw at once that he had entered the torture-chamber, and hastily surveying these horrible contrivances, was about to withdraw, when he noticed a trap-door in one corner. Advancing towards it, he perceived a flight of steps, and thinking they might lead him to the cell he was in search of, he descended, and came to a passage still narrower and gloomier than that he had quitted. As he proceeded along it, he thought he heard a low groan, and hurrying in the direction of the sound, arrived at a small door, and knocking against it, called "Alexia," but was answered in the feeble voice of a man.

"I am not Alexia, but whoever you are, liberate me from this horrible torture, or put me to death, and so free me from misery."

After some search, Cholmondeley discovered the key of the dungeon and unlocking it, beheld an old man in a strange stooping posture, with his head upon his breast, and his back bent almost double. The walls of the cell, which was called the Little Ease, were so low, and so contrived, that the wretched inmate could neither stand, walk, sit, nor he at full length within them.

With difficulty,—for the poor wretch's limbs were too much cramped by his long and terrible confinement, to allow him to move,—Cholmondeley succeeded in dragging him forth.

"How long have you been immured here?" he inquired.

"I know not," replied the old man. "Not many weeks perhaps—but to me it seems an eternity. Support me—oh! support me! I am sinking fast!"

"A draught of water will revive you," cried Cholmondeley. "I will bring you some in a moment."

And he was about to hurry to his cell for the pitcher, when the old man checked him..

"It is useless," he cried. "I am dying—nothing can save me. Young man," he continued, fixing his glazing eyes on Cholmondeley. "When I was first brought to the Tower, I was as young as you. I have grown old in captivity. My life has been passed in these dismal places. I was imprisoned by the tyrant Henry VIII. for my adherence to the religion of my fathers—and I have witnessed such dreadful things, that, were I to relate them, it would blanch your hair like mine. Heaven have mercy on my soul!" And, sinking backwards, he expired with a hollow groan.

Satisfied that life was wholly extinct, Cholmondeley continued his search for the scarcely less unfortunate Alexia. Traversing the narrow gallery, he could discover no other door, and he therefore returned to the torture-room, and from thence retraced his steps to the cell. As he approached it, Nightgall, who heard his footsteps, called out to him, and entreated to be set at liberty.

"I will do so, provided you will conduct me to the dungeon of Alexia," replied the esquire.

"You have not found her?" rejoined the jailor.

"I have not," replied Cholmondeley. "Will you guide me to it?"

Nightgall eagerly answered in the affirmative.

The esquire was about to unlock the chain, but as he drew near him, the jailor's countenance assumed so malignant an expression, that he determined not to trust him. Despite his entreaties, he again turned to depart.

"You will never get out without me," said Nightgall.

"I will make the attempt," rejoined Cholmondeley. And wrapping himself in the jailor's ample cloak, and putting on his cap, he quitted the dungeon.

This time, he shaped his course differently. Endeavouring to recall the road by which Nightgall had invariably approached, he proceeded for a short time along the onward passage, and presently reaching a spot where two avenues branched off—one to the right and the other to the left,—he struck into the latter, and found a second range of dungeons. He opened the doors of several, but they were untenanted; and giving up the idea of rescuing the ill-fated Alexia, he began to think it time to attend to his own safety.

The passage he had chosen, which, like all those he had previously traversed, was arched and flagged with stone, brought him to a low square chamber, from which a flight of steps ascended. Mounting these he came to two other passages, and without pausing to consider, hurried along the first. In a short time he was stopped by a strong iron door, and examining the lock tried every key, but could find none to fit it. Failing to procure egress in this quarter, he was obliged to return, and choosing his course at random, struck into an avenue on the right.

Greatly surprised at the extent of the passages he had tracked, he could not help admiring the extraordinary solidity of the masonry, and the freshness of the stone, which looked as if it had just come from the chisel. Arriving at a gate which impeded his further progress, he applied to his keys, and was fortunately able to open it. This did not set him free as he had anticipated, but admitted him into a spacious vault, surrounded by deep cavernous recesses, filled with stone coffins. Broken statues and tattered escutcheons littered the ground.

Wondering where he could have penetrated, he paused for a moment to consider whether he should return; but fearful of losing his way in the labyrinth he had just quitted, he determined to go on. A broad flight of stone steps led him to a large folding-door, which he pushed aside, and traversing a sort of corridor with which it communicated, he found himself at the foot of a spiral staircase. Mounting it, he came to an extremely narrow passage, evidently contrived in the thickness of the wall; and threading it, he reached a small stone door, in which neither bolt nor lock could be detected.

Convinced, however, that there must be some secret spring, he examined it more narrowly, and at length discovered a small plate of iron. Pressing this, the heavy stone turned as upon a pivot, and disclosed a narrow passage, through which he crept, and found himself to his great surprise in the interior of St. John's Chapel in the White Tower. At first, he thought he must be deceived, but a glance around convinced him he was not mistaken; and when he called to mind the multitude of passages he had traversed, his surprise was greatly diminished.

While he was thus musing, he heard footsteps approaching, and instantly extinguished the light. The masked door from which he had emerged, lay at the extremity of the northern aisle, and the parties (for there was evidently more than one) came from the other end of the chapel. Finding he had been noticed, Cholmondeley advanced towards them.

XIV.—HOW SIMON RENARD AND THE LORDS OF THE COUNCIL WERE ARRESTED BY LORD GUILFORD DUDLEY.

The brief and troubled reign of the ill-fated Queen Jane was fast drawing to a close. Every fresh messenger brought tidings of large accessions to the cause of the lady Mary, who was now at the head of thirty thousand men,—an army trebling the forces of Northumberland. Added to this, the metropolis itself was in a state of revolt. Immense mobs collected in Smithfield, and advanced towards the Tower-gates, commanding the warders to open them in the name of Queen Mary. These rioters were speedily driven off, with some bloodshed. But their leader, who was recognised as the prisoner Gilbert, escaped, and the next day larger crowds assembled, and it was feared that an attack would be made upon the fortress.

Meanwhile, Northumberland, whose order of march had been prescribed by the council, proceeded slowly on the expedition; and the fate that attended him fully verified the old proverb, that delay breeds danger. An accident, moreover, occurred, which, while it greatly disheartened his party, gave additional hope to that of the lady Mary. Six vessels, well manned with troops and ammunition, stationed off Yarmouth to intercept Mary in case she attempted to escape by sea, were driven into that port, where their commanders were immediately visited by Sir Henry Jerningham, who was levying recruits for the princess, and were prevailed upon by him to join her standard.

When the news of this defection reached the Tower, even the warmest partisans of Jane perceived that her cause was hopeless, and prepared to desert her. The Duke of Suffolk could not conceal his uneasiness, and despatched a secret messenger to Lord Guilford Dudley, who during the whole of this trying period had absented himself, commanding his instant return..

On receiving the summons, Dudley immediately answered it in person. Jane received him with the utmost affection, and their meeting, which took place in the presence of her father, the Duchess of Northumberland, and the Ladies Herbert and Hastings, was deeply affecting. Lord Guilford was much moved, and prostrating himself before the queen, besought her forgiveness for his ill-advised and ungenerous conduct—bitterly reproaching himself for having deserted her at a season of so much peril.

"I will not upbraid you, dear Dudley," rejoined Jane, "neither will I attempt to disguise from you that your absence has given me more anguish than aught else in this season of trouble. My crown you well know was your crown. But now, alas! I fear I have lost that which, though a bauble in my eyes, was a precious-jewel in yours."

"Oh, say not so, my queen," replied Lord Guilford, passionately. "Things are not so desperate as you imagine. I have letters full of hope and confidence from my father, who has reached Bury Saint Edmund's. He means to give battle to the rebels to-morrow. And the next messenger will no doubt bring news of their defeat."

"Heaven grant it may prove so, my dear lord!" rejoined Jane. "But I am not so sanguine. I have despatched missives to the sheriffs of the different counties, enjoining them to raise troops in my defence, and have summoned the Lord Mayor and the city-authorities to the council to-morrow, to decide upon what is best to be done in this emergency."

"Daughter," said the Duke of Suffolk, "it is my duty to, inform you that I have just received letters from his Grace of Northumberland, very different in purport from that which has reached Lord Guilford. In them he expresses himself doubtful, of the result of the conflict, and writes most urgently for further succour. His men, he says, are hourly deserting to the hostile camp. And, unless he speedily receives additional force and munition, it will be impossible to engage the enemy."

"This is bad news, indeed, my lord," replied Jane, mournfully.

"Have we not troops to send him?" cried Lord Guilford Dudley. "If a leader is wanted, I will set forth at once."

"We cannot spare another soldier from the Tower," replied Suffolk. "London is in a state of revolt. The fortress may be stormed by the rabble, who are all in favour of Mary. The Duke has already taken all the picked men. And, if the few loyal soldiers left, are removed, we shall not have sufficient to overawe the rebels."

"My lord," observed the Duchess of Northumberland, "you have allowed the council too much sway. They will overpower you. And your highness," she added, turning to Jane, "has suffered yourself to be deluded by the artful counsels of Simon Renard."

"Simon Renard has given me good counsel," replied Jane.

"You are deceived, my queen," replied her husband. "He is conspiring against your crown and life."

"It is too true," added Suffolk, "I have detected some of his dark practices."

"Were I assured of this," answered Jane, "the last act of my reign—the last exertion of my power should be to avenge myself upon him."

"Are the guards within the Tower true to us?" inquired Dudley.

"As yet," replied Suffolk. "But they are wavering. If something be not done to confirm them, I fear they will declare for Mary."

"And the council?"

"Are plotting against us, and providing for their own safety."

"Jane," said Lord Guilford Dudley, "I will not attempt to excuse my conduct. But if it is possible to repair the injury I have done you, I will do so. Everything now depends on resolution. The council are more to be feared than Mary and her forces. So long as you are mistress of the Tower, you are mistress of London, and Queen of England—even though the day should go against the Duke, my father. Give me a warrant under your hand for the arrest of the council, and the ambassadors Renard and De Noailles, and I will see it instantly executed."

"My lord!" she exclaimed.

"Trust me, my queen, it is the only means to save us," replied Dudley. "This bold step will confound them and compel them to declare their purposes. If they *are* your enemies, as I nothing doubt, you will have them in your power."

"I understand," replied Jane. "You shall have the warrant. It will bring matters to an issue."

At this moment, the door of the chamber was thrown open, and an usher announced "Monsieur Simon Renard."

"You are right welcome, M. Renard," said Lord Guilford, bowing haughtily. "I was about to go in search of you."

"Indeed," rejoined the ambassador, coldly returning the salutation. "I am glad to spare your lordship so much trouble,—and I am still more rejoiced to find you have recovered your temper, and returned to your royal consort."

"Insolent!" exclaimed Lord Guilford. "Guards!" he cried, motioning to the attendants—"Assure yourselves of his person."

"Ha!" exclaimed Renard, laying his hand upon his sword. "You have no authority for this."

"I have the Queens warrant," rejoined Dudley, sternly.

"The person of an ambassador is sacred," observed Renard.

"The emperor, Charles the Fifth, will resent this outrage as an insult to himself."

"I will take the consequences upon myself," replied Lord Guilford, carelessly.

"Your highness will not suffer this wrong to be done?" said Renard, addressing Jane.

"Monsieur Renard," replied the queen, "I have reason to believe you have played me false. If I find you have deceived me, though you were brother to the emperor, you shall lose your head."

"You will have cause to repent this step," rejoined Renard, furiously. "The council will command my instant release."

"The order must be speedy then," replied Dudley, "for I shall place them all in arrest. And here, as luck will have it, are your friends the Earls of Arundel and Pembroke. They will attend you to the White Tower."

So saying, he motioned to the guards to take them into custody.

"What means this?" cried Pembroke in astonishment.

"It means that Lord Guilford Dudley, who has been slumbering for some time in Sion House, has awakened at last, and fancies his royal consort's crown is in danger," rejoined Renard with a bitter sneer.

"This is some jest surely, my lord," observed Pembroke. "The council arrested at a moment of peril like this! Will you provoke us to manifest our power?"

"I will provoke you to manifest your treacherous designs towards her majesty," replied Dudley. "Away with them to the White Tower! Shrewsbury, Cecil, Huntingdon, Darcy, and the others shall soon join you there."

"One word before we go, gracious madam?" said Pembroke, addressing the queen.

"Not one, my lord," replied Jane. "Lord Guilford Dudley has my full authority for what he does. I shall hold early council to-morrow—which you shall be at liberty to attend, and you will then have ample opportunity to explain and defend yourself."

Upon this, the confederate nobles were removed.

"It is time to put an end to this farce," remarked Renard, as they were conducted along the gallery towards the White Tower.

"It is," answered Pembroke, "and my first address in the council to-morrow shall be to proclaim Queen Mary."

"The hair-brained Dudley imagines he can confine us in the White Tower," observed Renard, laughing. "There is not a chamber in it without a secret passage. And thanks to the jailor, Nightgall, I am familiar with them all. We will not be idle to-night."

XV.—HOW GUNNORA BRAOSE SOUGHT AN AUDIENCE OF QUEEN JANE.

Having seen the rest of the council conveyed to the White Tower, Lord Guilford Dudley returned to the palace. While discoursing on other matters with the queen, he casually remarked that he was surprised he did not perceive his esquire, Cuthbert Cholmondeley, in her highness's train, and was answered that he had not been seen since his departure for Sion House. Greatly surprised by the intelligence, Lord Guilford directed an attendant to make inquiries about him. After some time, the man returned, stating that he could obtain no information respecting him.

"This is very extraordinary," said Lord Guilford. "Poor Cholmondeley! What can have happened to him? As soon as this danger is past, I will make personal search for him."

"I thought he had left the Tower with you, my dear lord," observed Jane.

"Would he had!" answered her husband. "I cannot help suspecting he has incurred the enmity of the council, and has been secretly removed. I will interrogate them on the subject tomorrow."

While they were thus conversing, an usher appeared, and informed the queen that a young damsel supplicated an audience having somewhat to disclose of importance.

"You had better admit her, my queen," said Dudley. "She may have accidentally learned some plot which it is important for us to know."

Jane having signified her assent, the usher withdrew, and presently afterwards introduced Cicely. The young damsel, who appeared to have suffered much, greatly interested the queen by her extreme beauty and modesty. She narrated her story with infinite simplicity, and though she blushed deeply when she came to speak of the love professed for her by Cholmondeley, she attempted no concealment.

Both Jane and Lord Guilford Dudley were astonished beyond measure, when they learned that the young esquire had been incarcerated by Nightgall; and the latter was about to reproach Cicely for not having revealed the circumstance before, when she accounted for her silence by stating that she had been locked within her chamber, ever since the night in question, by her mother. Her story ended, Dudley declared his intention of seeking out the jailor without delay. "I will first compel him to liberate his prisoner," he said, "and will then inflict upon him a punishment proportionate to his offence."

"Alas!" exclaimed Cicely, bursting into tears, "I fear your lordship's assistance will come too late. Nightgall has visited me daily, and he asserts that Master

Cholmondeley has quitted the Tower by some secret passage under the moat. I fear he has destroyed him."

"If it be so, he shall die the death he merits," replied Dudley. "You say that the gigantic warders, whose lodging is in the By-ward Tower, are acquainted with the dungeon. I will proceed thither at once, be of good cheer, fair damsel. If your lover is alive he shall wed you on the morrow, and I will put it out of Nightgall's power to molest you further. Remain with the queen till I return."

"Ay, do so, child," said Jane, "I shall be glad to have you with me. And, if you desire it, you shall remain constantly near my person."

"It is more happiness than I deserve, gracious madam," replied Cicely, dropping upon her knee. "And though your majesty has many attendants more highly born, you will find none more faithful."

"I fully believe it," replied Jane, with a sigh. "Rise, damsel. Henceforth you are one of my attendants."

Cicely replied by a look of speechless gratitude, while summoning a guard, Dudley proceeded to the By-ward Tower. The giants informed him they had just returned from Nightgall's lodging, and that he was absent. He then commanded them to accompany him to the entrance of the subterranean dungeons beneath the Devilin Tower.

"It will be useless to attempt to gain admission without the keys, my lord," replied Og; "and they are in master Nightgall's keeping."

"Has no one else a key? demanded Dudley, impatiently.

"No one, unless it be Gillian Mauger, the headsman," replied Xit; "I will bring him to your lordship, instantly."

So saying, he hurried off in search of the executioner, while Dudley, attended by the two giants, proceeded slowly in the direction of the Beauchamp Tower. In a short time, the dwarf returned with Mauger, who limped after him as quickly as a lame leg would permit. He had no key of the dungeon, and on being questioned, declared there was no other entrance to it.

"Break open the door instantly, then," cried Dudley.

Mauger declared this was impossible, as it was cased with iron, and fastened with a lock of great strength.

Magog, who was standing at a little distance with his arms folded upon his breast, now stepped forward, and, without saying a word, lifted up a large block of stone placed there to repair the walls, and hurling it against the door, instantly burst it open.

"Bravely done," cried Lord Guilford. "How can I reward the service?"

"I scarcely know how to ask it of your lordship," rejoined Magog; "but if you could prevail upon her majesty to issue her commands to Dame Placida Paston to bestow her hand upon me, you would make me the happiest of mankind."

"If the dame be willing, surely she does not require enforcement," replied Dudley, laughing; "and if not"——

"She has half promised her hand to me, my lord," said Xit, "and your lordship can scarcely doubt to whom she would give the preference."

"She has indeed a fair choice betwixt giant and dwarf I must own," replied Dudley. "But bring torches and follow me. More serious business now claims my attention."

"I will guide your lordship through these dungeons," said Xit. "I have often accompanied Master Nightgall in his visits, and can conduct you to every cell."

"Lead on then," said Dudley.

After traversing a vast number of passages, and examining many cells, all of which were vacant, they at length came to the dungeon where Cholmondeley had been confined. Here they found Nightgall, who at first attempted to exculpate himself, and made a variety of wild accusations against the esquire, but when he found he was utterly disbelieved, he confessed the whole truth. Dismissing some of his companions in search of the esquire, who it was evident, if the jailor's statement was to be credited, must have lost himself in some of the passages. Dudley was about to follow them, when Nightgall flung himself at his feet, and offered, if his life were spared, to reveal all the secret practices of the Council which had come to his knowledge. Dudley then ordered the rest of his attendants to withdraw, and was so much astonished at Nightgall's communication, that he determined upon instantly conveying him to the palace. After a long, but ineffectual search for Chomondeley, whose escape has already been related, Dudley contented himself with leaving Xit and Og to look for him; and placing Nightgall in the custody of the two other giants, returned with him to the palace.

While this was passing, the queen had received an unexpected visit. She had retired to her closet with Cicely, and was listening to a recapitulation of the young damsel's love affair, when the hangings were suddenly drawn aside, and Simon Renard stepped from a masked door in the wall. Surprise for a moment held her silent, and Cicely was so much astonished by the appearance of the intruder, and so much alarmed by his stern looks, that she stood like one petrified. Renard's deportment, indeed, was most formidable, and could not fail to impress them both with terror. He said nothing for a moment, but fixed his black flaming eyes menacingly on the queen. As she remained speechless, he motioned Cicely to withdraw, and she would have obeyed had not Jane grasped her arm and detained her.

"Do not leave me!" she cried, "or summon the guard."

The words were no sooner spoken, than Renard drew his sword, and placed himself between her and the door.

"I have little to *say*," he observed;—"but I would have said it to you alone. Since you will have a witness, I am content."

By this time, Jane had recovered her confidence, and rising, she confronted Renard with a look as stern and haughty as his own.

"What brings you here, sir," she demanded; "and by what means have you escaped from the White Tower?—Are my guards false to their trust?"

"It matters not how I have escaped," replied Renard. "I am come hither to warn you."

"Of what?" asked Jane.

"Of the peril in which you stand,'" replied Renard. "You are no longer queen. The Duke of Northumberland has disbanded his army, and has himself proclaimed Mary."

"It is false," rejoined Jane.

"You will do well not to neglect my caution," replied Renard. "As yet the news is only known to me. To-morrow it will be known to all within the Tower. Fly! while it is yet time."

"No," replied Jane, proudly. "Were your news true, which I doubt, I would *not* fly. If I must resign my crown, it shall not be at your bidding. But I am still a queen; and you shall feel that I am so. Guards!" she cried in a loud voice, "Arrest this traitor."

But before the door could be opened, Renard had darted behind the arras and disappeared. Nor, upon searching the wall, could the attendants discover by what means he had contrived his escape. Soon after this, Lord Guilford Dudley returned, and his rage and consternation when he learned what had occurred was unbounded. He flew to the White Tower, where he found that Simon Renard, De Noailles, and the Earls of Pembroke and Arundel, who had been confined in a small room adjoining the council-chamber, had disappeared. The guards affirmed positively that they were not privy to their flight, and unable to obtain any clue to the mystery, Dudley returned in a state of great perplexity to the palace, where a fresh surprise awaited him.

Jane had scarcely recovered from the surprise occasioned by Renard's mysterious visit, when an usher presented himself, and delivering a ring to her, said that it had been given him by an old woman, who implored an audience. Glancing at the ornament, the queen instantly recognised it as that she had given to Gunnora Braose, and desired the attendant to admit her. Accordingly, the old woman was introduced, and approaching Jane, threw herself on her knees before her.

"What seek you, my good dame?" asked Jane. "I promised to grant any boon you might ask. Are you come to claim fulfilment of my promise?"

"Listen to me, gracious lady," said the old woman, "and do not slight my counsel,—for what I am about to say to you is of the deepest import. Your crown—your liberty—your life is in danger! The Council mean to depose you on the morrow, and proclaim Mary queen. Call to mind the warning I gave you before you entered this fatal fortress. My words have come to pass. You are betrayed—lost!"

"Rise, my good woman," said Jane, "and compose yourself. You may speak the truth. My enemies may prevail against me, but they shall not subdue me. It is now too late to retreat. Having accepted the crown, I cannot—will not lay it aside, till it is wrested from me."

"It will be wrested from you on the block, dear lady," cried Gunnora. "Listen to me, I beseech you. To-night you can make your retreat. To-morrow it will be too late."

"It is too late already," cried a stern voice behind them, and Renard again presented himself. He was accompanied by the Earl of Pembroke, and Cholmondeley who was muffled in the jailer's cloak. "Lady Jane Dudley," continued the ambassador, in an authoritative voice, "there is one means of saving your life, and only one. Sign this document," and he extended a parchment towards her. "It is your abdication. Sign it, and I will procure you a free pardon for yourself and your husband from Queen Mary."

"Mary is *not* queen,—nor will I sign it," replied Jane. "Then hear me," replied Renard. "In Queen Mary's name, I denounce you as an usurper. And if you further attempt to exercise the functions of royalty, you will not escape the block."

"He does not overrate your danger," interposed Gunnora.

"What make you here, old woman?" said Renard, addressing her.

"I have come on the same errand as yourself," she replied, "to warn this noble, but ill-advised lady of her peril."

"Have you likewise informed her why you were brought to the Tower?" demanded Renard, sternly.

"No," replied Gunnora.

"Then she shall learn it from me," continued the ambassador, "though it is not the season I would have chosen for the disclosure. This woman administered poison to your predecessor, Edward VI, by order of the Duke of Northumberland."

"It is false," cried Jane, "I will not believe it."

"It is true," said Gunnora.

"Wretch! you condemn yourself," said Jane.

"I know it," rejoined Gunnora; "but place me on the rack, and I will repeat the charge."

"What motive could the duke have for so foul a crime?" demanded the queen.

"This," replied Gunnora; "he wished to remove the king so suddenly, that the princesses Mary and Elizabeth might have no intelligence of his decease. But this is not all, madam."

"What more remains to be told?" asked Jane.

"You were to be the next victim," returned the old woman.

"Northumberland aimed at the supreme power. With this view, he wedded you to his son; with this view, he procured the letters patent from King Edward declaring you his successor; with this view, he proclaimed you queen, raised you to the throne, and would have made your husband king. His next step was to have poisoned you."

"Poisoned me!" exclaimed Jane, horror-stricken.

"Ay, poisoned you," repeated Gunnora. "I was to administer the fatal draught to you as I did to Edward. It was therefore I warned you not to enter the Tower. It was therefore I counselled you to resign a sceptre which I knew you could not sustain. I saw you decked out like a victim for the sacrifice, and I strove to avert the fatal blow—but in vain."

"Alas! I begin to find your words are true," replied Jane. "But if aught remains to me of power, if I am not a queen merely in name, I will now exert it. My lord of Pembroke, I command you to summon the guard, and arrest this traitor," pointing to Simon Renard. "I will not sleep till I have had his head. How, my lord, do you refuse to obey me? Hesitate, and you shall share his doom."

At this moment, Cholmondeley threw off his cloak, and advancing towards the ambassador, said, "M. Simon Renard, you are the queen's prisoner."

"Cholmondeley!" exclaimed Renard, starting; "can it be?"

"It is, traitor," replied the esquire; "but I will now unmask you and your projects."

"Back, sir!" cried Renard, in a tone so authoritative that all were overawed by it. "Lay hands upon me, and I give a signal which will cause a general massacre, in which none of Queen Mary's enemies will be spared. Lady Jane Dudley," he continued, addressing her, "I give you till to-morrow to reflect upon what course you will pursue. Resign the crown you have wrongfully assumed, and I pledge my word to obtain your pardon. But Northumberland's life is forfeited, and that of all his race."

"Think you I will sacrifice my husband, traitor?" cried Jane. "Seize him," she added, to Cholmondeley.

But before the young man could advance, Renard had unsheathed his sword, and placed himself in a posture of defence. "Lady Jane Dudley," he ejaculated, "I give you till to-morrow. Your own conduct will decide your fate."

"Call the guard," cried Jane.

The young esquire vainly endeavoured to obey this command, but he was attacked and beaten off by the ambassador and the Earl of Pembroke, who quickly retreating towards the masked door, passed through it, and closed it after them. At this juncture, Lord Guilford Dudley returned at the head of the guard. The occurrences of the last few minutes were hastily explained to him, and he was about to break open the secret door, when Nightgall said, "If I have a free pardon, I will conduct your lordship to the secret retreat of the Council, and unravel a plot which shall place them in your power."

"Do this," replied Lord Guilford, "and you shall not only have a free pardon, but a great reward."

"Take a sufficient guard with you, and follow me," rejoined Nightgall.

Dudley complied, and the party proceeded on their errand, while Cholmondeley remained with the queen and Cicely; and although his transports at beholding her again were somewhat alloyed by the perilous position in which Jane stood, he nevertheless tasted sufficient happiness to recompense him in some degree for his recent misery. Withdrawing to another apartment, Jane awaited in the utmost anxiety her husband's return. This did not occur for some hours, and when he appeared she saw at once, from his looks, that his search had been unsuccessful.

The remainder of the night was passed between the queen and her consort in anxious deliberation. Cholmondeley was entrusted with the command of the guard, and after a few hours' rest and other refreshment, of which he stood greatly in need, he proceeded with Lord Clinton, who still apparently remained firm in his adherence, to make the rounds of the Tower. Nothing unusual was noticed: the sentinels were at their posts. But as Cholmondeley looked towards Tower-hill, he fancied he observed a great crowd assembled, and pointed out the appearance to Lord Clinton, who seemed a little confused, but declared he could perceive nothing. Cholmondeley, however, was satisfied that he was not deceived; but apprehending no danger from the assemblage, he did not press the point. Towards daybreak he again looked out in the same quarter, but the mob had disappeared. Meanwhile, Gunnora Braose had been conducted to the Bowyer Tower, and locked within the chamber she had occupied, while Nightgall was placed in strict confinement.

XVI.—HOW THE COUNCIL DEPOSED QUEEN JANE; AND HOW SHE FLED FROM THE TOWER.

At length, the last morning which was to behold Jane queen dawned, and after an agitated and sleepless night, she addressed herself to her devotions, and endeavoured to prepare for the dangerous and difficult part she had to play. The Duke of Suffolk tried to persuade her to abdicate. But her husband, who, it has been already observed, inherited his father's ambitious nature, besought her not to part with the crown.

"It has been dearly purchased," he urged, "and must be boldly maintained. Let us meet the Council courageously, and we shall triumph."

To this Jane assented. But it was evident from her manner she had but slight hopes.

At an early hour the lord mayor, the aldermen, and all the civic authorities who had been summoned, arrived. Cranmer and Ridley came soon after. The Council were then summoned, and by ten o'clock all were assembled, excepting the Earls of Pembroke and Arundel, Simon Renard, and De Noailles. As soon as Jane was seated beneath the state canopy, she ordered a pursuivant to summon them. Proclamation being made, a stir was heard at the lower end of the council-chamber, and the absentees presented themselves. All four advanced boldly towards the throne, and took their place among the Council. Jane then arose, and with great dignity and self-possession thus-addressed the assemblage:—

"My lords," she said, "I have summoned you it may be for the last time, to deliberate on the course to be pursued to check the formidable tumults and rebellions that have been moved against me and my crown. Of that crown I cannot doubt I have lawful possession, since it was tendered me by your lordships, who have all sworn allegiance to me. Fully confiding, therefore, in your steadiness to my service, which neither with honour, safety, nor duty, you can now forsake, I look to you for support in this emergency."

Here a murmur arose among the Council.

"What!" exclaimed Jane: "do you desert me at the hour of need? Do you refuse me your counsel and assistance?"

"We do," replied several voices.

"Traitors!" exclaimed Lord Guilford Dudley: "you have passed your own sentence."

"Not so, my lord," replied Simon Renard. "It is you who have condemned yourself. Lady Jane Dudley," he continued in a loud voice, "you who have wrongfully usurped the title and station of queen,—in your presence I proclaim Mary, sister to the late king Edward the Sixth, and daughter of Henry the Eighth of famous memory, Queen of England and Ireland, and very owner of the crown, government, and title of England and Ireland, and all things thereunto belonging."

"God save Queen Mary!" cried the Council.

A few dissentient voices were raised. But the Earl of Pembroke drew his sword, and cried in a loud voice, "As heaven shall help me, I will strike that man dead who refuses to shout for Queen Mary." And he threw his cap in the air.

"Hear me," continued Renard, "and learn that resistance is in vain. I hereby proclaim a free pardon, in Queen Mary's name, to all who shall freely acknowledge her,—excepting always the family of the Duke of Northumberland, who is a traitor, and upon whose head a price is set. I require your Grace," he added to Suffolk, "to deliver up the keys of the Tower."

"They are here," replied the Duke, pointing to Magog who bore them.

"Do you yield, my lord?" cried Lord Guilford, passionately.

"It is useless to contend further," replied Suffolk. "All is lost."

"True," replied Jane. "My lords, I resign the crown into your hands; and Heaven grant you may prove more faithful to Mary than you have been to me. In obedience to you, my lord," she continued, addressing her husband, "I acted a violence on myself, and have been guilty of a grievous offence. But the present is my own act. And I willingly abdicate the throne to correct another's fault, if so great a fault can be corrected by my resignation and sincere acknowledgment."

"You shall not abdicate it, Jane," cried Dudley, fiercely. "I will *not* yield. Stand by me, Cholmondeley, and these audacious traitors shall find I am still master here. Let those who are for Queen Jane surround the throne."

As he spoke, he glanced round authoritatively, but no one stirred.

"Speak!" he cried, in accents of rage and disappointment. "Are ye all traitors? Is no one true to his allegiance?"

But no answer was returned.

"They are no traitors, my lord," said Simon Renard. "They are loyal subjects of Queen Mary."

"He speaks truly, my dear lord," replied Jane. "It is useless to contend further. I am no longer queen."

So saying, she descended from the throne.

"My lords," she continued, addressing the Council, "you are now masters here. Have I your permission to retire?"

"You have, noble lady," replied Pembroke. "But it grieves me to add, that you must perforce remain within the Tower till the pleasure of her Highness respecting you has been ascertained."

"A prisoner!" exclaimed Jane, trembling. "And my husband, you will suffer him to accompany me?"

"It cannot be," interposed Simon Renard, harshly; "Lord Guilford Dudley must be separately confined."

"You cannot mean this cruelty, sir?" cried Jane, indignantly. "Do not sue for me, Jane," rejoined Dudley. "I will not accept the smallest grace at his hands."

"Guards!" cried Renard, "I command you, in Queen Mary's name, to arrest Lord Guilford Dudley, and convey him to the Beauchamp Tower."

The order was instantly obeyed. Jane then took a tender farewell of her husband, and accompanied by Cicely and Cholmondeley, and others of her attendants, was escorted to the palace.,

She had no sooner taken her departure, than letters were despatched by the Council to the Duke of Northumberland, commanding him instantly to disband his army. And the Earl of Arundel was commissioned to proceed with a force to arrest him.

"I have a brave fellow who shall accompany your lordship," said Renard, motioning to Gilbert, who stood among his followers.

"Hark'ee, sirrah!" he added, "you have already approved your fidelity to Queen Mary. Approve it still further by the capture of the Duke, and, in the Queen's name, I promise you a hundred pounds in lands to you and your heirs, and the degree of an esquire. And now, my lords, to publicly proclaim Queen Mary."

With this the whole train departed from the Tower, and proceeded to Cheapside, where, by sound of trumpet, the new sovereign was proclaimed by the title of "Mary, Queen of England, France, and Ireland, Defender of the Faith."

Shouts rent the air, and every manifestation of delight was exhibited. "Great was the triumph," writes an eye-witness of the ceremony; "for my part, I never saw the like, and, by the report of others, the like was never seen. The number of caps that were thrown up at the proclamation was not to be told. The Earl of Pembroke threw away his cap full of angels. I saw myself money thrown out of the windows for joy. The bonfires were without number; and what with shouting and crying of the people, and ringing of bells, there could no man hear almost what another said—besides banquetting, and skipping the streets for joy."

The proclamation over, the company proceeded to St. Paul's, where Te Deum was solemnly sung. It is a curious illustration of the sudden change of feeling, that the Duke of Suffolk himself proclaimed Mary on Tower Hill.

The utmost confusion reigned throughout the Tower. Some few there were who regretted the change of sovereigns, but the majority were in favour of Mary. Northumberland in fact was so universally hated by all classes, and it was so notorious that the recent usurpation was contrived only for his own aggrandisement, that though Jane was pitied, no commiseration was felt for her husband or her ambitious father-in-law. Great rejoicings were held in the Tower-green, where an immense bonfire was lighted, and a whole ox roasted. Several casks of ale were also broached, and mead and other liquors were distributed to the warders and the troops. Of these good things the three gigantic warders and Xit partook; and Magog was so elated, that he plucked up courage to propose to Dame Placida, and, to the dwarf's infinite dismay and mortification, was accepted. Lord Guilford Dudley witnessed these rejoicings from the windows of the Beauchamp Tower, in which he was confined; and as he glanced upon the citadel opposite his prison, now lighted up by the gleams of the fire, he could not help reflecting with bitterness what a change a few days had effected. The voices which only nine days ago had shouted for Jane, were now clamouring for Mary; and of the thousands which then would have obeyed his slightest nod, not one would acknowledge him now.

From a prince he had become a captive, and his palace was converted into a dungeon. Such were the agonizing thoughts of Northumberland's ambitious son,—and such, or nearly such, were those of his unhappy consort, who, in her chamber in the palace was a prey to the bitterest reflection.

Attended only by Cholmondeley and Cicely, Jane consumed the evening in sad, but unavailing lamentations. About midnight, as she had composed her thoughts by applying herself to her wonted solace in affliction—study, she was aroused by a noise in the wall, and presently afterwards a masked door opened, and Gunnora Braose presented herself. Jane instantly rose, and demanded the cause of the intrusion. Gunnora laid her finger on her lips, and replied in a low tone, "I am come to liberate you."

"I do not desire freedom," replied Jane, "neither will I trust myself to you. I will abide here till my cousin Mary makes her entrance into the Tower, and I will then throw myself upon her mercy."

"She will show you no mercy," rejoined Gunnora. "Do not, I implore of you, expose yourself to the first outbreak of her jealous and vindictive nature. Queen Mary inherits her father's inexorable disposition, and I am well assured if you tarry here, you will fall a victim to her displeasure. Do not neglect this opportunity, sweet lady. In a few hours it may be too late."

"Accept her offer, gracious madam," urged Cicely, "it may be your last chance of safety. You are here surrounded by enemies."

"But how am I to escape from the fortress, if I accede to your wishes?" replied Jane.

"Follow me, and I will conduct you," answered Gunnora. "I have possessed myself of the key of a subterranean passage which will convey you to the other side of the moat."

"But my husband?" hesitated Jane.

"Do not think of him," interrupted Gunnora, frowning. "He deserted you in the hour of danger. Let him perish on the scaffold with his false father."

"Leave me, old woman," said Jane authoritatively; "I will not go with you."

"Do not heed her, my gracious mistress," urged Cholmondeley, "your tarrying here cannot assist Lord Guilford, and will only aggravate his affliction. Besides, some means may be devised for his escape."

"Pardon what I have said, dear lady," said Gunnora. "Deadly as is the hatred I bear to the house of Northumberland, for your sweet sake I will forgive his son. Nay more, I will effect his deliverance. This I swear to you. Come with me, and once out of the Tower make what haste you can to Sion House, where your husband shall join you before the morning."

"You promise more than you can accomplish," said Jane.

"That remains to be seen, madam," replied Gunuora: "but were it not that he is your husband, Lord Guilford Dudley should receive no help from me. Once more, will you trust me?"

"I will," replied Jane.

Cholmondeley then seized a torch, and fastening the door of the chamber, on the outside of which a guard was stationed, assisted Jane through the masked door. Preceded by the old woman, who carried a lamp, they threaded a long narrow passage built in the thickness of the wall, and presently arrived at the head of a flight of stairs, which brought them to a long corridor arched and paved with stone. Traversing this, they struck into an avenue on the right, exactly resembling one of those which Cholmondeley had recently explored. Jane expressed her surprise at the vast extent of the passages she was threading, when Gunnora answered—"The whole of the Tower is undermined with secret passages and dungeons, but their existence is known only to few."

A few minutes' rapid walking brought them to a stone staircase, which they mounted, traversed another gallery, and finally halted before a low gothic-arched door, which admitted them to the interior of the Bowyer Tower. Requesting Cholmondeley to assist her, Gunnora, with his help, speedily raised a trap-door of stone, and disclosed a flight of steps. While they were thus employed, a strange and unaccountable terror took possession of Jane. As she glanced timidly towards the doorway she had just quitted, she imagined she saw a figure watching her, and in the gloom almost fancied it was the same muffled object she had beheld in St. John's Chapel. A superstitious terror kept her silent. As she looked more narrowly at the figure, she thought it bore an axe upon its shoulder, and she was about to point it out to her companions, when making a gesture of silence it disappeared. By this time the trap-door being raised, Cholmondeley descended the steps with the torch, while Gunnora holding back the flag, begged her to descend. But Jane did not move.

Queen Jane's flight from the Tower

"Do not lose time," cried the old woman, "we may be followed, and retaken."

Still Jane hesitated. She cast another look towards the doorway, and the idea crossed her, that from that very outlet she should be led to execution. A deadly chill pervaded her frame,-and her feet seemed nailed to the ground. Seeing her irresolution, Cicely threw herself on her knees before her, and implored her to make an effort. Jane advanced a step, and then paused. After remaining a moment in deep abstraction, she turned to Cicely, and said,—.

"Child, I thank you for your zeal, but I feel it is useless. Though I may escape from the Tower, I *cannot* escape my fate." Cicely, however, renewed her entreaties, and seconded by Chomondeley she at length prevailed. Pursuing the same course which Gunnora had taken on the night she was brought to the Tower by Simon Renard, they at length arrived at the shed at the further side of the moat.

"You are now safe," said Gunnora. "Hasten to Sion House, and if my plan does not fail, your husband shall join you there before many hours have passed."

So saying, she departed. Jane and her attendants crossed Tower Hill, from which she turned to gaze at the scene of her greatness, indistinctly visible in the gloom—and so agonizing were the thoughts occasioned by the sight that she burst into tears. As soon as she had recovered from her paroxysm of grief, they proceeded to the river side, where they fortunately procured a boat, and were rowed towards Sion House.

XVII.-IN WHAT MANNER JANE WAS BROUGHT BACK TO THE TOWER OF LONDON.

Gunnora Braose kept her word. Before daybreak, Lord Guilford Dudley joined his afflicted consort. Their meeting was passionate and sad. As Jane ardently returned her husband's fond embrace, she cried—"Oh, my dear lord, that we had never been deluded by the false glitter, of greatness to quit this calm retreat! Oh that we may be permitted to pass the remainder of our days here!"

"I have not yet abandoned all hopes of the throne," replied Dudley. "Our fortunes may be retrieved."

"Never," returned Jane, gravely—"never so far as I am concerned. Were the crown to be again offered to me—were I assured I could retain it, I would not accept it. No, Dudley, the dream of ambition is over; and I am fully sensible of the error I have committed."

"As you please, my queen, for I will still term you so," rejoined Dudley—"but if my father is in arms, I will join him, and we will make one last effort for the prize, and regain it, or perish in the attempt."

"Your wild ambition will lead you to the scaffold—and will conduct me there, also," replied Jane. "If we could not hold the power when it was in our own hands—how can you hope to regain it?"

"It is *not* lost—I will not believe it, till I am certified under my father's own hand that he has abandoned the enterprise," rejoined Dudley. "You know him not, Jane. With five thousand men at his command—nay, with a fifth of that number, he is more than a match for all his enemies. We shall yet live to see him master of the Tower—of this rebellious city, we shall yet see our foes led to the scaffold. And if I see the traitors, Renard, Pembroke and Arundel, conducted thither I will excuse Fortune all her malice."

"Heaven forgive them their treason as I forgive them!" exclaimed Jane. "But I fear their enmity will not be satisfied till they have brought us to the block to which you would doom them."

"This is not a season for reproaches, Jane," said Dudley, coldly; "but if you had not trusted that false traitor, Renard,—if you had not listened to his pernicious counsels,—if you had not refused my suit for the crown, and urged my father to undertake the expedition against Mary,—all had been well. You had been queen—and I king."

"Your reproaches are deserved, Dudley," replied Jane, "and you cannot blame me more severely than I blame myself. Nevertheless, had I acceded to your desires,—had I raised you to the sovereignty,—had I turned a deaf ear to Renard's counsel, and not suffered myself to be duped by his allies Arundel and Pembroke,—had I retained your father in the Tower,—my reign would not have been of much longer duration."

"I do not understand you, madam," said Lord Guilford, sternly.

"To be plain, then," replied Jane,—"for disguise is useless now—I am satisfied that your father aimed at the crown himself,—that I was merely placed on the throne to prepare it for him,—and that when the time arrived, he would have removed me."

"Jane!" exclaimed her husband, furiously.

"Have patience, dear Dudley!" she rejoined. "I say not this to rouse your anger, or to breed further misunderstanding between us. Heaven knows we have misery enough to endure without adding to it. I say it to reconcile you to your lot. I say it to check the spirit of ambition which I find is yet smouldering within your bosom. I say it to prevent your joining in any fresh attempt with your father, which will assuredly end in the destruction of both."

"But you have brought a charge so foul against him, madam," cried her husband, "that as his son, I am bound to tell you you are grievously in error."

"Dudley," replied Jane, firmly, "I have proofs that the Duke poisoned my cousin, King Edward. I have proofs also, that he would have poisoned me."

"It is false," cried her husband, furiously—"it is a vile calumny fabricated by his enemies. You have been imposed upon."

"Not so, my lord," cried Gunnora Braose, who had been an unseen listener to the conversation. "It is no calumny. The royal Edward was poisoned by me at your 'father's instigation. And you and your consort would have shared the same fate."

"False hag! thou liest," cried Lord Guilford.

"Read that," replied Gunnora, placing a document in his hands. "It is my order in the Duke's own writing. Do you credit me now."

Dudley hastily cast his eyes over the scroll. His countenance fell, and the paper dropped from his grasp.

"And now hear my news," continued the old woman, with a smile of exultation. "Your father has proclaimed Queen Mary at Cambridge."

"Impossible!" cried Dudley.

"I tell you it is true," replied Gunnora—"a messenger arrived at midnight with the tidings, and it was during the confusion created by the intelligence that I contrived to effect your escape. The Earl of Arundel is despatched to arrest him, and, ere to-morrow night, he will be lodged within the Tower. Yes," she continued with a ferocious laugh—"I shall see him placed in the same dungeon in which he lodged my foster-son, the great Duke of Somerset. I shall see his head stricken off by the same axe, and upon the same scaffold, and I shall die content."

"Horrible!" cried Jane. "Leave us, wretched woman. Your presence adds to my affliction."

"I will leave you, dear lady," replied Gunnora—"but though absent from you, I will not fail to watch over you. I have powerful friends within the Tower, and if any ill be designed you, I will give you timely warning. Farewell!"

A miserable and anxious day was passed by Jane and her husband. Lord Guilford would fain have departed with Chol-mondeley to join his father at Cambridge, but suffered himself to be dissuaded from the rash undertaking, by the tears and entreaties of his consort. As to Cicely and her lover, their sympathies were so strongly excited for the distresses of Jane, that the happiness they would otherwise have experienced in each other's society, was wholly destroyed. At night, as the little party were assembled, Gunnora Braose again made her appearance, and her countenance bespoke that some new danger was at hand.

"What ill tidings do you bring?" cried Dudley, starting to his feet.

"Fly!" exclaimed Gunnora. "You have not a moment to lose. Simon Renard has discovered your retreat, and Lord Clinton, with a body of men, is hastening hither to convey you to the Tower. Fly!"

"Whither?" exclaimed Lord Guilford. "Whither shall we fly?"

"It is useless, my dear lord," replied Jane, calmly, "to contend further. I resign myself to the hands of Providence, and I counsel you to do the same."

"Come then with me, Cholmondeley," cried Dudley, snatching up his cloak, and girding on his sword, "we will to horse at once, and join my father at Cambridge. If he has a handful of men left we can yet make a gallant defence."

"The Duke is arrested, and on his way to the Tower," said Gunnora.

"Ha!" exclaimed Dudley, "when did this occur?"

"Yesterday," replied the old woman. "He was taken within his chamber by my grandson, Gilbert Pot, who has received a hundred pounds in lands, and the degree of an esquire, for the deed. He submitted himself to the Earl of Arundel, and his deportment was as abject as it formerly was arrogant. When he saw the Earl, he fell on his knees, and desired him to have pity on him for the love of God. 'Consider.' he said, 'I have done nothing but by the order of you and the whole Council.' Then the Earl of Arundel replied, 'I am sent hither by the Queen's majesty, and in her name I arrest you.' 'And I obey it, my lord.' answered the Duke. 'I beseech you use mercy towards me, knowing the case as it is.' 'My lord,' rejoined the Earl, 'you should have sought mercy sooner. I must do according to my commandment. You are my prisoner!' And he committed him in charge to my grandson and others of the guard."

"How learnt you this?" inquired Lord Guilford.

"From a messenger who has just arrived at the Tower," replied the old woman—"and this is the last act of the great Duke of Northumberland. We shall soon see how he comports himself on the scaffold."

"Begone," cried Jane, "and do not stay here to deride our misery.".

"I am not come hither to deride it," replied the old woman, "but to warn you."

"I thank you for your solicitude," replied Jane—"but, it is needless. Retire all of you, I entreat, and leave me with my husband."

Her injunctions were immediately complied with, and her attendants withdrew. The unfortunate pair were not, however, allowed much time for conversation. Before they had been many minutes alone, the door was burst open, and a troop of armed men headed by Lord Clinton, the lieutenant of the Tower, rushed in.

"I am aware of your errand, my lord," said Jane; "you are come to convey me to the Tower. I am ready to attend you."

"It is well," replied Lord Clinton. "If you have any preparations to make, you shall have time for them."

"I have none, my lord," she replied.

"Nor I," replied Lord Guilford.

"My sole request is, that I may take one female attendant with me," said Jane, pointing to Cicely.

"I am sorry I cannot comply with the request," answered Lord Clinton, "but my orders are peremptory."

"Will my esquire be permitted to accompany me?" inquired Dudley.

"If he chooses to incur the risk of so doing, assuredly," replied Clinton. "But he will go into captivity."

"I will follow my Lord Guilford to death," cried Cholmondeley.

"You are a faithful esquire, indeed!" observed Lord Clinton, with a slight sneer.

While this was passing, Cicely hastily threw a surcoat of velvet over her mistress's shoulders, to protect her from the night air, and then prostrating herself before her, clasped her hand, and bedewed it with tears.

"Rise, child," said Jane, raising her and embracing her—"Farewell! may you be speedily united to your lover, and may your life be happier than that of your unfortunate mistress!"

"My barge awaits you at the stairs," observed Lord Clinton.

"We will follow you, my lord," said Dudley.

Leaning upon Cicely, Jane, who was scarcely able to support herself, was placed in the stern of the boat. Her husband took his seat near her, and two men-at-arms, with drawn swords, were stationed as a guard on either side of them. Bidding a hasty adieu to the weeping Cicely, Cholmondeley sprang into the boat, and was followed by Clinton, who immediately gave the signal to the rowers. Cicely lingered till the bark disappeared, and as two halberdiers bearing torches were placed in the fore part of the vessel, she was enabled to track its course far down the river. When the last glimmer of light vanished, her heart died within her, and she returned to indulge her grief in solitude.

Meanwhile, the boat with its unhappy occupants pursued a rapid course. The tide being in their favour they shortly reached London, and as they swept past Durham House—whence, only twelve days ago, she had proceeded in so much pomp to the Tower—Jane's feelings became too poignant almost for endurance. The whole pageant rose before her in all its splendour. Again she heard the roar of the cannon announcing her departure. Again she beheld the brilliant crowd of proud nobles, gaily-dressed cavaliers, lovely and high-born dames, grave prelates, judges and ambassadors. Again she beheld the river glistening with golden craft. Again she heard the ominous words of Gunnora, '*Go not to the Tower!*' Again she beheld the fierce lightning flash, again heard the loud thunder roll—and she felt she had received a deep and awful warning. These thoughts affected her so powerfully, that she sank half fainting on her husband's shoulder.

In this state she continued till they had shot London Bridge, and the first object upon which her gaze rested, when she opened her eyes, was the Tower.

Here again other harrowing recollections arose. How different was the present, from her former entrance into the fortress! Then a deafening roar of ordnance welcomed her. Then all she passed saluted her as Queen. Then drawbridges were lowered, gates opened, and each vied with the other to show her homage. Then a thousand guards attended her. Then allegiance was sworn—fidelity vowed—but how kept? Now all was changed. She was brought a prisoner to the scene of her former grandeur, unattended, unnoted.

Striving to banish these reflections, which, in spite of her efforts, obtruded themselves upon her, she strained her gaze to discover through the gloom the White Towder, but could discern nothing but a sombre mass like a thunder-cloud. St. Thomas's, or Traitor's Tower was, however, plainly distinguishable, as several armed men carrying flambeaux were stationed on its summit.

Queen Jane & Lord Guilford Dudley brought back to the Tower through Traitors Gate

The boat was now challenged by the sentinels—merely as a matter of form, for its arrival was expected,—and almost before the answer could be returned by those on board, a wicket, composed of immense beams of wood, was opened, and the boat shot beneath the gloomy arch. Never had Jane experienced a feeling of such horror as now assailed her—and if she had been crossing the fabled Styx she could not have felt greater dread. Her blood seemed congealed within her veins as she gazed around. The lurid light of the torches fell upon the black dismal arch—upon the slimy walls, and upon the yet blacker tide. Nothing was heard but the sullen ripple of the water, for the men had ceased rowing, and the boat impelled by their former efforts soon struck against the steps. The shock recalled Jane to consciousness. Several armed figures bearing torches were now seen to descend the steps.

The customary form of delivering the warrant, and receiving an acknowledgement for the bodies of the prisoners being gone through, Lord Clinton, who stood upon the lowest step, requested Jane to disembark. Summoning all her resolution, she arose, and giving her hand to the officer, who stood with a drawn sword beside her, was assisted by him and a warder to land. Lord Clinton received her as she set foot on the step. By his aid she slowly ascended the damp and slippery steps, at the summit of which, two personages were standing, whom she instantly recognised as Renard and De Noailles. The former regarded her with a smile of triumph, and said in a tone of bitter mockery as she passed him—"So—Epiphany is over. The Twelfth Day Queen has played her part."

"My lord," said Jane, turning disdainfully from him to Lord Clinton—"will it please you to conduct me to my lodging?"

"What he! warders," cried Lord Clinton, addressing the gigantic brethren who were standing near—"Conduct Lady Jane Dudley to Master Partridge's dwelling till her chamber within the Brick Tower is prepared. Lord Guilford Dudley must be taken to the Beauchamp Tower."

"Are we to be separated?" cried Jane.

"Such are the Queen's commands," replied Lord Clinton, in a tone of deep commiseration.

"The Queen's!" exclaimed Jane.

"Ay! the Queen's!" repeated Renard. "Queen Mary of England, whom Heaven long preserve!"

THUS FAR THE FIRST BOOK OF THE CHRONICLE OF THE TOWER OF LONDON.

BOOK THE SECOND

I.—OF THE ARRIVAL OF QUEEN MARY IN LONDON; OF HER ENTRANCE INTO THE TOWER; AND OF HER RECEPTION OF THE PRISONERS ON THE GREEN.

MARY made her public entry into the city of London, on the 3d of August, 1553. The most magnificent preparations were made for her arrival, and as the procession of the usurper—for such Jane was now universally termed,— to the Tower, had been remarkable for its pomp and splendour, it was determined, on the present occasion, to surpass it. The Queen's entrance was arranged to take place at Aldgate, and the streets along which she was to pass were covered with fine gravel from thence to the Tower, and railed on either side. Within the rails stood the crafts of the city, in the dresses of their order; and at certain intervals were stationed the officers of the guard and their attendants, arrayed in velvet and silk, and having great staves in their hands to keep off the crowd.

Hung with rich arras, tapestry, carpets, and, in some instances, with cloths of tissue gold and velvet, the houses presented a gorgeous appearance. Every window was filled with richly-attired dames, while the roofs, walls, gables, and steeples, were crowded with curious spectators. The tower of the old church of Saint Botolph, the ancient walls of the city, westward as far as Bishopgate, and eastward to the Tower postern, were thronged with beholders. Every available position had its occupant. St. Catherine Coleman's in Fenchurch Street—for it was decided that the royal train was to make a slight detour—Saint Dennis Backchurch; Saint Benedict's; All Hallows, Lombard Street; in short, every church, as well as every other structure, was covered.

The Queen, who had passed the previous night at Bow, set forth at noon, and in less than an hour afterwards, loud acclamations, and still louder discharges of ordnance, announced her approach. The day was as magnificent as the spectacle—the sky was deep and cloudless, and the sun shone upon countless hosts of bright and happy faces. At the bars without Aldgate, on the Whitechapel road, Queen Mary was met by the Princess Elizabeth, accompanied by a large cavalcade of knights and dames. An affectionate greeting passed between the royal sisters, who had not met since the death of Edward, and the usurpation of Jane, by which both their claims to the throne had been set aside. But it was noted by those who closely observed them, that Mary's manner grew more grave as Elizabeth rode by her side. The Queen was mounted upon a beautiful milk-white palfrey, caparisoned in crimson velvet, fringed with golden thread. She was habited in a robe of violet-coloured velvet, furred with powdered ermine, and wore upon her head a caul of cloth of tinsel set with pearls, and above this a massive circlet of gold covered with gems of inestimable value. Though a contrary opinion is generally entertained, Mary was not without some pretension to beauty. Her figure was short and slight, but well proportioned; her complexion rosy and delicate; and her eyes bright and piercing, though, perhaps, too stern in their expression. Her mouth was small, with thin compressed lips, which gave an austere and morose character to an otherwise-pleasing face. If she had not the commanding port of her father, Henry the Eighth, nor the proud beauty of her mother, Catherine of Arragon, she inherited sufficient majesty and grace from them to well fit her for her lofty station.

No one has suffered more from misrepresentation than this queen. Not only have her failings been exaggerated, and ill qualities, which she did not possess, attributed to her, but the virtues that undoubtedly belonged to her, have been denied her. A portrait, perhaps too flatteringly coloured, has been left of her by Michele, but still it is nearer the truth than the darker presentations with which we are more familiar. "As to the more important qualities of her mind, with a few trifling exceptions, (in which, to speak the truth, she is like other women, since besides being hasty and somewhat resentful, she is rather more parsimonious and miserly than is fitting a munificent and liberal sovereign,) she has in other respects no notable imperfection, and in some things she is without equal; for not only she is endowed with a spirit beyond other women who are naturally timid, but is so courageous and resolute that no adversity nor danger ever caused her to betray symptoms of pusillanimity. On the contrary, she has ever preserved a greatness of mind and dignity that is admirable, knowing as well what is due to the rank she holds as the wisest of her councillors, so that in her conduct and proceedings during the whole of her life, it cannot be denied she has always proved herself to be the offspring of a truly royal stock. Of her humility, piety, and observance of religious duties, it is unnecessary to speak, since they are well known, and have been proved by sufferings little short of martyrdom; so that we may truly say of her with the Cardinal, that amidst the darkness and obscurity which overshadowed this kingdom, she remained like a faint flame strongly agitated by winds which strove to extinguish it, but always kept alive by her innocence and true faith, in order that she might one day shine to the world, as she now does." Other equally strong testimonies to her piety and virtue might be adduced. By Camden she is termed a "lady never sufficiently to be praised for her sanctity, charity, and liberality." And by Bishop Godwin—"a woman truly pious, benign, and of most chaste manners, and to be lauded, if *you do not regard her failure in religion*." It was this "failure in religion" which has darkened her in the eyes of her Protestant posterity. With so many good qualities it is to be lamented that they were overshadowed by bigotry.

If Mary did not possess the profound learning of Lady Jane Grey, she possessed more than ordinary mental acquirements. A perfect mistress of Latin, French, Spanish and Italian, she conversed in the latter language with fluency. She had extraordinary powers of eloquence when roused by any great emotion, and having a clear logical understanding, was well fitted for argument. Her courage was undaunted; and she possessed much of the firmness of character—obstinacy it might perhaps be termed, of her father. In the graceful accomplishment of the dance, she excelled, and was passionately fond of music, playing with skill on three instruments, the virginals, the regals, and the lute. She was fond of equestrian exercise, and would often indulge in the chace. She revived all the old sports and games which had been banished as savouring of mummery by the votaries of the reformed faith. One of her sins in their eyes was a fondness for rich apparel. In the previous reign female attire was remarkable for its simplicity. She introduced costly stuffs, sumptuous dresses, and French fashions.

In personal attractions the Princess Elizabeth far surpassed her sister. She was then in the bloom of youth, and though she could scarcely be termed positively beautiful, she had a very striking appearance, being tall, portly, with bright blue eyes, and exquisitely formed hands, which she took great pains to display.

As soon as Elizabeth had taken her place behind the Queen, the procession set forward. The first part of the cavalcade consisted of gentlemen clad in doublets of blue velvet, with sleeves of orange and red, mounted on chargers trapped with close housings of blue sarsenet powdered with white crosses. After them rode esquires and knights, according to their degree, two and two, well mounted, and richly apparelled in cloth of gold, silver, or embroidered velvet, "fresh and goodlie to behold." Then came the trumpeters, with silken pennons fluttering from their clarions, who did their devoir gallantly. Then a litter covered with cloth of gold, drawn by richly-caparisoned horses, and filled by sumptuously-apparelled dames. Then an immense retinue of nobles, knights, and gentlemen, with their attendants, all dressed in velvets, satins, taffeties, and damask of all colours, and of every device and fashion—there being no lack of cloths of tissue, gold, silver, embroidery, or goldsmith's work. Then came forty high-born damsels mounted on steeds, trapped with red velvet, arrayed in gowns and kirtles of the same material. Then followed two other litters covered with red satin. Then came the Queen's body guard of archers, clothed in scarlet, bound with black velvet, bearing on their doublets a rose woven in gold, under which was an imperial crown. Then came the judges; then the doctors; then the bishops; then the council; and, lastly, the knights of the Bath in their robes.

Before the Queen rode six lords, bare-headed, four of whom carried golden maces. Foremost amongst these rode the Earls of Pembroke and Arundel, bearing the arms and crown. They were clothed in robes of tissue, embroidered with roses of fine gold, and each was girt with a baldrick of massive gold. Their steeds were trapped in burnt silver, drawn over with cords of green silk and gold, the edges of their apparel being fretted with gold and damask. The Queen's attire has been already described. She was attended by six lacqueys habited in vests of gold, and by a female attendant in a grotesque attire, whom she retained as her jester, and who was known among her household by the designation of Jane the Fool. The Princess Elizabeth followed, after whom came a numerous guard of archers and arquebussiers. The retinue was closed by the train of the ambassadors, Noailles and Renard. A loud discharge of ordnance announced the Queen's arrival at Aldgate. This was immediately answered by the Tower guns, and a tremendous and deafening shout rent the air. Mary appeared greatly affected by this exhibition of joy, and as she passed under the ancient gate which brought her into the city, and beheld the multitudes assembled to receive her, and heard their shouts of welcome, she was for a moment overcome by her feelings. But she speedily recovered herself, and acknowledged the stunning cries with a graceful inclination of her person.

Upon a stage on the left, immediately within the gate, stood a large assemblage of children, attired like wealthy merchants, one of whom—who represented the famous Whittington—pronounced an oration to the Queen, to which she vouchsafed a gracious reply. Before this stage was drawn up a little phalanx, called the "Nine children of honour." These youths were clothed in velvet, powdered with flowers-de-luce, and were mounted on great coursers, each of which had embroidered on its housing a scutcheon of the Queen's title—as of England, France, Gascony, Guienne, Normandy, Anjou, Cornwall, Wales and Ireland. As soon as the oration was ended, the Lord Mayor, Aldermen, Sheriffs, and their officers and attendants, rode forth to welcome the Queen to the city. The Lord Mayor was clothed in a gown of crimson velvet, decorated with the collar of SS., and carried the mace. He took his place before the Earl of Arundel, and after some little delay the cavalcade was again set in motion. First marched the different civic crafts, with bands of minstrelsy and banners; then the children who had descended from the stage; then the nine youths of honour; then the city guard; and then the Queen's cavalcade as before described.

Mary was everywhere received with the loudest demonstrations of joy. Prayers, wishes, welcomings, and vociferations attended her progress. Nothing was heard but "God save your highness—God send you a long and happy reign." To these cries, whenever she could make herself heard, the Queen rejoined, "God save you, all my people. I thank you with all my heart." Gorgeous pageants were prepared at every corner. The conduits ran wine. The crosses and standards in the city wore newly painted and burnished. The bells pealed, and loud-voiced cannon roared. Triumphal arches covered with flowers, and adorned with banners, targets, and rich stuffs, crossed the streets. Largesse was showered among the crowd with a liberal hand, and it was evident that Mary's advent was hailed on all hands as the harbinger of prosperity. The train proceeded along Fenchurch Street, where was a "marvellous cunning' pageant, representing the fountain of Helicon, made by the merchants of the Stillyard; the fountain ran abundantly-racked Rhenish wine till night." At the corner of Gracechurch Street there was another pageant, raised to a great height, on the summit of which were four pictures; above these stood an angel robed in green, with a trumpet to its mouth, which was sounded at the Queen's approach, to the "great marvelling of many ignorant persons." Here she was harangued by the Recorder; after which the Chamberlain presented her with a purse of cloth of gold, containing a thousand marks. The purse she graciously received, but the money she distributed among the assemblage. At the corner of Gracechurch Street another stage was erected. It was filled with the loveliest damsels that could be found, with their hair loosened and floating over their shoulders, and carrying large branches of white wax. This was by far the prettiest spectacle she had witnessed, and elicited Mary's particular approbation. Her attention, however, was immediately afterwards attracted to the adjoining stage, which was filled with Romish priests in rich copes, with crosses and censers of silver, which they waved as the Queen approached, while an aged prelate advanced to pronounce a solemn benediction upon her. Mary immediately dismounted, and received it on her knees. This action was witnessed with some dislike by the multitude, and but few shouts were raised as she again mounted her palfrey. But it was soon forgotten, and the same cheers that had hitherto attended her accompanied her to the Tower. Traversing East-cheap, which presented fresh crowds, and offered fresh pageants to her view, she entered Tower Street, where she was welcomed by larger throngs than before, and with greater enthusiasm than ever. In this way she reached Tower Hill, where a magnificent spectacle burst upon her.

The vast area of Tower Hill was filled with spectators. The crowds who had witnessed her entrance into the city had now flocked thither, and every avenue had poured in its thousands, till there was not a square inch of ground unoccupied. Many were pushed into the moat, and it required the utmost exertion of the guards, who were drawn out in lines of two deep, to keep the road which had been railed and barred from the end of Tower Street to the gates of the fortress clear for the Queen. As Mary's eye ranged over this sea of heads—as she listened to their stunning vociferations, and to the loud roar of the cannon which broke from every battlement in the Tower, her heart swelled with exultation. It was an animating spectacle. The day, it has been said, was bright and beautiful. The sun poured down its rays upon the ancient fortress, which had so lately opened its gates to an usurper, but which now like a heartless rake had cast off one mistress to take another. The whole line of ramparts on the west was filled with armed men. On the summit of the White Tower floated her standard, while bombard and culverin kept up a continual roar from every lesser tower.

After gazing for a few moments in the direction of the lofty citadel, now enveloped in the clouds of smoke issuing from the ordnance, and, excepting its four tall turrets and its standard, entirely hidden from view, her eyes followed the immense cavalcade, which, like a swollen current, was pouring its glittering tide beneath the arch of the Bulwark Gate; and as troop after troop disappeared, and she gradually approached the fortress, she thought she had never beheld a sight so grand and inspiriting. Flourishes of trumpets, almost lost in the stunning acclamations of the multitude, and the thunder of artillery, greeted her arrival at the Tower. Her entrance was conducted with much ceremony. Proceeding through closely-serried ranks of archers and arquebussiers, she passed beneath the Middle Gate and across the bridge. At the By-ward Tower she was received by Lord Clinton and a train of nobles. On either side of the gate, stood Gog and Magog. Both giants made a profound obeisance as she passed. A few steps further, her course was checked by. Og and Xit. Prostrating himself before her, the elder giant assisted his diminutive companion to clamber upon his back, and as soon as he had gained this position, the dwarf knelt down, and offered the keys of the fortress to the Queen. Mary was much diverted at the incident, nor was she less surprised at the vast size of Og and his brethren—than at the resemblance they presented to her royal father. Guessing what was passing through her mind, and regardless of consequences as of decorum, Xit remarked,—

"Your majesty, I perceive, is struck with the likeness of my worthy friend Og to your late sire King Henry VIII., of high and renowned memory. You will not, therefore, be surprised, when I inform you that he is his—"

Before another word could be uttered, Og, who had been greatly alarmed at the preamble, arose with such suddenness, that Xit was precipitated to the ground.

"Pardon me, your majesty," cried the giant, in great confusion, "it is true what the accursed imp says. I have the honour to be indirectly related to your highness. God's death, sirrah, I have half a mind to set my foot upon thee and crush thee. Thou art ever in mischief."

The look and gesture, which accompanied this exclamation, were so indescribably like their royal parent, that neither the Queen nor the Princess Elizabeth could forbear laughing.

As to Xit, the occurrence gained him a new friend in the person of Jane the Fool, who ran up as he was limping off with a crestfallen look, and begged her majesty's permission to take charge of him. This was granted, and the dwarf proceeded with the royal cortege. On learning the name of his protectress, Xit observed,—

"You are wrongfully designated, sweetheart. Jane the Queen was Jane the Fool—you are Jane the Wise."

While this was passing, Mary had given some instructions in an under tone to Lord Clinton, and he immediately departed to fulfil them. The cavalcade next passed beneath the arch of the Bloody Tower, and the whole retinue drew up on the Green. A wide circle was formed round the queen, amid which, at intervals, might be seen the towering figures of the giants, and next to the elder of them, Xit, who having been obliged to quit his new friend had returned to Og and was standing on his tip-toes to obtain a peep at what was passing. No sooner had Mary taken up her position, than Lord Clinton re-appeared, and brought with him several illustrious persons who having suffered imprisonment in the fortress, for their zeal for the religion of Rome, wore now liberated by her command. As the first of the group, a venerable nobleman, Approached her and bent the knee before her, Mary's eyes filled with tears, and she exclaimed, in a voice of much emotion,—

"Arise, my Lord Duke of Norfolk. The attainder pronounced against you in my father's reign is reversed. Your rank, your dignities, honours, and estates shall be restored to you."

Queen Mary receiving the Prisoners on the Tower Green.

As the Duke retired, Gardiner, Bishop of Winchester, advanced.

"Your Grace shall not only have your bishoprick again," said Mary, "but you shall have another high and important office.—I here appoint you Lord Chancellor of the realm."

"Your highness overwhelms me with kindness," replied Gardiner, pressing her hand to his lips.

"You have no more than your desert, my lord," replied Mary. "But I pray you stand aside a moment. There are other claimants of our attention."

Gardiner withdrew, and another deprived bishop took his place. It was Bonner.

"My lord," said Mary, as he bowed before her, "you are restored to the see of London, and the prelate who now so unworthily fills that high post, Bishop Ridley, shall make room for you. My lord," she added to Lord Clinton, "make out a warrant, and let him be committed to the Tower."

"I told you how it would be," observed Renard to Lord Pembroke. "Ridley's last discourse has cost him his liberty. Cranmer will speedily follow."

Other prisoners, amongst whom was Tunstall, Bishop of Durham, and the Duchess of Somerset, now advanced, and were warmly welcomed by the Queen. The last person who approached her was a remarkably handsome young man, with fine features and a noble figure. This was Edward Courtenay, son of the Marquess of Exeter, who was beheaded in 1538. Since that time Courtenay had been a close prisoner in the Tower. He was of the blood-royal, being grandson of Catherine, youngest daughter of Edward the Fourth, and his father had been declared heir to the throne.

"You are right welcome, my cousin," said Mary, extending her hand graciously to him, which he pressed to his lips. "Your attainder shall be set aside, and though we cannot restore your father to life, we can repair the fortunes of his son, and restore him to his former honours. Henceforth, you are Earl of Devonshire. Your patent shall be presently made out, and such of your sire's possessions as are in our hands restored."

Courtenay warmly thanked her for her bounty, and the Queen smiled upon him in such gracious sort, that a suspicion crossed more than one bosom that she might select him as her consort.

"Her majesty smiles upon Courtenay as if she would bestow her hand upon him in right earnest," observed Pembroke to Renard.

"Hum!" replied the ambassador. "This must be nipped in the bud. I have another husband in view for her."

"Your master, Philip of Spain, I'll be sworn," said Pembroke—"a suitable match, if he were not a Catholic."

Renard made no answer, but he smiled an affirmative.

"I am glad this scheme has reached my ears," observed De Noailles, who overheard the conversation—"it will not suit my master, Henry II., that England should form an alliance with Spain. I am for Courtenay, and will thwart Renard's plot."

Having received the whole of the prisoners, Mary gave orders to liberate all those within the Tower who might be confined for their adherence to the Catholic faith.

"My first care," she said, "shall be to celebrate the obsequies of my brother, Edward VI.,—whose body, while others have been struggling for the throne, remains uninterred according to the forms of the Romish church. The service shall take place in Westminster Abbey."

"That may not be, your highness," said Cranmer, who formed one of the group. "His late majesty was a Protestant prince."

"Beware how you oppose me, my lord," rejoined Mary, sternly. "I have already committed Ridley to prison, and shall not hesitate to commit your Grace."

"Your highness will act as it seems best to you," rejoined Cranmer, boldly; "but I shall fulfil my duty, even at the hazard of incurring your displeasure. Your royal brother professed the Protestant faith, which is, as yet,—though Heaven only knows how long it may continue so,—the established religion of this country, and he must, therefore, be interred according to the rites of that church. No other ceremonies, but those of the Protestant church, shall be performed within Westminster Abbey, as long as I maintain a shadow of power."

"It is well," replied Mary. "We may find means to make your Grace more flexible. To-morrow, we shall publish a decree proclaiming our religious opinions. And it is our sovereign pleasure, that the words 'Papist' and 'Heretic' be no longer used as terms of reproach."

"I have lived long enough," exclaimed the Duke of Norfolk, falling on his knees—"in living to see the religion of my fathers restored."

"The providence which watched over your Grace's life, and saved you from the block, when your fate seemed all but sealed, reserved you for this day," rejoined Mary.

"It reserved me to be a faithful and devoted servant of your majesty," replied the Duke.

"What is your highness's pleasure touching the Duke of Northumberland, Lord Guilford Dudley, and Lady Jane Dudley?" inquired Clinton.

"The two latter will remain closely confined till their arraignment," replied Mary. "Lady Jane, also, will remain a prisoner for the present. And now, my lords, to the palace."

With this, she turned her palfreys head, and passing under the Bloody Tower, proceeded to the principal entrance of the ancient structure, where she dismounted, and accompanied by a throng of nobles, dames, and attendants, entered the apartments so lately occupied by the unfortunate Jane.

II.—HOW JANE WAS IMPRISONED IN THE BRICK TOWER.

The first shock over, Jane bore her reverse of fortune with the utmost patience and resignation, uttering no complaints, but making, in the language of Fuller, "misery itself amiable by her pious behaviour." She then reaped the full benefit of the religious education she had received, and her time was wholly passed in meditation, prayer, or profound study. Her demeanour was gentle and calm—graver and more thoughtful than it had been, but by no means cast down. If she had not regained her cheer-.fulness, she had fully recovered her composure; and the warder, Partridge, in whose habitation she was confined in the first instance, described her "as looking more like a queen than when she sat upon the throne."

In this way, some days were spent, when word was brought her by an attendant, that a chamber had been prepared for her in the Brick Tower, and that a guard was without to conduct her to it. She received the intimation with composure, and immediately rose to obey it, requesting only that her books might be sent after her. The attendant, whose eyes were blinded with tears, promised to fulfil her wishes. On going forth, she found an officer and the three gigantic warders waiting to escort her to her prison. The party moved forward in silence, and at a slow pace. While crossing the Green, she perceived another group advancing towards her, and as it drew nearer, she found it was her husband attended by a guard. Uttering a loud cry, she would have rushed and thrown herself into his arms, if she had not been prevented by the officer. Dudley, whose eyes had been bent on the ground, heard the cry, and immediately knew by whom it was uttered. He made a movement similar to that of Jane, but like her he was checked by his attendants. So deeply, however, were the guards on either side moved by the anguish of the unfortunate pair, that, although expressly enjoined to the contrary, they suffered them to approach and embrace each other. The meeting drew tears from all eyes that beheld it; and the susceptible heart of Magog was so touched, that he had much ado to hide his grief. From the few hasty words she was able to exchange with her husband, Jane learnt that his prison had been changed, and that an order had been issued for his removal from the Beauchamp to the Bowyer Tower.

"Every dungeon in the Tower," he said, "is filled with our friends and partisans. Your father, the Duke of Suffolk, is confined in the Martin Tower. And I have been just removed from the Beauchamp Tower to make room for my father, the Duke of Northumberland, my two brothers, Ambrose and Robert, and their faithful followers, Sir John Gates, Sir Henry Gates, and Sir Thomas Palmer."

"Alas!" cried Jane, "we are all equally culpable, and must all suffer alike. But we shall be speedily released."

"On the scaffold," rejoined Dudley, bitterly.

"Ay, on the scaffold," repeated Jane. "And I trust though the remainder of our mortal life may be separated, that we shall meet above to part no more. Pray for this, my dear lord. It is my own constant prayer. And it is my firm reliance upon it that enables me to endure the agony of this meeting, which otherwise would kill me."

"I will strive to do so, Jane," replied her husband. "But I still cling to life and hope."

"Divest yourself of these vain desires, my Lord," cried Jane, earnestly, "and turn your thoughts from earth to heaven. There indeed we shall inherit an everlasting kingdom, undisturbed by misery and calamity."

"Madam," said the officer, advancing; "I grieve to abridge this short meeting. But my duty admits of no alternative. You must follow me."

"It is well, sir," she replied—"Farewell, dear Dudley. My prayers shall be for you."

"And mine for you, dear Jane," replied her husband, pressing her to his bosom—"Heaven grant me your patience and resignation!"

"Amen!" she fervently ejaculated. And with another embrace, they parted.

For a short distance the two escorts walked close together, during which the afflicted pair kept their eyes fondly fixed on each other. After passing the north-west corner of the White Tower, Lord Guilford's attendants took a straight-forward course, while Jane's guards proceeded to the right. Still but a short distance intervened between them, until Jane beheld her husband disappear beneath the low-arched entrance of the Bowyer Tower. A convulsive movement passed over her frame; but the next moment she was apparently as calm as ever, and followed the officer into the structure destined for her reception.

This, as has already been intimated, was the Brick Tower, the next turret on the east of the Bowyer Tower. The upper story, which is of brick—whence its name—was erected in the reign of Edward the Fourth, or Richard the Third: the basement story is of stone, and of much greater antiquity.

Entering a narrow passage, she was ushered by the officer into a small room, which he informed her was prepared for her reception. Everything that circumstances would admit appeared to have been done to lessen the rigour of her confinement. The stone walls were hung with arras; and much of the furniture a carved oak table, and velvet-covered seats, placed in the deep embrasures of the windows—had been brought from Jane's late chamber in the palace.

"This seat, said the officer, pointing to a curiously-carved chair, * was used by Queen Anne Boleyn during her imprisonment. I had it brought hither for your ladyship's accommodation."

"I thank you for your consideration, sir," replied Jane; "it will serve to support one as unhappy as that ill-fated princess." Having inquired whether she had any further commands with which it was possible for him to comply, and being answered in the negative, the officer took his departure, and Jane was left alone.

THE BRICK TOWER.

Alone! the thought struck chill to her heart. She was now a solitary captive. She heard the door of her prison bolted—she examined its stone walls, partly concealed by the tapestry—she glanced at its iron-barred windows, and her courage forsook her. She had no bosom to lean upon—no ear to which she could impart her sorrows. Her husband, though not far from her, was, like her a prisoner. She pictured him in his solitary room—and she would have given worlds to be near him—if only for a few moments. The thought occasioned her so much anguish, that she burst into tears, and for some time was a prey to despair. She then knelt down beside the chair, and burying her face in her clasped hands, prayed deeply and fervently for support through her trial. And she prayed not in vain. She soon afterwards arose tranquil and refreshed.

* *This curious piece of furniture, authenticated to have*

belonged to the unfortunate queen above-named, is now in the possession of Mr. Cottenham, the architect, of Waterloo Road.

Jane Imprisoned in the Brick Tower.

III.-HOW SIMON RENARD ASCENDED TO THE ROOF OF THE WHITE TOWER; AND OF THE GOODLY PROSPECT HE BEHELD THEREFROM.

The night of Queen Mary's entrance into the Tower was spent by Simon Renard, the Duke of Norfolk, Gardiner (the new Lord Chancellor), Courtenay, Arundel, Pembroke, and other noble and honourable persons composing her council, in framing a public declaration of her religious opinions, to be proclaimed on the morrow, and in deliberating on other mighty matters connected with the establishment of her government. Throughout this consultation, when any difference of opinion arose, the matter was invariably deferred to the judgment of the imperial ambassador, whose decision was regarded as final; and as he was looked upon as the chief instrument in crushing the late rebellion, so it was supposed he could, by his sagacity and influence, establish Mary upon her throne.

It was late when the council separated, and instead of returning to his apartments in the palace, Renard, fevered and wearied by the protracted discussion at which he had assisted, preferred refreshing himself by a stroll in the open air. Accordingly, he proceeded to the green, and began to pace backwards and forwards, at a brisk pace, between the lieutenant's lodgings and the chapel. He continued this exercise for nearly an hour, pondering upon recent events, and revolving future schemes within his plotting brain, when just as day was breaking, and the hoary walls of the White Tower began to reveal themselves in all their grandeur, he perceived a man, armed with a caliver, advancing to meet him. Renard stood still, and throwing his ample cloak over his shoulder, awaited the new comers approach. It proved to be a warder, who, having seen him as he was going his rounds, at first supposed he had some ill designs in view, but finding out his mistake, as he drew nearer and recognised the Spanish ambassador, with whose person he was familiar, he was about to withdraw, when Renard called him back and demanded his name.

"I am called Gervase Winwike, worshipful sir," readied the man, "and am one of the senior warders of the Tower.

"Whither are you going, friend?" inquired Renard. "To the summit of the White Tower," answered Winwike; "to see that the sentinels are at their posts."

"Is it inconsistent with your duty to take me with you?" asked the ambassador.

"By no means," rejoined the warder. "I shall feel honoured by your presence. We shall reach the roof just at sunrise, and the view from thence, on a fine clear morning like the present, is magnificent beyond compare, and will amply repay your worship for climbing up so many steps as you will have to scale to obtain it."

"Let us make what haste we can, then," said Renard, "I am impatient to behold it."

Thus exhorted, Winwike led the way to the north-west turret of the ancient structure, before a door in which a sentinel was stationed, who, on receiving the pass-word, lowered his halbert, and suffered them to enter. They were now within a small circular chamber, from which a flight of spiral stone steps ascended. Followed by Renard, the warder commenced the ascent. Light was admitted at intervals through loop-holes, gradually diminishing in width as they approached the exterior of the walls, and serving to reveal their immense thickness. As they mounted, Winwike pointed out to his companion the entrance of a passage communicating with the Council-chamber. Renard was much struck with the substantial and beautiful masonry of the turret; but being anxious to gain the roof as soon as possible, he urged his companion to quicken his pace, and they soon arrived at an arched door, which Winwike threw open, and they stepped upon the roof..

Springing upon the platform, Renard was about to rush to the battlements, when Winwike offered to lead him to the best point of view. As he followed his conductor towards the southwest angle, Renard cast his eye over the roof. Cannon were placed on the raised platform, while armed men were stationed at twenty paces distant from each other. In the centre of the building stood a tall staff, from which floated the royal banner.

Depositing his caliver against the wall of the turret, Winwike told his companion to look around. Renard obeyed, and a glorious panorama met his gaze. Immediately beneath him lay the fortress, with its chain of flowers—its ramparts—its fortifications—its bridges, and its broad deep moat. Beyond was spread out old and picturesque London, with its numerous steeples, above which rose the massive tower of St. Paul's. A little on the left was old London Bridge, covered with out-houses—the noise of the falling water, and the mills, being distinctly audible where they stood. Nearer, was the river glittering in the sunbeams, and filled with a forest of masts. Renard contemplated this prospect for some time in silent admiration.

"There you behold the Tower of London," said Winwike, pointing downwards.

"And there I read the history of England," replied Renard.

"If it is written in those towers it is a dark and bloody history," replied the warder—"and yet your worship says truly. The building on which we stand, and those around us, are the best chronicles of our country. I can recount to your worship their foundation, and the chief events that have happened within them, if you are disposed to listen to me."

"Proceed then," replied Renard, "and when I have had enough I will interrupt you."

Simon Renard and Winwike the warder on the Roof of the White Tower

INTERIOR OF THE CRADLE TOWER.

IV.—OF THE TOWER OF LONDON; ITS ANTIQUITY AND FOUNDATION; ITS MAGNITUDE AND EXTENT; ITS KEEP, PALACE, GARDENS, FORTIFICATIONS, DUNGEONS, AND CHAPELS; ITS WALLS, BULWARKS, AND MOAT; ITS ROYAL INMATES; ITS CONSTABLES,

JAILORS, WARDERS, AND OTHER OFFICERS; ITS PRISONERS, EXECUTIONS, AND SECRET MURDERS.

In 1078, (for, instead of following the warder's narrative to Simon Renard, it appears advisable in this place to offer a slight sketch of the renowned fortress, under consideration, especially as such a course will allow of its history being brought down to a later period than could otherwise be accomplished,) the Tower of London was founded by William the Conqueror, who appointed Gundulph, Bishop of Exeter, principal overseer of the work. By this prelate, who seems to have been a good specimen of the church militant, and who, during the progress of his operations, was lodged in the house, of Edmere, a burgess of London, a part of the city wall, adjoining the northern banks of the Thames, which had been much injured by the incursions of the tide, was taken down, and a "great square tower," since called the White Tower, erected on its site.

Some writers have assigned an earlier date to this edifice, ascribing its origin to the great Roman invader of our shores, whence it has been sometimes denominated Cæsar's Tower; and the hypothesis is supposed to be confirmed by Fitz Stephens, a monkish historian of the period of Henry the Second, who states, that "the city of London hath in the east a very great and most strong Palatine Tower, whose turrets and walls do rise from a deep foundation, the mortar thereof being tempered with the blood of beasts." On this authority, Dr. Stukeley has introduced a fort, which he terms the *Arx Palatina*, in his plan of Londinium Augusta. But, though it is not improbable that some Roman military station may have stood on the spot now occupied by the White Tower,—certain coins and other antiquities having been found by the workmen in sinking the foundations of the Ordnance Office in 1777,—it is certain that no part of the present structure was erected by Julius Cæsar; nor can he, with propriety, be termed the founder of the Tower of London. As to its designation, that amounts to little, since, as has been shrewdly remarked by M. Dulaure, in his description of the Grand Châtelet at Paris—"every old building, the origin of which is buried in obscurity, is attributed to Cæsar or the devil."

Fourteen years afterwards, in the reign of William Rufus, who, according to Henry of Huntingdon, "pilled and shaved the people with tribute, especially about the Tower of London," the White Tower was greatly damaged by a violent storm, which, among other ravages, carried off the roof of Bow Church, and levelled above six hundred habitations with the ground. It was subsequently repaired, and an additional tower built on the south side near the river.

Strengthened by Geoffrey de Magnaville, Earl of Essex, and fourth constable of the fortress, who defended it against the usurper Stephen, but was, nevertheless, eventually compelled to surrender it; repaired in 1155, by Thomas à Becket, then Chancellor to Henry the Second; greatly extended and enlarged in 1190, the second year of the reign of Richard Cour de Lion, by William Longchamp, Bishop of Ely and Chancellor of the realm, who, encroaching to some distance upon Tower Hill, and breaking down the city wall as far as the first gate called the postern, surrounded it with high embattled walls of stone, and a broad deep ditch, thinking, as Stowe observes, "to have environed it with the river Thames;"—the Tower of London was finished by Henry the Third, who, in spite of the remonstrances of the citizens, and other supernatural warnings, if credit is to be attached to the statement of Matthew of Paris, completely fortified it.

A gate and bulwark having been erected on the west of the Tower, we are told by the old chronicler above-mentioned, "that they were shaken as it had been with an earthquake and fell down, which the king again commanded to be built in better sort, which was done. And yet, again, in the year 1241, the said wall and bulwarks that were newly builded, whereon the king had bestowed more than twelve thousand marks, were irrecoverably quite thrown down as before; for the which chance the citizens of London were nothing sorry, for they were threatened, that the said wall and bulwarks were builded, to the end, that if any of them would contend for the liberties of the city, they might be imprisoned. And that many might be laid in divers prisons, many lodgings were made, that no one should speak with another." These remarkable accidents (if accidents they were,) were attributed by the popular superstition of the times, to the miraculous interference of Thomas à Becket, the guardian saint of the Londoners.

By the same monarch the storehouse was strengthened and repaired, and the keep or citadel whitened, (whence probably it derived its name, as it was afterwards styled in Edward the Third's reign "*La Blanche Tour*") as appears by the following order still preserved in the Tower Rolls:—"We command you to repair the garner within the said tower, and well amend it throughout, wherever needed. And also concerning all the leaden gutters of the Great Tower, from the top of the said tower, through which the rain water must fall down, to lengthen them, and make them come down even to the ground;

so that the wall of the said tower, lately whitened anew, may by no means decay, nor easily break out, by reason of the rain water dropping down. But to make upon the said towers *alures* of good and strong timber, and throughout to be well leaded; by which people might see even to the foot of the said tower, and better to go up and down, if need be." Further orders were given in this reign for the beautifying and fitting up the chapels of Saint John and Saint Peter, as already mentioned in the account of those structures.

The same monarch planted a grove, or orchard of "perie trees," as they are described in his mandate to Edward of Westminster, in the vicinity of the Tower, and surrounded it with a wall of mud, afterwards replaced by another of brick, in the reign of Edward the Fourth. He likewise established a menagerie within the fortress, allotting a part of the bulwark at the western entrance since called the Lions' Tower, for the reception of certain wild beasts, and as a lodging for their keeper. In 1235, the Emperor Frederick sent him three leopards, in allusion to his scutcheon, on which three of those animals were emblazoned; and from that time, down to a very recent date, a menagerie has been constantly maintained within the Tower. To support it, Edward the Second commanded the Sheriffs of London to pay the keeper of his lions sixpence a day for their food, and three half-pence a-day for the man's own diet, out of the fee farm of the city.

Constant alterations and reparations wero made to the ramparts and towers during subsequent reigns. Edward the Fourth encroached still further on Tower Hill than his predecessors, and erected an outer gate called the Bulwark Tower. In the fifth year of the reign of this monarch, a scaffold and gallows having been erected on Tower Hill, the citizens, ever jealous of their privileges and liberties, complained of the step; and to appease them, a proclamation was made to the effect, "that the erection, and setting up of the said gallows be not a precedent or example thereby hereafter to be taken, in hurt, prejudice, or derogation, of the franchises, liberties, and privileges of the city."

Richard the Third repaired the Tower, and Stow records a commission to Thomas Daniel, directing him to seize for use within this realm, as many masons, bricklayers, and other workmen, as should be thought necessary for the expedition of the king's works within the Tower. In the twenty-third of Henry the Eighth, the whole of the fortress appears to have undergone repair—a survey being taken of its different buildings, which is is still preserved in the Chapter-house at Westminster. In the second of Edward the Sixth, the following strange accident occurred, by which one of the fortifications was destroyed. A Frenchman, lodged in the Middle Tower, accidentally set fire to a barrel of gunpowder, which blew up the structure, fortunately without damage to any other than the luckless causer of it.

At the period of this chronicle, as at the present time, the Tower of London comprehended within its walls a superficies of rather more than twelve acres, and without the moat a circumference of three thousand feet and upwards. Consisting of a citadel or keep, surrounded by an inner and outer ward, it was approached on the west by an entrance called the Bulwark Gate, which has long since disappeared. The second entrance was formed by an embattled tower, called the Lion's Gate, conducting to a strong tower flanked with bastions, and defended by a double portcullis, denominated the Middle Tower. The outworks adjoining these towers, in which was kept the menagerie, were surrounded by a smaller moat, communicating with the main ditch. A large drawbridge then led to another portal, in all respects resembling that last described, forming the principal entrance to the outer ward, and called the By-ward or Gate Tower. The outer ward was defended by a strong line of fortifications; and at the north-east corner stood a large circular bastion, called the Mount.

The inner ward or ballium was defended by thirteen towers, connected by an embattled stone wall about forty feet, high and twelve feet thick, on the summit of which was a footway for the guard. Of these towers, three were situated at the west, namely, the Bell, the Beauchamp and the Devilin Towers; four at the north, the Flint, the Bowyer, the Brick, and the Martin Towers; three at the east, the Constable, the Broad Arrow, and Salt Towers; and three on the south, the Well, the Lanthorn, and the Bloody Tower. The Flint Tower has almost disappeared; the Bowyer Tower only retains its basement story; and the Brick Tower has been so much modernized as to retain little of its pristine character. The Martin Tower is now denominated the Jewel Tower, from the circumstance of its being the depositary of the regalia. The Lanthorn Tower has been swept away with the old palace.

Returning to the outer ward, the principal fortification on the south was a large square structure, flanked at each angle by an embattled tower. This building, denominated Saint Thomas's, or Traitor's Tower, was erected across the moat, and masked a secret entrance from the Thames, through which state prisoners, as has before been related, were brought into the Tower. It still retains much of its original appearance, and recals forcibly to the mind of the observer the dismal scenes that have occurred beneath its low-browed arches. Further on the east, in a line with Traitor's Tower, and terminating a wing of the old palace, stood the Cradle Tower. At the eastern angle of the outer ward was a small fortification over-looking the moat, known as the Tower leading to the Iron Gate. Beyond it a draw-bridge crossed the moat, and led to the Iron Gate, a small portal protected by a tower, deriving its name from the purpose for which it was erected.

At this point, on the patch of ground intervening between the moat and the river, and forming the platform or wharf, stood a range of mean habitations, occupied by the different artisans and workmen employed in the fortress. At the south of the By-ward Tower, an arched and embattled gateway opened upon a drawbridge which crossed the moat at this point. Opposite this drawbridge were the main stairs leading to the edge of the river. The whole of the fortress, it is scarcely necessary to repeat, was (and still is) encompassed by a broad deep moat, of much greater width at the sides next to Tower Hill and East Smithfield, than at the south, and supplied with water from the Thames by the sluice beneath Traitor's Gate.

Having now made a general circuit of the fortress, we shall return to the inner ballium, which is approached on the south by a noble gateway, erected in the reign of Edward the Third. A fine specimen of the architecture of the fourteenth century, this portal is vaulted with groined arches adorned with exquisite tracery springing from grotesque heads. At the period of this chronicle, it was defended at each end by a massive gate clamped with iron, and a strong portcullis. The gate and portcullis at the southern extremity still exist, but those at the north have been removed. The structure above it was anciently called the Garden Tower; but subsequently acquired the appellation of the Bloody Tower, from having been the supposed scene of the murder of the youthful princes, sons of Edward the Fourth, by the ruthless Duke of Gloucester, afterwards Richard the Third. Without pausing to debate the truth of this tragical occurrence, it may be sufficient to mention that tradition assigns it to this building.

Proceeding along the ascent leading towards the green, and mounting a flight of stone steps on the left, we arrive in front of the ancient lodgings allotted to the lieutenant of the Tower. Chiefly constructed of timber, and erected at the beginning of the sixteenth century, this fabric has been so much altered, that it retains little of its original character. In one of the rooms, called, from the circumstance, the Council-chamber, the conspirators concerned in the Gunpowder Plot were interrogated; and in memory of the event, a piece of sculpture, inscribed with their names, and with those of the commissioners by whom they were examined, has been placed against the walls.

Immediately behind the lieutenant's lodgings stands the Bell Tower,—a circular structure, surmounted by a small wooden turret containing the alarm-bell of the fortress. Its walls are of great thickness, and light is admitted through narrow loopholes. On the basement floor is a small chamber, with deeply-recessed windows, and a vaulted roof of very curious construction. This tower served as a place of imprisonment to John Fisher, the martyred bishop of Rochester, beheaded on Tower Hill for denying Henry the Eighth's supremacy; and to the Princess Elizabeth, who was confined within it by her sister, Queen Mary.

Traversing the green, some hundred and forty feet brings us to the Beauchamp, or Cobham Tower, connected with the Bell Tower by means of a footway on the top of the ballium wall. Erected in the reign of Henry the Third, as were most of the smaller towers of the fortress, this structure appears, from the numerous inscriptions, coats of arms, and devices that crowd its walls, to have been the principal state-prison. Every room, from roof to vault, is covered with melancholy memorials of its illustrious and unfortunate occupants.

Over the fire-place in the principal chamber, (now used as a mess-room by the officers of the garrison,) is the autograph of Philip Howard, Earl of Arundel, beheaded in 1572, for aspiring to the hand of Mary Queen of Scots. On the right of the fire-place, at the entrance of a recess, are these words:— "Dolor Patientia vincitur. G. Gyfford. August 8, 1586." Amongst others, for we can only give a few as a specimen of the rest, is the following enigmatical inscription. It is preceded by the date 1568, April 28, but is unaccompanied by any signature.

NO HOPE IS BARD OR BAYNE

THAT HAPP DOTH OUS ATTAYNE.

The next we shall select is dated 1581, and signed Thomas Myagh.

THOMAS MIAGII WHICH LIETHE HERE ALONE

THAT FAYNE WOLD FROM HENCE BEGON

BY TORTURE STRAUNGE MI TROVTH WAS TRYED

YET OF MY LIBERTIE DENIED.

Of this unfortunate person the following interesting account is given by Mr. Jardine, in his valuable treatise on the *Use of Torture in the Criminal Law of England*. "Thomas Myagh was an Irishman who was brought over by the command of the Lord Deputy of Ireland, to be examined respecting a treasonable correspondence with the rebels in arms in that country. The first warrant for the torture of this man was probably under the sign-manual, as there is no entry of it in the council register. The two reports made by the Lieutenant of the Tower and Dr. Hammond, respecting their execution of this warrant, are, however, to be seen at the State-Paper Office. The first of these, which is dated the 10th of March, 1580-1, states that they had twice examined Myagh, but had forborne to put him in Skevington's Irons, because they had been charged to examine him with secrecy, 'which they could not do, that manner of dealing requiring the presence and aid of one of the jailors all the time that he should be in those irons,' and also because they 'found the man so resolute, as in their opinions little would be wrung out of him but by some sharper torture.' The second report, which is dated the 17th of March, 1580, merely states that they had again examined Myagh, and could get nothing from him, 'notwithstanding that they had made trial of him by the torture of Skevington's irons, and with so much sharpness, as was in their judgment for the man and his cause convenient.' How often Myagh was tortured does not appear; but Skevington's irons seem to have been too mild a torture, for on the 30th of July, 1581, there is an entry in the council books of an authority to the Lieutenant of the Tower and Thomas Norton, to deal with him with the rack in such sort as they should see cause."

From many sentences expressive of the resignation of the sufferers, we take the following, subscribed A. Poole, 1564:—"Deo. servire. penitentiam. inire. fato. ohedire. regnare. est." Several inscriptions are left by this person—one four years later than the foregoing, is as follows: "*A passage perillus maketh a port pleasant.*" Here is another sad memento: "*O miser Hyon, che pensi od essero.*" Another: "*Reprens le: sage: et: il: te: aimera: J. S. 1538.*" A third: "*Principium sapientio timor Domini, I. h. s. x. p. s. Be friend to one. Be ennemye to none. Anno D. 1571, 10 Sept. The most unhappy man in the world is he that is not patient in adversities: For men are not killed with the adversities they have, but with the impatience they suffer. Tout vient apoint, quy peult attendre. Gli sospiri ne son testimoni veri dell angoscia mia. Æt. 20. Charles Bailly.*".

Most of these records breathe resignation. But the individual who carved the following record, and whose naine has passed away, appears to have numbered every moment of his captivity: "*Close prisoner 8 months, 32 wekees, 224 dayes, 5376 houres.*" How much of anguish is comprised in this brief sentence!

We could swell out this list, if necessary, to a volume, but the above may suffice to show their general character. Let those who would know how much their forefathers have endured cast their eyes over the inscriptions in the Beauchamp Tower. In general they are beautifully carved, ample time being allowed the writers for their melancholy employment. It has been asserted that Anne Boleyn was confined in the uppermost room of the Beauchamp Tower. But if an inscription may be trusted, she was imprisoned in the Martin Tower (now the Jewel Tower) at that time a prison lodging.

Postponing the description of the remaining towers until we have occasion to speak of them in detail, we shall merely note, in passing, the two strong towers situated at the southwestern extremity of the White Tower, called the

Coal Harbour Gate, over which there was a prison denominated the Nun's Bower, and proceed to the palace, of which, unluckily for the lovers of antiquity, not a vestige now remains.

Erected at different periods, and consisting of a vast range of halls, galleries, courts and gardens, the old palace occupied, in part, the site of the modern Ordnance Office. Commencing at the Coal Harbour Gate, it extended in a south-easterly direction to the Lanthorn Tower, and from thence branched off in a magnificent pile of building, called the Queen's Gallery, to the Salt Tower. In front of this gallery, defended by the Cradle Tower and the Well Tower, was the privy garden. Behind it stretched a large quadrangular area, terminated at the western angle by the Wardrobe Tower, and at the eastern angle by the Broad Arrow Tower. It was enclosed on the left by a further range of buildings, termed the Queen's Lodgings, and on the right by the inner ballium wall. The last-mentioned buildings were also connected with the White Tower, and with a small embattled structure flanked by a circular tower, denominated the Jewel House where the regalia were then kept. In front of the Jewel House stood a large decayed hall, forming part of the palace; opposite which was a court, planted with trees, and protected by the ballium wall.

This ancient palace—the scene of so many remarkable historical events,—the residence, during certain portions of their reigns, of all our sovereigns, from William Rufus down to Charles the Second—is now utterly gone. Where is the glorious hall which Henry the Third painted with the story of Antiochus, and which it required thirty fir-trees to repair,—in which Edward the Third and all his court were feasted by the captive John,—in which Richard the Second resigned his crown to Henry of Lancaster,—in which Henry the Eighth received all his wives before their espousals,—in which so many royal councils and royal revels have been held;—where is that great hall? Where, also, is the chamber in which Queen Isabella, consort of Edward the Second, gave birth to the child called, from the circumstance, Joan of the Tower? They have vanished, and other structures occupy their place. Demolished in the reign of James the Second, an ordnance office was erected on its site; and this building being destroyed by fire in 1788, it was succeeded by the present edifice bearing the name.

Having now surveyed the south of the fortress, we shall return to the north. Immediately behind Saint Peter's Chapel stood the habitations of the officers of the then ordnance department, and next to them an extensive range of storehouses, armouries, granaries, and other magazines, reaching to the Martin Tower. On the site of these buildings was erected, in the reign of William the Third, that frightful structure, which we trust the better taste of this, or some future age will remove—the Grand Storehouse. Nothing can be imagined more monstrous or incongruous than this ugly Dutch toy, (for it is little better,) placed side by side with a stern old Norman donjon, fraught with a thousand historical associations and recollections. It is the great blot upon the Tower. And much as the destruction of the old palace is to be lamented, the erection of such a building as this, in such a place, is infinitely more to be deplored. We trust to see it rased to the ground.

In front of the Constable Tower stood another range of buildings appropriated to the different officers and workmen connected with the Mint, which, until the removal of the place of coinage to its present situation on Little Tower Hill, it is almost needless to say, was held within the walls of the fortress.

The White Tower once more claims our attention. Already described as having walls of enormous thickness, this venerable stronghold is divided into four stories including the vaults. The latter consist of two large chambers and a smaller one, with a coved termination at the east, and a deeply-recessed arch at the opposite extremity. Light is admitted to this gloomy chamber by four semicircular-headed loopholes. At the north is a cell ten feet long by eight wide formed in the thickness of the wall, and receiving no light except from the doorway. Here tradition affirms that Sir Walter Raleigh was confined, and composed his History of the World.

Amongst other half-obliterated inscriptions carved on the arched doorway of this dungeon, are these: *He that indvreth* TO THE ENDE SHALL BE SAVID. M. 10. R. REDSTON. DAR. KENT. Ano. 1553.—Be feithful to the death and I will give the a crown of life. T. Fane. 1554. Above stands Saint John's Chapel, and the upper story is occupied by the council-chamber and the rooms adjoining. A narrow vaulted gallery, formed in the thickness of the wall, communicating with the turret stairs, and pierced with semicircular-headed openings for the admission of light to the interior, surrounds this story. The roof is covered with lead, and crowned with four lofty turrets, three angular and one square, surmounted with leaden cupolas, each terminated with a vane and crown.

We have spoken elsewhere, and shall have to speak again of the secret and subterranean passages, as well as of the dungeons of the Tower; those horrible and noisome receptacles, deprived of light and air, infested by legions of rats, and flooded with water, into which the wretched captives were thrust to perish by famine, or by more expeditious means; and those dreadful contrivances, the Little Ease—and the Pit;—the latter a dark and gloomy excavation sunk to the depth of twenty feet.

To the foregoing hasty sketch, in which we have endeavoured to make the reader acquainted with the general outline of the fortress, we would willingly, did space permit, append a history of the principal occurrences that have happened within its walls. We would tell how in 1234, Griffith, Prince of

Wales, in attempting to escape from the White Tower, by a line made of hangings, sheets, and table-cloths, tied together, being a stout heavy man, broke the rope, and falling from a great height, perished miserably—his head and neck being driven into his breast between the shoulders. How Edward the Third first established a Mint within the Tower, coining florences of gold. How in the reign of the same monarch, three sovereigns were prisoners there;—namely, John, King of France, his son Philip, and David, King of Scotland. How in the fourth year of the reign of Richard the Second, during the rebellion of Wat Tyler, the insurgents having possessed themselves of the fortress, though it was guarded by six hundred valiant persons, expert in arms, and the like number of archers, conducted themselves with extraordinary licence, bursting into the king's chamber, and that of his mother, to both of whom they offered divers outrages and indignities; and finally dragged forth Simon Sudbury, Archbishop of Canterbury, and hurrying him to Tower Hill, hewed off his head at eight strokes, and fixed it on a pole on London Bridge, where it was shortly afterwards replaced by that of Wat Tyler.

How, in 1458, jousts were held on the Tower-Green by the Duke of Somerset and five others, before Queen Margaret of Anjou. How in 1471, Henry the Sixth, at that time a prisoner, was said to be murdered within the Tower; how seven years later, George Duke of Clarence, was drowned in a butt of Malmsey in the Bowyer Tower; and how five years after that, the youthful Edward the Fifth, and the infant Duke of York, were also *said*, for the tradition is more than doubtful, to be smothered in the Blood Tower. How in 1483, by command of the Duke of Gloucester, who had sworn he would not dine till he had seen his head off, Lord Hastings was brought forth to the green before the chapel, and after a short shrift, "for a longer could not be suffered, the protector made so much haste to dinner, which he might not go to until this were done, for saving of his oath," his head was laid down upon a large log of timber, and stricken off.

How in 1512, the woodwork and decorations of Saint John's chapel in the White Tower were burnt. How in the reign of Henry the Eighth, the prisons were constantly filled, and the scaffold deluged with blood. How Sir Richard Empson and Edmund Dudley, the hither of John Dudley, Duke of Northumberland, were beheaded. How the like fate attended the Duke of Buckingham, destroyed by Wolsey, the martyred John Fisher, Bishop of Rochester, the wise and witty Sir Thomas More, Anne Boleyn, her brother Lord Rochford, Norris, Smeaton, and others; the Marquis of Exeter, Lord Montacute, and Sir Edward Neville; Thomas, Lord Cromwell, the counsellor of the dissolution of the monasteries; the venerable and courageous Countess of Salisbury; Lord Leonard Grey; Katherine Howard and Lady Rochford; and Henry, Earl of Surrey.

How, in the reign of Edward the Sixth, his two uncles, Thomas Seymour, Baron Sudley, and Edward Seymour, Duke of Somerset, were brought to the block; the latter, as has been before related, by the machinations of Northumberland.

Passing over, for obvious reasons, the reign of Mary, and proceeding to that of Elizabeth, we might relate how Thomas Howard, Duke of Norfolk, was beheaded; how the dungeons were crowded with recusants and seminary priests; amongst others, by the famous Jesuits, fathers Campion and Persons; how Lord Stourton, whose case seems to have resembled the more recent one of Lord Ferrers, was executed for the murder of the Hartgills; how Henry Percy, Earl of Northumberland, shot himself in his chamber, declaring that the jade Elizabeth should not have his estate; and how the long catalogue was closed by the death of the Earl of Essex.

How, in the reign of James the First, Sir Walter Raleigh was beheaded, and Sir Thomas Overbury poisoned. How in that of Charles the First, Thomas Wentworth, Earl of Strafford, and Archbishop Laud, underwent a similar fate. How in 1656, Miles Sunderland, having been condemned for high treason, poisoned himself; notwithstanding which, his body, stripped of all apparel, was dragged at the horse's tail to Tower Hill, where a hole had been digged under the scaffold, into which it was thrust, and a stake driven through it. How, in 1661, Lord Monson and Sir Henry Mildmay suffered, and in the year following Sir Henry Vane. How in the same reign Blood attempted to steal the crown; and how Algernon Percy and Lord William Russell were executed.

How, under James the Second, the rash and unfortunate Duke of Monmouth perished. How, after the rebellion of 1715, Lords Derwentwater and Kenmuro were decapitated; and after that of 1745, Lords Kilmarnock, Bahnerino, and Lovat. How in 1760, Lord Ferrers was committed to the Tower for the murder of his steward, and expiated his offence at Tyburn. How Wilkes was imprisoned there for a libel in 1762; and Lord George Gordon for instigating the riots of 1780. How, to come to our own times, Sir Francis Burdett was conveyed thither in April 1810; and how, to close the list, the Cato-street conspirators, Thistlewood, Ings, and others, were confined there in 1820.

The chief officer appointed to the custody of the royal fortress, is termed the Constable of the Tower;—a place, in the words of Stowe, of "high honour and reputation, as well as of great trust, many earls and one duke having been constable of the Tower." Without enumerating all those who have filled this important post, it maybe sufficient to state, that the first constable was Geoffrey de Mandeville, appointed by William the Conqueror; the last, Arthur, Duke of Wellington. Next in command is the lieutenant, after whom come the deputy-lieutenant, and major, or resident governor. The civil establishment consists of a chaplain, gentleman-porter, physician, surgeon, and apothecary; gentleman-jailer, yeoman porter, and forty yeomen warders. In addition to these, though in no way connected with the government or custody of the Tower, there are the various officers belonging to the ordnance department; the keepers of the records, the keeper of the regalia; and formerly there were the different officers of the Mint.

The lions of the Tower—once its chief attraction with the many,—have disappeared. Since the establishment of the Zoological Gardens, curiosity having been drawn in that direction, the dens of the old menagerie are deserted, and the sullen echoes of the fortress are no longer awakened by savage yells and howling. With another and more important attraction—the armories—it is not our province to meddle.

To return to Simon Renard and the warder. Having concluded his recital, to which the other listened with profound attention, seldom interrupting him with a remark, Winwike proposed, if his companion's curiosity was satisfied, to descend.

"You have given me food for much reflection." observed Renard, aroused from a reverie into which he had fallen; "but before we return I would gladly walk round the buildings. I had no distinct idea of the Tower till I came hither."

The warder complied, and led the way round the battlements, pausing occasionally to point out some object of interest.

Viewed from the summit of the White Tower, especially on the west, the fortress still offers a striking picture. In the middle of the sixteenth century, when its outer ramparts were strongly fortified—when the gleam of corslet and pike was reflected upon the dark waters of its moat—when the inner ballium walls were entire and unbroken, and its thirteen towers reared their embattled fronts—when within each of those towers state prisoners were immured—when its drawbridges were constantly raised, and its gates closed—when its palace still lodged a sovereign—when councils were held within its chambers—when its secret dungeons were crowded—when Tower Hill boasted a scaffold, and its soil was dyed with the richest and best blood of the land—when it numbered among its inferior officers, jailors, torturers, and an executioner—when all its terrible machinery was in readiness, and could be called into play at a moment's notice—when the steps of Traitor's

Gate wore worn by the feet of those who ascended, them—when, on whichever side the gazer looked, the same stern prospect was presented—the palace, the fortress, the prison,—a triple conjunction of fearful significance—when each structure had dark secrets to conceal—when beneath all these ramparts, towers, and bulwarks, were subterranean passages and dungeons—*then*, indeed, it presented a striking picture both to the eye and mind.

Slowly following his companion, Renard counted all the towers, which, including that whereon he was standing, and these connected with the bulwarks and palace, amounted to twenty-two,—marked their position—commented upon the palace, and the arrangement of its offices and outbuildings—examined its courts and gardens—inquired into the situation of the queen's apartments, and was shown a long line of buildings with a pointed roof, extending from the south-east angle of the keep to the Lanthorn Tower—admired the magnificent prospect of the heights of Surrey and Kent—traced the broad stream of the Thames as far as Greenwich—suffered his gaze to wander over the marshy tract of country towards Essex—noted the postern gate in the ancient city walls, standing at the edge of the north bank of the moat—traced those walls by their lofty entrances from Aldgate to Cripplegate, and from thence returned to the church of All Hallows Barking, and Tower Hill. The last object upon which his gaze rested was the scaffold. A sinister smile played upon his features as he gazed on it.

"There," he observed, "is the bloody sceptre by which England is ruled. From the palace to the prison is a step—from the prison to the scaffold another."

"King Henry the Eighth gave it plenty of employment," observed Winwike.

"True," replied Renard; "and his daughter, Queen Mary, will not suffer it to remain idle."

"Many a head will, doubtless, fall (and justly), in consequence of the late usurpation," remarked the warder.

"The first to do so now rests within that building," rejoined Renard, glancing at the Beauchamp Tower.

"Your worship, of course, means the Duke of Northumberland, since his grace is confined there," returned the warder. "Well, if she is spared who, though placed foremost in the wrongful and ill-advised struggle, was the last to counsel it, I care not what becomes of the rest. Poor lady Jane! Could our eyes pierce yon stone walls," he added, pointing to the Brick Tower, "I make no doubt we should discover her on her knees. She passes most of her time, I am informed, in prayer."

"Humph!" ejaculated Renard. And he half muttered, "She shall either embrace the Romish faith, or die by the hand of the executioner."

Winwike made no answer to the observation, and affected not to hear it, but he shuddered at the look that accompanied it—a look that brought to mind all he heard of the mysterious and terrible individual at his side.

By this time, the sun was high in heaven, and the whole fortress astir. A flourish of trumpets was blown on the Green, and a band of minstrels issued from the portal of the Coalharbour Tower. The esquires, retainers, pages, and servitors of the various noblemen, lodged within the palace, were hurrying to and fro, some hastening to their morning meal, others to different occupations. Everything seemed bright and cheerful. The light laugh and the merry jest reached the ear of the listeners. Rich silks and costly stuffs, mixed with garbs of various-coloured serge, with jerkins and caps of steel, caught the eye. Yet how much misery was there near this smiling picture! What sighs from those in captivity responded to the shouts and laughter without! Queen Mary arose and proceeded to matins in Saint John's Chapel. Jane awoke and addressed herself to solitary prayer; while Northumberland, who had passed a sleepless night, pacing his dungeon like a caged tiger, threw himself on his couch, and endeavoured to shut out the light of day and his own agonizing reflections.

Meanwhile, Renard and the warder had descended from the White Tower and proceeded to the Green.

"Who is that person beneath the Beauchamp Tower gazing so inquisitively at its barred windows?" demanded the former.

"It is the crow scenting the carrion—it is Mauger the headsman," answered Winwike.

"Indeed?" replied Renard; "I would speak with him."

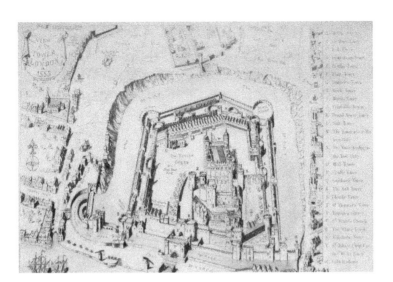

V.—HOW THE DUKE OF NORTHUMBERLAND WAS ARRAIGNED OF HIGH TREASON IN WESTMINSTER HALL; AND HOW HE MADE FOUR REQUESTS AFTER THE JUDGMENT.

Closely confined within the Beauchamp Tower, and treated with great rigour, it was almost a satisfaction to the Duke of Northumberland to be informed, after nearly a fortnight's immediate prisonment, that his trial would take place on the 18th of August. Though he anticipated the result, and had no hope of escaping the block, the near approach of death did not cast him down, but on the contrary served to reassure his firmness, which of late, shaken by his altered state of health, and intense mental anxiety, had in some degree failed him. The last few weeks had wonderfully changed his appearance. Heretofore, though past the middle term of life, he exhibited no symptom of decay. His frame was strong and muscular—his deportment lofty and majestic—his eye piercing as the eagle's. He was now shrunken—bent—with the gait and look of an old man. On the intelligence above mentioned being communicated to him, he all at once shook off this feebleness. His eye regained its fire, his frame its strength and lofty bearing; and if his figure was wasted and his brow furrowed, it detracted nothing from his dignity. Aware that his enemies would sit in judgment upon him, he determined to confront them boldly.

When the day appointed for the arraignment arrived, the Duke prepared himself betimes. He was habited in a doublet of black velvet, and wore the collar of the order of the garter. His eldest son, John Dudley, Earl of Warwick, and the Marquess of Northampton, were to be tried with him, and on the morning in question the three noblemen met for the first time since their imprisonment. The meeting took place in a spacious chamber on the first floor, now used, as has been already observed, as a mess-room, but then as a hall in which the prisoners were separately introduced at stated intervals to take exercise.

Throwing his arms round his son's neck, and with difficulty repressing his emotion, the Duke implored his forgiveness.

"For what, my lord?" demanded the young nobleman.

"For the great wrong I have done you in placing you in this fearful jeopardy," answered Northumberland.

"You have done me no wrong, my lord," replied his son. "My wishes were as strongly in favour of the cause as yours, and I am therefore as culpable as yourself. And as I should have been the first to congratulate you on its success, so I ought to be the last to reproach you with its failure."

"Nevertheless the fault *is* mine, and mine only," replied the Duke. "I was the originator of the scheme—the planner of the snare into which we have fallen—and if you perish, your death will be at my door."

"Think not of me, father," replied the young man. "The life I received from you, I will gladly lay down for you. If you desire my forgiveness you shall have it. But I ought rather to ask your's. And, at all events, I entreat your blessing."

"Heaven bless you, my son, and have mercy on us both," exclaimed Northumberland, fervently. "If the humblest supplication could move our judges in your favour it should not be wanting. But I well know they are inexorable."

"I would rather die a thousand deaths than you so demeaned yourself," replied Warwick. "Ask nothing from them but a speedy judgment. We go to a condemnation, not a trial."

"True, my lord," added Northampton; "we have nothing to hope, and therefore nothing to fear. The game is lost, and we must pay the penalty."

"Right, my lord," rejoined Northumberland, embracing him, "and we will discharge it to the uttermost. Would that my life could pay for all."

"Since it cannot be, my lord," replied Northampton, "e'en let us meet our fate like men, and give our enemies no additional triumph. To see your grace so well reconciled to your fate, must encourage those who have lost so little in comparison."

"I am so well reconciled to it," replied the Duke, "that I scarcely desire to be restored to my former condition. And yet," he added, sternly, "I would gladly enjoy my former power for an hour, to be avenged on one man.".

"His name?" inquired the Earl of Warwick, quickly.

"Simon Renard," replied the Duke.

A deep silence ensued, which was broken at length by Northumberland, who inquired from the officer in attendance if he knew aught of the Queen's intentions towards Lady Jane Dudley.

"Her highness, it is said, is inclined to pardon her, in consideration of her youth," replied the officer, "but her councillors are averse to such leniency."

"They are my enemies," rejoined the Duke—"Again my crimes are visited on an innocent head."

At this moment, a small arched door near one of the recesses was opened, and a warder announced that the escort was ready to convey the prisoners to Westminster Hall.

Preceded by the officer, the Duke and his companions descended a short spiral stone staircase, and, passing under an arched doorway, on either side of which was drawn up a line of halberdiers, entered upon the Green. The whole of this spacious' area, from Saint Peter's Chapel to the Lieutenant's lodgings—from the walls of the tower they had quitted, to those of the White Tower, was filled with spectators. Every individual in the fortress, whose duty did not compel his attendance elsewhere, had hastened thither to see the great Duke of Northumberland proceed to his trial; and so intense was the curiosity of the crowd, that it was with great difficulty that the halberdiers could keep them from pressing upon him. On the Duke's appearance something like a groan was uttered, but it was instantly checked. Northumberland was fully equal to this trying moment. Aware of his own unpopularity,—aware that amid that vast concourse he had not one well-wisher, but that all rejoiced in his downfall,—he manifested no discomposure, but marched with a step so majestic, and glanced around with a look, so commanding, that those who were near him involuntarily shrunk before his regards. The deportment of Northampton was dignified and composed—that of the Earl of Warwick fierce and scornful. Lord Clinton, the Constable of the Tower, and the Lieutenant, Sir John Gage, now advanced to meet them, and the former inquired from Northumberland whether he had any request to make that could be complied with. Before an answer could be returned by the Duke, an old woman broke through the ranks of the guard, and regardless of the menaces with which she was assailed confronted him.

"Do you know me?" she cried.

"I do," replied the Duke, a shudder passing over his frame. "You are Gunnora Braose."

"I am," she answered. "I am, moreover, foster-mother to the Duke of Somerset—the great, the good Lord Protector, whom you, murderer and traitor, destroyed eighteen months ago. By your false practices, he was imprisoned in the tower you have just quitted; he was led forth as you are, but he was not received like you with groans and hootings, but with tears. He was taken to Westminster Hall where you sat in judgment upon him, and condemned him, and where he will this day testify against you. Tremble! perfidious Duke, for a fearful retribution is at hand. He, whom you have destroyed, sleeps in yon chapel. Ere many days have passed, you will sleep beside him."

"Peace! woman," cried Lord Clinton, interfering.

"I *will* speak," continued Gunnora, "were they the last words I had to utter. Behold!" she cried, waving a handkerchief before the Duke, "this cloth was dipped in thy victim's blood. It is now beginning to avenge itself upon thee. Thou goest to judgment—to death—to death—ha! ha!"

"Remove her!" cried Lord Clinton.

"To judgment!—to judgment!—to death!" reiterated the old woman with a wild exulting laugh, as she was dragged away.

Order being restored, the procession set forth. First, marched a band of halberdiers; then came a company of arquebussiers, armed with calivers. Immediately before the Duke walked the gentleman-jailor, who, according to a custom then observed towards those charged with high treason, carried the axe with the edge turned *from* the prisoner. On either side of Northumberland and his companions walked an officer of the guard, with a drawn sword in his hand. The rear of the cortege was brought up by two other bands of halberdiers and arquebussiers. Taking its course across the green, and passing beneath the gloomy portal of the Bloody Tower, the train entered an archway at the left of the By-ward Tower, and crossing the drawbridge, drew up at the head of the stairs leading to the river. Here several boats were in readiness to convey them to their destination. As soon as the Duke and his companions had embarked, the gentleman-jailor followed them, and stationed himself at the head of the boat, holding the gleaming instrument of death in the same position as before.

In this way, surrounded by the escort, and attended by a multitude of smaller vessels, filled with curious spectators, the prisoners were conveyed to Westminster. No sympathy was exhibited for the Duke's fallen state; but, on the contrary, the spectacle seemed to afford more satisfaction to the observers than the gorgeous pageant he had so recently devised for their entertainment. Northumberland was not insensible to this manifestation of dislike, though he made no remark upon it; but he could not avoid noticing, with a sensation of dread, one boat following in his wake, as near as the escort would permit, in which was seated an old woman, waving a bloodstained handkerchief, and invoking vengeance upon his head. Many of the wherries pressed round her to ascertain the cause of her vociferations, and as soon as it was understood who she was, other voices were added to hers. On landing at the stairs near Westminster Hall, the escort first disembarked, and then the Duke and his companions, who, preceded by the gentleman-jailor in the same order as before, were conducted to the place of trial. In the midst of this magnificent and unrivalled hall, which William Rufus, who built it, affirmed was "but a bedchamber in comparison of what he meant to make," was erected an immense scaffold, hung with black cloth. At the upper extremity was a canopy of state, embroidered with the royal escutcheon in gold; and on either side were twenty-seven seats, each emblazoned with armorial bearings woven in silver. The canopy was reserved for the Duke of

Norfolk, Lord High Steward of England; the chairs for the different peers appointed to hear the arraignment of the prisoners. At the lower extremity was the bar. On entering the hall, the Duke and his companions were conducted into a small chamber on the right, where they were detained till the arrival of the judges.

After some time, they were summoned by an usher, and following the attendant through two long files of halberdiers, the Duke slowly but firmly ascended the steps of the scaffold. On arriving at the bar, he bowed profoundly to the assemblage, and every peer, except the Duke of Norfolk, immediately arose, and acknowledged the salutation. Drawing himself up to his full height. Northumberland then glanced sternly around the tribunal. Not one of those upon whom his gaze fell but—scarcely a month ago—had trembled at his nod. Wherever be looked, his glance encountered an enemy. There sat Arundel, Pembroke, Shrewsbury, Rich, Huntingdon, Darcy,—the abettors in his treason, now his judges. On the right of the Lord High Steward sat Bishop Gardiner, in his capacity of Lord Chancellor: on the left, Lord Paget.

Northumberland's indictment having been read, he thus addressed the court:—

"My lords," he said, "I here profess my faith and obedience to the Queen's highness, whom I confess to have most grievously offended, and beyond the hope of pardon. I shall not attempt to say anything in my own defence. But I would willingly have the opinion of the court in two points."

"State them,'" said the Duke of Norfolk.

"First then," replied Northumberland, "I desire to know, whether the performance of an act by the authority of the sovereign and the council, and by warrant of the great seal of England, can be construed as treason?"

"Most undoubtedly, in your grace's case," replied the Duke of Norfolk; "inasmuch as the great seal whence your authority was derived was not the seal of the lawful Queen of the realm, but that of a usurper, and therefore no warrant." Northumberland bowed.

"I am answered," he said. "And now to the second point on which I would be resolved. Is it fitting or right," he continued, glancing fiercely around, "that those persons who are equally culpable with myself, and by whose letters and commandments I have been directed in all I have done, should be my judges, or pass upon my trial at my death?"

"Grant that others are as deeply implicated in this case as your Grace," replied the Duke of Norfolk; "yet so long as no attainder is of record against them, they are able in the law to pass upon any trial, and cannot be challenged, except at the Queen's pleasure."

"I understand," replied Northumberland, bowing coldly; "and since it is useless to urge any reasonable matter, I will at once confess the indictment, entreating your Grace to be a means of mercy for me unto the Queen."

Judgment was then pronounced.

The Duke once more addressed them.

"I beseech you, my lords," he said, "all to be humble suitors for me to the queens highness, that she grant me four requests." Most of the peers having signified their assent by a slight inclination of the head, he proceeded:—

"First, that I may have that death which noblemen have had in times past, and not the other. Secondly," and his voice faltered, "that her highness will be gracious to my children, who may hereafter do her good service, considering that they went by my commandment, who am their father, and not of their own free wills."

"Do not include me in your solicitation, my lord," interrupted the Earl of Warwick, haughtily. "I neither ask mercy, nor would accept it at the Queen's hands; and prefer death to her service. What I have done, I have done on no authority save my own, and were it to do again, I would act in like manner."

"Rash boy, you destroy yourself," cried the Duke.

"Proceed, my lord," observed the Duke of Norfolk, compassionately; "your son's indiscreet speech will not weigh with us."

"Thirdly, then," rejoined Northumberland, "I would entreat that I may have appointed to me some learned man for the instruction and quieting of my conscience. And fourthly, that her highness will send two of the council to commune with me, to whom I will declare such matters as shall be expedient for her and the state. And thus I beseech you all to pray for me."

"Doubt it not, my lord," rejoined Norfolk; "and doubt not, also, that your requests shall be duly represented to the Queen."

"Add, if it please your grace," pursued Northumberland, "a few words in favour of the unhappy Lady Jane Dudley, who, as is well known to many now sitting in judgment upon me, so far from aspiring to the crown, was by enticement and force compelled to accept it."

The Duke then retired, and the Marquess of Northampton having advanced to the bar, and pleaded to his indictment, sentence was passed on him likewise.

His example was followed by the Earl of Warwick, who heard his condemnation pronounced with a smile.

"I thank you, my lords," he said, when the sentence was uttered, "and crave only this favour of the Queen, that as the goods of those condemned to death are totally confiscated, her highness will be pleased to let my debts be paid."

Upon this, he bowed to the tribunal and withdrew.

During the trial, an immense concourse had assembled in the open space in front of the hall, waiting in breathless impatience for the result. It was not till towards evening that this was known. The great doors were then thrown open, and a troop of halberdiers came forth to clear the way for the prisoners. A deep dead silence prevailed, and every eye was bent upon the doorway. From beneath it marched the gentleman-jailor, carrying the axe with its edge *towards* the prisoners. This was enough. The mob knew they were condemned, and expressed their satisfaction by a sullen roar.

Suddenly, the voice of a woman was heard exclaiming, "See ye not the axe? See ye not the edge turned towards him? He is condemned. The slayer of the good Duke of Somerset is condemned. Shout! Shout!"

And in obedience to her commands, a loud cry was raised by the mob. Amid this clamour and rejoicing, Northumberland and his companions were conveyed to their boat, and so to the Tower.

VI.—BY WHAT MEANS THE DUKE OF NORTHUMBERLAND WAS RECONCILED TO THE CHURCH OF ROME.

Several days having elapsed since the trial, and no order made for his execution, the Duke of Northumberland, being of a sanguine temperament, began to indulge hopes of mercy. With hope, the love of life returned, and so forcibly, that he felt disposed to submit to any humiliation to purchase his safety. During this time, he was frequently visited by Bishop Gardiner, who used every persuasion to induce him to embrace the Romish faith. Northumberland, however, was inflexible on this point, but, professing the most, sincere penitence, he besought the Bishop, in his turn, to intercede with the Queen in his behalf. Gardiner readily promised compliance, in case his desires were acceded to; but as the Duke still continued firm in his refusal, he declined all interference. "Thus much I will promise," said Gardiner, in conclusion; "your grace shall have ample time for reflection, and if you place yourself under the protection of the Catholic church, no efforts shall be wanting on my part to move the Queen's compassion towards you."

That night, the officer on guard suddenly threw open the door of his cell, and admitting an old woman, closed it upon them. The Duke, who was reading at the time by the light of a small lamp set upon a table, raised his eyes and beheld Gunnora Braose.

"Why have you come hither?" he demanded. "But I need no task. You have come to gratify your vengeance with a sight of my misery. Now you are satisfied, depart."

"I am come partly with that intent, and partly with another," replied Gunnora. "Strange as it may sound, and doubtful, I am come to save you."

"To save me!" exclaimed Northumberland, starting. "How?—But—no!—no! This is mockery. Begone, accursed woman."

"It is no mockery," rejoined Gunnora. "Listen to me, Duke of Northumberland. I love vengeance well, but I love my religion better. Your machinations brought my foster-son, the Duke of Somerset, to the block, and I would willingly see you conducted thither. But there is one consideration that overcomes this feeling. It is the welfare of the Catholic church. If you become a convert to that creed, thousands will follow your example; and for this great good I would sacrifice my own private animosity. I am come hither to tell you your life will be spared, provided you abandon the Protestant faith, and publicly embrace that of Rome."

"How know you this?" demanded the Duke.

"No matter," replied Gunnora. "I am in the confidence of those, who, though relentless enemies of yours, are yet warmer friends to the Church of Rome."

"You mean Simon Renard and Gardiner!" observed Northumberland.

G minora nodded assent.

"And now my mission is ended," she said. "Your grace will do well to weigh what I have said. But your decision must be speedy, or the warrant for your execution will be signed. Once within the pale of the Catholic church, you are safe."

"If I should be induced to embrace the offer!" said the Duke. "If"—cried Gunnora, her eye suddenly kindling with vindictive fire.

"Woman," rejoined the Duke, "I distrust you. I will die in the faith I have lived."

"Be it so," she replied. "I have discharged the only weight I had upon my conscience, and can now indulge my revenge freely. Farewell! my lord. Our next meeting will be on Tower Hill."

"Hold!" cried Northumberland. "It may be as you represent, though my mind misgives me."

"It is but forswearing yourself," observed Gunnora, sarcastically. "Life is cheaply purchased at such a price."

"Wretch!" cried the Duke. "And yet I have no alternative. I accede."

"Sign this then," returned Gunnora, "and it shall be instantly conveyed to her highness."

Northumberland took the paper, and casting his eye hastily over it, found it was a petition to the Queen, praying that he might be allowed to recant his religious opinions publicly, and become reconciled to the church of Rome. "It is in the hand of Simon Renard," he observed.

"It is," replied Gunnora.

"But who will assure me if I do this, my life will be spared!"

"*I* will," answered the old woman.

"You!" cried the Duke.

"I pledge myself to it," replied Gunnora. "Your life would be spared, even if your head were upon the block. I swear to you by this cross," she added, raising the crucifix that hung at her neck, "if I have played you falsely, I will not survive you."

"Enough," replied the Duke, signing the paper.

"This shall to the Queen at once," said Gunnora, snatching it with a look of ill-disguised triumph. "To-morrow will be a proud day for our church."

And with this she quitted the cell.

The next morning, the Duke was visited by Gardiner, on whose appearance he flung himself on his knees. The bishop immediately raised him, and embraced him, expressing his delight to find that he at last saw through his errors. It was then arranged that the ceremonial of the reconciliation should take place at midnight in Saint John's Chapel in the White Tower. When the Duke's conversion was made known to the other prisoners, the Marquess of Northampton, Sir Andrew Dudley, (Northumberland's brother,) Sir Henry Gates, and Sir Thomas Palmer; they all—with the exception of the Earl of Warwick, who strongly and indignantly reprobated his father's conduct,—desired to be included in the ceremonial. The proposal being readily agreed to, priests were sent to each of them, and the remainder of the day was spent in preparation for the coming rites.

At midnight, as had been arranged, they were summoned. Preceded by two priests, one of whom bore a silver cross, and the other a large flaming wax candle, and escorted by a band of halberdiers, carrying lighted torches, the converts proceeded singly, at a slow pace, across the Green, in the direction of the White Tower. Behind them marched the three gigantic warders, Og, Gog, and Magog, each provided with a torch. It was a solemn and impressive spectacle, and as the light fell upon the assemblage collected to view it, and upon the hoary walls of the keep. The effect was peculiarly striking. Northumberland walked with his arms folded, and his head upon his breast, and looked neither to the right nor to the left.

Passing through Coalharbour Gate, the train entered an arched door-way in a structure then standing at the south-west of the White Tower. Traversing a long winding passage, they ascended a broad flight of steps, at the head of which was a gallery leading to the western entrance of the chapel. Here, before the closed door of the sacred structure, beneath the arched and vaulted roof, surrounded by priests and deacons in rich copes, one of whom carried the crosier, while others bore silver-headed staves, attired in his amice, stole, pluvial and alb, and wearing his mitre, sat Gardiner upon a faldstool. Advancing slowly towards him, the Duke fell upon his knees, and his example was imitated by the others. Gardiner then proceeded to interrogate them in a series of questions appointed by the Romish formula for the reconciliation of a heretic; and the profession of faith having been duly made, he arose, took off his mitre, and delivering it to the nearest priest, and extended his arms over the converts, and pronounced the absolution. With his right thumb he then drew the sign of the cross on the Duke's forehead, saying, "*Accipe signum crucis.*" and being answered, "*Accepi.*" he went through the same form with the rest. Once more assuming the mitre, with his left hand he took the Duke's right, and raised him, saying, "*Ingredere in ceclesiam Dei à qua incaute alerrasti. Horicsce idola. Respite omnes gravitates et super superstitiones hereticus. Cole Deum oninipotcntem et Jesum fillimm ejus, et Spiritum Sanctum.*"

Upon this, the doors of the chapel were thrown open, and the bishop led the chief proselyte towards the altar. Against the massive pillars at the east end of the chapel, reaching from their capitals to the base, was hung a thick curtain of purple velvet, edged with a deep border of gold. Relieved against this curtain stood the altar, covered with a richly-ornaincnted antipendium, sustaining a large silver crucifix, and six massive candlesticks of the same metal. At a few paces from it, on either side, were two other colossal silver candlesticks, containing enormous wax lights. On either side were grouped priests with censers, from which were diffused the most fragrant odours.

INTERIOR OF SAINT JOHN'S CHAPEL IN THE WHITE TOWER.

As Northumberland slowly accompanied the bishop along the nave, he saw, with some misgiving, the figures of Simon Renard and Gunnora emerge from behind the pillars of the northern aisle. His glance met that of Renard, and there was something in the look of the Spaniard that made him fear he was the dupe of a plot—but it was now too late to retreat. When within a few paces of the altar, the Duke again knelt down, while the bishop removed his mitre as before, and placed himself in front of him.

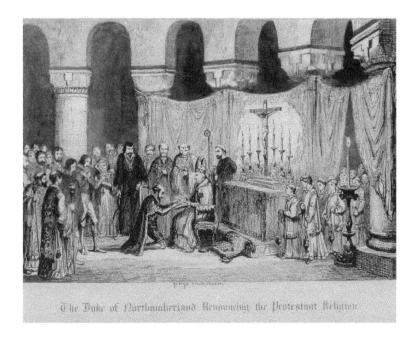

The Duke of Northumberland Renouncing the Protestant Religion

Meanwhile, the whole nave of the church, the aisles, and the circular openings of the galleries above, were filled with spectators. A wide semicircle was formed around the converts. On the right stood several priests. On the left Simon Renard had planted himself, and near to him stood Gunnora; while, on the same side against one of the pillars, was reared the gigantic frame of Magog. A significant look passed between them as Northumberland knelt before the altar. Extending his arms over the convert, Gardiner now pronounced the following exhortation:— *"Omnipotens sempiterne Deus hanc ovem tuam de faucibus lupi tua virtute subtractam paterna recipe, pietate et gregi tuo reforma piâ benignitate ne de familiâ tua damno inimicus exultet; sed de conversione et liberatione jus ecclesiam ut pia mater de filio reperto gratuletur per Christum Dominum nostrum."*

"Amen!" ejaculated Northumberland.

After uttering another prayer, the bishop resumed his mitre, and seating himself upon the faldstool, which, in the interim, had been placed by the attendants in front of the altar, again interrogated the proselyte:—

"Homo, abrenuncias Sathanas et angelos ejus?"

"Abrenuncio," replied the Duke.

"Abrenuncias etiam omnes sectas hereticæ pravitatis?" continued the bishop.

"Abrenuncio," responded the convert.

"Vis esse et vivere in imitate sancto fidei Catholico?" demanded Gardiner.

"Volo," answered the Duke.

Then again taking off his mitre, the bishop arose, and laying his right hand upon the head of the Duke, recited another prayer, concluding by signing him with the cross. This done, he resumed his mitre, and seated himself on the faldstool, while Northumberland, in a loud voice, again made a profession of his faith, and abjuration of his errors—admitting and embracing the apostolical ecclesiastical traditions, and all others—acknowledging all the observances of the Roman church——purgatory—the veneration of saints and relics—the power of indulgences—promising obedience to the Bishop of Rome,—and engaging to retain and confess the same faith entire and invio-lated to the end of his life. *"Ago talis,"* he said, in conclusion, *"cognoscens veram Catholicam et Apostolicum fidem. Anathematizo hic publiée omnem heresem, procipuè illam de qua hactenus extiti."This he affirmed by placing both hands upon the book of the holy gospels, proffered him by the bishop, exclaiming, "Sic me Deus adjunct, et hoc sancta Dei evangelia!"*

The ceremony was ended, and the proselyte arose. At this moment, he met the glance of Renard—that triumphant and diabolical glance—its expression was not to be mistaken. Northumberland shuddered, he felt that he had been betrayed.

VII.-HOW THE DUKE OF NORTHUMBERLAND WAS BEHEADED ON TOWER HILL.

Three days after Northumberland's reconciliation with the Church of Rome, the warrant for his execution was signed by Queen Mary. The fatal intelligence was brought him by the lieutenant, Sir John Gage, and though he received it with apparent calmness, his heart sank within him. he simply inquired when it was to take place, and, being informed on the following day at an early hour, he desired to be left alone. As soon as the lieutenant was gone, he abandoned himself wholly to despair, and fell into a state bordering on distraction. While he was in this frenzied state, the door of his cell opened, and the jailor introduced Gunnora Braose and a tall man muffled in the folds of an ample black cloak.

"Wretch!" cried the Duke, regarding the old woman fiercely. "You have deceived me. But the device shall avail you little. From the scaffold I will expose the snare in which I have been taken. I will proclaim my Protestant opinions; and my dying declaration will be of more profit to that faith than my recent recantation can be to yours."

"Your grace is mistaken," rejoined Gunnora. "I do not deserve your reproaches, as I will presently show. I am the bearer of a pardon to you."

"A pardon!" exclaimed Northumberland, incredulously.

"Ay, a pardon," replied the old woman. "The Queen's highness will spare your life. But it is her pleasure that her clemency be as public as your crime. You will be reprieved on the scaffold."

"Were I assured of this," cried Northumberland, eagerly grasping at the straw held out to him, "I would exhort the whole multitude to embrace the Catholic faith."

"Rest satisfied of it, then," replied Gunnora. "May I perish at the same moment as yourself if I speak not the truth!"

"Whom have we here?" inquired the Duke, turning to the muffled personage. "The headsman?"

"Your enemy," replied the individual, throwing aside his mantle, and disclosing the features of Simon Renard.

"It is but a poor revenge to insult a fallen foe," observed Northumberland, disdainfully.

"Revenge is sweet, however obtained," rejoined Renard. "I am not come, however, to insult your grace, but to confirm the truth of this old woman's statement. Opposed as I am to you, and shall ever be, I would not have you forfeit your life by a new and vile apostacy. Abjure the Catholic faith, and you will die unpitied by all. Maintain it; and at the last moment, when the arm of the executioner is raised, and the axe gleams in the air—when the eyes of thousands are fixed on it—sovereign mercy will arrest the blow."

"You awaken new hope in my bosom," rejoined the Duke.

"Be true to the faith you have embraced, and fear nothing," continued Renard. "You may yet be restored to favour, and a new career of ambition will open to you."

"Life is all I ask," replied the Duke; "and if that be spared, it shall be spent in her majesty's service. My pride is thoroughly humbled. But the language you hold to me, M. Renard, is not that of an enemy. Let me think that our differences are ended."

"They will be ended to-morrow," replied Renard, coldly.

"Be it so," replied Northumberland. "The first act of the life I receive from her highness shall be to prostrate myself at her feet: the next, to offer my thanks to you, and entreat your friendship."

"Tush," returned Renard, impatiently. "My friendship is more to be feared than my enmity."

"If there is any means of repairing the wrong I have done you," said the Duke, turning to Gunnora, "be assured I will do it."

"I am content with what your grace has done already," rejoined Gunnora, sternly. "You cannot restore the Duke of Somerset to life. You cannot give back the blood shed on the scaffold—"

"But I can atone for it," interrupted the Duke.

"Ay," cried Gunnora, her eyes flashing with vindictive fire, "you *can*—fearfully atone for it."

"Ha!" exclaimed the Duke.

"Your grace will not heed her raving," remarked Renard, seeing that Northumberland's suspicions were aroused by the old woman's manner.

"You can atone for it," continued Gunnora, aware of the impression she had produced, and eager to remove it, "by a life of penance. Pass the night in prayer for the repose of his soul, and do not omit to implore pardon for yourself, and to-morrow I will freely forgive you."

"I will do as you desire," replied the Duke.

"I must now bid your grace farewell," said Renard. "We shall meet to-morrow—on the scaffold."

"But not part there, I hope," replied Northumberland, forcing a smile.

"That will rest with your grace—not me," replied Renard, in a freezing tone.

"Will you accept this from me?" said Northumberland, detaching a jewelled ornament from his dress, and offering it to Gunnora.

"I will accept nothing from you," replied the old woman. "Yes,—one thing," she added quickly.

"It is yours," rejoined the Duke. "Name it?"

"You shall give it me to-morrow," she answered evasively.

"It is his head you require," observed Renard, with a sinister smile, as they quitted the Beauchamp Tower.

"You have guessed rightly," rejoined the old woman, savagely. "We have him in our toils," returned Renard. "He cannot escape. You ought to be content with your vengeance, Gunnora. You have destroyed both body and soul."

"I am content," she answered.

"And now to Mauger," said Renard, "to give him the necessary instructions. You should bargain with him for Northumberland's head, since you are so anxious to possess it."

"I shall not live to receive it," rejoined Gunnora.

"Not live!" he exclaimed. "What mean you?"

"No matter," she replied. "We lose time. I am anxious to finish this business. I have much to do to-night."

Taking their way across the Green, and hastening down the declivity they soon arrived at the Bloody Tower. Here they learnt from a warder that Manger, since Queen Mary's accession, had taken up his quarters in the Cradle Tower, and thither they repaired. Traversing the outer ward in the direction of the Lantern Tower, they passed through a wide portal and entered the Privy gardens, on the right of which stood the tower in question.

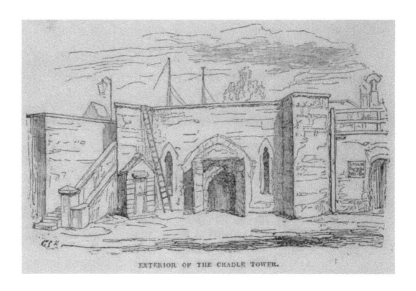

EXTERIOR OF THE CRADLE TOWER.

As they drew near, they heard the shrill sound produced by the sharpening of some steel instrument. Smiling significantly at Gunnora, Renard instead of opening the door proceeded to a narrow loop-hole, and looked in. He beheld a savage-looking individual seated on a bench near a grindstone. He had an axe in one hand, which he had just been sharpening, and was trying its edge with his thumb. His fierce blood-shot eyes, peering from beneath his bent and bushy brows, were fixed upon the weapon. His dress consisted of a doublet of red serge with tight black sleeves, and hose of the same colour. His brow was lowering and wrinkled—the summit of his head perfectly bald, but the sides were garnished with long black locks, which together with his immense grizzled moustaches, bristling like the whiskers of a cat-a-mountain, and ragged beard, imparted a wild and forbidding look to his physiognomy. Near him rested a square, solid piece of wood, hollowed out on either side to admit the shoulder and head of the person laid upon it. This was the block. Had Renard not known whom he beheld, instinct would have told him it was the headsman.

Manger sharpening his Axe.

Apparently satisfied with the sharpness of the implement, Manger was about to lay it aside, when the door opened, and Renard and Gunnora entered the chamber. The executioner rose to receive them. He had received a wound in his left leg which had crippled the limb, and he got up with difficulty.

"Do not disturb yourself," said Renard. "My business will be despatched in a few seconds. You are preparing I see for the execution to-morrow. What I have to say relates to it. The moment the Duke's head is laid upon this block," he added, pointing to it, "strike. Give him not a moment's pause. Do you hear?"

"I do," replied Mauger. "But I must have some warrant?"

"Be this your warrant," replied Renard, flinging him a heavy purse. "If you require further authority, you shall have it under the Queen's own hand."

"I require nothing further, worshipful sir," replied Mauger, smiling grimly. "Ere the neck has rested one second upon the block, the head shall be off."

"I have also a boon to offer, and an injunction to give," said Gunnora taking off the ring given her by the unfortunate Lady Jane, and presenting it to him.

"Your gift is the richer of the two, or I am mistaken, good mistress," said Mauger, regarding the glittering gem with greedy eyes. "What am I to do for it? I cannot behead him twice."

"I shall stand in front of the scaffold to-morrow," replied Gunnora, "in some conspicuous place where you will easily discern me. Before you deal the fatal blow, make a sign to me—thus—do you understand?"

"Perfectly," replied the headsman. "I will not fail you."

Upon this, Renard and the old woman quitted the Cradle Tower, and walked together as far as the outer ward, where each took a separate course.

The last night of his existence was passed by the Duke of Northumberland in a most miserable manner. Alternately buoyed up by hope, and depressed by fear, he could neither calm his agitation, nor decide upon any line of conduct. Allowed, as a matter of indulgence, to remain within the large room, he occupied himself in putting the finishing touches to a carving on the wall, which he had commenced on his first imprisonment, and had wrought at at intervals. This curious sculpture may still be seen on the right hand of the fireplace of the mess-room in the Beauchamp Tower, and contains his cognizance, a bear and lion supporting a ragged staff surrounded by a border of roses., acorns and flowers intermingled with foliage.

NORTHUMBERLAND'S INSCRIPTION IN THE BEAUCHAMP TOWER.

Northumberland was employed upon the third line of the quatrain below his name, which remains unfinished to the present day, when he was interrupted by the entrance of a priest, sent to him by Gardiner. The holy man found him in no very favourable frame of mind, but succeeded after some time in awakening him to a due sense of his awful situation. The Duke then made a full confession of his guilt, and received his shrift. At daybreak, the priest departed, with a promise to attend him to the place of execution.

Much tranquillised, the Duke now prepared himself for his last trial. He pondered over what he should say on the scaffold, and nerved himself to meet his fate, whatever it might be. The Duke of Warwick was then introduced to him to receive his blessing, and to take an everlasting farewell. After he had received the Duke's embrace, the Earl observed, "Would I could change places with you, father. I would say that on the scaffold which would shake the bigot Mary on the throne."

The Duke then partook of some refreshment, and wrapped himself in a loose robe of grain-coloured damask. At eight o'clock, the Sheriffs of London arrived at the Bulwark Gate, and demanded the body of the prisoner. Upon this, the Lieutenant, accompanied by four warders, proceeded to the Beauchamp Tower, and informed the Duke that all was in readiness.

"I am ready, too," replied Northumberland, once more embracing his son, whose firmness did not desert him at this trying juncture. And he followed the Lieutenant to the Green. Here they found the priest, and a band of halberdiers waiting to escort him to the scaffold. Among the by-standers stood Simon Renard, who immediately advanced towards him.

"How fares your grace!" he asked.

"Well enough, sir, I thank you," answered the Duke, bowing. "I shall be better anon."

The train then set forward, passing through lines of spectators, until it reached the Middle Tower, where it halted, to allow the Lieutenant to deliver the prisoner to the Sheriffs and their officers. This ceremony over, it again set forward, and passed through the Bulwark Gate.

Prepared as the Duke was for some extraordinary sight, he was yet taken completely by surprise. The whole area of Tower Hill seemed literally paved with human heads. A line of scaffoldings was erected on the brink of the moat, and every seat in them was occupied. Never before had so vast an assemblage been collected in the same place. The whole of the western ramparts of the fortress—the roof and battlements of the White Tower—every point from which a view of the spectacle could be obtained, was thronged. On the Duke's appearance, a murmur of satisfaction pervaded the immense host, and he then felt that even if the Queen's pardon should arrive, his personal safety was more than questionable.

Preceded by a band of arquebussiers, armed with calivers, and attended by the sheriffs, the priest, and Simon Renard, Northumberland marched slowly forward. At length, he reached the scaffold. It was surrounded by seats, set aside for persons of distinction; and among its occupants were many of his former friends and allies. Avoiding their gaze, the Duke mounted the scaffold with a firm foot; but the sight of the vast concourse from this elevated point almost unmanned him. As he looked around, another murmur arose, and the mob undulated like the ocean. Near the block stood Manger, leaning on his axe; his features concealed by a hideous black mask. On the Duke's appearance, he fell on his knees, and, according to custom, demanded forgiveness, which was granted. Throwing aside his robe, the Duke then advanced to the side of the scaffold, and leaning over the eastern rail, thus addressed the assemblage:

"Good people. I am come hither this day to die, as ye know. Indeed, I confess to you all that I have been an evil liver, and have done wickedly all the days of my life; and, of all, most against the Queen's highness, of whom I here openly ask forgiveness," and he reverentially bent the knee. "But I alone am not the original doer thereof, I assure you, for there were some others who procured the same. But I will not name them, for I will now hurt no man. And the chief occasion that I have erred from the Catholic faith and true doctrine of Christ, has been through false and seditious preachers. The doctrine, I mean, which has continued through all Christendom since Christ. For, good people, there is, and hath been ever since Christ, one Catholic church; which church hath continued from him to his disciples in one unity and concord, and so hath always continued from time to time until this day, and yet doth throughout all Christendom, ourselves alone excepted. Of this church I openly profess myself to be one, and do steadfastly believe therein. I speak unfeignedly from the bottom of my heart. And I beseech you all bear witness that I die therein. Moreover, I do think, if I had had this belief sooner, I never should have come to this pass: wherefore I exhort you all, good people, take example of me, and forsake this new doctrine betimes. Defer it not long, lest God plague you as he hath me, who now suffer this vile death most deservedly."

Concluding by desiring the prayers of the assemblage, he returned slowly, and fixing an inquiring look upon Renard, who was standing with his arms folded upon his breast, near the block, said in a low tone, "It comes not."

"It is not yet time," replied Renard.

The Duke was about to kneel down, when he perceived a stir amid the mob in front of the scaffold, occasioned by some one waving a handkerchief to him. Thinking it was the signal of a pardon, he paused. But he was speedily undeceived. A second glance showed him that the handkerchief was waved by Gunnora, and was spotted with blood.

Casting one glance of the bitterest anguish at Renard, he then prostrated himself, and the executioner at the same moment raised his hand. As soon as the Duke had disposed himself upon the block, the axe flashed like a gleam of lightning in the sunshine,—descended,—and the head was severed from the trunk.

Seizing it with his left hand, Mauger held it aloft, almost before the eyes were closed, crying out to the assemblage, in a loud voice, "Behold the head of a traitor!"

Amid the murmur produced by the released respiration of the multitude, a loud shriek was heard, and a cry followed that an old woman had suddenly expired. The report was true. It was Gunnora Braose.

Execution of the Duke of Northumberland upon Tower Hill

WEST VIEW OF THE BEAUCHAMP TOWER.

VIII.—OF QUEEN MARY'S ATTACHMENT TO COURTENAY.

Mary still continued to hold her court within the Tower. Various reasons were assigned for this choice of residence; but her real motive was that her plans for the restoration of the Catholic religion could be more securely concerted within the walls of the fortress than elsewhere. Simon Renard, who had become her confidential adviser, and through whom she carried on an active correspondence with her cousin, the Emperor Charles the Fifth, could here visit her unobserved. Here, also, she secretly received the envoy of Pope Julius the Third, Francisco Commendone (afterwards the celebrated Cardinal of that name,) and detained him until after the Duke of Northumberland's execution, that he might convey intelligence of the event, and of the effect produced by it upon the populace, to the Pontiff. To Commendone she gave the strongest assurances of her attachment to the Church of Rome, and of her fixed determination to restore its worship. But at the same time she declared that the change must be gradual, and that any undue precipitation would be fatal. In this opinion both Gardiner and Renard, who were admitted to the conference, concurred. And satisfied with their representations, the envoy departed, overjoyed at the success of his mission.

Other and gentler thoughts, however, than those connected with her government, occupied the bosom of the queen. We have already spoken of the impression produced upon her at their first interview on the Tower-Green, by the striking figure and noble features of Edward Courtenay, whom she on that occasion created Earl of Devonshire, and of the speculations it gave rise to among the by-standers. The interest she then felt had been subsequently strengthened. And it appeared certain to all who had any means of observation, that if she selected a husband, her choice would fall upon Courtenay.

The progress of her attachment was jealously watched by Renard, who having other designs in view, secretly opposed it. But aware that Mary, like many of her sex, was possessed of a spirit, which would be apt, if thwarted, to run into the opposite extreme, he was obliged to proceed with the utmost caution. He had, moreover, a strong party against him. From the moment it became evident that the Queen regarded the Earl of Devonshire with the eyes of affection, all were eager to pay court to him. Among his warmest supporters were Gardiner and De Noailles; the latter being mainly influenced in his conduct by distrust of the Court of Spain. Renard, therefore, stood alone. But though everything appeared against him, he did not despair of success. Placing reliance upon Mary's jealous and suspicious character, he felt certain of accomplishing his purpose. Accordingly, he affected to approve her choice; and with the view of carrying out his scheme more effectually, took care to ingratiate himself with Courtenay.

Inexperienced as the latter was in the arts of a court, being then only twenty-one, and having passed fourteen years of his life in close captivity in the Tower, he was easily duped by the wily ambassador; and though repeatedly warned against him by De Noailles, who saw through Renard's design, he disregarded the caution. Satisfied of the Queen's favourable disposition towards him, which was evinced by the most marked attention on her part, this young nobleman conceived himself wholly beyond the reach of rivalry; and trusting to his personal advantages, and the hold he had obtained over the affections of his royal mistress, he gave himself little concern about an opposition which he regarded as futile. He looked upon himself as certain of the Queen's hand; and but for his own imprudence, he would have been actually possessed of it.

Mary's meditated alliance was agreeable to all parties, except, as just intimated, that of Spain. Already nearly related to the crown by his descent from Edward the Fourth, no objection could be raised against her favourite on the score of rank; while his frank and conciliating manner, combined with his rare endowments of mind and person, won him universal regard. Doctor Thomas Wilson, in the funeral oration pronounced over Courtenay at Padua in 1556, states, that during his long imprisonment in the Tower, "he wholly devoted himself to study, and that neither the *augustia loci, nec solitudo, nec amissio libertatis, ilium à literis avocarent*; that he made such progress in philosophy, that no nobleman was equal to him in it; that he also explored the *mysteria naturae*; that he entered into the *mathematicorum labyrintha*; that he was so fond of painting, that he could easily and laudably make any one's portrait on a *tabula*; that he was equally attached to music, and had attained in it *absolutam perfectionem*; and that to these acquisitions he added the Spanish, French, and Italian languages. In manners he was grave without pride; pleasant without levity; prudent in speech; cautious in answering; modest in disputing; never boasting of himself, nor excluding others; and though familiar with many, yet intimately known to few." Allowing for the drawbacks which must necessarily be made from such an *éloge*, enough will remain to prove that his accomplishments were of no common order.

On the onset of his career, however, Courtenay was assailed by temptations which it required more experience of the world to resist. Strictly confined from his earliest youth, it may be conceived that when first exposed to female fascination, his heart was speedily melted. Hitherto, he had only read of beauty. He now felt its full force, and placed no bounds to the admiration which the charms of the dames of honour excited within his breast. It was upon this point of his character, that Renard justly grounded his hopes of alienating the Queen's affections. Encouraging his new-born licentiousness, he took care that none of his gallantries should fail to reach the ears of his royal mistress. Though of a staid and severe character, Mary was not indisposed to make allowances for one so utterly inexperienced as Courtenay; and her first direction to Renard was to check him. So far from doing this, the artful ambassador incited him to further irregularities, and contrived to place new objects in his way. In vain De Noailles remonstrated, entreating him at least to be more guarded in his conduct. In vain Gardiner sternly rebuked him. He turned a deaf ear alike to remonstrance and reproof; and hurried on by the unbridled impetuosity of youth, passed from one excess to another. Renard witnessed his conduct with secret satisfaction; but he was not prepared for the calmness with which the Queen viewed it. She was greatly displeased, yet as her lover still seemed passionately devoted to her, she looked upon his conduct as resulting from the circumstances of his previous life, and trusting he would soon open his eyes to its folly, was content to pardon it.

Renard then saw that he must have recourse to stronger measures. As Mary's jealousy was not to be easily aroused, he resolved to bring a more formidable rival into the held. There was one ready made to his hand. It was the Princess Elizabeth. On no one point was the Queen's vanity more easily touched than by any reference to the superior charms of her sister. Any compliment paid the latter she construed into a slight to herself; and she watched with an uneasy glance the effect produced by her in public. So sensible was Elizabeth of the Queen's foible, that she kept in the back ground as much as possible. Unaware of the mortification he inflicted upon his royal mistress, and of the injury he did himself, Courtenay often praised the Princess's beauty in terms so rapturous as to call a blush into her cheek, while the blood was driven from that of Mary. So undisguised was his admiration, that the Queen resolved to remove the object of it from her court; and would have done so, but for the artful management of Renard, who felt that such a step would ruin his plans.

Long before Courtenay had noticed it, the subtle ambassador, well skilled in woman's feelings, ascertained the state of Elizabeth's heart, and saw that she was not proof against the captivating manners and personal graces of the handsome young nobleman. It was not difficult for one possessed of so many opportunities as himself to heighten this feeling into a passion; and before long he had the satisfaction to find that the princess was deeply enamoured of her sister's suitor. Nor was Courtenay less easily enthralled. Apprised of his conquest by Renard, instead of resisting it, he at once surrendered himself to the snare. Again De Noailles, who saw his dangerous position, came to his aid. Again Gardiner rebuked him more severely than before. He derided their remonstrances; and heedless of the changing manner of the Queen— heedless also of the peril to which he exposed the princess, he scarcely attempted to disguise his passion, or to maintain the semblance of love for his royal mistress. Consumed by jealousy, Mary meditated some blow which should satisfy her outraged feelings; while Renard only waited a favourable opportunity to bring matters to a crisis.

Affairs being in this state, it chanced one day that Courtenay received a summons to the Queen's presence, and instantly repairing thither, he found her alone. His reception was so cold, that he was at no loss to understand she was deeply offended; and he would have thrown himself at her feet, if she had not prevented him by impatiently waving her hand.

"I have sent for you, my lord," she said, "for the last time——."

"For the last time, my gracious mistress!" exclaimed Courtenay.

"Do not interrupt me," rejoined Mary, severely. "I have sent for you to tell you that whatever were the feelings I once entertained for you, they are now entirely changed. I will not remind you of the favours I have shown you—of the honours I have bestowed on you—or of the greater honours I intended you. I will simply tell you that your ingratitude equals your perfidy; and that I banish you henceforth from my presence."

"How have I offended your highness?" demanded Courtenay, panic-stricken.

"*How?*" cried Mary, fiercely—her eyes kindling, and her countenance assuming the terrible expression she inherited from her father. "Do you affect ignorance of the cause? I have overlooked your indiscretions, though I have not been ignorant of them, imputing them to youth and inexperience. I have overlooked them, I say, because I thought I discovered amid all this vice and folly the elements of a noble nature—and because," and her voice faltered—"I persuaded myself that you loved me."

"Have you no faith in my adjurations of attachment?" cried Courtenay, prostrating himself, and endeavouring to take her hand.

"None," rejoined the queen, withdrawing her hand; "none whatever. Arise, my lord, and do not further degrade yourself. You may love the queen, but you do not love the woman.—You may prize my throne, but you do not prize me."

"You wrong me, gracious madam. On my soul you do," rejoined Courtenay. "I may have trifled with others, but I have given my heart wholly to you."

"It is false!" cried Mary, furiously. "You love the princess, my sister."

Courtenay turned very pale. But he instantly recovered himself.

"Your highness is mistaken," he answered.

"What!" cried the queen, her anger increasing each moment. "Dare you persist in the denial of your falsehood? Dare you tell me to my face that you have not breathed words of passion to her? Dare you assert that you have not lamented your engagement to me? Dare you say this?"

"I dare, madam."

"Then your own words shall give you the lie, traitor," replied the queen. "Here is your letter to her," she added, producing a paper, "wherein you tell her so."

"Confusion!" uttered Courtenay, "Renard has betrayed me."

"Is this letter your writing?" demanded the queen.

"I will not prevaricate, madam," replied Courtenay; "it is."

"And in the face of this you declare you have not deceived me?"

"I *have* deceived you, gracious madam," replied Courtenay. "But I have never ceased to love you."

"My lord!—my lord!" exclaimed Mary, in a menacing tone. "Beware how you attempt to deceive me further, or as God shall judge me, you shall find that the daughter of Henry the Eighth is not to be offended with impunity."

"I know you are terrible in anger, gracious madam," replied Courtenay; "but you are also just. Judge me—condemn me, if you please, but hear me: he who gave you that letter,—Simon Renard,—counselled me to write it."

"Ha!" exclaimed the queen.

"I have been guilty of folly—madness—" rejoined Courtenay—"but not the black perfidy your highness imagines. Dismiss me from your presence—send me into exile—I deserve any punishment—but do not believe that I have ceased to love you."

"I know not what *you* term love, my lord," replied Mary; "but I have no idea of sharing the affection of any man with another. Grant, however, that you speak the truth, why have you addressed this passionate epistle to the Princess Elizabeth?"

"I have already said I was deceived," replied Courtenay. "I cannot excuse my conduct—though I lament it."

"Are you sincere?" said Mary, who began to be softened by her lover's apparent penitence.

"By what oath shall I confirm my truth?" he replied, fervently.

"I will test it more surely," rejoined the queen, as if struck by a sudden idea.

"In any way your highness thinks proper," returned Courtenay.

"Summon the Princess Elizabeth to our presence instantly," said Mary, striking a small bell, the sound of which brought an usher before her.

"The Princess Elizabeth!" exclaimed Courtenay.

"Ay, the Princess," repeated the queen. "I will confront you with her. Bid the lord chancellor and the ambassadors of Spain and France attend us," she continued to the usher.

"I know not what your highness intends," said Courtenay, as the attendant departed. "But I will die rather than do aught to prejudice the princess."

"I doubt it not, my lord," rejoined Mary, bitterly. "But though I cannot punish the perfidy of a lover, I can the disobedience of a subject. If you refuse to obey my commands, you will take the consequences."

Courtenay bit his lips to repress the answer that rose to them.

In a few minutes, the usher returned and announced the Princess Elizabeth, as well as Gardiner, Renard, and De Noailles. Instantly perceiving how matters stood, the imperial ambassador deemed his own triumph complete, and Courtenay's disgrace certain.

"My lord," said Mary, addressing Gardiner, "it is no secret to you, neither to you, M. Renard, nor to you, M. De Noailles—that of all those proposed to me in marriage—the Princes of Spain and Portugal, the King of the Romans, Cardinal Pole, and others—I have preferred this man, whom I myself have raised to the rank he now holds, and enriched with the estates he enjoys."

"We know it, gracious Madam," replied Gardiner, alarmed at the ominous commencement, "and we think your highness has made a happy choice, and one most acceptable to your subjects. Do we not, M. Renard?"

The ambassador bowed, but said nothing.

"The alliance is in all respects agreeable to my sovereign, Henry the Second of France," observed De Noailles.

"What then if I inform you," pursued Mary, "that the Earl of Devonshire has rejected my proposal? What if he has broken his oath of fidelity? What if he has cast aside the crown offered him, and smitten by the charms of a youthful beauty, abandoned the Queen, who has stooped to raise him to her throne!"

"Impossible!" exclaimed Gardiner and De Noailles.

"You are mistaken," rejoined Mary, sternly. "You shall hear him avow his perfidy with his own lips."

"When I *do* hear it," replied De Noailles, looking steadily at Courtenay, "I will believe it. But I cannot think him capable of such madness."

"Nor I," said Gardiner, glancing significantly from beneath his bent brows.

Elizabeth, who on the commencement of the Queen's address had turned very pale, could with difficulty maintain her composure. Her agitation did not escape the notice of Mary, whose jealousy was increased by the sight.

"What if I tell you," she continued, "that this false earl has transferred his affections to our sister?"

"Your highness!" exclaimed Elizabeth.

"Peace!" cried the Queen, fiercely. "And she, well knowing his engagement to ourself, has dared to encourage his suit."

"Whoever told your majesty this, lied in his throat," cried Courtenay. "I own myself guilty, but the Princess Elizabeth is no partner to my folly."

"You do well to shield her, my lord," retorted Mary. "But you cannot deceive me. She is equally culpable."

"Nay, more so, if it comes to this," interposed Elizabeth, whose spirit, which was quite equal to her sisters, was aroused. "If I had repressed my admiration for the Earl of Devonshire, he would have made no advances to me. I am the most to blame in this matter."

"Not so;" replied Courtenay. "Let my folly and presumption be visited on my own head. I pray your highness to pass sentence on me at once. But do not let the Princess suffer for my fault."

"So, so!" exclaimed Mary, with a bitter laugh, "I have brought you to your confessions at last. If I had before doubted your love for each other, your present conduct would have convinced me of it. You shall have your request, my lord," she added, turning to Courtenay. "I *will* pass sentence upon you."

"Hold, madam," cried Gardiner. "Before the sentence is passed and irrevocable, reflect—if only for one moment. You are a great queen, and the daughter of a great king. But the rashness of one moment may annihilate all your future peace, destroy the hopes of your people, and the prosperity of your reign. The conduct of the Earl of Devonshire is unpardonable, I allow. But for your own sake—for the sake of your kingdom—not for his—I beseech you to overlook it. That he loves you, I am assured."

"Let him declare as much," said Renard.

"Hear me, then," replied Courtenay, throwing himself at the Queen's feet. "I bitterly repent my rashness; and though I can never hope to be restored to the place I once held in your Majesty's affections, I shall never cease to reproach myself—never cease to love you."

Mary was visibly moved.

"If I thought you sincere?" she said.

"I will answer for his sincerity," said Gardiner.

"And I," added De Noailles. "She relents," he continued in a whisper to Courtenay. "Improve the advantage you have gained."

"Grant me an instant's private audience with your Majesty," implored Courtenay; "and I feel certain I can remove all your doubts."

"No, my lord," rejoined Mary. "As our rupture has been public, our reconciliation (if it takes place,) shall be public, also."

"It must never take place," remarked Renard, in an under tone.

"Peace, sir," said the Queen, aloud. "As far as our government is concerned, we are content to follow your counsel. But in matters of the heart we shall follow its dictates alone."

"Your Majesty is in the right," observed Gardiner.

"Declare, my lord," pursued Mary, addressing Courtenay, "in the presence of these gentlemen, in that of our sister—*rival* we ought to say,—that you have deceived her, and, though your conduct may have misled her,—have never swerved from your devotion to ourself."

While the Queen pronounced these words, Renard's keen glance wandered from Courtenay to Elizabeth. The latter was violently agitated, and seemed to await the Earl's answer as if her fate hung upon it.

"Do you assert this, my lord?" demanded Mary.

"Hesitate, and you are lost, and so is the Princess," whispered De Noailles.

Before Courtenay could reply, Elizabeth fainted and would have fallen, if Renard had not flown to her assistance.

"Summon our maids of honour, and let her be instantly cared for," said Mary, with a look of ill-disguised satisfaction. "My lord," she added to Courtenay, "you are forgiven."

The Earl hastily, and with some confusion, expressed his thanks, while, in obedience to the Queen's mandate, Elizabeth was removed.

"And now, my lord," said Mary to him, "I must pass from my own affairs to those of my kingdom. I will not detain you further—nor you, M. De Noailles.

But I must crave your attendance, my lord, for a few minutes," she added, turning to Gardiner, "and yours, M. Renard."

"Your highness may always command my best counsel," replied the latter, in a slightly sarcastic tone—"provided you will act upon it."

"Farewell, my lord," said Mary, extending her hand to Courtenay, which he pressed to his lips. "I shall walk upon the Tower Green in an hour, and shall expect you there."

"I will attend your Majesty," replied Courtenay. And accompanied by De Noailles, he quitted the chamber.

"You have had a narrow escape, my lord," remarked the French Ambassador, as they traversed the long gallery together.

"So narrow that I thought I had lost all chance of the crown," replied Courtenay. "It is the work of that perfidious Simon Renard. But if I live an hour, I will requite him."

"You are the victor, my lord," returned De Noailles. "Maintain your present position, and you may defy his utmost malice."

"Tarry with me a moment, M. De Noailles," said Courtenay, "and you shall see how I will avenge myself upon him."

"Prudence, my good lord—prudence," replied De Noailles. "Your rashness has already put you once in his power. Do not let it do so a second time."

"I will punish his treachery, if it costs me my life," replied Courtenay.

IX.—OF THE DUEL BETWEEN COURTENAY AND SIMON RENARD; AND HOW IT WAS INTERRUPTED.

M eanwhile, a long discussion was carried on between Mary and her councillors, as to the best means of effecting the entire restoration of the Romish religion.

"I have a letter from Cardinal Pole," observed the Queen, "wherein his Eminence urges me to adopt no half measures."

"It will not be safe to do so as matters now stand, gracious madam," replied Gardiner. "You must proceed cautiously. The noxious weed, heresy, has taken too deep a root in this country to be forcibly extirpated. I need not remind you of the murmurs that followed the celebration of mass in the chapel in the White Tower, for the repose of the King your brothers soul— of Cranmer's vehement opposition—of the lord mayor's remonstrance, because mass was sung in another chapel in the city—of the riot for a similar cause in Smithfield—of the dagger thrown at Doctor Bourne, when he preached at Saint Paul's Cross, and inveighed against the deprivation of our prelates during the late reign. Your Majesty did wisely to declare, at my suggestion, that although your conscience is stayed in matters of religion, yet you meant not to compel and constrain other men's consciences. Abide by this declaration a little longer. The two chief opponents of our religion, Ridley and Latimer, are already prisoners in the fortress, and Cranmer will be speedily brought hither."

"So speedily, my lord, that he shall be lodged within it today," replied Mary. "The order is already signed for his committal on a charge of high treason for counselling our disinheritance, and aiding the Duke of Northumberland with horse and men against us in the revolt of the Lady Jane Grey."

"When will your highness have him arraigned?" asked Gardiner.

"After our coronation," replied Mary; "when Lady Jane Grey and her husband shall also be tried."

"Suffolk is already liberated," remarked Renard; "and yet he was more deeply implicated than Cranmer."

"True," replied Mary; "but he is not so dangerous."

"The counsel of my master, the emperor," rejoined Renard, "as I have more than once stated to your Highness, is to spare none of the rebels—above all, the Lady Jane Grey, who, though she may have been the instrument of others, is yet in the eyes of the people the principal offender."

"Poor Lady Jane!" exclaimed Mary, in a compassionate tone. "She is very young—very beautiful. I would rather reconcile her to our church than doom her to the block."

"I do not despair of being able to accomplish her conversion," said Gardiner, "though she is an obstinate heretic. I have appointed to-morrow for a conference with her on the subject of her religion, and I trust to be able to convince her of her errors."

"With your lordship's permission, I will attend the conference," said Renard.

"By all means," replied Gardiner. "It will take place in the Beauchamp Tower. Her husband, Lord Guilford Dudley, has become a proselyte, and they will be both present at the disputation."

"I leave the care of her soul in your hands, my lord," replied Mary. "And now I must to my own devotions."

So saying, she dismissed them, and proceeded to an oratory, where she was joined by her confessor, Feckenham.

On issuing from the audience-chamber, Renard perceived De Noailles and Courtenay pacing the gallery.

"I have waited for you, sir," said the latter, advancing to meet him.

"I am sorry to have detained your lordship so long," replied Renard.

"Apologies are needless," rejoined Courtenay. "M. Renard, you are a double-faced villain."

"Rail on my lord, and welcome," replied Renard, contemptuously. "Your ill-humour has no effect on me!"

"Coward! will not that move you?" cried Courtenay, taking off his glove, and striking him with it in the face.

"Ha!" exclaimed Renard fiercely, and half-unsheathing his sword. "Follow me, my lord, and you shall find me as prompt to avenge an insult as you can be to offer one."

"My lord," interposed De Noailles, "and you, M. Renard, I warn you before you proceed further in this quarrel, that it will deeply offend the queen."

"It was not my seeking," replied Renard, sternly. "But since it is forced upon me, I will not be stayed. As his lordship has found no difficulty in duping her majesty with a feigned passion, so, if he survives, he may readily make out his case by an equally false statement that I was the aggressor."

"Insolent!" cried Courtenay. "Fool that I was to place any faith in one in whom the whole perfidy of his country seems concentred. Follow me, and quickly, or I will repeat the blow—unless," he added with bitter scorn, "like your own arrogant but cowardly nation you prefer avenging it by assassination."

"The cowardice will be yours, my lord," rejoined Renard, haughtily, "if you attempt to repeat the blow—nay, if you tarry here longer, I shall think you desire to attract the attention of some of her majesty's attendants, and by causing us to be arrested, contrive to escape my vengeance."

"Trust me, sir, I have no such intention," replied Courtenay. "An Englishman never deals a blow without allowing his adversary to return it. M. De Noailles, I request your attendance at the duel. It will be a mortal combat—for I will neither give mercy nor receive it from this perfidious villain."

"Pardon me, my lord, if I refuse your request," replied De Noailles. "I pledge my word that I will not interrupt you, nor cause you to be interrupted during the adjustment of your differences. But I will be no party to the duel."

"As you please," replied Courtenay. "Come then, sir," he added, turning to Renard, "and let the recollection of the insult I have offered you be fresh in your memory."

"M. De Noailles," said Renard, "I take you to witness before I depart, that I have not sought this quarrel. Whatever ensues, you will avouch the truth."

"Undoubtedly," replied De Noailles. "Whither are you going?" he demanded.

"To the palace-garden," replied Courtenay. "It is the only place in the Tower, where we can be free from interruption. Beneath the trees we shall be unobserved."

"Lead on then, my lord," cried Renard, impatiently. "The affair ought to have been arranged by this time."

Hastily quitting the corridor, they descended the grand staircase, and traversing with rapid steps a long suite of apartments, passed through a small door opening from the range of building called the Queen's gallery, upon the privy garden. At the western angle of this garden stood a grove of trees, and thinking themselves unobserved they hastened towards it.

It chanced however at this moment that Xit was passing along one of the walks, and struck by their furious looks he immediately conjectured their errand, and being, as has before been shown, of an inquisitive turn, determined to watch them, and with this view struck into a shrubbery, which effectually screened him from observation.

On reaching the grove, Renard instantly divested himself of his cloak, and drawing his rapier and dagger, placed himself in an attitude of defence.

Courtenay did not remove his mantle, and therefore he was in readiness before his adversary. The preliminary forms always observed by the combatants of the period, being gone through, the conflict commenced with great fury on the side of Courtenay, and with equal animosity, but more deliberation, on that of Renard. As the latter was the most perfect swordsman of his time, he felt little doubt as to the result of the combat—but still the fury of the Earl was so irresistible that he broke through his surest wards. In one of these furious passes Renard received a slight wound in the arm, and roused by the pain, he forgot his cautious system, and returned Courtenay's thrusts with others equally desperate.

Feeling that he was no match for his antagonist, who was evidently his superior both in force and skill, the Earl now determined to bring the combat to a close, before his strength should be further exhausted. Collecting all his energies, he dashed upon Renard with such impetuosity, that the latter was compelled to retreat, and his foot catching against the root of a tree, he fell, and lay at the mercy of his antagonist.

"Strike!" he cried. "I will never yield."

"No," replied Courtenay. "I will not take this advantage. Arise, and renew the combat."

"Your courtesy is like your attachment, misplaced, my lord," replied Renard, springing to his feet, and preparing to attack him. "Look to yourself."

The combat recommenced with fresh fury, and must have speedily terminated fatally, if a sudden interruption had not occurred. Alarmed by the deadly nature of the strife, and thinking he should gain credit with the queen if he prevented any accident to her favourite, Xit no sooner beheld the swords drawn, than he ran off as swiftly as he could to the garden-gate, near the Lanthorn Tower, where he know Og was stationed. The giant did not require to be bid twice to accompany him; but grasping his immense halbert, hurried in the direction of the fight, and reached the grove just as it had recommenced.

The combatants were so occupied with each other, and so blinded with rage, that they did not hear his approach. Og, however, soon made them sensible of his presence. Bidding them in a voice of thunder lay down their arms, and finding himself wholly disregarded, he rushed between them, and seizing each by the doublet, hurled them forcibly backwards—swearing lustily that if either advanced another footstep, he would fell him to the ground with his partizan. By this time Xit, who had come up, drew his sword, and seconded the giant's threat, adding with his usual coxcombical dignity, "My lords, I command you, in the Queen's name, to deliver up your weapons to me."

Upon this, he took off his cap, and strutting up to Courtenay, demanded his sword.

"What if I refuse it, sirrah?" said the earl, who in spite of his indignation, could scarcely help laughing at the dwarf's assurance.

"Your lordship, I am assured, will not compel me to enforce its delivery," replied Xit.

"I will not," replied Courtenay, delivering the weapon to him.

"I shall not fail to report your magnanimity to my royal mistress," returned Xit. "Now yours, worshipful sir," he added, to Renard.

"Take it," replied the ambassador, flinging his rapier on the ground. "It is fit that an affair so ridiculously begun, should have such a ridiculous termination."

"It is not ended, sir," rejoined Courtenay.

"You will note that, Magog," interposed Xit. "His lordship says it is not ended. Her Majesty must hear of this. I take upon myself to place you both in arrest. Attach their persons, Magog."

"This insolence shall not go unpunished," cried Courtenay, angrily.

"Heed him not, Magog," whispered Xit. "I am sure her highness will approve our conduct. At all events, I take the responsibility of the arrest upon myself—though I promise thee, if there is any reward, thou shalt share it. I arrived at a critical minute for your lordship," he added, in an under tone to Courtenay. "Your adversary's blade was within an inch of your breast."

"Peace, knave," cried Courtenay.

"Bring them along, Magog," said Xit, "while I run to the palace to apprise her Majesty of the occurrence, and ascertain her pleasure concerning them.'

"Hold!" exclaimed Courtenay. "Take this purse, and keep silence on the subject."

"No, my lord," replied Xit, with an offended look, "I am above a bribe. Had your lordship—but no matter. Magog, you will answer for their peaceable conduct. I am off to the palace."

And he hurried away, while the giant followed at a slow pace with Courtenay and Renard.

X.—OF THE CONFERENCE HELD BETWEEN BISHOP GARDINER AND LADY JANE GREY IN THE BEAUCHAMP TOWER.

During all this time, Jane was kept a close prisoner in the Brick Tower, and neither allowed to hold any intercourse with her husband, nor to correspond with him. Heart-breaking as the deprivation was to her in the first instance, she became in some degree reconciled to it, on learning from her jailor,— who displayed as much humanity towards her as was consistent with his office,—that he bore his fate with the utmost fortitude and resignation.

Entertaining no hopes of mercy, Jane's whole time was past in preparation for her end. Except the few hours of refreshment actually required by nature, every moment was devoted to the most intense application, or to fervent prayer. By degrees, all trace of sorrow vanished from her features, and they assumed a spiritualized and almost angelic expression. Lovely as she was before, she looked far more lovely now—or rather her beauty was of a more refined and exalted character. She was frequently visited by the queen's confessor, Feckenham, who used every effort to induce her to renounce her religion,—but in vain. When told that the sure way to her Majesty's favour would be to embrace the faith of Rome—she replied that, anxious as she was to obtain the queen's forgiveness, she could not purchase it at the price of her salvation, and that the only favour she desired was to pass the brief residue of her days unmolested. Northumberland's apostacy was a terrible shock to her. Feckenham brought the intelligence, and boasted of the convert the Catholic Church had gained.

"You may have induced the Duke to recant with his lips, sir," replied Jane; "but of this I am assured, he died a Protestant in heart."

"It may be so," rejoined Feckenham. "He was hypocrite enough to act thus. It is enough for us that he publicly abjured his errors. And before long, others of his house will follow his example."

"What mean you, sir?" demanded Jane, anxiously. "You do not surely allude to my husband?"

Feckenham made no reply, but with a significant smile departed. The insinuation was not lost upon Jane. And now she more than ever lamented that she was not near her husband, to strengthen his wavering faith, and confirm his resolution. Well knowing that his character in a great measure resembled his father's, she feared that the inducement held out by his enemies might be too much for his resistance. Unable to communicate her fears to him—or to offer any of the counsel her heart suggested, she could only relieve her distresses by earnest supplications in his behalf. But even prayer did not on this occasion afford her the consolation it was wont to do. The Duke of Northumberland's recantation perpetually haunted her; and the thought that her husband might be made a similar example filled her with inexpressible dread..

While suffering from these agonising reflections, she received another visit from Feckenham. The expression of his countenance, which was triumphing and sinister, alarmed her, and she almost felt unwilling, though at the same time anxious, to question him.

After enjoying her suspense for a few minutes, he said, "Daughter, you blamed the Duke of Northumberland for being reconciled to our church. What, if I inform you that Lord Guilford Dudley has been likewise converted?"

"I should indeed be grieved to hear it," replied Jane, in a tone of anguish; "but I trust it is not so."

"It is as I have said," answered Feckenham.

"Heaven pardon him!" exclaimed Jane. "You bring me ill news, indeed. I had far rather you came to tell me the executioner was waiting for me—nay, that my husband was about to be led to the block—than this fatal intelligence. I thought our separation would be short. But now I find it will be eternal."

"You are in error, daughter," rejoined Feckenham, sternly. "You will neither be separated from your husband in this world, nor the next, if you are equally conformable."

"Am I to understand, then, that his apostasy, for I can give it no milder term, has been purchased by an offer of pardon?" demanded Jane.

"I said not so, daughter," replied Feckenham; "but I now tell you that his hopes of grace rest with yourself."

"With me?" cried Jane, with a look of agony.

"With you, daughter," repeated the confessor. "Much as it rejoices our pious Queen to win over one soul like that of Lord Guilford Dudley to the true faith—gladly as she will receive his recantation, she will pledge herself to mercy only on one condition."

"And that is—"

"Your conversion."

"A safe promise, for her clemency will never be exhibited," replied Jane. "Not even to purchase my husband's life would I consent. I would willingly die to bring him back to the paths from which he has strayed. But I will not surrender myself to Rome and her abominations."

"Your firmness, in a good cause, daughter, would elicit my approbation," replied Feckenham. "As it is, it only excites my compassion. I am deeply concerned to see one so richly gifted so miserably benighted—one so fair so foully spotted with heresy. I should esteem it a glorious victory over Satan to rescue your soul from perdition, and will spare no pains to do so."

"It is in vain, sir," replied Jane; "and if I have hitherto repressed my anger at these solicitations, it is because feeling firm in myself, I look upon them merely as an annoyance, to which it is my duty to submit with patience. But when I perceive the mischief they have done to others, I can no longer contain my indignation. Yours is a pernicious and idolatrous religion,—a religion founded on the traditions of men, not on the word of God—a religion detracting from the merits of our Saviour—substituting mummery for the simple offices of prayer,—and though I will not be uncharitable enough to assert that its sincere professors will not be saved,—yet I am satisfied, that no one to whom the true light of heaven has once been vouchsafed, can believe in it, or be saved by it."

"Since you are thus obstinate, daughter," replied Feckenham, "let us dispute point by point, and dogma by dogma, of our creeds, and I think I can convince you of the error in which you rest. Do not fear wearying me. I cannot be better employed."

"Pardon me, then, sir, if I reply, than I *can* be far better employed," returned Jane; "and, though I would not shrink from such a discussion—were it useful,—and do not fear its result, yet, as no good can arise from it, I must decline it."

"As you please, daughter," rejoined Feckenham. "But I must own that your refusal to accept my challenge seems a tacit admission of the weakness of your cause."

"Put what construction you please upon it, sir,—so you leave me in peace," replied Jane. "I will fight the good fight when called upon to do so. But I will not waste the little time that remains to me in fruitless disputation."

"Before I depart, however, daughter," rejoined Feckenham, "let me deliver your husband's message to you."

"What is it?" inquired Jane, eagerly,—"and yet, I almost dread to ask."

"He implored you not to be his executioner," answered Feckenham.

"*His* executioner!—my husband's executioner!—oh, no!—no! that I can never be!" cried Jane, bursting into tears.

"That you *will* be, unless you consent," replied the priest, coldly.

"I beseech you, sir, urge me no further," rejoined Jane.

"I would lay down my life for my husband a thousand times, but I cannot save him thus. Tell him that I will pray for him night and day,—and oh! tell him that his swerving from his faith has wounded me more severely than the axe will ever do."

"I shall tell him that I left you in the same obstinate state I found you—deaf to the voice of truth—inaccessible to natural affection, and besotted with heresy. Daughter, you love not your husband."

"Not love him!" echoed Jane, passionately. "But no,—you shall not shake my firmness. I thought to die calmly, and I looked forward to death as to a certain restoration to my husband. This hope is now at an end. It is you, sir, who are his true executioner. Not content with robbing him of his eternal happiness, you impute his destruction to me. Tell him I love him too well to grant his request—and if he loves me, and hopes to be reunited to me in the bonds of unceasing happiness, he will remain unshaken in his adherence to the Protestant faith."

"Then you absolutely refuse compliance?" demanded Fecken-ham.

"Absolutely," replied Jane.

"Your husband's blood be upon your head!" exclaimed the confessor, in a menacing voice.

And without another word, he departed.

As soon as the door of her chamber was locked, and Jane felt herself alone, she threw herself on her knees, and was about to pour out her heart in earnest supplication for her husband, but the shock had been too great for her, and she fainted. On reviving, she was scarcely able to move, and it was some time before she entirely regained her strength.

Repairing to the palace, Feckenham detailed the interview to the queen, observing in conclusion, "I still do not despair of her conversion, and shall leave no means untried to accomplish it." The next day, he again visited Jane, but with no better success. He found her in great affliction, and she earnestly implored to be allowed to see her husband, if only for a few minutes, and in the presence of witnesses. The confessor replied that in her present frame of mind her request could not be granted. But that if she showed herself conformable she should no longer be separated from him, and he would answer for their ultimate pardon. "I have already acquainted you with my determination, sir," rejoined Jane, "and you will seek in vain to move me. The rack should not shake my constancy; neither shall the mental torture to which you subject me."

When Feckenham reported the result of his mission to Gardiner, the bishop decided upon holding a religious conference with the captive, feeling confident that notwithstanding her boasted learning and zeal, he could easily overcome her in argument. To induce her to assent to the plan, it was agreed that a meeting should be allowed between her and her husband on the occasion. When the matter was announced to Jane, she readily expressed her acquiescence, and begged that it might not be delayed, as she had no preparation to make. "Take heed," she observed, in conclusion, "lest I win back from you the treasure you have gained."

"We shall add to it a greater treasure—yourself, madam," replied the confessor.

On the following day, she was summoned by an officer of the guard to attend the Bishop in the Beauchamp Tower. Taking up a volume of the Holy Scriptures lying on a table beside her, and wrapping herself in an ermined surcoat, she arose and followed the officer—quitting her chamber for the first time for nearly two months. On issuing into the open air, the effect was almost overpowering, and she could not repress her tears.

It was a bright, sunshiny morning, and everything looked so beautiful—so happy, that the contrast with her recent sufferings was almost too much for her. Bearing up resolutely against her feelings, in order forcibly to divert her attention she fixed her eyes upon the reverend walls of the White Tower, which she was at that moment passing. Near it she perceived the three gigantic warders, all of whom doffed their caps as she approached. Og coughed loudly, as if to clear his throat; Gog hastily brushed the moisture from his eyes with his sleeve; while Magog, who was the most tender-hearted of the three, fairly blubbered aloud. Xit, who formed one of the group, but who was the least affected, bade her be of good cheer.

This encounter was so far of service to Jane, that it served to distract her thoughts, and she had in a great measure regained her composure, when another incident occurred, which had nearly upset her altogether. As she passed near the porch of Saint Peter's Chapel, she beheld Simon Renard emerge from it. And if she felt her blood chilled by the sight of her implacable foe, her alarm was not diminished on hearing him call to her guards to bring her within the chapel. At a loss to comprehend the meaning of this mysterious summons, Jane entered the sacred structure. Coldly saluting her, Renard informed her that her husband was within the chapel. Trembling at the intimation, Jane looked eagerly round. At first, she could discern nothing; but, guided by the ambassador's malignant glance, she perceived a figure kneeling in front of the altar. Instantly recognising her husband, with an exclamation of delight that made him spring to his feet, she rushed forward and threw herself into his arms.

After the first passionate emotion had subsided, Jane inquired how he came to be there.

"Do you not know?" replied Lord Guilford. "Or have you been kept in ignorance of the terrible tragedy which has been recently enacted? Look there!" And he pointed downwards.

Jane obeyed, and saw that she was standing upon a gravestone, on which was inscribed in newly-cut letters—

JOHN DUDLEY, DUKE OF NORTHUMBERLAND.
—DECAPITATED AUGUST 22, 1553

Jane trembled and leaned upon her husband for support. "Here is the victim—there the executioner," said Lord Guilford, pointing from the grave to Renard.

"Three months ago," said the Ambassador, who stood with folded arms at a little distance from them, "within this very chapel, I told the Duke of Northumberland he would occupy that grave. My words have been fulfilled. And I now tell you, Lord Guilford Dudley, and you Lady Jane, that unless you are reconciled with our holy Church, you will rest beside him."

With these words he quitted the chapel, and the guards closing round the captives, they were compelled to follow. During their short walk, Jane passionately implored her husband not to yield to the persuasions of his enemies. He hung his head and returned no answer, and she inferred from his silence, that he was not disposed to yield to her solicitations. They were now close upon the Beauchamp Tower, when Dudley, pointing to a barred window in the upper story of one of its turrets, observed—"Within that room my father parsed the last few weeks of his existence."

BEAUCHAMP TOWER FROM THE EAST.

Ascending the spiral stone stairs of the tower, they passed beneath the arched doorway, and entered the principal chamber—now used—as has more than once been observed—as the mess-room of the garrison. Here they found Gardiner awaiting their arrival, he was seated on a high backed arm chair between Bonner and Feckenham, who occupied stools on either side of him, while behind him stood the friar who had attended the Duke of Northumberland on the scaffold. Across one of the deep and arched embrazures of the room looking towards the south, a thick curtain was drawn, and before it, at a small table covered with a crimson cloth, on which writing materials were placed, sat a secretary prepared to take down the heads of the disputation. On Jane's appearance, Gardiner and the other ecclesiastics arose and gravely saluted her.

"You are welcome, daughter," said the bishop. "You have come hither an unbeliever in our doctrines. I trust you will depart confirmed in the faith of Rome."

"I am come to vanquish, not to yield, my lord," replied Jane, firmly. "And as I shall give you no quarter, so I expect none."

"Be it so," rejoined the bishop. "To you, my son," he continued, addressing Lord Guilford, "I can hold very different language. I can give you such welcome as the prodigal son received, and rejoice in your reconciliation with your heavenly father. And I sincerely trust that this noble lady, your consort, will not be a means of turning aside that mercy which her most gracious Majesty is desirous of extending towards you."

"My lord," said Jane, stepping between them, and steadfastly regarding the bishop, "if I am wrong and my husband is right, the Queen will do well not to punish the innocent with the guilty. And you, dear Dudley," she continued, taking his hand, and gazing at him with streaming eyes, "grant me one favour—the last I shall ever ask of you."

"Daughter!" observed Gardiner, severely, "I cannot permit this interference. I must interpose my authority to prevent your attempting to shake your husband's determination."

"All I ask, my lord, is this," rejoined Jane, meekly; "that he will abide the issue of the disputation before he renounces his faith for ever. It is a request, which I am sure neither he, nor *you* will refuse."

"It is granted, daughter," replied Gardiner; "the rather that I feel so certain of convincing you that I doubt not you will then as strongly urge his reconciliation as you now oppose it."

"I would that not my husband alone, but that all Christendom could be auditors of our conference, my lord," replied Jane. "In this cause I am as strong, as in the late on which I was engaged I was weak. With this shield," she continued, raising the Bible which she carried beneath her arm, "I cannot sustain injury." Advancing towards the table at which the secretary was seated, she laid the sacred volume upon it. She then divested of her surcoat, and addressed a few words, in an under tone, to her husband, while the ecclesiastics conferred together. While this was passing, Lord Guilford's eye accidentally fell upon his father's inscription on the wall, and he called Jane's attention to it. She sighed as she looked, and remarked, "Do not let your name be stained like his."

Perceiving Simon Renard gazing at them with malignant satisfaction, she then turned to Gardiner and said, "My lord, the presence of this person troubles me. I pray you, if he be not needful to our conference, that you will desire him to withdraw."

The bishop acquiesced, and having signified his wishes to the ambassador, he feigned to depart. But halting beneath the arched entrance, he remained an unseen witness of the proceedings.

A slight pause ensued, during which Jane knelt beside the chair, and fervently besought heaven to grant her strength for the encounter. She then arose, and fixing her eye upon Gardiner, said in a firm tone, "I am ready, my lord, I pray you question me, and spare me not."

Bishop Gardiner's conference with Jane in the Beauchamp Tower

No further intimation was necessary to the bishop, who immediately proceeded to interrogate her on the articles of her faith; and being a man of profound learning, well versed in all the subtleties of scholastic dispute, he sought in every way to confound and perplex her. In this he was likewise assisted by Bonner and Feckenham, both of whom were admirable theologians, and who proposed the most difficult questions to her. The conference lasted several hours, during which Jane sustained her part with admirable constancy—never losing a single point—but retorting upon her opponents questions, which they were unable to answer—displaying such a fund of erudition—such powers of argument—such close and clear reasoning—and such profound knowledge of the tenets of her own faith and of theirs, that they were completely baffled and astounded. To a long and eloquent address of Gardiner's she replied at equal length, and with even more eloquence and fervour, concluding with these emphatic words—"My lord, I have lived in the Protestant faith, and in that faith I will die. In these sad times, when the power of your church is in the ascendant, it is perhaps needful there should be martyrs in ours to prove our sincerity. Amongst these I shall glory to be numbered—happy in the thought that my firmness will be the means in after ages, of benefiting the Protestant church. On this rock," she continued, pointing to the Bible, which lay open before her—"my religion is built, and it will endure, when yours, which is erected on sandy foundations, shall be utterly swept away. In this sacred volume, I find every tenet of my creed, and I desire no other mediator between my Maker and myself."

As she said this, her manner was so fervid, and her look so full of inspiration, that all her listeners were awe-stricken, and gazed at her in involuntary admiration. The secretary suspended his task to drink in her words; and even Simon Renard, who ensconced beneath the door-way, seemed no inapt representation of the spirit of evil, appeared confounded.

After a brief pause, Gardiner arose, saying, "the conference is ended, daughter. You are at liberty to depart. If I listen longer," he added, in an under tone to his companions, "I shall be convinced against my will."

"Then you acknowledge your defeat, my lord," said Jane, proudly.

"I acknowledge that it is in vain to make any impression on you," answered the bishop.

"Jane," cried her husband, advancing towards her, and throwing himself on his knees before her, "you have conquered, and I implore your forgiveness. I will never change a religion of which you are so bright an ornament."

"This is indeed a victory," replied Jane, raising him and clasping him to her bosom. "And now, my lord," she added to Gardiner, "conduct us to prison or the scaffold as soon as you please. Death has no further terrors."

After a parting embrace, and an assurance from her husband, that he would now remain constant in his faith, Jane was removed by her guard to the Brick Tower, while Lord Guilford was immured in one of the cells adjoining the room in which the conference had taken place.

MESS-ROOM IN THE BEAUCHAMP TOWER.

XI.—HOW CUTHBERT CHOLMONDELEY REVISITED THE STONE KITCHEN; AND HOW HE WENT IN SEARCH OF CICELY.

Cuthbert Cholmondeley, who, it may be remembered, attended Lord Guilford Dudley, when he was brought from Sion House to the Tower, was imprisoned at the same time as that unfortunate nobleman, and lodged in the Nun's Bower—a place of confinement so named, and situated, as already mentioned, in the upper story of the Coal Harbour Tower. Here he was detained until after the Duke of Northumberland's execution, when, though he was not restored to liberty, he was allowed the range of the fortress. The first use he made of his partial freedom was to proceed to the Stone Kitchen, in the hope of meeting with Cicely; and his bitter disappointment may be conceived on finding that she was not there, nor was anything known of her by her foster-parents.

"Never since the ill-fated Queen Jane, whom they now call a usurper, took her into her service, have I set eyes upon her," said Dame Potentia, who was thrown into an agony of affliction, by the sight of Cholmondeley. "Hearing from old Gunnora Braose, that when her unfortunate mistress was brought back a captive to the Tower she had been left at Sion House, and thinking she would speedily return, I did not deem it necessary to send for her; but when a week had elapsed, and she did not make her appearance, I desired her father to go in search of her. Accordingly, he went to Sion House, and learnt that she had been fetched away, on the morning after Queen Jane's capture, by a man who stated he had come from us. This was all Peter could learn. Alas! Alas!"

"Did not your suspicions alight on Nightgall?" asked Cholmondeley.

"Ay, marry, did they," replied the pantler's wife; "but he averred he had never quitted the Tower. And as I had no means of proving it upon him, I could do nothing more than tax him with it."

"He still retains his office of jailer, I suppose?" said Cholmondeley.

"Of a surety," answered Potentia; "and owing to Simon Renard, whom you may have heard, is her Majesty's right hand, he has become a person of greater authority than ever, and affects to look down upon his former friends."

"He cannot look down upon me at all events," exclaimed a loud voice behind them. And turning at the sound, Cholmondeley beheld the bulky figure of Gog darkening the door-way.

A cordial greeting passed between Cholmondeley and the giant, who in the same breath congratulated him upon his restoration to liberty, and condoled with him on the loss of his mistress.

"In the midst of grief we must perforce eat," observed the pantler, "and our worthy friends, the giants, as well as Xit, have often enlivened our board, and put care to flight. Perhaps you are not aware that Magog has been married since we last saw you."

"Magog married!" exclaimed Cholmondeley, in surprise.

"Ay. indeed!" rejoined Gog, "more persons than your worship have been astonished by it. And shall I let you into secret—if ever husband was henpecked, it is my unfortunate brother. Your worship complains of losing your mistress. Would to heaven he had had any such luck! And the worst of it is that before marriage she was accounted the most amiable of her sex."

"Ay, that's always the case," observed Peter Trusbut; "though I must do my dame the justice to say that she did not disguise her qualities during my courtship."

"I will not hear a word uttered in disparagement of Dame Potentia," cried Ribald, who at that moment entered the kitchen, "even by her husband. Ah! Master Cholmondeley I am right glad to see you. I heard of your release to-day. So, the pretty bird is flown you find—and whither none of us can tell, though I think I could give a guess at the fowler."

"So could I," replied Cholmondeley.

"I dare say both our suspicions tend to the same mark," said Ribald—"but we must observe caution now—for the person I mean is protected by Simon Renard, and others in favour with the queen."

"He is little better than an assassin," said Cholmondeley; "and has detained a wretched woman whom he has driven out of her senses by his cruelty a captive in the subterranean dungeons beneath the Devilin Tower."

And he proceeded to detail all he knew of the captive Alexia.

"This is very dreadful, no doubt," remarked Ribald, who had listened to the recital with great attention. "But as I said before, Nightgall is in favour with persons of the greatest influence, and he is more dangerous and vindictive than ever. What you do, you must do cautiously."

By this time, the party had been increased by the arrival of Og and Xit, both of whom, but especially the latter, appeared rejoiced to meet with the young esquire.

"Ah! Master Cholmondeley," said the elder giant, heaving a deep sigh. "Times have changed with us all since we last met. Jane is no longer Queen. The Duke of Northumberland is beheaded. Cicely is lost. And last and worst of all, Magog is married."

"So I have heard from Gog," replied Cholmondeley, "and I fear not very much to your satisfaction.1'

"Nor his own either," replied Og, shrugging his shoulders. "However it can't be helped. He must make the best of a bad bargain."

"It *might* be helped though," observed Xit. "Magog seems to have lost all his spirit since he married. If I had to manage her, I'd soon let her see the difference."

"You, forsooth!" exclaimed Dame Potentia, contemptuously. "Do you imagine any woman would stand in awe-of you!"

And before the dwarf could elude her grasp, she seized him by the nape of the neck, and regardless of his cries, placed him upon the chimney-piece, amid a row of shining pewter plates.

"There you shall remain," she added, "till you beg pardon for your impertinence."

Xit looked piteously around, but seeing no hand extended to reach him down, and being afraid to spring from so great a height, he entreated the dame's forgiveness in a humble tone; and she thereupon set him upon the ground.

"A pretty person you are to manage a wife," said Dame Potentia, with a laugh, in which all, except the object of it, joined.

It being Cholmondeley's intention to seek out a lodging at one of the warder's habitations, he consulted Peter Trusbut on the subject, who said, that if his wife was agreeable, he should be happy to accommodate him in his own dwelling. The matter being referred to Dame Potentia she at once assented, and assigned him Cicely's chamber.

On taking possession of the room, Cholmondeley sank upon a chair, and for some time indulged the most melancholy reflections, from which he was aroused by a tremendous roar of laughter, such as he knew could only be uttered by the gigantic brethren, proceeding from the adjoining apartment. Repairing thither, he found the whole party assembled round the table, which was, as usual, abundantly, or rather superabundantly, furnished. Amongst the guests were Magog and his wife, and the laughter he had heard was occasioned by a box administered by the latter to the ears of her spouse, because he had made some remark that sounded displeasing in her own.

Magog bore the blow with the utmost philosophy, and applied himself for consolation to a huge pot of metheglin, which he held to his lips as long as a drop remained within it.

"We had good doings in Queen's Jane's reign," remarked Peter Trusbut, offering the young esquire a seat beside him, "but we have better in those of Queen Mary."

And, certainly, his assertion was fully borne out by the great joints of beef, the hams, the pasties, and pullets with which the table groaned, and with which the giants were making their accustomed havoc. In the midst stood what Peter Trusbut termed a royal pasty, and royal it was, if size could confer dignity. It contained two legs of mutton, the pantler assured his guests, besides a world of other savoury matters, enclosed in a wall of rye-crust, and had taken twenty-four hours to bake.

"Twenty-four hours!" echoed Magog. "I will engage to consume it in the twentieth part of the time."

"For that observation you shall not even taste it," said his arbitrary spouse.

Debarred from the pasty, Magog made himself some amends by attacking a gammon of Bayonne bacon, enclosed in a paste, and though he found it excellent, he had the good sense to keep his opinion to himself. In this way, the supper passed off—Ribald jesting as usual, and devoting himself alternately to the two dames—Peter Trusbut carving the viands and assisting his guests—and the giants devouring all before them.

Towards the close of the repast, Xit, who always desired to be an object of attention, determined to signalise himself by some feat. Brandishing his knife and fork, he therefore sprang upon the table, and striding up to the royal pasty, peeped over the side, which was rather higher than himself, to take a survey of the contents.

While he was thus occupied, Dame Placida, who was sitting opposite to the pasty, caught him by the skirts of his doublet, and tossed him into the pie, while Peter Trusbut instantly covered it with the thick lid of crust, which had been removed when it was first opened. The laughter which followed this occurrence was not diminished, as the point of Xit's knife appeared through the wall of pastry—nor was it long before he contrived to cut a passage out.

His re-appearance was hailed with a general shout of merriment. And Magog was by no means displeased at seeing him avenge himself by rushing towards his plump partner, and before she could prevent him, throw his arms round her, and imprint a sounding kiss upon her lips, while his greasy habiliments besmeared her dress.

Xit would have suffered severely for this retaliation, if it had not been for the friendly interference of Ribald, who rescued him from the clutches of the offended dame, and contrived with a tact peculiar to himself not only to appease her anger, but to turn it into mirth. Order being once more restored, the dishes and plates were removed, and succeeded by flagons and pots of ale and wine. The conversation then began to turn upon a masque about to be given to the Queen by the Earl of Devonshire, at which they were all to assist, and arrangements were made as to the characters they should assume. Though this topic was interesting enough to the parties concerned, it was not so to Cholmondeley, who was about to retire to his own chamber to indulge his grief unobserved, when his departure was arrested by the sudden entrance of Lawrence Nightgall.

At the jailor's appearance, the merriment of the party instantly ceased, and all eyes were bent upon him.

"Your business here, master Nightgall?" demanded Peter Trusbut, who was the first to speak.

"My business is with Master Cuthbert Cholmondeley," replied the jailor.

"State it then at once," replied the esquire, frowning. "It is to ascertain where you intend to lodge, that I may report it to the lieutenant," said Nightgall.

"I shall remain here," replied Cholmondeley, sternly—"in Cicely's chamber."

"Here!" exclaimed Nightgall, starting, but instantly recovering himself, he turned to Peter Trusbut, and in a voice of forced composure, added—"You will be responsible then for him, Master Pantler, with your life and goods to the Queen's highness, which, if he escapes, will both be forfeited."

"Indeed!" cried Trusbut, in dismay. "I—I—"

"Yes—yes—my husband understands all that," interposed Dame Potentia; "he will be answerable for him—and so will I."

"You will understand still further," proceeded Nightgall, with a smile of triumph, "that he is not to stir forth except for one hour at mid-day, and then that his walks are to be restricted to the green."

While this was passing, Og observed in a whisper to Xit—"If I were possessed of that bunch of keys at Nightgall's girdle, I could soon find Cicely."

"Indeed!" said Xit. "Then you shall soon have them." And the next minute he disappeared under the table.

"You have a warrant for what you do, I suppose?" demanded Og, desirous of attracting the jailor's attention.

"Behold it," replied Nightgall, taking a parchment from his vest. He then deliberately seated himself, and producing an ink-horn and pen, wrote Peter Trusbut's name upon it.

"Master Pantler," he continued, delivering it to him, "I have addressed it to you. Once more I tell you, you will be responsible for the prisoner. And with this I take my leave."

"Not so fast, villain," said Cholmondeley, seizing his arm with a firm grasp,— "where is Cicely?"

"You will never behold her more," replied Nightgall. "What have you done with the captive Alexia?" pursued the esquire, bitterly.

"She likewise is beyond your reach," answered the jailor, moodily. And shaking off Cholmondeley's grasp, he rushed out of the chamber with such haste as nearly to upset Xit, who appeared to have placed himself purposely in his path.

This occurrence threw a gloom over the mirth of the party.

The conversation flagged, and even an additional supply of wine failed to raise the spirits of the guests. Just as they were separating, hasty steps were heard on the stairs, and Night-gall again presented himself. Rushing up to Cholmondeley, who was sitting apart wrapt in gloomy thought, he exclaimed in a voice of thunder—"My keys!—my keys!—you have stolen my keys."

"What keys?" demanded the esquire, starting to his feet. "Those of Alexia's dungeon."

"Restore them instantly," cried Nightgall, furiously—"or I will instantly carry you back to the Nun's Bower."

"Were they in my possession," replied Cholmondeley, "nothing should force them from me till I had searched your most secret hiding-places."

"'Tis therefore you stole them," cried Nightgall. "See where my girdle has been cut," he added, appealing to Peter Trusbut. "If they are not instantly restored, I will convey you all before the lieutenant, and you know how he will treat the matter."

Terrified by this threat, the pantler entreated the esquire, if he really had the keys, to restore them. But Cholmondeley positively denied the charge, and after a long and fruitless search, all the party except Xit, who had disappeared, having declared their ignorance of what had become of them, Nightgall at last departed, in a state of the utmost rage and mortification.

Soon after this, the party broke up, and Cholmondeley retired to his own room. Though the pantler expressed no fear of his escaping, he did not neglect the precaution of locking the door. Throwing himself on a couch, the esquire, after a time, fell into a sort of doze, during which he was haunted by the image of Cicely, who appeared pale and suffering, and as if imploring his aid. So vivid was the impression, that he started up, and endeavoured to shake it off. In vain. He could not divest himself of the idea that he was at that moment subjected to the persecutions of Nightgall. Having endured this anguish for some hours, and the night being far advanced, he was about to address himself once more to repose, when he heard the lock turned, and glancing in the direction of the door, perceived it cautiously opened by Xit. The mannikin placed his finger to his lips in token of silence, and held up a huge bunch of keys, which Cholmondeley instantly conjectured were those lost by Nightgall. Xit then briefly explained how he had possessed himself of them, and offered them to Cholmondeley.

"I love the fair Cicely," he said, "hate Nightgall, and entertain a high respect for your worship. I would gladly make you happy with your mistress if I can. You have now at least the means of searching for her, and heaven grant a favourable issue to the adventure. Follow me, and tread upon the points of your feet, for the pantler and his spouse occupy the next room."

As they crossed the kitchen, they heard a sound proceeding from an adjoining room, which convinced them that neither Peter Trusbut nor Dame Potentia were on the watch.

"They don't snore *quite* so loud as my friends the giants," whispered Xit; "but they have tolerably good lungs.'"

Having, at Xit's suggestion, armed himself with a torch and materials to light it, and girded on a sword which he found reared against the wall, the esquire followed his dwarfish companion down a winding stone staircase, and speedily issued from the postern.

The night was profoundly dark, and they were therefore unobserved by the sentinels on the summit of the Byward Tower, and on the western ramparts. Without delaying a moment, Cholmondeley hurried towards the Devilin Tower. Xit accompanied him, and after some little search they found the secret door, and by a singular chance Cholmondeley, on the first application, discovered the right key. He then bade farewell to the friendly dwarf, who declined attending him further, and entering the passage, and locking the door withinside, struck a light and set fire to the torch.

Scarcely knowing whither to shape his course, and fully aware of the extent of the dungeons he should have to explore, Cholmondeley resolved to leave no cell unvisited, until he discovered the object of his search. For some time, he proceeded along a narrow arched passage, which brought him to a stone staircase, and descending it, his further progress was stopped by an iron door.

Unlocking it, he entered another passage, on the right of which was a range of low cells, all of which he examined, but they were untenanted, except one, in which he found a man whom he recognized as one of the Duke of Northumberland's followers. He did not, however, dare to liberate him, but with a few words of commiseration passed on.

Turning off on the left, he proceeded for some distance, until being convinced by the hollow sound of the floor that there were vaults beneath, he held his torch downwards, and presently discovered an iron ring in one of the stones. Raising it, he beheld a flight of steps, and descending them, found himself in a lower passage about two feet wide, and apparently of considerable length. Hastily tracking it, he gradually descended until he came to a level, where both the floor and ceiling were damp and humid. His torch now began to burn feebly, and threw a ghastly light upon the slimy walls and dripping roof.

While he was thus pursuing his way, a long and fearful shriek broke upon his ear, and thinking it might proceed from the captive Alexia, he hastened forward as quickly as the slippery path would allow him. It was evident, from the increasing humidity of the atmosphere, that he was approaching the river. As he advanced the cries grew louder, and he became aware, from the noise around, that legions of rats were fleeing before him. These loathsome animals were in such numbers, that Cholmondeley, half-fearing an attack from them, drew his sword.

After proceeding about fifty yards, the passage he was traversing terminated in a low wide vault, in the centre of which was a deep pit. From the bottom of this abyss the cries resounded, and hurrying to its edge, he held down the torch, and discovered, at the depth of some twenty feet, a miserable half-naked object up to his knees in water, and defending himself from hundreds of rats that were swarming around him. While he was considering how he could accomplish the poor wretch's deliverance, who continued his shrieks more loudly than ever, asserting that the rats were devouring him, Cholmondeley perceived a ladder in a corner of the vault, and lowering it into the pit, the sides of which were perpendicular and flagged, instantly descended.

If he had been horrified at the vociferations of the prisoner, he was now perfectly appalled by the ghastly spectacle he presented. The unfortunate person had not exaggerated his danger when he said that the rats were about to devour him. His arms, body, and face were torn and bleeding, and as Cholmondeley approached he beheld numbers of his assailants spring from him and swim off. More dead than alive, the sufferer expressed his thanks, and taking him in his arms, Cholmondeley carried him up the ladder.

As soon as he had gained the edge of the pit, the esquire, who had been struck with the man's voice, examined his features by the light of the torch, and was shocked to find that he was one of the attendants of the Duke of Northumberland, with whom he was well acquainted. Addressing him by his name, the man instantly knew him, and informed him that he had been ordered into confinement by the council, and having given some offence to Nightgall, had been tortured and placed in this horrible pit.

"I have been here two days and nights," he said, "as far as I can guess, without food or light, and should soon have perished, had it not been for your aid; and, though I do not fear death,—yet to die by inches—a prey to those horrible animals—was dreadful."

"Let me support you," returned Cholmondeley, taking his arm, "and while you have strength left, convey you to a more wholesome part of the dungeon, where you will be free from these frightful assailants, till I can procure you further assistance."

The poor prisoner gratefully accepted his offer, and lending him all the assistance in his power, Cholmondeley slowly retraced his course. Having reached the flight of stone steps, leading to the trap-door, the esquire dragged his companion up them, and finding it in vain to carry him further, and fearing he should be disappointed in the main object of his search, he looked around for a cell in which he could place him for a short time.

Perceiving a door standing ajar on the left, he pushed it open, and, entering a small cell, found the floor covered with straw, and, what was still more satisfactory to him, discovered a loaf on a shelf, and a large jug of water. Placing the prisoner on the straw, he spread the provisions before him, and having seen him partake of them, promised to return as soon as possible.

"Bestow no further thought on me," said the man. "I shall die content now."

Cholmondeley then departed, and proceeding along the passage he had just traversed, came to a wide arched opening on the left, which he entered, and pursuing the path before him, after many turnings, arrived at another low circular vault, about nineteen feet in diameter, which, from the peculiar form of its groined arches, he supposed (and correctly) must be situated beneath Devereux Tower.

DUNGEON BENEATH THE DEVILIN TOWER.

Of a style of architecture of earlier date than the Beauchamp Tower, the Devilin, or, as it is now termed, the Devereux Tower, from the circumstance of Robert Devereux, Earl of Essex, the favourite of Queen Elizabeth, having been confined within it in 1601, has undergone less alteration than most of the other fortifications, and except in the modernising of the windows, retains much of its original character. In the dungeon into which Cholmondeley had penetrated, several curious spear-heads of great antiquity, and a gigantic thigh-bone, have been recently found.

At the further end of the vault Cholmondeley discovered a short flight of steps, and mounting them unlocked a door, which admitted him to another narrow winding stone staircase. Ascending it, he presently came to a door on the left, shaped like the arched entrance in which it was placed. It was of strong oak, studded with nails, and secured by a couple of bolts.

INTERIOR OF THE DEVILIN TOWER.—BASEMENT.

Drawing back the fastenings, he unsheathed his sword, and pushing aside the door with the blade, raised his torch, and beheld a spectacle that Idled him with horror. At one side of the cell, which was about six feet long and three wide, and contrived in the thickness of the wall, upon a stone seat rested the dead body of a woman, reduced almost to a skeleton. The face was turned from the door, but rushing forward he instantly recognised its rigid features. On the wall close to where she lay, and evidently carved by her own hand, was traced her name—ALEXIA.

Cholmondeley discovering the body of Alexia in the Devilin Tower

NORTH VIEW OF THE SALT TOWER.

XII.—-HOW EDWARD UNDERHILL, THE "HOT-GOSPELLER," ATTEMPTED TO ASSASSINATE QUEEN MARY; AND HOW SHE WAS PRESERVED BY SIR HENRY BEDINGFELD.

Among those who viewed Mary's accession to the throne with the greatest dissatisfaction, was the Hot-Gospeller. Foreseeing the danger with which the Protestant church was menaced, he regarded the change of sovereigns as one of the most direful calamities that could have befallen his country. The open expression of these sentiments more than once brought him into trouble, and he was for some time placed in durance. On his liberation, he observed more caution; and though his opinions were by no means altered, but rather strengthened, he no longer gave utterance to them.

During his imprisonment, he had pondered deeply upon the critical state of his religion; and having come to the conclusion that there was no means but one of averting the threatened storm, he determined to resort to that desperate expedient. Underhill's temporal interests had been as much affected as his spiritual, by the new government. He was dismissed from the post he had hitherto held of gentleman-pensioner; and this circumstance, though he was, perhaps, scarcely conscious of it, contributed in no slight degree to heighten his animosity against the queen. Ever brooding upon the atrocious action he was about to commit, he succeeded in persuading himself, by that pernicious process of reasoning by which religious enthusiasts so often delude themselves into the commission of crime, that it was not only justifiable, but meritorious.

Though no longer a prisoner, or employed in any office, the Hot-Gospeller still continued to linger within the Tower, judging it the fittest place for the execution of his purpose. He took up his abode in a small stone cell, once tenanted by a recluse, and situated at the back of Saint Peter's chapel, on the Green; devoting his days to prayer, and his nights to wandering, like a ghost, about the gloomiest and least-frequented parts of the fortress. He was often challenged by the sentinels,—often stopped, and conveyed to the guard-room by the patrol; but in time they became accustomed to him, and he was allowed to pursue his ramblings unmolested. By most persons he was considered deranged, and his wasted figure—for he almost denied himself the necessaries of life, confining his daily meal to a crust of bread, and a draught of water,—together with his miserable attire, confirmed the supposition.

Upon one occasion, Mary herself, who was making the rounds of the fortress, happened to notice him, and ordered him to be brought before her. A blaze of fierce delight passed over the enthusiast's face when the mandate was conveyed to him. But his countenance fell the next moment, on recollecting that he was unarmed. Bitterly reproaching himself for his want of caution, he searched his clothes. He had not even a knife about him. He then besought the halberdiers who came for him to lend him a cloak and a sword, or even a partizan, to make a decent appearance before the queen. But laughing at the request, they struck him with the poles of their weapons, and commanded him to follow them without delay.

Brought into the royal presence, he with difficulty controlled himself. And nothing but the conviction that such a step would effectually defeat his design, prevented him from pouring forth the most violent threats against the queen. As it was, he loudly lamented her adherence to the faith of Rome, entreating her to abjure it, and embrace the new and wholesome doctrines,— a course, which he predicted, would ensure her a long and prosperous reign, whereas, a continuance in her present idolatrous creed would plunge her kingdom in discord, endanger her crown, and, perhaps, end in her own destruction.

Regarding him as a half-crazed, but harmless enthusiast, Mary paid little attention to his address, which was sufficiently wild and incoherent to warrant the conclusion that his intellects were disordered. Pitying his miserable appearance, and inquiring into his mode of life, she ordered him better apparel, and directed that he should be lodged within the palace.

Underhill would have refused her bounty, but, at a gesture from Mary, he was removed from her presence.

This interview troubled him exceedingly. He could not reconcile the queen's destruction to his conscience so easily as he had heretofore done. Despite all his reasoning to the contrary, her generosity affected him powerfully. He could not divest himself of the idea that she might yet be converted; and persuading himself that the glorious task was reserved for him, he resolved to make the attempt, before resorting to a darker mode of redress. Managing to throw himself, one day, in her way, as she was proceeding along the grand gallery, he immediately commenced a furious exhortation. But his discourse was speedily interrupted by the queen, who ordered her attendants to remove him into the court yard, and cudgel him soundly; directing that any repetition of the offence should be followed by severer chastisement. This sentence was immediately carried into effect. The Hot-Gospeller bore it without a murmur. But he internally resolved to defer no longer his meditated design.

His next consideration was how to execute it. He could not effect his purpose by poison; and any attempt at open violence would, in all probability, (as the queen was constantly guarded,) be attended by failure. He therefore determined, as the surest means, to have recourse to fire-arms. And, being an unerring marksman, he felt certain of success in this way.

Having secretly procured an arquebuss and ammunition, he now only awaited a favourable moment for the enterprise. This soon occurred. It being rumoured one night in the Tower, that the queen was about to proceed by water to Whitehall on the following morning, he determined to station himself at some point on the line of road, whence he could take deliberate aim at her. On inquiring further, he ascertained that the royal train would cross the drawbridge leading from the south of the Byward Tower to the wharf, and embark at the stairs. Being personally known to several officers of the guard, he thought he should have no difficulty in obtaining admittance to Saint Thomas's Tower, which, while it commanded the drawbridge, and was within shot, was yet sufficiently distant not to excite suspicion. Accordingly, at an early hour, on the next day, he repaired thither, wrapped in a cloak, beneath which he carried the implement of his treasonable intent.

As he anticipated, he readily procured admission, and, under pretence of viewing the passage of the royal train, was allowed a place at a narrow loophole in the upper story of one of the western turrets. Most of the guard being required on the summit of the fortification, Underhill was left alone in the small chamber. Loud shouts, and the discharge of artillery from the ramparts of the fortress, as well as from the roofs of the different towers, proclaimed that Mary had set forth. A few embers were burning on the hearth in the chamber occupied by the enthusiast. With these he lighted his tow-match, and offering up a prayer for the success of his project, held himself in readiness for its execution.

Unconscious of the impending danger, Mary took her way towards the By-ward Tower. She was attended by a numerous retinue of nobles and gentlemen. Near her walked one of her councillors, Sir Henry Bedingfeld, in whom she placed the utmost trust, and whose attachment to her had been often approved in the reigns of her father and brother, as well as during the late usurpation of Lady Jane Grey. Sir Henry was a grave-looking, dignified personage, somewhat stricken in years. He was attired in a robe of black velvet, of the fashion of Henry the Eighth's time, and his beard was trimmed in the same bygone mode. The venerable knight walked bare-headed, and carried a long staff, tipped with gold.

By this time, Mary had reached the gateway opening upon the scene of her intended assassination. The greater part of her train had already passed over the drawbridge, and the deafening shouts of the beholders, as well as the renewed discharges of artillery, told that the queen was preparing to follow. This latter circumstance created a difficulty, which Underhill had not foreseen. Confined by the ramparts and the external walls of the moat, the smoke from the ordnance completely obscured the view of the drawbridge. Just, however, as Mary set foot upon it, and Underhill had abandoned the attempt in despair, a gust of wind suddenly dispersed the vapour. Conceiving this a special interposition of Providence in his favour, who had thus placed his royal victim in his hands, the Hot-Gospeller applied the match to the arquebuss, and the discharge instantly followed.

The queen's life, however, was miraculously preserved. Sir Henry Bedingfeld, who was walking a few paces behind her, happening to cast his eye in the direction of Traitor's Tower, perceived the barrel of an arquebuss thrust from a loop-hole in one of the turrets, and pointed towards her. Struck with the idea that some injury might be intended her, he sprung forward, and interposing his own person between the queen and the discharge, drew her forcibly backwards. The movement saved her. The ball passed through the knight's mantle, but without harming him further than ruffling the skin of his shoulder; proving by the course it took, that, but for his presence of mind, its fatal effect must have been certain.

All this was the work of an instant. Undismayed by the occurrence, Mary, who inherited all her father's intrepidity, looked calmly round, and pressing Bedingfeld's arm in grateful acknowledgment of the service he had rendered her, issued her commands that the assassin should be secured, strictly examined, and, if need be, questioned on the rack. She then proceeded to the place of embarkation as deliberately as if nothing had happened. Pausing before she entered the barge, she thus addressed her preserver:—

"Sir Henry Bedingfeld, you have ever been my loyal servant. You were the first, during the late usurpation, to draw the sword in my defence—the first to raise troops for me—to join me at Framlingham—to proclaim me at Norwich. But you have thrown all these services into the shade by your last act of devotion. I owe my life to you. What can I do to evince my gratitude?"

"You have already done more than enough in thus acknowledging it, gracious madam," replied Sir Henry; "nor can I claim any merit for the action. Placed in my situation, I am assured there is not one of your subjects, except the miscreant who assailed you, who would not have acted in the same manner. I have done nothing, and deserve nothing."

"Not so, sir," returned Mary. "Most of my subjects, I believe, share your loyalty. But this does not lessen your desert. I should be wanting in all gratitude were I to let the service you have rendered me pass unrequited. And since you refuse to tell me how I can best reward you, I must take upon myself to judge for you. The custody of our person and of our fortress shall be entrusted to your care. Neither can be confided to worthier hands. Sir

John Gage shall receive another appointment. Henceforth, you are Lieutenant of the Tower."

This gracious act was followed by the acclamations of the bystanders; and the air resounded with cries of "God save Queen Mary!—a Bedingfeld!—a Bedingfeld!"

"Your majesty has laid an onerous duty upon me, but I will endeavour to discharge it to your satisfaction," replied Sir Henry, bending the knee, and pressing her hand devotedly to his lips. And amid the increased acclamations of the multitude, Mary entered her barge.

Edward Underhill, meanwhile, whose atrocious purpose had been thus providentially defeated, on perceiving that his royal victim had escaped, uttered an ejaculation of rage and disappointment, flung down the arquebuss, and folding his arms upon his bosom, awaited the result. Fortunately, an officer accompanied the soldiers who seized him, or they would have hewn him in pieces.

The wretched man made no attempt to fly, or to defend himself, but when the soldiers rushed into the room, cried, "Go no further. I am he you seek."

"We know it, accursed villain," rejoined the foremost of their number, brandishing a sword over his head. "You have slain the queen."

"Would I had!" rejoined Underhill. "But it is not the truth. The Lord was not willing I should be the instrument of his vengeance."

"Hear the blasphemer!" roared another soldier, dealing him a blow in the mouth with the pummel of his dagger, that made the blood gush from his lips. "He boasts of the villany he has committed."

"If my arm had not been stayed, I had delivered the land from idolatry and oppression," returned Underhill. "A season of terrible persecution is at hand, when you will lament as much as I do, that my design has been frustrated. The blood of the righteous would have been spared; the fagots at the stake un-lighted; the groans of the martyrs unheard. But it is the Lord's will that this should be. Blessed be the name of the Lord!"

"Silence, hell-dog!" vociferated a third soldier, placing the point of his halbert at his breast. "Host think Heaven would approve the foul deed thou meditatedst? Silence! I say, or I will drive my pike to thy heart."

"I will *not* be silent," rejoined Underhill, firmly. "So long as breath is left me, I will denounce the idolatrous queen by whom this unhappy land is governed, and pray that the crown may be removed from her head."

"Rather than thou shalt do so in my hearing, I will pluck out thy traitorous tongue by the roots," returned the soldier who had last spoken.

"Peace," interposed the officer. "Secure him, but harm him not. He may have confederates. It is important that all concerned in this atrocious attempt should be discovered."

"I have no accomplice," replied Underhill. "My own heart dictated what my hand essayed."

"May that hand perish in everlasting fire for the deed!" rejoined the officer. "But if there be power in torture to make you confess who set you on, it shall not be left untried."

"I have already spoken the truth," replied the enthusiast; "and the sharpest engine ever devised by ruthless man shall not make me gainsay it, or accuse the innocent. I would not have shared the glory of the action with any one. And since it has failed, my life alone shall pay the penalty."

"Gag him," cried the officer. "If I listen longer, I shall be tempted to anticipate the course of justice, and I would not one pang should be spared him."

The command was obeyed. On searching him, they found a small powder-flask, a few bullets, notched, to make the wound they inflicted more dangerous, a clasp-knife, and a bible, in the first leaf of which was written a prayer for the deliverance and restoration of Queen Jane,—a circumstance afterwards extremely prejudicial to that unfortunate lady.

After Underhill had been detained for some hours in the chamber where he was seized, an order arrived to carry him before the council. Brought before them, he answered all their interrogations firmly, confessed his design, related how he had planned it, and denied as before, with the strongest asseverations, that he had any accomplice. When questioned as to the prayer for Lady Jane Grey, whom he treasonably designated "Queen Jane," he answered that he should ever regard her as the rightful sovereign, and should pray with his latest breath for her restoration to the throne—a reply, which awakened a suspicion that some conspiracy was in agitation in Jane's favour. Nothing further, however, could be elicited, and he was ordered to be put to the rack.

Delivered by the guard to Lawrence Nightgall and his assistants, he was conveyed to the torture-chamber. The sight of the dreadful instruments there collected, though enough to appal the stoutest breast, appeared to have no terror for him. Scrutinizing the various engines with a look of curiosity, he remarked that none of them seemed to have been recently used; and added, that they would soon be more frequently employed. He had not been there many minutes, when Mauger, the headsman, Wolfytt, the sworn tormentor, and Sorrocold the chirurgeon, arrived, and preparations were made for administering the torture.

The rack has already been described as a large oaken frame, raised about three feet from the ground, having a roller at each end, moved by a lever. Stripped, and placed on his back on the ground, the prisoner was attached by strong cords to the rollers. Stationing themselves at either extremity of the frame, Mauger and Wolfytt each seized a lever, while Nightgall took up his position at the small table opposite, to propose the interrogations, and write down the answers. The chirurgeon remained near the prisoner, and placed his hand upon his wrist. Those preparations made, Nightgall demanded, in a stern tone, whether the prisoner would confess who had instigated him to the crime he had committed.

"I have already said I have no accomplices," replied Underhill.

Nightgall made a sign to the assistants, and the rollers were turned with a creaking sound, extending the prisoners limbs in opposite directions, and giving him exquisite pain. But he did not even groan.

After the lapse of a few moments, Nightgall said, "Edward Underhill, I again ask you who were your accomplices?"

No answer being returned, the jailor waved his hand, and the levers were again turned. The sharpness of the torture forced an involuntary cry from the prisoner. But beyond this expression of suffering, he continued silent.

The interrogation was a third time repeated; and after some effort on the part of the assistants, the levers were again turned. Nightgall and the chirurgcon both watched this part of the application with some curiosity. The strain upon the limbs was almost intolerable. The joints started from their sockets, and the sinews were drawn out to their utmost capability of tension.

After the wretched man had endured this for a few minutes, Sorrocold informed Nightgall, in a low tone, that nature was failing. The cords were then gradually relaxed, and he was unbound. His temples being bathed with vinegar, he soon afterwards revived.

But he was only recovered from one torture to undergo another. The next step taken by his tormentors was to place him in a suit of irons, called the Scavenger's Daughter—a hideous engine devised by Sir William Skevington, lieutenant of the Tower, in Henry the Eighth's reign, and afterwards corrupted into the name above mentioned. By this horrible machine, which was shaped like a hoop, his limbs were compressed so closely together that he resembled a ball; and being conveyed to an adjoining dungeon, he was left in this state without light or food for further examination.

XIII.—HOW MAGOG NEARLY LOST HIS SUPPER; HOW HIS BEARD WAS BURNT; HOW XIT WAS PLACED IN A BASKET; AND HOW HE WAS KICKED UPON THE RAMPARTS.

Congratulations, rejoicings, and public thanksgivings followed the queen's preservation from the hand of the assassin. Courtenay, who had long planned a masque to be exhibited for her amusement within the Tower, thought this a fitting occasion to produce it. And the utmost expedition being used, on the day but one after Underhill's attempt, all was in readiness.

Great mystery having been observed in the preparations for the pageant, that it might come upon the spectators as a surprise, none, except those actually concerned in it, knew what was intended to be represented. Even the actors, themselves, were kept in darkness concerning it, and it was only on the night before, when their dresses were given them, that they had any precise notion of the characters they were to assume. A sort of rehearsal then took place in one of the lower chambers of the palace; at which the Earl of Devonshire assisted in person, and instructed them in their parts. A few trials soon made all perfect, and when the rehearsal was over, Courtenay felt satisfied that the pageant would go off with tolerable eclat.

As may be supposed, the three gigantic warders and their diminutive follower were among the mummers. Indeed, the principal parts wore assigned them; and on no previous occasion had Xit's characteristic coxcombry been more strongly called forth than during the rehearsal. No consequential actor of modern times could give himself more airs. Perceiving he was indispensable, he would only do exactly what pleased him, and, when reprimanded for his impertinence, refused to perform at all, and was about to walk off with an air of offended dignity. A few conciliatory words, however, from the Earl of Devonshire induced him to return; and when all was arranged to his satisfaction, he began to exhibit a fun and humour that bid fair to outshine all his competitors.

The rehearsal over, a substantial repast was provided by the earl for his troop. And here, as usual, the giants acquitted themselves to admiration. Unfortunately, however, for Magog, his spouse was present, and his dull apprehension of his part at the rehearsal, having excited her displeasure, she now visited it upon his devoted head. Whenever he helped himself to a piece of meat, or a capon, she snatched it from his plate, and transferred it to those of his brethren.

Supper was nearly over, and the hen-pecked giant, who as yet had tasted nothing, was casting wistful glances at the fast-vanishing dishes, when Dame

Placida arose, and saying she was greatly fatigued, expressed her determination to return home immediately. In vain Magog remonstrated. She was firm, and her hapless spouse was arising with a most rueful countenance to accompany her, when Ribald very obligingly offered to take his place and escort her. Dame Placida appeared nothing loth, and Magog, having eagerly embraced the proposal, the pair departed.

"And now brother," said Gog, "you can do as you please. Make up for lost time."

"Doubt it not," replied Magog, "and by way of commencing, I will trouble you for that sirloin of beef. Send me the dish and the carving-knife, I pray you, for with this puny bit of steel I can make no progress at all."

His request was immediately complied with, and it was pleasant to behold with what inconceivable rapidity slice after slice disappeared. In a brief space, a few bare bones were all that remained of the once-lordly joint. Magog's brethren watched his progress with truly fraternal interest. Their own appetites being satisfied, they had full leisure to minister to his wants; and most sedulously did they attend to them. A brisket of veal, steeped in verjuice, supplied the place of the sirloin, and a hare-pie, in due season, that of the veal.

Magog acknowledged these attentions with grateful murmurings.

He was too busy to speak. When the hare-pie, which was of a somewhat savoury character, was entirely consumed, he paused for a moment, and pointed significantly to a large measure of wine at some little distance from him. Og immediately stretched out his arm, and handed it to him. Nodding to his brother, the married giant drained its contents at a draught, and then applied himself with new ardour to the various dishes with which his plate was successively laden.

"What would your wife say, if she could see you now?" observed Peter Trusbut, who sat opposite to him, and witnessed his proceedings with singular satisfaction.

"Don't mention her," rejoined Magog, bolting a couple of cheesecakes which he had crammed, at the same time, into his capacious mouth; "don't mention her, or you will take away my appetite."

"No fear of that," laughed the pantler; "but what say you to a glass of distilled waters? It will be a good wind-up to your meal, and aid digestion."

"With all my heart," rejoined the giant.

The pantler then handed him a stone bottle, holding perhaps a quart, and knowing his propensities, thought it needful to caution him as to the strength of the liquid. Disregarding the hint, Magog emptied the greater part of the spirit into a flagon, and tossed it off, as if it had been water. Peter Trusbut held up his hands in amazement, and expected to see the giant drop senseless under the table. But no such event followed. The only consequence of the potent draught being that it brought the water into his eyes, and made him gasp a little to recover his breath.

"How do you feel after it, brother?" inquired Og, slapping him on the shoulder.

"So valiant," hiccupped Magog, "that I think when I get home, I shall assert my proper position as a lord of the creation."

"Act up to that resolution, Master Magog," observed the pantler, laughing, "and I shall not think my liquor thrown away."

"If such be its effect," said Xit, who; it has before been remarked, had an unconquerable tendency to imitate, and, if possible, exceed the extravagancies of his companions, "I will e'en try a drop of it myself."

And before he could be prevented, the mannikin applied the stone bottle to his lips, and drained it to the last drop. If Magog's brain was sufficiently stolid to resist the effect of the fiery liquid, Xit's was not. Intoxication speedily displayed itself in the additional brilliancy of his keen sparkling little orbs, and in all his gestures. At first, his antics created much diversion, and he was allowed to indulge them freely; but before long he became so outrageous and mischievous, that it was found necessary to restrain him. Springing upon the table, he cut the most extraordinary capers among the dishes, breaking several of them, upsetting the flagons and pots of wine, tweaking the noses of the male guests, kissing the females, and committing a hundred other monkey tricks.

On being called to order, he snapped his fingers in the face of the reprover, and conceiving himself especially affronted by Gog, he threw a goblet at his head. Luckily, the missile was caught before it reached its mark. He next seized a torch, and perceiving that Magog had fallen asleep, set fire to his beard, to arouse him. Starting to his feet, the giant clapped his hand to his chin—too late however, to save a particle of his hirsute honours. His rage was terrific. Roaring like a wild bull, he vowed he would be the death of the offender; and would have kept his word, if it had not been for his brethren, who, seizing each an arm, restrained him by main strength, and forced him into his seat, where, after a few minutes, his anger gave way to laughter.

This was mainly attributable to an accident that befel Xit in his hurry to escape. Not being particular where he set his feet, the dwarf plumped into an open plum tart, the syrup of which was so thick and glutinous that it detained him as effectually as birdlime. In his terror, he dragged the dish after him to a considerable distance, and his grimaces were so irresistibly ludicrous that they convulsed the beholders with laughter. No one attempted to assist him, and it was only by the loss of both shoes that he could extricate himself from his unpleasant situation. Peter Trusbut then seized him, and thrusting him into a basket, fastened down the lid to prevent further mischief.

This occurrence served as the signal for separation. Og and Gog took their way to the By-ward Tower, the latter carrying the basket containing Xit under his arm, while Magog, bemoaning the loss of his beard, and afraid of presenting himself to his wife under such untoward circumstances, accompanied them as far as the gateway of the Bloody Tower. Here he paused to say good night.

"Would I could anticipate a good night, myself!" he groaned "But I can neither eat, drink, nor sleep in comfort now. Ah! brothers, if I had but listened to your advice! But repentance comes too late."

"It does—it does," replied Gog; "But let us hope your dame will amend."

"That she never will," screamed Xit from the basket. "What a lucky escape *I* had—ha! ha!"

"Peace! thou stinging gadfly," roared Magog. "Am I ever to be tormented by thee!"

But as Xit, who imagined himself secure, only laughed the louder, he grew at last so enraged, that snatching the basket from Og, he placed it on the ground, and gave it such a kick, that it flew to the top of the ramparts beyond Traitor's Tower, where it was picked up by a sentinel, and the dwarf taken out more dead than alive.

On reaching his habitation—which was the same Dame Placida had formerly occupied during her state of widowhood, at the right of the road leading from the Bloody Tower to the Green,—Magog found she had not retired to rest as he expected, but was engaged in conversation with Ribald, who had been prevailed upon to remain for a few minutes to taste the ale for which she was so much, and so justly, celebrated. One cup had led to another, and the jovial warder seemed 'in no hurry to depart. The giant was delighted to see him, and, forgetting his misfortune, was about to shake him heartily by the hand, when his wife screamed out—"Why Magog, what is the matter with your chin? You have lost your beard!"

Humbly deprecating her resentment, the giant endeavoured to explain. But as nothing would satisfy her, he was fain to leave her with Ribald, and betake himself to his couch, where he speedily fell asleep, and forgot his troubles.

XIV.—OF THE MASQUE GIVEN BY COURTENAY IN HONOUR OF QUEEN MARY; AND HOW XIT WAS SWALLOWED BY A SEA-MONSTER.

During the early part of the next day, the majority of the inmates of the Tower were on the tiptoe of expectation for the coming pageant, which was fixed to take place in the evening in the large court lying eastward of that wing of the palace, denominated the Queen's Lodgings. The great hall, used on the previous night for the rehearsal, was allotted as a dressing-room to those engaged in the performance, and thither they repaired a few hours before the entertainment commenced.

As the day declined, multitudes flocked to the court, and stationed themselves within the barriers, which had been erected to keep off the crowd. In addition to these defences, a warder was stationed at every ten paces, and a large band of halberdiers was likewise in attendance to maintain order. Banners were suspended from the battlements of the four towers flanking the corners of the court,—namely, the Salt Tower, the Lanthorn Tower, the Wardrobe Tower, and the Broad Arrow Tower. The summits of these fortifications were covered with spectators, as were the eastern ramparts, and the White Tower. Such windows of the palace as overlooked the scene, were likewise thronged.

At the southern extremity of the court, stretching from the Lanthorn Tower to the Salt Tower, stood a terrace, raised a few feet above the level of the inclosure, and protected by a low-arched balustrade of stone. This was set apart for the Queen, and beneath a mulberry-tree, amid the branches of which a canopy of crimson velvet was disposed, her chair was placed.

About six o'clock, when every inch of standing-room was occupied, and expectation raised to its highest pitch, a door in the palace leading to the terrace was thrown open, and the Queen issued from it. Stunning vociferations welcomed her, and these were followed, or rather accompanied, by a prolonged flourish of trumpets. It was a moment of great excitement, and many a heart beat high at the joyous sounds. Every eye was directed towards Mary, who bowing repeatedly in acknowledgment of her enthusiastic reception, was saluted with—"God save your highness! Confusion to your enemies! Death to all traitors!" and other exclamations referring to her late providential deliverance.

The Queen was attired in a rich gown of raised cloth of gold. A partlet, decorated with precious stones, surrounded her throat, and her stomacher literally blazed with diamonds. Upon her head she wore a caul of gold, and over it, at the back, a round cap, embroidered with orient pearls. In front, she wore a cornet of black velvet, likewise embroidered with pearls. A couple of beautiful Italian greyhounds, confined by a silken leash, accompanied her. She was in excellent spirits, and, whether excited by the promised spectacle, or by some secret cause, appeared unusually animated. Many of the beholders, dazzled by her gorgeous attire, and struck by her sprightly air, thought her positively beautiful. Smilingly acknowledging the greetings of her subjects, she gave her hand to the Earl of Devonshire, and was conducted by him to the seat beneath the mulberry-tree.

They were followed by a numerous train of dames and nobles, foremost among whom came Sir Henry Bedingfeld,—who as lieutenant of the Tower, claimed the right of standing behind the royal chair. Next to the knight stood the Princess Elizabeth, who viewed with the bitterest jealousy the devoted attention paid by Courtenay to her sister; and, next to the princess, stood Jane the Fool. Simon Renard also was among the crowd. But he kept aloof, resolved not to show himself, unless occasion required it.

As soon as the Queen was seated, another flourish of trumpets was blown, and from the great gates at the further end of the court issued a crowd of persons clothed in the skins of wild animals, dragging an immense machine, painted to resemble a rocky island. On reaching the centre of the inclosure, the topmost rock burst open, and discovered a beautiful female seated upon a throne, with a crown on her head, and a sceptre in her hand. While the spectators expressed their admiration of her beauty by loud plaudits, another rock opened, and discovered a fiendish-looking figure, armed with a strangely-formed musket, which he levelled at the mimic sovereign. A cry of horror pervaded the assemblage, but at that moment another rock burst asunder, and a fairy arose, who placed a silver shield between the Queen and the assassin; while a gauze drapery, wafted from beneath, enveloped them in its folds.

Masque in the Palace Garden of the Tower

At the appearance of the fairy, the musket fell from the assassin's grasp. Uttering a loud cry, a troop of demons issued from below, and seizing him with their talons bore him out of eight. The benignant fairy then waved her sword; the gauzy drapery dropped to her feet; and four other female figures arose, representing Peace, Plenty, Justice, and Clemency. These figures ranged themselves round the Queen, and the fairy addressed her in a speech, telling her that these were her attributes;—that she had already won her people's hearts, and ended by promising her a long and prosperous reign. Each word, that applied to Mary, was followed by a cheer from the bystanders, and when it was ended, the applauses were deafening. The mimic queen then arose, and taking off her crown, tendered it to the real sovereign. The four attributes likewise extended their arms towards her, and told her they belonged to her. And while the group was in this position, the machine was borne away.

Fresh flourishes of trumpets succeeded; and several lively airs were played by bands of minstrels stationed at different points of the court-yard.

A wild and tumultuous din was now heard; and the gates being again thrown open, forth rushed a legion of the most grotesque and fantastic figures ever beheld. Some were habited as huge, open-jawed sea-monsters; others as dragons, gorgons, and hydras; others, as satyrs and harpies; others, as gnomes and salamanders. Some had large hideous masks, making them look all head,—some monstrous wings,—some long coiled tails, like serpents many were mounted on hobby-horses,—and all whose garbs would permit them, were armed with staves, flails, or other indescribable weapons.

When this multitudinous and confused assemblage had nearly filled the inclosure, loud roarings were heard, and from the gateway marched Gog and Magog, arrayed like their gigantic namesakes of Guildhall. A long artificial beard, of a blue tint, supplied the loss which Magog's singed chin had sustained. His head was bound with a wreath of laurel leaves. Gog's helmet precisely resembled that worn by his namesake, and he carried a curiously-formed shield, charged with the device of a black eagle, like that with which the wooden statue is furnished. Magog was armed with a long staff, to which a pudding-net, stuffed with wool, was attached; while Gog bore a long lathen spear. The appearance of the giants was hailed with a general roar of delight. But the laughter and applauses were increased by what followed.

Once more opened to their widest extent, the great gates admitted what, at first, appeared to be a moving fortification. From its sides projected two enormous arms, each sustaining a formidable club. At the summit stood a smaller turret, within which, encircled by a wreath of roses and other flowers, decorated with silken pennoncels, sat Xit, his pigmy person clothed in tight silk fleshings. Glittering wings fluttered on his shoulders, and he was armed with the weapons of the Paphian God. The tower, which, with its decorations, was more than twenty feet high, was composed of basket-work, covered with canvass, painted to resemble a round embattled structure. It was tenanted by Og, who moved about in it with the greatest case. A loophole in front enabled him to see what was going forward, and he marched slowly towards the centre of the inclosure. An edging of loose canvass, painted like a rocky foundation, concealed his feet. The effect of this moving fortress was highly diverting, and elicited shouts of laughter and applause from the beholders.

"That device," observed Courtenay to the queen, "represents a tower of strength—or rather, I should say, the Tower of London. It is about to be attacked by the rabble rout of rebellion, and, I trust, will be able to make good its defence against them."

"I hope so," replied Mary, smiling. "I should be grieved to think that my good Tower yielded to such assailants. But who is that I perceive? Surely, it is Cupid?"

"Love is at present an inhabitant of the Tower," replied Courtenay, with a passionate look.

Raising his eyes, the next moment, he perceived Elizabeth behind Sir Henry Bedingfeld. She turned from him with a look of reproach.

A seasonable interruption to his thoughts was offered by the tumultuous cry arising from the mummers. Gog and Magog having placed themselves on either side of the Tower as its defenders, the assault commenced. The object of the assailants was to overthrow the fortress. With this view, they advanced against it from all quarters, thrusting one another forward, and hurling their weapons against it. This furious attack was repelled by the two giants, who drove them back as fast as they advanced, hurling some head over heels, trampling others under foot, and exhibiting extraordinary feats of strength and activity. The Tower, itself, was not behind-hand in resistance. Its two arms moved about like the sails of a windmill, dealing tremendous blows.

The conflict afforded the greatest amusement to the beholders; but while the fortress and its defenders maintained their ground against all the assailants, there was one person who began to find his position somewhat uncomfortable. This was Xit. So long as Og contented himself with keeping off his enemies, the dwarf was delighted with his elevated situation, and looked round with a smile of delight. But when the giant, animated by the sport, began to attack in his turn, the fabric in which he was encased swayed to and fro so violently, that Xit expected every moment to be precipitated to the ground. In vain he attempted to communicate his fears to Og. The giant was unconscious of his danger, and the din and confusion around them was so great, that neither Gog nor Magog could hear his outcries. As a last resource, he tried to creep into the turret, but this he found impracticable.

"The god of love appears in a perilous position, my lord," observed the queen, joining in the laughter of the spectators.

"He does, indeed," replied Courtenay; "and though the Tower may defend itself, I fear its chief treasure will be lost in the struggle."

"You speak the truth, my lord," remarked the deep voice of Simon lienard, from behind.

If Courtenay intended any reply to this observation of his mortal foe, it was prevented by an incident which at that moment occurred. Combining their forces, the rabble rout of dragons, gorgons, imps, and demons had made a desperate assault upon the Tower. Og whirled around his clubs with increased rapidity, and dozens were prostrated by their sweep. Gog and Magog likewise plied their weapons vigorously, and the assailants were driven back completely discomfited.

But, unluckily, at this moment, Og made a rush forward to complete his conquest, and in so doing pitched Xit out of the turret. Falling head-foremost into the yawning jaws of an enormous goggle-eyed sea-monster, whose mouth seemed purposely opened to receive him, and being moved by springs, immediately closed, the dwarf entirely disappeared. A scream of delight arose from the spectators, who looked upon the occurrence as part of the pageant.

The queen laughed heartily at Xit's mischance, and even Courtenay, though discomposed by the accident, could not help joining in the universal merriment.

"I might take it as an evil omen," he remarked in an under tone to Mary, "that love should be destroyed by your majesty's enemies."

"See! he re-appears," cried the queen, calling the earl's attention to the monster, whose jaws opened and discovered the dwarf. "He has sustained no injury."

Xit's disaster, meanwhile, had occasioned a sudden suspension of hostilities among the combatants. All the mummers set up a shout of laughter, and the echoing of sound produced by their masks was almost unearthly. Gog and Magog, grinning from ear to ear, now approached the dwarf, and offered to restore him to his turret. But he positively refused to stir, and commanded the monster, in whose jaws he was seated, to carry him to the queen. After a little parley, the order was obeyed; and the huge pasteboard monster, which was guided within-side by a couple of men, wheeled round, and dragged its scaly length towards the terrace.

Arrived opposite the royal seat, the mimic Cupid sprang out of the monster's jaws, and fluttering his gauzy wings (which were a little the worse for his recent descent) to give himself the appearance of flying, ran nimbly up the side of the terrace, and vaulted upon the balustrade in front of her majesty. He had still possession of his bow and arrows, and poising himself with considerable grace on the point of his left foot, fitted a silver shaft to the string, and aimed it at the queen.

"Your highness is again threatened," observed Sir Henry Bedingfeld, advancing and receiving the arrow, which, winged with but little force, dropped harmlessly from his robe.

"You are ever faithful, Sir Henry," observed Mary, to the knight, whose zeal in this instance occasioned a smile among the attendants; "but we have little fear from the darts of Cupid."

Xit, meanwhile, had fitted another arrow, and drawing it with greater force, struck Courtenay on the breast. Not content with this, the mischievous urchin let fly a third shaft at the Princess Elizabeth, who had advanced somewhat nearer the queen, and the arrow chancing to stick to some of the ornaments on her stomacher, appeared to have actually pierced her bosom. Elizabeth coloured deeply as she plucked the dart from her side, and threw it angrily to the ground. A cloud gathered on the queen's brow, and Courtenay was visibly disconcerted.

Xit, however, either unconscious of the trouble he had occasioned, or utterly heedless of it, took a fourth arrow from his quiver, and affecting to sharpen its point upon the stone balustrade, shot it against Jane the Fool. This last shaft likewise hit its mark, though Jane endeavoured to ward it off with her marotte; and Xit Completed the absurdity of the scene by fluttering towards her, and seizing her hand, pressed it to his lips,—a piece of gallantry for which he was rewarded by a sound cuff on the ears.

"Nay, mistress," cried Xit, "that is scarcely fair. Love and Folly were well matched."

"If Love mate with Folly, he must expect to be thus treated," replied Jane.

"Nay, then, I will bestow my favours on the wisest woman I can find," replied Xit.

"There thou wilt fail again," cried Jane; "for every wise woman will shun thee."

"A truce to thy rejoinders, sweetheart," returned Xit. "Thy wit is as keen as my arrows, and as sure to hit the mark."

"My wit resembles thy godship's arrows in one particular only," retorted Jane. "It strikes deepest where it is most carelessly aimed. But, hie away! Thou wilt find Love no match for Folly."

"So I perceive," replied Xit, "and shall therefore proceed to Beauty. I must have been blinder than poets feign, to have come near thee at all. In my pursuit of Folly, I have forgot the real business of Love. But thus it is ever with me and my minions!"

With this, he fluttered towards the queen, and prostrating himself before her, said—"Your majesty will not banish Love from your court?"

"Assuredly not," replied Mary; "or if we did banish thee, thou wouldst be sure to find some secret entrance."

"Your majesty is in the right," replied the mimic deity, "I should. And disdain not this caution from Cupid. As long as you keep my two companions, Jealousy and Malice, at a distance, Love will appear in his own rosy hues. But the moment you admit them, he will change his colours, and become a tormentor."

"But if thou distributest thy shafts at random, so that lovers dote on more than one object, how am I to exclude Jealousy?" asked the queen.

"By cultivating self-esteem," replied Cupid. "The heart I have wounded for your highness can never feel disloyalty."

"That is true, thou imp," observed Courtenay; "and for that speech, I forgive thee the mischief thou hast done."

"And so thou assurest me against infidelity?" said Mary.

"Your highness may be as inconstant as you please," replied Cupid, "since the dart I aimed at you has been turned aside by Sir Henry Bedingfeld. But rest easy. He who loves you can love no other."

"I am well satisfied," replied Mary, with a gratified look.

"And since I have thy permission to love whom I please, I shall avail myself largely of it, and give all my heart to my subjects."

"Not *all* your heart, my gracious mistress," said Courtenay, in a tender whisper.

At this juncture, Xit, watching his opportunity, drew an arrow from his quiver, and touched the queen with it near the heart.

"I have hit your majesty at last, as well as the Earl of Devonshire," he cried gleefully. "Shall I summon my brother Hymen to your assistance? He is among the crowd below."

A half-suppressed smile among the royal attendants followed this daring remark.

"That knave's audacity encourages me to hope, gracious madam," whispered Courtenay, "that this moment may be the proudest—the happiest of my life."

"No more of this—at least not now, my lord," replied Mary, whose notions of decorum were somewhat scandalised at this public declaration. "Dismiss this imp. He draws too many eyes upon us."

"I have a set of verses to recite to your majesty," interposed Xit, whose quick ears caught the remark, and who was in no hurry to leave the royal presence.

"Not now," rejoined Mary, rising. "Fear nothing, thou merry urchin. We will take care Love meets its desert. We thank you, my lord," she added, turning to Courtenay, "for the pleasant pastime you have afforded us."

As the queen arose, loud and reiterated shouts resounded from the spectators, in which all the mummers joined. Amid these acclamations she returned to the palace. Courtenay again tendered her his hand, and the slight pressure which he hazarded was sensibly returned.

Just as she was about to enter the window, Mary turned round to bow for the last time to the assemblage, when there arose a universal cry—"Long live Queen Mary!—Long live the Earl of Devonshire!"

Mary smiled. Her bosom palpitated with pleasure, and she observed to her lover—"You are the people's favourite, my lord. I should not deserve to be their queen if I did not share in their affection."

"May I then hope?" asked the Earl, eagerly.

"You may," replied Mary, softly.

The brilliant vision which these words raised before Courtenay's eyes, was dispersed by a look which he at that moment received from Elizabeth.

The festivities in the court did not terminate with the departure of the royal train. Xit was replaced in the turret, whence he aimed his darts at the prettiest damsels he could perceive, creating infinite merriment among the crowd. An immense ring was then formed by all the mummers, who danced round the three giants, the minstrels accompanying the measure with appropriate strains. Nothing more grotesque can be imagined than the figures of Gog and Magog, as engaged in the dance, in their uncouth garbs. As to Og, he flourished his clubs, and twirled himself round with great rapidity in the opposite direction to the round of dancers, until at last, becoming giddy, he lost his balance, and fell with a tremendous crash, upsetting Xit for the second time.

Ever destined to accidents, the dwarf, from his diminutive stature, seldom sustained any injury, and upon this occasion, though a good deal terrified, he escaped unhurt. Og was speedily uncased, and, glad to be set at liberty, joined the ring of dancers, and footed it with as much glee as the merriest of them.

As the evening advanced, fire-works were discharged, and a daring rope-dancer, called Peter the Dutchman, ascended the cupola of the south-east turret of the White Tower, and got upon the vane, where he lighted a couple of torches. After standing for some time, now upon one foot—now on the other, he kindled a firework placed in a sort of helmet on his head, and descended amid a shower of sparks by a rope, one end of which was fastened in the court where the masquers were assembled. A substantial supper, of which the mummers and their friends partook, concluded the diversions of the evening, and all departed well satisfied with their entertainment.

XV.—BY WHOSE INSTRUMENTALITY QUEEN MARY BECAME CONVINCED OF COURTENAY'S INCONSTANCY; AND HOW SHE AFFIANCED HERSELF TO PHILIP OF SPAIN.

While the festivities above described occurred without the palace, within, all was confusion and alarm. The look, which Elizabeth had given Courtenay, sank into his very soul. All his future greatness appeared valueless in his eyes, and his only desire was to break off the alliance with Mary, and reinstate himself in the affections of her sister. For the queen, it is almost needless to say, he felt no real love. But he was passionately enamoured of Elizabeth, whose charms had completely captivated him.

As soon as she could consistently do so, after her return to the palace, the princess retired to her own apartments, and though her departure afforded some relief to the earl, he still continued in a state of great perturbation. Noticing his altered manner, the queen inquired the cause with great solicitude. Courtenay answered her evasively. And putting her own construction upon it, she said in a tone of encouragement—"It was a strange remark made by the little urchin who enacted Cupid. Was he tutored in his speech?"

"Not by me, gracious madam," replied Courtenay, distractedly.

"Then the knave hath a ready wit," returned the queen. "He has put thoughts into my head which I cannot banish thence."

"Indeed!" exclaimed the earl. "I trust his boldness has not offended you."

"Do I look so?" rejoined Mary, smiling. "If I do, my countenance belies my feelings. No, Courtenay, I have been thinking that no woman can govern a great kingdom, like mine, unaided. She must have some one, to whom she can ever apply for guidance and protection,—some one to whom she can open her whole heart,—to whom she can look for counsel, consolation, love. In whom could she find all this?"

"In no one but a husband, gracious madam," replied Courtenay, who felt he could no longer affect to misunderstand her.

"You are right, my lord," she replied playfully. "Can you not assist our choice?"

"If I dared,"—said Courtenay, who felt he was standing upon the verge of a precipice.

"Pshaw!" exclaimed Mary. "A queen must ever play the wooer. It is part of her prerogative. Our choice is already made—so we need not consult you on the subject."

"May I not ask whom your majesty has so far distinguished?" demanded the earl, trembling.

"You shall learn anon, my lord," replied the queen. "We choose to keep you a short time in suspense, for here comes Simon Renard, and we do not intend to admit him to our confidence."

"That man is ever in my path," muttered the earl, returning the ambassador s stern glance with one equally menacing. "I am half reconciled to this hateful alliance by the thought of the mortification it will inflict upon him."

It would almost seem from Renard's looks, that he could read what was passing in the other's breast; for his brow grew each instant more lowering.

"I must quit your majesty for a moment," observed Courtenay, "to see to the masquers. Besides, my presence might be a restraint to your councillor. He shall not want an opportunity to utter his calumnies behind my back."

Renard smiled bitterly.

"Farewell, my lord," said the queen, giving him her hand to kiss. "When you return, you shall have your answer."

"It is the last time his lips shall touch that hand," muttered Renard, as the earl departed.

On quitting the royal presence, Courtenay wandered in a state of the utmost disquietude to the terrace. He gazed vacantly at the masquers, and tried to divert his thoughts with their sports; but in vain. He could not free himself from the idea of Elizabeth. He had now reached the utmost height of his ambition. He was all but affianced to the queen, and he doubted not that a few hours—perhaps moments—would decide his fate. His bosom was torn with conflicting emotions. On one side stood power, with all its temptations—on the other passion, fierce, irrepressible passion. The struggle was almost intolerable.

After debating with himself for some time, he determined to seek one last interview with Elizabeth, before he finally committed himself to the queen, vainly imagining it would calm his agitation. But, like most men under the influence of desperate emotion, he acted from impulse, rather than reflection. The resolution was no sooner formed, than acted upon. Learning that the Princess was in her chamber, he proceeded thither, and found her alone.

Elizabeth was seated in a small room, partially hung with arras, and over the chair she occupied, were placed the portraits of her sire, Henry the Eighth, and two of his wives, Anne Boleyn and Catharine of Arragon. Greatly surprised by the earl's visit, she immediately arose, and in an authoritative tone commanded him to withdraw.

"How is this?" she cried. "Are you not content with what you have already done, but must add insult to perfidy!"

"Hear me, Elizabeth," said Courtenay, advancing towards her, and throwing himself on his knee. "I am come to implore your forgiveness."

"You have my compassion, my lord," rejoined Elizabeth; "but you shall not have my forgiveness. You have deeply deceived me."

"I have deceived myself," replied Courtenay.

"A paltry prevarication, and unworthy of you," observed the Princess, scornfully. "But I have endured this long enough. Arise, and leave me."

"I will *not* leave you, Elizabeth," said Courtenay, "till I have explained the real motives of my conduct, and the real state of my feelings, which, when I have done, I am persuaded you will not judge me as harshly, as you do now."

"I do not desire to hear them," replied tho Princess. "But since you are determined to speak, be brief."

"During my captivity in this fortress," began Courtenay, "when I scarcely hoped for release, and when I was an utter stranger, except from description, to the beauties of your sex, I had certain vague and visionary notions of female loveliness, which I have never since found realized except in yourself."

Elizabeth uttered an exclamation of impatience.

"Do not interrupt me," proceeded Courtenay. "All I wish to show is, that long before I had seen you, my heart was predisposed to love you. On my release from imprisonment, it was made evident in many ways, that the Queen, your sister, regarded me with favourable eyes. Dazzled by the distinction—as who would not be?—I fancied I returned her passion. But I knew not then what love was—nor was it till I was bound in this thraldom that I became acquainted with its pangs."

"This you have said before, my lord," rejoined Elizabeth, struggling against her emotion. "And if you had not, it is too late to say it now."

"Your pardon, dearest Elizabeth," rejoined Courtenay, "for such you will ever be to me. I know I do not deserve your forgiveness. But I know, also, that I shall not the less on that account obtain it. Hear the truth from me, and judge me as you think proper. Since I knew that I had gained an interest in your eyes, I never could love your sister. Her throne had no longer any temptation for me—her attachment inspired me with disgust. You were, and still *are*, the sole possessor of my heart."

"Still are! my lord," exclaimed Elizabeth, indignantly. "And you are about to wed the Queen. Say no more, or *my* pity for you will be changed into contempt."

"It is my fate," replied the earl. "Oh! if you knew what the struggle has cost me, to sacrifice love at the shrine of ambition, you would indeed pity me."

"My lord," said Elizabeth, proudly, "if you have no respect for me, at least have some for yourself, and cease these unworthy lamentations."

"Tell me you no longer love me—tell me you despise—hate me—anything to reconcile myself to my present lot," cried Courtenay.

"Were I to say I no longer loved you, I should belie my heart," rejoined Elizabeth; "for, unfortunately for my peace of mind, I have formed a passion which I cannot conquer. But were I also to say that your abject conduct does not inspire me with contempt—with scorn for you, I should speak falsely. Hear me, in my turn, my lord. To-morrow, I shall solicit permission from the Queen to retire from the court altogether, and I shall not return till my feelings towards yourself are wholly changed." "Say not so," cried Courtenay. "I will forego all the brilliant expectations held out to me by Mary. I cannot endure to part with you."

"You have gone too far to retreat, my lord," said Elizabeth. "You are affianced to my sister."

"Not so," replied Courtenay, "and I never will be. When I came hither, it was to implore your forgiveness, and to take leave of you for ever. But I find that wholly impossible. Let us fly from this fortress, and find either in a foreign land, or in some obscure corner of this kingdom, a happiness, which a crown could not confer."

As he pronounced these words with all the ardour of genuine passion, he pressed her hand to his lips. Elizabeth did not withdraw it.

"Save me from this great crime," he cried—"save me from wedding one whom I have never loved—save me from an union, which my soul abhors."

"Are you sincere?" asked Elizabeth, much moved.

"On my soul I am," replied Courtenay fervently. "Will you fly with me—this night—this hour,—now?"

Queen Mary surprising Courtenay and the Princess
Elizabeth.

"I will answer that question," cried a voice, which struck them both as if a thunderbolt had fallen at their feet. "I will answer that question," cried Mary, forcibly throwing aside the arras and gazing at them with eyes that literally seemed to flash fire,—"she will *not*."

"Had I not heard this with my own ears," she continued in a terrible tone, addressing her faithless lover, who still remained in a kneeling posture, regarding her with a look of mingled shame and defiance—"had I not heard this with my own ears, and seen it with my own eyes, I could not have believed it! Perfidious villain! you have deceived us both. . But you shall feel what it is to incur the resentment of a queen—and that queen the daughter of Henry the Eighth. Come in, sir," she added to some one behind the arras, and Simon Renard immediately stepped forth. "As I owe the discovery of the Earl of Devonshire's perfidy to you, the least I can do is to let you witness his disgrace."

"I will not attempt to defend myself, gracious madam," said Courtenay, rising.

"Defend yourself!" echoed the Queen, bitterly. "Not a word of your conversation to the Princess has escaped my ears. I was there—behind that curtain—almost as soon as you entered her chamber. I was acquainted with your treachery by this gentleman. I disbelieved him. But I soon found he spoke the truth. A masked staircase enabled me to approach you unobserved. I have heard all—all, traitor, all."

"To play the eaves-dropper was worthy of Simon Renard," returned Courtenay, with a look of deadly hatred at the ambassador, "but scarcely, I think, befitting the Queen of England."

"Where the Queen of England has unworthy persons to deal with, she must resort to unworthy means to detect them," returned Mary. "I am deeply indebted to M. Renard for his service—more deeply than I can express. An hour more, and it had been too late. Had I affianced myself to you, I should have considered the engagement binding. As it is, I can unscrupulously break it. I am greatly beholden to you, sir."

"I am truly rejoiced to be the instrument of preventing your majesty from entering into this degrading alliance," said Renard.—"Had it taken place, you would have unceasingly repented it."

"For you, minion," continued the Queen, turning to Elizabeth, who had looked silently on, "I have more pity than anger. You have been equally his dupe."

"I do not desire your highness's pity," rejoined the Princess, haughtily. "Your own case is more deserving of compassion than mine."

"Ah! God's death! derided!" cried the Queen, stamping her foot with indignation. "Summon the guard, M. Renard. I will place them both in confinement. Why am I not obeyed?" she continued, seeing the ambassador hesitated.

"Do nothing at this moment, I implore you, gracious madam." said Renard, in a low voice. "Disgrace were better than imprisonment. You punish the Earl sufficiently in casting him off."

"Obey me, sir," vociferated Mary, furiously, "or I will fetch the guard myself. An outraged woman may tamely submit to her wrongs—an outraged Queen can revenge them. Heaven be thanked! I have the power to do so, as I have the will. Down on your knees, Edward Courtenay, whom I have made Earl of Devonshire, and *would* have made King of England—on your knees, I say. Now, my lord, your sword."

"It is here," replied the Earl, presenting it to her, "and I entreat your majesty to sheathe it in my bosom."

"His crime does not amount to high treason," whispered Renard, "nor can your highness do more than disgrace him."

"The guard! the guard, sir!" cried Mary, authoritatively. "Our father, Henry the Eighth, whose lineaments frown upon us from that wall, had not authority for all he did. He was an absolute king, and we are absolute queen. Again, I say, the guard! and bid Sir Henry Bedingfeld attend us."

"Your majesty shall be obeyed," replied Renard, departing. "Do with me what you please, gracious madam," said Courtenay, as soon as they were alone. "My life is at your disposal. But, I beseech you, do not visit my faults upon the Princess Elizabeth. If your majesty tracked me hither, you must be well aware that my presence was as displeasing to her as it could be to yourself."

"I will not be sheltered under this plea," replied Elizabeth, whose anger was roused by her sister's imperious conduct. "That the interview was unsought on my part, your highness well knows. But that I lent a willing ear to the Earl of Devonshire's suit is equally true. And if your highness rejects him, I see nothing to prevent my accepting him."

"This to my face!" cried Mary, in extremity of indignation.

"And wherefore not?" returned Elizabeth, maliciously.

"Anger me no further," cried Mary, "or by my father's soul! I will not answer for your head." Her manner was so authoritative, and her looks so terrible, that even Elizabeth was awed.

"Again," interposed Courtenay, humbly, "let me, who am the sole cause of your majesty's most just displeasure, bear the weight of it. The Princess Elizabeth, I repeat, is not to blame."

"I am the best judge in my own cause, my lord," replied the Queen. "I will not hear a word more."

A deep silence then ensued, which was broken by the entrance of the Lieutenant of the Tower and the guard. Renard brought up the rear.

"Sir Henry Bedingfeld," said Mary, "I commit the Princess Elizabeth and the Earl of Devonshire to your custody."

"I can scarcely credit my senses, gracious Madam," replied Bedingfeld, gazing at the offenders with much concern, "and would fain persuade myself it is only a part of the pastime I have so recently witnessed."

"It is no pastime, Sir Henry," replied the Queen, sternly. "I little thought, when I entrusted you with the government of this fortress, how soon, and how importantly, you would have to exercise your office. Let the prisoners be placed in close confinement."

"This is the first time in my life," replied the old knight, "that I have hesitated to obey your majesty. And if I do so now, I beseech you to impute it to the right motive."

"How, sir!" cried the Queen fiercely. "Do you desire to make me regret that I have removed Sir John Gage? *He* would not have hesitated."

"For your own sake, gracious madam," said Sir Henry, falling on his knees before her, "I beseech you pause. I have been a faithful servant of your high and renowned father. Henry the Eighth—of your illustrious mother, Catherine of Arragon, who would almost seem,—from their pictures on that wall,—to be present now. In *their* names, I beseech you pause. I am well aware your feelings have been greatly outraged. But they may prompt you to do that which your calmer judgment may deplore."

"Remonstrance is in vain," rejoined the Queen. "I am inexorable. The Princess Elizabeth may remain a close prisoner in her own apartments. The Earl of Devonshire must be removed elsewhere. You will be answerable for their safe custody."

"I will," replied Bedingfeld, rising; "but I would that I had never lived to see this day!"

With this, he commanded his attendants to remove Courtenay, and when the order was obeyed, he lingered for a moment at the door, in the hope that the Queen would relent. But, as she continued immoveable, he departed with a sorrowful heart, and conveyed the Earl to his own lodgings.

Courtenay gone, Elizabeth's proud heart gave way, and she burst into a hood of tears. As Mary saw this, a feeling of compassion crossed her, which Renard perceiving, touched her sleeve, and drew her away.

"It were better to leave her now," he observed. Yielding to his advice, Mary was about to quit the room, when Elizabeth arose and threw herself at her feet.

"Spare him!" she cried.

"She thinks only of her lover," thought the Queen; "those tears are for him. I will *not* pity her."

And she departed without returning an answer.

Having seen two halberdiers placed at the door of the chamber, and two others at the foot of the masked staircase by which she and Renard had approached, Mary proceeded with the ambassador to her own apartments.

On thinking over the recent occurrences, her feelings were so exasperated, that she exclaimed aloud, "Oh! that I could avenge myself on the perjured traitor."

"I will show you how to avenge yourself," replied Renard.

"Do so, then," returned the queen.

"Unite yourself to my master, Philip of Spain," rejoined the ambassador. "Your cousin, the Emperor, highly desires the match. It will be an alliance worthy of you, and acceptable to your subjects. The Prince is a member of your own religion, and will enable you to restore its worship throughout your kingdom."

"I will think of it," replied Mary, musingly.

"Better *act* upon it," rejoined Renard. "The prince, besides his royal birth, is in all respects more richly endowed by nature than the Earl of Devonshire."

"So I have heard him accounted," replied Mary.

"Your majesty shall judge for yourself," rejoined Renard, producing a miniature. "Here is his portrait. The likeness is by no means flattering."

"He must be very handsome," observed Mary, gazing at the miniature.

"He is," replied Renard; "and his highness is as eager for the alliance as his imperial father. I have ventured to send him your majesty's portrait, and you shall hear in what rapturous terms he speaks of it."

And taking several letters from his doublet, he selected one sealed with the royal arms of Spain, from which he read several highly complimentary remarks on Mary's personal appearance.

"Enough, sir," said Mary, checking him. "More unions are formed from pique than from affection, and mine will be one of them. I am resolved to affiance myself to the Prince of Spain, and that forthwith. I will not allow myself time to change my mind."

"Your highness is in the right," observed Renard, eagerly.

"Meet me at midnight in Saint John's Chapel in the White Tower," continued the queen, "where in your presence, and in the presence of Heaven, I will solemnly affiance myself to the prince."

"Your majesty transports me by your determination," replied the ambassador. And full of joy at his unlooked-for success, he took his departure.

At midnight, as appointed, Renard repaired to Saint John's Chapel. He found the Queen, attended only by Feckenham, and kneeling before the altar, which blazed with numerous wax-lights. She had changed her dress for the ceremony, and was attired in, a loose robe of three-piled crimson velvet, trimmed with swansdown. Renard remained at a little distance, and looked on with a smile of Satanic triumph.

After she had received the sacrament, and pronounced the *"Veni Creator,"* Mary motioned the ambassador towards her, and placing her right hand on a parchment lying on the altar, to which were attached the broad seals of England, addressed him thus:—"I have signed and sealed this instrument, by which I contract and affiance myself in marriage to Philip, Prince of Spain, son of his imperial majesty, Charles the Fifth. And I further give you, Simon Renard, representative of the prince, my irrevocable promise, in the face of the living God and his saints, that I will wed him and no other."

Queen Mary at the instance of Simon Renard affiancing herself to Philip of Spain.

"May Heaven bless the union!" exclaimed Feckenham.

"There is the contract," pursued Mary, giving the parchment to Renard, who reverentially received it. "On my part, it is a marriage concluded."

"And equally so on the part of the prince, my master," replied Renard. "In his name I beg to express to your highness the deep satisfaction which this union will afford him."

"For the present this contract must be kept secret, even from our privy councillors," said the queen.

"It shall never pass my lips," rejoined Renard.

"And mine are closed by my sacred calling," added the confessor.

"Your majesty, I am sure, has done wisely in this step," observed Renard, "and, I trust, happily."

"I trust so too, sir," replied the Queen—"but time will show. These things are in the hands of the Great Disposer of events."

XVI.—WHAT BEFEL CICELY IN THE SALT TOWER.

Horror-stricken by the discovery he had made of the body of the ill-fated Alexia, and not doubting from its appearance that she must have perished from starvation, Cholmondeley remained for some time in a state almost of stupefaction in the narrow chamber where it lay. Rousing himself, at length, he began to reflect that no further aid could be rendered her,—that she was now, at last, out of the reach of her merciless tormentor,—and that his attention ought, therefore, to be turned towards one who yet lived to suffer from his cruelty.

Before departing, he examined the corpse more narrowly to ascertain whether it bore any marks of violence, and while doing so, a gleam of light called his attention to a small antique clasp fastening her tattered hood at the throat. Thinking it not impossible this might hereafter furnish some clue to the discovery of her real name and condition, he removed it. On holding it to the light, he thought he perceived an inscription upon it, but the characters were nearly effaced, and reserving the solution of the mystery for a more favourable opportunity, he carefully secured the clasp, and quitted the cell. He then returned to the passages he had recently traversed, explored every avenue afresh, reopened every cell-door, and after expending several hours in fruitless search, was compelled to abandon all hopes of finding Cicely.

Day had long dawned when he emerged from the dungeon; and as he was slowly wending his way towards the Stone Kitchen, he descried Lawrence Nightfall advancing towards him. From the furious gestures of the jailor, he at once knew that he was discovered, and drawing his sword, he stood upon his defence. But a conflict was not what Nightgall desired. He shouted to the sentinels on the ramparts, and informing them that his keys had been stolen, demanded their assistance to secure the robber. Some half-dozen soldiers immediately descended, and Cholmondeley finding resistance in vain, thought fit to surrender. The keys being found upon him, were delivered to Nightgall, while he himself was conveyed to the guard-room near the By-ward Tower.

After he had been detained there for some hours in close captivity,—not even being allowed to communicate with his friends in the Stone-kitchen,—Nightgall returned with an order from the council for his imprisonment in the Nun's Bower, whither he was forthwith removed. On the way to his place of confinement, he encountered Xit, and the friendly dwarf would fain have spoken with him, but he was kept at a distance by the halberts of the guard. He contrived, however, to inform him by sundry nods, winks, and expressive gestures, that he would keep a sharp watch upon the proceedings of Nightgall.

Having seen Cholmondeley safely bestowed, the jailor repaired to the entrance of the subterranean dungeons, and lighting a torch, opened the door of a small recess, from which he took a mattock and spade. Armed with these implements, he proceeded to the vault, beneath the Devilin Tower, where he commenced digging a grave. After labouring hard for a couple of hours, he attained a sufficient depth for his purpose, and taking the torch, ascended to the small chamber. Lifting the skeleton frame in his arms, he returned to the vault. In placing the torch on the ground it upset, and rolling into the grave was extinguished, leaving him in profound darkness. His first impulse was to throw down the body, but having, in his agitation, placed the hands, which were clasped together, over his neck, he found it impossible to free himself from it. His terror was so great that he uttered a loud cry, and would have fled, but his feet were rooted to the spot. He sank at last on his knees, and the corpse dropped upon him, its face coming into contact with his own. Grown desperate, at length, he disengaged himself from the horrible embrace, and threw the body into the grave. Relieved by this step from much of his fear, he felt about for the spade, and having found it, began to shovel in the mould.

SECRET STAIRCASE IN THE SALT TOWER.

While thus employed, he underwent a fresh alarm. In trampling down the mould, a hollow groan issued from the grave, trembling in every limb, he desisted from his task. His hair stood erect, and a thick damp gathered on his brow. Shaking off his terrors, he renewed his exertions, and in a short time his task was completed.

He then groped his way out of the vault, and having become by long usage familiarized with its labyrinths, soon reached the entrance, where he struck a light, and having found a lantern, set fire to the candle within it. This done, he returned to the vault, where, to his great horror, he perceived that the face of the corpse was uncovered. Averting his gaze from it, he heaped the earth over it, and then flattened the mass with repeated blows of the spade. All trace of his victim being thus removed, and the vault restored to its original appearance, he took back the implements he had used, and struck into a passage leading in another direction.

Pursuing it for some time, he came to a strong door; unlocked it; and, ascending a flight of stone steps, reached another arched passage, which he swiftly traversed. After threading other passages with equal celerity, he came to a wider avenue, contrived under the eastern ramparts, and tracked it till it brought him to a flight of steps leading to a large octangular chamber, surrounded by eight deep recesses, and forming the basement story of the Salt Tower, at that time, and for upwards of a century afterwards, used as one of the prison lodgings of the fortress. In a chamber in the upper story of this fortification, now occupied as a drawing-room, is a curious sphere, carved a few years later than the date of this chronicle, by Hugh Draper, an astrologer, who was committed to the Tower on suspicion of sorcery.

CHAMBER IN THE SALT TOWER.

Quitting this chamber, Nightgall ascended a winding stone staircase which brought him to an arched door, leading to the room just described. Taking a key from the bunch at his girdle, he unlocked it, and entered the room. A female was seated in one corner with her face buried in her hands. Raising her head at his approach, she disclosed the features of Cicely. Her eyes were red with weeping—and her figure attenuated by long suffering. Conceiving from the savage expression of the jailor's countenance that he meditated some further act of cruelty, she uttered a loud shriek, and tried to avoid him.

ARCHED DOOR IN THE SALT TOWER, COMMUNICATING WITH SECRET STAIRCASE.

"Peace!" cried Nightgall, "I will do you no harm. Your retreat has been discovered. You must go with me to the tower leading to the Iron Gate."

"I will never go thither of my accord," replied Cicely. "Release me, villain. I will die sooner than become your bride."

"We shall see that," growled the jailer. "Another month's captivity will make you alter your tone. You shall never be set free, unless you consent to be mine."

"Then I shall die a prisoner like your other victims," cried Cicely.

"Who told you I had other victims?" cried Nightgall, moodily.

"No matter who told me. I have heard Cuthbert Cholmondeley, whom I love as much as I hate you, speak of one—Alexia, I think she was named."

"No more of this," cried Nightgall, fiercely, "come along, or—"

"Never!" shrieked Cicely—"I will not go. You will murder me,"—And she filled the chamber with her screams.

"Confusion!" cried Nightgall, "we shall be heard. Come along, I say."

In struggling to free herself from him, Cicely fell upon the ground, regardless of this, Nightgall dragged her by main, force through the doorway, and so down the secret staircase. She continued her screams, until her head striking against the stones, she was stunned by the blow, and became insensible. He then raised her in his arms, and descending another short flight of steps, traversed a narrow passage, and came to a dark chamber beneath the Tower leading to the Iron Gate.

TOWER LEADING TO THE IRON GATE.

Lawrence Nightgall dragging Cicely down the secret
stairs in the Salt Tower.

WEST VIEW OF TRAITOR'S TOWER.

XVII.—OF THE CONSPIRACY FORMED BY DE NOAILLES; AND HOW XIT DELIVERED A LETTER TO ELIZABETH, AND VISITED COURTENAY IN THE LIEUTENANT'S LODGINGS.

As soon as it was known that the Princess Elizabeth and Courtenay were placed under arrest, the greatest consternation prevailed throughout the Tower. While some few rejoiced in the favourite's downfall, the majority deplored it; and it was only the idea that when Mary's jealous indignation subsided, he would be restored to his former position, that prevented open expression being given to their sentiments. On being made acquainted with what had occurred, Gardiner instantly sought an audience of the Queen, and without attempting to defend Courtenay's conduct, he besought her earnestly to pause before she proceeded to extremities,—representing the yet unsettled state of her government, and how eagerly advantage would be taken of the circumstances to stir up dissension and rebellion. Mary replied that her feelings had been so greatly outraged that she was resolved upon vengeance, and that nothing but the Earl's life would satisfy her.

"If this is your determination, madam," returned Gardiner,

"I predict that the crown will not remain upon your head a month. Though the Earl of Devonshire has grievously offended your highness, his crime is not treason. And if you put him to death for this offence, you will alienate the hearts of all your subjects."

"Be it so," replied Mary, sternly. "No personal consideration shall deter me from my just revenge."

"And what of the Princess Elizabeth?" asked the Bishop.

"She shall share his fate," answered the Queen.

"This must not be, my gracious mistress," cried Gardiner, throwing himself at her feet. "Hero I will remain till I have driven these dark and vindictive feelings from your breast. Banish the Earl—take his life, if nothing else will content you,—but do not raise your hand against your sister."

"Bishop of Winchester," replied the Queen, "how many hours have you knelt before my father, Henry the Eighth, and have yet failed to turn him from his purpose! I am by nature as jealous—as firm—as obstinate, if you will—as he was. Arise."

"No, madam," replied Gardiner, "I will not rise till I have convinced you of your error. Your august father was a prince of high and noble qualities, but the defects that clouded his royal nature would show to double disadvantage in one of your sex. Dismiss all thought of this faithless Earl from your heart,—banish him from your presence, from your kingdom,—nay, keep him in durance if you will, but use no harsh measures against the Princess Elizabeth. Every step taken against her will be fearfully resented by the Protestant party, of which, I need not remind you, she is the representative."

"And what matter if it be, my lord?" rejoined Mary. "I am strong enough to maintain my own authority, and shall be right glad of some plea to put down heresy and schism by fire and sword. You are not wont to advocate this cause."

"Nor do I advocate it now, madam," returned Gardiner. "All I counsel is prudence. You are not yet strong enough to throw off the mask of toleration which you have hitherto worn. Your first parliament has not yet met. The statutes establishing the Reformed religion are yet unrepealed,—nay, though I shame to speak it, the marriage of your illustrious parents has not yet been confirmed."

"You *should* shame to speak it, my lord," rejoined Mary, fiercely; "for it is mainly by your machinations that the divorce was obtained."

"I own it to my sorrow," replied Gardiner, "but I then owed the same obedience to your illustrious sire that I now owe to your highness. I did your injured mother great wrong, but if I live I will repair it. This, however, is foreign to the subject. Your majesty may believe me when I tell you, your worst enemies could not desire you to take a more injudicious step, or one more fraught with danger to yourself, than to strain your prerogative against Courtenay and Elizabeth."

"Were I to assent to your request and set them free," replied

Mary, after a moment's reflection, "the first act of the princess would be to unite herself to this perfidious villain."

"I do not think it," replied Gardiner. "But what if she were to do so?"

"*What!*" exclaimed Mary, furiously. "The thought revives all my indignation. Am I so tame of spirit that I can bear to see him whom I have loved united to a rival I hate? No, my lord, I am not. This is no doubtful case. I have heard his treachery with my own ears—seen it with my own eyes—and I will terribly avenge myself. Courtenay never again shall behold Elizabeth. He has breathed his last false sigh—uttered his last perjured profession of love— exchanged his last look, unless they meet upon the scaffold. You know not what an injured woman feels. I *have* the power of avenging myself, and, by my father's head, I will use it!"

"And when you have gratified this fell passion, madam," returned Gardiner, "remorse will succeed, and you will bitterly regret what you have done. Since nothing better may be,—and if you will not nobly, and like yourself, pardon the offenders,—at least reflect before you act. If you persist in your present intention, it will be the duty of all your faithful subjects to prepare for a rebellion, for such will certainly ensue."

"Make what preparations you deem fitting, my lord," replied Mary. "In my father's time the people did not dare to resist his decrees, however arbitrary."

"The people are no longer what they were, madam, nor are you—for I must make bold to say so—in the position, or backed by the power of your dread father. What he did is no rule for you. I am no advocate for Courtenay—nor for the princess Elizabeth. Could you avenge yourself upon them with safety, though I should lament it, I would not oppose you. But you cannot do so. Others must bleed at the same time. Remember the Lady Jane Gray and her husband yet live. You will revive their faction—and must of necessity doom them to death to prevent another rebellion. Once begun, there will be no end to bloodshed."

"These are cogent reasons, my lord," returned Mary, after a moment's reflection,—"supposing them well-founded."

"And trust me, they *are* well-founded, gracious madam," replied the Bishop. "Do not sacrifice your kingdom—do not sacrifice the holy Catholic church which looks to you for support—to an insane thirst of vengeance."

"Gardiner," replied Mary, taking his hand and looking at him earnestly, "you know not how I have loved this man. Put yourself in my position. How would you act?"

"As I am assured your highness would, if you were not under the dominion of passion," replied the bishop—"forgive him."

"I would do so," rejoined Mary, "but oh! if he were to wed Elizabeth, I should die. I would rather yield them my crown,—my life,—than consent to their espousals. But I will not think for myself. Arise, my lord. Give me your counsel, and what you recommend I will follow."

"Spoken like yourself, gracious madam," replied the bishop.

"I was sure your noble nature could soon triumph over unworthy thoughts. Since your highness thinks it possible Courtenay may wed Elizabeth, I would advise you to detain him for the present a captive in the Tower. But instantly liberate the princess—dismiss her from your court—and let her retire to Ashbridge."

"I like your advice well, my lord," replied the Queen, "and will act upon it. The princess shall set out to-day."

"I cannot too highly applaud your highness's determination," replied Gardiner; "but as you have spoken thus frankly, may I venture to ask whether the earl's case is utterly hopeless?—whether, after he has sufficiently felt the weight of your displeasure you will not restore him to your favour—to your affections?"

"Never," replied Mary, firmly, "never. And could you counsel it?"

"He is inexperienced, madam," urged the bishop; "and after this salutary lesson——"

"No more, my lord," interrupted the Queen, a shade passing over her features, "it is too late."

"Too late!" echoed Gardiner. "Am I to understand your highness has made another engagement?"

"You are to understand nothing more than you are told, my lord," replied Mary, angrily. "In due season you shall know all."

As Gardiner bowed in acquiescence, he perceived the miniature of Philip of Spain lying on the table, and a sudden apprehension of the truth crossed him.

"There is one person upon whom I should chiefly desire your highness's choice *not* to fall,1' he said.

"And that is—?" interrupted Mary.

"Philip of Spain," answered Gardiner.

"What objections have you to him, my lord?" demanded the queen, uneasily.

"My objections are threefold," rejoined Gardiner. "First, I dislike the tyrannical character of the prince, which would be ill-suited to render your highness's union a happy one. Secondly, I am assured that the match would be disagreeable to your subjects—the English nation not being able to brook a foreign yoke; and of all dominations none being so intolerable as that of Spain. Thirdly, the alliance would plunge us in endless wars with France—a country that would never tamely submit to such a formidable extension of power, as this would prove, on the part of its old enemy, Charles the Fifth."

"If not Philip of Spain, whom would you recommend me?" asked Mary, who was anxious to mislead him.

"One of your own nobles," replied Gardiner; "by which means your authority would be unabridged. Whereas, if you wed a prince, odious for his tyranny in the eyes of all Europe"———

"No more of this, my lord," interrupted Mary, hastily.

"Madam," said Gardiner, "however I may risk displeasing you, I should be wanting in duty, in loyalty, and in sincerity, were I not strongly to warn you against a match with Philip of Spain. It will be fatal to your own happiness— fatal to the welfare of your people."

"I have already said it is too late," sighed Mary.

"Your Majesty has not affianced yourself to him," cried Gardiner, anxiously..

"Question me no further," rejoined Mary. "What is done is done."

"Alas! madam," cried Gardiner, "I understand your words too well. You have taken a perilous step, at the instigation of evil counsellors, and under the influence of evil passions. God grant good may come of it!"

"These are mere surmises on your part, my lord," returned Mary. "I have not told you I have taken any step."

"But your majesty leads me to infer it," answered the bishop. "For your own sake, and for the sake of your kingdom, I trust my fears are unfounded."

As he spoke, an usher approached, and informed the queen that the imperial ambassador, Simon Renard, desired an audience.

"Admit him," said Mary. "Farewell, my lord," she added, turning to Gardiner; "I will weigh what you have said."

"Act upon it, gracious madam, if you *can*," rejoined the bishop. "But if you are so far committed as to be unable to retreat, count upon my best services to aid you in the difficulty." At this moment, Simon Renard entered the audience-chamber, and the expression of his countenance was so exulting, that Gardiner was convinced his conjectures were not far wide of the truth. His first object, on quitting the royal presence, was to seek out Feckenham, from whom he succeeded in eliciting the fact of the betrothment in Saint John's chapel; and with a breast full of trouble he returned to his own apartments. On the way thither, he encountered De Noailles.

"Well met, my lord," cried the ambassador. "I was about to seek you. So, it seems all our projects are ruined. Courtenay is disgraced and imprisoned."

"His folly has destroyed the fairest chance that ever man possessed," observed the bishop. "He is now irretrievably lost."

"Not irretrievably, I trust, my good lord," replied Do Noailles. "A woman's mind is proverbially changeful. And when this jealous storm is blown over, I doubt not he will, again bask in the full sunshine of royal favour."

"Your excellency is in the wrong," rejoined Gardiner. "The queen will never forgive him, or, what is equally to be lamented, will never unite herself to him."

"You speak confidently, my lord," returned Do Noailles gravely. "I trust nothing has occurred to warrant what you say."

"M. De Noailles," said the bishop significantly, "look to yourself. The party of France is on the decline. That of Spain is on the ascendant."

"What mean you, my lord?" cried the ambassador, eagerly. "Renard has not succeeded in his aim? Mary has not affianced herself to the Prince of Spain?"

"I know nothing positively," replied Gardiner evasively. "I merely throw out the hint. It is for you to follow it up."

"This were a blow, indeed!" cried De Noailles. "But subtle as Renard is, and with all the advantage he has gained, I will yet countermine him."

"You shall not want my aid," returned Gardiner, "provided you hatch no treason against the queen. And that you may the better know how to act, learn that her majesty *is* affianced to Philip of Spain."

"Curses on the crafty Spaniard!" exclaimed De Noailles, furiously. "But I will yet defeat him."

"The princess Elizabeth will be liberated to-day, and sent with a strong guard to Ashbridge," remarked Gardiner. "Courtenay will be kept a prisoner in the Tower."

"We must find means to liberate him," rejoined the ambassador.

"In this you must proceed without my aid," said the bishop. "If it be possible to reinstate the earl in Mary's favour, it shall be done. But I can take no part in aiding his flight."

"Leave it to me, my lord," rejoined De Noailles. "All I require is your voice with the queen."

"That you may rely on," answered the bishop.

With this, they separated; Gardiner proceeding to his own apartments, and De Noailles bending his steps towards the green, debating with himself, as he wended thither, what course it would be best to pursue in the emergency. Nothing occurred to him but expedients so hazardous that he instantly dismissed them. While resolving these matters, as he walked to and fro beneath the avenue, he was accosted by Xit, who, doffing his cap, and making a profound bow, inquired whether the rumour was correct that the Earl of Devonshire had incurred the queen's displeasure and was imprisoned.

"Ay, marry is it," replied De Noailles.

"I am truly concerned to hear it," replied the mannikin; "and I make no doubt his lordship's disgrace is owing to the machinations of his mortal foe, Simon Renard."

"Thou art in the right," replied De Noailles. "And let it be known throughout the Tower that this is the case."

"I will not fail to spread it among my fellows," replied Xit. "But none can lament it more than myself. I would lay down my life for his lordship."

"Indeed!" exclaimed De Noailles. "This knave may be useful," he muttered. "Harkee, sirrah! Canst thou devise some safe plan by which a letter may be conveyed to the earl, who is imprisoned in the lieutenant's lodgings?"

"Your excellency could not have chanced upon one more able or willing to serve you," replied Xit. "Give me the letter, and I will engage it shall reach its destination."

"Come to my lodgings this evening," said De Noailles, "and it shall be ready for thee. As yet, my plan is not matured."

"Your excellency may depend upon me," replied the dwarf.

"But I conclude, if I perform my task to your satisfaction, I shall be rewarded?"

"Amply," replied De Noailles. "Take this purse in earnest of what is to follow."

"I do not desire gold," returned the dwarf, restoring the purse. "What I aspire to is rank. I am tired of being attendant to three gluttonous giants. If the Earl of Devonshire is restored by my means to liberty and to the position he has lost with the queen, I trust the service will not be unremembered, but that I may be promoted to some vacant post."

"Doubt it not," replied De Noailles, who could scarcely help laughing at the dwarfs overweening vanity. "I will answer for it, if thou performest thy part well, thou shalt be knighted ere a month be past. But I will put thy skill further to the test. The princess Elizabeth will be removed from the Tower to-day. Thou must find some means of delivering a letter to her, unperceived by her attendants."

"I will do it," replied Xit, unhesitatingly. "Knighted, did your excellency say?"

"Ay, knighted," returned De Noailles,—"within a month. Follow me. I will prepare the letter."

It being the ambassador's wish to carry on a secret correspondence with the princess, he pondered upon the safest means of accomplishing his object; and chancing to notice a guitar, which had been lent him by Elizabeth, it occurred to him that it would form an excellent medium of communication. Accordingly, he set to work; and being well versed in various state ciphers, speedily traced a key to the system beneath the strings of the instrument. He then despatched it by a page to the princess, who, immediately comprehending that some mystery must be attached to it, laid it aside to take with her to Ashbridge. Do Noailles, meanwhile, wrote a few hasty lines on a piece of paper, explaining his motive in sending the guitar, and delivering it to Xit, charged him, as he valued his life, not to attempt to give it the princess, unless he could do so unobserved.

About noon, Elizabeth, escorted by Sir Edward Hastings, and a large guard, left the palace. She was on horseback, and as she rode through the gateway of the By-ward Tower, Xit, who had stationed himself on Og's shoulder, took off his bonnet, and let it fall as if by accident, on her steed's head. Startled by the blow, the animal reared, and in the confusion that ensued, the dwarf contrived to slip the billet unperceived into her hand. As soon as the cavalcade had passed on, and the dwarf had undergone a severe rebuke from Og and the other warders for his supposed carelessness, he hastened to the ambassador's room, to relate the successful issue of his undertaking. De Noailles was overjoyed by the intelligence; complimented him on his skill; promised him still higher dignities in case of success; and bade him return in the evening for further orders.

The remainder of the day was consumed by the ambassador in revolving his project. The more he reflected upon the matter, the more convinced he became, that in the present critical state of affairs, nothing could be done without some daring conspiracy; and after a long debate, he conceived a scheme which would either overthrow Mary's government altogether, and place Elizabeth on the throne, or reduce the former to such an abject state that he could dictate his own terms to her. On consideration, thinking it better not to write to the Earl for fear of mischance, he entrusted Xit with a message to him, earnestly impressing upon the dwarf the necessity of caution.

The subject of all this plotting, it has been stated, was confined in the lieutenant's lodgings. Every consideration due to his rank and peculiar position was shown him by Sir Henry Bedingfeld. He was permitted to occupy the large chamber on the second floor, since noted as the scene of the examinations of the Gunpowder Plot conspirators. He was, however, strictly guarded. No one was allowed to hold any communication with him, either personally or by letter, except through the medium of the lieutenant. And every article either of attire or furniture that was brought him was carefully inspected before it was delivered to him.

Xit, who, as a privileged person, went and came where he pleased, found little difficulty in obtaining admittance to the lieutenant's lodgings. But all his cunning could not procure him a sight of the prisoner, and after wasting several hours in fruitless attempts, being fearful of exciting suspicion, he was compelled for that night to relinquish the design. The next day, he was equally unsuccessful, and he was almost driven to his wits' end with perplexity, when as he was passing beneath a tree at the southern extremity of the green, he chanced to cast his eye upwards, and saw a cat spring from one of the topmost branches on to the roof of the Bloody Tower.

"Wherever a cat can go, I can," thought Xit; "That roof reached, I could pass along the summits of the ramparts and fortifications connecting it with the lieutenant's lodgings; and on arriving there, it were easy to descend the chimney, and get into the earl's chamber. Bravo! That will do."

The plan so enchanted him, that he was in a fever to put it in execution. This, however, could not take place till night, and retiring to a little distance to survey the premises, he satisfied himself, after some consideration, that he had discovered the chimney communicating with the earl's room. When the proper time arrived, he cautiously approached the tree, and looking round to make sure no one observed him, he clambered up it with the agility of a squirrel. Notwithstanding his caution, a serious accident had nearly befallen him. Just as he was about to spring upon the wall, the bough on which he stood broke. Luckily he caught hold of a projection of the building, and saved himself. But he was some minutes before he recovered from the fright. The noise, too, had nearly betrayed him to the sentinels, who approached within a few paces of him. But the darkness was so profound, that he escaped observation. When they returned to their posts he proceeded along the ridge of the battlements, and dropping upon the ballium wall, proceeded with the utmost caution to the edge of the ramparts. He then passed on tip-toe close to the guard, and hastening forward, reached the tiled roof of the lieutenant's house, up which he clambered, as noiselessly and actively as the animal he emulated.

On gaining the chimney he was in search of, he untied a cord with which he had provided himself, and securing it to the brickwork, let one end drop down the aperture. He then descended, and soon came to a level with the chamber, and perceiving a light within it, resolved to reconnoitre before he ventured further. Courtenay was asleep on a couch in the corner, while two attendants were likewise slumbering upon seats near the door. At a loss how to act, as he could scarcely awaken the earl without disturbing the guards, Nit got out of the chimney, and crept cautiously towards the couch. He would fain have extinguished the lamp, but it was out of his reach. Planting himself on the further side of the couch, so as to conceal himself from the attendants, he ventured at length slightly to shake the sleeper. Courtenay started, and uttered an exclamation which immediately aroused his guards.

"Who touched me?" he demanded angrily.

"No one, my lord," replied the foremost of the men, glancing at the door and round the chamber. "Your lordship must have been dreaming."

"I suppose it must be so," replied the carl, looking round, and perceiving nothing. "And yet—"

At this moment a slight pressure on the hand warned him to be silent.

"If your lordship wishes it, we will search the room," observed the second soldier.

"No, no, it is needless," replied Courtenay. "I have no doubt it was a dream."

In a few minutes, the soldiers were again snoring, and Xit popping his head from beneath the coverlet, in a low tone delivered his message. The earl expressed his satisfaction, and proceeded to make inquiries respecting the Princess Elizabeth. On learning that she had quitted the Tower the day before, he had much ado to restrain his joy. And when he ascertained by what means the dwarf had obtained access to the chamber, he was desirous to attempt an escape by the same way, but was dissuaded by Xit, who represented to him the risk he would incur, adding that even if he escaped from his present prison, he would be unable to quit the Tower.

The dwarf then departed as he came. Climbing up the chimney, he drew the rope after him, retraced his course over the fortifications; and on reaching the Bloody Tower, contrived, with much exertion, and no little risk, to lay hold of a branch of the tree, down which he clambered. The next day, he related the successful issue of his trip to his employer.

De Noailles did not remain idle. He had already mentioned his project to the Duke of Suffolk, Lord Thomas Grey, Sir Nicholas Throckmorton, Sir James Croft, Sir Peter Carew, and Sir Thomas Wyat, all of whom eagerly joined in it. With most of these, but especially with Wyat,—afterwards the leader of the rebellion against Mary,—the main inducement to conspire was aversion to the Queen's meditated alliance with the Prince of Spain. With the Duke of Suffolk and his ambitious brother, Lord Thomas Grey, it was, (as De Noailles had foreseen,) the hope that in the tumult the Lady Jane Grey might be restored, that purchased their compliance. The conspirators had frequent secret meetings in the apartments of the French ambassador, where they conferred upon their plans. Suffolk, though pardoned for his late treason by Mary, was yet detained a prisoner on parole within the Tower. His brother had not taken a sufficiently prominent part to bring him into trouble. The bravest of their number was Wyat, of whom it may be necessary to say a few words.

Inheriting the wit and valour of his father, the refined and courtly poet of the same name, Sir Thomas Wyat of Allingham Castle in Kent, had already earned for himself the highest character as a military leader. His father's friend, the chivalrous and poetical Earl of Surrey, in one of his despatches to Henry the Eighth, thus describes his conduct at the siege of Boulogne:—"I assure your Majesty, you have framed him to such towardness and knowledge in the war, that (none other dispraised) your Majesty hath not many like him within your realm, for hardiness, painfulness, circumspection, and natural disposition for the war." Wyat was in the very flower of his age. But his long service,—for from his earliest youth, he had embraced the profession of arms,—had given him an older look than his years warranted. He was of middle-size, strongly but symmetrically proportioned, with handsome boldly-carved features, of a somewhat stern expression. His deportment partook of his frank soldier-like character. In swordsmanship, horsemanship, and all matters connected with the business of war, he was, as may be supposed, eminently skilful.

After much deliberation, it was agreed among the conspirators to have all in readiness for a general insurrection, but to defer their project until the meeting of parliament, when the Queen's intentions respecting her alliance with Spain would be declared, and if what they anticipated should prove true, the whole nation would favour their undertaking.

XVIII.—HOW COURTENAY ESCAPED FROM THE TOWER.

While the great outbreak was thus deferred, it was deemed expedient to liberate Courtenay as soon as possible. Such were the precautions taken by the vigilant Sir Henry Bedingfeld, that this was not so easy of accomplishment as it appeared on the onset. At length, however, all was arranged, and Xit was despatched to the earl to tell him the attempt might be made on the following night, when unluckily, just as the mannikin had entered the chimney, one of the guards awakened, and hearing a noise, flew to see what occasioned it. Exerting his utmost agility, the dwarf was soon out of reach, and the attendant could not distinguish his person, but he instantly gave the alarm.

Flying for his life, Xit got out of the chimney, hurried along the tops of the ramparts, and jumping at the hazard of his neck, into the tree, reached the ground just as the alarm was given to the sentinels. It was past midnight. But Sir Henry Bedingfeld, aroused from his couch, instantly repaired to the chamber of his prisoner. Nothing could be found but the rope by which Xit had descended, and which in his hasty retreat he had not been able to remove. Courtenay refused to answer any interrogations respecting his visiter, and after a long and fruitless search, the lieutenant departed.

The next day, the occurrence was made known to the queen, and at her request Simon Renard visited the prisoner. Not thinking his place of confinement secure enough, Renard suggested that he should be removed to the Bell Tower,—a fortification flanking the lieutenant's habitation on the west, and deriving its name, as has already been mentioned, from the alarm-bell of the fortress, which was placed in a small wooden belfry on its roof. This tower is still in existence, and devoted to the same purpose as of old,— though its chambers, instead of being used as prison-lodgings, form the domestic offices of the governor. In shape it is circular, like all the other towers, with walls of great thickness pierced by narrow loopholes, admitting light to the interior. Courtenay was confined in a small room on the basement floor, having a vaulted roof supported by pointed arches of curious construction, with deep recesses in the intervals. From this strong and gloomy cell it seemed impossible he could escape; and having seen him placed within it, Renard departed fully satisfied.

THE BELL TOWER.

When the intelligence of the earl's removal was brought to De Noailles, he was greatly disheartened; but Xit bade him be of good cheer, as he still felt certain of effecting his deliverance. Some time, however, elapsed before any new scheme could be devised; when one night Xit appeared with a smiling countenance, and said he had found means of communicating with the prisoner. On being questioned as to how he had contrived this, he replied that he had crept up to a loophole opening into the earl's chamber, and filed away one of the iron bars; and though the aperture was not large enough to allow a full-grown man to pass through it, he had done so without inconvenience, and under cover of night without being perceived. He then proceeded to detail a somewhat hazardous plan of flight, which Courtenay had determined to risk, provided his friends would second the attempt. All the earl required was, that a well-manned boat should be in waiting for him near the Tower-wharf, to put off the instant he reached it.

After some consideration, this plan was held feasible, and Sir Thomas Wyat undertook the command of the boat. A dark night being indispensable for the enterprise, the third from that time, when there would be no moon, was chosen; and this arrangement was communicated by the dwarf to Courtenay. Measures were then concerted between the earl and his assistant, and all being settled, it was agreed, to avoid heedless risk, that the latter should not return again till the appointed night.

On its arrival, Xit, as soon as it grew dark, crept through the loophole, and found the earl impatiently expecting him. He was alone, for since his removal to so strong a prison it was deemed needless to have an attendant constantly with him. Xit brought him a rapier and dagger, and a long coil of rope, and when he had armed himself with the weapons, they proceeded to the execution of their project. Knocking at the door, the earl summoned the warder who was stationed outside. The man immediately obeyed the call, and as he opened the door Xit crept behind it, and while Courtenay engaged the warder's attention, he slipped out, and concealed himself behind a projection in the winding stairs. The earl having made a demand which he knew would compel the warder to proceed to Sir Henry Bedingfeld, dismissed him.

Quitting the cell, the warder, who had no suspicions, locked the door, leaving the key,—as had been foreseen,—within it. He then ascended the stairs, and passed close to Xit without perceiving him. As soon as he was gone, the dwarf unlocked the door, and made good his own retreat through the loophole; it being necessary he should give the signal to the party on the river.

Courtenay then hurried up the winding steps. On reaching the upper chamber, he perceived it was vacant—but the open door showed him that the warder had just passed through it. Hastily shutting it, and barring it withinside, he mounted a short flight of steps leading to the roof, where he knew a sentinel who had charge of the alarm-bell was stationed. Before the man, who was leaning upon his partizan, could utter an exclamation, Courtenay snatched the weapon from him, and dealt him a blow that stretched him senseless at his feet. He then quickly fastened the rope to one of the stout wooden supporters of the belfry, and flinging the coil over the battlements, prepared to descend by it.

Possessed of great strength and activity, and materially aided by the roughened surface of the old walls, and other irregularities in the structure, against which he placed his feet, the earl reached the ground in safety. He was now in the outer ward, near the By-ward Tower. It was so dark that his descent had not been noticed, but he perceived several soldiers passing at a little distance from him, from whose remarks he gathered that they were about to convey the keys of the fortress to the lieutenant.

As soon as they had passed him, he rushed across the ward in the direction of the arched passage leading to the drawbridge. Here he encountered Og, who was on guard at the time. The gigantic warder immediately challenged him, and presented his huge halbert at his breast. But the earl, without making any reply, stooped down, and before he could be prevented, darted through his legs. Og, in a voice of thunder, gave the alarm, and was instantly answered by a party of halberdiers, who rushed out of the adjoining guard-room. They were all armed, some with pikes, some with arquebusses, and snatching a torch from the soldier nearest him, Og darted after the fugitive.

By this time, the earl's flight from the Bell Tower had been discovered. On his return, finding the door barred withinside, the warder suspected something wrong, and gave the alarm. A few seconds sufficed to the men-at-arms to break down the door with their bills, and they then found what had occurred. The alarm-bell was instantly rung, and word passed to the sentinels on the By-ward Tower, and on the other fortifications, that the Earl of Devonshire had escaped. In an instant, all was in motion. Torches gleamed along the whole line of ramparts; shouts were heard in every direction; and soldiers hastened to each point whence it was conceived likely he would attempt to break forth.

Before relating the result of the attempt, it may be proper to advert to what had been done in furtherance of it by Xit. Having got through the loophole as before related, the dwarf pursued the course subsequently taken by Courtenay, made a hasty excuse to Og, and crossed the drawbridge just before it was raised. Approaching the side of the river, he drew a petronel, and flashing it, the signal was immediately answered by the sound of muffled oars; and Xit, whose gaze was steadfastly bent upon the stream, could just detect a boat approaching the strand. The next moment, Sir Thomas Wyat sprang ashore, and as Xit was explaining to him in a whisper what had occurred, the alarm was given as above related.

It was a moment of intense interest to all concerned in the enterprise, and Wyat held himself in readiness for action. On reaching the drawbridge and finding it raised, Courtenay without hesitation bounded over the rails, and plunging into the moat, struck out towards the opposite bank.

Courtenay's escape from the Tower

At this juncture, Og and his companions arrived at the outlet. The giant held his torch over the moat, and perceived the earl swimming across it. A soldier beside him levelled his arquebuss at the fugitive, and would have fired, but Og checked him, crying, "Beware how you harm the queen's favourite. It is the Earl of Devonshire. Seize him, but injure him not—or dread her majesty's displeasure."

The caution, however, was unheeded by those on the summit of the By-ward Tower. Shots were fired from it, and the balls speckled the surface of the water, but without doing any damage. One of Wyat's crew hastened to the edge of the moat, and throwing a short line into the water, assisted the earl to land.

While this was passing, the drawbridge was lowered, and Og and his companions rushed across it—too late, however, to secure the fugitive. As soon as Courtenay had gained a footing on the wharf, Sir Thomas Wyat seized his hand, and hurried him towards the boat, into which they leaped. The oars were then plunged into the water, and before their pursuers gained the bank, the skiff had shot to some distance from it. Another boat was instantly manned and gave chase, but without effect. The obscurity favoured the fugitives. Wyat directed his men to pull towards London Bridge, and they soon disappeared beneath its narrow arches.

XIX.—HOW QUEEN MARY VISITED THE LIONS' TOWER; HOW MAGOG GAVE HIS DAME A LESSON; AND HOW XIT CONQUERED A MONKEY, AND WAS WORSTED BY A BEAR.

Courtenay's escape from the Tower created almost as much sensation as his imprisonment had done; and while his partisans were cheered by it, his enemies were proportionately discouraged. Several bands of soldiers, headed by trusty leaders, were sent in pursuit of him in different directions; but no trace could be discovered of the course he had taken; nor could all the vigilance of Sir Henry Bedingfeld detect who had assisted him in his flight. After some time, as no tidings were heard of him, it was concluded he had embarked for France. Inspired by jealousy, Mary immediately sent an order to Ashbridge to double the guard over her sister; and she secretly instructed Sir Edward Hastings, in case of any attempt to set her free, to convey her instantly to the Tower. Elizabeth either was severely indisposed, or feigned to be so, and it was bruited abroad that poison had been given her. This rumour, which obtained general credence, as well as others to the effect that her life had been attempted by different means, at length reached the queen's ears, and occasioned her great distress and annoyance. To remove the suspicion, she commanded Elizabeth's appearance at court. And though the princess would fain have refused, she was compelled to obey.

Some weeks had now elapsed since Courtenay's flight, and during that time the queen's anger had so much abated, that Gardiner thought he might venture to solicit his pardon, he-presenting to her, that she had already punished him sufficiently by the disgrace she had inflicted upon him, and that it was desirable to give no pretext for tumult during the momentous discussions which would take place on the meeting of parliament,—then immediately about to be assembled,—he urged his suit so warmly, that in the end Mary consented to pardon the carl, provided he appeared at court within three days.

Intelligence of the queen's change of feeling was soon conveyed to Courtenay, who had been concealed in an obscure lodging in London, and on the second day he presented himself before her. Mary received him graciously but coldly, and in such a manner as to convince him and his friends, if they still indulged any such hopes, that a restoration to the place he had once held in her affections was out of the question.

"If you are disposed to travel, my lord," she said, sarcastically, "I will take care you have such appointments to foreign courts as will best suit your age and inclination."

"Your Majesty has perchance some delicate mission at the Court of Madrid, which you desire me to execute," replied the earl, significantly.

"Had I any mission to that court," replied the Queen, repressing her emotion, "it is not to your hands I should entrust it. You have offended me once, Courtenay. Beware how you do so a second time. Abandon all hopes of Elizabeth. She never can be—never *shall be* yours."

"That remains to be seen," muttered Courtenay as he quitted the presence.

The interview over, Courtenay was joined by De Noailles, and, from that moment, he surrendered himself unresistingly to the designs of the artful ambassador.

Mary had now removed her court to Whitehall. But she frequently visited the Tower, and appeared to prefer its gloomy chambers to the gorgeous halls in her other palaces. One night, an order was received by Hairun, the bearward, who had charge of the wild animals, that, on the following day, the Queen would visit the menagerie. Preparations were accordingly made for her reception; and the animals were deprived of their supper, that they might exhibit an unusual degree of ferocity. But though Hairun starved the wild beasts, he did not act in like manner towards himself. On the contrary, he deemed it a fitting occasion to feast his-friends, and accordingly invited Magog, his dame, the two other giants, Xit, Ribald, and the pantler and his spouse, to take their evening meal with him. The invitation was gladly accepted; and about the hour of a modern dinner, the guests repaired to the bearward's lodgings, which were situated in the basement chamber of the Lions' Tower. Of this structure, nothing but an arched embrasure, once overlooking the lesser moat, and another subterranean room, likewise boasting four deep arched recesses, but constantly flooded with water, now remain. A modern dwelling-house, tenanted by the former keeper of the menagerie in the fortress, occupies the site of the ancient fabric.

Aware of the appetites of his friends, and being no despicable trencherman himself, Hairun had provided accordingly. The principal dish was a wild boar, a present to the bearward from Sir Henry Bedingfeld, which having been previously soaked for a fortnight, in a mixture of vinegar, salt, bruised garlic, and juniper-berries, was roasted whole under the personal superintendence of Peter Trusbut, who predicted it would prove delicious eating—and the result proved him no false prophet. On the appearance of this magnificent dish, which succeeded the first course of buttered stock-fish, and mutton pottage, a murmur of delight pervaded the company. The eyes of the giants glistened, their mouths watered, and they grasped their knives and forks like men preparing for a combat to the utterance. Magog had seated himself as far from his wife as possible. But she was too much engrossed by the assiduous attention, of Ribald, to take any particular notice of him.

Peter Trusbut, as usual, officiated as carver. And the manner in which he distributed slices of the savoury and juicy meat, which owing to the preparation it had undergone, had a tenderness and mellowness wholly indescribable, with modicums of the delicate fat, elicited the host's warmest approbation. The giants spoke not a word; and even the ladies could only express their delight by interjections. Reserving certain delicate morsels for himself, Peter Trusbut, with a zeal worthy of the cause in which he was engaged, continued to ply his knife so unremittingly, that no one's plate was for a moment empty, and yet with all this employment, he did not entirely forget himself. Hairun was in ecstacies; and while the giants were still actively engaged, he placed before them enormous goblets filled with bragget, a drink composed of strong ale sweetened with honey, spiced and flavoured with herbs. At the first pause, the gigantic brethren drained their cups; and they were promptly replenished by the hospitable bearward. By this time, the greater part of the boar had disappeared. Its well-flavoured back and fattened flanks were gone, and the hams and head alone remained. Seeing that the other guests were satisfied, the pantler, with some little labour, hewed off the two legs, and giving one to each of the unmarried giants, assigned the head to Magog.

"Mauger himself never did his office with greater dexterity than you have displayed in decapitating that wild boar, master pantler," observed Magog, smiling as he received the welcome gift.

"You are not going to eat all that, you insatiable cormorant," cried his dame, from the other end of the table.

"Indeed, but I am, sweetheart," replied Magog, commencing operations on the cheek; "wherefore not?"

"Wherefore not," screamed Dame Placida, "because you'll die of an apoplexy, and I shall be a second time a widow."

"No matter," replied the giant, "I'm weary of life, and cannot end it more comfortably.—I'll eat in spite of her," he added, half aloud.

This last remark, in spite of Ribald's interference, might have called forth some practical rejoinder on the part of his wife, had not her attention and that of the rest of the company been drawn, at the moment, towards Xit. Amongst other animals allowed to range about the bearward's house, was a small mischievous ape. This creature had seated itself behind Xit's chair, where it made the most grotesque grimaces in imitation of the mannikin. The guests were at first too much occupied to take any notice of its proceedings, and Xit, wholly unconscious of its presence, pursued his repast in tranquillity. The more substantial viands disposed of, he helped himself to some roasted chesnuts, and was greedily munching them, when the monkey stretched its arm over his shoulder, and snatched a handful.

Astonished and alarmed at the occurrence, Xit turned to regard the intruder. But when he perceived the ape's grinning face close to his own, and heard the shouts and laughter of the assemblage, his fear changed to anger, and he immediately attempted to regain what had been pilfered from him. But the monkey was not inclined to part with his spoil, and a struggle of a very comical kind ensued. Xit seized the monkey's paws, and tried to get back the chesnuts, while the latter, gibbering and grinning horribly, laid hold of the mannikin's shock head of hair, and after lugging him tremendously, tore up a large lock by the roots. Enraged by the pain, Xit tried to draw his sword, but finding it impossible, he grasped the beast by both ears, and despite its struggling, squealing, and attempts to bite, succeeded in keeping it at bay.

What might have been the result of the conflict it is impossible to say. But just as Xit's strength was failing, Hairun flew to his assistance, and partly by threats, partly by the application of a switch to its back, drove the monkey into a corner. Xit was highly complimented for his courage, and though he occasionally rubbed his head, these encomiums entirely reconciled him to the loss of his hair. Magog, who cherished some little resentment for his former tricks, laughed immoderately at the incident, and said, "My beard is already grown again, but it will be a long time before thy rough poll regains its accustomed appearance. Ha! ha!"

In this way, the meal was concluded, and it was followed by a plentiful supply of ale, hydromel, bragget, and wine. Nor did Peter Trusbut forget to slip the stone bottle of distilled water into Magog's hand, recommending him on no account to let Xit taste it—a suggestion scrupulously observed by the giant. His guests having passed a merry hour over their cups, Hairun proposed to conduct them over the menagerie, that they might see what condition the animals were in.

The proposal was eagerly accepted, and providing torches, the bearward led them into a small court, communicating by a low arched door with the menagerie. It was then as now, (for the modern erection, which is still standing though wholly unused, followed the arrangement of the ancient structure, and indeed retains some of the old stone arches), a wide semicircular fabric, in which were contrived, at distances of a few feet apart, a number of arched cages, divided into two or more compartments, and secured by strong iron bars.

THE MENAGERIE.

A high embattled wall of the same form as the inner structure faced on the west a small moat, now filled up, which flowed round these outworks from the base of the Middle Tower to a fortification, now also removed, called, from its situation, the Lions' Gate, where it joined the larger moat.

Opposite the dens stood a wide semicircular gallery, defended by a low stone parapet, and approached by a flight of steps from the back. It was appropriated exclusively to the royal use.

The idea of maintaining a menagerie within the Tower, as an appendage to their state, was, in all probability derived by our monarchs, as has been previously intimated, from the circumstance of the Emperor Frederick having presented Henry the Third with three leopards, in allusion to his coat of arms, which animals were afterwards carefully kept within the fortress. Two orders from this sovereign to the sheriffs of London, in reference to a white bear, which formed part of his live stock, are preserved; the first, dated 1253, directing that fourpence a day (a considerable sum for the period) be allowed for its sustenance; and tho second, issued in the following year, commanding "that for the keeper of our white bear, lately sent us from Norway, and which is in our Tower of London, ye cause to be had one muzzle and one iron chain, to hold that bear without the water; and one long and strong cord to hold the same bear when fishing in the river of Thames." Other mandates relating to an elephant appear in the same reign, in one of which it is directed—"that ye cause without delay to be built at our Tower of

London one house of forty feet long, and twenty feet deep, for our elephant; providing that it be so made and so strong, that when need be, it may be fit and necessary for other uses. And the cost shall be computed at the Exchequer." A fourth order appoints that the animal and his keeper shall be found with such necessaries "as they shall reasonably require." The royal menagerie was greatly increased by Edward the Third, who added to it, amongst other animals, a lion and lioness, a leopard, and two wild cats; and in the reign of Henry the Sixth the following provisions was made for the keeper:—"We of our special grace have granted to our beloved servant, Robert Mansfield, esquire, marshall of our hall, the office of keeper of the lions, with a certain place which hath been appointed anciently within our said Tower for them; to have and to occupy the same, by himself or by his sufficient deputy, for the term of his life, with the wages of sixpence per day for himself, and with the wages of sixpence per day for the maintenance of every lion or leopard now being in his custody, or that shall be in his custody hereafter." From this it will appear that no slight importance was attached to the office, which was continued until recent times, when the removal of the menagerie rendered it wholly unnecessary.

Dazzled by the lights, and infuriated with hunger, the savage denizens of the cages set up a most terrific roaring as the party entered the flagged space in front of them. Hairun, who was armed with a stout staff, laid about him in right earnest, and soon produced comparative tranquillity. Still, the din was almost deafening. The animals were numerous, and fine specimens of their kind. There were lions in all postures,—couchant, dormant, passant, and guardant; tigers, leopards, hyaenas, jackals, lynxes, and bears. Among the latter, an old brown bear, presented to Henry the Eighth by the Emperor Maximilian, and known by the name of the imperial donor, particularly attracted their attention, from its curious tricks. At last, after much solicitation from Dames Placida and Potentia, the bearward opened the door of the cage, and old Max issued forth. At first, he was all gentleness, sat upon his hind legs, and received the apples and biscuits given him like a lap-dog, when all at once, his master having stepped aside to quell a sudden disturbance which had arisen in one of the adjoining cages, he made a dart at Dame Placida, who was standing near him, and devouring the fruit and cakes she held in her hand at a mouthful, would have given her a formidable hug, if she had not saved herself by running into his cage, the door of which stood open. Here she would certainly have been caught, if her husband had not rushed to the entrance. Max warily eyed his new opponent, and uttered a menacing growl, but seemed to decline the attack. Dame Placida filled the cage with her shrieks, and alarmed by the cries, all the wild animals renewed their howling. Hairun would have flown to Magog's assistance, but the latter called to him in a voice of thunder to desist.

"I will have no interference," he roared, "old Max and I understand each other perfectly."

As if he comprehended what was said, the bear replied by a hoarse growl, and displayed his enormous fangs in a formidable manner. Dame Placida renewed her cries, and besought Ribald to come to her assistance.

"Stay where you are," thundered Magog, "I will settle this matter in my own way."

"Help! for mercy's sake, help!" shrieked Dame Placida,—"never mind him!—help! good Hairun—dear Ribald—help! or I shall be torn in pieces."

Thus exhorted, Ribald and Hairun would have obeyed. But they were prevented by Og and Gog, who began to sec through their brother's design.

"Leave him alone," they cried, laughing loudly. "He is about to give his dame a lesson."

"Is that all?" replied Hairun. "Then he shall have no interruption from me."

"Barbarian!" cried Dame Placida, appealing to her husband. "Do you mean that I should be devoured! Oh! if ever I *do* get out, you shall bitterly repent your cruel conduct."

"You never *shall* get out, unless you promise to amend your own conduct," rejoined Magog.

"I will die sooner than make any such promise," replied Placida.

"Very well, then," rejoined Magog, "I shall give free passage to Max."

And he slightly moved his person, while the animal uttered another growl. The giants laughed loudly, and encouraged their brother to proceed.

"Make her promise, or let Max take his course," they shouted.

"Fear it not," answered Magog.

"Monster!" shrieked Dame Placida, "you cannot mean this—help! help!"

But no one stirred. And above the roaring of the animals and the angry growling of Max, which Magog had provoked with a sly kick or two, was heard the loud laughter of the gigantic brethren.

"I give you two minutes to consider," said Magog. "If you do not resolve to amend in that time, I leave you to your fate.'"

And he again goaded Max into a further exhibition of fury. Dame Placida became seriously alarmed, and her proud spirit began to give way.

"I promise," she uttered faintly.

"Speak up!" bellowed Magog. "I can't hear you for the noise."

"I promise," replied Placida, in a loud and peevish voice. "That won't do," rejoined her husband. "Speak as you used to do before I married you, and let the others hear you."

"Yes—yes," cried Og, drawing near with the rest, "we must all hear it, that we may be witnesses hereafter. You promise to amend your conduct, and let our brother live peaceably?"

"I do—I do," replied Placida, in a penitential tone.

"Enough," replied Magog. And putting out his arm behind to his wife he covered her retreat, and then suddenly turning upon Max, kicked him into the cage, and fastened the door.

Much laughter among the male portion of the company ensued. But Dame Potentia looked rather grave, and privately intimated to her husband her desire, or rather command, that he should go home. As Peter Trusbut took his departure, he whispered to Hairun, "If ever you think of marrying, I advise you to take good care of old Max. I wish I could borrow him for a day or two."

"You shall have him, and welcome," returned the bearward, laughing.

"Thank you—thank you," answered the pantler, dejectedly. "Mine is a hopeless case."

Dame Placida appeared so much subdued, that at last Magog took compassion upon her, and led her away, observing to the bearward, "For my sake bestow a plentiful supper on Max. He has done me a good turn, and I would fain requite it."

The rest of the party speedily followed their example, and as Xit took his leave, he remarked to his host, "Nothing but Magog's desire to terrify his dame prevented me from attacking Max. I am certain I could master him."

"Say you so?" replied Hairun; "then you may have an opportunity of displaying your prowess before the queen tomorrow."

"I will certainly avail myself of it," replied Xit. "Give him a good supper, and he will be in better condition for the fight."

Early on the following day, Mary arrived at the Tower. She came by water, and was received at the landing-place by Sir Henry Bedingfeld, who conducted her with much ceremony to the palace, where a sumptuous banquet was prepared, at which the knight assisted as chief sewer, presenting each dish to the queen on his bended knee, and placing a silver ewer filled with rosewater, and a napkin, before her between the courses. Mary looked grave and thoughtful, nor could the liveliest sallies of De Noailles, who was one of the guests, call a smile to her lips. Renard, also, was present, and looked more gloomy than usual. The banquet ended, Sir Henry Bedingfeld approached, and laid a parchment before the queen.

"What is this, sir?" she demanded.

"The warrant for the burning of Edward Underhill, the miscreant who attempted your highness's life," replied Bedingfeld.

"How!—burned! and I had pardoned him," exclaimed Mary.

"He has been delivered over by the council to the ecclesiastical authorities, and such is the sentence pronounced against him," returned the knight.

Mary sighed, and attached her signature to the scroll.

"The hour of execution, and the place?" demanded Bedingfeld.

"To-morrow at midnight, on the Tower-green," replied Mary.

Soon after this, it being intimated to the queen that all was in readiness at the Lion's Tower, she arose and proceeded thither, attended by a large retinue of nobles and dames. On the way a momentary interruption occurred, and Simon Renard, who walked a few paces behind her, stepped forward, and whispered in her ear, "I beseech your highness to remain to-night in the Tower. I have somewhat of importance to communicate to you, which can be more safely revealed here than elsewhere."

Mary bowed assent, and the train set forward. A large assemblage was collected within the area in front of the Lions' Tower, but a passage was kept dear for the royal party by two lines of halberdiers drawn up on either side. Og and Magog were stationed at the entrance, and reverentially doffed their caps as she passed. Mary graciously acknowledged the salute, and inquired from the elder giant what had become of his diminutive companion.

"He is within, an' please your majesty," replied Og, "waiting to signalize himself by a combat with a bear."

"Indeed!" rejoined Mary smiling. "It is a hardy enterprise for so small a champion. However, large souls oft inhabit little bodies."

"Your highness says rightly," observed Og. "But your illustrious father, to whom I have the honour to be indirectly related," and he inclined his person, "was wont to observe that he had rather have a large frame and small wit, than much wit and a puny person."

"My father loved to look upon a *man*," replied Mary, "and better specimens of the race than thee and thy brethren he could not well meet with."

"We are much beholden to your highness," replied Og; "and equally, if not more so, to your royal father. Whatever we can boast of strength and size is derived from him. Our mother—"

"Some other time," interrupted Mary, hastily passing on.

"Have I said aught to offend her highness?" asked Og of his brother, as soon as they wero alone.

"I know not," returned Magog. "But you fetched the colour to her cheeks."

On reaching the steps, Mary tendered her hand to Sir Henry Bcdingfeld, and he assisted her to ascend. A temporary covering had been placed over the gallery, and the stone parapet was covered with the richest brocade, and velvet edged with gold fringe. The queen's chair was placed in the centre of the semicircle, and as soon as she was seated, Sir Henry Bcdingfeld stationed himself at her left hand, and waved his staff. The signal was immediately answered by a flourish of trumpets; and a stout, square-built man, with large features, an enormous bushy beard, a short bull throat, having a flat cap on his head, and a stout staff in his hand, issued from a side-door and made a profound obeisance. It was Hairun. His homage rendered, the bearward proceeded to unfasten the door of the central cage, in which a lion of the largest size was confined; and uttering a tremendous roar that shook the whole building, the kingly brute leaped forth. As soon as he had reached the ground, he glared furiously at his keeper, and seemed to meditate a spring. But the latter, who had never removed his eye from him, struck him a severe blow on the nose with his pole, and he instantly turned tail like a beaten hound, and fled howling to the further extremity of the area. Quickly pursuing him, Hairun seized him by the mane, and, in spite of his resistance, compelled him to arise, and bestriding him, rode him backwards and forwards for some time; until the lion, wearying of the performance, suddenly dislodged his rider, and sprang back to his den. This courageous action elicited great applause from the beholders, and the queen loudly expressed her approbation. It was followed by other feats equally daring, in which the bearward proved that he had attained as complete a mastery over the savage tribe as any lion-tamer of modern times. Possessed of prodigious personal strength, he was able to cope with any animal, while his knowledge of the habits of the beast rendered him perfectly fearless as to the result. He unloosed a couple of leopards, goaded them to the utmost pitch of fury, and then defended himself from their combined attack. A tiger proved a more serious opponent. Springing against him, he threw the bearward to the ground, and for a moment it appeared as if his destruction was inevitable. But the brute's advantage was only momentary. In this unfavourable position, Hairun seized him by the throat, and nearly strangling him with his gripe, pulled him down, and they rolled over each other. During the struggle,

Hainin dealt his antagonist a few blows with his fist, which deprived him of his wind, and glad to retreat, he left the bearward master of the field.

Hairun immediately arose, and bowed to the queen, and, excepting a few scratches in the arms, and a gash in the cheek, from which the blood trickled down his beard, appeared none the worse for the contest. So little, indeed, did he care for it, that without tarrying to recover breath, he opened another cage and brought out a large hyæna, over whom he obtained an easy conquest. At last, having finished his performance to the queen's entire satisfaction, he stepped to a side-door, and introduced Gog and Xit. The latter was arrayed in his gayest habiliments, and strutting into the centre of the area with a mincing step, made a bow to the gallery that drew a smile to the royal lips, and addressing Hairun, called in a loud voice, "Bring forth Maximilian, the imperial bear, that I may combat with him before the queen."

The bearward proceeded to the cage, and unfastening it, cried, "Come forth, old Max." And the bear obeyed.

Xit, meanwhile, flung his cap on the ground, and drawing his sword, put himself in a posture of defence.

"Shall I stand by thee?" asked Gog.

"On no account," replied Xit, in an offended tone, "I want-no assistance. I can vanquish him alone."

"Spare thy adversary's life," observed Hairun, laughingly.

"Fear nothing," replied Xit, "the brave are ever merciful."

"True," laughed Hairun, "I must give a like caution to Max." And feigning to whisper in the bear's ear, who was sitting on its hind legs, lolling out its tongue, and looking round in expectation of some eatables, he laughingly withdrew.

Seeing that Max paid no attention to him, Xit drew nearer, and stamping his foot furiously on the ground several times, made a lunge at him, screaming— "Sa-ha! sa-ha! sirrah,—to the combat!—to the combat."

Still, Max did not notice him, but kept his small red eyes fixed on the gallery, expecting that something would be thrown to him. Enraged at this contemptuous treatment of his defiance, Xit snatched up his cap, flung it in the bear's face, and finding even this insult prove ineffectual, began to prick him with the point of his sword, crying, "Rouse thee, craven beast! Defend thy life, or I will slay thee forthwith."

Thus provoked, Max at length condescended to regard his opponent. He uttered a fierce growl, but would not perhaps have retaliated, if Xit had not persevered in his annoyances. Gesticulating and vociferating fiercely, the dwarf made a number of rapid passes, some of which took effect in his antagonist's hide. All at once, Max made a spring so suddenly, that Xit could not avoid it, struck down the sword, and catching the dwarf in his arms, hugged him to his bosom. All Xit's courage vanished in a breath. He screamed loudly for help, and kicked and struggled to free himself from the terrible grasp in which he was caught. But Max was not disposed to let him off so cheaply, and the poor dwarfs terror was excessive when he beheld those formidable jaws, and that terrible array of teeth ready to tear him in pieces. It had been all over with him, if Gog, who stood at a little distance, and narrowly watched the fray, thinking he had suffered enough, had not run to his assistance.

Gog extricating Xit from the Bear in the Lions Tower

Grasping the bear's throat with his right hand, the giant forced back his head so as to prevent him from using his teeth, while planting his knee against the animal's side, he tore asunder its gripe with the other hand. Hairun, who was likewise flying to the rescue, seeing how matters stood, halted, and burst into a loud laugh. The next moment, Gog gave Max a buffet on the ears that laid him sprawling on his back, and Xit escaped from his clutches. As soon as the bear regained his legs, he uttered a low angry growl, and scrambled off to his cage. For a few seconds, Xit looked completely crest-fallen. By degrees, however, he recovered his confidence, and bowing to the gallery, said,—"I can scarcely with propriety lay claim to the victory, as if it had been for my friend Gog—"

"Nay, thou art welcome to my share of it," interrupted the giant.

"If so," rejoined Xit, "I must be pronounced the conqueror, for Max has acknowledged himself vanquished by beating a retreat." As he spoke, the bear growled fiercely, and putting his head out of his cage, seemed disposed to renew the fight—a challenge so alarming to Xit, that he flew to Gog for protection, amid the laughter of the assemblage. Mary then arose, and giving a purse of gold to Sir Henry Bedingfeld, to be bestowed upon the bearward, took her departure for the palace.

As Xit was conversing with his friends, maintaining that he should have vanquished the bear, if Hairun had not most unfairly instructed the beast what to do, and offering to renew the combat on an early occasion, Lawrence Nightgall, accompanied by two halberdiers, entered the court, and approaching him, directed his companions to attach his person. Xit drew his sword, and called upon Gog to defend him.

"What is the meaning of this, master jailor?" demanded the giant, sternly.

"He is arrested by order of the council. There is the warrant," replied Nightgall.

"Arrested!" exclaimed Xit. "For what?"

"For conspiring against the queen," replied Nightgall.

"I am innocent of the charge," replied Xit.

"That remains to be proved," replied Nightgall.

"I have no fears," rejoined Xit, recovering his composure,—"but if I must lose my head, like his grace of Northumberland, I will make a better figure on the scaffold. I shall be the first dwarf that ever perished by the axe. Farewell, Gog. Comfort thyself, I am innocent. Lead me away, thou caitiff jailor."

So saying, he folded his arms upon his breast, and preceded by Nightgall, marched at a slow and dignified pace between his guards.

XX.—HOW EDWARD UNDERHILL WAS BURNT ON TOWER GREEN.

It was the policy of the Romish priesthood, at the commencement of Mary's reign, to win, by whatever means, as many converts as possible to their church. With this view, Gardiner, by the queen's desire, offered a free pardon to the Hot-Gospeller, provided he would publicly abjure his errors, and embrace the Catholic faith; well knowing, that as general attention had been drawn to his crime, and strong sympathy was excited on account of his doctrines, notwithstanding the heinous nature of his offence, among the Protestant party, that his recantation would be far more available to their cause than his execution. But the enthusiast rejected the offer with disdain. Worn down by suffering, crippled with torture, his spirit still burnt fiercely as ever. And the only answer that could be wrung from him by his tormentors was, that he lamented his design had failed, and rejoiced he should seal his faith with his blood.

On one occasion, he was visited in his cell by Bonner, who desired that the heavy irons with which he was loaded should be removed, and a cup of wine given him. Underhill refused to taste the beverage, but Nightgall and Wolfytt, who were present, forced him to swallow it. A brief conference then took place between the bishop and the prisoner, wherein the former strove earnestly to persuade him to recant. But Underhill was so firm in his purpose, and so violent in his denunciations against his interrogator, that Bonner lost all patience, and cried, "If my words do not affright thee, thou vile traitor and pestilent heretic, yet shall the fire to which I will deliver thee."

"There thou art mistaken, thou false teacher of a false doctrine," rejoined Underhill sternly. "The fire may consume my body, but it hath no power over my mind, which shall remain as unscathed as the three children of Israel, Shadrach, Meshach, and Abed-nego, when they stood in the midst of the fiery furnace. For as the apostle saith—'The fire shall try every man's work what it is. If any man's work, that he hath builded upon, abide, he shall receive a reward. If any man's work burn, he shall suffer loss. But he shall be saved himself, nevertheless, yet as it were through fire.' Even so shall I, despite my manifold transgressions, be saved: while ye, idolatrous priests and prophets of Baal, shall be consumed in everlasting flames."

"Go to,—go to, thou foolish boaster," retorted Bonner angrily; "a season will come when thou wilt bitterly lament thou hast turned aside the merciful intentions of thy judges."

"I have already said that the fire has no terrors for me," replied Underhill. "When the spirit has once asserted its superiority over the flesh, the body can feel no pain. Upon the rack—in that dreadful engine, which fixes the frame in such a posture that no limb or joint can move—I was at ease. And to prove that I have no sense of suffering, I will myself administer the torture."

So saying, and raising with some difficulty his stiffened arm, he held his hand over the flame of a lamp that stood upon the table before him, until the veins shrunk and burst, and the sinews cracked. During this dreadful trial, his countenance underwent no change. And if Bonner had not withdrawn the lamp, he would have allowed the limb to be entirely consumed.

"Peradventure, thou wilt believe me now," he cried triumphantly; "and wilt understand that the Lord will so strengthen me with his holy spirit that I may be 'one of the number of those blessed, which, enduring to the end, shall reap a heavenly inheritance.'"

"Take him away," replied Bonner. "His blood be upon his own head. He is so blinded and besotted, that he does not perceive that his death will lead to damnation."

"No, verily," rejoined Underhill, exultingly; "for as Saint Paul saith, There is no damnation to them that are in Christ Jesus, which walk not after the flesh, but after the spirit. Death, where is thy sting? Hell, where is thy victory?"

"Hence with the blasphemer," roared Bonner; "and spare him no torments, for he deserves the severest ye can inflict."

Upon this, Underhill was removed, and the bishop's injunctions in respect to the torture literally fulfilled.

Brought to trial for the attempt upon the queen's life, he was found guilty, and received the royal pardon. Nothing could be elicited as to his having any associates or instigators to his crime. And the only matter that implicated another was the prayer for the restoration of Jane, written in a leaf of the bible found upon his person at the time of his seizure. But though he was pardoned by Mary, he did not escape. He was claimed as a heretic by Bonner; examined before the ecclesiastical commissioners; and adjudged to the stake. The warrant for his execution was signed, as above related, by the queen.

On the night before this terrible sentence was carried into effect, he was robed in a loose dress of flame-coloured taffeta, and conveyed through the secret passages to Saint John's Chapel in the White Tower, which was brilliantly illuminated, and filled with a large assemblage. As he entered the sacred structure, a priest advanced with holy water, but he turned aside with a scornful look. Another, more officious, placed a consecrated wafer to his lips, but he spat it out; while a third forced a couple of tapers into his hands, which he was compelled to carry, in this way, he was led along the aisle by his guard, through the crowd of spectators who divided as he moved towards the altar, before which, as on the occasion of the Duke of Northumberland's reconciliation, Gardiner was seated upon the faldstool, with the mitre on his head. Priests and choristers were arranged on either side in their full habits. The aspect of the chancellor-bishop was stern and menacing, but the miserable enthusiast did not quail before it. On the contrary, he seemed inspired with new strength; and though he had with difficulty dragged his crippled limbs along the dark passages, he now stood firm and erect. His limbs were wasted, his cheeks hollow, his eyes deep sunken in their sockets, but flashing with vivid lustre. At a gesture from Gardiner, Nightgall and Wolfytt, who attended him, forced him upon his knees.

Edward Underhill, demanded the bishop, in a stern voice, "for the last time, I ask thee dost thou persist in thy impious and damnable heresies?"

"I persist in my adherence to the Protestant faith, by which alone I can be saved," replied Underhill, firmly. "I deserve and desire death for having raised my hand against the queens life. But as her highness has been graciously pleased to extend her mercy towards me, if I suffer death it will be in the cause of the gospel. And I take all here present to witness that I am right willing to do so, certain that I shall obtain by such means the crown of everlasting life. I would suffer a thousand deaths—yea all the rackings, torments, crucifyings, and other persecutions endured by the martyrs of old, rather than deny Christ and his gospel, or defile my faith and conscience with the false worship of the Romish religion."

"Then perish in thy sins, unbeliever," replied Gardiner sternly.

And he arose, and taking off his mitre, the whole assemblage knelt down, while the terrible denunciation of the Catholic church against a heretic was solemnly pronounced. This done, mass was performed, hymns were chanted, and the prisoner was conducted to his cell.

The brief remainder of his life was passed by Underhill in deep but silent devotion; for his jailors, who never left him, would not suffer him to pray aloud, or even to kneel; and strove, though vainly, to distract him, by singing ribald songs, plucking his beard and garments, and offering other interruptions.

The place appointed as the scene of his last earthly suffering was a square patch of ground, marked by a border of white flint stones, then, and even now, totally destitute of herbage, in front of Saint Peter's Chapel on the Green, where the scaffold for those executed within the Tower was ordinarily erected, and where Anne Boleyn and Catherine Howard were beheaded.

On this spot a strong stake was driven deeply into the ground, and at a little distance from it was piled a large stack of fagots. An iron ring was fixed to the centre of the stake, and to the ring was attached a broad iron girdle, destined to encircle the body of the victim.

As night set in, a large band of halberdiers marched into the green, and stationed themselves round the stake. Long before this, sombre groups had gathered together at various points, and eyed the proceedings in moody silence. None of the curiosity—none of the excitement ordinarily manifested upon such occasions—was now exhibited. Underhills crime had checked the strong tide of sympathy which would otherwise have run in his favour. Still, as he had been pardoned by the queen, and was condemned for his religious opinions only, deep commiseration was felt for him. It was not, however, for him that the assemblage looked grave, but for themselves. Most of them were of the Reformed faith, and they argued—and with reason,—that this was only the commencement of a season of trouble; and that the next victim might be one of their own family. With such sentiments, it is not to be wondered at, that they looked on sternly and suspiciously, and with the strongest disposition—though it was not manifested, otherwise than by looks—to interrupt the proceedings. As it grew dark, and faces could no longer be discerned, loud murmurings arose, and it was deemed expedient to double the guard, and to place in custody some of the most clamorous. By this means, all disposition to tumult was checked, and profound silence ensued. Meanwhile, numbers continued to flock thither, until, long before the appointed hour arrived, the whole area from the lieutenant's lodgings to Saint Peters Chapel was densely thronged.

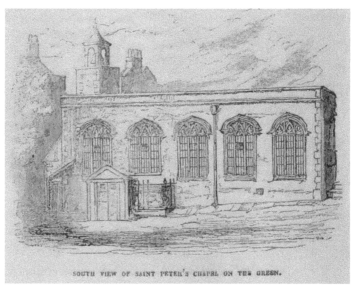

SOUTH VIEW OF SAINT PETER'S CHAPEL ON THE GREEN.

As the bell ceased tolling the hour of midnight, a lugubrious procession slowly issued from beneath the gloomy archway of the Coalharbour Gate.

First came four yeomen of the guard walking two and two, and bearing banners of black silk, displaying large white crosses. Then twelve deacons in the same order, in robes of black silk and flat caps, each carrying a long lighted wax taper. Then a priest's assistant, in a white surplice, with a red cross in front, bareheaded, and swinging a large bell heavily to and fro. Then two young priests, likewise bareheaded, and in white surplices, each holding a lighted taper in a massive silver candlestick. Then an old priest with the mitre. Then two chantry-priests in their robes singing the Miserere. Then four Carmelite monks, each with a large rosary hanging from his wrist, supporting a richly gilt square canopy, decorated at each corner with a sculptured cross, beneath which walked Bonner, in his scarlet chimere and white rochet. Then came Feckenham and other prelates, followed by two more chantry-priests singing the same doleful hymn as their predecessors. Then came a long train of halberdiers. Then the prisoner, clothed in sackcloth and bare-footed, walking between two friars of the lowly order of Saint Francis, who besought him, in piteous tones, to repent ere it was too late. And lastly, the rear was brought up by a company of archers of the queen's body guard.

As soon as the procession had formed in the order it arrived round the place of execution, the prisoner was brought forward by the two friars, who for the last time earnestly exhorted him to recant, and save his soul alive. But he pushed them from him, saying, "Get hence ye popish wolves! ye raveners of Christ's faithful flock! Back to the idolatrous Antichrist of Rome who sent ye hither. I will have none of your detestable doctrines. Get hence, I say, and trouble me no more."

When the friars drew back, he would have addressed the assemblage. But a halberdier, by Bonner's command, thrust a pike into his mouth and silenced him. A wild and uncouth figure, with strong but clumsily-formed limbs, coarse repulsive features, lighted up by a savage smile, now stepped forward. It was Wolfytt, the sworn tormentor. He was attired in a jerkin and hose of tawny leather. His arms and chest were bare, and covered with a thick pile of red hair. His ragged locks and beard, of the same disgusting colour, added to his hideous and revolting appearance. He was armed with a long iron pitchfork, and had a large hammer and a pair of pincers stuck in his girdle. Behind him came Mauger and Nightgall.

A deep and awful silence now prevailed throughout the concourse. Not a breath was drawn, and every eye was bent upon the victim. He was seized and stripped by Mauger and Wolfytt, the latter of whom dragged him to the stake, which the poor zealot reverently kissed as he reached it, placed the iron girdle round his waist, and riveted it to the post. In this position, Underhill cried with a loud voice, "God preserve Queen Jane! and speedily restore her to the throne, that she may deliver this unhappy realm from the popish idolaters who would utterly subvert it."

Several voices cried "Amen!" and Wolfytt, who was nailing the girdle at the time, commanded him to keep silence, and enforced the order by striking him a severe blow on the temples with the hammer.

"You might have spared me that, friend," observed Underhill, meekly. And he then added, in a lower tone, "Have mercy upon me, O Lord, for I am weak! O Lord heal me, for all my bones are vexed!"

While the fagots were heaped around him by Mauger and Nightgall, he continued to pray fervently; and when all was made ready, he cried, "Dear Father, I beseech thee to give once more to this realm the blessing of thy word, with godly peace. Purge and purify me by this fire in Christ's death and passion through thy spirit, that I may be an acceptable burnt-offering in thy sight. Farewell, dear friends. Pray for me, and pray with me."

As he spoke, Nightgall seized a torch and applied it to the fagots. His example was imitated by Mauger and Wolfytt, and the pile was speedily kindled. The dry wood crackled, and the smoke rose in thick volumes. the flames then burst forth, and burning fast and fiercely, cast a lurid light upon the countenances of the spectators, upon the windows of Saint Peter's chapel, and upon the grey walls of the White Tower. As yet, the fire had not reached the victim; the wind blowing strongly from the west, carried it aside. But in a few seconds it gained sufficient ascendancy, and his sufferings commenced. For a short space, he endured them without a groan. But as the flames mounted, notwithstanding all his efforts, the sharpness of the torment overcame him. Placing his hands behind his neck, he made desperate attempts to draw himself further up the stake, out of the reach of the devouring element. But the iron girdle effectually restrained him. He then lost all command of himself; and his eyes starting from their sockets—his convulsed features—his erected hair, and writhing frame—proclaimed the extremity of his agony. He sought relief by adding to his own torture. Crossing his hands upon his breast, and grasping either shoulder, he plunged his nails deeply into the flesh. It was a horrible sight, and a shuddering groan burst from the assemblage. Fresh fagots were added by Nightgall and his companions, who moved around the pyre like fiends engaged in some impious rite. The flames again arose brightly and fiercely. By this time, the lower limbs were entirely consumed; and throwing back his head, and uttering a loud and lamentable yell which was heard all over the fortress, the wretched victim gave up the ghost. A deep and mournful silence succeeded this fearful cry. It found an heco in every breast.

The Burning of Edward Underhill on the Tower Green.

GATEWAY OF THE BLOODY TOWER.

XXI.—HOW LORD GUILFORD DUDLEY AND LADY JANE WERE ARRAIGNED AND ATTAINTED OF HIGH TREASON; AND HOW THEY WERE PARDONED BY QUEEN MARY.

More than three months had now been passed by Jane in solitary confinement in the Brick Tower. Long as was the interval, it appeared brief to her—her whole time being devoted to intense mental application, or to prayer. She lived only in her books; and addressed herself with such ardour to her studies, that her thoughts were completely abstracted.

Sometimes, indeed, in spite of all her efforts, recollections of the past would obtrude themselves upon her—visions of earlier days and of the events and scenes connected with them would rise before her. She thought of Bradgate and its green retreats,—of her beloved preceptor, Roger Ascham,—of the delight with which she had become acquainted, through him, with the poetry, the philosophy, the drama of the ancient world. She recalled their long conversations, in which he had painted to her the vanities and vexations of the world, and the incomparable charms of a life of retirement and meditation, and she now felt the truth of his assertions. Had it been permitted her to pass her quiet and blameless career in that tranquil place, how happy would she have been! And yet she did not repine at her lot, but rather rejoiced at it. "Whatever my own sufferings may be," she murmured—"however severely I may be chastened, I yet feel I shall not endure in vain, but that others will profit by my example. If heaven will vouchsafe me grace and power, not one action of my life but shall redound to the honour of the faith I profess."

One thought she ever checked, feeling that the emotions it excited, threatened to shake her constancy. This was the idea of her husband; and whenever it arose she soothed the pang it occasioned by earnest prayer. The reflection that he was now as firm an adherent to the tenets of the gospel as herself, and that by her own resolution she had wrought this beneficial change in him, cheered and animated her, and almost reconciled her to her separation.

So fully prepared did she now feel for the worst shock of fate, that the only thing she regretted was that she was not speedily brought to trial. But she repressed even this desire as inconsistent with her duty, and unworthy of her high and holy calling. "My part is submission," she murmured, "and whether my term of life is long or short, it becomes me to feel and act in like manner. Whenever I am called upon, I am ready,—certain, if I live devoutly, to attain everlasting happiness, and rejoin my husband where he will never be taken from me."

In this way, she thoroughly reconciled herself to her situation. And though in her dreams old scenes and faces would often revisit her—though her husband's image constantly haunted her—and on waking her pillow was bedewed with her tears—still, she maintained her cheerfulness, and by never allowing one moment to pass unemployed, drove away all distressing thoughts.

Not so her husband. Immured in the Beauchamp Tower, he bore his confinement with great external fortitude; but his bosom was a prey to vain regrets and ambitious hopes. Inheriting, as has before been observed, the soaring aspirations of his father, but without his genius or daring, his mind was continually dwelling upon the glittering bauble he had lost, and upon the means of regaining it. Far from being warned by the duke's fate,—far from considering the fearful jeopardy in which he himself stood—he was ever looking forward to the possibility of escape, and to the chance of reinstating himself in his lost position.

Sincerely attached to Jane, he desired to be restored to her rather from the feeling which had led him to seek her hand—namely, a desire to use her as a means of aggrandizement,—than from any deep regret at the loss of her society. Not that misfortune had lessened his attachment, but that his ruling passion was ambition, which no reverse could quench, no change subdue. "He who has once nearly grasped a sceptre can never lose all thoughts of it," he exclaimed to himself. "I may perish—but while I live I shall indulge the hope of being king of England. And if I should ever obtain my liberty, I will never rest till I have won back the crown. Jane's name shall be my watchword—the Protestant cause my battle-cry; and if the victory is mine, she shall share my throne, but not, as heretofore, occupy it alone. Had I been king, this would never have happened. But my father's ambition ruined all. He aimed at the throne himself, and used me as his stepping-stone. Well, he has paid the penalty of his rashness, and I may perchance share his fate. Yet what if I do? Better die on the scaffold, than linger out a long inglorious life. Oh! that I could make one effort more! If I failed I would lay my head upon the block without a murmur."

The *long* delay that occurred before his trial encouraged his hopes, and a secret communication made to him by the Duke of Suffolk, who had leave to visit him, that a plot was in agitation to restore Jane to the throne, so raised his expectations, that he began to feel little apprehension for the future, confident that ere long the opportunity he sighed for would present itself.

Ever since Jane's conference with Gardiner, Dudley had resisted all overtures from the Romish priesthood to win him over to their religion, and if his own feelings had not prompted him to this course, policy would have now dictated it. Slight as was the information he was able to obtain, he yet gathered that Mary's determination to restore the Catholic religion was making her many enemies, and giving new spirits to her opponents. And when he found, from the communication of De Noailles, that a plot, having for its basis the preservation of the Reformed religion, now menaced by the proposed alliance with Spain, was being formed, he became confirmed in his opinions.

It was not deemed prudent by the conspirators to attempt any communication with Jane. They doubted much whether she could be prevailed upon to join them;—whether she might not even consider it her duty to reveal it;—and they thought there would be ample time to make it known to her when the season for outbreak arrived. Jane's partisans consisted only of her father, her uncle, and ostensibly Do Noailles, who craftily held out hopes to Suffolk and his brother to secure their zealous co-operation. In reality, the wily Frenchman favoured Courtenay and Elizabeth, But he scarcely cared which side obtained the mastery, provided he thwarted his adversary, Simon Renard.

During the early part of her imprisonment, Jane's solitude was disturbed by Feckenham, who, not content with his own discomfiture and that of his superiors, Gardiner and Bonner, returned again and again to the charge, but with no better success than before. Worsted in every encounter, he became, at length, convinced of the futility of the attempt, and abandoned it in despair. At first, Jane regarded his visits as a species of persecution, and a waste of the few precious hours allowed her, which might be far more profitably employed than in controversy. But when they ceased altogether, she almost regretted their discontinuance, as the discussions had led her to examine her own creed more closely than she otherwise might have done; and the success she invariably met with, inspired her with new ardour and zeal.

Thus time glided on. Her spirits were always equable; her looks serene; and her health, so far from being affected by her captivity, appeared improved. One change requires to be noticed. It was remarked by her jailor that when first brought to the Brick Tower, she looked younger than her age, which was scarcely seventeen; but that ere a month had elapsed, she seemed like a matured woman. A striking alteration had, indeed, taken place in her appearance. Her countenance was grave, but so benignant, that its gravity had no displeasing effect. Her complexion was pale but clear,—so clear that the course of every azure vein could be traced through the wax-like skin. But that which imparted the almost *angelic* character to her features, was their expression of perfect purity, unalloyed by any taint of earth. What with her devotional observances, and her intellectual employments, the mind had completely asserted its dominion over the body; and her seraphic looks and beauty almost realized the Catholic notion of a saint.

She had so won upon her jailor by her extraordinary piety, and by her gentleness and resignation, that he could scarcely offer her sufficient attention. He procured her such books as she desired—her sole request; and never approached her but with the profoundest reverence. From him she learned the fate of Edward Underhill, and during the dreadful sufferings of the miserable enthusiast, when the flames that were consuming him lighted up her prison-chamber, and his last wild shriek rang in her ears, her lips were employed in pouring forth the most earnest supplications for his release.

It was a terrible moment to Jane; and the wretched sufferer at the stake scarcely endured more anguish. Like many others, she saw in his fate a prelude of the storm that was to follow; and passed the whole of the night in prayer, that the danger might be averted. She prayed also, earnestly and sincerely, that a like death might be hers, if it would prove beneficial to her faith, and prevent further persecution.

One day, shortly after this event, the jailor made his appearance at an unwonted hour, and throwing himself at her feet, informed her that after a severe struggle with himself, he was determined to liberate her; and that he would not only throw open her prison-door that night, but would find means to set her free from the Tower. When he concluded, Jane, who had listened to his proposal with extreme surprise, at once, though with the utmost thankfulness, declined it. "You would break *your* trust, and I *mine*," she observed, "were I to accept your offer. But it would be useless. Whither should I fly—what should I do were I at large? No, friend, I cannot for a moment indulge the thought. If that door should be opened to me, I would proceed to the queen's presence, and beseech her highness to bring me to speedy trial. That is all the favour I deserve, or desire."

"Well, madam," replied the jailor, in accents of deep disappointment, "since I may not have my wish and set you free, I will at once resign my post."

"Nay, do not so, I beseech you, good friend," returned Jane, "that were to do me an unkindness, which I am sure you would willingly avoid, by exposing me to the harsh treatment of some one less friendly-disposed towards me than yourself, from whom I have always experienced compassion and attention."

"Foul befal me if I did not show you such, sweet lady!" cried the jailor.

"Your nature is kindly, sir," pursued Jane; "and as I must needs continue a captive, so I pray you show your regard by continuing my jailor. It gladdens me to think I have a friend so near."

"As you will, madam," rejoined the man, sorrowfully. "Yet I beseech you, pause ere you reject my offer. An opportunity of escape now presents itself, which may never occur again. If you will consent to fly, I will attend you, and act as your faithful follower."

"Think me not insensible to your devotion, good friend, if I once more decline it," returned Jane, in a tone that showed that her resolution was taken. "I cannot fly—I have ties that bind me more securely than those strong walls and grated windows. Were the queen to give me the range of the fortress— nay, of the city without it, I should consider myself equally her captive. No, worthy friend, we must remain as we are."

Seeing remonstrance was in vain, the man, ashamed of the emotion he could neither control nor conceal, silently withdrew. The subject was never renewed, and though he acted with every consideration towards his illustrious captive, he did not relax in any of his duties.

Full three months having elapsed since Jane's confinement commenced, on the first of November her jailor informed her that her trial would take place in Guildhall on the day but one following. To his inquiry whether she desired to make any preparations, she answered in the negative.

"The offence I have committed," she said, "is known to all. I shall not seek to palliate it. Justice will take its course. Will my husband be tried with me?"

"Undoubtedly, madam," replied the jailor.

"May I be permitted to confer with him beforehand?" she asked.

"I grieve to say, madam, that the queen's orders are to the contrary." returned the jailor. "You will not meet him till you are placed at the bar before your judges."

"Since it may not be, I must resign myself contentedly to her majesty's decrees. Leave me, sir. Thoughts press upon me so painfully that I would fain be alone."

"The queen's confessor is without, madam. He bade me say he would speak with you."

"He uses strange ceremony, methinks," replied Jane. "He would formerly enter my prison without saying, By your leave: but since he allows me a choice in the matter, I shall not hesitate to decline his visit. If I may not confer with my husband, there is none other whom I desire to see."

"But he is the bearer of a message from her majesty," urged the jailor.

"If he is resolved to see me, I cannot prevent it," replied Jane. "But if I have the power to hinder his coming, he shall not do so."

"I will communicate your wish to him, madam," replied the jailor, retiring.

Accordingly, he told Feckenham that his charge was in no mood to listen to him, and the confessor departed.

The third of November, the day appointed for Jane's trial, as well as for that of her husband, and of Cranmer, archbishop of Canterbury, was characterized by unusual gloom, even for the season. A dense fog arose from the river and spread itself over the ramparts, the summits of which could scarcely be discerned by those beneath them. The sentinels pacing to and fro looked like phantoms, and the whole fortress was speedily enveloped in a tawny-coloured vapour. Jane had arrayed herself betimes, and sat in expectation of the summons with a book before her, but it became so dark that she was compelled to lay it aside. The tramp of armed men in front of the building in which she was lodged, and other sounds that reached her, convinced her that some of the prisoners were being led forth; but she had to wait long before her own turn came. She thought more—much more—of beholding her husband, than of the result of the trial, and her heart throbbed as any chance footstep reached her ear, from the idea that it might be his.

An hour after this, the door of her chamber was unbarred, and two officers of the guard in corslets and steel caps appeared and commanded her to follow them. Without a moment's hesitation she arose, and was about to pass through the door when the jailor prostrated himself before her, and pressing the hand she kindly extended to him to his lips, expressed, in faltering tones, a hope that she might not be brought back to his custody. Jane shook her head, smiled faintly, and passed on.

Issuing from the structure, she found a large band of halberdiers drawn out to escort her. One stern figure arrested her attention, and recalled the mysterious terrors she had formerly experienced. This was Nightgall, who by Renard's influence had been raised to the post of gentleman-jailor. He carried the fatal axe,—its handle supported by a leathern pouch passed over his shoulders. The edge was turned from her, as was the custom on proceeding to trial. A shudder passed over her frame as her eye fell on the implement of death, connected as it was with her former alarms; but she gave no further sign of trepidation, and took the place assigned her by the officers. The train was then put in motion, and proceeded at a slow pace past the White Towner, down the descent leading to the Bloody Tower. Nightgall marched a few paces before her, and Jane, though she strove to reason herself out of her fears, could not repress a certain misgiving at his propinquity.

The gateway of the Bloody Tower, through which the advanced guard was now passing, is perhaps one of the most striking remnants of ancient architecture to be met with in the fortress. Its dark and gloomy archway, bristling with the iron teeth of the portcullis, and resembling some huge ravenous monster, with jaws wide-opened to devour its prey, well accords with its ill-omened name, derived, as before stated, from the structure above it being the supposed scene of the murder of the youthful princes.

Erected in the reign of Edward the Third, this gateway is upwards of thirty feet in length, and fifteen in width. It has a vaulted roof, supported by groined arches, and embellished with moulded tracery of great beauty. At the period of this chronicle, it was defended at either extremity by a massive oak portal, strengthened by plates of iron and broad-headed nails, and a huge portcullis. Of these defences those at the south are still left. On the eastern side, concealed by the leaf of the gate when opened, is an arched doorway, communicating with a flight of spiral stone steps leading to the chambers above, in which is a machine for working the portcullis.

By this time, Jane had reached the centre of the arch, when the gate was suddenly pushed aside, and Feckenham stepped from behind it. On his appearance, word was given by the two captains, who marched with their drawn swords in hand on either side of the prisoner, to the train to halt. The command was instantly obeyed. Nightgall paused a few feet in advance of Jane, and grasping his fatal weapon, threw a stealthy glance over his left shoulder to ascertain the cause of the interruption.

"What would you, reverend sir?" said Jane, halting with the others, and addressing Feckenham, who advanced towards her, holding in his hand a piece of parchment to which a large seal was attached.

"I would save you, daughter," replied the confessor. "I here bring you the queen's pardon."

"Is it unconditional, reverend sir?" demanded Jane, coldly.

"The sole condition annexed to it is your reconciliation with the church of Rome," replied Feckenham.

"Then I at once reject it," rejoined Jane, firmly. "I have already told you I should prefer death a thousand-fold to any violation of my conscience; and neither persuasion nor force shall compel me to embrace a religion opposed to the gospel of our Saviour, and which, in common with all his true disciples, I hold in utter abhorrence. I take all here to witness that such are my sentiments—that I am an earnest and zealous, though unworthy member of the Protestant church—and that I am fully prepared to seal my faith with my blood."

A slight murmur of approbation arose from the guard, which, however, was instantly checked by the officers.

"And I likewise take all here to witness," rejoined Feckenham, in a loud voice, "that a full and free pardon is offered you by our gracious queen, whom you have so grievously offended, that no one except a princess of her tender and compassionate nature would have overlooked it; coupled only with a condition which it is her assured belief will conduce as much to your eternal welfare as to your temporal. It has been made a reproach to our church by its enemies, that it seeks to win converts by severity and restraint. That the charge is unfounded her highness's present merciful conduct proves. We seek to save the souls of our opponents, however endangered by heresy, alive; and our first attempts are ever gentle. If these fail, and we are compelled to have recourse to harsher measures, is it our fault, or the fault of those who resist us? Thus, in your own case, madam—here, on the way to a trial the issue of which all can foresee, the arm of mercy is stretched out to you and to your husband, on a condition which, if you were not benighted in error, you would recognize as an additional grace,—and yet you turn it aside."

"The sum of her majesty's mercy is this," replied Jane; "she would kill my soul to preserve my body. I care not for the latter, but I regard the former.

Were I to embrace your faith, I should renounce all hopes of heaven. Are you answered, sir?"

"I am," replied Feckenham. "But oh! madam," he added, falling at her feet; "believe not that I urge you to compliance from any unworthy motive. My zeal for your salvation is hearty and sincere."

"I doubt it not, sir," rejoined Jane. "And I thank you for your solicitude."

"Anger not the queen by a refusal," proceeded Feckenham:—"anger not heaven, whose minister I am, by a blind and obstinate rejection of the truth, but secure the favour of both your earthly and your celestial judge by compliance."

"I should indeed anger heaven were I to listen to you further," replied Jane. "Gentlemen," she added, turning to the officers, "I pray you proceed. The tribunal to which you are about to conduct me waits for us."

Feckenham arose, and would have given utterance to the denunciation that rose to his lips, had not Jane's gentle look prevented him. Bowing his head upon his breast, he withdrew, while the procession proceeded on its course, in the same order as before.

On reaching the bulwark gate, Jane was placed in a litter, stationed there for her reception, and conveyed through vast crowds of spectators, who, however, were unable to obtain even a glimpse of her, to Guildhall, where she was immediately brought before her judges. The sight of her husband standing at the bar, guarded by two halberdiers, well nigh overpowered her; but she was immediately re-assured by his calm, collected, and even haughty demeanour. He cast a single glance of the deepest affection at her, and then fixed his gaze upon the Marquis of Winchester, high treasurer of the realm, who officiated as chief judge.

On the left of Lord Guilford Dudley, on a lower platform, stood his faithful esquire, Cuthbert Cholmondeley, charged with abetting him in his treasonable practices. A vacant place on this side of her husband was allotted to Jane. Cranmer, having already been tried and attainted, was removed. The proceedings were soon ended, for the arraigned parties confessed their indictments, and judgment was pronounced upon them. Before they were removed, Lord Guilford turned to his consort, and said in a low voice—"Be of good cheer, Jane. No ill will befal you. Our judges will speedily take our places."

Jane looked at him for a moment, as if she did not comprehend his meaning, and then replied in the same tone—"I only required to see you so resigned to your fate, my dear lord, to make me wholly indifferent to mine. May we mount the scaffold together with as much firmness!"

"We shall mount the throne together—not the scaffold, Jane," rejoined Dudley, significantly.

"Ha!" exclaimed Jane, perceiving from his speech that he meditated some new project.

Further discourse was not, however, allowed her, for at this moment she was separated from her husband by the halberdiers, who led her to the litter in which she was carried back to the Tower.

Left to herself within her prison-chamber, she revolved Dudley's mysterious words; and though she could not divine their precise import, she felt satisfied that he cherished some hope of replacing her on the throne. So far from this conjecture affording her comfort, it deeply distressed her—and for the first time for a long period her constancy was shaken. When her jailor visited her, he found her in the deepest affliction.

"Alas! madam," he observed, in a tone of great commiseration, "I have heard the result of your trial, but the queen may yet show you compassion."

"It is not for myself I lament," returned Jane, raising her head, and drying her tears, "but for my husband."

"Her majesty's clemency may be extended towards him likewise," remarked the jailor.

"Not so," returned Jane, "we have both offended her too deeply for forgiveness, and justice requires that we should expiate our offence with our lives. But you mistake me, friend. It is not because my husband is condemned as a traitor, that I grieve; but because he still nourishes vain and aspiring thoughts. I will trust you, knowing that you are worthy of confidence. If you can find means of communicating with Lord Guilford Dudley for one moment, tell him I entreat him to abandon all hopes of escape, or of restoration to his fallen state, and earnestly implore him to think only of that everlasting kingdom which we shall soon inherit together. Will you do this?"

"Assuredly, madam, if I can accomplish it with safety," replied the jailor.

"Add also," pursued Jane, "that if Mary would resign her throne to me, I would not ascend it."

"I will not fail, madam," rejoined the jailor.

Just as he was about to depart, steps were heard on the staircase, and Sir Henry Bedingfeld, attended by a couple of halberdiers, entered the chamber. He held a scroll of parchment in his hand.

"You are the bearer of my death-warrant, I perceive, sir," said Jane, rising at his approach, but without displaying any emotion.

"On the contrary, madam," returned Sir Henry, kindly, "it rejoices me to say that I am a bearer of her majesty's pardon."

"Clogged by the condition of my becoming a Catholic, I presume?" rejoined Jane, disdainfully.

"Clogged by no condition," replied Bedingfeld, "except that of your living in retirement."

Jane could scarcely credit her senses, and she looked so bewildered that the knight repeated what he had said.

"And my husband?" demanded Jane, eagerly.

"He too is free," replied Bedingfeld; "and on the same terms as yourself. You are both at liberty to quit the Tower as soon as you think proper. Lord Guilford Dudley has already been apprised of her highness's clemency, and will join you here in a few' minutes."

Jane heard no more. The sudden revulsion of feeling produced by this joyful intelligence, was too much for her; and uttering a faint cry, she sank senseless into the arms of the old knight.

XXII.—OF JANE'S RETURN TO SION HOUSE; AND OF HER ENDEAVOURS TO DISSUADE HER HUSBAND FROM JOINING THE CONSPIRACY AGAINST QUEEN MARY.

That night Lord Guilford Dudley and Jane, attended by Cholmondeley, who was included in the pardon, left the Tower, and repaired to Sion House. On finding herself once more restored to freedom, and an inmate of the house she loved so well, Jane was completely prostrated. Joy was more difficult to bear than affliction; and the firmness that had sustained her throughout her severest trials now altogether forsook her. But a few days brought back her calmness, and she poured forth her heartfelt thanks to that beneficent Being, who had restored her to so much felicity. Measureless content seemed hers, and as she traversed the long galleries and halls of the ancient mansion—as she wandered through its garden walks,—or by the river's side—she felt that even in her proudest moment she had never known a tithe of the happiness she now experienced.

Day after day flew rapidly by, and pursuing nearly the same course she had adopted in prison, she never allowed an hour to pass that was not profitably employed. But she observed with concern that her husband did not share her happiness. He grew moody and discontented, and became far more reserved than she had heretofore known him. Shunning her society, he secluded himself in his chamber, to which he admitted no one but Cholmondeley.

This conduct Jane attributed in some degree to the effect produced upon his spirits by the reverse of fortune he had sustained, and by his long imprisonment. But she could not help fearing, though he did not confide the secrets of his bosom to her, that he still cherished the project he had darkly hinted at. She was confirmed in this opinion by the frequent visits of her father, who like her husband, had an anxious look, and by other guests who arrived at nightfall, and departed as secretly as they came.

As soon as this conviction seized her, she determined, at the hazard of incurring his displeasure, to speak to her husband on the subject; and accordingly, one day, when he entered her room with a moodier brow than usual, she remarked, "I have observed with much uneasiness, dear Dudley, that ever since our release from imprisonment, a gradually-increasing gloom has taken possession of you. You shun my regards, and avoid my society,—nay, you do not even converse with me, unless I wring a few reluctant answers from you. To what must I attribute this change?"

"To anything but want of affection for you, dear Jane," replied Dudley, with a melancholy smile, while he fondly pressed her hand. "You had once secrets from me, it is my turn to retaliate, and be mysterious towards you."

"You will not suppose me influenced by idle curiosity if I entreat to be admitted to your confidence, my dear lord," replied Jane. "Seeing you thus oppressed with care, and knowing how much relief is afforded by sharing the burthen with another, I urge you, for your own sake, to impart the cause of your anxiety to me. If I cannot give you counsel, I can sympathy."

Dudley shook his head, and made a slight effort to change the conversation.

"I will not be turned from my purpose," persisted Jane; "I am the truest friend you have on earth, and deserve to be trusted."

"I *would* trust you, Jane, if I dared," replied Dudley.

"Dared!" she echoed. "What is there that a husband dares not confide to his wife?"

"In this instance much," answered Dudley; "nor can I tell you what occasions the gloom you have noticed, until I have your plighted word that you will not reveal aught I may say to you. And further, that you will act according to my wishes."

"Dudley," returned Jane gravely, "your demand convinces me that my suspicions are correct. What need of binding me to secrecy, and exacting my obedience, unless you are acting wrongfully, and desire me to do so likewise? Shall I tell why you fear I should divulge your secret—why you are apprehensive I should hesitate to obey your commands? You are plotting against the queen, and dread I should interfere with you."

"I have no such fears," replied Dudley, sternly.

"Then you own that I am right?" cried Jane, anxiously.

"You are so far right," replied Dudley, "that I am resolved to depose Mary, and restore you to the throne, of which she has unjustly deprived you."

"Not unjustly, Dudley, for she is the rightful queen, and I was an usurper," replied Jane. "But oh! my dear, dear lord, can you have the ingratitude—for I will use no harsher term, to requite her clemency thus?" *

"I owe her no thanks," replied Dudley, fiercely. "I have solicited no grace from her, and if she has pardoned me, it was of her own free will. It is part of her present policy to affect the merciful. But she showed no mercy towards my father."

"And does not your present conduct, dear Dudley, prove how necessary it is for princes, who would preserve their government undisturbed, to shut their hearts to compassion?" returned Jane. "You will fail in this enterprise if you proceed in it. And even I, who love you most, and am most earnest for your happiness and honour, do not desire it to succeed. It is based upon injustice, and will have no support from the right-minded."

"Tush!" cried Dudley, impatiently. "I well knew you would oppose my project, and therefore I would not reveal it to you. You shall be queen in spite of yourself."

"Never again," rejoined Jane, mournfully;—"never again shall my brow be pressed by that fatal circlet. Oh! if it is for me you are about to engage in this wild and desperate scheme, learn that even if it succeeded, it will be futile. Nothing should ever induce me to mount the throne again; nor, if I am permitted to occupy it, to quit this calm retreat. Be persuaded by me, dear Dudley. Abandon your project. If you persist in it, I shall scarcely feel justified in withholding it from the queen."

"How, madam," exclaimed Dudley, sternly; "would you destroy your husband?"

"I would save him," replied Jane.

"A plague upon your zeal!" cried Dudley, fiercely. "If I thought you capable of such treachery, I would ensure your silence."

"And if I thought *you* capable, dear Dudley, of such black treason to a sovereign to whom you owe not merely loyalty and devotion, but life itself, no consideration of affection, still less intimidation, should prevent me from disclosing it, so that I might spare you the commission of so foul a crime."

"Do so, then," replied Dudley, in a taunting tone. "Seek Mary's presence. Tell her that your husband and his brothers are engaged in a plot to place you on the throne. Tell her that your two uncles, the Lords John and Thomas Grey, are conspiring with them—that your father, the Duke of Suffolk, is the promoter, the leader, of the design."

"My father!" exclaimed Jane, with a look of inexpressible anguish.

"Add that the Earl of Devon, Sir Thomas Wyat, Throckmorton, Sir Peter Carew, and a hundred others, are leagued together to prevent the spread of popery in this country—to cast off the Spanish yoke, with which the people are threatened, and to place a Protestant monarch on the throne. Tell her this, and bring your husband—your father—your whole race—to the block. Tell her this, and you, the pretended champion of the gospel, will prove yourself its worst foe. Tell her this—enable her to crush the rising rebellion, and England is delivered to the domination of Spain—to the inquisition—to the rule of the pope—to idolatrous oppression. Now, go and tell her this."

"Dudley, Dudley," exclaimed Jane, in a troubled tone, "you put evil thoughts into my head—you tempt me sorely."

"I tempt you only to stand between your religion and the danger with which it is menaced," returned her husband. "Since the meeting of parliament, Mary's designs are no longer doubtful; and her meditated union with Philip of Spain has stricken terror into the hearts of all good Protestants. A bloody and terrible season for our church is at hand, if it be not averted. And it *can* only be averted by the removal of the bigoted queen who now fills the throne."

"There is much truth in what you say, Dudley," replied Jane, bursting into tears. "Christ's faithful flock are indeed in fearful peril; but bloodshed and rebellion will not set them right. Mary is our liege mistress, and if we rise against her we commit a grievous sin against heaven, and a crime against the state."

"Crime or not," replied Dudley, "the English nation will never endure a Spanish yoke nor submit to the supremacy of the see of Rome. Jane, I now tell you that this plot may be revealed—may be defeated; but another will be instantly hatched, for the minds of all true Englishmen are discontented, and Mary will never maintain her sovereignty while she professes this hateful faith, and holds to her resolution of wedding a foreign prince."

"If this be so, still I have no title to the throne," rejoined Jane. "The Princess Elizabeth is next in succession, and a Protestant."

"I need scarcely remind you," replied Dudley, "that the act just passed, annulling the divorce of Henry the Eighth from Catherine of Arragon, has annihilated Elizabeth's claims, by rendering her illegitimate. Besides, she has, of late, shown a disposition to embrace her sister's creed."

"It may be so given out—nay, she may encourage the notion herself," replied Jane; "but I know Elizabeth too well to believe for a moment she could abandon her faith."

"It is enough for me she has *feigned* to do so," replied Dudley, "and by this means alienated her party. On *you*, Jane, the people's hopes are fixed. Do not disappoint them."

"Cease to importune me further, my dear lord. I cannot govern myself—still less, a great nation."

"You shall occupy the throne, and entrust the reins of government to me," observed Dudley.

"There your ambitious designs peep forth, my lord," rejoined Jane. "It is for yourself, not for me you are plotting. You would be king!"

"I would," returned Dudley. "There is no need to mask my wishes now."

"Sooner than this shall be," rejoined Jane, severely, "I will hasten to Whitehall, and warn Mary of her danger."

"Do so," replied Dudley, "and take your last farewell of me. You are aware of the nature of the plot—of the names and object of those concerned in it. Reveal all—make your own terms with the queen. But think not you can check it. We have gone too far to retreat. When the royal guards come hither to convey me to the Tower, they will not find their prey, but they will soon hear of me. You will precipitate measures, but you will not prevent them. Go, madam."

"Dudley," replied Jane, falling at his feet—"by your love or me—by your allegiance to your sovereign—by your duty to your Maker—by every consideration that weighs with you—I implore you to relinquish your design."

"I have already told you my fixed determination, madam," he returned, repulsing her. "Act as you think proper."

Jane arose and walked slowly towards the door. Dudley laid his hand upon his sword, half drew it, and then thrusting it back into the scabbard, muttered between his ground teeth, "No, no—let her go. She dares not betray me."

As Jane reached the door, her strength failed her, and she caught against the hangings for support. "Dudley," she murmured, "help me—I faint."

In an instant, he was by her side.

"You cannot betray your husband he said, catching her in his arms.

"I cannot—I cannot," she murmured, as her head fell upon his bosom.

Jane kept her husband's secret. But her own peace of mind was utterly gone. Her walks—her studies—her occupations had no longer any charms for her. Even devotion had lost its solace. She could no longer examine her breast as heretofore—no longer believe herself reproachless! She felt she was an accessary to the great crime about to be committed; and with a sad presentiment of the result, she became a prey to grief,—almost to despair.

XXIII.—HOW XIT WAS IMPRISONED IN THE CONSTABLE TOWER; AND HOW HE WAS WEDDED TO THE "SCAVENGER'S DAUGHTER."

Persuading himself that his capture was matter of jest, Xit kept up his braggadocio air and gait, until he found himself within a few paces of the Constable Tower,—a fortification situated on the east of the White Tower, and resembling in its style of architecture, though somewhat smaller in size, the corresponding structure on the west, the Beauchamp Tower. As Nightgall pointed to this building, and told him with a malicious grin that it was destined to be his lodging, the dwarf's countenance fell. All his heroism forsook him; and casting a half-angry, half-fearful look at his guards, who were laughing loudly at his terrors, he darted suddenly backwards, and made towards a door in the north-east turret of the White Tower.

Nightgall and the guards, not contemplating any such attempt, were taken completely by surprise, but immediately started after him. Darting between the legs of the sentinel stationed at the entrance of the turret, who laughingly presented his partizan at him, Xit hurried up the circular staircase leading to the roof. His pursuers were quickly after him, shouting to him to stop, and threatening to punish him severely when they caught him. But the louder they shouted, the swifter the dwarf fled; and, being endowed with extraordinary agility, arrived, in a few seconds, at the doorway leading to the roof. Here half-a-dozen soldiers, summoned by the cries, were assembled to stop the fugitive. On seeing Xit, with whose person they were well acquainted—never supposing he could be the runaway,—they inquired what was the matter.

"The prisoner! the prisoner!" shouted Xit, instantly perceiving their mistake, and pushing through them, "Where is he? What have you done with him?"

"No one has passed us," replied the soldiers. "Who is it?"

"Lawrence Nightgall," replied Xit, keeping as clear of them as he could. "He has been arrested by an order from the privy-council, and has escaped."

At this moment, Nightgall made his appearance, and was instantly seized by the soldiers. An explanation quickly ensued, but, in the meantime, Xit had flown across the roof, and reaching the opposite turret at the south-east angle, sprang upon the platform, and clambering up the side of the building at the hazard of his neck, contrived to squeeze himself through a loophole.

"We have him safe enough," cried one of the soldiers, as he witnessed Xit's manoeuvre. "Here is the key of the door opening into that turret, and he cannot get below."

So saying, he unlocked the door and admitted the whole party into a small square chamber, in one corner of which was the arched entrance to a flight of stone steps. Up these they mounted, and as they gained the room above, they perceived the agile mannikin creeping through the embrazure.

"Have a care!" roared Nightgall, who beheld this proceeding with astonishment; "You will fall into the court below and be dashed to pieces."

Xit replied by a loud laugh, and disappeared. When Nightgall gained the outlet, he could see nothing of him, and after calling to him for some time and receiving no answer, the party adjourned to the leads, where they found he had gained the cupola of the turret, and having clambered up the vane, had seated himself in the crown by which it was surmounted. In this elevated, and as he fancied, secure position, he derided his pursuers, and snapping off a piece of the iron-work, threw it at Nightgall, and with so good an aim that it struck him in the face.

A council of war was now held, and it was resolved to summon the fugitive to surrender; when, if he refused to comply, means must be taken to dislodge him. Meanwhile, the object of this consultation had been discovered from below. His screams and antics had attracted the attention of a large crowd, among whom were his friends the giants. Alarmed at his arrest, they had followed to see what became of him, and were passing the foot of the turret at the very moment when he had reached its summit. Xit immediately recognized them, and hailed them at the top of his voice. At first, they were unable to make out whence the noise proceeded; but at length, Gog chancing to look up, perceived the dwarf, and pointed him out to his companions.

Xit endeavoured to explain his situation, and to induce the giants to rescue him; but they could not hear what he said, and only laughed at his gestures and vociferations. Nightgall now called to him in a peremptory tone to come down. Xit refused, and pointing to the crown in which he was seated, screamed, "I have won it, and am determined not to resign it. I am now in the loftiest position in the Tower. Let him bring me down who can."

"I will be no longer trifled with," roared Nightgall. "Lend me your arquebuss, Winwike. If there is no other way of dislodging that mischievous imp, I will shoot him as I would a jackdaw."

Seeing he was in earnest, Xit thought fit to capitulate. A rope was thrown him which he fastened to the vane, and after bowing to the assemblage, waving his cap to the giants, and performing a few other antics, he slided down to the leads in safety. He was then seized by Nightgall, and though he promised, to march as before between his guards, and make no further attempt to escape, he was carried, much to his discomfiture,—for even in his worst scrapes he had an eye to effect,—to the Constable Tower, and locked up in the lower chamber.

"So, it has come to this," he cried, as the door was barred outside by Nightgall. "I am now a state prisoner in the Tower. Well, I only share the fate of all court favourites and great men—of the Dudleys, the Rochfords, the Howards, the Nevills, the Courtenays, and many others whose names do not occur to me. I ought rather to rejoice than be cast down that I am thus distinguished. But what will be the result of it? Perhaps, I shall be condemned to the block. If I am, what matter? I always understood from Mauger that decapitation was an easy death—and then what a crowd there will be to witness *my* execution—Xit's execution—the execution of the famous dwarf of the Tower! The Duke of Northumberland's will be nothing to it. With what an air I shall ascend the steps—how I shall bow to the assemblage— how I shall raise up Mauger when he bends his lame leg to ask my forgiveness—how I shall pray with the priest—address the assemblage— take off my ruff and doublet, and adjust my head on the block! One blow and all is over. One blow—sometimes, it takes two or three—but Mauger understands his business, and my neck will be easily divided. That's one advantage, among others, of being a dwarf. But to return to my execution. It will be a glorious death, and one worthy of me. I have half a mind to con over what I shall say to the assembled multitude. Let me see. Hold! it occurs to me that I shall not be seen for the railing. I must beg Mauger to allow me to stand on the block. I make no doubt he will indulge me—if not, I will not forgive him. I have witnessed several executions, but I never yet beheld what I should call a really good death. I must try to realize my own notions. But I am getting on a little too fast. I am neither examined, nor sentenced yet. Examined! that reminds me of the rack. I hope they won't torture me. To be beheaded is one thing—to be tortured another. I could bear anything in public, where there are so many people to look at me, and applaud me—but in private it is quite another affair. The very sight of the rack would throw me into fits. And then suppose I should be sentenced to be burnt like Edward Underhill—no, I *won't* suppose that for a moment. It makes me quite hot to think of it. Fool that I was, to be seduced by the hope of rank and dignity held out to me by the French ambassador, to embark in plots which place me in such jeopardy as this! However, I will reveal nothing. I will be true to my employer."

Communing thus with himself, Xit paced to and fro within his prison, which was a tolerably spacious apartment, semi-circular in form, and having deep recesses in the walls, which were of great thickness.

LOWER CHAMBER IN THE CONSTABLE TOWER.

As he glanced around, an Idea occurred to him. "Every prisoner of consequence confined within the Tower carves his name on the walls," he said. "I must carve mine, to serve as a memorial of my imprisonment."

The only implement left him was his dagger, and using it instead of a chisel, he carved, in a few hours, the following inscription in characters nearly as large as himself:—

X I T.

1553.

By the time he had finished his work, he was reminded by a clamorous monitor within him, that he had had no supper, and he recalled with agonizing distinctness the many glorious meals he had consumed with his friends the giants. He had not even the common prisoners fare, a loaf and a cup of water, to cheer him.

"Surely they cannot intend to starve me," he thought. "I will knock at the door and try whether any one is without." But though he thumped with all his might against it, no answer was returned. Indignant at this treatment, he began to rail against the giants, as if they had been the cause of his misfortunes.

"Why do they not come to deliver me?" he cried, in a peevish voice. "The least they could do would be to bring me some provisions. But, I warrant me, they have forgotten their poor famishing dwarf, while they are satisfying their own inordinate appetites. What would I give for a slice of Hairun's wild boar now! The bare idea of it makes my mouth water. But the recollection of a feast is a poor stay for a hungry stomach. Cruel Og! barbarous Gog! inhuman Magog! where are ye now? Insensible that ye are to the situation of your friend, who would have been the first to look after you had ye been similarly circumstanced! Where are ye, I say—supping with Peter Trusbut, or Ribald, or at our lodging in the By-ward Tower? Wherever ye are, I make no doubt you have plenty to eat, whereas I, your best friend, who would have been your patron, if I had been raised to the dignity promised by De Noailles—am all but starving. It cannot be—hilloah! hilloah! help!" And he kicked against the door as if his puny efforts would burst it open. "The queen cannot be aware of my situation. She shall hear of it—but how?"

Perplexing himself how to accomplish this, he flung himself on a straw mattress in one corner, which, together with a bench and a small table constituted the sole furniture of the room, and in a short time fell asleep. He was disturbed by the loud jarring of a door, and, starting to his feet, perceived that two men had entered the room, one of whom bore a lantern, which he hold towards him. In this person Xit at once recognised Nightgall; and in the other, as he drew nearer, Wolfytt the sworn tormentor. The grim looks of the latter so terrified Xit, that he fell back on the mattress in an ecstacy of apprehension. His fright seemed to afford great amusement to the cause of it, for he burst into a coarse loud laugh that made the roof ring again. His merriment rather restored the dwarf, who ventured to inquire, in a piteous accent, whether they had brought him any supper.

"Ay, ay!" rejoined Wolfytt, with a grin. "Follow us, and you shall have a meal that shall serve you for some days to come."

"Readily," replied Xit. "I am excessively hungry, and began to think I was quite forgotten."

"We have been employed in making all ready for you," rejoined Wolfytt. "We were taken a little by surprise. It is not often we have such a prisoner as you."

"I should think not," returned Xit, whose vanity was tickled by the remark. "I was determined to let posterity know that *one* dwarf had been confined within the Tower. Bring your lantern this way, Master Nightgall, and you will perceive I have already carved my name on the wall."

"So I see," growled Nightgall, holding the light to the inscription. "Bring him along, Wolfytt."

"He will not need, sir," returned Xit, with dignity. "I am ready to attend you."

"Good!" exclaimed Wolfytt. "Supper awaits us, he! he!" They then passed through the door, Xit strutting between the pair. Descending a short flight of stone steps, they came to another strong door, which Nightgall opened. It admitted them to a dark narrow passage, which, so far as it could be discerned, was of considerable extent. After pursuing a direct course for some time, they came to an opening on the left, into which they struck. This latter passage was so narrow that they were obliged to walk singly. The roof was crusted with nitrous drops, and the floor was slippery with moisture.

"We are going into the worst part of the Tower," observed Xit, who began to feel his terrors revive. "I have been here once before. I recollect it leads to the Torture Chamber, the Little-Ease, and the Pit. I hope you are not taking me to one of those horrible places?"

"Poh! poh!" rejoined Wolfytt, gruffly. "You are going to Master Nightgall's bower."

"His bower!" exclaimed Xit, surprised by the term—"what! where he keeps Cicely?"

At the mention of this name, Nightgall, who had hitherto maintained a profound silence, uttered an exclamation of anger, and regarded the dwarf with a withering look.

"I can keep a secret if need be," continued Xit, in a deprecatory tone, alarmed at his own indiscretion. "Neither Cuthbert Cholmondeley, nor Dame Potentia, nor any one else, shall hear of her from me, if you desire it, good Master Nightgall."

"Peace!" thundered the jailor.

"You will get an extra turn of the rack for your folly, you crack-brained jackanapes," laughed Wolfytt.

Luckily the remark did not reach Xit's ears. He was too much frightened by Nightgall's savage look to attend to anything else.

They had now reached a third door, which Nightgall unlocked and fastened as soon as the others had passed through it. The passage they entered was even darker and damper than the one they had quitted. It contained a number of cells, some of which, as was evident from the groans that issued from them, were tenanted.

"Is Alexia here?" inquired Xit, whose blood froze in his veins as he listened to the dreadful sounds.

"Alexia!" vociferated Nightgall, in a terrible voice. "What do you know of her?"

"Oh, nothing, nothing," replied Xit. "But I have heard Cuthbert Cholmondeley speak of her."

"She is dead," replied Nightgall, in a sombre voice; "and I will bury you in the same grave with her, if her name ever passes your lips again."

"It shall not, worthy sir," returned Xit,—"it shall not. Curse on my unlucky tongue, which is for ever betraying me into danger!"

They had now arrived at an arched doorway in the wall, which being opened by Nightgall, discovered a flight of steps leading to some chamber beneath. Nightgall descended, but Xit refused to follow him.

"I know where you are taking me," he cried. "This is the way to the torture-chamber."

Wolfytt burst into a loud laugh, and pushed him forward.

"I won't go," screamed Xit, struggling with all his force against the tormentor. "You have no authority to treat me thus. Help! kind Og! good Gog! dear Magog!—help! or I shall be lamed for life. I shall never more be able to amuse you with my gambols, or the tricks that so much divert you. Help! help! I say."

"Your cries are in vain," cried Wolfytt, kicking him down the steps; "no one can save you now."

Precipitated violently downwards, Xit came in contact with Nightgall, whom he upset, and they both rolled into the chamber beneath, where the latter arose, and would have resented the affront upon his comrade, or, at all events, upon the dwarf, if he had not been in the presence of one of whom he stood in the greatest awe. This was Simon Renard, who was writing at a table. Disturbed by the noise, the ambassador glanced round, and on perceiving the cause immediately resumed his occupation. Near him stood the thin erect figure of Sorrocold,—his attenuated limbs appearing yet more meagre from the tight-fitting black hose in which they were enveloped, The chirurgcon wore a short cloak of sad-coloured cloth, and a doublet of the same material. His head was covered by a flat black cap, and a pointed beard terminated his hatchet-shaped, cadaverous face. His hands rested on a long staff, and his dull heavy eyes were fixed upon the ground.

At a short distance from Sorrocold, stood Mauger, bare-headed, and stripped to his leathern doublet, his arms folded upon his bosom, and his gaze bent upon Renard, whose commands he awaited. Nightgall's accident called a smile to his grim countenance, but it instantly faded away, and gave place to his habitual sinister expression.

Such were the formidable personages in whoso presence Xit found himself. Nor was the chamber less calculated to strike terror into his breast than its inmates. It was not the torture-room visited by Cholmondeley, when he explored the subterranean passages of the fortress, but another and larger chamber contiguous to the former, yet separated from it by a wall of such thickness that no sound could penetrate through it. It was square-shaped, with a deep round-arched recess on the right of the entrance, at the further end of which was a small cell, surmounted with a pointed arch. On the side where Renard sat, the wall was decorated with thumb-screws, gauntlets, bracelets, collars, pincers, saws, chains and other nameless implements of torture. To the ceiling was affixed a stout pulley with a rope, terminated by an iron hook, and two leathern shoulder-straps. Opposite the door-way stood a brasier, filled with blazing coals, in which a huge pair of pincers were thrust; and beyond it was the wooden frame of the rack, already described, with its ropes and levers in readiness. Reared against the side of the deep dark recess, previously mentioned, was a ponderous wheel, as broad in the felly as that of a waggon, and twice the circumference. This antiquated instrument of torture was placed there to strike terror into the breasts of those who beheld it—but it was rarely used. Next to it was a heavy bar of iron employed to break the limbs of the sufferers tied to its spokes.

Perceiving in whose presence he stood, and what preparations were made for him, Xit gave himself up for lost, and would have screamed aloud, had not his utterance failed him. His knees smote one another; his hair, if possible, grew more erect than ever; a thick damp burst upon his brow; and his tongue, ordinarily so restless, clove to the roof of his mouth.

"Bring forward the prisoner," cried Renard, with a stern voice, but without turning his head.

Upon this, Nightgall seized Xit by the hand, and dragged him towards the table. A quarter of an hour elapsed, during which Renard continued writing as if no one were present; and Xit, who at first was half dead with fright, began to recover his spirits.

"Your excellency sent for me." he ventured, at length.

"Ha!" ejaculated Renard, pausing and looking at him, "I had forgotten thee."

"A proof that my case is not very dangerous," thought Xit. "I must let this proud Spaniard see I am not so unimportant as he seems to imagine. Your excellency I presume, desires to interrogate me on some point," he continued aloud. "I pray you proceed without further delay."

"Is it your excellency's pleasure that we place him on the rack?" interposed Nightgall.

"Or shall we begin with the thumb-screws," observed Mauger, pointing to a pair upon the table; "I dare say they will extort all he knows. It would be a pity to stretch him out."

"I would not be an inch taller for the world," rejoined Xit, raising himself on his tiptoes.

"I have a suit of irons that will exactly fit him," observed Wolfytt, going to the wall, and taking down an engine that looked like an exaggerated pair of sugar-tongs. "These were made as a model, and have never been used before, except on a monkey belonging to Hairun the bearward. We will wed you to the 'Scavenger's Daughter,' my little man."

Xit wedded to the "Scavenger's Daughter"

Xit knew too well the meaning of the term to take any part in the merriment that followed this sally.

"The embraces of the spouse you offer me are generally fatal," he observed. "I would rather decline the union, if his excellency will permit me.1' *

"What is your pleasure?" asked Nightgall, appealing to Renard.

"Place him in the irons," returned the latter. "If these fail, we can have recourse to sharper means."

Xit would have flung himself at the ambassador's feet, to ask for mercy, but he was prevented by Wolfytt, who slipping a gag into his mouth, carried him into the dark recess, and, by the help of Mauger, forced him into the engine. Diminished to half his size, and bent into the form of a hoop, the dwarf was then set on the ground, and the gag taken out of his mouth.

"How do you like your bride?" demanded Wolfytt, with a brutal laugh.

"So little," answered Xit, "that I care not how soon I am divorced from her. After all," he added, "uncomfortable as I am, I would not change places with Magog."

This remark was received with half-suppressed laughter by the group around him, and Wolfytt was so softened that he whispered in his ear, that if he was obliged to put him on the rack, he would use him as tenderly as he could. "Let me advise you as a friend," added the tormentor, "to conceal nothing."

"Rely upon it," replied Xit, in the same tone. "I'll tell all I know—and more."

"That's the safest plan," rejoined Wolfytt, drily.

By this time, Renard having finished his despatch, and delivered it to Nightgall, he ordered Xit to be brought before him. Lifting him by the nape of his neck, as he would have carried a lap-dog, Wolfytt placed him on the edge of the rack, opposite the ambassador's seat. He then walked back to Manger, who was leaning against the wall near the door, and laid his hand on his shoulder, while Nightgall seated himself on the steps. All three looked on with curiosity, anticipating much diversion. Sorrocold, who had never altered his posture, only testified his consciousness of what was going forward by raising his lacklustre eyes from the ground, and fixing them on the dwarf.

Wheeling round on the stool, and throwing one leg indolently over the other, Renard regarded the mannikin with apparent sternness, but secret entertainment. The expression of Xit's countenance, as he underwent this scrutiny, was so ludicrous, that it brought a smile to every face except that of the chirurgeon.

After gazing at the dwarf for a few minutes in silence, Renard thus commenced—"You conveyed messages to the Earl of Devonshire when he was confined in the Bell Tower?"

"Several," replied Xit.

"And from whom?" demanded Renard.

"Your excellency desires me speak the truth, I conclude?" rejoined Xit.

"If you attempt to prevaricate, I will have you questioned by that engine," returned Renard, pointing to the rack. "I again ask you by whom you were employed to convey these messages?"

"Your excellency and your attendants will keep the secret if I tell you?" replied Xit. "I was sworn not to reveal my employer's name."

"No further trifling, knave," cried Renard, "or I shall deliver you to the tormentors. Who was it?"

"The Queen," replied Xit.

"Impossible!" exclaimed Renard, in surprise.

"Nothing is impossible to a woman in love," replied Xit; "and her highness, though a queen, is still a woman."

"Beware how you trifle with me, sirrah," rejoined Renard. "It was M. De Noailles who employed you."

"He employed me on the part of her majesty, I assure your excellency," returned Xit.

"He deceived you if he told you so," replied Renard. "But now, repeat to me the sum of your conversations with the earl."

"Our conversations all related to his escape," replied Xit.

"Hum!" exclaimed Renard. "Now mark me, and answer me truly as you value a whole skin. Was nothing said of the princess Elizabeth, and of a plot to place her on the throne, and wed her to Courtenay?"

"Nothing that I remember," answered Xit.

"Think again!" cried Renard.

"I *do* recollect that upon one occasion his lordship alluded to the princess," answered Xit, after a moment's pretended reflection.

"Well, what did he say?" demanded Renard.

"That he was sorry he had ever made love to her," replied Xit.

"And well he might be," observed Renard. "But was that all?"

"Every syllable," replied Xit.

"I must assist your memory, then," said Renard. "What ho! tormentors."

"Hold!" cried the dwarf; "I will hide nothing from you."

"Proceed, then," rejoined Renard, "or I give the order."

"Well, then," returned Xit, "since I must needs confess the whole truth, the reason why the Earl of Devonshire was sorry he had made love to the princess was this. Her majesty sent him a letter through me, promising to forgive him, and restore him to her affections."

"You have been either strangely imposed upon, or you are seeking to impose upon me, knave," cried Renard. "But I suspect the latter."

"I carried the billet myself, and saw it opened," returned Xit, "and the earl was so transported with its contents, that he promised to knight me on the day of his espousals."

"A safe promise, if he ever made it," rejoined Renard; "but the whole story is a fabrication. If her majesty desired to release the earl, why did she not issue her orders to that effect to Sir Henry Bedingfeld?"

"Because—but before I proceed, I must beg your excellency to desire your attendants to withdraw. You will perceive my motives, and approve them, when I offer you my explanation."

Renard waved his hand, and the others withdrew, Wolfytt observing to Mauger, "I should like to hear what further lies the little varlet will invent. He hath a ready wit."

"Now, speak out—we are alone," commanded Renard.

"The reason why her majesty did not choose to liberate the Earl of Devonshire was the fear of offending your excellency," replied Xit.

"How?" exclaimed Renard, bending his brows.

"In a moment of pique she had affianced herself to Prince Philip of Spain," continued Xit. "But in her calmer moments she repented her precipitancy, and feeling a return of affection for the earl, she employed M. De Noailles to make up the matter with him. But the whole affair was to be kept a profound secret from you."

"Can this be true?" cried Renard. "But no—no—it is absurd. You are abusing my patience."

"If your excellency will condescend to make further inquiries you will find I have spoken the truth," rejoined the dwarf.

"But I pray you not to implicate me with the queen. Her majesty, like many of her sex, has changed her mind, that is all. And she may change it again for aught I know."

"It is a strange and improbable story," muttered Renard; "yet I am puzzled what to think of it."

"It was no paltry hope of gain that induced me to act in the matter," pursued Xit; "but, as I have before intimated, a promise of being knighted."

"If I find, on inquiry, you have spoken the truth," rejoined Renard, "and you will serve me faithfully on any secret service on which I may employ you, I will answer for it you shall attain the dignity you aspire to."

"I will do whatever your excellency desires," returned Xit, eagerly. "I *shall* be knighted by somebody, after all."

"But if you have deceived me," continued Renard, sternly, "every bone in your body shall be broken upon that wheel. Your examination is at an end." With this, he clapped his hands together, and at the signal the attendants returned.

"Am I to remain in these irons longer?" inquired Xit.

"No," replied Renard. "Release him, and take him hence. I shall interrogate him at the same hour to-morrow night."

"I pray your excellency to desire these officials to treat me with the respect due to a person of my anticipated dignity," cried Xit, as he was unceremoniously seized and thrown on his back by Wolfytt; "and above all, command them to furnish me with provisions. I have tasted nothing to-night."

Renard signified a wish that the latter request should be complied with, and the dwarf's irons being by this time removed, he was led back, by the road he came, to his chamber in the Constable Towrer, where some provisions and a flask of wine were placed before him, and he was left alone.

XXIV.—HOW XIT ESCAPED FROM THE CONSTABLE TOWER; AND HOW HE FOUND CICELY.

While satisfying his appetite, Xit could not help reflecting upon the probable consequences of the ridiculous statement he had made to Renard, and the idea of the anger of the ambassador when he discovered the deception practised upon him, occasioned him much internal trepidation. It did not, however, prevent him from doing full justice to the viands before him, nor from draining to the last drop the contents of the flask. Inspired by the potent liquid, he laughed at his former fears, sprang upon the bench, and committed a hundred other antics and extravagancies. But as the fumes of the wine evaporated, his valour declined; until, like Acres's, it fairly "oozed out at his fingers' ends."

He then began to consider whether it might not be possible to escape. With this view, he examined the embrazures, but they were grated, and defied his efforts to pass through. He next tried the door, and to his great surprise found it unfastened; having, most probably, been left open intentionally by Wolfytt. As may be supposed, Xit did not hesitate to avail himself of the chance thus unexpectedly offered him. Issuing forth, he hurried up a small spiral stone staircase, which brought him to the entrance of the upper chamber. The door was ajar, and peeping cautiously through it, he perceived Nightgall and Wolfytt, both asleep; the former reclining with his face on the table, which was covered with fragments of meat and bread, goblets, and a large pot of wine; and the latter, extended at full length, on the floor. It was evident, from their heavy breathing and disordered attire, they had been drinking deeply.

Stepping cautiously into the chamber, which in size and form exactly corresponded with that below, Xit approached the sleepers. A bunch of keys hung at Nightgall's girdle—the very bunch he had taken once before,—and the temptation to possess himself of them was irresistible. Creeping up to the jailor, and drawing the poignard suspended at his right side from out its sheath, he began to sever his girdle. While he was thus occupied, the keys slightly jingled, and Nightgall, half-awakened by the sound, put his hand to his belt. Finding all safe, as he imagined, he disposed himself to slumber again, while Xit who had darted under the table at the first alarm, as soon as he thought it prudent, recommenced his task, and the keys were once more in his possession.

As he divided the girdle, a piece of paper fell from it; and glancing at it, he perceived it was an order from the council to let the bearer pass at any hour whithersoever he would, through the fortress. Thrusting it into his jerkin, and carrying the keys as carefully as he could to prevent their clanking, he quitted the room, and mounted another short staircase, which brought him to the roof.

It was just getting light as Xit gained the battlements, and he was immediately challenged by the sentinel. On producing the order, however, he was allowed to pass, and crossing the roof towards the south, he descended another short spiral staircase, and emerged from an open door on the ballium wall, along which he proceeded.

On the way, he encountered three more sentinels, all of whom allowed him to pass on sight of the order. Passing through an arched door-way he mounted a flight of steps, and reached the roof of the Broad Arrow Tower.

ROOF OF THE BROAD ARROW TOWER.

Here he paused to consider what course he should pursue. The point upon which he stood commanded a magnificent view on every side of the ramparts and towers of the fortress. Immediately before him was the Wardrobe Tower—now removed, but then connected by an irregular pile of buildings with the Broad Arrow Tower,—while beyond it frowned the grey walls of the White Tower.

On the left was the large court where the masque had been given by the Earl of Devonshire, at which he had played so distinguished a part, surrounded on the west and the south by the walls of the palace. On the right, the view comprehended the chain of fortifications as far as the Flint Tower, with the range of store-houses and other buildings in front of them. At the back ran the outer line of ramparts, leading northward to the large circular bastion, still existing, and known as the Brass Mount; and southward to the structure denominated the Tower leading to the Iron Gate, and now termed the Devil's Battery. Further on, was to be seen London Bridge with its pile of houses, and the tower of Saint Saviour's Church formed a prominent object in the picture..

But Xit's attention was not attracted to the view. He only thought how he could make good his escape, and where he could hide himself in case of pursuit. After debating with himself for some time, he determined to descend to the lowest chamber of the fortification on which he stood and see whether it had any communication with the subterranean passages of which he possessed the keys.

Accordingly, he retraced the steps he had just mounted, and continued to descend till he reached an arched door. Unlocking it with one of the keys from his bunch, he entered a dark passage, along which he proceeded at a swift pace. His course was speedily checked by another door, but succeeding in unfastening it, he ran on as fast as his legs could carry him, till he tumbled headlong down a steep flight of steps. Picking himself up he proceeded more cautiously, and arrived, after some time, without further obstacle, at a lofty, and as he judged from the sound, vaulted chamber.

To his great dismay, though he searched carefully round it, he could find no exit from this chamber, and he was about to retrace his course, when he discovered a short ladder laid against the side of the wall. It immediately occurred to him that this might be used as a communication with some secret door, and rearing it against the wall, he mounted, and feeling about, to his great joy encountered a bolt.

Drawing it aside, a stone door slowly revolved on its hinges, and disclosed a small cell in which a female was seated before a table with a lamp burning upon it. She raised her head at the sound, and revealed the features of Cicely.

Xit uttered an exclamation of astonishment, and rushing towards her, expressed his joy at seeing her. Cicely was equally delighted at the sight of the dwarf, and explained to him that she had been thus long forcibly detained a prisoner by Nightgall.

"Your captivity is at an end," said Xit, as her relation was concluded. "I am come to deliver you, and restore you to your lover. I am afraid he won't think your beauty improved—but I am sure he won't like you the worse for that. Come along. Lean on me. I will support you."

They were just emerging from the cell, when hasty footsteps were heard approaching, and a man entered the vaulted chamber, bearing a torch. It was Nightgall. His looks were wild and furious, and on seeing the dwarf and his companion, he uttered an exclamation of rage, and hurried towards them. Cicely ran screaming to the cell, while Xit, brandishing Night-gall's own poniard, threatened to stab him if he dared to mount the ladder.

XXV.—OF THE ARRIVAL OF THE IMPERIAL AMBASSADORS; AND OF THE SIGNING OF THE MARRIAGE-TREATY BETWEEN MARY AND PHILIP OF SPAIN.

On the 2nd of January, 1554, a solemn embassy from the emperor Charles the Fifth, consisting of four of his most distinguished nobles, the Count D'Egmont, the Count Lalaing, the Seigneur De Courrieres, and the Sieur De Nigry, chancellor of the order of the Toison D'Or, arrived in London to sign the marriage-treaty between Philip and Mary which had been previously agreed upon by the courts of England and Spain.

Gardiner, who as long as he found it possible to do so, had strenuously opposed the match, and had recommended Mary to unite herself to Courtenay, or at least to some English nobleman, finding her resolutely bent upon it, consented to negociate the terms of marriage with Renard, and took especial care that they were favourable to his royal mistress.

They were as follows:—The queen was to have for her jointure thirty thousand ducats a year, with all the Low Countries of Flanders,—her issue was to be heir as well to the kingdom of Spain as to the Low Countries,—her government was to continue in all things as before,—and no stranger was to be member of the council, nor have custody of any forts of castles, nor bear any rule or office in the queen's household, or elsewhere in all England.

To these terms Renard, on behalf of his sovereign, readily assented, and the subject was brought before the Parliament where it met with violent opposition from all parties. In spite of this, Mary asserted her privilege to wed whom she pleased, and after a long and stormy discussion the measure, chiefly through the management of Arundel, Paget and Rochester, was carried.

During the agitation of the question, Mary deemed it prudent to feign indisposition to avoid receiving an address intended to be presented to her from the Commons imploring her to marry one of her own countrymen. But when at length she could no longer decline giving them an audience, she dismissed them with these words:—

"I hold my crown from God, and I beseech him to enlighten me as to the conduct I ought to pursue in a matter so important as my marriage. I have not yet determined to wed, but since you say in your address that it is for the welfare of the state that I should choose a husband, I will think of it—nothing doubting I shall make a choice as advantageous as any you may propose to me, having as strong an interest in the matter as yourselves."

While this was going forward, De Noailles and his party had not been idle. Many schemes were devised, but some were abandoned from the irresolution and vacillation of Courtenay; others were discovered and thwarted by Renard. Still, the chief conspirators, though suspected, escaped detection, or rather their designs could not be brought home to them, and they continued to form their plans as the danger grew more imminent with greater zeal than ever.

At one time, it was determined to murder Arundel, Paget, Rochester, and the chief supporters of the Spanish match, to seize the person of the queen and compel her to marry Courtenay, or depose her and place Elizabeth on the throne. This plan not suiting the views of Lord Guilford Dudley and Suffolk, was opposed by them; and owing to the conflicting interests of the different parties that unity of purpose indispensable to success could not be obtained.

Elizabeth, as has before been intimated, had dissembled her religious opinions, and though she formed some excuse for not being present at the performance of mass, she requested to have an instructor in the tenets of the Catholic faith, and even went so far as to write to the emperor to send a cross, a chalice, and other ornaments for the celebration of the religious rites of Rome, to decorate her chapel.

As to Courtenay, he appeared to have become sensible of the perilous position in which he stood, and was only prevented from withdrawing from the struggle by his unabated passion for Elizabeth. Lord Guilford Dudley still cherished his ambitious views, and Jane still mourned in secret.

Matters were in this state at the commencement of the new year, when as above related, the ambassadors arrived from the court of Spain. Shortly after their arrival, they had an audience of the queen in the council-chamber of the White Tower; and when they had declared in due form that the Prince of Spain demanded her in marriage, she replied with great dignity, but some little prudery:—

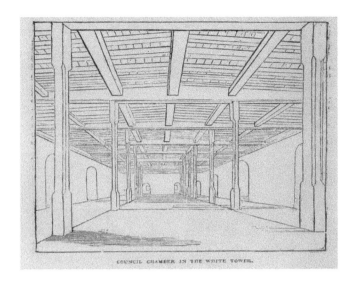

COUNCIL CHAMBER IN THE WHITE TOWER.

"It does not become one of my sex to speak of her marriage, nor to treat of it herself. I have therefore charged my council to confer with you on the matter, and, by the strictest conditions, to assure all rights and advantages to my kingdom, which I shall ever regard as my first husband."

As she pronounced the last words she glanced at the ring placed on her finger by Gardiner on the day of her coronation.

On the following day, the four ambassadors held a conference with Gardiner, Arundel, and Paget. The terms were entirely settled; and on the 12th of January, the treaty was signed, and delivered on both sides.

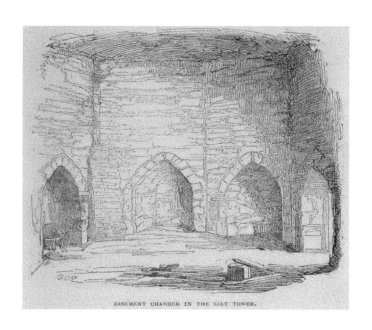

BASEMENT CHAMBER IN THE SALT TOWER.

XXVI.—BY WHAT MEANS GARDINER EXTRACTED THE SECRET OF THE CONSPIRACY FROM COURTENAY; AND OF THE CONSEQUENCES OF THE DISCLOSURE.

Three days after the marriage-treaty was signed,—namely, on the 15th of January, 1554, the lords of the council, the lord mayor, the aldermen, and forty of the head commoners of the city, were summoned to the Tower, where they were received in the presence-chamber of the palace by Gardiner and Renard; the former of whom, in his capacity of chancellor, made them a long oration, informing them that an alliance was definitively concluded between the queen and Philip of Spain; and adding, "that they were bound to thank God that so noble, worthy, and famous a prince would so humble himself in his union with her highness, as to take upon him rather the character of a subject, than of a monarch of equal power."

The terms of the treaty were next read, and the chancellor expatiated upon the many important concessions made by the imperial ambassadors; endeavouring to demonstrate that England was by far the greatest gainer by the alliance, and stating, "that it was her highness's pleasure and request, that like good subjects they would, for her sake, most lovingly receive her illustrious consort with reverence, joy, and honour."

No plaudits followed this announcement, nor was the slightest expression of joy manifested, except by the lords Arundel, Paget, and Rochester,—the main supporters of the match, as has been previously stated, when it was brought before Parliament. Gardiner glanced at the council—at the civic authorities—as if in expectation of a reply, but none was attempted, unless their very silence could be so construed. Whatever his real sentiments might be, the chancellor assumed an air of deep displeasure, and turning to Renard, who, with arms folded on his breast, scanned the assemblage with a cold scrutinizing gaze, asked in an under tone, whether he should dismiss them?

"On no account," replied the ambassador. "Compel them to give utterance to their thoughts. We shall the better know how to deal with them. My project once carried, and Philip united to Mary," he muttered to himself, "we will speedily cudgel these stubborn English bull-dogs into obedience."

"Renard does not appear to relish the reception which the announcement of her majesty's proposed alliance has met with," observed De Noailles, who stood in one corner of the chamber with Courtenay. "It will give him a foretaste of what is to follow. Had your lordship been proposed to the assembly, their manner would have been widely different."

"Perhaps so," returned Courtenay, with a gratified smile; "and yet I know not."

"It may be shortly put to the proof," answered De Noailles. "Never," replied Courtenay; "I will never wed Mary."

"But Elizabeth?" cried the ambassador.

"Ay, Elizabeth," echoed the earl passionately, "with, or without a throne, she would be equally dear to me."

"You shall have her and the crown as well," replied De Noailles.

"I care not for the latter, provided I can obtain the former," returned the earl.

"One is dependent upon the other," rejoined De Noailles. "While Mary reigns, you must give up all hopes of Elizabeth."

"It is that conviction alone that induces me to take part in the conspiracy," sighed Courtenay. "I am neither ambitious to rule this kingdom, nor to supplant Philip of Spain. But I would risk fortune, title, life itself, for Elizabeth."

"I know it," ejaculated De Noailles to himself, "and therefore I hold her out as a lure to you, weak, wavering fool! I will use you as far as I find necessary, but no further. Rash and harebrained as he is, Lord Guilford Dudley would make the better leader, and is the more likely to succeed. Jane's party is hourly gaining strength. Well, well, I care not who wins the day, provided I foil Renard, and that I will do at any cost."

"A thousand marks that I read your excellency's thoughts!" cried a martial-looking personage, approaching them. He was attired in a coat of mail, with quilted sleeves, a velvet cassock, cuisses, and buff boots drawn up above the knee; and carried in his hand a black velvet cap, ornamented with broad bone-work lace. His arms were rapier and dagger, both of the largest size. "Is the wager accepted?" he added, taking the ambassador's arm within his own, and drawing him aside.

"My thoughts are easily guessed, Sir Thomas Wyat," replied De Noailles, "I am thinking how prosperously all goes for us."

"Right," rejoined Wyat; "out of that large assemblage three only are favourable to the imperialists. If you approve it, I will myself—though not a member of the council—answer Gardiner's speech, and tell him we will not suffer this hateful alliance to take place."

"That were unwise," rejoined De Noailles, "do not meddle in the matter. It will only attract suspicion towards us."

"I care not if it does," replied Wyat; "we are all ready and sure of support. I will go further, if need be, and add, if the queen weds not Courtenay, a general insurrection will follow."

"Courtenay will never wed the queen," observed the earl, who had followed them, and overheard the remark.

"How?" exclaimed Wyat, in surprise.

"No more at present," interposed De Noailles, hastily. "Renard's eyes are upon us.";

"What if they are?" cried Wyat, glancing fiercely in the direction of the imperial ambassador. "His looks—basilisk though they be—have no power to strike us dead. Oh that I had an opportunity of measuring swords with him! He should soon perceive the love I bear his prince and him."

"I share in your hatred towards him," observed Courtenay. "The favour Mary shows him proves the ascendancy he has obtained over her."

"If he retains his power, farewell to the liberty of Englishmen," rejoined Wyat; "we shall become as abject as the Flemings. But I, for one, will never submit to the yoke of Spain."

"Not so loud!" cried De Noailles, checking him. "You will effectually destroy our scheme. Renard only seeks some plea to attack us. Have a moment's patience, and some one not connected with the plot will take the responsibility upon himself."

The prudence of the ambassador's counsel was speedily exemplified. While the conversation above related occurred, a few words passed between the principal members of the council, and the heads of the civic authorities, and, at their instance, the Earl of Pembroke stepped forward.

"We are aware, my lord," he said, addressing Gardiner, "that we ought on the present occasion, to signify our approval of the queen's choice—to offer her our heartfelt congratulations—our prayers for her happiness. But we shall not seek to disguise our sentiments. We do *not* approve this match; and we have heard your lordship's communication with pain—with sorrow—with displeasure—displeasure, that designing counsellors should have prevailed upon her highness to take a step fatal to her own happiness, and to the welfare of her kingdom. Our solicitations are, therefore—and we earnestly entreat your lordship to represent them to her majesty, that she will break off this engagement, and espouse some English nobleman. And we further implore of her to dismiss from her councils the imperial ambassador, M. Simon Renard, by whose instrumentality this match has been contrived, and whose influence we conceive to be prejudicial to the interests of our country."

"You do me wrong, Lord Pembroke," replied Renard; "and I appeal to the lord chancellor, whether, in negotiating this treaty, I have made any demands on the part of my sovereign calculated to detract from the power or authority of yours."

"On the contrary," replied Gardiner, "your excellency has conceded more than we had any right to expect."

"And more than my brother-ambassadors deemed fitting," rejoined Renard. "But I do not repent what I have done,—well knowing how anxious the emperor Charles the Fifth is to unite his son to so wise, so excellent, and so religious a princess as the queen of this realm, and that no sacrifice could be too great to insure him her hand."

"I am bound to add that your excellency has advanced nothing but the truth," acquiesced Gardiner; "and though, at first, as is well known to Lord Pembroke and others of the council, I was as averse to the match as he or they could be, I am now its warmest advocate. But I will not prolong the discussion. Her highness's word is passed to the prince—the contract signed—the treaty concluded. Your remonstrances, therefore, are too late. And if you will suffer me to point out to you the only course that can with propriety be pursued, I would urge you to offer her majesty your loyal congratulations on her choice—to prepare to receive her consort in the manner she has directed—and to watch over the interests of your country so carefully, that the evils you dread may never arise."

"If my solemn assurance will satisfy the Earl of Pembroke and the other honourable persons here present," remarked Renard, "I will declare, in the prince my master's name, that he has not the remotest intention of interfering with the government of this country—of engaging it in any war—or of placing his followers in any office or post of authority."

"Whatever may be the prince's intentions," rejoined Gardiner, "he is precluded by the treaty from acting upon them. At the same time, it is but right to add, that these terms were not wrung from his ambassador, but voluntarily proposed by him."

"They will never be adhered to," cried Sir Thomas Wyat, stepping forward, and facing Renard, whom he regarded with a look of defiance.

"Do you dare to question my word, sir?" exclaimed Renard.

"I do," replied Wyat, sternly. "And let no Englishman put faith in one of your nation, or he will repent his folly. I am a loyal subject of the queen, and would shed my heart's blood in her defence. But I am also a lover of my country, and will never surrender her to the domination of Spain!"

"Sir Thomas Wyat," rejoined Gardiner, "you are well known as one of the queen's bravest soldiers; and it is well you are so, or your temerity would place you in peril."

"I care not what the consequences are to myself, my lord," replied Wyat, "if the queen will listen to my warning. It is useless to proceed further with this match. The nation will never suffer it to take place; nor will the prince be allowed to set foot upon our shores."

"These are bold words, Sir Thomas," observed Gardiner, suspiciously. "Whence do you draw your conclusions?"

"From sure premises, my lord," answered Wyat, "the very loyalty entertained by her subjects towards the queen makes them resolute not to permit her to sacrifice herself. They have not forgotten the harsh treatment experienced by Philip's first wife, Maria of Portugal. Hear me, my lord chancellor, and report what I say to her highness. If this match is persisted in, a general insurrection will follow."

"This is a mere pretext for some rebellious design, Sir Thomas," replied Gardiner, sternly. "Sedition ever masks itself under the garb of loyalty. Take heed, sir. Your actions shall be strictly watched, and if aught occurs to confirm my suspicions, I shall deem it my duty to recommend her majesty to place you in arrest."

"Wyat's rashness will destroy us," whispered De Noailles to Courtenay.

"Before we separate, my lords," observed Renard, "I think it right to make known to you that the emperor, deeming it inconsistent with the dignity of so mighty a queen as your sovereign to wed beneath her own rank, is about to resign the crown of Naples and the dukedom of Milan to his son, prior to the auspicious event."

A slight murmur of applause arose from the council at this announcement.

"You hear that," cried the Earl of Arundel. "Can you longer hesitate to congratulate the queen on her union?"

The earl was warmly seconded by Paget and Rochester, but no other voice joined them.

"The sense of the assembly is against it," observed the Earl of Pembroke.

"I am amazed at your conduct, my lords," cried Gardiner, angrily. "You deny your sovereign the right freely accorded to the meanest of her subjects—the right to choose for herself a husband. For shame!—for shame! Your sense of justice, if not your loyalty, should prompt you to act differently. The prince of Spain has been termed a stranger to this country, whereas his august sire is not merely the queen's cousin, but the oldest ally of the crown. So far from the alliance being disadvantageous, it is highly profitable, ensuring, as it does, the emperor's aid against our constant enemies the Scots and the French. Of the truth of this you may judge by the opposition it has met with, overt and secret, from the ambassador of the King of France. But without enlarging upon the advantages of the union, which must be sufficiently apparent to you all, I shall content myself with stating that it is not your province to dictate to the queen whom she shall marry, or whom she shall not marry, but humbly to acquiesce in her choice. Her majesty, in her exceeding goodness, has thought fit to lay before you—a step altogether needless—the conditions of her union. It pains me to say you have received her condescension in a most unbecoming manner. I trust, however, a better feeling has arisen among you, and that you will now enable me to report you, as I desire, to her highness."

The only assenting voices were those of three lords constituting the imperial party in the council.

Having waited for a short time, Gardiner bowed gravely, and dismissed the assemblage.

As he was about to quit the presence-chamber, he perceived Courtenay standing in a pensive attitude in the embrasure of a window. Apparently, the room was entirely deserted, except by the two ushers, who, with white wands in their hands, were stationed on either side of the door. It suddenly occurred to Gardiner that this would be a favourable opportunity to question the Earl respecting the schemes in which he more than suspected he was a party, and he accordingly advanced towards him.

"You have heard the reception which the announcement of her majesty's marriage has met with," he said. "I will frankly own to you it would have been far more agreeable to me to have named your lordship to them. And you have to thank yourself that such has not been the case."

"True," replied Courtenay, raising his eyes, and fixing them upon the speaker. "But I have found love more powerful than ambition."

"And do you yet love Elizabeth?" demanded Gardiner, with a slight sneer. "Is it possible that an attachment can endure with your lordship longer than a month?"

"I never loved till I loved her," sighed Courtenay.

"Be that as it may, you must abandon her," returned the chancellor. "The queen will not consent to your union."

"Your lordship has just observed, in your address to the council," rejoined Courtenay, "that it is the privilege of all—even of the meanest—to choose in marriage whom they will. Since her highness would exert this right in her own favour, why deny it to her sister?"

"Because her sister has robbed her of her lover," replied Gardiner. "Strong-minded as she is, Mary is not without some of the weaknesses of her sex. She could not bear to witness the happiness of a rival."

Courtenay smiled.

"I understand your meaning, my lord," pursued Gardiner sternly; "but if you disobey the queen's injunctions in this particular, you will lose your head, and so will the princess."

"The queen's own situation is fraught with more peril than mine," replied Courtenay. "If she persists in her match with the prince of Spain, she will lose her crown, and then who shall prevent my wedding Elizabeth?"

Gardiner looked at him as he said this so fixedly, that the earl involuntarily cast down his eyes.

"Your words and manner, my lord," observed the chancellor, after a pause, "convince me that you are implicated in a conspiracy, known to be forming against the queen."

"My lord!" cried Courtenay.

"Do not interrupt me," continued Gardiner,—"the conduct of the council to-day, the menaces of Sir Thomas Wyat, your own words, convince me that decided measures must be taken. I shall therefore place you in arrest. And this time, rest assured, care shall be taken that you do not escape."

Courtenay laid his hand upon his sword, and looked uneasily at the door.

"Resistance will be in vain, my lord," pursued Gardiner; "I have but to raise my voice, and the guard will immediately appear."

"You do not mean to execute your threats, my lord?" rejoined Courtenay.

"I have no alternative," returned Gardiner, "unless by revealing to me all you know respecting this conspiracy, you will enable me to crush it. Not to keep you longer in the dark, I will tell you that proofs are already before us of your connection with the plot. The dwarf Xit, employed by M. de Noailles to convey messages to you, and who assisted in your escape, has, under threat of torture, made a full confession. From him we have learnt that a guitar, containing a key to the cipher to be used in a secret correspondence, was sent to Elizabeth by the ambassador. The instrument has been found in the princess's possession at Ashbridge, and has furnished a clue to several of your own letters to her, which we have intercepted. Moreover some of the French ambassador's agents, under the disguise of Huguenot preachers, have been arrested, and have revealed his treasonable designs. Having thus fairly told you the nature and extent of the evidence against you, I would recommend you to plead guilty, and throw yourself upon the queen's mercy."

"If you are satisfied with the information you have obtained, my lord," returned Courtenay, "you can require nothing further from me."

"Yes!—the names of your associates," rejoined Gardiner.

"The rack should not induce me to betray them," replied Courtenay.

"But a more persuasive engine may," rejoined the chancellor. "What if I offer you Elizabeth's hand provided you will give up all concerned in this plot?"

"I reject it," replied the earl, struggling between his sense of duty and passion.

"Then I must call the guard," returned the chancellor.

"Hold!" cried Courtenay, "I would barter my soul to the enemy of mankind to possess Elizabeth. Swear to me she shall be mine, and I will reveal all."

Gardiner gave the required pledge.

"Yet if I confess, I shall sign my own condemnation, and that of the princess," hesitated Courtenay.

"Not so," rejoined the chancellor. "In the last session of parliament it was enacted, that those only should suffer death for treason, who had assisted at its commission, either by taking arms themselves, or aiding directly and personally those who *had* taken them. Such as have simply known or approved the crime are excepted—and your case is among the latter class. But do not let us tarry here. Come with me to my cabinet, and I will resolve all your scruples."

"And you will ensure me the hand of the princess?" said Courtenay.

"Undoubtedly," answered Gardiner. "Have I not sworn it?"

And they quitted the presence-chamber.

No sooner were they gone, than two persons stepped from behind the arras where they had remained concealed during the foregoing conversation. They were De Noailles and Sir Thomas Wyat.

"Perfidious villain!" cried the latter, "I breathe more freely since he is gone. I had great difficulty in preventing myself from stabbing him on the spot."

"It would have been a useless waste of blood," replied De Noailles. "It was fortunate that I induced you to listen to their conversation. We must instantly provide for our own safety, and that of our friends. The insurrection must no longer be delayed."

"It shall not be delayed an hour," replied Wyat. "I have six thousand followers in Kent, who only require to see my banner displayed to flock round it. Captain Bret and his company of London trainbands are eagerly expecting our rising. Throckmorton will watch over the proceedings in the city. Vice-Admiral Winter, with his squadron of seven sail, now in the river, under orders to escort Philip of Spain, will furnish us with ordnance and ammunition; and, if need be, with the crews under his command."

"Nothing can be better," replied De Noailles. "We must get the Duke of Suffolk out of the Tower, and hasten to Lord Guilford Dudley, with whom some plan must be instantly concerted. Sir Peter Carew must start forthwith for Devonshire,—Sir James Croft for Wales. Your destination is Kent. If Courtenay had not proved a traitor, we would have placed him on the throne. As it is, my advice is, that neither Elizabeth nor Jane should be proclaimed, but Mary Stuart."

"There the policy of France peeps out," replied Wyat. "But I will proclaim none of them. We will compel the queen to give up this match, and drive the Spaniard from our shores."

"As you will," replied De Noailles, hastily. "Do not let us remain longer here, or it maybe impossible to quit the fortress."

With this, they left the palace, and seeking the Duke of Suffolk, contrived to mix him up among their attendants, and so to elude the vigilance of the warders. As soon as they were out of the Tower, Sir Thomas Wyat embarked in a wherry, manned by four rowers, and took the direction of Gravesend. De Noailles and the Duke of Suffolk hastened to Sion House, where they found Lord Guilford Dudley seated with Jane and Cholmondeley. On their appearance, Dudley started to his feet, and exclaimed, "We are betrayed!"

"We are," replied De Noailles. "Courtenay has played the traitor. But this is of no moment, as his assistance would have been of little avail, and his pretensions to the crown might have interfered with the rights of your consort. Sir Thomas Wyat has set out for Kent. We must collect all the force we can, and retire to some place of concealment till his messengers arrive with intelligence that he is marching towards London. We mean to besiege the Tower, and secure the queen's person."

"Dudley," cried Jane, "if you have one spark of honour, gratitude, or loyalty left, you will take no part in this insurrection."

"Mary is no longer queen," replied her husband, bending the knee before her. "To you, Jane, belongs that title; and it will be for you to decide whether she shall live or not."

"The battle is not yet won," observed the Duke of Suffolk. "Let us obtain the crown before we pass sentence on those who have usurped it."

"The lady Jane must accompany us," whispered De Noailles to Dudley. "If she falls into the hands of our enemies, she may be used as a formidable weapon against us."

"My lord," cried Jane, kneeling to the Duke of Suffolk; "if my supplications fail to move my husband, do not you turn a deaf ear to them. Believe me, this plot will totally fail, and conduct us all to the scaffold."

"The duke cannot retreat if he would, madam," interposed Do Noailles. "Courtenay has betrayed us all to Gardiner, and ere now I doubt not officers are despatched to arrest us."

"Jane, you must come with us," cried Dudley.

"Never," she replied, rising. "I will not stir from this spot. I implore you and my father to remain here likewise, and submit yourselves to the mercy of the queen."

"And do you think such conduct befitting the son of the great Duke of Northumberland?" replied Dudley. "No, madam, the die is cast. My course is taken. You *must* come with us. There is no time for preparation. M. De Noailles, I place myself entirely in your hands. Let horses be brought round instantly," he added, turning to his esquire.

"They shall be at the gate almost before you can reach it, my lord," returned Cholmondeley. "There are several ready-saddled within the stables."

"It is well," replied Dudley.

And the esquire departed.

"Father, dear father," cried Jane, "you will not go. You will not leave me."

But the duke averted his gaze from her, and rushed out of the room.

De Noailles made a significant gesture to Dudley, and followed him.

"Jane," cried Dudley, taking her hand, "I entreat—nay command you—to accompany me."

"Dudley," she replied, "I cannot—will not—obey you in this. If I could, I would detain you. But as I cannot, I will take no part in your criminal designs."

"Farewell for ever, then," rejoined Dudley, breaking from her. "Since you abandon me in this extremity, and throw off my authority, I shall no longer consider myself bound to you by any ties."

"Stay!" replied Jane. "You overturn all my good resolutions. I am no longer what I was. I cannot part thus."

"I knew it," replied Dudley, straining her to his bosom. "You will go with me."

"I will," replied Jane, "since you will have it so."

"Come, then," cried Dudley, taking her hand, and leading her towards the door—"to the throne!"

"No," replied Jane, sadly—"to the scaffold!"

XXVII.—OF THE INSURRECTION OF SIR THOMAS WYAT.

The party had not quitted Sion House more than an hour, when a band of soldiers, headed by Sir Edward Hastings, master of the horse, and one of the privy council, arrived to arrest them. But no traces of their retreat could be discovered; and after an unsuccessful search, Hastings was compelled to return to Gardiner with the tidings that their prey had escaped. Not one of the conspirators charged by Courtenay could be found, and it was evident they had received timely warning, though from what quarter the chancellor could not divine. At first, his suspicions fell upon the Earl of Devonshire, but the utter impossibility of this being the case speedily made him reject the idea.

A council was immediately held; at which several resolutions, founded upon the information obtained from Courtenay, were passed. Fresh troops were ordered into the Tower, and active preparations made for its defence, in case of a siege. The chancellor himself deemed it prudent to wear a coat of mail beneath his robes; and quitting his palace, old Winchester House, situated on the Surrey side of the river, a little to the west of Saint Saviour's, he took up his abode within the fortress. Mary was also advised to remove thither from Whitehall, and, at the instance of Renard, she reluctantly complied.

On the day after her return to the Tower, the imperial ambassadors, D'Egmont, Lalaing, De Courrieres, and De Nigry, were conducted by the Earl of Arundel to Saint John's Chapel, where they found the whole of the council assembled, and the queen kneeling before the altar. The sacrament was administered by Gardiner, and high mass performed; after which Mary, kneeling with her face to the assemblage, said: "I take God to witness that I have not consented to wed the prince of Spain from any desire of aggrandizement, or carnal affection; but solely for the honour and profit of my kingdom, and the repose and tranquillity of my subjects. Nor shall my marriage prevent me from keeping inviolably the oath I have made to the crown, on the day of my coronation." Uttered with great earnestness and dignity, these words produced a strong effect upon the hearers. Ratifications of the treaty were then exchanged, and the customary oaths taken on both sides.

This ceremony over, the queen arose, and glancing at the council, observed: "I have heard, my lords, that most of you highly disapprove my match with the prince of Spain; but I feel confident, when you have well considered the matter, you will see cause to alter your opinion. However this may be, I am well assured that your loyalty will remain unchanged, and that I may fully calculate upon your services for the defence and protection of my person, in case the rebellion with which I am threatened should take place."

"Your highness may rely upon us all," replied the Duke of Norfolk.

And the assurance was reiterated by the whole assemblage.

At this moment, an attendant stepped forward, and informed the queen that a messenger who had ridden for his life, was arrived from Kent, bringing intelligence of an insurrection in that county.

"Let him approach," replied Mary. "You shall hear, my lords, what danger we have to apprehend. Well, fellow," she continued, as the man was ushered into her presence, "thy news?"

"I am the bearer of ill tidings, your majesty," replied the messenger, bending the knee before her. "Sir Thomas Wyat yesterday, by sound of trumpet published, in the market-place at Maidstone a proclamation against your highness's marriage; exhorting all Englishmen wishing well to their country to join with him and others, to defend the realm from the threatened thraldom of Spain."

"Ah! traitor!" exclaimed the queen. "And how was the proclamation received?—Speak out—and fear not."

"With universal acclamations," replied the messenger, "and shouts of 'A Wyat! A Wyat! No Spanish match—no inquisition! I and such treasonable vociferations. Sir Thomas had fifteen hundred men in arms with him, but before he quitted Maidstone, above five hundred more joined him, and multitudes were flocking to his standard when I left the place."

Scarcely had the messenger concluded his recital, when another was introduced.

"What further news hast thou, good fellow?1' demanded the queen.

"I am come to inform your highness," replied the man, "that Sir Thomas Wyat and his followers have taken possession of the castle of Rochester, and fortified it as well as the town. Moreover, they have broken down the bridge across the Medway, and stop all passengers, by land or water, taking from them their arms."

"Now by our lady!" exclaimed the queen, "this Wyat is a hardy traitor. But he shall meet with the punishment due to his offences. Your grace," she added, turning to the Duke of Norfolk, "shall march instantly against him with a sufficient force to dislodge him from his hold. And for your better defence, you shall take with you the trained bands of our good city of London, under the command of Captain Bret."

With this, she quitted the chapel, and returned to the palace.

As soon as he could collect his forces, amounting to about a thousand men, the Duke of Norfolk, accompanied by Bret and the trained bands, set out on his expedition, and arrived at Stroud the same night, where he made preparations to besiege Rochester castle at daybreak.

Meantime, the utmost anxiety prevailed within the Tower, and tidings of the issue of the expedition were eagerly looked for. Towards the close of the day after Norfolk's departure, a messenger arrived, bringing the alarming intelligence that Bret and his band had revolted to Wyat, shouting, "We are all Englishmen!—we are all Englishmen!—We will not fight against our countrymen." It was added, that the duke, who had just planted his cannon against the castle, seeing how matters stood, and being uncertain of the fidelity of the troops remaining with him, had made a hasty retreat, leaving his ammunition and horses in the hands of the enemy.

This intelligence struck terror into the hearts of all who heard it, and it was the general impression that the insurgents would be victorious—an opinion considerably strengthened, a few hours afterwards, by the arrival of other messengers, who stated that Wyat had besieged and taken Cowling castle, the residence of Lord Cobham, and was marching towards London. It was also affirmed that he had been joined by Lord Guilford Dudley, the Duke of Suffolk, Lord Thomas Grey, and others, with a considerable force, and that their object was to depose Mary, and replace Jane upon the throne. Humours of insurrections in other parts of the country as well as in London were added; but these could not be so well authenticated.

On the following day, it being ascertained that the rebels had reached Dartford, Sir Edward Hastings and Sir Thomas Cornwallis were sent to hold a parley with the rebels. The army of the insurgents was stationed at the west of the town, before which their ordnance was planted. Dismounting, the two knights sent forward a herald to Wyat, who was standing with Dudley, Suffolk, and Bret, near the outworks; and on learning their business, he immediately advanced to meet them. After a haughty salutation on both sides, Sir Edward Hastings spoke.

"Sir Thomas Wyat," he said, "the queen desires to know why you, who style yourself, in your proclamations, her true subject, act the part of a traitor in gathering together her liege subjects in arms against her?"

"I am no more a traitor than yourself, Sir Edward Hastings," replied Wyat, "and the reason why I have gathered together the people, is to prevent the realm from being overrun by strangers, which must happen, if her highness's marriage with Philip of Spain takes place."

"No strangers are yet arrived," replied Hastings, "and the mischief you apprehend is yet far off. But if this is your only grievance, are you content to confer on the matter with the council?"

"I am," replied Wyat; "but I will be trusted rather than trust. I will treat with whomsoever the queen desires; but in surety of her good faith, I must have delivered to me the custody of the Tower of London, and of her highness's person. Furthermore, I require the head of Simon Renard, the originator of this tumult.".

"Insolent!" cried Hastings. "Rather than your traitorous demands shall be complied with, you and all your rabble rout shall be put to the sword."

With these words, he sprang upon his steed, and accompanied by Cornwallis and his attendants, rode back to the Tower, to declare the ill success of his mission to Mary.

Wyat's successes created the greatest consternation among the queen's party. Though the Tower was filled with armed men, its inmates did not feel secure, being in constant apprehension of a rising in London. The imperial ambassadors were not less alarmed, as it was generally thought they would be sacrificed to the popular fury. Gardiner counselled them to make good their retreat to Brussels; and they all, with the exception of Simon Renard, who declared he would remain upon his post, decided upon following the advice.

They would not, however, depart without taking leave of Mary, who desired them to recommend her to the emperor, and to assure him she was under no alarm for her personal safety. Costly presents were offered them; but, under the circumstances, they were declined. The ambassadors quitted the Tower at dead of night, embarking at Traitor's Gate, and were compelled to leave their horses, attendants, and baggage, behind them.

In spite of the secrecy of their departure, it was discovered, and an attempt was made to capture them by some watermen, who in all probability would have succeeded, if they had not been driven off by the batteries of the fortress. Fortunately, the fugitives found a fleet of merchantmen, armed with a few guns, ready to sail for Antwerp; in one of which they embarked, and under cover of night, got safely down the river.

On the following morning, news was brought that Wyat was within a few miles of London; and it was added that his appearance before the walls of the fortress would be the signal for the rising of the citizens,—that the gates of the city would be thrown open to him, and perhaps those of the Tower itself. Every possible precaution was taken by Sir Henry Bedingfeld. He visited the whole line of ramparts and fortifications, and ascertained that all the men were at their posts, and in readiness, in case of a sudden attack. By his directions, the drawbridges on London Bridge were broken down—the craft moored on the Middlesex side of the river—the ferry-boats staved and sunk—and the bridges for fifteen miles up the river destroyed. While this was going on, Gardiner, seriously alarmed by the aspect of things, sought the queen's presence, and endeavoured to persuade her to fly to France. But Mary, who, it has been more than once observed, inherited all the lion spirit of her father, and whose courage rose in proportion to the danger by which she was surrounded, at once, and disdainfully, rejected the proposal.

"My people may abandon *me*," she said, "but I will never abandon *them*. I have no fear of the result of this struggle, being well assured I have plenty of loyal English hearts to serve and defend me. If need be, I will take up arms myself, and try the truth of this quarrel; for I would rather die with those who will stand by me, than yield one jot to such a traitor as Wyat."

"Your majesty is in the right," replied Renard, who was present on the occasion, "if you fly, all is lost. My counsel to you is to resort to the severest measures. Since Lady Jane Grey has disappeared, and you cannot avenge yourself upon her, let the Princess Elizabeth be brought from Ashbridge to the fortress, and on the appearance of Wyat, have a scaffold erected on the summit of Traitor's Tower, and if the arch-rebel will not withdraw his forces, put her and Courtenay to death in his sight."

"I like not your proposal, sir," replied the queen, "I have no thirst for Courtenay's blood. Nay, the love I once bore him would prevent my taking his life—and it should only be at the last extremity that I would deal severely with Elizabeth. Neither do I think your counsel politic. Such a course might answer in Spain, but not in England. It would only inflame still more the minds of the seditious, and excite them to a state of ungovernable fury."

"You judge wisely, madam," replied Gardiner. "Besides, I have made myself answerable for the safety of the Earl of Devonshire. The blow that falls upon his head, must strike mine also. Since your majesty, with a resolution worthy of the daughter of your great sire, decides on maintaining your ground against these rebels, I nothing fear for the result. Let the worst come to the worst, we can but die; and we will die fighting in your cause."

"My lord," rejoined the queen, after a moment's reflection, "bid Sir Henry Bedingfeld, and the whole of the officers and men not required on duty on the ramparts, attend high mass within Saint John's chapel an hour hence. You yourself will officiate with all the prelates and priesthood in the fortress. The service over, I shall repair to the council-chamber, where it is my purpose to address them."

Gardiner bowed and retired to execute her commands, and the queen enjoining Renard's attendance at the chapel, retired to her closet with her dames of honour.

XXVIII.—OF THE QUEEN'S SPEECH IN THE COUNCIL-CHAMBER; AND OF HER INTERVIEW WITH SIR THOMAS WYAT.

At the appointed time, Saint John's chapel was thronged with armed men; and as the royal train passed along the upper gallery, and glanced down upon them, Mary was inexpressibly struck by the scene. Banners waved from the arched openings of the gallery, and the aisles and nave gleamed with polished steel. For fear of a sudden surprise, the soldiers were ordered to carry their weapons, and this circumstance added materially to the effect of the picture. Around the columns of the southern aisle were grouped the arquebussiers with their guns upon their shoulders; around those of the north stood the pike-men, in their steel caps and corslets; while the whole body of the nave was filled with archers, with their bows at their backs. Immediately in front of the altar stood the Duke of Norfolk, the Earls of Arundel and Pembroke, the lords Paget and Rochester; Sir Henry Bedingfeld; Sir Henry Jerningham, master of the horse; Sir Edward Bray, master of the ordnance, all in full armour. On the queen's appearance all these personages bent the knee before her; and Bedingfeld, in virtue of his office, advancing a step before the others, drew his sword, and vowed he would never yield up the fortress but with life. He then turned to the troops, and repeated his determination to them. And the walls of the sacred structure rang with the shouts of the soldiers.

"You have yet loyal followers enow who will shed their last drop of blood in your defence," he added to Mary.

"I nothing doubt it, dear Sir Henry," she replied, in a voice of deep emotion. "I will share your danger, and, I trust, your triumph."

Solemn mass was then performed by Gardiner, who was attended by Bonner, Tunstal, Feckenham, and other prelates and priests in their full robes. On its conclusion, the queen gave her hand to Sir Henry Bedingfeld, and followed by the whole assemblage, proceeded to the council-chamber, and took her seat beneath the state canopy.

As soon as the whole party was assembled, silence was commanded, and Mary spoke as follows: "I need not acquaint you that a number of Kentish rebels have seditiously and traitorously gathered together against us and you. Their pretence, as they at first asserted, was to resist a marriage between us and the prince of Spain. To this pretended grievance, and to the rest of their evil-contrived complaints, you have been made privy. Since then, we have caused certain of our privy council to confer with the rebels, and to demand the cause of their continuance in their seditious enterprise; and by their own avowal it appears that our marriage is the least part of their quarrel. For they now, swerving from their first statement, have betrayed the inward treason of their hearts, arrogantly demanding the possession of our person, the keeping of our Tower of London, and not only the placing and displacing of our council, but also the head of one who is an ambassador at our court, and protected by his office from injury."

Here a murmur of indignation arose among the assemblage.

"Now, loving subjects," continued Mary, "what I am you right well know. I am your queen, to whom, at my coronation, when I was wedded to the realm, and to the laws of the realm, (the spousal ring whereof I hold on my finger, never as yet left off, nor hereafter to be so), you promised your allegiance and obedience. And that I am the right and true inheritor of the crown of England, I not only take all Christendom to witness, but also your own acts of parliament confirming my title. My father, as you all know, possessed the regal estate by right of inheritance; and by the same right it descended to me. To him you always showed yourselves faithful subjects, and obeyed and served him as your liege lord and king. And, therefore, I doubt not you will show yourselves equally loyal to me, his daughter."

"God save your highness!" cried the whole assemblage. "Long live Queen Mary!"

"If you are what I believe you," pursued Mary, energetically; "you will not suffer any rebel to usurp the governance of our person, nor to occupy our estate, especially so presumptuous a traitor as this Wyat, who having abused our subjects to be adherents to his traitorous quarrel, intends, under some plea, to subdue the laws to his will, and to give scope to the rascal and forlorn persons composing his army to make general havoc and spoil of our good city of London.

"Down with Wyat!" cried several voices. "Down with the rebels!"

"Never having been a mother," continued Mary, "I cannot tell how naturally a parent loves her children: but certainly a queen may as naturally and as tenderly love her subjects as a mother her child. Assure yourselves, therefore, that I, your sovereign lady, do as tenderly love and favour you; and thus loving you, I cannot but think that you as heartily and faithfully love me again. And so, joined together in a knot of love and of concord, I doubt not we shall be able to give these rebels a short and speedy overthrow."

Here she was again interrupted by the most enthusiastic expressions of loyalty and devotion.

"On the word of a queen I promise you," concluded Mary, "if it shall not appear to the nobility and commons in parliament assembled, that my intended marriage is for the benefit of the whole realm, I will not only abstain from it, but from any other alliance. Pluck up your hearts, then, and like true men stand fast with your lawful queen against these rebels, both my enemies and yours, and fear them not, for I fear them nothing at all."

Thundering plaudits followed Mary's oration, which, it was evident, had produced the desired effect upon the assemblage; and if any one entered the council-chamber wavering in his loyalty, he returned confirmed in his attachment to the throne. Mary's intrepid demeanour was sufficient to inspire courage in the most faint-hearted; and her spirit imparted an expression of beauty to her countenance which awakened the warmest admiration among all the beholders.

"You have proved yourself a worthy daughter of your august sire, madam," observed Bedingfeld.

"I *will* prove myself so before I have done, Sir Henry," rejoined Mary, smiling. "I trust myself wholly to you."

"Your majesty may depend upon me," replied the old knight. "And now, with your permission, I will withdraw my forces, and visit the ramparts. After your address no one will forsake his post."

So saying, he departed with the troops, and, after making his rounds, returned to his lodgings.

THE LIEUTENANT'S LODGINGS.

Mary then appointed Lord William Howard, in conjunction with the Lord Mayor, Sir Thomas White, to the government of the city, and the Earl of Pembroke to the command of the army. These arrangements made, she continued for some time in conference with Gardiner and Renard. Just as she was about to retire, Sir Henry Bedingfeld came to apprise her that Wyat's army had reached Southwark, and had taken up a position at the foot of London Bridge. After mature deliberation, it was resolved that the rebel-leader should be invited to an interview with the queen; and Bedingfeld was intrusted with the mission.

Proceeding to Traitor's Gate, the old knight embarked in a wherry with four soldiers and a herald, and was rowed towards the hostile party. As he drew near the Surrey side of the water, Wyat's sentinels presented their calivers at him; but as soon as they perceived he was attended by a herald, they allowed him to approach. On learning his errand, Wyat, contrary to the advice of the Duke of Suffolk and Lord Guilford Dudley, determined to accompany him.

"You will fall into some snare," observed Dudley, "and lose the day when you have all but gained it."

"Have no fears," replied Wyat. "We shall conquer without striking a blow. Mary would not have made this proposal to me had she not felt certain of defeat."

"But dare you trust her?" demanded Suffolk.

"Sir Henry Bedingfeld has pledged his word for my safe return, and I know him too well to doubt it. Farewell, my lords. We shall meet again in an hour."

"I much doubt if we shall meet again at all," observed Dudley to the duke, as Wyat stepped into Bedingfeld's wherry, which was rowed swiftly across the river, and presently disappeared beneath the gloomy arch of Traitor's Gate.

Ushered into the council-chamber, Wyat found Mary seated on a chair of state placed at the head of a row of chairs near a partition dividing the vast apartment, and covered with arras representing various naval engagements. The wooden pillars supporting the roof were decorated with panoplies; and through an opening on the right of the queen, Wyat perceived a band of armed men, with their leader at their head, cased in steel, and holding a drawn sword in his hand. Noticing these formidable preparations with some uneasiness, he glanced inquiringly at Bedingfeld.

"Fear nothing," observed the old knight. "My head shall answer for yours."

Thus re-assured, Wyat advanced more confidently towards the queen, and when within a few paces of her, paused and drew himself up to his full height. Bedingfeld took up a station on the right of the royal chair, and supported himself on his huge two-handed sword. On the left stood Gardiner and Renard.

"I have sent for you, traitor and rebel that you are," commenced Mary, "to know why you have thus incited my subjects to take up arms against me?"

"I am neither traitor nor rebel, madam," replied Wyat, "as I have already declared to one of your council, and I but represent the mass of your subjects, who being averse to your union with the prince of Spain, since you refuse to listen to their prayers, are determined to make themselves heard."

"Ha! God's death! sir," cried Mary, furiously, "do you, or do any of my subjects think they can dispose of me in marriage as they think proper? But this is an idle pretext. Your real object is the subversion of my government, and my dethronement. You desire to place the princess Elizabeth on the throne—and in default of her, the Lady Jane Grey."

"I desire to uphold your majesty's authority," replied Wyat, "provided you will comply with my demands."

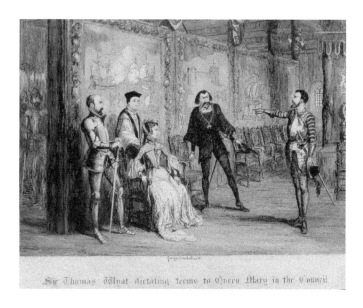

Sir Thomas Wyat dictating terms to Queen Mary in the Council

"*Demands!*" cried Mary, stamping her foot, while her eyes flashed fire. "It is the first time such a term has been used to me, and it shall be the last. In God's name, what are your demands? Speak, man."

"These, madam," replied Wyat, firmly. "I demand the custody of the Tower,—the care of your royal person,—the dismissal of your council,—and the head of your false counsellor, Simon Renard."

"Will nothing less content you?" inquired Mary, sarcastically.

"Nothing," returned Wyat.

"I pray your majesty to allow me to punish the insolence of this daring traitor," cried Renard, in extremity of fury.

"Peace, sir," rejoined Mary, majestically. "Now hear me in turn, thou traitor Wyat. No man ever dictated terms to my father, and, by his memory! none shall do so to me. At once, and peremptorily, I reject your conditions; and had not Sir Henry Bedingfeld pledged his word for your safety, my guards should have led you from hence to the scaffold. Quit my presence, and as I would rather be merciful than severe, and spare the lives of my subjects than destroy them, if you disperse your host, and submit yourself to my mercy, I will grant you a free pardon. Otherwise, nothing shall save you."

"When we next meet your majesty may alter your tone," rejoined Wyat; "I take my leave of your highness."

So saying, he bowed and retired with Sir Henry Bedingfeld.

"Your majesty will not let him escape?" cried Renard.

"In sooth but I shall sir," replied Mary; "my word must be kept even with a traitor."

"You are over-scrupulous, madam," rejoined Renard; "there is no faith to be kept with such a villain. Beseech you, let me follow him. His head, displayed to his companions, will disperse them more speedily than your whole army."

"I have already said it must not be," replied Mary.

"Nay then," rejoined Renard, "I will take the responsibility of the act upon myself."

"Disobeyed!" exclaimed Mary, authoritatively. "I command you not to leave the presence."

"Your majesty will repent this mistaken clemency," cried Renard, chafing with fury.

"I shall never repent adhering to my word," returned Mary. "And see here comes our lieutenant. How now, Sir Henry? Is the traitor gone?"

"He is, your highness," replied Bedingfeld; "and it required all my authority to prevent the infuriated guard from falling upon him, and cutting him in pieces."

"I am glad you were with him," replied Mary; "I would not for the best jewel in my crown that any harm had happened to him. Give me your hand, Sir Henry. I will myself visit the ramparts, and cheer the soldiers with my presence."

"Your majesty will expose yourself," returned Bedingfeld.

"To whom?" replied Mary,—"only to my subjects. They will not dare to assail their queen. The daughter of your old master, Henry the Eighth, should have no fear."

XXIX.—THE SIEGE OF THE TOWER.

On Wyat's return, it was resolved that, under cover of darkness, the Duke of Suffolk and Lord Guilford Dudley should march with two detachments of men to Deptford, where a squadron of seven sail commanded by Admiral Winter, together with a number of lesser craft, awaited them. Dudley and his party were then to cross the river in Winter's boats, and proceed to East Smithfield; while Suffolk was to embark his men in the larger vessels, and to sail up the river with the tide. Wyat determined to attempt a passage across London Bridge, and if this could not be accomplished, to abide the arrival of Winter's squadron.

It was then arranged that the attack should take place two hours before dawn. The fortress was to be assailed simultaneously at three different points, so as to distract the attention of its defenders. To Lord Guilford Dudley was assigned the Brass Mount, and the north-east angle of the ramparts; to the Duke of Suffolk Traitor's Tower, and the southern fortifications; and to Wyat the Middle Tower, and the By-ward Tower,—two of the strongest defences of the fortress. If the attack proved successful, the three leaders were to concentrate their forces before the gateway of the Bloody Tower.

When it was sufficiently dark, Suffolk and Dudley placed themselves at the head of their detachments and set out. Though they moved along with the utmost caution, they were heard by the soldiers on the ramparts, who reported their suspicions to Bedingfeld, and precautions were taken accordingly, though it was the opinion of many that the rebels had beat a retreat.

At midnight, Wyat prepared to cross London Bridge. Aware that the drawbridges were cut away—that it was barricaded, and strongly defended— he provided himself with planks and ropes, and issuing instructions to his men, set forward. They were allowed to proceed without molestation to the first drawbridge, but here a sharp fire was opened upon them. In spite of this, Wyat succeeded in laying down a plank, and, at the head of a dozen men, crossed it. Dislodging their opponents, several other planks were laid down, and the passage being rendered secure, the whole party crossed, and carried over their ammunition in safety.

The report of the attack soon reached the city-guard. Drums were beaten, trumpets sounded, and shouts heard in every direction. While this was passing, a well-contested fight took place at the barricades in the centre of the bridge, between their defenders and the insurgents. Having broken down these obstacles, Wyat drove all before him. Still, another and wider chasm lay between him and the Middlesex shore. In front of it, the assailed party made a desperate stand; but their resistance was unavailing. Many were precipitated into the yawning gulf, and drowned; while others threw down their arms, and besought mercy.

On the further side of the chasm, a formidable array of soldiery opposed the progress of the rebel-army, and a piece of ordnance did terrible execution amongst them. Two planks were hewn asunder as soon as they were thrust across the abyss; but the moment the third was laid down, Wyat dashed across it, and drove back two men with hatchets in their hands who were about to sever it. He was followed by half-a-dozen soldiers. In this instance, his fiery courage had well nigh proved fatal to him for no sooner had the small band crossed it, than the plank was hurled into the chasm, and Wyat left, with his trifling party, to contend against the whole host of his foes. His destruction appeared inevitable, but his self-possession stood him in good stead.

"Fellow-countrymen," he shouted, "I am your friend, not your enemy. I would deliver you from thraldom and oppression. You ought rather to aid than oppose me. You are upholding Spain—and the inquisition—while I am fighting for England and liberty."

These few words, vociferated while he made a desperate stand against his opponents, turned the tide of affairs. In vain the royalist leaders shouted "Down with the rebels! the queen!—the queen!" They were answered by deafening cries of "A Wyat! a Wyat! No Philip of Spain—no Popish supremacy—no inquisition!"

Amid this tumult, the insurgents, who had witnessed with dismay the perilous position of their leader, redoubled their exertions; and placing several planks across the gulf, crossed them, and flew to his assistance. Following up the advantage he had gained, Wyat, without difficulty, routed his opponents. He then paused to cover the passage of the remainder of his troops and artillery across the chasm, which was safely accomplished.

At the foot of Fish-street-hill, they were checked by a company of horse under the command of the Earl of Pembroke, and a skirmish took place, in which the royalists were worsted with severe loss, and many prisoners taken, as well as arms and horses. Pembroke however, escaped and retreated to the Tower, bringing the news of his own defeat and of the successes of the rebels.

The citizens showed little disposition to take part in the struggle. All they were uneasy about was the security of their property; but Wyat, having prohibited his men from plunder or riot, and Captain Bret proclaiming that no mischief should be done, they remained tranquil. In this way, the insurgents marched, without further interruption, to Cornhill, where Wyat marshalled his forces, distributed rations of meat and liquors among them, and awaited the appointed time for his attack upon the Tower.

Within the fortress all was consternation. The extraordinary success which had hitherto attended Wyat, well nigh paralysed the queen's party. The council again urged Mary to escape privately, but she peremptorily refused, and forbade the subject to be mentioned again, on pain of her severest displeasure. Some of the more timid then ventured to advise that she should assent to Wyat's terms—that Renard should be given up, and the match with the Prince of Spain abandoned. "I will sooner abandon my crown," rejoined Mary. Her courage never for one instant forsook her, and her spirit and resolution sustained the wavering minds of her adherents.

Long before this, Suffolk and Dudley had reached Dartford. As agreed, the duke and his detachment embarked on board Winter's squadron, while the others were transported across the river in smaller boats. At Poplar, Dudley ordered his men to nail together a number of stout boards, to serve as rafts. These were fastened with ropes to such horses as they could procure, and on reaching East Smithfield were unharnessed and held in readiness, until the signal of attack should be given. Besides the rafts, two or three wherries had been brought up from the river, and several long scaling-ladders provided.

Dudley's detachment consisted of about a thousand men, archers and arquebussiers, all of whom were well armed and eager for the attack. As yet, all was involved in profound darkness, and so far as they could judge, no suspicion of their presence was entertained by those within the fortress.

Scouts were despatched towards the postern gate,—a fortification terminating the city wall, and situated, as has before been stated, at the north side of the moat,—and from one of them, who had contrived to scramble along the edge of the fosse, it was ascertained that a detachment of Sir Thomas Wyat's party was creeping stealthily along, with the intention of surprising the postern gate.

It had been Cholmondeley's intention to search for the entrance to the secret communication through which he had passed beneath the moat, but the almost certainty that it would be stopped, induced him to abandon the idea.

All at once, a blaze of light was seen at the south of the fortress, in the direction of the river. It was followed by the roar of artillery, and the sharper discharge of fire-arms, accompanied by the beating of drums, the loud braying of trumpets, the clashing of swords, and other martial sounds.

THE BRASS MOUNT.

Attack upon the Brass Mount by Lord Guilford Dudley.

On hearing this, Dudley gave the signal of assault. Dashing down the sides of the moat, his men launched their rafts on the water, and pushed them across with long poles. The noise they made betrayed them to the sentinels. The alarm was instantly given, and a tremendous fire opened upon them from the batteries and casemate of the Brass Mount, as well as from the eastern and western line of ramparts.

The Brass Mount has already been described as the largest bastion of the Tower, standing at the north-east angle of the fortress, and its walls were, and still are, of such immense thickness, and it was so well fortified, that it was regarded as impregnable. Notwithstanding this impression, it formed the main object of the present attack. Amid a slaughterous fire from the besieged, Dudley embarked with Cholmondeloy, who carried his standard, in a small skiff, and waving his sword above his head, pointed to the Brass Mount, and urged his men to the assault. They wanted no encouragement; but in some degree protected by the showers of arrows discharged by the archers stationed on the sides of the moat, and the constant fire of the arquebussiers, succeeded in placing two ladders against that part of the eastern ramparts immediately adjoining the bastion.

These were instantly covered with men, who mounted sword in hand, but were attacked and hurled backwards by the besieged. Another ladder was soon planted against the Brass Mount, while two more were reared against the northern ramparts opposite the postern gate, which had been stormed and taken by Wyat's party, several of whom were descending the banks of the moat, and firing upon the fortress, assisted by three culverins placed in a temporary battery composed of large baskets filled with sand.

All this had not been executed without severe loss on the part of the insurgents. Several of the rafts were swamped, and their occupants, embarrassed by the weight of their arms, drowned. One of the ladders planted against the northern battlements was hurled backwards with its living load; and such was the vigour and determination of the besieged, that none of the assailants could set a foot on the ramparts.

Considerable execution, however, was done by the showers of arrows from archers, as well as by the discharges of the arquebussiers. But success did not, as yet, declare itself for either side. Constantly repulsed, the insurgents still resolutely returned to the charge; and though numbers fell from the ladders, others were instantly found to take their place.

Seeing how matters stood, and aware that some desperate effort must be made, Dudley, who had hitherto watched the progress of the fight from the moat, exposing himself to the full fire of the batteries, resolved to ascend the ladder placed against the Brass Mount. Cholmondeley agreed to follow him; and amid the cheers of the assailants and the unrelaxing fire of the besieged, the boat was run in to the side of the bastion.

At this juncture, a loud explosion, succeeded by a tremendous shout, was heard at the south side of the fortress. For a brief space, both royalists and insurgents ceased fighting; and taking advantage of the pause, Dudley swiftly mounted the ladder, and reaching the summit, shouted "God save Queen Jane!"

"God save Queen Jane!" echoed Cholmondeley, who was close behind him. "God save Queen Jane!" he repeated, waving the banner.

The cry was reiterated from below, and the firing recommenced more furiously than ever.

It was rumoured among Dudley's men, and the report stimulated their ardour, that the Duke of Suffolk had taken Saint Thomas's Tower. This, however, was not the case. After the embarkation of the troops as before related, the squadron under the command of Admiral Winter, accompanied by a number of galleys, and wherries, made its way slowly to the Tower. Owing to the necessary delay, the tide had turned, and the larger vessels had to be towed up the river by the smaller craft.

Attack upon Saint Thomas's Tower by the Duke of Suffolk.

On their arrival they were immediately perceived by the sentinels, who opened a fire upon them, which was instantly returned. This was the commencement of the siege, and served as the signal to Dudley, and likewise to Wyat, of whose movements it will be necessary to speak hereafter.

Before the squadron came up, the Duke of Suffolk embarked in a small galley, and accompanied by several wherries filled with soldiers, contrived, by keeping close under the wall of the wharf, to effect a landing, unperceived, at the stairs. Taken by surprise, the guard fell an easy prey to their assailants, who seizing the cannon placed there, turned them against the fortress.

While this was passing, several boats landed their crews at the eastern end of the wharf, and many others speeded towards it from all quarters. In a short time, it was crowded by the insurgents; and notwithstanding the tremendous fire kept up against them from the whole line of battlements—from Traitor's Tower—and from all the fortifications within shot, they resolutely maintained their ground.

Directing the attack in person, and exposing himself to every danger, the Duke of Suffolk displayed the utmost coolness and courage. The fight raged furiously on both sides. Several boats, and one of the larger vessels, were sunk by the guns of the batteries, and the ranks of the insurgents were greatly thinned. Still there was no symptom of irresolution exhibited; nor did they relax for a moment in their efforts.

Scaling-ladders were placed against the walls of Traitor's Tower, and crowded with climbers, while a gun-boat entered the dark arch beneath it, and its crew commenced battering with axes, halberds, and poles, against the portcullis and water-gate. Another party had taken possession of the buildings opposite the By-ward Tower, and were trying to reach the drawbridge, which, it is almost needless to say, was raised. Added to these, a strong body of Essex men, having congregated at Limehouse, approached the fortress by Saint Catherine's, and the lane leading to the Flemish church, and were striving to force the Iron Gate and the eastern outlet of the wharf.

At this juncture, an occurrence took place, which, while it disheartened the besieged, tended greatly to animate the assailing party. At the south-west corner of the wharf stood a row of small habitations separating it from Petty Wales. One of these was presently observed to be on fire, and the flames rapidly spread to the others. Shortly afterwards, a tremendous explosion took place. A building was blown up, and the fiery fragments tossed into the river and moat; while across the blazing ruins, with loud shouts, rushed a party of men from the troops under Sir Thomas Wyat.

This was the explosion that reached the ears of Dudley and his band. Rushing to the assistance of their friends, the new-comers seemed determined to carry all before them, and such was the effect of their sudden appearance, that the besieged for a moment gave way, and a small body of the insurgents gained a footing on the roof of Traitor's Tower. But the next moment, the royalists rallied, drove off their assailants, and the fight continued as obstinately as before.

It was a sublime but terrific spectacle, and one not easily effaced from the remembrance of those who beheld it. The ruddy light cast upon the water by the burning houses, and serving to reveal the tall vessels—the armed boats—the sinking craft and struggling figures with which it was covered—the towers and battlements of the fortress pouring forth fire and smoke—the massive pile of the ancient citadel, which added its thunder to the general din,—the throng of warlike figures engaged in active strife on the wharf, or against Traitor's Tower—constituted a scene of intense, though fearful interest—nor did the roar of the cannon, the clash of arms, the shouts and cheers of the combatants and the groans of the wounded, detract from its effect.

There was yet another scene, which though unwitnessed, except by those actually concerned in it equalled, if not surpassed it, in gloomy power. This was a conflict under Saint Thomas's Tower. It has been already mentioned that a party, manning a gun-boat, had penetrated beneath the arch leading to Traitor's Tower, where they endeavoured, with such weapons as they possessed, to effect an entrance. While they were thus employed, the portcullis was suddenly raised, and the Watergate opened; and the men supposing their own party had gained possession of the fortification above them, dashed forward.

They were speedily undeceived. Before they reached the steps, a number of armed figures, some of whom bore torches, appeared, while a thundering splash behind told that the portcullis had been let down, so as to cutoff their retreat. Nothing remained but to sell their lives as dearly as they could. Quarter was neither asked nor granted. Some leaped overboard, and tried, sword in hand, to force a way up the steps; others prepared to follow them; and the gunner discharged a falconet planted at the prow of the boat, occasioning fearful havoc among their opponents.

But this availed nothing. They were driven back, and their assailants pursuing them into the recesses of the arch, put them to death. The light of the few torches that illumined the scene, fell upon figures fearfully struggling, while the arches rang with the reports of musquetry, groans, and curses. In a short time, all was still and dark as heretofore. But when the watersgate was afterwards opened, fourteen mangled corpses floated out to the Thames.

While the siege was thus vigorously carried on, on the north and south, the western side of the fortress was not neglected. Remaining at Cornhill for some hours, Wyat divided his forces into two detachments, and committed one to Captain Bret, whom he directed to proceed to the upper part of Tower Hill, along Lombard-street, Fenchurch-street, and Tower-street, and to place his men within the churchyard of All-Hallows Barking, and at the rear of the scaffold on Tower Hill; while with the other he himself marched down

Gracechurch-street, along Thames-street, taking up a position before the Bulwark Gate.

As soon as he had reached this point, and arranged his men, he rode off to Bret, and ordered a party, commanded by Captain Cobliam, to attack the postern-gate, as before related. Bret was to hold himself in readiness to march down to the Bulwark Gate, or to attack the Leg Mount, a bastion at the north-west angle of the fortress, corresponding (though of somewhat smaller size,) with the Brass Mount, as he should receive instructions.

Having issued these directions, Wyat rode back to his troops—he was now mounted, as were several of his officers, on the steeds captured in the recent skirmish with the Earl of Pembroke—and commanded them to remain perfectly quiet till Admiral Winter's squadron should arrive off the Tower. His injunctions were strictly obeyed, and such perfect silence was observed, that though his men were drawn up within a few yards of the fortress, they were not discovered by the sentinels.

On the arrival of the squadron, Wyat immediately commenced an attack upon the Bulwark Gate—one of the weakest outworks of the fortress,—and while directing his engines against it, some half-dozen wooden houses adjoining it on the side of the moat, were fired by his men; and the flames quickly extending to the buildings immediately contiguous to the Bulwark Gate, that defence was at once surrendered.

The first point gained, Wyat despatched a messenger to Bret ordering him to join him instantly; and while a handful of his men, rushing round the semicircular wall, heretofore described as protecting the lesser moat, attacked the embattled gateway fronting the Lion's Tower, with the intention of joining Suffolk's party on the wharf, he directed his main force against the Lion's Gate. This fortification was stoutly defended, and the insurgents were twice repulsed before they could bring their engines to bear against it.

Bret and his party having arrived, such an irresistible attack was made upon the gate, that in a short time it was carried. With loud shouts, the insurgents drove the royalists before them along the narrow bridge facing the Lion's Tower, and leading to the Middle Tower, putting some to the sword, and throwing others over the walls into the moat.

WEST VIEW OF THE MIDDLE TOWER.

The movement was so expeditious, and the rout so unexpected, that the portcullis of the Middle Tower, which was kept up to allow the flying men to pass through it, could not be lowered, and hastily directing those around him to prop it up with a piece of timber, Wyat continued the pursuit to the By-ward. Tower.

Sir Thomas Wyat attacking the By Ward Tower

Hitherto, complete success had attended his efforts; and if he had passed the fortification he was approaching, in all probability he would have been master of the Tower. Nothing doubting this, he urged his men onwards. On his left rode Bret, and behind them, at a short distance, came Captain Knevet, and two other leaders, likewise on horseback.

As they arrived within a few paces of the By-ward Tower, three tremendous personages issued from it, and opposed their further progress. They were equipped in corslets of polished steel and morions; and two of them were armed with bucklers and enormous maces, while the third wielded a partizan of equal size. These, it is almost needless to state, were the three giants. The bearer of the partizan was Gog. Behind them came their diminutive attendant, who, it appeared, had been released from his thraldom, particulars of which, and of his adventures subsequent to his meeting with Cicely in the cell beneath the Salt Tower, will be related at a more convenient opportunity.

Like his gigantic companions, Xit was fully armed, in a steel corslet, cuisses, and gauntlets. His head was sheltered by a helmet, shaded by an immense plume of feathers, which, being considerably too large for him, almost eclipsed his features. He was furthermore provided with a sword almost as long as himself, and a buckler.

Taking care to keep under the shelter of the giants, Xit strutted about, and brandishing his sword in a valiant manner, shouted, or rather screamed,—

"Upon them Og!—attack them Gog!—why do you stand still, Magog? Let me pass, and I will show you how you should demean yourselves in the fight!"

At the sight of the giants, the flying royalists rallied, and a fierce but ineffectual struggle took place. During it, Bret was dismounted and thrown into the moat. Urged by their leader, the insurgents pressed furiously forward. But the giants presented an impassable barrier. Og plied his mace with as much zeal as he did the clubs when he enacted the part of the Tower at Courtenay's masque, and with far more terrible effect. All avoided the sweep of his arm.

Not content with dealing blows, he dashed among the retreating foe, and hurled some dozen of them into the moat. His prowess excited universal terror and astonishment. Nor was Gog much behind him. Wherever his partizan descended, a foe fell beneath its weight; and as he was incessantly whirling it over his head, and bringing it down, a space was speedily cleared before him.

Seeing the havoc occasioned by the gigantic brethren, and finding that they completely checked his further advance, Wyat struck spurs into his charger, and dashing upon Magog, tried to hew him down. If the married giant had not caught the blow aimed at him upon his shield, Dame Placida had been made a widow for the second time. Again plunging the spurs rowel-deep into his horse's flanks, Wyat would have ridden over his gigantic antagonist, if the latter, perceiving his intention, had not raised his mace, and with one tremendous blow smashed the skull of the noble animal.

"Yield you, Sir Thomas Wyat," cried Magog, rushing up to the knight, who was borne to the ground with his slaughtered charger—"you are my prisoner."

"Back, caitiff!" cried Wyat, disengaging himself and attacking the giant; "I will never yield with life."

Wyat, however, would have been speedily captured by the giant, if Knevet, seeing his perilous situation, had not pressed forward with several others to his assistance, and rescued him. This accident, however, enabled the retreating party to pass beneath the archway of the By-ward Tower, the portcullis of which was instantly lowered.

Meanwhile, a body of the insurgents having taken possession of the Middle Tower, had planted themselves at the various loop-holes, and on the roof, and kept up a constant fire on the soldiers stationed on the summit of the By-Ward Tower.

Among those who contrived to distinguish themselves in the action was Xit. Finding his position one of more danger than he had anticipated, he scrambled upon the wall on the right of the By-ward Tower, where, being out of the rush, he could defy at his ease those who were swimming in the moat.

While he was in this situation, Bret, who, it has been mentioned, was thrown into the moat, swam to the wall, and endeavoured to ascend it. Xit immediately attacked him, and adopting the language of Magog to Wyat, threatened to throw him back again if he did not yield.

"I do yield," replied Bret.

"Your name and rank?" demanded the dwarf, in an authoritative tone.

"Alexander Bret, captain of the London Trained Bands, second in command to Sir Thomas Wyat," replied the other.

"Here, Magog—Gog—Og—help!" shouted Xit—"I have taken a prisoner. It is Captain Bret, one of the rebel leaders—help him out of the moat, and let us carry him before the queen! I am certain to be knighted for my valour. Mind, *I* have taken him. He has yielded to me. No one else has had a hand in his capture."

Thus exhorted, Magog pulled Bret out of the moat. As soon as he ascertained who he was, he bore him in his arms towards the By-Ward Tower—Xit keeping near them all the time, screaming, "he is *my* prisoner. You have nothing to do with it. I shall certainly be knighted."

At Magog's command, the portcullis was partially raised, and Xit and Bret thrust under it, while the two other giants repelled the assailants.

CASEMATE IN THE BRASS MOUNT.

SOUTH-EAST VIEW OF THE JEWEL TOWER.

XXX.—HOW QUEEN MARY COMPORTED HERSELF DURING THE SIEGE; HOW LORD GUILFORD DUDLEY WAS CAPTURED; AND HOW SIR THOMAS WYAT AND THE DUKE OF SUFFOLK WERE ROUTED.

Throughout the whole of the siege, the queen maintained her accustomed firmness; and to her indomitable courage, and the effect produced by it upon her followers, the successful issue of the conflict to the royalist party is mainly to be attributed. Startled from her slumbers by the roar of the artillery, Mary arose, and hastily arraying herself, quitted the palace with Gardiner, Renard, and a few other attendants, who had flown to her on the first rumour of the attack, and repaired to the lieutenant's lodgings, where she found Sir Henry Bedingfeld in the entrance hall, surrounded by armed men, busied in giving them instructions, and despatching messages to the officers in command of the different fortifications.

At the queen's appearance, the old knight would have flung himself at her feet, but she motioned him not to heed her, and contented herself with saying, as each messenger departed:—"Tell my soldiers, that I will share their danger. I will visit every fortification in turn, and I doubt not I shall find its defenders at their posts. No courageous action shall pass unrequited: and as I will severely punish these rebels, so I will reward those who signalise themselves in their defeat. Bid them fight for their queen—for the daughter of the Eighth Henry, whose august spirit is abroad to watch over and direct them. He who brings me Wyat's head, shall receive knighthood at my hands, together with the traitor's forfeited estates. Let this be proclaimed. And now fight—and valiantly—for you fight for the truth."

Charged with animating addresses like these, the soldiers hurried to their various leaders. The consequence may be easily imagined. Aware that they were under the immediate eye of their sovereign, and anticipating her coming each moment, the men, eager to distinguish themselves, fought with the utmost ardour; and such was the loyalty awakened by Mary's energy and spirit, that even those secretly inclined towards the opposite party, of whom there were not a few, did not dare to avow their real sentiments.

While Mary remained in the lieutenant's lodgings, word was brought that the fortress was attacked on all sides, and the thunder of the ordnance now resounding from the whole line of ramparts, and answered by the guns of the besiegers, confirmed the statement. As she heard these tidings, and listened to the fearful tumult without, her whole countenance underwent a change; and those who remembered her kingly sire, recognised his most terrible expression, and felt the same awe they had formerly experienced in his presence.

"Oh! that I had been born a man!" she cried, "that with my own hand I might punish these traitors. But they shall find though they have a woman to deal with, they have no feeble and faint-hearted antagonist. I cannot wield a sword; but I will stand by those who can. Sir Henry Bedingfeld, take these orders from me, and they are final. Let the siege go how it may, I will make no terms with the rebels, nor hold further parley with them. Show them no quarter—exterminate them utterly. I no longer regard them as subjects—children; but as aliens—foes. Deal with them as such. And look you yield not this fortress—for by God's grace! *I* never will yield it. Where is your own post, Sir Henry?"

"At the By-ward Tower, your highness," replied Bedingfeld. "The traitor Wyat directs the attack in that quarter; and he is most to be feared of all our opponents. I will not quit the fortification with my life. But who shall succeed me, if I fall?"

"The queen," replied Mary. "But you will *not* fall, good Bedingfeld. You are appointed by Heaven to be my preserver. Go to your post; and keep it, in my name. Go, and fight for your royal mistress, and for the holy Catholic faith which we both of us profess, and which these rebels—these heretics, would overthrow. Go, and the Virgin prosper you, and strengthen your arm.".

"I obey your majesty," replied Bedingfeld; "and yet I cannot but feel that my place is by your side."

"Ah! do you loiter, sir?" cried Mary fiercely. "You have tarried here too long already. Do you not hear yon loud-voiced cannon summon you hence? Are you deaf to those cries? To your post, sir—and quit it not for your head. Stay!" she added, as the knight was about to obey her. "I meant not this. I have been over-hasty. But you will bear with me. Go. I have no fears—and have much to do. Success be with you. We meet again as victors, or we meet no more."

"We shall meet ere day-break," replied the knight. And quitting the presence, he hurried to the By-ward Tower.

"In case fate declares itself against your highness, and the insurgents win the fortress," observed Renard, "I can convey you beyond their reach. I am acquainted with a subterranean passage communicating with the further side of the moat, and have stationed a trusty guard at its entrance."

"In the event your excellency anticipates," returned Mary, sternly, "but which I am assured will never occur, I will not fly. While one stone of that citadel stands upon another it shall never be surrendered: and while life remains to her, Mary of England will never desert it. In your next despatch to the prince your master, tell him his proposed consort proved herself worthy—in resolution, at least—of the alliance."

"I will report your intrepid conduct to the prince," replied Renard. "But I would, for his sake, if not for your own, gracious madam, that you would not further expose yourself."

"To the ramparts!" cried Mary, disregarding him. "Let those follow me, who are not afraid to face these traitors."

Quitting the entrance-hall, she mounted a broad staircase of carved oak, and traversing a long gallery, entered a passage leading to the Bell Tower—a fortification already described as standing on the west of the lieutenant's lodgings, and connected with them. The room to which the passage brought her, situated on the upper story, and now used as part of the domestic offices of the governor, was crowded with soldiers, busily employed in active defensive preparations. Some were discharging their calivers through the loopholes at the besiegers, while others were carrying ammunition to the roof of the building..

Addressing a few words of encouragement to them, and, crossing the room, Mary commanded an officer to conduct her to the walls. Seeing from her manner that remonstrance would be useless, the officer obeyed. As she emerged from the low arched doorway opening upon the ballimn wall, the range of wooden houses on the opposite side of the moat burst into flames, and the light of the conflagration, while it revealed the number of her enemies and their plan of attack, rendered her situation infinitely more perilous, inasmuch as it betrayed her to general observation. Directed by the shouts, the besiegers speedily discovered the occasion of the clamour; and though Sir Thomas Wyat, who was engaged at the moment in personally directing the assault on the Bulwark Gate, commanded his men to cease firing in that quarter, his injunctions were wholly disregarded, and several shots struck the battlements close to the queen. Seriously alarmed, Gardiner earnestly entreated her to retire, but she peremptorily refused, and continued her course as slowly as if no danger beset her—ever and anon pausing to watch the movements of the besiegers, or to encourage and direct her own-men. Before she reached the Beauchamp Tower, the Bulwark Gate was carried, and the triumphant shouts of the insurgents drew from her an exclamation of bitter anger.

"It is but a small advantage gained, your highness," remarked the officer; "they will be speedily repulsed."

"Small as it is, sir," rejoined the queen, "I would rather have-lost the richest jewel from my crown than they had gained so much. Look! they are gathering

- 383 -

together before the Lion's Gate. They are thundering against it with sledge-hammers, battering-rams, and other engines. I can hear the din of their blows above all this tumult. And see! other troops are advancing to their aid. By their banners and white coats, I know they are the London trained-bands, headed by Bret. Heaven confound the traitor! He who will bring him to me dead or alive, shall have whatever he asks. Ah, God's death! they have forced the Lion's Gate—they drive all before them. Recreants! why do you not dispute it inch by inch, and you may regain what you have lost? Confusion! Wyat and his rebel band press onward, and the others fly. They pass through the Middle Tower. Ah! that shout, those fearful cries! They put my faithful subjects to the sword. They are in possession of the Middle Tower, and direct its guns on the By-ward Tower. Wyat and his band are on the bridge. They press forward, the others retreat. Retreat! ah, caitiffs, cowards that you are, you *must* fight now, if you have a spark of loyalty left. They fly. They have neither loyalty nor valour. Where is Bedingfeld?—where is my lieutenant? why does he not sally forth upon them? If I were there, I would myself lead the attack."

"Your majesty's desires are fulfilled," remarked the officer; "a sally is made by a party from the gate—the rebels are checked."

"I see it!" exclaimed the queen, joyfully—"but what valiant men are they who thus turn the tide? Ah! I know them now, they are my famous giants—my loyal warders. Look how the rebel ranks are cleared by the sweep of their mighty arms. Brave yeomen! you have fought as no belted knights have hitherto fought, and have proved the truth of your royal descent. Ah! Wyat is down. Slay him! spare him not, brave giant! his lands, his title are yours. Heaven's curse upon him, the traitor has escaped! I can bear this no longer." she added, turning to her conductor. "Lead on: I would see what they are doing elsewhere." The command was obeyed, but the officer had not proceeded many yards when a shot struck him, and he fell mortally wounded at the queen's feet.

"I fear you are hurt, sir," said Mary, anxiously.

"To death, madam," gasped the officer. "I should not care to die, had I lived to see you victorious. When all others were clamouring for the usurper Jane, my voice was raised for you, my rightful queen; and now my last shout shall be for you."

"Your name?" demanded Mary, bending over him.

"Gilbert," replied the officer—"I am the grandson of Gunora Braose."

"Live, Gilbert," rejoined Mary—"live for my sake!"

Raising himself upon one arm, with a dying effort, Gilbert waved his sword over his head, and cried, "God save Queen Mary, and confusion to her enemies!" And with these words, he fell backwards, and instantly expired. The queen gazed for a moment wistfully at the body.

"How is it," she mused, as she suffered herself to be led onward by Renard, "that, when hundreds of my subjects are perishing around me, this man's death should affect me so strongly?—I know not. Yet, so it is."

Her attention, however, was speedily attracted to other matters. Passing through the Beauchamp Tower, she proceeded to the next fortification.

The main attacks of the besiegers, as has been previously stated, were directed against the Brass Mount, Saint Thomas's Tower, and the By-ward Tower;—the western and north-western ramparts, including the Leg Mount, a large bastion corresponding with the Brass Mount, being comparatively unmolested, faking up a position on the roof of the Devilin Tower, which flanked the north-west angle of the ballium wall, Mary commanded two sides of the fortress, and the view on either hand was terrific and sublime. On the left, the blazing habitations, which being of highly-combustible material were now, in a great measure, consumed, cast a red and lurid glare on the moat, lighting up the ramparts, the fortifications behind them, and those on the bridge,—two of which, she was aware, were in the possession of the besiegers. In this quarter the firing had ceased; and it seemed that both parties had by mutual consent suspended hostilities, to renew them in a short time with greater animosity than ever. On the right, however, the assault continued with unabated fury. A constant fire was kept up from the temporary batteries placed before the postern gate; clouds of arrows whizzed through the air, shot by the archers stationed on the banks of the moat; and another ladder having been placed against the ramparts, several of the scaling party had obtained a footing, and were engaged hand to hand with the besieged. Ever and anon, amid this tumultuous roar was heard a loud splash, proclaiming that some miserable wretch had been hurled into the moat.

After contemplating the spectacle for some time in silence, Mary proceeded to the Flint Tower—a fortification about ninety feet nearer the scene of strife. Here the alarming intelligence was brought her that Lord Guilford Dudley was in possession of the Brass Mount, and that other advantages had been gained by the insurgents in that quarter. The fight raged so fiercely, it was added, that it would be tempting Providence in her majesty to proceed further. Yielding, at length, to the solicitations of her attendants, Mary descended from the walls, and shaped her course towards the White Tower; while Renard, by her command, hastened to the Martin Tower (now the Jewel Tower) to ascertain how matters stood. His first step was to ascend the roof of this structure, which, standing immediately behind the Brass Mount, completely overlooked it.

It must be borne in mind that the Tower is surrounded by a double line of defences, and that the ballium wall and its fortifications are much loftier than the outer ramparts. Renard found the roof of the Martin Tower thronged with soldiers, who were bringing their guns to bear upon the present possessors of the Brass Mount. They were assisted in their efforts to dislodge them by the occupants of the Brick Tower and the Constable Tower; and notwithstanding the advantage gained by the insurgents, they sustained severe loss from the constant fire directed against them. Bernard's glance sought out Lord Guilford Dudley; and after a few moments' search, guided by the shouts, he perceived him with Cholmondeley driving a party of royalists before him down the steps leading to the eastern ramparts. Here he was concealed from view, and protected by the roofs of a range of habitations from the guns on the ballium wall.

A few moments afterwards, intelligence was conveyed by the soldiers on the Broad Arrow Tower to those on the Constable Tower, and thence from fortification to fortification, that Dudley having broken into one of the houses covering the ramparts, was descending with his forces into the eastern ward.

Renard saw that not a moment was to be lost. Ordering the soldiers not to relax their fire for an instant, he put himself at the head of a body of men, and hurrying down a spiral stone-staircase, which brought him to a subterranean chamber, unlocked a door in it, and traversing with lightning swiftness a long narrow passage, speedily reached another vaulted room. At first no outlet was perceptible; but snatching a torch from one of his band, Renard touched a knob of iron in the wall, and a stone dropping from its place discovered a flight of steps, up which they mounted. These brought them to a wider passage, terminated by a strong door clamped with iron, and forming a small sally-port opening upon the eastern ward, a little lower down than Lord Guilford Dudley and his party had gained admittance to it. Commanding his men to obey his injunctions implicitly, Renard flung open the sally-port, and dashed through it at their head.

Dudley was pressing forward in the direction of the Iron Gate when Renard appeared. Both parties were pretty equally matched in point of number, though neither leader could boast more than twenty followers. Still, multitudes were hastening to them from every quarter. A detachment of royalists were issuing from a portal near the Salt Tower; while a host of insurgents were breaking through the house lately forced by Lord Guilford Dudley, and hurrying to his assistance. In a few seconds, the opposing parties met. By the light of the torches, Dudley recognized Renard; and, uttering a shout of exultation, advanced to the attack.

As soon as it was known to the insurgents that the abhorred Spanish ambassador was before them, with one accord they turned their weapons against him, and if their leader had not interposed, would have inevitably slain him.

"Leave him to me," cried Dudley, "and I will deliver my country from this detested traitor. Fellow soldiers," he added, addressing Renard's companions, "will you fight for Spain, for the Inquisition, for the idolatries of Rome, when swords are drawn for your country—and for the Reformed religion? We are come to free you from the yoke under which you labour. Join us, and fight for your liberties, your laws,—for the gospel, and for Queen Jane."

"Ay, fight for Jane, and the gospel!" shouted Cholmondeley. "Down with Renard and the See of Rome. No Spanish match! no Inquisition!"

"Who are you fighting for? Who is your leader?" continued Dudley;—"a base Spanish traitor. Who are you fighting against?—Englishmen, your friends, your countrymen, your brothers—members of the same faith, of the same family."

This last appeal proved effectual. Most of the royalists went over to the insurgents, shouting, "No Spanish match! no Inquisition! Down with Renard!"

"Ay, down with Renard!" cried Dudley. "I will no longer oppose your just vengeance. Slay him, and we will fix his head upon a spear. It will serve to strike terror into our enemies."

Even in this extremity, Renard's constitutional bravery did not desert him; and, quickly retreating, he placed his back against the wall. The few faithful followers who stood by him, endeavoured to defend him, but they were soon slain, and he could only oppose his single sword against the array of partizans and pikes raised against him. His destruction appeared inevitable, and he had already given himself up for lost, when a rescue arrived.

The detachment of soldiers, headed by Sir Thomas Brydges, already described as issuing from the gate near the Salt Tower, seeing a skirmish taking place, hurried forward, and reached the scene of strife just in time to save the ambassador, whose assailants were compelled to quit him to wield their weapons in their own defence. Thus set free, Renard sprang like a tiger upon his foes, and, aided by the new-comers, occasioned fearful havoc among them. But his deadliest fury was directed against those who had deserted him, and he spared none of them whom he could reach with his sword.

Lord Guilford Dudley and his esquire performed prodigies of valour. The former made many efforts to reach Renard, but, such was the confusion around him, that he was constantly foiled in his purpose. At length, seeing it was in vain to contend against such superior force, and that his men would be speedily cut in pieces, and himself captured, he gave the word to retreat, and fled towards the north-east angle of the ward. The royalists started after them; but such was the speed at which the fugitives ran, that they could not overtake them. A few stragglers ineffectually attempted to check their progress, and the soldiers on the walls above did not dare to fire upon them, for fear of injuring their own party. In this way, they passed the Martin Tower, and were approaching the Brick Tower, when a large detachment of soldiers were seen advancing towards them.

"Long live Queen Jane!" shouted Dudley and his companions, vainly hoping they were friends.

"Long live Queen Mary, and death to the rebels!" responded the others.

At the cry, Dudley and his little band halted. They were hemmed in on all sides, without the possibility of escape; and the royalists on the fortifications above being now able to mark them, opened a devastating fire upon them. By this time, Renard and his party had turned the angle of the wall, and the voice of the ambassador was heard crying—"Cut them in pieces! Spare no one but their leader. Take him alive."

Hearing the shout, Dudley observed to Cholmondeley—"You have ever been my faithful esquire, and I claim one last service from you. If I am in danger of being taken, slay me. I will not survive defeat."

"Nay, my lord, live," cried Cholmondeley. "Wyat or the Duke of Suffolk may be victorious, and deliver you."

"No," replied Dudley, "I will not run the risk of being placed again in Mary's power. Obey my last injunctions. Should you escape, fly to Jane. You know where to find her. Bid her embark instantly for France, and say her husband with his last breath blessed her."

At this moment, he was interrupted by Cholmondeley, who pointed out an open door in the ramparts opposite them. Eagerly availing himself of the chance, Dudley called to his men to follow him, and dashed through it, uncertain whither it led, but determined to sell his life dearly. The doorway admitted them into a low vaulted chamber, in which were two or three soldiers and a stand of arms and ammunition. The men fled at their approach along a dark, narrow passage, and endeavoured to fasten an inner door, but the others were too close upon them to permit it. As Dudley and his band advanced, they found themselves at the foot of a short flight of steps, and rushing up them, entered a semi-circular passage, about six feet wide, with a vaulted roof, and deep embrazures in the walls, in which cannon were planted. It was, in fact, the casemate of the Brass Mount. By the side of the cannon stood the gunners, and the passage was filled with smoke. Alarmed by the cries of their companions, and the shouts of Dudley and his band, these men, who were in utter ignorance of what had passed, except that they had been made aware that the summit of the bastion was carried, threw down their arms, and sued for quarter.

"You shall have it, friends," cried Dudley, "provided you will fight for Queen Jane."

"Agreed!" replied the gunners. "Long live Queen Jane."

"Stand by me," returned Dudley, "and these stout walls shall either prove our safeguard, or our tomb."

The gunners then saw how matters stood, but they could not retract; and they awaited a favourable opportunity to turn against their new masters.

Perceiving the course taken by Dudley and his companions, Henard felt certain of their capture, and repeated his injunctions to the soldiers to take him alive if possible, but on no account to suffer him to escape.

Dudley, meanwhile, endeavoured with Cholmondeley to drag one of the large pieces of ordnance out of the embrasure in which it was placed, with the view of pointing it against their foes. But before this could be accomplished, the attack commenced. Darting to the head of the steps, Dudley valiantly defended the pass for some time; and the royalist soldiers, obedient to the injunctions of Renard, forbore to strike him, and sought only his capture. The arched roof rang with the clash of weapons, with the reports of shot, and with the groans of the wounded and dying. The floor beneath them soon became slippery with blood. Still, Dudley kept his ground. All at once, he staggered, and fell. A blow had been dealt him from behind by one of the gunners, who had contrived to approach him unawares.

"It is over," he groaned to his esquire, "finish me, and fly, if you can, to Jane."

Cholmondeley raised his sword to comply with his lord's injunctions, but the blow was arrested by the strong arm of Renard, who bestriding his prey, cried, in a voice of exultation, "He is mine! Bear him to the Queen before he expires."

Cholmondelcy heard no more, but darting backwards, sprang into the embrazure whence he had endeavoured to drag the cannon, and forcing himself through the aperture, dropped from the dizzy height into the moat.

While this was passing, Mary proceeded to Saint John's-Chapel in the White Tower. It was brilliantly illuminated, and high mass was being performed by Bonner and the whole of the priesthood assembled within the fortress. The transition from the roar and tumult without to this calm and sacred scene was singularly striking, and calculated to produce a strong effect on the feelings. There, all was strife and clamour; the air filled with smoke was almost stifling; and such places as were not lighted up by the blaze of the conflagration or the flashing of the ordnance and musquetry, were buried in profound gloom. Here, all was light, odour, serenity, sanctity. Without, fierce bands were engaged in deathly fight—nothing was heard but the clash of arms, the thunder of cannon, the shouts of the victorious, the groans of the dying. Within, holy men were celebrating their religious rites, undisturbed by the terrible struggle around them, and apparently unconscious of it; tapers shone from every pillar; the atmosphere was heavy with incense; and the choral, hymn mingled with the scarce-heard roar of cannon. Mary was so affected by the scene, that for the first time she appeared moved. Her bosom heaved, and a tear started to her eye.

"How peaceful is the holy place," she observed to Gardiner, "and what a contrast it presents to the scene we have just quitted! I could almost wish that Heaven had destined me to the cloister instead of the throne, that I might pass my days in the exercise of my religion."

"Heaven has destined you to be the restorer and defender of our religion, madam," replied Gardiner. "Had you not been called to the high station you occupy, the Catholic worship, so long discontinued in these holy walls, would not now be celebrated. To you we owe its restoration;—to you we must owe its continuance."

As Mary advanced to the altar, the anthem ceased, and silence prevailed throughout the sacred structure. Prostrating herself, she prayed for a few moments fervently, and in an audible voice. She then arose, and observed to Gardiner, "I feel so much comforted, that I am assured Heaven will support me and our holy religion."

As she spoke, solemn music resounded through the chapel, the anthem was again chanted, and the priests resumed their holy rites. With a heart strengthened and elated, Mary ascended the staircase behind the altar, and passing through the gallery proceeded to the council-chamber, where she was informed that Xit, having captured a prisoner of importance, waited without to ascertain her pleasure concerning him. Mary ordered the dwarf to be brought into her presence with his captive, and in a few moments he was introduced with Bret, who was guarded by a couple of halberdiers.

On no previous occasion had Xit exhibited so much consequence as the present, and his accoutrements and fantastically-plumed casque added to his ludicrous appearance. He advanced slowly and majestically towards the chair of state in which Mary was seated, ever and anon turning his head to see that Bret was close behind him, and when within a short distance of the royal person, he made a profound salutation. Unluckily, in doing so, his helmet fell from his head, and rolled to the queen's feet. Slightly discomposed by the accident, and still more by Mary's frowns, he picked up his helmet, and stammered forth,—

"I am come to inform your highness that I have taken a prisoner—taken him with my own hands——"

"Who is it?" interrupted Mary, glancing sternly at the captive, who remained with his arms folded upon his breast, and his eyes cast upon the floor. "Who is it?" she asked, in an imperious tone.

"The arch-traitor Bret," answered Xit,—"the captain of the London Trained Bands, who revolted from the Duke of Norfolk, and joined the rebels at Rochester."

"Bret!" ejaculated Mary, in a tone that made Xit recoil several steps with fright, while the prisoner himself looked up. "Aha! is the traitor then within our power? Take him without, and let the headsman deal with him."

"Your highness!" cried Bret, prostrating himself.

"Away with him!" interrupted Mary. "Do you, my lord," she added, to Gardiner, "see that my commands are obeyed." The prisoner was accordingly removed, and Xit, who was completely awed by the queen's furious looks, was about to slink off, when she commanded him to remain.

"Stay!" she cried. "I have promised on my queenly word, that whoso brought this traitor Bret to me, should have whatever he demanded. Art thou in good truth his captor? Take heed thou triflest not with me. I am in no mood for jesting."

"So I perceive, gracious madam," replied Xit. "But I swear to you, I took him with my own hand, in fair and open combat. My companion Magog, if he survives the fray, will vouch for the truth of my statement—nay, Bret himself will not gainsay it.

"Bret will gainsay little more," rejoined Mary sternly; "his brain will contrive no further treason against us, nor his tongue give utterance to it. But I believe thee—the rather that I am persuaded thou darest not deceive me. Make thy request—it is granted.".

"If I dared to raise my hopes so high," said Xit, bashfully "What means the knave?" cried Mary. "I have said the request shall be granted."

"Whatever I ask?" inquired Xit.

"Whatever thou mayest ask in reason, sirrah!" returned Mary, somewhat perplexed.

"Well, then," replied Xit, "I should have claimed a dukedom. But as your highness might possibly think the demand unreasonable, I will limit myself to knighthood."

In spite of herself, Mary could not repress a smile at the dwarf's extravagant request, and the terms in which it was couched.

"I have made many efforts to obtain this distinction," pursued Xit,—"and for a while unsuccessfully. But fortune, or rather my bravery, has at length favoured me. I desire knighthood at your Majesty's hands."

"Thou shalt have it," replied Mary; "and it will be a lesson to me to make no rash promises in future. Hereafter, when affairs are settled, thou wilt not fail to remind me of my promise."

"Your highness may depend upon it, I will not fail to do so," replied Xit, bowing and retiring. "Huzza!" he cried, as soon as he gained the antechamber. "Huzza!" he repeated, skipping in the air, and cutting as many capers as his armour would allow him, "at length, I have reached the height of my ambition. I shall be knighted. The queen has promised it. Aha! my three noble giants, I am now a taller man than any of you. My lofty title will make up for my want of stature. Sir Xit!—that does not sound well. I must change my name for one more euphonious, or at least find out my surname. Who am I? It is strange I never thought of tracing out my history before. I feel I am of illustrious origin. I must clear up this point before I am knighted. Stand aside, base grooms," he continued to the grinning and jeering attendants, "and let me pass."

While pushing through them, a sudden bustle was heard behind, and he was very unceremoniously thrust back by Simon Renard, who was conducting Dudley to the queen's presence.

"Another prisoner!" exclaimed Xit. "I wonder what Renard will get for his pains. If I could but take Wyat, my fortune were indeed made. First, I will go and see what has become of Bret; and then, if I can do so without much risk, I will venture outside the portcullis of the By-ward Tower. Who knows but I may come in for another good thing!"

Thus communing with himself, Xit went in search of the unfortunate captain of the Trained Bands, while Renard entered the council-chamber with Dudley. The latter, though faint from loss of blood, on finding himself in the queen's presence, exerted all his strength, and stood erect and unsupported.

"So far your highness is victorious," said Renard; "one of the rebel-leaders is in your power, and ere long all will be so: Will it please you to question him—or shall I bid Mauger take off his head at once?"

"Let me reflect a moment," replied Mary, thoughtfully, "He shall die," she added, after a pause; "but not yet."

"It were better to behead him now," rejoined Renard.

"I do not think so," replied Mary. "Let him be removed to some place of safe confinement—the dungeon beneath Saint John's Chapel."

"The only grace I ask from your highness is speedy death," said Dudley.

"Therefore I will not grant it," replied Mary. "No, traitor! you shall perish with your wife."

"Ah!" exclaimed Dudley, "I have destroyed her."

And as the words were pronounced, he reeled backwards, and would have fallen, if the attendants had not caught him.

"Your Majesty has spared Mauger a labour," observed Renard, sarcastically.

"He is not dead," replied Mary; "and if he were so, it would not grieve me. Remove him; and do with him as I have commanded."

Her injunctions were obeyed, and the inanimate body of Dudley was carried away.

Renard was proceeding to inform the queen that the insurgents had been driven from the Brass Mount, when a messenger arrived, with tidings that another success had been gained—Sir Henry Jerningham having encountered the detachment under the Duke of Suffolk, and driven them back to their vessels, was about to assist the Earl of Pembroke and Sir Henry Bedingfeld in a sally upon Sir Thomas Wyat's party. This news so enchanted Mary, that she took a valuable ring from her finger and presented it to the messenger, saying—"I will double thy fee, good fellow, if thou wilt bring me word that Wyat is slain, and his traitorous band utterly routed."

Scarcely had the messenger departed, when another appeared. He brought word that several vessels had arrived off the Tower, and attacked the squadron under the command of Admiral Winter; that all the vessels, with the exception of one, on board which the Duke of Suffolk had taken refuge, had struck; and that her majesty might now feel assured of a speedy conquest. At this news, Mary immediately fell on her knees, and cried—"I thank thee, O Lord! not that thou hast vouchsafed me a victory over my enemies, but that thou hast enabled me to triumph over thine."

"The next tidings your highness receives will be that the siege is raised," observed Renard, as the queen arose; "and, with your permission, I will be the messenger to bring it."

"Be it so," replied Mary. "I would now gladly be alone."

As Renard issued from the principal entrance of the White

Tower, and was about to cross the Green, he perceived a small group collected before Saint Peter's Chapel, and at once guessing its meaning, he hastened towards it. It was just beginning to grow light, and objects could be imperfectly distinguished. As Renard drew nigh, he perceived a circle formed round a soldier whose breast-plate, doublet, and ruff had been removed, and who was kneeling with his arms crossed upon his breast beside a billet of wood. Near him, on the left, stood Manger, with his axe upon his shoulder, and on the right, Gardiner holding a crucifix towards him, and earnestly entreating him to die in the faith of Rome; promising him, in case of compliance, a complete remission of his sins. Bret, for he it was, made no answer, but appeared, from the convulsive movement of his lips, to be muttering a prayer. Out of patience, at length Gardiner gave the signal to Mauger, and the latter motioned the rebel captain to lay his head upon the piece of timber. The practised executioner performed his task with so much celerity that a minute had not elapsed before the head was stricken from the body, and placed on the point of a spear. While the apparatus of death and the blood-streaming trunk were removed, Xit, who was one of the spectators, seized the spear with its grisly burden, and, bending beneath the load, bore it towards the By-ward Tower. A man-at-arms preceded him, shouting in a loud voice, "Thus perish all traitors."

Having seen this punishment inflicted, Renard hastened towards the By-ward Tower, and avoiding the concourse that flocked round Xit and his sanguinary trophy, took a shorter cut, and arrived there before them. He found Pembroke and Bedingfeld, as the messenger had stated, prepared with a large force to make a sally upon the insurgents. The signal was given by renewed firing from the roof and loopholes of the Middle Tower. Wyat, who had retired under the gateway of that fortification, and had drawn up his men in the open space behind it, now advanced at their head to the attack. At this moment, the portcullis of the By-ward Tower was again raised, and the royalists issued from it. Foremost among them were the giants. The meeting of the two hosts took place in the centre of the bridge, and the shock was tremendous. For a short time, the result appeared doubtful. But the superior numbers, better arms, and discipline, of the queen's party, soon made it evident on which side victory would incline.

If conquest could have been obtained by personal bravery, Wyat would have been triumphant. Wherever the battle raged most fiercely he was to be found.

He sought out Bedingfeld, and failing in reaching him, cut his way to the Earl of Pembroke, whom he engaged and would have slain, if Og had not driven him off with his exterminating mace. The tremendous prowess of the gigantic brethren, indeed, contributed in no slight degree to the speedy termination of the fight. Their blows were resistless, and struck such terror into their opponents, that a retreat was soon begun, which Wyat found it impossible to check. Gnashing his teeth with anger, and uttering ejaculations of rage, he was compelled to follow his flying forces. His anger was vented against Gog. He aimed a terrible blow at him, and cut through his partizan, but his sword shivered against his morion. A momentary rally was attempted in the court between the Lion's Gate and the Bulwark Gate; but the insurgents were speedily, driven out. On reaching Tower Hill, Wyat succeeded in checking them; and though he could not compel them to maintain their ground; he endeavoured, with a faithful band, to cover the retreat of the main body to London Bridge. Perceiving his aim, Pembroke sent off a detachment under Bedingfeld, by Tower-street, to intercept the front ranks while he attacked the rear. But Wyat beat off his assailants, made a rapid retreat down Thames-street, and after a skirmish with Bedingfeld at the entrance of the bridge, in which he gained a decided advantage, contrived to get his troops safely across it, with much less loss than might have been anticipated. Nor was this all. He destroyed the planks which had afforded him passage, and took his measures so well and so expeditiously on the Southwark side, that Pembroke hesitated to cross the bridge and attack him. >

The Tower, however, was delivered from its assailants. The three giants pursued the flying foe to the Bulwark Gate, and then returned to the Middle Tower, which was yet occupied by a number of Wyat's party, and summoned them to surrender! The command was refused, unless accompanied by a pardon. The giants said nothing more, but glanced significantly at each other. Magog seized a ram, which had been left by the assailants, and dashed it against the door on the left of the gateway. A few tremendous blows sufficed to burst it open. Finding no one within the lower chamber, they ascended the winding stone staircase, their progress up which was opposed, but ineffectually, by the insurgents. Magog pushed forward like a huge bull, driving his foes from step to step till they reached the roof, where a short but furious encounter took place. The gigantic brethren fought back to back, and committed such devastation among their foes, that those who were left alive threw down their arms, and begged for quarter. Disregarding their entreaties, the giants hurled them over the battlements. Some were drowned in the moat, while others wore dashed to pieces in the court below. "It is thus," observed Magog with a grim smile to his brethren, as the work of destruction was ended, "that the sons of the Tower avenge the insults offered to their parent."

On descending, they found Xit stationed in the centre of the bridge, carrying the spear with Bret's head upon it. The dwarf eagerly inquired whether they had taken Wyat; and being answered in the negative, expressed his satisfaction.

"The achievement is reserved for me," he cried; "no more laughter, my masters,—no more familiarity. I am about to receive knighthood from the queen." This announcement, however, so far from checking the merriment of the giants, increased it to such a degree, that the irascible mannikin dashed the gory head in their faces, and would have attacked them with the spear, if they had not disarmed him.

By this time, Sir Henry Bedingfeld had returned from the pursuit of the rebels. Many prisoners had been taken, and conveyed, by his directions, to a secure part of the fortress. Exerting-himself to the utmost, and employing a large body of men in the work, the damages done to the different defences of the fortress were speedily repaired, the bodies of the slain thrown into the river, and all rendered as secure as before. The crews on board Winter's squadron had surrendered; but their commander, together with the Duke of Suffolk, had escaped, having been put ashore in a small boat. Conceiving all lost, and completely panic-stricken, the Duke obtained horses for himself and a few companions, and riding to Shene, where he had appointed a meeting with his brother, Lord Thomas Grey, set off with him, at full speed, for Coventry, the inhabitants of which city he imagined were devoted to him. But he soon found out his error. Abandoned by his adherents, and betrayed into the hands of the Earl of Huntingdon, who had been sent after him, he was shortly afterwards brought a prisoner to the Tower.

Not to anticipate events, such was the expedition used, that in less than an hour, Bedingfeld conveyed to the queen the intelligence that all damage done by the besiegers was repaired, and that her loss had been trifling compared with that of her enemies. He found her surrounded by her nobles; and on his appearance she arose, and advanced a few steps to meet him.

"You have discharged your office right well, Sir Henry," she said; "and if we deprive you of it for a while, it is because we mean to intrust you with a post of yet greater importance."

"Whatever office your majesty may intrust me with, I will gladly accept it," replied Bedingfeld.

"It is our pleasure, then, that you set out instantly with the Earl of Sussex to Ashbridge," returned Mary, "and attach the person of the Princess Elizabeth. Here is your warrant. Bring her alive or dead." #

"Alas!" exclaimed Bedingfeld, "is this the task your highness has reserved for me?"

"It is," replied Mary; and she added in a lower tone, "you are the only man to whom I could confide it."

"I must perforce obey, since your majesty wills it—but—"

"You must set out at once," interrupted Mary—"Sir Thomas Brydges shall be lieutenant of the Tower in your stead. We reserve you for greater dignities."

Bedingfeld would have remonstrated, but seeing the queen was immoveable, he signified his compliance, and having received further instructions, quitted the presence to make preparations for his departure.

The last efforts of the insurgents must be briefly told. After allowing his men a few hours' rest, Wyat made a forced march to Kingston, and hastily repairing the bridge, which had been broken down, with planks, ladders, and beams tied together, passed over it with his ordnance and troops in safety, and proceeded towards London. In consequence of a delay that occurred on the road, his plan was discovered, and the Earl of Pembroke, having by this time collected a considerable army, drew up his forces in Saint James's fields to give him battle.

A desperate skirmish took place, in which the insurgents, disheartened by their previous defeat, were speedily worsted. Another detachment, under the command of Knevet, were met and dispersed at Charing Cross, by Sir Henry Jerningham, and would have been utterly destroyed, but that they could not be distinguished from the royalists, except by their muddy apparel, which occasioned the cry among the victors of "Down with the draggle-tails."

Wyat himself, who was bent upon entering the city, where he expected to meet with great aid from Throckmorton, dashed through all opposition, and rode as far as the Belle Sauvage (even then a noted hostel), near Ludgate. Finding the gate shut, and strongly defended, he rode back as quickly as he came to Temple Bar, where he was encountered by Sir Maurice Berkeley, who summoned him to surrender, and seeing it was useless to struggle further, for all his companions had deserted him, he complied. His captor carried him to the Earl of Pembroke; and as soon as it was known that the rebel-leader was taken, the army was disbanded, and every man ordered to return to his home. Proclamation was next made that no one, on pain of death, should harbour any of Wyat's faction, but should instantly deliver them up to the authorities.

That same night Wyat, together with Knevet, Cobham, and ethers of his captains, were taken to the Tower by water. As Wyat, who was the last to disembark, ascended the steps of Traitor's Gate, Sir Henry Brydges, the new lieutenant, seized him by the collar, crying, "Oh! thou base and unhappy traitor! how could'st thou find in thy heart to work such detestable treason against the queen's majesty? Were it not that the law must pass upon thee, I would stab thee with my dagger."

Holding his arms to his side, and looking at him, as the old chroniclers report, "grievously, with a grim look," Wyat answered, "It is no mastery now." Upon which, he was conveyed with the others to the Beauchamp Tower.

XXXI.—HOW JANE SURRENDERED HERSELF A PRISONER; AND HOW SHE BESOUGHT QUEEN MARY TO SPARE HER HUSBAND.

Towards the close of the day following that on which the rebels were defeated, a boat, rowed by a single waterman, shot London Bridge, and swiftly approached the Tower wharf. It contained two persons, one of whom, apparently a female, was so closely muffled in a cloak that her features could not be discerned; while her companion, a youthful soldier, equipped in his full accoutrements, whose noble features were clouded with sorrow, made no attempt at concealment. As they drew near the stairs, evidently intending to disembark, the sentinels presented their arquebusses at them, and ordered them to keep off; but the young man immediately arose, and said that having been concerned in the late insurrection, they were come to submit themselves to the queen's mercy. This declaration excited some surprise among the soldiers, who were inclined to discredit it, and would not have suffered them to land, if an officer of the guard, attracted by what was passing, had not interfered, and granted the request. By his command, they were taken across the draw-bridge opposite the stairs, and placed within the guard-room near the By-ward Tower. Here the officer who had accompanied them demanded their names and condition, in order to report them to the lieutenant.

"I am called Cuthbert Cholmondeley," replied the young man, "somewhile esquire to Lord Guilford Dudley."

"You bore that rebel lord's standard in the attack on the Brass Mount—did you not?" demanded the officer, sternly.

"I did," replied Cholmondeley.

"Then you have delivered yourself to certain death, young man," rejoined the officer. "What madness has brought you hither? The queen will show you no mercy, and blood enough will-flow upon the scaffold without yours being added to the stream."

"I desire only to die with my master," replied Cholmondeley.

"Where is Lord Guilford Dudley?" demanded the muffled' female, in a tone of the deepest emotion.

"Confined in one of the secret dungeons—but I may not answer you further, madam," replied the officer.

"Are his wounds dangerous?" she continued, in a tone of the deepest anxiety.

"They are not mortal, madam," he answered. "He will live long enough to expiate his offences on the scaffold."

"Ah!" she exclaimed with difficulty, repressing a scream.

"No more of this—if you are a man," cried Cholmondeley, fiercely. "You know not whom you address." *

"I partly guess." replied the officer, with a compassionate look. "I respect your sorrows, noble lady—but oh! why—why are you here? I would willingly serve you—nay, save you—but it is out of my power."

"My presence here must show you, sir, that I have no wish to avoid the punishment I have incurred," she replied. "I am come to submit myself to the queen. But if you would serve me—serve me without danger to yourself, or departure from your duty—you will convey this letter without delay to her highness's own hand."

"It may be matter of difficulty," rejoined the officer, "for her majesty is at this moment engaged in a secret conference in the Hall Tower, with the chancellor and the Spanish ambassador. Nay, though I would not further wound your feelings, madam, she is about to sign the death-warrants of the rebels."

"The more reason, then," she replied, in accents of supplicating eagerness, "that it should be delivered instantly. Will you take it?"

The officer replied in the affirmative.

"Heaven's blessing upon you!" she fervently ejaculated. Committing the captives to the guard, and desiring that every attention, consistent with their situation, should be shown them, the officer departed. Half an hour elapsed before his return, and during the interval but few words were exchanged between Cholmondeley and his companion. When the officer reappeared, she rushed towards him, and inquired what answer he brought.

"Your request is granted, madam," he replied. "I am commanded to bring you to the queen's presence; and may your suit to her highness prove as successful as your letter! You are to be delivered to the chief jailor, sir," he added to Chol-mondeley, "and placed in close custody."

As he spoke, Nightgall entered the guard-room. At the sight of his hated rival, an angry flush rose to the esquire's countenance—nor was his wrath diminished by the other's exulting looks.

"You will not have much further power over me," he observed, in answer to the jailor's taunts. "Cicely, like Alexia, is out of the reach of your malice. And I shall speedily join them."

"You are mistaken," retorted Nightgall, bitterly. "Cicely yet lives; and I will wed her on the day of your execution. Bring him away," he added, to his assistants. "I shall take him, in the first place, to the torture-chamber, and thence to the subterranean dungeons. I have an order to rack him."

"Farewell, madam," said the esquire, turning from him, and prostrating himself before his companion, who appeared in the deepest anguish; "we shall meet no more on earth."

"I have destroyed you," she cried. "But for your devotion to me, you might be now in safety."

"Think not of me, madam—I have nothing to live for," replied the esquire, pressing her hand to his lips. "Heaven support you in this your last, and greatest, and—as I can bear witness—most unmerited trial. Farewell, for ever!"

"Ay, for ever!" repeated the lady. And she followed the officer; while Cholmondeley was conveyed by Nightgall and his assistants to the secret entrance of the subterranean dungeons near the Devilin Tower.

Accompanied by his charge, who was guarded by two halberdiers, the officer proceeded along the southern ward, in the direction of the Hall Tower—a vast circular structure, standing on the east of Bloody Tower.

INTERIOR OF THE HALL TOWER.

This fabric, (sometimes called the Wakefield Tower from the prisoners confined within it, after the battle of that name in 1460, and more recently the Record Tower, from the use to which it has been put,) is one of the oldest in the fortress, and though not coeval with the White Tower, dates back as far as the reign of William Rufus, by whom it was erected. It contains two large octagonal chambers,—that on the upper story being extremely lofty, with eight deep and high embrazures, surmounted by pointed arches, and separated by thin columns, springing from the groined arches formerly supporting the ceiling, which though unfortunately destroyed, corresponded, no doubt, with the massive and majestic character of the apartment. In this room tradition asserts that

—the aspiring blood of Lancaster

Sank in the ground:—

—it being the supposed scene of the murder of Henry the Sixth by the ruthless Gloster. And whatever doubts may be entertained as to the truth of that dark legend, it cannot be denied that the chamber itself seems stamped with the gloomy character of the occurrence. In recent times, it has been devoted to a more peaceful purpose, and is now fitted up with presses containing the most ancient records of the kingdom. The room on the basement floor is of smaller dimensions, and much less lofty. The recesses, however, are equally deep, though not so high, and are headed by semicircular arches. At high tides it is flooded, and a contrivance for the escape of the water has been made in the floor.

Passing through an arched doorway on the east of this structure, where the entrance to the Record Office now stands, the officer conducted his prisoner up a spiral stone staircase, and left her in a small antechamber, while he announced her arrival. The unhappy lady still kept herself closely muffled. But though her features and figure were hidden, it was evident she trembled violently. In another moment, the officer reappeared, and motioning her to follow him, led the way along a narrow passage, at the end of which hangings were drawn aside by two ushers, and she found herself in the presence of the queen.

Mary was seated at a table, near which stood Gardiner and Renard, and at the new-comer's appearance she instantly arose.

The interview about to be related took place in the large octangular chamber previously described. It was sumptuously furnished: the walls were hung with arras from the looms of Flanders, and the deep recesses occupied with couches, or sideboards loaded with costly cups and vessels.

Hastily advancing towards the queen, the lady prostrated herself at her feet, and, throwing aside her disguise, revealed the features of Jane. She extended her hands supplicatingly towards Mary, and fixed her streaming eyes upon her, but was for some moments unable to speak.

Jane imploring Mary to spare her Husband's life

"I am come to submit myself to your highness's mercy," she said, as soon as she could find utterance.

"Mercy!" exclaimed Mary, scornfully. "You shall receive justice, but no mercy."

"I neither deserve, nor desire it," replied Jane. "I have deeply, but not wilfully—Heaven is my witness!—offended your majesty, and I will willingly pay the penalty of my fault."

"What would you with me?" demanded Mary. "I have acceded to this interview in consideration of your voluntary submission. But be brief. I have important business before me, and my heart is steeled to tears and supplications."

"Say not so, gracious madam," rejoined Jane. "A woman's heart can never be closed to the pleadings of the unfortunate of her own sex, still less the heart of one so compassionate as your highness. I do not sue for myself."

"For whom, then?" demanded the queen.

"For my husband," replied Jane.

"I am about to sign his death-warrant,1' replied Mary, in a freezing tone.

"I will not attempt to exculpate him, madam," returned Jane, restraining her emotion by a powerful effort, "for his offence cannot be extenuated. Nay, I deplore his rashness as much as your highness can condemn it. But I am well assured that vindictiveness is no part of your royal nature—that you disdain to crush a fallen foe—and that, when the purposes of justice are answered, no sentiments but those of clemency will sway your bosom. I myself, contrary to my own wishes, have been the pretext for the late insurrection, and it is right I should suffer, because while my life remains, your highness may not feel secure. But my husband has no claims, pretended or otherwise, to the throne, and when I am removed, all fear of him will be at an end. Let what I have done speak my sincerity. I *could* have escaped to France, if I had chosen. But I did not choose to accept safety on such terms. Well knowing with whom I had to deal—knowing also that my life is of more importance than my husband's, I have come to offer myself for him. If your highness has any pity for me, extend it to him, and heap his faults on my head."

"Jane," said Mary, much moved—"you love your husband devotedly."

"I need not say I love him better than my life, madam," replied Jane, "for my present conduct will prove that I do so. But I love him so well, that even his treason to your highness, to whom he already owes his life, cannot shake it. Oh, madam! as you hope to be happy in your union with the Prince of Spain—as you trust to be blessed with a progeny which shall continue on the throne of this kingdom—spare my husband—spare him for my sake."

"For *your* sake, Jane, I would spare him," replied Mary, in a tone of great emotion, "but I cannot."

"Cannot, madam!" cried Jane—"you are an absolute queen, and who shall say you nay? Not your council—not your nobles—not your people—not your own heart. Your majesty *can* and *will* pardon him. Nay, I read your gracious purpose in your looks. You will pardon him, and your clemency shall do more to strengthen your authority than the utmost severity could do."

"By Saint Paul!" whispered Renard to Gardiner, who had listened with great interest to the conference, and now saw with apprehension the effect produced on Mary, "she will gain her point, if we do not interfere."

"Leave it to me," replied Gardiner. "Your majesty will do well to accede to the Lady Jane's request," he remarked aloud to the queen, "provided she will comply with your former proposition, and embrace the faith of Rome."

"Ay," replied Mary, her features suddenly lighting up, "on these terms I will spare him. But your reconciliation with our holy church," she added to Jane, "must be public."

"Your highness will not impose these fatal conditions upon me," cried Jane, distractedly.

"On no other will I accede," replied Mary, peremptorily. "Nay, I have gone too far already. But my strong sympathy for you as a wife, and my zeal for my religion, are my inducements. Embrace our faith, and I pardon your husband."

"I cannot," replied Jane, in accents of despair; "I will die for him, but I cannot destroy my soul alive."

"Then you shall perish together," replied Mary, fiercely. "What ho! guards. Let the Lady Grey be conveyed to the Brick Tower, and kept a close prisoner during our pleasure." And, waving her hand, Jane was removed by the attendants, while Mary seated herself at the table, and took up some of the papers with which it was strewn, to conceal her agitation.

"You struck the right key, my lord,—bigotry," observed Renard, in an under tone to Gardiner.

XXXII.—HOW THE PRINCESS ELIZABETH WAS BROUGHT A PRISONER TO THE TOWER.

Charged with the painful and highly-responsible commission imposed upon him by the queen, Sir Henry Bedingfeld, accompanied by the Earl of Sussex and three others of the council, Sir Richard Southwell, Sir Edward Hastings, and Sir Thomas Cornwallis, with a large retinue, and a troop of two hundred and fifty horse, set out for Ashbridge, where Elizabeth had shut herself up previously to the outbreak of Wyat's insurrection. On their arrival, they found her confined to her room with real or feigned indisposition, and she refused to appear; but as their mission did not admit of delay, they were compelled to force their way to her chamber. The haughty princess, whose indignation was roused to the highest pitch by the freedom, received them in such manner as to leave no doubt how she would sway the reins of government, if they should ever come within her grasp.

"I am guiltless of all design against my sister," she said, "and I shall easily convince her of my innocence. And then look well, sirs—you that have abused her authority—that I requite not your scandalous treatment."

"I would have willingly declined the office," replied Bedingfeld; "but the queen was peremptory. It will rejoice me to find you can clear yourself with her highness, and I am right well assured, when you think calmly of the matter, you will acquit me and my companions of blame."

And he formed no erroneous estimate of Elizabeth's character. With all her proneness to anger, she had the strongest sense of justice. Soon after her accession, she visited the old knight at his seat, Oxburgh Hall, in Norfolk;—still in the possession of his lineal descendant, the present Sir Henry Bedingfeld, and one of the noblest mansions in the county,—and, notwithstanding his adherence to the ancient faith, manifested the utmost regard for him, playfully terming him "her jailor."

Early the next morning, Elizabeth was placed in a litter, with her female attendants; and whether from the violence of her passion, or that she had not exaggerated her condition, she swooned, and on her recovery appeared so weak that they were obliged to proceed slowly. During the whole of the journey, which occupied five days, though it might have been easily accomplished in one, she was strictly guarded;—the greatest apprehension being entertained of an attempt at rescue by some of her party. On the last day, she robed herself in white, in token of her innocence; and on her way to Whitehall, where the queen was staying, she drew aside the curtains of her litter, and displayed a countenance, described in Renard's despatches to the Emperor, as "proud, lofty, and superbly disdainful,—an expression assumed to disguise her mortification." On her arrival at the palace, she earnestly entreated an audience of her majesty, but the request was refused.

That night Elizabeth underwent a rigorous examination by Gardiner and nineteen of the council, touching her privity to the conspiracy of De Noailles, and her suspected correspondence with Wyat. She admitted having received letters from the French ambassador on behalf of Courtenay, for whom, notwithstanding his unworthy conduct, she still owned she entertained the warmest affection, but denied any participation in his treasonable practices, and expressed the utmost abhorrence of Wyat's proceedings. Her assertions, though stoutly delivered, did not convince her interrogators, and Gardiner told her that Wyat had confessed on the rack that he had written to her, and received an answer.

"Ah! says the traitor so?" cried Elizabeth. "Confront me with him, and if he will affirm as much to my face, I will own myself guilty."

"The Earl of Devonshire has likewise confessed, and has offered to resign all pretensions to your hand, and to go into exile, provided the queen will spare his life," rejoined Gardiner.

"Courtenay faithless!" exclaimed the princess, all her haughtiness vanishing, and her head, declining upon her bosom, "then it is time I went to the Tower. You may spare yourselves the trouble of questioning me further, my lords, for by my faith I will not answer you another word—-no, not even if you employ the rack."

Upon this, the council departed. Strict watch was kept over her during the night. Above a hundred of the guard were stationed within the palace-gardens, and a great fire was lighted in the hall, before which Sir Henry Bedingfeld and the Earl of Sussex, with a large band of armed men, remained till day-breaks At nine o'clock, word was brought to the princess that the tide suited for her conveyance to the Tower. It was raining heavily, and Elizabeth refused to stir forth on the score of her indisposition. But Bedingfeld told her the queen's commands were peremptory, and besought her not to compel him to use force. Seeing resistance was in vain, she consented with an ill grace, and as she passed through the garden to the water-side, she cast her eyes towards the windows of the palace, in the hope of seeing Mary, but was disappointed.

The rain continued during the whole of her passage, and the appearance of every thing on the river was as dismal and depressing as her own thoughts. But Elizabeth was not of a nature to be easily subdued. Rousing all her latent energy, she bore up firmly against her distress. An accident had well nigh occurred as they shot London Bridge. She had delayed her departure so long that the fall was considerable, and the prow of the boat struck upon the ground with such force as almost to upset it, and it was some time before it righted. Elizabeth was wholly unmoved by their perilous situation, and only remarked that "She would that the torrent had sunk them." Terrible as the stern old fortress appeared to those who approached it under similar circumstances, to Elizabeth it assumed its most appalling aspect. Gloomy at all times, it looked gloomier than usual now, with the rain driving against it in heavy scuds, and the wind, whistling round its ramparts and fortifications, making the flag-staff and the vanes on the White Tower creak, and chilling the sentinels exposed to its fury to the bone. The storm agitated the river, and the waves more than once washed over the sides of the boat.

"You are not making for Traitors Gate," cried Elizabeth, seeing that the skiff was steered in that direction; "it is not fit that the daughter of Henry the Eighth should land at those steps."

"Such are the queen's commands," replied Bedingfeld, sorrowfully. "I dare not for my head disobey."

"I will leap overboard sooner," rejoined Elizabeth.

"I pray your highness to have patience," returned Bedingfeld, restraining her. "It would be unworthy of you—of your great father, to take so desperate a step."

Elizabeth compressed her lips and looked sternly at the old knight, who made a sign to the rowers to use their utmost despatch; and, in another moment, they shot beneath the gloomy gateway. The awful effect of passing under this dreadful arch has already been described, and Elizabeth, though she concealed her emotion, experienced its full horrors. The Water-gate revolved on its massive hinges, and the boat struck against the foot of the steps. Sussex and Bedingfeld, and the rest of the guard and her attendants, then landed, while Sir Thomas Brydges, the new lieutenant, with several warders, advanced to the top of the steps to receive her. But she would not move, but continued obstinately in the boat, saying, "I am no traitor, and do not choose to land here."

"You shall *not* choose, madam,'" replied Bedingfeld, authoritatively. "The queen's orders must, and *shall* be obeyed. Disembark, I pray you, without more ado, or it will go hardly with you."

"This from von, Bedingfeld," rejoined Elizabeth, reproachfully, "and at such a time, too?"

"I have no alternative,'" replied the knight.

"Well then, I will not put you to further shame," replied the princess, rising.

"Will it please you to take my cloak as a protection against the rain?" said Bedingfeld, offering it to her. But she pushed it aside "with a good dash," as old Fox relates; and springing on the steps, cried in a loud voice, "Here lands as true a subject, being prisoner, as ever set foot on these stairs. And before thee, O God, I speak it, having no other friend but thee." *

"Your highness is unjust," replied Bedingfeld, who stood bare-headed beside her; "you have many friends, and amongst them none more zealous than myself. And if I counsel you to place some restraint upon your conduct, it is because I am afraid it may be disadvantageous reported to the queen."

"Say what you please of me, sir," replied Elizabeth; "I will not be told how I am to act by you, or any one."

"At least move forward, madam," implored Bedingfeld; "you will be drenched to the skin if you tarry here longer, and will fearfully increase your fever."

"What matters it if I do?" replied Elizabeth, seating herself on the damp step, while the shower descended in torrents upon her. "I will move forward at my own pleasure—not at your bidding. And let us see whether you will dare to use force towards me."

"Nay, madam, if you forget yourself, I will not forget what is due to your father's daughter," replied Bedingfeld, "you shall have ample time for reflection."

The deeply-commiserating and almost paternal tone in which this reproof was delivered touched the princess sensibly; and glancing round, she was further moved by the mournful looks of her attendants, many of whom were deeply affected, and wept audibly. As soon as her better feelings conquered, she immediately yielded to them; and, presenting her hand to the old knight, said, "You are right, and I am wrong, Bedingfeld. Take me to my dungeon."

Elizabeth brought Prisoner to the Tower.

XXXIII.—HOW NIGHTGALL WAS BRIBED BY DE NOAILLES TO ASSASSINATE SIMON RENARD; AND HOW JANE'S DEATH-WARRANT WAS SIGNED.

The Tower was now thronged with illustrious prisoners. All the principal personages concerned in the late rebellion, with the exception of Sir Peter Carew, who had escaped to France, were confined within its walls; and the queen and her council wore unremittingly employed in their examinations. The Duke of Suffolk had written and subscribed his confession, throwing himself upon the royal mercy; Lord Guilford Dudley, who was slowly recovering from his wound, refused to answer any interrogatories; while Sir Thomas Wyat, whose constancy was shaken by the severity of the torture to which he was exposed, admitted his treasonable correspondence with Elizabeth and Courtenay, and charged De Noailles with being the originator of the plot. The latter was likewise a prisoner. But as it was not the policy of England, at that period, to engage in a war with France, he was merely placed under personal restraint until an answer could be received from Henry the Second, to whom letters had been sent by Mary.

Well instructed as to the purport of these despatches, and confident of his sovereigns protection, De Noailles felt little uneasiness as to his situation, and did not even despair of righting himself by some master-stroke. His grand object was to remove Renard; and as he could not now accomplish this by fair means, he determined to have recourse to foul; and to procure his assassination. Confined, with certain of his suite, within the Flint Tower, he was allowed, at stated times, to take exercise on the Green, and in other parts of the fortress, care being taken to prevent him from holding communication with the other prisoners, or, indeed, with any one except his attendants. De Noailles, however, had a ready and unsuspected instrument at hand. This was his jailor, Lawrence Nightgall, with whom he had frequent opportunities of conversing, and whom he had already sounded on the subject. Thus, while every dungeon in the fortress was filled with the victims of his disastrous intrigues; while its subterranean chambers echoed with the groans of the tortured; while some expired upon the rack, others were secretly executed, and the public scaffold was prepared for sufferers of the highest rank; while the axe and the block were destined to frequent and fearful employment, and the ensanguined ground thirsted for the best and purest blood in England; while such was the number of captives that all the prisons in London were insufficient to contain them, and they were bestowed within the churches; while twenty pairs of gallows were erected in the public places of the city, and the offenders with whom they were loaded left to rot upon them as a terrible example to the disaffected; while universal dread and lamentation prevailed,—the known author of all this calamity remained, from prudential reasons, unpunished, and pursued his dark and dangerous machinations as before.

One night, when he was alone, Nightgall entered his chamber, and, closing the door, observed, with a mysterious look,—"Your excellency has thrown out certain dark hints to me of late. You can speak safely now, and I pray you do so plainly. What do you desire me to do?"

Do Noailles looked scrutinizingly at him, as if he feared some treachery. But at length, appearing satisfied, he said abruptly, "I desire Renards assassination. His destruction is of the utmost importance to my king."

"It is a great crime," observed Nightgall, musingly.

"The reward will be proportionate," rejoined De Noailles.. "What does your excellency offer?" asked Nightgall.

"A thousand angels of gold," replied the ambassador, "and a post at the court of France, if you will fly thither when the deed is done."

"By my troth, a tempting offer," rejoined Nightgall. "But I am under great obligations to M. Simon Renard. He appointed me to my present place. It would appear ungrateful to kill him."

"Pshaw!" exclaimed De Noailles, contemptuously. "You are not the man to let such idle scruples stand in the way of your fortune. Renard only promoted you because you were useful to him. And he would sacrifice you as readily, if it suited his purpose. He will serve you better dead than living."

"It is a bargain," replied Nightgall. "I have the keys of the subterranean passages, and can easily get out of the Tower when I have despatched him. Your excellency can fly with me if you think proper."

"On no account," rejoined De Noailles. "I must not appear in the matter. Come to me when the deed is done, and I will furnish you with means for your flight, and with a letter to the king of France, which shall ensure you your reward when you reach Paris. But it must be done quickly."

"It shall be done to-morrow night," replied Nightgall. "Fortunately, M. Renard has chosen for his lodgings the chamber in the Bloody Tower in which the two princes were murdered."

"A fitting spot for his own slaughter," remarked De Noailles, drily. "It is so, in more ways than one," replied Nightgall; "for I can approach him unawares by a secret passage, through which, when all is over, escape will be easy."

"Good!" exclaimed De Noailles, rubbing his hands gleefully. "I should like to be with you at the time. Mortdieu! how I hate that man. He has thwarted all my schemes. But I shall now have my revenge. Take this ring and this purse in earnest of what is to follow, and mind you strike home."

"Fear nothing," replied Nightgall, smiling grimly, and playing his dagger; "the blow shall not need to be repeated. Your excellency's plan chimes well with a project of my own. There is a maiden whom I have long sought, but vainly, to make my bride. I will carry her off with me to France."

"She will impede your flight," observed De Noailles, hastily. "On all difficult occasions, women are sadly in the way."

"I cannot leave her," rejoined Nightgall.

"Take her, then, in the devil's name," rejoined De Noailles, peevishly; "and if she brings you to the gallows, do not forget my warning."

"My next visit shall be to tell you your enemy is no more," returned Nightgall. "Before midnight to-morrow, you may expect me." And he quitted the chamber.

While his destruction was planned in the manner above-related, Simon Renard was employing all his art to crush by one fell stroke all the heads of the Protestant party. But he met with opposition from quarters where he did not anticipate it. Though the queen was convinced of Elizabeth's participation in the plot, as well from Wyat's confession, who owned that he had written to her during his march to London, offering to proclaim her queen, and had received favourable answers from her,—as from the declaration of a son of Lord Russell, to the effect, that he had delivered the despatches into her own hand, and brought back her replies;—notwithstanding this, Mary refused to pass sentence upon her, and affected to believe her innocent. Neither would she deal harshly with Courtenay, though equally satisfied of his guilt; and Renard, unable to penetrate her motives, began to apprehend that she still nourished a secret attachment to him. The truth was, the princess and her lover had a secret friend in Gardiner, who counteracted the sanguinary designs of the ambassador. Baffled in this manner, Renard determined to lose no time with the others. Already, by his agency, the Duke of Suffolk, Lord Thomas Grey, and Wyat, were condemned—Dudley and Jane alone were wanting to the list.

Touched, by a strong feeling of compassion for their youth, and yet more by the devotion Jane had exhibited to her husband, Mary hesitated to sign their death-warrant. She listened to all Renard's arguments with attention, but they failed to move her. She could not bring herself to put a period to the existence of one whom she knew to be so pure, so lovely, so loving, so blameless, as Jane. But Renard was determined to carry his point.

"I will destroy them all," he said; "but I will begin with Dudley and Jane, and end with Courtenay and Elizabeth."

During the examination of the conspirators, the queen, though she had moved her court to Whitehall, passed much of her time at the Tower, occupied in reading the depositions of the prisoners, or in framing interrogatories to put to them. She also wrote frequent despatches to the emperor, whose counsel she asked in her present difficulties; and while thus occupied, she was often closeted for hours with Renard.

Whether by accident, or that the gloomy legend connected with it, harmonising with his own sombre thoughts, gave it an interest in his eyes, Renard had selected for his present lodging in the Tower, as intimated by Nightgall, the chamber in which the two youthful princes were destroyed. It might be that its contiguity to the Hall Tower, where Mary now for the most part held her conferences with her council, and with which it was connected by a secret passage, occasioned this selection—or he might have been influenced by other motives—suffice it to say he there took up his abode; and was frequently visited within it by Mary. Occupying the upper story of the Bloody Tower, this mysterious chamber looks on the north upon the ascent leading to the Green, and on the south upon Saint Thomas's Tower. It is now divided into two rooms by a screen—that to the south being occupied as a bed-chamber; and tradition asserts, that in this part of the room the "piece of ruthless butchery," which stamps it with such fearful interest, was perpetrated. On the same side, between the outer wall and the chamber, runs a narrow passage, communicating on the west with the ballium wall, and thence with the lieutenant's lodgings, by which the murderers are said to have approached; and in the inner partition is a window, through which they gazed upon their sleeping victims. On the east, the passage communicates with a circular staircase, descending to a small vaulted chamber at the right of the gateway, where the bodies were interred. In later times, this mysterious room has been used as a prison-lodging. It was occupied by Lord Ferrers during his confinement in the Tower, and more recently by the conspirators Watson and Thistlewood.

SOUTH SIDE OF THE ROOM IN WHICH THE YOUNG PRINCES WERE MURDERED.

On the evening appointed by Nightgall for the assassination of Renard, the proposed victim and the queen were alone within this chamber. The former had renewed all his arguments, and with greater force than ever, and seeing he had produced the desired impression, he placed before her the warrant for the execution of Jane and her husband.

"Your majesty will never wear your crown easily till you sign that paper," he said.

"I shall never wear it easily afterwards," sighed Mary. "Do you not remember Jane's words? She told me, I should be fortunate in my union, and my race should continue upon the throne, if I spared her husband. They seem to me prophetic. If I sign this warrant, I may destroy my own happiness."

"Your highness will be not turned from your purpose by such idle fears," rejoined Renard, in as sarcastic a tone as he dared assume. "Not only your throne may be endangered, if you suffer them to live, but the Catholic religion."

"True," replied Mary, "I will no longer hesitate."

And she attached her signature to the warrant.

Renard watched her with a look of such fiendish exultation, that an unseen person who gazed at the moment into the room, seeing a tall dark figure, dilated by the gloom, for it was deepening twilight, and a countenance from which everything human was banished, thought he beheld a demon, and, fascinated by terror, could not withdraw his eyes. At the same moment, too, the queen's favourite dog, which was couched at her feet, and for a short time previously had been uttering a low growl, now broke into a fierce bark, and sprang towards the passage-window. Mary turned to ascertain the cause of the animal's disquietude, and perceived that it had stiffened in every joint, while its barking changed to a dismal howl. Not without misgiving, she glanced towards the window—and there, at the very place whence she had often heard that the murderers had gazed upon the slumbering innocents before the bloody deed was done—there, between those bars, she beheld a hideous black mask, through the holes of which glared a pair of flashing orbs.

PASSAGE IN THE BLOODY TOWER BY WHICH THE MURDERERS APPROACHED.

Repressing a cry of alarm, she called Renard's attention to the object, when she was equally startled by his appearance. He seemed transfixed with horror, with his right hand extended towards the mysterious object, and clenched, while the left grasped his sword. Suddenly, he regained his consciousness, and drawing his rapier, dashed to the door,—but ere he could open it, the mask had disappeared. He hurried along the passage in the direction of the lieutenant's lodgings, when he encountered some one who appeared to be advancing towards him. Seizing this person by the throat and presenting his sword to his breast, he found from the voice that it was Nightgall.

NORTH SIDE OF THE ROOM IN WHICH THE PRINCES WERE MURDERED.

The Death Warrant.

NORTH VIEW OF THE BLOODY TOWER.

XXXIV.—HOW THE PRINCESS ELIZABETH WAS CONFRONTED WITH SIR THOMAS WYAT IN THE TORTURE-CHAMBER.

As Elizabeth passed beneath the portal of the Bloody Tower, on her way to the lieutenant's lodgings, whither she was conducted after quitting Traitor's Gate, by Bedingfeld and Sussex, she encountered the giants, who doffed their caps at her approach, and fell upon their knees. All three were greatly affected, especially Magog, whose soft and sensitive nature was completely overcome. Big tears rolled down his cheeks, and in attempting to utter a few words of consolation, his voice failed him. Touched by his distress, Elizabeth halted for a moment, and laying her hand on his broad shoulder, said in a tone, and with a look calculated to enforce her words, "Bear up, good fellow, and like a man. If I shed no tears for myself, those who love me need shed none. It is the duty of my friends to comfort—not to dishearten me. My ease is not so hopeless as you think. The queen will never condemn the innocent, and unheard. Get up, I say, and put a bold face on the matter, or you are not your father's son."

Roused by this address, Magog obeyed, and rearing his bulky frame to its full height, so that his head almost touched the spikes of the portcullis, cried in a voice of thunder, "Would your innocence might be proved by the combat, madam, as in our—" and he hesitated,—"I mean your royal father's time! I would undertake to maintain your truth against any odds. Nay, I and my brethren would bid defiance to the whole host of your accusers."

"Though I may not claim you as champions," replied Elizabeth; "I will fight my own battle, as stoutly as you could fight it for me."

"And your grace's courage will prevail," rejoined Og.

"My innocence will," returned Elizabeth.

"Right," cried Gog. "Your grace, I am assured, would no more harbour disloyalty against the queen than we should; seeing that—"

"Enough," interrupted the princess, hastily. "Farewell, good friends," she continued, extending her hand to them, which they eagerly pressed to their lips, "farewell! be of good cheer. No man shall have cause to weep for me."

"This is a proud, though a sad day," observed Og, who was the last honoured by the princess's condescension, "and will never be obliterated from my memory. By my father's beard!" he added, gazing rapturously at the long, taper fingers he was permitted to touch, "it is the most beautiful hand I ever beheld, and whiter than the driven snow."

Pleased by the compliment—for she was by no means insensible to admiration,—Elizabeth forgave its unseasonableness for its evident sincerity, and smilingly departed. But she had scarcely ascended the steps leading to the Green, when she was chilled by the sight of Renard, who was standing at the northern entrance of the Bloody Tower, wrapped in his cloak, and apparently waiting to see her pass.

As she drew near, he stepped forward, and made her a profound, but sarcastic salutation. His insolence, however, failed in its effect upon Elizabeth. Eyeing him with the utmost disdain, she observed to Bedingfeld, "Put that Spanish knave out of my path. And he who will remove him from the queen's councils will do both her and me a good turn."

"Your grace has sufficient room to pass," returned Renard, with bitter irony, and laying his hand upon the hilt of his sword, as if determined to resist any attempt to remove him. "Your prison within the Bell Tower is prepared, and if my counsels have any weight with her majesty, you will quit it only to take the same path, and ascend the same scaffold as your mother, Anne Boleyn."

"Another such taunt," cried Sussex, fiercely, "and neither the sacred character of your office, nor the protection of the queen, shall save you from my sword."

And he thrust him forcibly backwards.

Elizabeth moved on at a slow and stately pace, while the guard closing round her and Sussex, opposed the points of their halberds to the infuriated ambassador.

"Your highness has increased Renard's enmity," observed Bedingfeld, with a troubled look.

"I fear him not," replied Elizabeth, dauntlessly. "Let him do his worst. English honesty will ever prove more than a match for Spanish guile."

Entering the lieutenant's lodgings, and traversing the long gallery already described as running in a westerly direction, Elizabeth soon reached the upper chamber of the Bell Tower, which, she was informed by Sir Thomas Brydges, was appointed for her prison.

"It is a sorry lodging for a king's daughter," she observed, "and for one who may be queen of this realm. But since my sister will have it so, I must make shift with it. How many attendants are allowed me?"

"One female," replied Brydges.

"Why not deprive me of all?" cried the princess, passionately. "This chamber will barely accommodate me. I will be alone."

"As your grace pleases,'" replied Brydges, "but I cannot exceed my authority."

"Can I write to the queen?" demanded Elizabeth.

"You will be furnished with writing-materials, if it is your purpose to prepare your confession," returned the lieutenant. "But it must be delivered to the council, who will exercise their discretion as to transmitting it to her highness."

"Ah!" exclaimed the princess, "am I at *their* mercy?"

"Alas! madam, you are so," replied Bedingfeld; "but the chancellor is your friend."

"I am not sure of it," returned Elizabeth. "Oh! that I could see the queen, were it but for one minute. My mother perished because she could not obtain a hearing of my royal sire, whose noble nature was abused in respect to her; and the Duke of Somerset himself told me, that if his brother the Admiral had been allowed speech of him, he would never have consented to his death.

But it is ever thus. The throne is surrounded by a baneful circle, whose business is to prevent the approach of truth. They keep me from my sister's presence, well knowing that I could clear myself at once, while they fill her ears with false reports. Bedingfeld, you are her faithful servant, and, therefore, not my enemy. Tell her, if she will grant me an audience alone, or before her councillors, I will either approve my innocence, or consent to lose my head. Above all, implore her to let me be confronted with Wyat, that the truth may be extorted from him."

"The interview would little benefit your grace," remarked Brydges. "Wyat confesses your privity to the rebellion."

"He lies," replied Elizabeth, fiercely. "The words have been put into his mouth with the vain hope of pardon. But he will recant them if he sees me. He dare not—will not look me in the face, and aver that I am a partner in his foul practices. But I will not believe it of him. Despite his monstrous treason, he is too brave, too noble-minded, to act so recreant a part."

"Wyat has undergone the question ordinary, and extraordinary, madam," replied Brydges; "and though he endured the first with surprising constancy, his fortitude sank under the severity of the latter application."

"I forgive him," rejoined Elizabeth, in a tone of deep commiseration. "But it proves nothing. He avowed thus much to escape further torture."

"It may be," returned Brydges, "and for your grace's sake I hope it is so. But his confession, signed with his own hand, has been laid before the queen."

"Ah!" exclaimed Elizabeth, sinking into the only seat which the dungeon contained.

"I beseech your highness to compose yourself," cried Bedingfeld, compassionately. "We will withdraw and leave you to the care of your attendant."

"I want no assistance," replied Elizabeth, recovering herself. "Will you entreat her majesty to grant me an audience on the terms I have named, and in the presence of Wyat?"

"It must be speedy, then," remarked Brydges, "for he is adjudged to die to-morrow."

"To-morrow!" echoed Elizabeth. "Nay, then, good Bedingfeld, seek the queen without delay. Implore her by the love she once bore me—by the love I am assured she bears me still—to interrogate me before this traitor. If he perishes with this confession uncontradicted, I am lost."

"Your words shall be repeated to her highness," replied Bedingfeld, "and I will not fail to add my entreaties to your own. But I cannot give a hope that your request will be granted."

"It is fortunate for your highness that the queen visits the Tower to-day," observed Brydges. "Her arrival is momently expected. As I live!" he exclaimed, as the bell was rung overhead, and answered by the beating of drums and the discharge of cannon from the batteries, "she is here!"

"It is Heaven's interposition in my behalf," cried Elizabeth, "Go to her at once, Bedingfeld. Let not the traitor, Renard, get the start of you. I may live to requite the service. Go—go." #

The old knight obeyed, and the others immediately afterwards retired, closing the door upon the princess, and placing a guard outside.

Left alone, Elizabeth flew to the narrow, and strongly-grated loophole, commanding the southern ward, through which the queen must necessarily pass on her way to the palace, in the hope of catching a glimpse of her. She had not to wait long. Loud fanfares of trumpets resounded from the gate of the By-ward Tower. These martial flourishes were succeeded by the trampling of steeds, and fresh discharges of ordnance, and the next moment, a numerous retinue of horse and foot emerged from the gateway. Just as the royal litter appeared, it was stopped by Sir Henry Bedingfeld, and the curtains were drawn aside by Mary's own hand. It was a moment of intense interest to Elizabeth, and she watched the countenance of the old knight, as if her life depended upon each word he uttered. At first, she could not see the queen's face, but as Bedingfeld concluded, Mary leaned forward, and looked up at the Bell Tower. Uncertain whether she could be seen, Elizabeth determined to make her presence known, and thrusting her hand through the bars, waved her kerchief. Mary instantly drew back. The curtains of the litter were closed; Bedingfeld stepped aside; and the cavalcade moved on.

"She will not see me!" cried Elizabeth, sinking back in despair. "I shall perish like my mother."

The princess's agitation did not subside for some time. Expecting Bedingfeld to return with the tidings that Mary had refused her request, she listened anxiously to every sound, in the hope that it might announce his arrival. Hour after hour passed by and he came not, and concluding that he did not like to be the bearer of ill news, or what was yet more probable, that he was not allowed to visit her, she made up her mind to the worst. Elizabeth had not the same resources as Jane under similar circumstances. Though sincerely religious, she had not the strong piety that belonged to the other, nor could she, like her, divorce herself from the world, and devote herself wholly to God. Possessing the greatest fortitude, she had no resignation, and while capable of enduring any amount of physical suffering, could not controul her impatience. Her thoughts were bitter and mortifying enough, but she felt no humiliation; and the only regrets she indulged were at having acted so unwise a part. Scalding tears bedewed her cheeks—tears that would never have been shed, if any one had been present; and her mingled emotions of rage and despair were so powerful, that she had much ado to overcome them. Ungovernable fury against Mary took possession of her, and she pondered upon a thousand acts of revenge. Then came the dreadful sense of her present situation—of its hopelessness—its despair. She looked at the stone walls by which she was inclosed, and invoked them to fall upon her and crush her—and she rushed towards the massive and iron-girded door, as if she would dash herself against it with impotent fury. Her breast was ravaged by fierce and conflicting passions; and when she again returned to her seat, she grasped it convulsively to prevent herself from executing the desperate deeds that suggested themselves to her. In after years, when the crown was placed upon her head, and she grasped one of the most powerful sceptres ever swayed by female hand—when illustrious captives were placed in that very dungeon by her command, and one royal victim, near almost to her as a sister, lingered out her days in hopeless captivity, only to end them on the block— at such seasons, she often recalled her own imprisonment—often in imagination endured its agonies, but never once with a softened or relenting heart. The sole thought that now touched her, and subdued her violence, was that of Courtenay. Neither his unworthiness nor his inconstancy could shake her attachment. She loved him deeply and devotedly—with all the strength and fervour of her character; and though she had much difficulty in saving him from her contempt, this feeling did not abate the force of her regard. The idea that he would perish with her, in some degree reconciled her to her probable fate.

Thus meditating, alternately roused by the wildest resentment, and softened by thoughts of love, Elizabeth passed the remainder of the day without interruption. Worn out, at length, she was about to dispose herself to slumber, when the door was opened, and Sir Thomas Brydges, accompanied by two serving-men and a female attendant, entered the room. Provisions were placed before her by the men, who instantly withdrew, and Brydges was about to follow, leaving the female attendant behind, when Elizabeth stopped him, and inquired what answer Sir Henry Bedingfeld had brought from the queen.

"My orders are to hold no communication with your grace," replied the lieutenant.

"At least, tell me when I am to be examined by the council?" rejoined Elizabeth. "The meanest criminal has a right to be so informed!"

But Brydges shook his head, and quitting the chamber, closed the door, and barred it outside.

Controlling her feelings, as she was now no longer alone, Elizabeth commanded her attendant to awaken her in an hour, and threw herself upon the couch. Her injunctions were strictly complied with, and she arose greatly refreshed. A lamp had been left her, and taking up a book of prayers, she addressed herself to her devotions, and while thus occupied her mind gradually resumed its composure. About midnight, the door was opened by the lieutenant, who entered the room attended by Nightgall, and two other officials in sable robes, while a guard of halberdiers, bearing torches, remained without.

"I must request your grace to follow me," said Brydges.

"Whither?" demanded Elizabeth, rising. "To the queen's presence?"

The lieutenant made no answer.

"To the council?" pursued the princess,—"or to execution? No matter. I am ready." And she motioned the lieutenant to lead on.

Sir Thomas Brydges obeyed, and followed by the princess, traversed the gallery, descended the great staircase, and entered a spacious chamber on the ground floor. Here he paused for a moment, while a sliding panel in the wall was opened, through which he and his companion passed.

A short flight of stone steps brought them to a dark narrow passage, and they proceeded silently and slowly along it, until their progress was checked by a strong iron door, which was unfastened and closed behind them by Nightgall. The jarring of the heavy bolts, as they were shot into their sockets, resounded hollowly along the arched roof of the passage, and smote forcibly upon Elizabeth's heart, and she required all her constitutional firmness to support her.

They were now in one of those subterranean galleries, often described before, on either side of which were cells, and the clangour called forth many a dismal response. Presently afterwards, they arrived at the head of a staircase, which Elizabeth descended, and found herself, in the torture-chamber. A dreadful spectacle met her gaze. At one side of the room, which was lighted by a dull lamp from the roof, and furnished as before with numberless hideous implements—each seeming to have been recently employed—sat, or rather was supported, a wretched man upon whom every refinement of torture had evidently been practised. A cloak was thrown over his lower limbs, but his ghastly and writhen features proved the extremity of suffering to which he had been subjected. Elizabeth could scarcely believe that in this miserable object, whom it would have been a mercy to despatch, she beheld the once bold and haughty Sir Thomas Wyat.

Placed on the corner of a leathern couch, and supported by Wolfytt and Sorrocold, the latter of whom bathed his temples with some restorative, Wyat fixed his heavy eyes upon the princess. But her attention was speedily diverted from him to another person, whose presence checked her feelings. This was the queen, who stood on one side, with Gardiner and Renard. Opposite them was Courtenay, with his arms folded upon his breast. The latter looked up as Elizabeth entered the chamber; and after gazing at her for a moment, turned his regards, with an irrepressible shudder, to Wyat. Knowing that her safety depended upon her firmness, though her heart bled for the tortured man, Elizabeth disguised all appearance of compassion, and throwing herself at the queen's feet, cried, "Heaven bless your highness, for granting me this interview! I can now prove my innocence."

"In what way?" demanded Mary coldly. "It would indeed rejoice me to find I have been deceived. But I cannot shut my ears to the truth. Yon traitor," she continued, pointing to Wyat, "who dared to rise in arms against his sovereign, distinctly charges you with participation in his rebellious designs. I have his confession, taken from his own lips, and signed with his own hand, wherein he affirms, by his hopes of mercy from the Supreme Judge before whom he will shortly appear to answer for his offences, that you encouraged his plans for my dethronement, and sought to win the crown for yourself, in order to bestow it with your hand upon your lover, Courtenay."

"It is false," cried Elizabeth;—"false as the caitiff who invented it—false as the mischievous councillor who stands beside you, and who trusts to work my ruin,—but, by our father's soul it shall go hard if I do not requite him! Your majesty has not a more loyal subject than myself, nor has any of your subjects a more loving sister. This wretched Wyat, whose condition would move my pity were he not so heinous a traitor, may have written to me, but, on my faith, I have never received his letters."

"Lord Russell's son declares that he delivered them into your own hands," observed Mary.

"Another he, as false as the first," replied Elizabeth. "It is a plot, your highness—a contrivance of my enemy, Simon Renard. Where is Lord Russell's son? Why is he not here?"

"You shall see him anon, since you desire it," replied Mary. "Like yourself, he is a prisoner in the Tower. But these assertions do not clear you."

"Your highness says you have Wyat's confession," rejoined Elizabeth. "What faith is to be attached to it? It has been wrung from him by the severity of the torture to which he has been subjected. Look at his shattered frame, and say whether it is not likely he would purchase relief from such suffering as he must have endured at any cost. The sworn tormentors are here. Let them declare how often they have stretched him on the rack—how often applied the thumbscrew,—how often delivered him to the deadly embraces of the scavenger's daughter, before this false charge was wrung from him. Speak, fellows! how often have you racked him?"

But the tormentors did not dare to reply. A stifled groan broke from Wyat, and a sharp convulsion passed over his frame.

"The question has only extorted the truth," observed Mary.

"If the accusation so obtained be availing, the retraction must be equally so," replied Elizabeth. "Sir Thomas Wyat," she exclaimed, in aloud and authoritative tone, and stepping towards him, "if you would not render your name for ever infamous, you will declare my innocence."

Elizabeth confronted with Wyat in the Torture Chamber.

The sufferer gazed at her, as if he did not clearly comprehend what was said to him.

Elizabeth repeated the command, and in a more peremptory tone.

"What have I declared against you?" asked Wyat, faintly.

"You have accused me of countenancing your traitorous practices against the queen's highness, who now stands before you," rejoined Elizabeth. "You well know it is false. Do not die with such a stain upon your knighthood and your honour. The worst is over. Further application of the rack would be fatal, and it will not be resorted to, because you would thus escape the scaffold. You can have, therefore, no object in adhering to this vile fabrication of my enemies. Retract your words, I command you, and declare my innocence."

"I do," replied Wyat, in a firm tone. "I have falsely accused you, and was induced to do so in the hope of pardon. I unsay all I have said, and will die proclaiming your innocence."

"It is well," replied Elizabeth, with a triumphant glance at the queen.

"Place me at the feet of the princess," said Wyat to his supporters. "Your pardon, madam," he added, as the order was obeyed.

"You have it," replied Elizabeth, scarcely able to repress her emotion. "May God forgive you, as I do."

"Then your former declaration was false, thou perjured traitor?" cried Mary, in amazement.

"What I have said, I have said," rejoined Wyat; "what I now say is the truth." And he motioned the attendants to raise him, the pain of kneeling being too exquisite for endurance.

"And you will adhere to your declaration?" pursued Mary.

"To my last breath," gasped Wyat.

"At whose instigation were you induced to charge the princess with conspiring with you?" demanded Renard, stepping forward.

"At yours," returned Wyat, with a look of intense hatred. "You, who have deceived the queen—deceived me—and would deceive the devil your master, if you could—you urged me to it—you—ha! ha!" And with a convulsive attempt at laughter, which communicated a horrible expression to his features, he sank into the arms of Wolfytt, and was conveyed to a cell at the back of the chamber, the door of which was closed.

"My innocence is established," said Elizabeth, turning to the queen.

"Not entirely," answered Mary. "Wyat's first charge was supported by Lord Russell's son."

"Take me to him, or send for him hither," rejoined Elizabeth. "He has been suborned, like Wyat, by Renard. I will stake my life that he denies it."

"I will not refute the idle charge brought against me," observed Renard, who had been for a moment confounded by Wyat's accusation. "Your majesty will at once discern its utter groundlessness."

"I ask no clemency for myself," interposed Courtenay, speaking for the first time; "but I beseech your highness not to let the words of that false and crafty Spaniard weigh against your sister. From his perfidious counsels all these disasters have originated."

"You would screen the princess in the hope of obtaining her hand, my lord," replied Mary. "I see through your purpose, and will defeat it."

"So far from it," replied the Earl, "I here solemnly renounce all pretensions to her."

"Courtenay!" exclaimed Elizabeth, in a tone of anguish.

"Recent events have cured me of love and ambition," pursued the Earl, without regarding her. "All I desire is freedom."

"And is it for one so unworthy that I have entertained this regard?" cried Elizabeth. "But I am rightly punished."

"You are so," replied Mary, bitterly. "And you now taste some of the pangs you inflicted upon me."

"Hear me, gracious madam," cried Courtenay, prostrating himself before the queen. "I have avowed thus much, that you may attach due credit to what I am about to declare concerning Renard. My heart was yours, and yours only, till I allowed myself to be influenced by him. I knew not then his design, but it has since been fully revealed. It was to disgust you with me that he might accomplish the main object of his heart—the match with the prince of Spain. He succeeded too well. Utterly inexperienced, I readily yielded to the allurements he spread before me. My indiscretions were reported to you. But, failing in alienating me from your regard, he tried a deeper game, and chose out as his tool, the princess Elizabeth."

"Ha!" exclaimed Mary.

"He it was," pursued Courtenay, "who first attracted my attention towards her—who drew invidious comparisons between her youthful charms and your Majesty's more advanced age. He it was, who hinted at the possibility of an alliance between us—who led me on step by step till I was completely enmeshed. I will own it, I became desperately enamoured of the princess. I thought no more of your highness—of the brilliant prospects lost to me; and, blinded by my passion, became reckless of the perilous position in which I placed myself. But now that I can look calmly behind me, I see where, and why I fell—and I fully comprehend the tempter's motives."

"What says your excellency to this?" demanded Mary, sternly.

"Much that the Earl of Devonshire has asserted is true," replied Renard. "But in rescuing your majesty, at any cost, from so unworthy an alliance, I deserve your thanks, rather than your reprobation. And I shall ever rejoice that I have succeeded."

"You have succeeded at my expense, and at the expense of many of my bravest and best subjects," replied Mary, severely. "But the die is cast, and cannot be recalled."

"True," replied Renard, with a smile of malignant satisfaction.

"Will your highness pursue your investigations further tonight?" demanded Gardiner.

"No," replied the queen, who appeared lost in thought. "Let the Princess Elizabeth be taken back to the Bell Tower, and Courtenay to his prison in the Bowyer Tower. I will consider upon their sentence. Wyat is respited for the present. I shall interrogate him further."

With this, she quitted the torture-chamber with her train, and the prisoners were removed as she had directed.

XXXV.—-HOW XIT DISCOVERED THE SECRET OF HIS BIRTH; AND HOW HE WAS KNIGHTED UNDER THE TITLE OF SIR NARCISSUS LE GRAND.

Life is full of the saddest and the strongest contrasts. The laugh of derision succeeds the groan of despair—the revel follows the funeral—the moment that ushers the new-born babe into existence, is the last, perchance, of its parent—without the prison walls, all is sunshine and happiness—within, gloom and despair. But throughout the great city which it commanded, search where you might, no stronger contrasts of rejoicing and despair could be found, than were now to be met with in the Tower of London. While, on the one hand, every dungeon was crowded, and scarcely an hour passed that some miserable sufferer did not expire under the hand of the secret tormentor, or the public executioner; on the other, there was mirth, revelry, and all the customary celebrations of victory. As upon Mary's former triumph over her enemies, a vast fire was lighted in the centre of the Tower Green, and four oxen, roasted whole at it, were distributed, together with a proportionate supply of bread, and a measure of ale or mead, in rations, to every soldier in the fortress; and as may be supposed, the utmost joviality prevailed. To each warder was allotted an angel of gold, and a dish from the royal table; while to the three giants were given the residue of a grand banquet, a butt of Gascoign wine, and, in consideration of their valiant conduct during the siege, their yearly fee, by the queen's command, was trebled. On the night of these festivities, a magnificent display of fireworks took place on the Green, and an extraordinary illumination was effected by means of a row of barrels filled with pitch, ranged along the battlements of the White Tower, which being suddenly lighted, cast forth a glare that illumined the whole fortress, and was seen at upwards of twenty miles' distance.

Not unmindful of the queen's promise, Xit, though unable to find a favourable opportunity of claiming it, did not fail to assume all the consequence of his anticipated honours. He treated those with whom he associated with the utmost haughtiness; and though his arrogant demeanour only excited the merriment of the giants, it drew many a sharp retort, and not a few blows, from such as were not disposed to put up with his insolence. The subject that perpetually occupied his thoughts, was the title he ought to assume;—for he was thoroughly dissatisfied with his present appellation. "Base and contemptible name!" he exclaimed. "How I loathe it!—and how did I acquire it? It was bestowed upon me, I suppose, in my infancy, by Og, to whose care I was committed. A mystery hangs over my birth. I must unravel it. Let me see:—Two-and-twenty years ago, (come Martinmas,) I was deposited at the door of the Byward Tower in a piece of blanket!—unworthy swaddling-cloth for so illustrious an infant—a circumstance which fully proves that my noble parents were anxious for concealment. Stay! I have heard of changelings—of elfin children left by fairies in the room of those they steal. Can I be such a one? A shudder crosses my frame at the bare idea. And yet my activity, my daring, my high mental qualities, my unequalled symmetry of person, small though it be—all these seem to warrant the supposition. Yes! I am a changeling. I am a fairy child. Yet hold! this will not do. Though I may entertain these notions in secret of my alliance with the invisible world, they will not be accepted by the incredulous multitude. I must have some father, probable, or improbable. Who could he have been? Or who *might* he have been? Let me see. Sir Thomas More was imprisoned in the Tower about the time of my birth. Could I not be his son? It is more than probable. So was the Bishop of Rochester. But to claim descent from him would bring scandal, upon the church. Besides, he was a Catholic prelate. No, it must be Sir Thomas More. That will account for my wit. Then about the same time there were the Lord Darcy; and Robert Salisbury, Abbot of Vale Crucis; the Prior of Doncaster; Sir Thomas Percy; Sir Francis Bygate; and Sir John Bulmer. All these were prisoners, so that I have plenty to choose from. I will go and consult Og. I wonder whether he has kept the piece of blanket in which I was wrapped. It will be a gross omission if he has not."

The foregoing soliloquy occurred in one of the galleries of the palace, where the vain-glorious mannikin was lingering in the hope of being admitted to the royal presence. No sooner did the idea of consulting Og on the subject of his birth occur to him, than he set off to the By-ward Tower, where he found the two unmarried giants employed upon a huge smoking dish of baked meat, and, notwithstanding his importunity, neither of them appeared willing to attend to him. Thus baffled, and his appetite sharpened by the savoury odour of the viands, Xit seized a knife and fork, and began to ply them with great zeal. The meal over, and two ponderous jugs that flanked the board emptied of their contents, Og leaned his huge frame against the wall, and in a drowsy tone informed the dwarf that he was ready to listen to him.

"No sleeping, then, my master," cried Xit, springing upon his knee, and tweaking his nose. "I have a matter of the utmost importance to consult you about. You must be wide awake."

"What is it? replied the good-humoured giant, yawning as if he would have swallowed the teazing mannikin.

"It relates to my origin," replied Xit. "Am I the son of a nobleman?"

"I should rather say you were the offspring of some ape escaped from the menagerie," answered Og, bursting into a roar of laughter, in which he was joined by Gog, much to the discomfiture of the cause of their merriment. "You have all the tricks-of the species."

"Dare to repeat that insinuation, base Titan," cried Xit, furiously, and drawing his sword, "and I will be thy death. I am as illustriously descended as thyself, and on both sides too, whereas thy mother was a frowzy fish-wife. Know that I am the son of Sir Thomas More."

"Sir Thomas More!" echoed both giants, laughing more immoderately than ever. "What has put that notion into thy addle pate?"

"My better genius," replied Xit, "and unless you can show me who *was* my father, I shall claim descent from him."

"You will only expose yourself to ridicule," returned Og, patting the mannikin's shock head—a familiarity which he resented,—"and though I and my brethren laugh at you, and make a jest of you, we do not desire others to do so."

"Once graced by knighthood, no man, be he of my stature or of yours, my overgrown master, shall make a jest of me with impunity," replied Xit, proudly. "But since you think I am *not* the son of Sir Thomas More, from whom can I safely claim descent?"

"I would willingly assist you to a father," replied Og, smothering a laugh, "but on my faith, I can think of none more probable than Hairun's pet monkey, or perhaps old Max."

"Anger me not," shrieked Xit, in extremity of fury, "or you will rue it. What has become of the blanket in which I was wrapped?"

"The blanket!" exclaimed Og, "why, it was a strip scarcely bigger than my hand."

"Is it lost?" demanded Xit, eagerly.

"I fear so," replied Og. "Stay! now I recollect, I patched an old pair of hose with it."

"Patched a pair of hose with it!" cried Xit. "You deserve to go in tatters during the rest of your days. You have destroyed the sole clue to my origin."

"Nay, if that blanket will guide you, I have taken the best means of preserving it," rejoined Og;—"for I think I have the hose still."

"Where are they?" inquired Xit. "Let me see them instantly."

"If they still exist, they are in a large chest in the upper chamber," replied Og. "But be not too much elated, for I fear we shall be disappointed."

"At all events, let us search without a moment's delay," rejoined Xit, jumping down, and hurrying up the staircase.

He was followed somewhat more leisurely by the two giants, and the trunk was found crammed under a heap of lumber into an embrasure. The key was lost, but as Xit's impatience would not allow him to wait to have it unfastened by a smith, Og forced it open with the head of a halbert. It contained a number of old buskins, cloaks of all hues and fashions, doublets, pantoufles, caps, buff-boots and hose. Of the latter there were several pair, and though many were threadbare enough, it did not appear that any were patched.

Xit, who had plunged into the trunk to examine each article, was greatly disappointed.

"I fear they are lost," observed Og.

"It would seem so," replied Xit, "for there are only a doublet and cloak left. Oh! that a worshipful knight's history should hang on so slight a tenure!"

"Many a knight's history has hung on less," replied Gog. "But what have we rolled up in that corner?"

"As I live, a pair of watchet-coloured hose," cried Xit.

"The very pair we are in quest of," rejoined Og. "Unfold them, and you will find the piece of blanket in the seat."

Xit obeyed, and mounting on the side of the box held out the huge garments, and there, undoubtedly in the region intimated by Og, was a piece of dirty flannel.

"And this, then, was my earliest covering," apostrophised Xit. "In this fragment of woollen cloth my tender limbs were swathed!"

"Truly were they," replied Og, laughing. "And when I first beheld thee it was ample covering. But what light does it throw upon thy origin?"

"That remains to be seen," returned Xit. And unsheathing his dagger he began to unrip the piece of flannel from the garment in which it was stitched.

The two giants watched his proceedings in silence, and glanced significantly at each other. At length, Xit tore it away.

"It is a labour in vain," observed Og.

"Not so," replied Xit. "See you not that this corner is doubled over. There is a name worked within it."

"The imp is right," cried Og. "How came I to overlook it." And he would have snatched the flannel from Xit, but the dwarf darted away, crying, "No one shall have a hand in the discovery but myself. Stand off!"

Trembling with eagerness, he then cut open the corner, and found, worked withinside, the words: *NARCISSUS LE GRAND.*

"Narcissus Le Grand!" exclaimed Xit, triumphantly. "That was my father's title. He must have been a nobleman."

"If that was your father's name," returned Gog, "and I begin to think you have stumbled upon the right person at last, he was a Frenchman, and groom of the pantry to Queen Anne Boleyn."

"He was a dwarf like yourself," added Og, "and though the ugliest being I ever beheld, had extraordinary personal vanity."

"In which respect he mightily resembled his son," laughed Gog; "and since we have found out the father, I think I can give a shrewd guess at the mother."

"I hope she was a person of distinction?" cried Xit, whose countenance had fallen at the knowledge he had acquired of his paternity.

"She was a scullion," replied Gog,—"by name Mab Leather-barrow."

"A scullion!" ejaculated Xit, indignantly. "I, the son of a scullion,—and of one so basely-named as Leatherbarrow—impossible!"

"I am as sure of it as of my existence," replied Og. "Your mother was not a jot taller, or more well-favoured than your father; and they both, I now remember, disappeared about the time you were found."

"Which name will you adopt—Le Grand, or Leatherbarrow?" demanded Gog, maliciously.

"This is an unlucky discovery," thought Xit. "I had better have left my parentage alone. The son of a groom of the pantry and a scullion. What a degrading conjunction! However, I will make the most of it, and not let them have the laugh against me. I shall assume my father's name," he added aloud—"Sir Narcissus Le Grand—and a good, well-sounding title it is, as need be desired."

"It is to be hoped all will have forgotten the former bearer of it," laughed Og.

"I care not who remembers it," replied Xit; "the name bespeaks noble descent. Call me in future Narcissus Le Grand. The title fits me exactly,— Narcissus expressing my personal accomplishments—Le Grand my majesty. For the present, you may put 'master' to my name. You will shortly have to use a more honourable style of address. Farewell, sirs."

And thrusting the piece of flannel into his doublet, he strutted to the door.

"Farewell, sweet Master Narcissus," cried Og.

"Farewell, Leatherbarrow," added Gog.

"Le Grand," corrected Xit, halting, with a dignified air; "Le Grand, henceforth, is my name." And he marched off with his head so erect that, unfortunately missing his footing, he tumbled down the staircase. Picking himself up before the giants, whose laughter enraged him, could reach him, he darted off, and did not return till a late hour, when they had retired to rest.

Two days after this discovery,—the queen being then at the Tower,—as he was pacing the grand gallery of the palace, according to custom, an usher tapped him on the shoulder, and desired him to follow him. With a throbbing heart Xit obeyed, and, putting all the dignity he could command into his deportment, entered the presence-chamber. On that very morning, as good luck would have it, his tailor had brought him his new habiliments; and arrayed in a purple velvet mantle lined with carnation-coloured silk, a crimson doublet slashed with white, orange-tawny hose, yellow buskins fringed with gold, and a green velvet cap, decorated with a plume of ostrich feathers, and looped with a diamond aigrette, he cut, in his own opinion, no despicable figure.

If the dwarf had entertained any doubts as to why he was summoned they would have been dispersed at once, as he advanced, by observing that the three giants stood at a little distance from the queen, and that she was attended only by a few dames of honour, her female jester, and the vice-chamberlain, Sir John Gage, who held a crimson velvet cushion, on which was laid a richly-ornamented sword. A smile crossed the queen's countenance as Xit drew nigh, and an irrepressible titter spread among the dames of honour. Arrived within a few yards of the throne, the mannikin prostrated himself as gracefully as he could. But he was destined to mishaps. And in this the most important moment of his life, his sword, which was of extraordinary length, got between his legs, and he was compelled to remove it before his knee would touch the ground.

"We have not forgotten our promise—rash though it was," observed Mary, "and have summoned thy comrades to be witness to the distinction we are about to confer upon thee. In the heat of the siege, we promised that whoso would bring us Bret, alive or dead, should have his request, be it what it might. Thou wert his captor, and thou askest—"

"Knighthood at your majesty's hands," supplied Xit.

"How shall we name thee?" demanded Mary.

"Narcissus Le Grand," replied the dwarf. "I am called familiarly Xit. But it is a designation by which I do not desire to be longer distinguished."

Mary took the sword from Sir John Gage, and placing it upon the dwarf's shoulder, said, "Arise, Sir Narcissus."

The new-made knight immediately obeyed, and making a profound reverence to the queen, was about to retire, when she checked him.

"Tarry a moment, Sir Narcissus," she said. "I have a further favour to bestow upon you."

"Indeed!" cried the dwarf, out of his senses with delight. "I pray your majesty to declare it."

"You will need a dame," returned the queen.

"Of a truth," replied Sir Narcissus, tenderly ogling the bevy of beauties behind the throne, "I need one sadly."

"I will choose for you," said the queen.

"Your highness's condescension overwhelms me," rejoined Sir Narcissus, wondering which would fall to his share.

"This shall be your bride," continued the queen, pointing to Jane the Fool, "and I will give her a portion."

Sir Narcissus had some ado to conceal his mortification. Receiving the announcement with the best grace he could assume, he strutted up to Jane, and taking her hand, said, "You hear her highness's injunctions, sweetheart. You are to be Lady Le Grand. I need not ask your consent, I presume?"

"You shall never have it," replied Jane the Fool, with a coquettish toss of the head, "if her highness did not command it."

"I shall require to exert my authority early," thought Sir Narcissus, "or I shall share the fate of Magog."

"I, myself, will fix the day for your espousals," observed Mary. "Meanwhile, you have my permission to woo your intended bride for a few minutes in each day."

"*Only* a few minutes!" cried Sir Narcissus, with affected disappointment. "I could dispense with even that allowance," he added to himself.

"I cannot reward your services as richly," continued Mary, addressing the gigantic brethren, "but I am not unmindful of them,—nor shall they pass unrequited. Whenever you have a boon to ask, hesitate not to address me."

The three giants bowed their lofty heads.

"A purse of gold will be given to each of you," continued the queen; "and on the day of his marriage, I shall bestow a like gift upon Sir Narcissus." She then waved her hand, and the new-made knight and his companions withdrew.

XXXVI.—HOW CHOLMONDELEY LEARNT THE HISTORY OF CICELY; HOW NIGHTGALL ATTEMPTED TO ASSASSINATE RENARD; AND OF THE TERRIBLE FATE THAT BEFEL HIM.

Cuthbert Cholmondeley, after upwards of a week's solitary confinement, underwent a rigorous examination by certain of the Council relative to his own share in the conspiracy, and his knowledge of the different parties connected with it. He at once admitted that he had taken a prominent part in the siege, but refused to answer any other questions. "I confess myself guilty of treason and rebellion against the queen's highness," he said, "and I ask no further mercy than a speedy death. But if the word of one standing in peril of his life may be taken, I solemnly declare, and call upon you to attest my declaration,—that the Lady Jane Grey is innocent of all share in the recent insurrection. For a long time, she was kept in total ignorance of the project, and when it came to her knowledge, she used every means, short of betraying it,—tears, entreaties, menaces,—to induce her husband to abandon the design."

"This declaration will not save her," replied Sir Edward Hastings, who was one of the interrogators, sternly,—"By not revealing the conspiracy, she acquiesced in it. Her first duty was to her sovereign."

"I am aware of it, and so is the unfortunate lady herself," replied Cholmondeley. "But I earnestly entreat you, in pity for her misfortunes, to report what I have said to the queen."

"I will not fail to do so," returned Hastings; "but I will not deceive you. Her fate is sealed. And now, touching the Princess Elizabeth's share in this unhappy affair. Do you know aught concerning it?"

"Nothing whatever," replied Cholmondeley; "and if I did, I would not reveal it."

"Take heed what you say, sir," rejoined Sir Thomas Brydges, who was likewise among the examiners, "or I shall order you to be more sharply questioned."

Nightgall heard this menace with savage exultation.

"The rack will wrest nothing from me," said Cholmondeley, firmly.

Brydges immediately sat down at a table, and writing out a list of questions to be put to the prisoner, added an order for the torture, and delivered it to Nightgall.

Without giving Cholmondeley time to reflect upon his imprudence, the jailor hurried him away, and he did not pause till he came to the head of the stairs leading to the torture-chamber. On reaching the steps, Nightgall descended first, but though he opened the door with great caution, a glare of lurid light burst forth, and a dismal groan smote the ears of the listener. It was followed by a creaking noise, the meaning of which the esquire too well divined.

Some little time elapsed before the door was again opened, and the voice of Nightgall was heard from below calling to his attendants to bring down the prisoner. The first object that caught Cholmondeley's gaze on entering the fatal chamber, was a figure, covered from head to foot in a blood-coloured cloth. The sufferer, whoever he was, had just been released from the torture, as two assistants were supporting him, while Wolfytt was arranging the ropes on the rack. Sorrocold, also, who held a small cup filled with some pungent-smelling liquid, and a sprinkling-brush in his hand, was directing the assistants.

Horror-stricken at the sight, and filled with the conviction from the mystery observed, and the stature of the veiled person, that it was Lord Guilford Dudley, Cholmondeley uttered his name in a tone of piercing anguish. At the cry, the figure was greatly agitated—the arms struggled—and it was evident that an effort was made to speak. But only an inarticulate sound could be heard. The attendants looked disconcerted, and Nightgall stamping his foot angrily, ordered them to take their charge away. But Cholmondeley perceiving their intention, broke from those about him, and throwing himself at the feet of him whom he supposed to be Dudley, cried—"My dear, dear lord, it is I, your faithful esquire, Cuthbert Cholmondeley. Make some sign, if I am right in supposing it to be you."

The figure struggled violently, and shaking off the officials, raised the cloth, and disclosed the countenance of the unfortunate nobleman—but oil! how changed since Cholmondeley had seen him last—how ghastly, how distorted, how death-like, were his features!

"You here!" cried Dudley. "Where is Jane? Has she fled? Has she escaped?"

"She has surrendered herself," replied Cholmondeley, "in the hope of obtaining your pardon.'"

"False hope!—delusive expectation!" exclaimed Dudley, in a tone of the bitterest anguish. "She will share my fate. I could have died happy—could have defied these engines, if she had escaped—but now!—"

"Away with him!" interposed Nightgall. "Throw the cloth over his head."

"Oh God! I am her destroyer!" shrieked Dudley, as the order was obeyed, and he was forced out of the chamber.

Cholmondeley was then seized by Wolfytt and the others, and thrown upon his back on the floor. He made no resistance, well knowing it would be useless; and he determined, even if he should expire under the torture, to let no expression of anguish escape him. He had need of all his fortitude; for the sharpness of the suffering to which he was subjected by the remorseless Nightgall, was such as few could have withstood. But not a groan burst from him, though his whole frame seemed rent asunder by the dreadful tension.

"Go on," cried Nightgall, finding that Wolfytt and the others paused. "Turn the rollers round once more."

"You will wrench his bones from their sockets,—he will expire if you do," observed Sorrocold.

"No matter," replied Nightgall; "I have an order to question him sharply, and I will do so, at all hazards."

"Do so at your own responsibility, then," replied Sorrocold, retiring. "I tell you he will die if you strain him further."

"Go on, I say," thundered Nightgall. But as he spoke, the sufferer fainted, and Wolfytt refused to comply with the jailor's injunctions.

Cholmondeley was taken off the engine. Restoratives were applied by Sorrocold, and the questions proposed by the lieutenant put to him by Nightgall. But he returned no answer; and uttering an angry exclamation at his obstinacy, the jailor ordered him to be taken back to his cell, where he was thrown upon a heap of straw, and left without light or food.

For some time, Cholmondeley remained in a state of insensibility, and when he recovered, it was to endure far greater agony than he had experienced on the rack. His muscles were so strained that he was unable to move, and every bone in his body appeared broken. The thought, however, that Cicely was alive, and in the power of his hated rival, tormented him more sharply than his bodily suffering. Supposing her dead, though his heart was ever constant to her memory, and though he was a prey to deep and severe grief, yet the whirl of events in which he had been recently engaged had prevented him from dwelling altogether upon her loss. But now, when he knew that she still lived, and was in the power of Nightgall, all his passion—all his jealousy, returned with tenfold fury. The most dreadful suspicions crossed him; and his mental anguish was so great as to be almost intolerable. While thus tortured in body and mind, the door of his cell was opened, and Nightgall entered, dragging after him a female. The glare of the lamp so dazzled Cholmondeley's weakened vision, that he involuntarily closed his eyes. But what was his surprise to hear his own name pronounced by well-known accents, and, as soon as he could steady his gaze, to behold the features of Cicely—but so pale, so emaciated, that he could scarcely recognise them.

"There," cried Nightgall, with a look of fiendish exultation, pointing to Cholmondeley. "I told you you should see your lover. Glut your eyes with the sight. The arms that should have clasped you are nerveless—the eyes that gazed so passionately upon you, dim—the limbs that won your admiration, crippled. Look at him—and for the last time. And let him gaze on you, and see whether in these death-pale features—in this wasted form, there are any remains of the young and blooming maiden that won his heart."

"Cicely," cried Cholmondeley, making an ineffectual attempt to rise, "do I indeed behold you? I thought you dead."

"Would I were so," she cried, kneeling beside him, "rather than what I am. And to see you thus—and without the power to relieve you."

"You *can* relieve me of the worst pang I endure," returned Cholmondeley. "You have been long in the power of that miscreant—exposed to his violence, his ill-usage, to the worst of villany. Has he dared to abuse his power? Do not deceive me! Has he wronged you?—Are you his minion? Speak! And the answer will either kill me at once, or render my death on the scaffold happy. Speak! Speak!"

"I am yours, and yours only—in life or death, dear Cholmondeley," replied Cicely. "Neither entreaties nor force should make me his."

"The time is come when I will show you no further consideration," observed Nightgall, moodily. "And if the question your lover has just asked, is repeated, it shall be differently answered. You shall be mine to-morrow, either by your own free consent, or by force. I have spared you thus long, in the hope that you would relent, and not compel me to have recourse to means I would willingly avoid. Now, hear me. I have brought you hither to gratify my vengeance upon the miserable wretch, writhing at my feet, who has robbed me of your affections, and whose last moments I would embitter by the certainty that you are in my power. But though it will be much to me to forego the promised gratification of witnessing his execution, or knowing that he will be executed, yet I will purchase your compliance even at this price. Swear to wed me to-morrow, and to accompany me unresistingly whithersoever I may choose to take you, and, in return, I swear to free him."

"He made a like proposal once before, Cicely," cried the esquire. "Reject it. Let us die together."

"It matters little to me how you decide," cried Nightgall. "Mine you shall be, come what will."

"You hear what he says, Cholmondeley," cried Cicely, distractedly. "I cannot escape him. Oh, let me save you!"

"Never!" rejoined Cholmondeley, trying to stretch his hands towards her. "Never! You torture me by this hesitation. Reject it, if you love me, positively—peremptorily!"

"Oh, Heaven direct me!" cried Cicely, falling upon her knees. "If I refuse, I am your destroyer."

"You will utterly destroy me, if you yield," groaned Cholmondeley.

"Once wedded to me," urged Nightgall, "you shall set him free yourself."

"Oh, no, no, no!" cried Cicely. "Death were better than that. I cannot consent. Cholmondelcy, you must die."

"You bid me live," returned the esquire.

"You have signed his death-warrant!" cried Nightgall, seizing her hand. "Come along."

"I will die here," shrieked Cicely, struggling.

"Villain!" cried Cholmondeloy, "your cruelty will turn her brain, as it did that of her mother Alexia."

"How do you know Alexia was her mother?" demanded Nightgall, starting, and relinquishing his grasp of Cicely.

"I am sure of it," replied Cholmondeley. "And, what is more, I am acquainted with the rightful name and title of your victim. She was the wife of Sir Alberic Mountjoy, who was attainted of heresy and high treason, in the reign of Henry the Eighth."

"I will not deny it," replied Nightgall. "She was so. But how did you learn this?"

"Partly, from an inscription upon a small silver clasp, which I found upon her hood when I discovered her body in the Devilin Tower," replied Cholmondeley; "and partly, from inquiries since made. I have ascertained that the Lady Mountjoy was imprisoned with her husband in the Tower; and that at the time of his execution she received a pardon. I would learn from you why she was subsequently detained?—why she was called Alexia?—and why her child was taken from her?"

"She lost her senses on the day of her husbands death," replied Nightgall. "I will tell you nothing more."

"Alas!" cried Cicely, who had listened with breathless interest to what was said, "hers was a tragical history."

"Yours will be still more tragical, if you continue obstinate," rejoined Nightgall. "Come along."

"Heaven preserve me from this monster!" she shrieked. "Help me, Cholmondeley."

"I am powerless as a crushed worm," groaned the esquire, in a tone of anguish.

Nightgall laughed exultingly, and twining his arms around Cicely, held his hand over her mouth to stifle her cries, and forced her from the cell.

The sharpest pang he had recently endured was light to Cholmondeley, compared with his present maddening sensations, and had not insensibility relieved him, his reason would have given way. How long he remained in this state he knew not, but, on reviving, he found himself placed on a small pallet, and surrounded by three men, in sable dresses. His attire had been removed, and two of these persons were chafing his limbs with an ointment, which had a marvellous effect in subduing the pain, and restoring pliancy to the sinews and joints; while the third, who was no other than Sorrocold, bathed his temples with a pungent liquid. In a short time, he felt himself greatly restored, and able to move; and when he thought how valuable the strength he had thus suddenly and mysteriously acquired would have been a short time ago, he groaned aloud.

"Give him a cup of wine,'" said an authoritative voice, which Cholmondeley fancied he recognised, from the further end of the cell. And glancing in the direction of the speaker, he beheld Renard.

"It may be dangerous, your excellency," returned Sorrocold.

"Dangerous or not, he shall have it," rejoined Renard.

And wine was accordingly poured out by one of the attendants, and presented to the esquire, who eagerly drained it.

"Now leave us," said Renard; "and return to the torture-chamber. I will rejoin you there."

Sorrocold and his companions bowed, and departed.

Renard then proceeded to interrogate Cholmondeley respecting his own share in the rebellion; and also concerning Dudley and Lady Jane. Failing in obtaining satisfactory answers, he turned his inquiries to Elizabeth's participation in the plot; and he shaped them so artfully, that he contrived to elicit from the esquire, whose brain was a good deal confused by the potent draught he had swallowed, some important particulars relative to the princess's correspondence with Wyat.

Satisfied with the result of the examination, the ambassador turned to depart, when he beheld, close behind him, a masked figure, which he immediately recognised as the same that had appeared at the window of his lodgings in the Bloody Tower, on the evening when Jane's death-warrant was signed by the queen.

No sound had proclaimed the mask's approach, and the door was shut. The sight revived all Renard's superstitious fears.

"Who, and what art thou?" he demanded.

"Your executioner," replied a hollow voice. And suddenly drawing a poniard, the mask aimed a terrible blow at Renard, which, if he had not avoided it, must have proved fatal.

Thus assaulted, Renard tried to draw his sword, but he was prevented by the mask, who grappled with him, and brought him to the ground. In the struggle, however, the assassin's vizard fell off, and disclosed the features of Nightgall.

"Nightgall!" exclaimed Renard. "You, then, were the mysterious visitant to my chamber in the Bloody Tower. I might have guessed as much when I met you in the passage. But you persuaded me I had seen an apparition."

"If your excellency took me for a ghost, I took you for something worse," replied Nightgall, keeping his knee upon the ambassador's chest, and searching for his dagger, which had dropped in the conflict.

"Release me, villain!" cried Renard. "Would you murder me?"

"I am paid to put your excellency to death," rejoined Nightgall, with the utmost coolness.

"I will give you twice the sum to spare me," rejoined Renard, who saw from Nightgall's looks that he had no chance, unless he could work upon his avarice.

"Hum!" exclaimed the jailor; who, not being able to reach his dagger, which had rolled to some distance, had drawn his sword, and was now shortening it, with intent to plunge it in the other's throat—"I would take your offer— but I have gone too far."

"Fear nothing," gasped Renard, giving himself up for lost. "I swear by my patron, Saint Paul, that I will not harm a hair of your head. Against your employer only will I direct my vengeance."

"I will not trust you," replied Nightgall, about to strike.

But just as he was about to deal the fatal blow—at the very moment that the point of the blade pierced the ambassador's skin, he was plucked backwards by Cholmondeley, and hurled on the ground. Perceiving it was his rival, who was more hateful to him even than Renard, Cholmondeley, on the onset, had prepared to take some part in the struggle, and noticing the poniard, had first of all possessed himself of it, and then attacked Nightgall in the manner above related.

Throwing himself upon his foe, Cholmondeley tried to stab him; but it appeared that he wore a stout buff jerkin, for the weapon glanced aside, without doing him any injury. As Cholmondeley was about to repeat the thrust, and in a part less defended, he was himself pushed aside by Renard, who, by this time, had gained his feet, and was threatening vengeance upon his intended assassin. But the esquire was unwilling to abandon his prey; and in the struggle, Nightgall, exerting all his strength, broke from them, and wresting the dagger from Cholmondeley, succeeded in opening the door. Renard, foaming with rage, rushed after him, utterly forgetful of Cholmondeley, who listened with breathless anxiety, to their retreating footsteps. Scarcely knowing what to do, but resolved not to throw away the chance of escape, the esquire hastily attired himself, and taking up a lamp which Renard had left upon the floor, quitted the cell.

"I will seek out Cicely," he cried, "and set her free; and then, perhaps, we may be able to escape together."

But the hope that for a moment arose within his breast was checked by the danger and difficulty of making the search. Determined, however to hazard the attempt, he set out in a contrary direction to that taken by Nightgall and Renard, and proceeding at a rapid pace soon reached a flight of steps, up which he mounted. He was now within a second passage, similar to the first, with cells on either side; but though he was too well convinced, from the sounds issuing from them, that they were occupied, he did not dare to open any of them. Still pursuing his headlong course, he now took one turn—now another, until he was completely bewildered and exhausted. While leaning against the wall to recruit himself, he was startled by a light approaching at a distance and, fearing to encounter the person who bore it, was about to hurry away, when, to his inexpressible joy, he perceived it was Cicely. With a wild cry, he started towards her, calling to her by name; but the young damsel, mistaking him probably for her persecutor, let fall her lamp, uttered a piercing scream, and fled. In vain, her lover strove to overtake her—in vain, he shouted to her, and implored her to stop—his cries were drowned in her shrieks, and only added to her terror. Cholmondeley, however, though distanced, kept her for some time in view; when all at once she disappeared.

On gaining the spot where she had vanished, he found an open trap-door, and, certain she must have descended by it, took the same course. He found himself in a narrow, vaulted passage, but could discover no traces of her he sought. Hurrying forward, though almost ready to drop with fatigue, he came to a large octagonal chamber. At one side, he perceived a ladder, and at the head of it the arched entrance to a cell. In an agony of hope and fear he hastened towards the recess, and as he approached, his doubt was made certainty by a loud scream. Quick as thought, he sprang into the cell, and found, crouched in the further corner, the object of his search.

"Cicely," he exclaimed. "It is I—your lover—Cholmondeley."

"You!" she exclaimed, starting up, and gazing at him as if she could scarcely trust the evidence of her senses; "and I have been flying from you all this time, taking you for Nightgall." And throwing herself into his arms, she was strained passionately to his bosom.

After the first rapturous emotions had subsided, Cicely hastily explained to her lover that after she had been borne away by Nightgall she had fainted, and on reviving, found herself in her accustomed prison. Filled with alarm by his dreadful threats, she had determined to put an end to her existence rather than expose herself to his violence; and had arisen with that resolution, when an impulse prompted her to try the door. To her surprise it was unfastened—the bolt having shot wide of the socket, and quitting the cell, she had wandered about along the passages, until they had so mysteriously encountered each other. This explanation given, and Cholmondeley having related what had befallen him, the youthful pair, almost blinded to their perilous situation by their joy at their unexpected reunion, set forth in the hope of discovering the subterranean passage to the further side of the moat.

Too much engrossed by each other to heed whither they were going, they wandered on;—Cicely detailing all the persecution she had experienced from Nightgall, and her lover breathing vengeance against him. The only person she had seen, she said, during her captivity was Xit. He had found his way to her dungeon, but was discovered while endeavouring to liberate her by Nightgall, who threatened to put him to death, if he did not take a solemn oath, which he proposed, not to reveal to the place of her captivity. And she concluded the dwarf had kept his vow, as she had seen nothing of him since; nor had any one been led to her retreat.

To these details, as well as to her professions of love for him, unshaken by time or circumstance, Cholmondeley listened with such absorbing attention, that, lost to everything else, he tracked passage after passage, unconscious where he was going. At last, he opened a door which admitted them to a gloomy hall, terminated by a broad flight of steps, down which several armed figures wore descending. Cholmondeley would have retreated, but it was impossible. He had been perceived by the soldiers, who rushed towards him, questioned him and Cicely, and not being satisfied with their answers, conveyed them up the stairs to the lower guard-room in the White Tower, which it appeared the wanderers had approached.

Here, amongst other soldiers and warders, were the three giants, and instantly addressing them, Cholmondeley delivered Cicely to their care. He would have had them convey her to the Stone Kitchen, but this an officer who was present would not permit, till inquiries had been made, and, meanwhile, the esquire was placed in arrest.

Shortly after this, an extraordinary bustle was heard at the door, and four soldiers entered carrying the body of a man upon a shutter. They set it down in the midst of the room. Amongst those, who flocked round to gaze upon it, was Cholmondeley. It was a frightful spectacle. But in the mutilated, though still breathing mass, the esquire recognized Nightgall. While he was gazing at the miserable wretch, and marvelling how he came in this condition, a tall personage strode into the room, and commanding the group to stand aside, approached the body. It was Renard. After regarding the dying man for a few moments with savage satisfaction, he turned to depart, when his eye fell upon Cholmondeley.

"I had forgotten you," he said. "But it seems you have not neglected the opportunity offered you of escape."

"We caught him trying to get out of the subterranean passages, your excellency," remarked the officer.

"Let him remain here till further orders," rejoined Renard. "You have saved my life, and shall find I am not ungrateful," he added to Cholmondeley.

"If your excellency would indeed requite me," replied the esquire, "you will give orders that this maiden, long and falsely, imprisoned by the wretch before us, may be allowed to return to her friends."

"I know her," rejoined Renard, looking at Cicely; "and I know that what you say is true. Release her," he added to the officer. And giving a last terrible look at Nightgall, he quitted the room.

"Is Cicely here? groaned the dying man.

"She is," replied Cholmondeley. "Have you aught to say to her!"

"Ay, and to you, too," replied Nightgall. "Let her approach, and bid the others stand off; and I will confess all I have done. Give me a draught of wine, for it is a long story, and I must have strength to tell it."

Before relating Nightgall's confession, it will be necessary to see what dreadful accident had befallen him; and in order to do this, his course must be traced, subsequently to his flight from Cholmondeley's dungeon.

Acquainted with all the intricacies of the passages, and running with great speed, Nightgall soon distanced his pursuer, who having lost trace of him, was obliged to give up the chase. Determined, however, not to be baulked of his prey, he retraced his steps to the torture-chamber, where he found Wolfytt, Sorro-cold, and three other officials, to whom he recounted the jailor's atrocious attempt.

"I will engage to find him for your excellency," said Wolfytt, who bore no very kindly feeling to Nightgall, "if he is anywhere below the Tower. I know every turn and hole in these passages better than the oldest rat that haunts them."

"Deliver him to my vengeance," rejoined Renard, "and you shall hold his place."

"Says your excellency so!" cried Wolfytt; "then you may account him already in your hands."

With this, he snatched up a halberd and a torch, and bidding two of the officials come with him, started off at a swift pace on the right. Neither he nor his companions relaxed their pace, but tracked passage after passage, and examined vault after vault—but still without success.

Renard's impatience manifested itself in furious exclamations, and Wolfytt appeared perplexed and disappointed.

"I have it!" he exclaimed, rubbing his shaggy head. "He must have entered Saint John's Chapel, in the White Tower, by the secret passage."

The party were again in motion; and, taking the least circuitous road, Wolfytt soon brought them to a narrow passage, at the end of which he descried a dark crouching figure.

"We have him!" he cried, exultingly. "There he is!"

Creeping quickly along, for the roof was so low that he was compelled to stoop, Wolfytt prepared for an encounter with Nightgall. The latter grasped his dagger, and appeared ready to spring upon his assailant. Knowing the strength and ferocity of the jailor, Wolfytt hesitated a moment, but goaded on by Renard, who was close behind, and eager for vengeance, he was about to commence the attack, when Nightgall, taking advantage of the delay, touched a spring in the wall behind him, and a stone dropping from its place, he dashed through the aperture. With a yell of rage and disappointment, Wolfytt sprang after him, and was instantly struck down by a blow from his opponent's dagger. Renard followed, and beheld the fugitive speeding across the nave of Saint John's Chapel, and, without regarding Wolfytt, who was lying on the floor, bleeding profusely, he continued the pursuit.

Nightgall hurried up the steps behind the altar, and took his way along one of the arched stone galleries opening upon the council-chamber. But, swiftly as he fled, Renard, to whom fury had lent wings, rapidly gained upon him.

It was more than an hour after day-break, but no one was astir in this part of the citadel, and as the pursued and pursuer threaded the gallery, and crossed the council-chamber, they did not meet even a solitary attendant. Nightgall was now within the southern gallery of the White Tower, and Renard shouted to him to stop; but he heeded not the cry. In another moment, he reached a door, opening upon the north-east turret. It was bolted, and the time lost in unfastening it, brought Renard close upon him. Nightgall would have descended, but thinking he heard voices below, he ran up the winding stairs.

STAIRCASE IN THE NORTH-EASTERN TURRET OF THE WHITE TOWER.

The Fate of Nightgall.

Renard now felt secure of him, and uttered a shout of savage delight. The fugitive would have gained the roof, if he had not been intercepted by a party of men, who at the very moment he reached the doorway communicating with the leads presented themselves at it. Hearing the clamour raised by Renard and his followers below, these men commanded Nightgall to surrender. Instead of complying, the miserable fugitive, now at his wits' end, rushed backwards, with the determination of assailing Renard. He met the ambassador at a turn in the stairs a little below, and aimed a desperate blow at him with his dagger. But Renard easily warded it off, and pressing him backwards, drove him into one of the deep embrasures at the side.

Driven to desperation, Nightgall at first thought of springing through the loophole; but the involuntary glance that he cast below, made him recoil. On seeing his terror, Renard was filled with delight, and determined to prolong his enjoyment. In vain, Nightgall endeavoured to escape from the dreadful snare in which he was caught. He was driven remorselessly back. In vain, he implored mercy in the most abject terms. None was shown him. Getting within the embrasure, which was about twelve feet deep, Renard deliberately pricked the wretched man with the point of his sword, and forced him slowly backwards.

Nightgall struggled desperately against the horrible fate that awaited him, striking at Renard with his dagger, clutching convulsively against the wall, and disputing the ground inch by inch. But all was unavailing. Scarcely a foot's space intervened between him and destruction, when Renard sprang forward, and pushed him by main force through the loophole. He uttered a fearful cry, and tried to grasp at the roughened surface of the wall. Renard watched his descent. It was from a height of near ninety feet.

He fell with a terrific smash upon the pavement of the court below. Three or four halberdiers, who were passing at a little distance, hearing the noise, ran towards him, but finding he was not dead, though almost dashed in pieces, and scarcely retaining a vestige of humanity, they brought a shutter, and conveyed him to the lower guard-room, as already related.

"I have no hope of mercy," gasped the dying man, as his request was complied with, and Cicely, with averted eyes, stood beside him, "and I deserve none. But I will make what atonement I can for my evil deeds. Listen to me, Cicely, (or rather I should say Angela, for that is your rightful name,) you are the daughter of Sir Alberic Mountjoy, and were born while your parents were imprisoned in the Tower. Your mother, the Lady Grace, lost her reason on the day of her husband's execution, as I have before stated. But she did not expire as I gave out. My motive for setting on foot this story, and for keeping her existence secret, was the hope of making her mine if she recovered her senses, as I had reason to believe would be the case."

"Wretch!" exclaimed Cholmondeley.

"You cannot upbraid me more than I now upbraid myself," groaned Nightgall; "but my purpose was thwarted. The ill-fated lady never recovered, and disappointment, acting upon my evil nature, made me treat her with such cruelty that her senses became more unsettled than ever."

"Alas! alas!" cried Cicely, bursting into tears; "my poor mother! what a fate was yours!"

"When all hope of her recovery was extinguished," continued Nightgall, "I thought, that if any change occurred in the sovereignty or religion of the country, I might, by producing her, and relating a feigned story, obtain a handsome reward for her preservation. But this expectation also passed by. And I must confess that, at length, my only motive for allowing her to exist was that she formed an object to exercise my cruelty upon."

"Heaven's curse upon you!" cried Cholmondeley.

"Spare your maledictions," rejoined Nightgall; "or heap them on my lifeless clay. You will soon be sufficiently avenged. Give me another draught of wine, for my lips are so dry I can scarcely speak, and I would not willingly expire till I have made known the sum of my wickedness."

The wine given him, he proceeded.

"I will not tell you all the devilish cruelties I practised upon the wretched Alexia, (for so, as you are aware, I called her, to conceal her real name,)—because from what you have seen you may guess the rest. But I kept her a solitary captive in those secret dungeons, for a term of nearly seventeen years—ever since your birth, in short," he added, to Cicely. "Sometimes, she would elude my vigilance, and run shrieking along the passages. But when any of the jailors beheld her, they fled, supposing her a supernatural being."

"Her shrieks were indeed dreadful," remarked Cholmondeley. "I shall never forget their effect upon me. But you allowed her to perish from famine at last?"

"Her death was accidental," replied Nightgall, in a hollow voice, "though it lies as heavy on my soul as if I had designed it. I had shut her up for security in the cell in the Devilin Tower, where you found her, meaning to visit her at night, as was my custom, with provisions. But I was sent on special business by the queen to the palace at Greenwich for three days; and on my return to the Tower, I found the wretched captive dead."

"She had escaped you, then," said Cholmondeley, bitterly. "But you have not spoken of her daughter?"

"First, let me tell you where I have hidden the body, that decent burial may be given it," groaned Nightgall. "It lies in the vault beneath the Devilin Tower—in the centre of the chamber—not deep—not deep."

"I shall not forget," replied Cholmondeley, noticing with alarm that an awful change had taken place in his countenance. "What of her child?"

"I must be brief," replied Nightgall, faintly; "for I feel that my end approaches. The little Angela was conveyed by me, to Dame Potentia Trusbut. I said she was the offspring of a lady of rank,—but revealed no name,—and what I told beside was a mere fable. The good dame, having no child of her own, readily adopted her, and named her Cicely. She grew up in years—in beauty; and as I beheld her dawning charms, the love I had entertained for the mother was transferred to the child—nay, it was ten times stronger. I endeavoured to gain her affections, and fancied I should succeed, till you"—looking at Cholmondeley—"appeared. Then I saw my suit was hopeless. Then evil feelings again took possession of me, and I began a fresh career of crime. You know the rest."

"I do," replied Cholmondeley. "Have you aught further to disclose?"

"Only this," rejoined Nightgall, who was evidently on the verge of dissolution. "Cut open my doublet; and within its folds you will find proofs of Angela's birth, together with other papers referring to her ill-fated parents. Lay them before the queen; and I make no doubt that the estates of her father, who was a firm adherent to the Catholic faith, and died for it, as well as a stanch supporter of Queen Catherine of Arragon, will be restored to her."

Cholmondeley lost not a moment in obeying the injunction. He cut open the blood-stained jerkin of the dying man, and found, as he had stated, a packet.

"That is it," cried Nightgall, fixing his glazing eyes on Angela,—"that will restore you to your wealth—your title. The priest by whom you were baptised was the queen's confessor, Feckenham. He will remember the circumstance—he was the ghostly counsellor of both your parents. Take the packet to him and he will plead your cause with the queen. Forget— forgive me—"

His utterance was suddenly choked by a stream of blood that gushed from his mouth, and with a hideous expression of pain he expired.

"Horrible!" cried Angela, placing her hands before her eyes.

"Think not of him," said Cholmondeley, supporting her, and removing her to a little distance,—"think of the misery you have escaped,—of the rank to which you will assuredly be restored. When I first beheld those proud and beautiful lineaments, I was certain they belonged to one of high birth. And I was not mistaken."

"What matters my newly-discovered birth—my title—my estates, if I obtain them,—if *you* are lost to me!" cried Angela, despairingly. "I shall never know happiness without you."

As she spoke, an usher, who had entered the guard-room, marched up to Cholmondeley, and said, "I am the bearer of the queen's pardon to you. Your life is spared, at the instance of the Spanish ambassador. But you are to remain a prisoner on parole, within the fortress, during the royal pleasure."

"It is now my turn to support you," said Angela, observing her lover stagger, and turn deadly pale.

"So many events crowd upon my brain," cried Cholmondeley, "that I begin to fear for my reason—Air!—air!"

Led into the open court, he speedily recovered, and in a transport of such joy as has seldom been experienced, he accompanied Angela to the Stone Kitchen, where they were greeted with mingled tears and rejoicings by Dame Potentia and her spouse.

In the course of the day, Cholmondeloy sought out Feckenham, and laid the papers before him. The confessor confirmed all that Nightgall had stated respecting the baptism of the infant daughter of Lady Mountjoy, and the other documents satisfied him that the so-called Cicely was that daughter. He undertook to lay the case at once before the queen, and was as good as his word. Mary heard his statement with the deepest interest, but made no remark; and at its conclusion desired that the damsel might be brought before her.

CHAMBER IN THE MARTIN, OR JEWEL TOWER.

BASEMENT CHAMBER IN THE FLINT TOWER.

XXXVII.—-HOW JANE WAS IMPRISONED IN THE MARTIN TOWER; HOW SHE WAS VISITED BY ROGER ASCHAM; HOW SHE RECEIVED FECKENHAM'S ANNOUNCEMENT THAT THE TIME OF HER EXECUTION WAS FIXED; AND HOW SHE WAS RESPITED FOR THREE DAYS.

The Martin Tower (or, as it is now termed, the Jewel Tower, from the purpose to which it is appropriated), where Jane was confined by the queen's commands, lies at the north-eastern extremity of the ballium wall, and corresponds in size and structure with the Develin, or Devereux Tower, at the opposite angle. Circular in form, like the last-mentioned building, and erected, in all probability, at the same period—the latter end of the reign of John, or the commencement of that of Henry the Third, it consists of two stories having walls of immense thickness, and containing, as is the case with every other fortification, deep recesses, terminated by narrow loop-holes. A winding stone staircase, still in a tolerable state of preservation, communicates with these stories, and with the roof, which was formerly embattled, and defended on either side by two small square turrets. Externally, on the west, the Martin Tower has lost its original character; the walls being new-fronted and modernized, and a flight of stops raised to the upper story, completely masking the ancient door-way, which now forms the entrance to the jewel-room. On the cast, however, it retains much of its ancient appearance, though in part concealed by surrounding habitations; and when the building now in progress, and intended for the reception of the regalia, is completed, it will be still further hidden. * While digging the foundations of the proposed structure, which were sunk much below the level of the ballium wall, it became apparent that the ground had been artificially raised to a considerable height by an embankment of gravel and sand; and the prodigious solidity and strength of the wall were proved from the difficulty experienced by the workmen in breaking through it, to effect a communication with the new erection.

Within, on the basement floor, on the left of the passage, and generally hidden by the massive portal, is a small cell constructed in the thickness of the wall; and further on, the gloomy chamber used as a depository for the crown ornaments, and which requires to be artificially lighted, is noticeable for its architecture, having a vaulted and groined roof of great beauty. The upper story, part of the residence of Mr. Swift, the keeper of the regalia, at present comprehends two apartments, with a hall leading to them, while the ceiling having been lowered, other rooms are gained. Here, besides the ill-fated and illustrious lady whose history forms the subject of this chronicle, was confined the lovely, and, perhaps guiltless, Anne Boleyn. The latter fact has, however, been doubted, and the upper chamber in the Beauchamp Tower assigned as the place of her imprisonment. But this supposition, from many circumstances, appears improbable, and the inscription bearing her name, and carved near the entrance of the hall, is conclusive as to her having been confined in this tower.

Here, in 1641, the twelve bishops, impeached of high treason by the revolutionary party in the House of Commons, for protesting against the force used against them, and the acts done in their absence, were imprisoned during their committal to the Tower:—at least, so runs the legend, though it is difficult to conceive how so many persons could be accommodated in so small a place. Here, also, Blood made his atrocious attempt (a story still involved in obscurity—it has been conjectured, with some show of probability, that he was prompted to the deed by Charles himself), to steal the crown jewels; and in this very chamber, the venerable Talbot Edwards made his gallant defence of the royal ensigns, receiving for his bravery and his wounds, a paltry grant of two hundred pounds, half of which, owing to vexatious delays, he only received, while the baffled robber was rewarded with a post at court, and a pension of five hundred pounds a-year in Ireland. Can it be doubted after this which of the two was the offender, in the eyes of the monarch?

The view of this fabric, at page 321, was taken from the

spot cleared out for the erection of the New Jewel Rooms;

and as the latter structure is already in a state of

forwardness, and will be probably finished before Christmas,

this aspect of the old tower can scarcely be said to exist

longer.

ENTRANCE HALL IN THE MARTIN, OR JEWEL TOWER.

It must not be omitted that the Jewel Tower enjoys, in common with its corresponding fortification, the Devereux Tower, the reputation of being haunted. Its ghostly visitant is a female figure robed in white—whether the spirit of Anne Boleyn, or the ill-fated Jane, cannot be precisely ascertained.

The Martin Tower acquired its present designation of the Jewel Tower, in the reign of James the First, when the crown ornaments were removed to it from a small building, where they had been hitherto kept, on the south side of the White Tower.

The regalia were first exhibited to the public in the reign of Charles the Second, when many of the perquisites of the ancient master of the Jewel House were abolished, and its privileges annexed to the office of the lord chamberlain.

Jane's present prison was far more commodious than her former place of confinement in the Brick Tower, and by Mary's express injunctions, every attention consistent with her situation was shown her. Strange as it may seem, she felt easier, if not happier, than she had done during the latter part of the period of her liberation. Then, she was dissatisfied with herself, anxious for her husband, certain of the failure of his enterprise, and almost desiring its failure,—now, the worst was past. No longer agitated by the affairs of the world, she could suffer with patience, and devote herself wholly to God. Alone within her prison-chamber, she prayed with more fervour than she had been able to do for months; and the soothing effect it produced, was such, that she felt almost grateful for her chastening. "I am better able to bear misfortune than prosperity," she murmured, "and I cannot be too thankful to Heaven, that I am placed in a situation to call forth my strength. Oh! that Dudley may be able to endure his trial with equal fortitude! But I fear his proud heart will rebel. Sustain him, Lord! I beseech thee, and bring him to a true sense of his condition."

Convinced that her days were now numbered, having no hope of pardon, scarcely desiring it, and determined to reject it, if coupled with any conditions affecting her faith, Jane made every preparation for her end. No longer giving up a portion of her time to study, she entirely occupied herself with her devotions. Influenced by the controversial spirit of the times, she had before been as anxious to overcome her opponents in argument, as they were to convince her of her errors. Now, though feeling equally strong in her cause, she was more lowly-minded. Reproaching herself bitterly with her departure from her duty, she sought by incessant prayer, by nightly vigil, by earnest and heart-felt supplication to wipe out the offence. "I have not sinned in ignorance," she thought, "but with my eyes open, and therefore my fault is far greater than if no light had been vouchsafed me. By sincere contrition alone can I hope to work out my salvation; and if sorrow, remorse, and shame, combined with the most earnest desire of amendment, constitute repentance, I am truly contrite. But I feel my own unworthiness, and though I know the mercy of Heaven is infinite, yet I scarcely dare to hope for forgiveness for my trespasses. I have trusted too much to myself already— and find that I relied on a broken reed. I will now trust only to God."

And thus she passed her time, in the strictest self-examination, fixing her thoughts above, and withdrawing them as much as possible from earth. The effect was speedily manifest in her altered looks and demeanour. When first brought to the Martin Tower, she was downcast and despairing. Ere three days had passed, she became calm, and almost cheerful, and her features resumed their wonted serene and seraphic expression. She could not, it is true, deaden the pangs that ever and anon shook her, when she thought of her husband and father. But she strove to console herself by the hope that they would be purified, like herself, by the trial to which they were subjected, and that their time of separation would be brief. To the duke she addressed that touching letter preserved among the few fragments of her writings, which after it had been submitted to Gardiner, was allowed to be delivered to him. It concluded with these words:—"And thus, good father, I have opened unto you the state wherein I presently stand,—my death at hand. Although to you it may seem woful, yet to me there is nothing that can be more welcome than to aspire from this Vale of Misery to that heavenly throne of all joy and pleasure with Christ, my Saviour. In whose steadfast faith (if it may be lawful for the daughter so to write to the father), the Lord who hath hitherto strengthened you so continue to keep you, that at the last we may meet in heaven."

With her husband she was allowed no communication; and in reply to her request to see him once more, she was told that their sole meeting would be on the scaffold:—a wanton insult, for it was not intended to execute them together. The room, or rooms, (for the large circular chamber was even then divided by a partition,) occupied by Jane in the Martin Tower, were those on the upper story, tenanted, as before-mentioned, by the keeper of the regalia, and her chief place of resort during the day-time was one of the deep embrasures looking towards the north. In this recess, wholly unobserved and undisturbed, she remained, while light lasted, upon her knees, with a book of prayers, or the bible before here, fearful of losing one of the precious moments which flew by so quickly—and now so tranquilly. At night, she withdrew, not to repose, but to a small table in the midst of the apartment, on which she placed the sacred volume and a lamp, and knelt down beside it. Had she not feared to disturb her calm condition, she would not have allowed herself more than an hour's repose, at the longest intervals nature could endure. But desirous of maintaining her composure to the last, she yielded to the demand, and from midnight to the third hour stretched herself upon her couch. She then arose, and resumed her devotions. The same rules were observed in respect to the food she permitted herself to take. Restricting herself to bread and water, she ate and drank sufficient to support nature, and no more.

On the fourth day after her confinement, the jailor informed her there was a person without who had an order from the queen to see her. Though Jane would have gladly refused admittance to the applicant, she answered meekly, "Let him come in."

Immediately afterwards a grave-looking middle-aged man, with a studious countenance overclouded with sorrow, appeared, he was attired in a black robe, and carried a flat velvet cap in his hand.

"What, Master Roger Ascham, my old instructor!" exclaimed Jane, rising as he approached, and extending her hand to him, "I am glad to see you."

Ascham was deeply affected. The tears rushed to his eyes, and it was some moments before he could speak.

"Do not lament for me, good friend," said Jane, in a cheerful tone, "but rejoice with me, that I have so profited by your instructions as to be able to bear my present lot with resignation."

"I do indeed heartily rejoice at it, honoured and dear madam," replied Ascham, subduing his emotion, "and I would gladly persuade myself that my instructions had contributed in however slight a degree to your present composure. But you derive your fortitude from a higher source than any on earth. It is your piety, not your wisdom that sustains you; and though I have pointed out the way to the living waters at which you have drunk, it is to that fountain alone that you owe the inestimable blessing of your present frame of mind. I came not hither to depress, but to cheer you—not to instruct, but be instructed. Your life, madam, will afford the world one of the noblest lessons it has ever received, and though your career may be closed at the point whence most others start, it will have been run long enough."

"Alas! good Master Ascham," rejoined Jane, "I once thought that my life and its close would be profitable to our church—that my conduct might haply be a model to its disciples—and my name enrolled among its martyrs. Let him who standeth take heed lest he fall. I had too much confidence in myself. I yielded to impulses, which, though not culpable in the eyes of men, were so in those of God."

"Oh madam! you reproach yourself far too severely," cried Ascham. "Unhappy circumstances have made you amenable to the laws of your country, it is true, and you give up your life as a willing sacrifice to justice. But this is all that can, or will be required of you, by your earthly or your supreme Judge. That your character might have been more absolutely faultless in the highest sense I will not deny, had you sacrificed every earthly feeling to duty. But I for one should not have admired—should not have loved you as I now love you, had you acted otherwise. What you consider a fault has proved you a true woman in heart and affection; and your constancy as a believer in the gospel, and upholder of its doctrines, has been equally strongly manifested. Your name in after ages will be a beacon and a guiding-star to the whole Protestant church."

"Heaven grant it!" exclaimed Jane, fervently. "I once hoped—once thought so."

"Hope so—think so still," rejoined Ascham. "Ah, dear madam, when I last took my leave of you before my departure for Germany, and found you in your chamber at Bradgate, buried in the Phædo of the divine philosopher, while your noble father and his friends were hunting, and disporting themselves in the park—when to my wondering question, as to why you did not join in their pastime, you answered, 'that all their sport in the park was but a shadow to the pleasure you found in Plato'—adding, 'alas! good folk, they never felt what true pleasure meant'—at that time, I little thought for what a sad, though proud destiny you were reserved."

"Neither did I, good Master Ascham," replied Jane; "but you now find me at a better study. I have exchanged him whom you term, and truly, in a certain sense, the 'divine' philosopher, for writings derived from the highest source of inspiration,—direct from heaven—and I find in this study more pleasure and far more profit than the other. And now farewell, good friend. Do me one last favour. Be present at my ending. And see how she, whom you have taught to live, will die. Heaven bless you!" <

"Heaven bless you too, noble and dear lady," replied Ascham, kneeling and pressing her hand to his lips. "I will obey your wishes." He then arose, and covering his face to hide his fast-falling tears, withdrew.

Jane, also, was much moved, for she was greatly attached to her old instructor; and to subdue her emotion, took a few turns within her chamber. In doing this, she noticed the various inscriptions and devices carved by former occupants; and taking a pin, traced with its point the following lines, on the wall of the recess where she performed her devotions:

Non aliéna putes homini quæ obtingere possunt;

Sors hodierna mihi, eras erit ilia tibi.

Underneath, she added the following, and subscribed them with her name:

Deo juvante, nil nocet livor malus;

Et non juvante, nil juvat labor gravis:

Post tenebras, spero lucem!

The lines have been effaced. But tradition has preserved them. How deeply affecting is the wish of the patient sufferer—"*Post tenebras, spero lucem!*"

Scarcely had Jane resumed her devotions, when she was a second time interrupted by the jailor, who, ushering a young female into the room, departed. Jane arose, and fixed her eyes upon the new-comer, but did not appear to recognise her; while the latter, unable to restrain her tears, tottered towards her, and threw herself at her feet.

"Do you not know me, dearest madam?" she cried, in a voice suffocated by emotion.

"Can it be Cicely?" inquired Jane, eagerly. "The tones are hers."

"It is—it is," sobbed the other.

Jane instantly raised her, and pressed her affectionately to her bosom.

"Poor child!" she exclaimed, gazing at her pale and emaciated features, now bedewed with tears, "you are as much altered as I am,—nay, more. You must have suffered greatly to rob you of your youth and beauty thus. But I should have known you at once, despite the change, had I not thought you dead. By what extraordinary chance do I behold you here?"

As soon as she could command herself, Angela related all that had befallen her since their last sad parting. She told how she had been betrayed into the hands of Nightgall by one of his associates, who came to Sion House with a forged order for her arrest,—carried her off, and delivered her to the jailor. How she was conveyed by the subterranean passage from Tower Hill to the secret dungeons beneath the fortress,—how she was removed from one cell to another by her inexorable captor, and what she endured from his importunities, threats, and cruel treatment,—and how at last, when she had abandoned all hope of succour, Providence had unexpectedly and mysteriously interposed to release her, and punish her persecutor. She likewise recounted the extraordinary discovery of her birth—Nightgall's confession—Cholmondeley's interview with Feckenham—and concluded her narration thus:—"The confessor having informed me that her majesty desired I should be brought before her, I yesterday obeyed the mandate. She received me most graciously—ordered me to relate my story—listened to it with profound attention—and expressed great sympathy with my misfortunes. 'Your sufferings are at an end, I trust,' she said, when I had finished, 'and brighter and happie days are in store for you. The title and estates of which you have been so long and so unjustly deprived, shall be restored to you. Were it for your happiness, I would place you near my person; but a life of retirement, if I guess your disposition rightly, will suit you best.' In this I entirely agreed, and thanking her majesty for her kindness, she replied:—'You owe me no thanks, Angela. The daughter of Sir Alberic Mountjoy—my mother's trusty friend—has the strongest claims upon my gratitude. Your lover has already received a pardon, and when these unhappy affairs are ended, he shall be at liberty to quit the Tower. May you be happy with him!'"

"I echo that wish with all my heart, dear Angela," cried Jane. "May heaven bless your union!—and it *will* bless it, I am assured, for you deserve happiness. Nor am I less rejoiced at your deliverance than at Cholmondeley's. I looked upon myself as in some degree the cause of his destruction, and unceasingly reproached myself with having allowed him to accompany me to the Tower. But now I find—as I have ever found in my severest afflictions,—that all was for the best."

"Alas! madam," returned Angela, "when I see you here, I can with difficulty respond to the sentiment."

"Do not question the purposes of the Unquestionable, Angela," replied Jane, severely. "I am chastened because I deserve it, and for my own good. The wind is tempered to the shorn lamb, and fortitude is given me to bear my afflictions. Nay, they are *not* afflictions. I would not exchange my lot—sad as it seems to you—for that of the happiest and the freest within the realm. When the bondage of earth is once broken,—when the flesh has no more power over the spirit—when the gates of heaven are open for admittance—can the world, or worldly joys, possess further charms? No. These prison walls are no restraint to me. My soul soars upwards, and holds communion with God and with his elect, among whom I hope to be numbered. The scaffold will have no terror for me. I shall mount it as the first step towards heaven; and shall hail the stroke of the axe as the signal to my spirit to wing its flight to the throne of everlasting joy."

"I am rebuked, madam," returned Angela, with a look of admiration. "Oh! that I might ever hope to obtain such a frame of mind."

"You may do so, dear Angela," replied Jane—"but your lot is cast differently from mine. What is required from me is not required from you. Such strong devotional feelings have been implanted in my breast, for a wise purpose, that they usurp the place of all other, and fit me for my high calling. The earnest and hearty believer in the gospel will gladly embrace death, even if accompanied by the severest tortures, at seasons perilous to his church, in the conviction that it will be profitable to it. Such have been the deaths of the martyrs of our religion—such shall be my death."

"Amen!" exclaimed Angela, fervently.

"Must we part now?" inquired Jane.

"Not unless you desire it," replied Angela. "I have obtained the queen's permission to remain with you to the last."

"I thank her for the boon," returned Jane. "It will be a great consolation to me to have you near me. Angela, you must not shrink from the last duty of a friend—you must accompany me to the scaffold. I may need you there."

"I will shrink from nothing you injoin, madam," replied Angela, shuddering. "But I had rather—far rather—suffer in your stead."

Jane made no reply, but pressed her hand affectionately.

"I have omitted to tell you, madam," continued Angela, "that the queen, before I was dismissed from the presence, urged me to embrace the faith of Rome,—that of my father, who perished for his adherence to it,—and to use my endeavours to induce you to become reconciled with that church."

"And what answer did you make?" demanded Jane, sternly.

"Such as you yourself, would have made, madam," replied Angela—"I refused both."

"It is well," rejoined Jane. "And now I must return to my devotions. You will have a weary office in attending me, Angela. Nor shall I be able to address more than a few words to you—and those but seldom."

"Think not of me, madam," replied the other; "all I desire is to be near you, and to join my prayers with yours."

Both then knelt down, and both prayed long and fervently. It would have been a touching sight to see those young and beautiful creatures with eyes upturned to heaven—hands clasped—and lips murmuring prayer. But the zeal that animated Jane far surpassed that of her companion. Long before the former sought her couch, fatigue overcame the latter, and she was compelled to retire to rest; and when she arose (though it was not yet daybreak), she found the unwearying devotee had already been up for hours. And so some days were spent—Jane ever praying—Angela praying too, but more frequently engaged in watching her companion.

On the morning of Thursday, the 8th of February, the jailor appeared, with a countenance of unusual gloom, and informed his captive that the lieutenant of the Tower and Father Feckenham were without, and desired to see her.

"Admit them," replied Jane. "I know their errand. You are right welcome, sirs," she added, with a cheerful look, as they entered. "You bring me good news."

"Alas! madam," replied Feckenham, sorrowfully, "we are the bearers of ill tidings. It is our melancholy office to acquaint you that your execution is appointed for to-morrow."

"Why that *is* good news," returned Jane, with an unaltered countenance. "I have long and anxiously expected my release, and am glad to find it so near at hand."

"I am further charged, by the queen's highness, who desires not to kill the soul as well as the body," pursued Feckenham, "to entreat you to use the few hours remaining to you in making your peace with heaven."

"I will strive to do so, sir,1' replied Jane meekly.

"Do not mistake me, madam," rejoined Feckenham, earnestly. "Her majesty's hope is that you will reconcile yourself with the holy Catholic church, by which means you can alone ensure your salvation. For this end, she has desired me to continue near you to the last, and to use my best efforts for your conversion—and by God's grace I will do so."

"You may spare yourself the labour, sir," replied Jane. "You will more easily overturn these solid walls by your arguments than my resolution."

"At least, suffer me to make the attempt," replied Feckenham. "That I have hitherto failed in convincing you is true, and I may fail now, but my very zeal must satisfy you that I have your welfare at heart, and am eager to deliver you from the bondage of Satan."

"I have never doubted your zeal, sir," returned Jane; "nor—and I say it in all humility,—do I doubt my own power to refute your arguments. But I must decline the contest now, because my time is short, and I would devote every moment to the service of God."

"That excuse shall not avail you, madam," rejoined Fecken-ham, significantly. "The queen and the chancellor are as anxious as I am, for your conversion, and nothing shall be left undone to accomplish it."

"I must submit, then," replied Jane, with a look of resignation. "But I repeat, you will lose your labour."

"Time will show," returned Feckenham.

"I have not yet dared to ask a question which has risen to my lips, but found no utterance," said Jane, in an altered tone. "My husband!—what of him?"

"His execution will take place at the same time with your own," replied Feckenham.

"I shall see him to-morrow, then?" cried Jane.

"Perhaps before," returned Feckenham.

"It were better not," said Jane, trembling. "I know not whether I can support the interview."

"I was right," muttered Feckenham to himself. "The way to move her is through the affections." And he made a sign to the lieutenant, who quitted the chamber.

"Prepare yourself, madam," he added to Jane.

"For what?" she cried.

"For your husband's approach. He is here."

As he spoke, the door was opened, and Dudley rushed forward, and caught her in his arms. Not a word was uttered for some moments by the afflicted pair. Angela withdrew weeping as if her heart would break, into one of the recesses, and Feckenham and the lieutenant into another. After the lapse of a short time, thinking it a favourable opportunity for his purpose, the confessor came forward. Jane and her husband were still locked in each other's embrace, and it seemed as if nothing but force could tear them asunder.

"I would not disturb you," said Feckenham, "but my orders are that this interview must be brief. I am empowered also to state, madam," he added to Jane, "that her majesty will even now pardon your husband, notwithstanding his heinous offences against her, provided you are publicly reconciled with the church of Rome."

"I cannot do it, Dudley," cried Jane, in a voice of agony—"I cannot—cannot."

"Neither do I desire it," he replied. "I would not purchase life on such terms. We will die together."

"Be it so," observed Feckenham, with a disconcerted look. "The offer will never be repeated."

"It would never have been made at all, if there had been a chance of its acceptance," returned Dudley, coldly. "Tell your royal mistress, that I love my wife too well to require such a sacrifice at her hands, and that she loves me too well to make it."

"Dudley," exclaimed Jane, gazing at him with tearful eyes, "I can now die without a pang."

"Have you aught more to say to each other?" demanded Feckenham. "You will meet no more on earth!"

"Yes, on the scaffold," cried Jane.

"Not so," replied Feckenham, gloomily. "Lord Guilford Dudley will suffer on Tower Hill—you, madam, will meet your sentence on the green before the White Tower, where Anne Boleyn and Catherine Howard perished."

"We shall meet in the grave, then," rejoined Dudley, bitterly, "where Mary's tyranny can neither reach us, nor the voice of juggling priest disturb us more."

"Your prisoner," cried Feckenham, turning angrily to the lieutenant.

"Farewell, dear Dudley," exclaimed Jane, straining him to her bosom—"Be constant."

"As yourself," he replied, gently disengaging himself from her. "I am ready, sir," he added, to Brydges. And without hazarding another look at Jane, who fell back in the arms of Angela, he quitted the chamber.

Half an hour after this, when Jane had in some degree recovered from the shock, Feckenham returned, and informed her that he had obtained from the queen a reprieve for herself and her husband for three days. "You can now no longer allege the shortness of the time allowed you, as a reason for declining a conference with me," he said: "and I pray you address yourself earnestly to the subject, for I will not desist till I have convinced and converted you."

"Then I shall have little of the time allotted me to myself," replied Jane. "But I will not repine. My troubles may benefit others—if not myself."

XXXVIII.—HOW THE PRINCESS ELIZABETH AND COURTENAY WERE DELIVERED OUT OF THE TOWER TO FURTHER DURANCE; AND HOW QUEEN MARY WAS WEDDED, BY PROXY, TO PHILIP OF SPAIN.

Elizabeth still continued a close prisoner in the Bell Tower. But she indulged the most sanguine expectations of a speedy release. Her affections had received a severe blow in Courtenay's relinquishment of his pretensions to her hand, and it required all her pride and mastery over herself to bear up against it. She did, however, succeed in conquering her feelings, and with her usual impetuosity, began now to hate him in the proportion of her former love. While his mistress was thus brooding over the past, and trying to regulate her conduct for the future within the narrow walls of her prison, Courtenay, who had been removed to the Flint Tower, where he was confined in the basement chamber, was likewise occupied in revolving his brief and troubled career. A captive from his youth, he had enjoyed a few months' liberty, during which, visions of glory, power, greatness, and love— such as have seldom visited the most exalted—opened upon him. The bright dream was now ended, and he was once more a captive. Slight as his experience had been, he was sickened of the intrigues and hollowness of court life, and sighed for freedom and retirement. Elizabeth still retained absolute possession of his heart, but he feared to espouse her, because he was firmly persuaded that her haughty and ambitious character would involve him in perpetual troubles. Cost what it might, he determined to resign her hand as his sole hope of future tranquillity. In this resolution he was confirmed by Gardiner, who visited him in secret, and counselled him as to the best course to pursue.

"If you claim my promise," observed the crafty chancellor, "I will fulfil it, and procure you the hand of the princess, but I warn you you will not hold it long. Another rebellion will follow, in which you and Elizabeth will infallibly be mixed up, and then nothing will save you from the block."

Courtenay acquiesced, and Gardiner having gained his point, left him with the warmest assurances that he would watch over his safety. Insincere as he was, the Chancellor was well-disposed towards Courtenay, but he had a difficult game to play. He was met on all hands by Renard, who was bent on the Earl's destruction and that of the princess; and every move he made with the queen was checked by his wary and subtle antagonist. Notwithstanding her belief in their treasonable practices, Mary was inclined to pardon the offenders, but Renard entreated her to suspend her judgment upon them, till the emperor's opinion could be ascertained. This, he well knew, if agreed to, would insure their ruin, as he had written secretly in such terms to Charles the Fifth as he was satisfied would accomplish his object. Extraordinary despatch was used by the messengers; and to Renard's infinite delight, while he and Gardiner were struggling for ascendancy over the queen, a courier arrived from Madrid. Renard's joy was converted into positive triumph as he opened his own letters received by the same hand, and found that the emperor acquiesced in the expediency of the severest measures towards Elizabeth and her suitor, and recommended their immediate execution. The same despatches informed him that Charles, apprehensive of some further difficulty in respect to his son's projected union with Mary, had written to the Count D'Egmont at Brussels, with letters of ratification and procuration, commissioning him to repair to the court of London without delay, and conclude the engagement by espousing the queen by proxy.

Not many hours later, the Count himself, who had set out instantly from Brussels on receiving his commission, arrived. He was received on the queen's part by the Earl of Pembroke, the Earl of Shrewsbury, comptroller of the household, and the Marquis of Winchester, high treasurer, and conducted to the state apartments within the palace of the Tower, where the court was then staying. Mary appointed an audience with him on the following day, and in the interim, to Renard's disappointment, remained closeted with Gardiner, and would see no one beside. The ambassador, however, consoled himself with the certainty of success, and passed the evening in consultation with D'Egmont, to whom he detailed all that had passed since the flight of the latter.

"The heretical faction in England," he observed, "is entirely crushed—or will be so, when Jane and Elizabeth are executed. And if his highness, Prince Philip, will follow up my measures, he may not only restore the old faith throughout the realm, but establish the inquisition in the heart of London within six months."

The next day, at the appointed hour, the Count D'Egmont attended by Renard and the whole of his suite, was conducted with much ceremony to the council-chamber in the White Tower. He found Mary surrounded by the whole of her ministers, and prostrating himself before the throne, acquainted her with his mission, and, presenting her with the letters of procuration he had received from the prince, entreated her to ratify on her side the articles already agreed upon. To this request, for which she was already prepared by the emperor's despatches, Mary vouchsafed a gracious answer, saying: "I am as impatient for the completion of the contract as the prince your master can be, and shall not hesitate a moment to comply with his wishes. But I would," she added, smiling, "that he had come to claim its fulfilment himself."

"His highness only awaits your majesty's summons, and an assurance that he can land upon your shores without occasioning further tumult," rejoined D'Egmont.

"He shall speedily receive that assurance," returned Mary. "Heaven be praised! our troubles are ended, and the spirit of disaffection and sedition checked, if not altogether extinguished. But I pray you hold me excused for a short time," she continued, motioning him to rise; "I have some needful business to conclude before I proceed with this solemnity."

Waving her hand to Sir Thomas Brydges, who stood among the group of nobles near the throne, he immediately quitted the presence, returning in a few moments with a guard of halberdiers in the midst of which were Elizabeth and Courtenay. At the approach of the prisoners, the assemblage divided into two lines to allow them passage; and preceded by the lieutenant, they advanced to within a short distance of the queen.

Marv, meantime, had seated herself; and her countenance, hitherto radiant with smiles, assumed a severe expression. A mournful silence pervaded the courtly throng, and all seemed as ominous and lowering as if a thunder-cloud had settled over them. This was not however the case with Renard. A sinister smile lighted up his features, and he observed in an under-tone to D'Egmont, "My hour of triumph is at hand."

"Wait awhile," replied the other.

Elizabeth looked in no wise abashed or dismayed by the position in which she found herself. Throwing angry and imperious glances around, and bending her brows on those who scanned her too curiously, she turned her back upon Courtenay, and seemed utterly unconscious of his presence.

At the queen's command, Gardiner stepped forward, and taking a roll of paper from an attendant, proceeded to read the charges against the prisoners, together with the depositions of those who had been examined, as to their share in the insurrection. When he concluded, Elizabeth observed in a haughty tone—"There is nothing in all that to touch me, my lord. Wyat has recanted his confession, and avowed he was suborned by Renard. And as to the rest of my accusers, they are unworthy of credit. The queen's highness must acquit me."

"What say you, my lord!" demanded Gardiner of Courtenay.

"Nothing," replied the earl.

"Do you confess yourself guilty of the high crimes and misdemeanours laid to your charge, then?" pursued the chancellor.

"No!" answered Courtenay, firmly. "But I will not seek to defend myself further. I throw myself on the queen's mercy."

"You do wisely, my lord," returned Gardiner; "and your grace," he added to Elizabeth, "would do well to abate your pride, and imitate his example."

"In my father's time, my lord," observed the princess, scornfully, "you would not, for your head, have dared to hold such language towards me."

"I dared to plead your mother's cause with him," retorted Gardiner with much asperity. "Your majesty will now pronounce such sentence upon the accused, as may seem meet to you," he added, turning to the queen.

"We hold their guilt not clearly proven," replied Mary. "Nevertheless, too many suspicious circumstances appear against them to allow us to set them at large till all chance of further trouble is ended. Not desiring to deal harshly with them, we shall not confine them longer within the Tower. Which of you, my lords, will take charge of the princess Elizabeth? It will be no slight responsibility. You will answer for her security with your heads. Which of you will take charge of her, I say?"

As she spoke, she glanced inquiringly round the assemblage, but no answer was returned.

"Had not your highness better send her grace under a sure guard to the emperor's court at Brussels," observed Renard, who could scarcely conceal his mortification at the queen's decision.

"I will think of it," returned Mary.

"Sooner than this shall be," interposed Sir Henry Bedingfeld, "since none worthier of the office can be found, I will undertake it."

"You are my good genius, Bedingfeld," replied Mary.—"To you, then, I confide her, and I will associate with you in the office, Sir John Williams, of Thame. The place of her confinement shall be my palace at Woodstock, and she will remain there till you receive further orders. You will set out with a sufficient guard for Oxfordshire."

"I am ever ready to obey your highness," replied Bedingfeld.

"Accursed meddler!" exclaimed Renard to D'Egmont, "he has marred my project."

"The Earl of Devonshire will be confined in Fotheringay Castle, in Northamptonshire," pursued Mary. "To you, Sir Thomas Tresham," she continued, addressing one of those near her, "I commit him."

"I am honoured in the charge," returned Tresham, bowing.

"Your majesty will repent this ill-judged clemency," cried Renard, unable to repress his choler; "and since my counsels are unheeded, I must pray your highness to allow me to resign the post I hold near your person."

"Be it so," replied Mary in a freezing tone; "we accept your resignation—and shall pray his imperial majesty to recal you."

"Is this my reward?" exclaimed Renard, as he retired, covered with shame and confusion. "Cursed is he that puts faith in princes!"

The prisoners were then removed, and as they walked side by side, Courtenay sought to address the princess, but she turned away her head sharply, according him neither look nor word in reply. Finding himself thus repulsed, the earl desisted, and they proceeded in silence as long as their way lay together.

And thus, without one farewell, they parted—to meet no more. Liberated at the instance of Philip of Spain, Courtenay journeyed to Italy, where he died two years afterwards, at Padua, obtaining, as Holinshed touchingly remarks, "that quiet, which in his life he could never have." Of the glorious destiny reserved for Elizabeth, nothing need be said.

The prisoners removed, the queen presented her hand to the Earl of Pembroke, and repaired with her whole retinue to Saint John's Chapel.

Arrived there, Mary stationed herself at the altar, around which were grouped Bonner, Tunstal, Feckenham, and a host of other priests and choristers, in their full robes. In a short time, the nave and aisles of the sacred structure were densely crowded by the lords of the council, together with other nobles and their attendants, the dames of honour, the guard, and the suite of the Count D'Egmont. Nor were the galleries above unoccupied, every available situation finding a tenant.

D'Egmont, as the representative of Philip of Spain, took up a position on the right of the queen, and sustained his part with great dignity. As soon as Gardiner was prepared, the ceremonial commenced. D'Egmont tendered his hand to Mary, who took it, and they both knelt down upon the cushion before the altar, while the customary oaths were administered, and a solemn benediction pronounced over them. This done, they arose, and Gardiner observed to the queen in a voice audible throughout the structure—"Your majesty is now wedded to the Prince of Spain. May God preserve you both, and bless your union!"

"God preserve Queen Mary!" cried the Earl of Pembroke, stepping forward.

And the shout was enthusiastically echoed by all within the chapel. But not a voice was raised, nor a blessing invoked for her husband.

Te Deum was then sung by the choristers, and mass performed by Bonner and the priests.

"His imperial majesty entreats your acceptance of this slight offering," said D'Egmont, when the sacred rites were concluded, presenting the queen with a diamond ring, of inestimable value.

"I accept the gift," replied Mary, "and I beg you to offer my best thanks to the emperor. For yourself, I hope you will wear this ornament in remembrance of me, and of the occasion." And detaching a collar of gold set with precious stones from her own neck, she placed it over that of D'Egmont.

"I now go to bring your husband, gracious madam," said the count.

"Heaven grant you a safe and speedy journey!" replied Mary.

"And to your highness a prosperous union!" rejoined the count; "and may your race long occupy the throne." So saying, he bowed and departed.

D'Egmont's wish did not produce a cheering effect on Mary. Jane's words rushed to her mind, and she feared that her union would not be happy— would not be blessed with offspring. And it need scarcely be added, her forebodings were realised. Coldly treated by a haughty and neglectful husband, she went childless to the tomb.

XXXIX.—OF THE WEDDING OF SIR NARCISSUS LE GRAND WITH JANE THE FOOL, AND WHAT HAPPENED AT IT; AND OF THE ENTERTAINMENT GIVEN BY HIM, ON THE OCCASION, TO HIS OLD FRIENDS AT THE STONE KITCHEN.

Sir Narcissus Le Grand made rapid strides in the royal favour, as well as in that of his mistress. He was now in constant attendance on the queen, and his coxcombry afforded her so much amusement, that she gave him a post near her person, in order to enjoy it. Jane the Fool, too, who had a secret liking for him, though she affected displeasure at Mary's command, became so violently enamoured, and so excessively jealous, if the slightest attentions were paid him by the dames of honour, that the queen thought it desirable to fix an early day for wedding.

The happy event took place on Saturday, the 10th of February, at Saint Peter's chapel on the green, and was honoured by the presence of the queen, and all her attendants. Never were merrier nuptials witnessed! And even the grave countenance of Feckenham, the officiating priest on the occasion, wore a smile, as the bridegroom, attired in his gayest habiliments, bedecked at all points with lace, tags, and fringe; curled, scented, and glistening with silver and gold, was borne into the chapel on the shoulders of Og,—who had carried him from the By-ward Tower, through a vast concourse of spectators,—and deposited at the altar near the bride. Behind Og, came his two brethren, together with Dames Placida and Potentia; while Peter Trusbut, Ribald, and Winwike, brought up the rear.

Arrived at the height of his ambition, graced with a title, favoured by the queen, and idolised by his bride, who was not altogether destitute of personal attractions, and was, at least, twice his own size, the poor dwarfs brain was almost turned, and he had some difficulty in maintaining the decorous and dignified deportment which he felt it necessary to maintain on the occasion. The ceremony was soon performed,—too soon for Sir Narcissus, who would willingly have prolonged it—The royal train departed,—not, however, before Mary had bestowed a well-filled purse of gold upon the bridegroom, and commanded him to bring his friends to the palace, where a supper would be provided for them. Sir Narcissus then offered his hand to his bride, and led her forth, followed by his companions.

A vast crowd had collected before the doors of the sacred edifice. But a passage having been kept clear by a band of halberdiers for the queen, the lines were unbroken when the wedding-party appeared. Loud acclamations welcomed Sir Narcissus, who paused for a moment beneath the porch, and taking off his well-plumed cap, bowed repeatedly to the assemblage. Reiterated shouts and plaudits succeeded, and the clamour was so great from those who could not obtain a glimpse of him, that the little knight entreated Og to take him once more upon his shoulder. The request was immediately complied with; and when he was seen in this exalted situation, a deafening shout rent the skies. The applauses, however, were shared by his consort, who placed on the shoulder of Gog, became equally conspicuous.

In this way, they were carried side by side along the green, and Sir Narcissus was so enchanted that he desired the bearers to proceed as slowly as possible. His enthusiasm became at length so great, that when several of those around him jestingly cried, "Largesse, largesse! Sir Narcissus," he opened the purse lately given him by the queen, and which hung at his girdle, and threw away the broad pieces in showers. "I will win more gold," he observed to Og, who remonstrated with him on his profusion; "but such a day as this does not occur twice in one's life."

"Happiness and long life attend you and your lovely dame, Sir Narcissus!" cried a bystander.

"There is not a knight in the Tower to be compared with you, worshipful sir!" roared another.

"You deserve the queen's favour!" vociferated a third.

"Greater dignities are in store for you!" added a fourth.

EASTERN DRAWBRIDGE.

Never was new-made and new-married knight so enchanted. Acknowledging all the compliments and fine speeches with smirks, smiles, and bows, he threw away fresh showers of gold. After making the complete circuit of the fortress, he crossed the drawbridge, and proceeded to the wharf, where he was hailed by different boats on the river: everywhere, his reception was the same. On the return of the party, Hairun invited them all to the Lions' Tower, and ushering them to the gallery, brought out several of the wild animals, and went through his performances as if the queen herself had been present. In imitation of the sovereign, Sir Narcissus bestowed his last few coins, together with the purse containing them, upon the bearward. During the exhibition, the knight had entertained his consort with an account of his combat with old Max; and before quitting the menagerie he led her into the open space in front of the cages, that she might have a nearer view of the formidable animal.

"It will not be necessary to read you such a lesson, sweetheart, as my friend Magog read his dame," he observed. "But it is as well you should know that I have a resource in case of need."

"I shall not require to be brought to obedience by a bear, chuck," returned Lady Le Grand, with a languishing look. "Your slightest word is law to me!"

"So she says now," observed Dame Potentia, who happened to overhear the remark, to Dame Placida. "But let a week pass over their heads, and she will alter her tone."

"Perhaps so," sighed Placida. "But I have never had my own way since my encounter with old Max. Besides, these dwarfs are fiery fellows, and have twice the spirit of men of larger growth."

"There *is* something in that, it must be owned," rejoined Potentia, reflectively.

Max, by Sir Narcissus's command, was let out of his cage, and when within a few yards of them, sat on his hind-legs, and opened his enormous jaws. At this sight, Lady Le Grand screamed, and took refuge behind her husband, who, bidding her fear nothing, drew his sword, and put himself in a posture of defence. Suppressing a laugh, Hairun informed the knight that Max only begged for something to eat; and sundry biscuits and apples being given him, he was driven back to his cage without any misadventure. Hairun then led the party to his lodging, where a collation was spread out for them, of which they partook-At its conclusion, Peter Trusbut observed, that if Sir Narcissus-and Lady Le Grand would honour him with their company at the Stone Kitchen on the following night, he would use his best endeavours to prepare a supper worthy of them.

"It will give me infinite pleasure to sup with thee, worthy Peter," replied the knight, with a patronising air; "but I must insist that the banquet be at my expense. Thou shalt cook it,—I will pay for it."

"As you please, worshipful sir," rejoined Trusbut. "But I can have what I please from the royal larder."

"So much the better," returned Sir Narcissus. "But mine the entertainment shall be. And I here invite you all to it."

"My best endeavours shall be used to content your worship," replied the pantler. "We have had some good suppers in the Stone Kitchen ere now, but this shall exceed them all."

"It is well," replied the knight. "Hairun, you had better bring your monkey to divert us."

"Right willingly, worshipful sir," replied the bearward; "and if you have a cast-off suit of clothes to spare, I will deck him in them for the occasion."

"You will find my last suit at the By-ward Tower," replied Sir Narcissus. "Og will give them to you; and you may, if you choose, confer upon him the name I have cast off with them."

"I will not fail to adopt your worship's suggestion," returned Hairun, smothering a laugh. "Henceforth, I shall call my ape Xit, and who knows whether in due season he may not attain the dignity of knighthood?"

Sir Narcissus did not exactly relish this remark, which made many of the guests smile; but he thought it better not to notice it, and taking a courteous leave of the hospitable bearward, proceeded to the palace, where a lodging was now given him, and where he passed the remainder of the day with his friends in jollity and carousing. Nor was it until the clock had chimed midnight, that he was left alone with his spouse.

At what hour Sir Narcissus arose on the following morning does not appear. But at eight in the evening, attired as on the previous day, and accompanied by his dame in her wedding-dress, he repaired to the Stone Kitchen. He found the whole party assembled, including, besides those he had invited, Win-wike, and his son, a chubby youth of some ten years old, Mauger, Wolfytt, and Sorrocold. Sir Narcissus could have dispensed with the company of the three latter; but not desiring to quarrel with them, he put the best face he could upon the matter, and bade them heartily welcome. He found, too, that Hairun had literally obeyed his injunctions, and brought his monkey with him, dressed up in his old clothes.

"Allow me to present Xit, the ape, to your worship," said the bearward.

"He is welcome," replied Sir Narcissus, laughing, to conceal his vexation at the absurd resemblance which the animal bore to him.

Sir Narcissus was then conducted to a seat at the head of the table. On the right was placed his lady, on the left, Dame Placida; while the pantler, who, as usual, filled the office of carver, faced him. The giants were separated by the other guests, and Ribald sat between Dames Placida and Potentia, both of whom he contrived to keep in most excellent humour. Peter Trusbut did not assert too much when he declared that the entertainment should surpass all that had previously been given in the Stone Kitchen; and not to be behindhand, the giants exceeded all their former efforts in the eating line. They did not, it is true, trouble themselves much with the first course, which consisted of various kinds of pottage and fish; though Og spoke in terms of rapturous commendation of a sturgeon's jowl, and Magog consumed the best part of a pickled tunny-fish.

But when these were removed, and the more substantial viands appeared, they set to work in earnest. Turning up their noses at the boiled capons, roasted bustards, stewed quails, and other light matters, they, by one consent, assailed a largo shield of brawn, and speedily demolished it. Their next incursion was upon a venison pasty—a soused pig followed,—and while Gog prepared himself for a copious draught of Rhenish by a dish of anchovies, Magog, who had just emptied a huge two-handed flagon of bragget, sharpened his appetite—the edge of which was a little taken off,—with a plate of pickled oysters. A fawn roasted, whole, with a pudding in its inside, now claimed their attention, and was pronounced delicious. Og, then, helped himself to a shoulder of mutton and olives; Gog to a couple of roasted ruffs; and Magog again revived his flagging powers with a dish of buttered crabs. At this juncture, the strong waters were introduced by the pantler, and proved highly acceptable to the labouring giants.

Xit, now Sir Narcissus Le Grand, entertaining his friends on his wedding day.

Peter Trusbut performed wonders. In the old terms of his art, he leached the brawn, reared the goose, sauced the capon, spoiled the fowls, flushed the chickens, unlaced the rabbits, winged the quails, minced the plovers, thighed the pigeons, bordered the venison pasty, tranched the sturgeon, under-tranched the tunny-fish, tamed the crab, and barbed the lobster.

The triumphs of the repast now appeared. They were a baked swan, served in a coffin of rye-paste; a crane, likewise roasted whole; and a peacock, decorated with its tail. The first of these birds,—to use his own terms,—was reared by the pantler; the second displayed; and the last disfigured. And disfigured it was, in more ways than one; for, snatching the gaudy plumes from its tail, Sir Narcissus decorated his dame's cap with them. The discussion of these noble dishes fully occupied the giants, and when they had consumed a tolerable share of each, they declared they had done. Nor could they be tempted with the marrow toasts, the fritters, the puddings, the wafers, and other cates and sweetmeats that followed,—though they did not display the like objection to the brimming cups of hippocras, which wound up the repast.

The only person who appeared to want appetite for the feast, or who, perhaps, was too busy to eat, was Sir Narcissus. For the first time in his life, he played the part of host, and he acquitted himself to admiration. Ever and anon, rising in his chair, with a goblet of wine in his hand, he would pledge some guest, or call out to Peter Trusbut to fill some empty plate. He had a jest for every one;—abundance of well-turned compliments for the ladies; and the tenderest glances and whispers for his dame, who looked more lovesick and devoted than ever. By the time the cloth was removed, and the dishes replaced by flagons and pots of hydromel and wine, Sir Narcissus was in the height of his glory. The wine had got a little into his head, but not more than added to his exhilaration, and he listened with rapturous delight to the speech made by Og, who in good set terms proposed his health and that of his bride. The pledge was drunk with the utmost enthusiasm; and in the heat of his excitement, Sir Narcissus mounted on the table, and bowing all round, returned thanks in the choicest phrases he could summon. His speech received several interruptions from the applauses of his guests; and Hairun, who was bent upon mischief, thought this a favourable opportunity for practising it. During the banquet, he had kept the monkey in the back-ground, but he now placed him on the table behind Sir Narcissus, whose gestures and posture the animal began to mimic. Its grimaces were so absurd and extraordinary, that the company roared with laughter, to the infinite astonishment of the speaker, who at the moment wras indulging in a pathetic regret, at the necessity he should be under of quitting his old haunts in consequence of his new dignities and duties; but his surprise was changed to anger, as he felt his sword suddenly twitched from the sheath, and beheld the grinning countenance of the ape close behind him. Uttering an exclamation of fury, he turned with the intention of sacrificing the cause of his annoyance on the spot; but the animal wras too quick for him, and springing on his shoulders, plucked off his cap, and twisted its fingers in his well-curled hair, lugging him tremendously. Screaming with pain and rage, Sir Narcissus ran round the table upsetting all in his course, but unable to free himself from his tormentor, who keeping fast hold of his head, grinned and chattered as if in mockery of his vociferations.

Lady Le Grand had not noticed the monkey's first proceedings, her attention being diverted by Ribald, who pressed her, with many compliments upon her charms, to take a goblet of malmsey which he had poured out for her. But she no sooner perceived what was going forward, than she flew to the rescue, beat off the monkey, and hugging her little lord to her bosom, almost smothered him with kisses and caresses. Nor were Dames Placida and Potcntia less attentive to him. At first, they had treated the matter as a joke, but seeing the diminutive knight was really alarmed, they rubbed his head, patted him on the back, embraced him as tenderly as Lady Le Grand would permit, and loudly upbraided Hairun for his misconduct. Scarcely able to conceal his laughter, the offender pretended the utmost regret, and instantly sent off the monkey by one of the attendants to the Lions' Tower.

It was some time before Sir Narcissus could be fully appeased; and it required all the blandishments of the dames, and the humblest apologies from Hairun, to prevent him from quitting the party in high dudgeon. At length, however, he was persuaded by Magog to wash down his resentment in a pottle of sack, brewed by the pantler—and the generous drink restored him to instant good-humour. Called upon by the company to conclude his speech, he once more ventured upon the table, and declaiming bitterly against the interruption he had experienced, finished his oration amid the loudest cheers. He then bowed round in his most graceful manner, and returned to his chair.

It has already been stated that Mauger, Sorrocold, and Wolfytt were among the guests. The latter had pretty nearly recovered from the wound inflicted by Nightgall, which proved, on examination, by no means dangerous; and, regardless of the consequences, he ate, drank, laughed, and shouted as lustily as the rest. The other two being of a more grave and saturnine character, seldom smiled at what was going forward; and though they did not neglect to fill their goblets, took no share in the general conversation, but sat apart in a corner near the chimney with Winwike, discussing the terrible scenes they had witnessed in their different capacities, with the true gusto of amateurs.

"And so Lady Jane Grey and her husband will positively be executed to-morrow?" observed Winwike. "There is no chance of further reprieve, I suppose."

"None whatever," replied Mauger. "Father Feckenham, I understand, offered her two days more, if she would prolong her disputation with him, but she refused. No—no. There will be no further respite. She will suffer on the Green—her husband on Tower Hill."

"So I heard," replied Sorrocold—"Poor soul! she is very young—not seventeen, I am told."

"Poll—poh!" cried Mauger, gruffly—"there's nothing in that. Life is as sweet at seventy as seventeen. However, I'll do my work as quickly as I can. If you wish to see a head cleanly taken off, get as near the scaffold as you can."

"I shall not fail to do so," returned Sorrocold. "I would not miss it for the world."

"As soon as the clock strikes twelve, and the Sabbath is ended," continued Mauger, "my assistants will begin to put up the scaffold. You know the spot before Saint Peter's chapel. They say the grass won't grow there. But that's an old woman's tale—he! he!"

"Old woman's tale, or not," rejoined Winwike, gravely—"it's true. I've often examined the spot, and never could find a blade of herbage there."

"Well, well," rejoined Mauger, "I won't dispute the point. Believe it, and welcome. I could tell other strange tales concerning that place. It's a great privilege to be beheaded there, and only granted to illustrious personages. The last two who fell there were Queen Catherine Howard, and her confidante, the Countess of Rochford. Lady Jane Grey would be beheaded on Tower Hill, with her husband, but they are afraid of the mob, who might compassionate the youthful pair, and occasion a riot. It's better to be on the safe side—he! he!"

"You said you had some other strange tales to tell concerning that place," observed Sorrocold. "What are they?"

"I don't much like talking about them," rejoined Mauger, reluctantly, "but since I've dropped a hint on the subject, I may as well speak out. You must know, then, that the night before the execution of the old Countess of Salisbury, who would not lay her head upon the block, and whom I was obliged to chase round the scaffold and bring down how I could—the night before she fell,—and a bright moonlight night it was,—I was standing on the scaffold putting it in order for the morrow, when all at once there issued from the church porch a female figure, shrouded from head to foot in white."

"Well!" exclaimed Sorrocold, breathlessly.

"Well," returned the headsman, "though filled with alarm, I never took my eyes from it, but watched it glide slowly round the scaffold, and finally return to the porch, where it disappeared."

"Did you address it?" asked Winwike.

"Not I," replied Mauger. "My tongue clove to the roof of my mouth. I could not have spoken to save my life."

"Strange!" exclaimed Sorrocold. "Did you ever see it again?"

"Yes, on the night before Catherine Howard's execution," replied Mauger; "and I have no doubt it will appear to-night."

"Do you think so?" cried Sorrocold. "I will watch for it."

"I shall visit the scaffold myself, an hour after midnight," returned Mauger—"you can accompany me if you think proper."

"Agreed!" exclaimed the chirurgeon.

They were here interrupted by a boisterous roar of merriment from the other guests. While their sombre talk was going on, Ribald, who had made considerable progress in the good graces of Lady Le Grand, had related a merry tale, and at its close, which was attended with shouts of laughter, Sir Narcissus ordered a fresh supply of wine, and the vast measures were promptly replenished by the pantier. Several pleasant hours were thus consumed, until at last Sir Narcissus arose, or rather attempted to rise, for his limbs refused their office, and his gaze was rather unsteady, and addressed his friends as follows:—"Farewell, my merry gossips," he hiccupped—

"farewell! As I am now a married man, I must keep go-o-o-d hours." (At this moment the clock struck twelve). "I have already trespassed too much on Lady Le Grand's good nature. She is getting sleepy. So, to speak truth, am! I shall often visit you again—as often, at least, as my dignities and duties will permit. Do not stand in awe of my presence. I shall always unbend with you—always. The truly great are never proud—at least to their inferiors. With their superiors it is a different matter. This alone would convince you of my illustrious origin."

"True," cried Gog, "no one would suspect you of being the son of a groom of the pantry, for instance."

"No one," repeated Xit, fiercely, and making an ineffectual attempt to draw his sword, "or if he *did* suspect it, he should never live to repeat it."

"Well, well," replied Gog, meekly. "*I* don't suspect it."

"None of us suspect it," laughed Og.

"I am qu-quito sa-sa-satisfied," replied Sir Narcissus. "More wine, old Trusbut. Fill the pots, pantler. I'll give you a r-r-r-rousing pledge."

"And so will I," cried his dame, who, like her lord, was a little the worse for the wine she had swallowed,—her goblet being kept constantly filled by the assiduous Ribald—"so will I, if you don't come home directly, you little sot."

"Lady Le Gr-r-and," cried Sir Narcissus, furiously, "I'll divorce you.—I'll behead you as Harry the Eighth did Anne Boleyn."

"No, chuck, you won't," replied the lady. "You will think better of it to-morrow." So saying, she snatched him up in her arms, and despite his resistance carried him off to his lodging in the palace, long before reaching which, he had fallen asleep, and when he awoke next morning, he had but a very confused recollection of the events of the preceding night.

And here, as it will be necessary to take leave of our little friend, we will give a hasty glance at his subsequent history. Within a year of his union, a son was born to him, who speedily eclipsed his sire in stature, and in due season became a stalwart, well-proportioned man, six feet in height, and bearing a remarkable resemblance to Ribald. Sir Narcissus was exceedingly fond of him; and it was rather a droll sight to see them together. The dwarfish knight continued to rise in favour with the queen, and might have been constantly with the court had he pleased, but as he preferred, from old habits and associations, residing within the Tower, he was allowed apartments in the palace, of which he was termed, in derision, the grand seneschal. On Elizabeth's accession, he was not removed, but retained his post till the middle of the reign of James the First, when he died full of years and honours—active, vain, and consequential to the last, and from his puny stature, always looking young. He was interred in front of Saint Peter's chapel on the green, near his old friends the giants, who had preceded him some years to the land of shadows, and the stone that marks his grave may still be seen.

As to the three gigantic warders, they retained their posts, and played their parts at many a feast and high solemnity during Elizabeth's golden rule, waxing in girth and bulk as they advanced in years, until they became somewhat gross and unwieldy. Og, who had been long threatened with apoplexy, his head being almost buried in his enormous shoulders, expired suddenly in his chair after a feast; and his two brethren took his loss so much to heart, that they abstained altogether from the flask, and followed him in less than six months, dying, it was thought, of grief, but more probably of dropsy. Their resting-place has been already indicated. In the same spot, also, the Lady Le Grand, Dame Placida, and the worthy pantler and his spouse. Magog was a widower during the latter part of his life, and exhibited no anxiety to enter a second time into the holy estate of matrimony. Og and Gog died unmarried.

XL.—OF THE VISION SEEN BY MAUGER AND SORROCOLD ON THE TOWER GREEN.

After the forcible abduction of Sir Narcissus by his spouse, the party broke up,—Og and Gog shaping their course to the By-ward Tower, Magog and his spouse, together with Ribald, who had taken up his quarters with them, to their lodging on the hill leading to the Green,—Hairun to the Lions' Tower, Win-wike and his son to the Flint Tower, while Mauger, Wolfytt, and Sorrocold proceeded to the Cradle Tower. Unfastening his door, the headsman struck a light, and setting fire to a lamp, motioned the others to a bench, and placed a stone jar of strong waters before them, of which Wolfytt took a long, deep pull, but the chirurgeon declined it.

"I have had enough," he said. "Besides, I want to see the spirit."

"I care for no other spirit but this," rejoined Wolfytt, again applying his mouth to the jar.

"Take care of yourselves, masters," observed Mauger. "I must attend to business."

"Never mind us," laughed Wolfytt, observing the executioner take up an axe, and after examining its edge, begin to sharpen it, "grind away."

"This is for Lord Guilford Dudley," remarked Mauger, as he turned the wheel with his foot. "I shall need two axes to-morrow."

"Sharp work," observed Wolfytt, with a detestable grin.

"You would think so were I to try one on you," retorted Mauger. "Ay, now it will do," he added laying aside the implement, and taking up another. "This is my favourite axe. I can make sure work with it. I always keep it for queens or dames of high degree—he! he! This notch, which I can never grind away, was made by the old Countess of Salisbury, that I told you about. It was a terrible sight to see her white hair dabbled with blood. Poor Lady Jane won't give me so much trouble, I'll be sworn. She'll die like a lamb."

"Ay, ay," muttered Sorrocold. "God send her a speedy death!"

"She's sure of it with me," returned Mauger, "so you may rest easy on that score." And as he turned the grindstone quickly round, drawing sparks from the steel, he chaunted; as hoarsely as a raven, the following ditty:—

The axe was sharp, and heavy as lead,

As it touched the neck, off went the head!

Wh i r—wh i r—wh i r—wh i r!

And the screaming of the grindstone formed an appropriate accompaniment to the melody.

Queen Anne laid her white throat upon the block,

Quietly waiting the fatal shock;

The axe it severed it right in twain,

And so quick—so true—that she felt no pain!

Whir—whir—whir—whir!

And he again set the wheel in motion.

Salisbury's countess, she would not die

As a proud dame should—decorously.

Lifting my axe, I split her skull,

And the edge since then has been notched and dull.

Whir—tvhir—whir—whir!

Queen Catherine Howard gave me a fee,—

A chain of gold—to die easily:

And her costly present she did not rue,

For I touched her head, and away it flew!

Whir—whir—whir—whir!

"A brave song, and well sung," cried Wolfytt, approvingly. "Have you any more of it?"

"No," replied Mauger, significantly. "I shall make another verse to-morrow. My axe is now as sharp as a razor," he added, feeling its edge. "Suppose we go to the scaffold? It must be up by this time.",

"With all my heart," replied Sorrocold, whose superstitious curiosity was fully awakened.

Shouldering the heavy block with the greatest ease, Mauger directed Wolfytt to bring a bundle of straw from a heap in the corner, and extinguishing the lamp, set forth. It was a sharp, frosty night, and the hard ground rang beneath their footsteps. There was no moon, but the stars twinkled brightly down, revealing every object with sufficient distinctness. As they passed Saint Thomas's Tower, Wolfytt laughingly pointed out Bret's head stuck upon a spike on the roof, and observed,—"That poor fellow made Xit a knight."

The Night before the Execution.

On reaching the Green, they found Manger's conjecture right—the scaffold was nearly finished. Two carpenters were at work upon it, nailing the planks to the posts, and the noise of their hammers resounded in sharp echoes from the surrounding habitations. Hurrying forward, Mauger ascended the steps, which were placed on the north, opposite Saint Peter's chapel, and deposited his burthen on the platform. He was followed more leisurely by Sorrocold; and Wolfytt, throwing the straw upon the ground, scrambled after them as well as he could.

"If I had thought it was so sold, I would have taken another pull at the stone bottle," he said, rubbing his hands.

"Warm yourself by helping the carpenter," replied Sorrocold gravely. "It will do you more good."

Wolfytt laughed, and dropping on his knees, grasped the block with both hands, and placed his neck in the hollowed space.

"Shall I try whether I can take your head off?" demanded Mauger, feigning to draw his dagger.

Apprehensive that the jest might be carried a little too far, Wolfytt got up, and imitated, as well as his drunken condition would allow, the actions of a person addressing the multitude and preparing for execution. In bowing to receive the blessing of the priest, he missed his footing a second time, and rolled off the scaffold. He did not attempt to ascend again, but supported himself against one of the posts near the carpenters. Mauger and Sorrocold took no notice of him, but began to converse in an under tone about the apparition. In spite of himself, the executioner could not repress a feeling of dread, and the chirurgeon half-repented his curiosity.

After a while, neither spoke, and Sorrocold's teeth chattered, partly with cold, partly with terror. Nothing broke the deathlike silence around, except the noise of the hammer, and ever and anon, a sullen and ominous roar proceeding from the direction of the Lions' Tower.

"Do you think it will appear?" inquired Sorrocold, whose blood ran cold at the latter awful sounds.

"I know not," replied Mauger—"All! there—there it is." And he pointed towards the church porch, from which a figure, robed in white, but unsubstantial almost as the mist, suddenly issued. It glided noiselessly along, and without turning its face towards the beholders. No one saw it except Mauger and Sorrocold, who followed its course with their eyes. The carpenters continued their work, and Wolfytt stared at his companions in stupid and inebriate wonderment. After making the complete circuit of the scaffold, the figure entered the church porch and disappeared.

"What think you of it?" demanded Mauger, as soon as he could find utterance.

"It is marvellous and incomprehensible, and if I had not seen it with my own eyes, I could not have believed it," replied the churgeon. "It must be the shade of Anne Boleyn, she is buried in that chapel."

"You are right," replied the executioner. "It is her spirit, there will be no further respite. Jane will die to-morrow."

XLI.—OF THE UNION OF CHOLMONDELEY WITH ANGELA.

The near approach of death found Jane as unshaken as before, or rather she rejoiced that her deliverance was at hand. Compelled to her infinite regret to hold a disputation with Fecken-ham, she exerted all her powers; and, as upon a former occasion, when opposed to a more formidable antagonist, Gardiner, came off victorious. But though defeated, the zealous confessor did not give up his point, trusting he should be able to weary her out. He, accordingly, passed the greater part of each day in her prison, and brought with him, at different times, Gardiner, Tunstal, Bonner, and other prelates, all of whom tried the effect of their reasoning upon her,—but with no avail. Bonner, who was of a fierce and intolerant nature, was so enraged, that on taking leave of her he said with much acrimony—"Farewell, madam. I am sorry for you and your obstinacy, and I am assured we shall never meet again."

"True, my lord," replied Jane; "we never *shall* meet again, unless it shall please God to turn your heart. And I sincerely pray that he may send you his holy spirit, that your eyes may be opened to his truth."

Nor had the others better success. Aware that whatever she said would be reported to the disadvantage of the Protestant faith, if it could be so perverted, she determined to give them no handle for misrepresentation, and fought the good fight so gallantly that she lost not a single point, and wrung even from her enemies a reluctant admission of defeat. Those best skilled in all the subtleties of scholastic argument, could not perplex her. United to the most profound learning, she possessed a clear logical understanding, enabling her at once to unravel and expose the mysteries in which they sought to perplex her, while the questions she proposed in her turn were unanswerable. At first, she found Feckenham's visits irksome, but by degrees they became almost agreeable to her, because she felt she was at once serving the cause of the Gospel, and taken from her own thoughts. During all this time, Angela never for a moment quitted her, and though she took no part in the conferences, she profited greatly by them.

Two days before she suffered, Jane said to Feckenham, "You have often expressed a wish to serve me, reverend sir. There is one favour you *can* confer upon me if you will."

"What is it, madam?" he rejoined.

"Before I die," returned Jane, "I would fain see Angela united to her lover, Cuthbert Cholmondeley. He was ever a faithful follower of my unfortunate husband, and he has exhibited a like devoted attachment to me. I know not whether you can confer this favour upon me, or whether you will do so if you can. But I venture, from your professions of regard for me, to ask it. If you consent, send, I pray you to Master John Bradford, pre bendary of Saint Paul's, and let him perform the ceremony in this chamber."

"Bradford!" exclaimed Feckenham, frowning. "I know the obstinate and heretical preacher well. If you are willing that I should perform the ceremony, I will undertake to obtain the queen's permission for it. But it must not be done by Bradford."

"Then I have nothing further to say," replied Jane.

"But how comes it that you, Angela," said Feckenham, addressing her in a severe tone, "the daughter of Catholic parents, both of whom suffered for their faith, abandon it?"

"A better light has been vouchsafed me," she replied, "and I lament that they were not equally favoured."

"Well, madam," observed Feckenham, to Jane, "you shall not say I am harsh with you. I desire to serve Angela, for her parents' sake—both of whom were very dear to me. I will make known your request to the queen, and I can almost promise it shall be granted on one condition."

"On no condition affecting my opinions," said Jane.

"Nay, madam," returned the confessor, with a half-smile, "I was about to propose nothing to which you can object. My condition is, that if Bradford is admitted to your prison, you exchange no word with him, except in reference to the object of his visit. That done, he must depart at once."

"I readily agree to it," replied Jane, "and I thank you for your consideration."

After some further conference, Feckenham departed, and Angela, as soon as they were alone, warmly thanked Jane for her kindness, saying—"But why think of me at such a time?"

"Because it will be a satisfaction to me to know that you are united to the object of your affections," replied Jane. "And now leave me to my devotions, and prepare yourself for what is to happen."

With this, she withdrew into the recess, and, occupied in fervent prayer, soon abstracted herself from all else. Three hours afterwards, Feckenham returned. He was accompanied by Cholmondeley, and a grave-looking divine in the habit of a minister of the Reformed Church, in whom Jane immediately recognised John Bradford,—the uncompromising preacher of the Gospel, who not long afterwards won his crown of martyrdom at Smithfield. Apparently, he knew why he was summoned, and the condition annexed to it, for he fixed an eye full of the deepest compassion and admiration upon Jane, but said nothing. Cholmondeley threw himself at her feet, and pressed her hand to his lips, but his utterance failed him. Jane raised him kindly and entreated him to command himself, saying, "I have not sent for you hero to afflict you, but to make you happy." <

"Alas! madam," replied Cholmondcley, "you are ever more thoughtful for others than yourself."

"Proceed with the ceremony without delay, sir," said Fleckenham.

"I rely upon your word, madam, that you hold no conference with him."

"You *may* rely upon it," returned Jane.

And the confessor withdrew.

Bradford then took from his vest a book of prayers, and in that prison-chamber, with Jane only as a witness, the ceremony was performed. At its conclusion, Angela observed to her husband—"We must separate as soon as united, for I shall never quit my dear mistress during her lifetime."

"I should deeply regret it, if you did otherwise," returned Cholmondcley. "Would I had like permission to attend on Lord Guilford. But that is denied me."

At the mention of her husband's name, a shade passed over Jane's countenance—but she instantly checked the emotion.

"My blessing upon your union!" she cried, extending her hands over the pair, "and may it be happy—happier than mine."

"Amen!" cried Bradford. "Before I take my leave, madam, I trust I shall not transgress the confessor's commands, if I request you to write your name in this book of prayers. It will stimulate me in my devotions, and may perchance cheer me in a trial like your own."

Jane readily complied, and taking the book, wrote a short prayer in the blank leaf, and subscribed it with her name.

"This is but a slight return for your compliance with my request, Master Bradford," she said, as she returned the book, "but it is all I have to offer."

"I shall prize it more than the richest gift," replied the preacher. "Farewell, madam, and doubt not I shall pray constantly for you."

"I thank you heartily, sir," she rejoined. "You must go with him, Cholmondeley," she continued, perceiving that the esquire lingered—"We must now part for ever."

"Farewell, madam," cried Cholmondeley, again prostrating himself before her, and pressing her hand to his lips.

"Nay, Angela, you must lead him forth," observed Jane, kindly, though a tear started to her eye. And she withdrew into an embrasure, while Cholmondeley, utterly unable to control his distress, rushed forth, and was followed by Bradford.

Jane's benediction did not fall to the ground. When the tragic event, which it is the purpose of this chronicle to relate, was over, Angela fell into a dangerous illness, during which her husband watched over her with the greatest solicitude. Long before her recovery, he had been liberated by Mary, and as soon as she was fully restored to health, they retired to his family seat, in Cheshire, where they passed many years of uninterrupted happiness,—saddened,—but not painfully,—by the recollection of the past.

XLII.—THE EXECUTION OF LADY JANE GREY.

Monday, the 12th of February, 1554, the fatal day destined to terminate Jane's earthly sufferings, at length, arrived. Excepting a couple of hours which she allowed to rest, at the urgent entreaty of her companion, she had passed the whole of the night in prayer. Angela kept watch over the lovely sleeper, and the effect produced by the contemplation of her features during this her last slumber, was never afterwards effaced. The repose of an infant could not be more calm and holy. A celestial smile irradiated her countenance; her lips moved as if in prayer; and if good angels are ever permitted to visit the dreams of those they love on earth, they hovered that night over the couch of Jane. Thinking it cruelty to disturb her from such a blissful state, Angela let an hour pass beyond the appointed time. But observing a change come over her countenance,—seeing her bosom heave, and tears gather beneath her eye-lashes, she touched her, and Jane instantly arose.

"Is it four o'clock?" she inquired.

"It has just struck five, madam," replied Angela. "I have disobeyed you for the first and last time. But you seemed so happy, that I could not find in my heart to waken you."

"I *was* happy," replied Jane, "for I dreamed that all was over—without pain to me—and that my soul was borne to regions of celestial bliss by a troop of angels who had hovered above the scaffold."

"It will be so, madam," replied Angela, fervently. "You will quit this earth immediately for heaven, where you will rejoin your husband in everlasting happiness."

"I trust so," replied Jane, in an altered tone, "but in that blessed place I searched in vain for him. Angela, you let me sleep too long, or not long enough."

"Your pardon, dearest madam," cried the other, fearfully.

"Nay, you have given me no offence," returned Jane, kindly. "What I meant was that I had not time to find my husband."

"Oh you *will* find him, dearest madam," returned Angela, "doubt it not. Your prayers would wash out his offences, even if his own could not."

"I trust so," replied Jane. "And I will now pray for him, and do you pray too."

Jane then retired to the recess, and in the gloom, for it was yet dark, continued her devotions until the clock struck seven. She then arose, and assisted by Angela attired herself with great care.

"I pay more attention to the decoration of my body now I am about to part with it," she observed, "than I would do, if it was to serve me longer. So joyful is the occasion to me, that were I to consult my own feelings, I would put on my richest apparel to indicate my contentment of heart. I will not, however, so brave my fate, but array myself in these weeds." And she put on a gown of black velvet, without ornament of any kind; tying round her slender throat (so soon alas! to be severed) a simple white falling collar. Her hair was left purposely unbraided, and was confined by a caul of black velvet. As Angela performed those sad services, she sobbed audibly.

"Nay, cheer thee, child," observed Jane. "When I was clothed in the robes of royalty, and had the crown placed upon my brow,—nay, when arrayed on my wedding-day,—I felt not half so joyful as now."

"Ah! madam!" exclaimed Angela, in a paroxysm of grief. "My condition is more pitiable than yours. You go to certain happiness. But I lose you."

"Only for a while, dear Angela," returned Jane. "Comfort yourself with that thought. Let my fate be a warning to you. Be not dazzled by ambition. Had I not once yielded, I had never thus perished. Discharge your duty strictly to your eternal and your temporal rulers, and rest assured we shall meet again,— never to part."

"Your counsel shall be graven on my heart, madam," returned Angela. "And oh! may my end be as happy as yours!"

"Heaven grant it!" ejaculated Jane, fervently. "And now," she added, as her toilette was ended, "I am ready to die."

"Will you not take some refreshment, madam?" asked Angela.

"No," replied Jane. "I have done with the body!"

The morning was damp and dark. A thaw came on a little before day-break, and a drizzling shower of rain fell. This was succeeded by a thick mist, and the whole of the fortress was for a while enveloped in vapour. It brought to Jane's mind the day on which she was taken to trial. But a moral gloom likewise overspread the fortress. Every one within it, save her few enemies, (and they were few indeed,) lamented Jane's approaching fate. Her youth, her innocence, her piety, touched the sternest breast, and moved the pity even of her persecutors. All felt that morning as if some dire calamity was at hand, and instead of looking forward to the execution as an exciting spectacle (for so such revolting exhibitions were then considered,) they wished it over. Many a prayer was breathed for the speedy release of the sufferer—many a sigh heaved—many a groan uttered: and if ever soul was wafted to Heaven by the fervent wishes of those on earth, Jane's was so.

It was late before there were any signs of stir and bustle within the fortress. Even the soldiers gathered together reluctantly—and those who conversed, spoke in whispers. Dudley, who it has been stated was imprisoned in the Beauchamp Tower, had passed the greater part of the night in devotion. But towards morning, he became restless and uneasy, and unable to compose himself, resorted to the customary employment of captives in such cases, and with a nail which he had found, carved his wife's name in two places on the walls of his prison. These inscriptions still remain.

At nine o'clock, the bell of the chapel began to toll, and an escort of halberdiers and arquebussiers drew up before the Beauchamp Tower, while Sir Thomas Brydges and Feckenham entered the chamber of the prisoner, who received them with an unmoved countenance.

"Before you set out upon a journey from which you will never return, my lord," said Feckenham, "I would ask you for the last time, if any change has taken place in your religious sentiments—and whether you are yet alive to the welfare of your soul?"

"Why not promise me pardon if I will recant on the scaffold, and silence me as you silenced the duke my father, by the axe!" replied Dudley, sternly. "No, sir, I will have naught to do with your false and idolatrous creed. I shall die a firm believer in the gospel, and trust to be saved by it."

"Then perish, body and soul," replied Feckenham, harshly. "Sir Thomas Brydges, I commit him to your hands."

"Am I to be allowed no parting with my wife?" demanded Dudley, anxiously.

"You have parted with her for ever,—heretic and unbeliever!" rejoined Feckenham.

"That speech will haunt your death-bed, sir," retorted Dudley, sternly. And he turned to the lieutenant, and signified that he was ready.

The first object that met Dudley's gaze, as he issued from his prison, was the scaffold on the green. He looked at it for a moment, wistfully.

"It is for Lady Jane," observed the lieutenant.

"I know it," replied Dudley, in a voice of intense emotion.—"I thank you for letting me die first."

"You must thank the queen, my lord," returned Brydges. "It was her order."

"Shall you see my wife, sir?" demanded Dudley, anxiously.

The lieutenant answered in the affirmative.

"Tell her I will be with her on the scaffold," said Dudley.

As he was about to set forward, a young man pushed through the lines of halberdiers, and threw himself at his feet. It was Cholmondeley. Dudley instantly raised and embraced him. "At least I see one whom I love," he cried.

"My lord, this interruption must not be," observed the lieutenant. "If you do not retire," he added, to Cholmondeley, "I shall place you in arrest."

"Farewell, my dear lord," cried the weeping esquire—"farewell!"

"Farewell, for ever!"—returned Dudley, as Cholmondeley was forced back by the guard.

The escort then moved forward, and the lieutenant accompanied the prisoner to the gateway of the Middle Tower, where he delivered him to the sheriffs and their officers, who were waiting there for him with a Franciscan friar, and then returned to fulfil his more painful duty. A vast crowd was collected on Tower Hill, and the strongest commiseration was expressed for Dudley, as he was led to the scaffold, on which Mauger had already taken his station.

On quitting the Beauchamp Tower, Feckenham proceeded to Jane's prison. He found her on her knees, but she immediately arose.

"Is it time?" she asked.

"It is, madam,—to repent," replied Feckenham, sternly. "A few minutes are all that now remain to you of life—nay, at this moment, perhaps, your husband is called before his Eternal Judge. There is yet time. Do not perish like him in your sins."

"Heaven have mercy upon him!" cried Jane, falling on her knees.

And notwithstanding the importunities of the confessor, she continued in fervent prayer, till the appearance of Sir Thomas Brydges. She instantly understood why he came, and rising, prepared for departure. Almost blinded by tears, Angela rendered her the last services she required. This done, the lieutenant, who was likewise greatly affected, begged some slight remembrance of her.

"I have nothing to give you but this book of prayers, sir," she answered— "but you shall have that, when I have done with it, and may it profit you."

"You will receive it only to cast it into the flames, my son," remarked Feckenham.

"On the contrary, I shall treasure it like a priceless gem," replied Brydges.

"You will find a prayer written in it in my own hand," said Jane.—"And again I say, may it profit you."

Brydges then passed through the door, and Jane followed him. A band of halberdiers were without. At the sight of her, a deep and general sympathy was manifested; not an eye was dry; and tears trickled down cheeks unaccustomed to such moisture. The melancholy train proceeded at a slow pace. Jane fixed her eyes upon the prayer-book, which she read aloud to drown the importunities of the confessor, who walked on her right, while Angela kept near her on the other side. And so they reached the green.

By this time, the fog had cleared off, and the rain had ceased; but the atmosphere was humid, and the day lowering and gloomy. Very few spectators were assembled,—for it required firm nerves to witness such a tragedy. A flock of carrion-crows and ravens, attracted by their fearful instinct, wheeled around overhead, or settled on the branches of the bare and leafless trees, and by their croaking added to the dismal character of the scene. The bell continued tolling all the time.

The sole person upon the scaffold was Wolfytt. He was occupied in scattering straw near the block. Among the bystanders was Sorrocold leaning on his staff; and as Jane for a moment raised her eyes as she passed along, she perceived Roger Ascham. Her old preceptor had obeyed her, and she repaid him with a look of gratitude.

By the lieutenant's directions, she was conducted for a short time into the Beauchamp Tower, and here Feckenham continued his persecutions, until a deep groan arose among those without, and an officer abruptly entered the room.

"Madam," said Sir John Brydges, after the new-comer had delivered his message, "we must set forth."

Jane made a motion of assent, and the party issued from the Beauchamp Tower, in front of which a band of halberdiers was drawn up. A wide open space was kept clear around the scaffold. Jane seemed unconscious of all that was passing. Preceded by the lieutenant, who took his way towards the north of the scaffold, and attended on either side by Feckenham and Angela as before, she kept her eyes steadily fixed on her prayer-book.

Arrived within a short distance of the fatal spot, she was startled by a scream from Angela, and looking up, beheld four soldiers, carrying a litter covered with a cloth, and advancing toward her. She knew it was the body of her husband, and unprepared for so terrible an encounter, uttered a cry of horror. The bearers of the litter passed on, and entered the porch of the chapel.

Jane meeting the body of her husband on her way to the Scaffold.

While this took place, Mauger, who had limped back as fast as he could after his bloody work on Tower I Till,—only tarrying a moment to exchange his axe,—ascended the steps of the scaffold, and ordered Wolfytt to get down. Sir Thomas Brydges, who was greatly shocked at what had just occurred, and would have prevented it if it had been possible, returned to Jane and offered her his assistance. But she did not require it. The force of the shock had passed away, and she firmly mounted the scaffold.

When she was seen there, a groan of compassion arose from the spectators, and prayers were audibly uttered. She then advanced to the rail, and, in a clear distinct voice, spoke as follows:—

"I pray you all to bear me witness that I die a true Christian woman, and that I look to be saved by no other means except the mercy of God, and the merits of the blood of his only son Jesus Christ. I confess when I knew the word of God I neglected it, and loved myself and the world, and therefore this punishment is a just return for my sins. But I thank God of his goodness that he has given me a time and respite to repent. And now good people, while I am alive, I pray you assist me with your prayers."

Many fervent responses followed, and several of the by-standers imitated Jane's example, as, on the conclusion of her speech, she fell on her knees and recited the *Miserere*.

At its close, Feckenham said in a loud voice, "I ask you, madam, for the last time, will you repent?"

"I pray you, sir, to desist," replied Jane, meekly. "I am now at peace with all the world, and would die so."

She then arose, and giving the prayer-book to Angela, said,—"When all is over, deliver this to the lieutenant. These," she added, taking off her gloves and collar, "I give to you."

"And to me," cried Mauger, advancing and prostrating himself before her according to custom, "you give grace."

"And also my head," replied Jane. "I forgive thee heartily, fellow. Thou art my best friend."

"What ails you, madam?" remarked the lieutenant, observing Jane suddenly start and tremble.

"Not much," she replied, "but I thought I saw my husband pale and bleeding."

"Where?" demanded the lieutenant, recalling Dudley's speech.

"There, near the block," replied Jane. "I see the figure still. But it must be mere fantasy."

Whatever his thoughts were, the lieutenant made no reply; and Jane turned to Angela, who now began, with trembling hands, to remove her attire, and was trying to take off her velvet robe, when Mauger offered to assist her, but was instantly repulsed.

He then withdrew, and stationing himself by the block, assumed his hideous black mask, and shouldered his axe.

Partially disrobed, Jane bowed her head, while Angela tied a kerchief over her eyes, and turned her long tresses over her head to be out of the way. Unable to control herself, she then turned aside, and wept aloud. Jane moved forward in search of the block, but fearful of making a false step, felt for it with her hands, and cried—"What shall I do?—Where is it?—Where is it?"

Sir Thomas Brydges took her hand and guided her to it. At this awful moment, there was a slight movement in the crowd, some of whom pressed nearer the scaffold, and amongst others Sorrocold and Wolfytt. The latter caught hold of the boards to obtain a better view. Angela placed her hands before her eyes, and would have suspended her being, if she could; and even Feckenham veiled his countenance with his robe. Sir Thomas Brydges gazed firmly on.

By this time, Jane had placed her head on the block, and her last words were, "Lord, into thy hands I commend my spirit!"

The axe then fell, and one of the fairest and wisest heads that ever sat on human shoulders, fell likewise.

THUS ENDS THE CHRONICLE OF THE TOWER OF LONDON

Thus ends the Chronicle of the Tower of London.

Milton Keynes UK
Ingram Content Group UK Ltd.
UKHW010805110624
444053UK00005B/498